IRISH FAIRY TALES

This is a FLAME TREE Book

Publisher & Creative Director: Nick Wells
Project Editors: Laura Bulbeck and Gillian Whitaker
Editorial Board: Josie Mitchell, Catherine Taylor, Taylor Bentley

Publisher's Note: Due to the historical nature of the classic text, we're aware that there may be some language used which has the potential to cause offence to the modern reader. However, wishing overall to preserve the integrity of the text, rather than imposing contemporary sensibilities, we have left it unaltered.

FLAME TREE PUBLISHING
6 Melbray Mews, Fulham,
London SW6 3NS, United Kingdom
www.flametreepublishing.com

First published 2018

The cover image is based on artwork by Arthur Rackham.
Contributors, authors, editors and sources for this series include: Loren Auerbach, Norman Bancroft-Hunt, E.M. Berens, Samuel Butler, Laura Bulbeck, Jeremiah Curtin, O.B. Duane, Dr Ray Dunning, W.W. Gibbings, H.A. Guerber, Jake Jackson, Judith John, Katharine Berry Judson, Charles Kingsley, Andrew Lang, J.W. Mackail, Chris McNab, Professor James Riordan, Rachel Storm, K.E. Sullivan.

A copy of the CIP data for this book is available from the British Library.

Printed and bound in China

See our new fiction list
FLAME TREE PRESS | FICTION WITHOUT FRONTIERS
New and original writing in Horror, Crime, SF and Fantasy

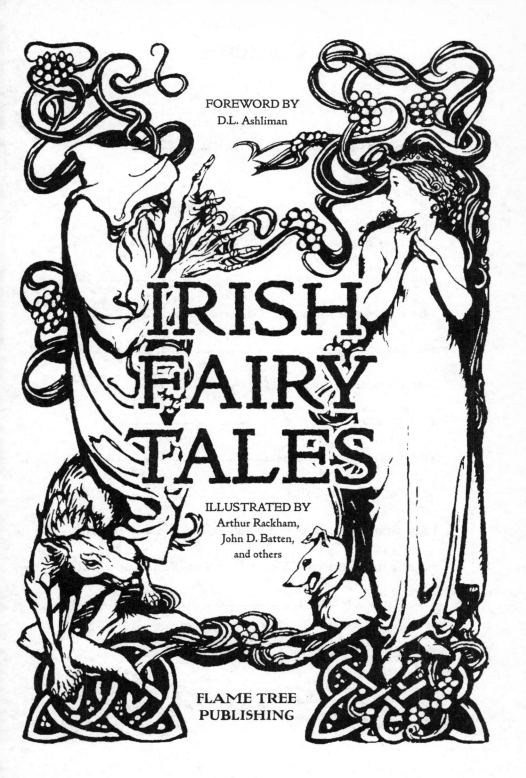

FOREWORD BY
D.L. Ashliman

IRISH
FAIRY
TALES

ILLUSTRATED BY
Arthur Rackham,
John D. Batten,
and others

FLAME TREE
PUBLISHING

Contents

Romance & Tragedy

Heroes & Giants

Fairies & Sea-Folk

Supernatural Forces

Foreword: Irish Fairy Tales

NO EUROPEAN COUNTRY has a richer storytelling heritage than does Ireland. Like their counterparts in other cultures, Irish fairy tales typically represent a half dozen different genres, four of which are included in the current collection.

Myths

IN COMMON USAGE the word *myth* carries a number of meanings, including the connotation of falsehood, for example: "Politicians' claims are only myths." Folklorists, anthropologists, and historians of culture assign a more dignified meaning to the term, designating with it a body of stories and beliefs that give meaning to some of life's greatest mysteries. The creation of the earth, the nature of good and evil, and the ambiguities of human existence are among the subjects covered by traditional myths. Their characters include deities, demons, superhuman heroes, and treacherous enemies. To the generations that create and disseminate them, myths both define and reflect a value system akin to religion.

Irish myths originated with the Celts, whose ancestors migrated to the British Isles from central Europe, beginning around 700 BC. Ireland's isolation shielded it from Roman colonization and other outside influences, thus helping to preserve Celtic traditions. However, most early Irish myths were not written down until the eighth century or later. The Christian monks who first recorded them undoubtedly removed or altered many of the stories' 'heathen' tenets.

Stories in the current anthology derived from ancient Irish myths include 'The Cattle-Raid of Cualnge' and 'The Knighting of Cuculain'. They feature one of Ireland's greatest mythological heroes: Cú Chulainn (variously spelled), who is often compared to Hercules and Siegfried of Greco-Roman and Germanic traditions.

Legends

AS USED BY FOLKLORISTS, the term *legend* refers to a narrative that claims to be true. Such accounts often assert credibility by including authentic place names and plausible personal names. For example, the 'Bewitched Butter' tale begins: "Not far from Rathmullen lived, last spring, a family called Hanlon; and in a farmhouse, some fields distant, people named Dogherty." Sometimes similar accounts are attributed to different locations and thus are known as *migratory legends*. For example: 'The Brewery of Eggshells' relates how a fairy changeling is exposed when he expresses surprise at the mother's feigned brewing of eggshells. Comparable tales are told throughout the British Isles, and across continental Europe, always claiming local authenticity.

The aforementioned legends are typical in that they offer supernatural solutions to real-life problems. A family cow ceases to give milk, due to theft by a witch. A human child fails to thrive, because it is actually a fairy changeling. In each instance the ostensible cause is discovered and a magical solution is effected. We no longer believe in witches that steal milk, and in fairies that replace healthy human children with misshapen imps, nor that there are magical charms offering protection against such misfortune. Previous generations found comfort in legends that described such relief, even if these tales were based more on hope than on fact.

Magic Tales

THE STORIES known as *fairy tales* do not necessarily feature fairies and might thus more appropriately be labelled *magic tales*. Unlike legends, magic tales do not typically claim to be true, but admittedly take place in a realm of make-believe. These stories often provide fantasy solutions to realistic problems. 'Smallhead and the King's Son' offers a good example. The heroine, nicknamed *Smallhead* by her stepsisters, with magical help survives their persecution and in the end marries a king. This plot resembles the universally loved tale 'Cinderella'. The magic tales of most countries have parallels in other cultures, and Irish stories are no exception. 'Fair, Brown, and Trembling' is another 'Cinderella' variant. Similarly, 'The Haughty Princess' echoes the basic plot of Shakespeare's *The Taming of the Shrew* and closely resembles the Grimm brothers' 'King Thrushbeard'.

Literary Fairy Tales

OUR FINAL CATEGORY is the *literary fairy tale*. Here the story is not drawn directly from oral tradition, but is instead the invention of a known author, for example Hans Christian Andersen, the famous Danish storyteller. Literary fairy tales, while drawing on traditional motifs and situations, are usually more finely crafted than their orally transmitted counterparts. Examples from the current collection include 'Princess Finola and the Dwarf' and 'The House in the Lake', both by Edmund Leamy.

D.L. Ashliman

Publisher's Note

STORIES FROM IRELAND have long captured the imagination of their audience with potent narratives that sweep the reader beyond the human realm. Fascinating examples of fireside stories of warriors, druids, giants, changelings, mermaids and more are gathered together in this book with fantastical images from Arthur Rackham's distinctive body of work, and illustrations by John D. Batten, George Denham, Corinne Turner, H.R. Heaton and S. Fazoin from the original publications more than a century ago. Where practical, textual notes that provide context to terms and names have been kept, as in L. Winifred's 1904 translation of the Cattle-Raid of Cualnge, where marks ('—') indicate an obscure portion of manuscript left untranslated. In the majority of cases though, we have removed footnotes to keep the text clean. Similarly, the variants of names from Celtic legend have been left as they appear in the source material, in order for the authenticity of the stories to be enjoyed in all its enchanting power.

IRISH FAIRY TALES

Romance
&
Tragedy

Introduction

FAIRY TALES are often grounded in the pursuit, and perils, of love. Not all of them end in happiness and wedded bliss, as demonstrated by the story of Deirdre, one of the most famous tragic heroines in Irish legend. The version of her story given here is joined by other stories of adventure, magic and young love, including an Irish version of the Cinderella story in 'Fair, Brown, and Trembling'.

Princess Finola and the Dwarf

A LONG, LONG TIME AGO there lived in a little hut in the midst of a bare, brown, lonely moor an old woman and a young girl. The old woman was withered, sour-tempered, and dumb. The young girl was as sweet and as fresh as an opening rosebud, and her voice was as musical as the whisper of a stream in the woods in the hot days of summer. The little hut, made of branches woven closely together, was shaped like a beehive. In the centre of the hut a fire burned night and day from year's end to year's end, though it was never touched or tended by human hand. In the cold days and nights of winter it gave out light and heat that made the hut cosy and warm, but in the summer nights and days it gave out light only. With their heads to the wall of the hut and their feet towards the fire were two sleeping-couches – one of plain woodwork, in which slept the old woman; the other was Finola's. It was of bog-oak, polished as a looking-glass, and on it were carved flowers and birds of all kinds, that gleamed and shone in the light of the fire. This couch was fit for a princess, and a princess Finola was, though she did not know it herself.

Outside the hut the bare, brown, lonely moor stretched for miles on every side, but towards the east it was bounded by a range of mountains that looked to Finola blue in the daytime, but which put on a hundred changing colours as the sun went down. Nowhere was a house to be seen, nor a tree, nor a flower, nor sign of any living thing. From morning till night, nor hum of bee, nor song of bird, nor voice of man, nor any sound fell on Finola's ear. When the storm was in the air the great waves thundered on the shore beyond the mountains, and the wind shouted in the glens; but when it sped across the moor it lost its voice, and passed as silently as the dead. At first the silence frightened Finola, but she got used to it after a time, and often broke it by talking to herself and singing.

The only other person beside the old woman Finola ever saw was a dumb dwarf who, mounted on a broken-down horse, came once a month to the hut, bringing with him a sack of corn for the old woman and Finola. Although he couldn't speak to her, Finola was always glad to see the dwarf and his old horse, and she used to give them cake made with her own white hands. As for the dwarf he would have died for the little princess, he was so much in love with her, and often and often his heart was heavy and sad as he thought of her pining away in the lonely moor.

It chanced that he came one day, and she did not, as usual, come out to greet him. He made signs to the old woman, but she took up a stick and struck him, and beat his horse and drove him away; but as he was leaving he caught a glimpse of Finola at the door of the hut, and saw that she was crying. This sight made him so very miserable that he could think of nothing else but her sad face that he had always seen so bright, and he allowed the old horse to go on without minding where he was going. Suddenly he heard a voice saying: "It is time for you to come."

The dwarf looked, and right before him, at the foot of a green hill, was a little man not half as big as himself, dressed in a green jacket with brass buttons, and a red cap and tassel.

"It is time for you to come," he said the second time; "but you are welcome, anyhow. Get off your horse and come in with me, that I may touch your lips with the wand of speech, that we may have a talk together."

The dwarf got off his horse and followed the little man through a hole in the side of a green hill. The hole was so small that he had to go on his hands and knees to pass through it, and when he was able to stand he was only the same height as the little fairyman. After walking three or four steps they were in a splendid room, as bright as day. Diamonds sparkled in the roof as stars sparkle in the sky when the night is without a cloud. The roof rested on golden pillars, and between the pillars were silver lamps, but their light was dimmed by that of the diamonds. In the middle of the room was a table, on which were two golden plates and two silver knives and forks, and a brass bell as big as a hazelnut, and beside the table were two little chairs covered with blue silk and satin.

"Take a chair," said the fairy, "and I will ring for the wand of speech."

The dwarf sat down, and the fairyman rang the little brass bell, and in came a little weeny dwarf no bigger than your hand.

"Bring me the wand of speech," said the fairy, and the weeny dwarf bowed three times and walked out backwards, and in a minute he returned, carrying a little black wand with a red berry at the top of it, and, giving it to the fairy, he bowed three times and walked out backwards as he had done before.

The little man waved the rod three times over the dwarf, and struck him once on the right shoulder and once on the left shoulder, and then touched his lips with the red berry, and said: "Speak!"

The dwarf spoke, and he was so rejoiced at hearing the sound of his own voice that he danced about the room.

"Who are you at all, at all?" said he to the fairy.

"Who is yourself?" said the fairy. "But come, before we have any talk let us have something to eat, for I am sure you are hungry."

Then they sat down to table, and the fairy rang the little brass bell twice, and the weeny dwarf brought in two boiled snails in their shells, and when they had eaten the snails he brought in a dormouse, and when they had eaten the dormouse he brought in two wrens, and when they had eaten the wrens he brought in two nuts full of wine, and they became very merry, and the fairyman sang 'Cooleen dhas', and the dwarf sang 'The little blackbird of the glen'.

"Did you ever hear the 'Foggy Dew?'" said the fairy.

"No," said the dwarf.

"Well, then, I'll give it to you; but we must have some more wine."

And the wine was brought, and he sang the 'Foggy Dew', and the dwarf said it was the sweetest song he had ever heard, and that the fairyman's voice would coax the birds off the bushes.

"You asked me who I am?" said the fairy.

"I did," said the dwarf.

"And I asked you who is yourself?"

"You did," said the dwarf.

"And who are you, then?"

"Well, to tell the truth, I don't know," said the dwarf, and he blushed like a rose.

"Well, tell me what you know about yourself."

"I remember nothing at all," said the dwarf, "before the day I found myself going along with a crowd of all sorts of people to the great fair of the Liffey. We had to pass by the king's palace on our way, and as we were passing the king sent for a band of jugglers to come and show their tricks before him. I followed the jugglers to look on, and when the play was over the king called me to him, and asked me who I was and where I came from. I was dumb then, and couldn't answer; but even if I could speak I could not tell him what he wanted to know, for I remember nothing of myself before that day. Then the king asked the jugglers, but they knew nothing about me, and no one knew anything, and then the king said he would take me into his service; and the only work I have to do is to go once a month with a bag of corn to the hut in the lonely moor."

"And there you fell in love with the little princess," said the fairy, winking at the dwarf.

The poor dwarf blushed twice as much as he had done before.

"You need not blush," said the fairy; "it is a good man's case. And now tell me, truly, do you love the princess, and what would you give to free her from the spell of enchantment that is over her?"

"I would give my life," said the dwarf.

"Well, then, listen to me," said the fairy. "The Princess Finola was banished to the lonely moor by the king, your master. He killed her father, who was the rightful king, and would have killed Finola, only he was told by an old sorceress that if he killed her he would die himself on the same day, and she advised him to banish her to the lonely moor, and she said she would fling a spell of enchantment over it, and that until the spell was broken Finola could not leave the moor. And the sorceress also promised that she would send an old woman to watch over the princess by night and by day, so that no harm should come to her; but she told the king that he himself should select a messenger to take food to the hut, and that he should look out for someone who had never seen or heard of the princess, and whom he could trust never to tell anyone anything about her; and that is the reason he selected you."

"Since you know so much," said the dwarf, "can you tell me who I am, and where I came from?"

"You will know that time enough," said the fairy. "I have given you back your speech. It will depend solely on yourself whether you will get back your memory of who and what you were before the day you entered the king's service. But are you really willing to try and break the spell of enchantment and free the princess?"

"I am," said the dwarf.

"Whatever it will cost you?"

"Yes, if it cost me my life," said the dwarf; "but tell me, how can the spell be broken?"

"Oh, it is easy enough to break the spell if you have the weapons," said the fairy.

"And what are they, and where are they?" said the dwarf.

"The spear of the shining haft and the dark blue blade and the silver shield," said the fairy. "They are on the farther bank of the Mystic Lake in the Island of the Western Seas. They are there for the man who is bold enough to seek them. If you are the man who will bring them back to the lonely moor you will only have to strike the shield three times with the haft, and three times with the blade of the spear, and the silence of the moor will be broken for ever, the spell of enchantment will be removed, and the princess will be free."

"I will set out at once," said the dwarf, jumping from his chair.

"And whatever it cost you," said the fairy, "will you pay the price?"

"I will," said the dwarf.

"Well, then, mount your horse, give him his head, and he will take you to the shore opposite the Island of the Mystic Lake. You must cross to the island on his back, and make your way through the water-steeds that swim around the island night and day to guard it; but woe betide you if you attempt to cross without paying the price, for if you do the angry water-steeds will rend you and your horse to pieces. And when you come to the Mystic Lake you must wait until the waters are as red as wine, and then swim your horse across it, and on the farther side you will find the spear and shield; but woe betide you if you attempt to cross the lake before you pay the price, for if you do, the black Cormorants of the Western Seas will pick the flesh from your bones."

"What is the price?" said the dwarf.

"You will know that time enough," said the fairy; "but now go, and good luck go with you."

The dwarf thanked the fairy, and said goodbye! He then threw the reins on his horse's neck, and started up the hill, that seemed to grow bigger and bigger as he ascended, and the dwarf soon found that what he took for a hill was a great mountain. After travelling all the day, toiling up by steep crags and heathery passes, he reached the top as the sun was setting in the ocean, and he saw far below him out in the waters the island of the Mystic Lake.

He began his descent to the shore, but long before he reached it the sun had set, and darkness, unpierced by a single star, dropped upon the sea. The old horse, worn out by his long and painful journey, sank beneath him, and the dwarf was so tired that he rolled off his back and fell asleep by his side.

He awoke at the breaking of the morning, and saw that he was almost at the water's edge. He looked out to sea, and saw the island, but nowhere could he see the water-steeds, and he began to fear he must have taken a wrong course in the night, and that the island before him was not the one he was in search of. But even while he was so thinking he heard fierce and angry snortings, and, coming swiftly from the island to the shore, he saw the swimming and prancing steeds. Sometimes their heads and manes only were visible, and sometimes, rearing, they rose half out of the water, and, striking it with their hoofs, churned it into foam, and tossed the white spray to the skies. As they approached nearer and nearer their snortings became more terrible, and their nostrils shot forth clouds of vapour. The dwarf trembled at the sight and sound, and his old horse, quivering in every limb, moaned piteously, as if in pain. On came the steeds, until they almost touched the shore, then rearing, they seemed about to spring on to it. The frightened dwarf turned his head to fly, and as he did so he heard the twang of a golden harp, and right before him who should he see but the little man of the hills, holding a harp in one hand and striking the strings with the other.

"Are you ready to pay the price?" said he, nodding gaily to the dwarf.

As he asked the question, the listening water-steeds snorted more furiously than ever.

"Are you ready to pay the price?" said the little man a second time.

A shower of spray, tossed on shore by the angry steeds, drenched the dwarf to the skin, and sent a cold shiver to his bones, and he was so terrified that he could not answer.

"For the third and last time, are you ready to pay the price?" asked the fairy, as he flung the harp behind him and turned to depart.

When the dwarf saw him going he thought of the little princess in the lonely moor, and his courage came back, and he answered bravely:

"Yes, I am ready."

The water-steeds, hearing his answer, and snorting with rage, struck the shore with their pounding hoofs.

"Back to your waves!" cried the little harper; and as he ran his fingers across his lyre, the frightened steeds drew back into the waters.

"What is the price?" asked the dwarf.

"Your right eye," said the fairy; and before the dwarf could say a word, the fairy scooped out the eye with his finger, and put it into his pocket.

The dwarf suffered most terrible agony; but he resolved to bear it for the sake of the little princess. Then the fairy sat down on a rock at the edge of the sea, and, after striking a few notes, he began to play the 'Strains of Slumber'.

The sound crept along the waters, and the steeds, so ferocious a moment before, became perfectly still. They had no longer any motion of their own, and they floated on the top of the tide like foam before a breeze.

"Now," said the fairy, as he led the dwarf's horse to the edge of the tide.

The dwarf urged the horse into the water, and once out of his depth, the old horse struck out boldly for the island. The sleeping water-steeds drifted helplessly against him, and in a short time he reached the island safely, and he neighed joyously as his hoofs touched solid ground.

The dwarf rode on and on, until he came to a bridle-path, and following this, it led him up through winding lanes, bordered with golden furze that filled the air with fragrance, and brought him to the summit of the green hills that girdled and looked down on the Mystic Lake. Here the horse stopped of his own accord, and the dwarf's heart beat quickly as his eye rested on the lake, that, clipped round by the ring of hills, seemed in the breezeless and sunlit air –

> *As still as death,*
> *And as bright as life can be.*

After gazing at it for a long time, he dismounted, and lay at his ease in the pleasant grass. Hour after hour passed, but no change came over the face of the waters, and when the night fell sleep closed the eyelids of the dwarf.

The song of the lark awoke him in the early morning, and, starting up, he looked at the lake, but its waters were as bright as they had been the day before.

Towards midday he beheld what he thought was a black cloud sailing across the sky from east to west. It seemed to grow larger as it came nearer and nearer, and when it was high above the lake he saw it was a huge bird, the shadow of whose outstretched wings darkened the waters of the lake; and the dwarf knew it was one of the Cormorants of the Western Seas. As it descended slowly, he saw that it held in one of its claws a branch of a tree larger than a full-grown oak, and laden with clusters of ripe red berries. It alighted at some distance from the dwarf, and, after resting for a time, it began to eat the berries and to throw the stones into the lake, and wherever a stone fell a bright red stain appeared in the water. As he looked more closely at the bird the dwarf saw that it had all the signs of old age, and he could not help wondering how it was able to carry such a heavy tree.

Later in the day, two other birds, as large as the first, but younger, came up from the west and settled down beside him. They also ate the berries, and throwing the stones into the lake it was soon as red as wine.

When they had eaten all the berries, the young birds began to pick the decayed feathers off the old bird and to smooth his plumage. As soon as they had completed their task, he rose slowly from the hill and sailed out over the lake, and dropping down on the waters, dived beneath them. In a moment he came to the surface, and shot up into the air with a joyous cry, and flew off to the west in all the vigour of renewed youth, followed by the other birds.

When they had gone so far that they were like specks in the sky, the dwarf mounted his horse and descended towards the lake.

He was almost at the margin, and in another minute would have plunged in, when he heard a fierce screaming in the air, and before he had time to look up, the three birds were hovering over the lake.

The dwarf drew back frightened.

The birds wheeled over his head, and then, swooping down, they flew close to the water, covering it with their wings, and uttering harsh cries.

Then, rising to a great height, they folded their wings and dropped headlong, like three rocks, on the lake, crashing its surface, and scattering a wine-red shower upon the hills.

Then the dwarf remembered what the fairy told him, that if he attempted to swim the lake, without paying the price, the three Cormorants of the Western Seas would pick the flesh off his bones. He knew not what to do, and was about to turn away, when he heard once more the twang of the golden harp, and the little fairy of the hills stood before him.

"Faint heart never won fair lady," said the little harper. "Are you ready to pay the price? The spear and shield are on the opposite bank, and the Princess Finola is crying this moment in the lonely moor."

At the mention of Finola's name the dwarf's heart grew strong.

"Yes," he said; "I am ready – win or die. What is the price?"

"Your left eye," said the fairy. And as soon as said he scooped out the eye, and put it in his pocket.

The poor blind dwarf almost fainted with pain.

"It's your last trial," said the fairy, "and now do what I tell you. Twist your horse's mane round your right hand, and I will lead him to the water. Plunge in, and fear not. I gave you back your speech. When you reach the opposite bank you will get back your memory, and you will know who and what you are."

Then the fairy led the horse to the margin of the lake.

"In with you now, and good luck go with you," said the fairy.

The dwarf urged the horse. He plunged into the lake, and went down and down until his feet struck the bottom. Then he began to ascend, and as he came near the surface of the water the dwarf thought he saw a glimmering light, and when he rose above the water he saw the bright sun shining and the green hills before him, and he shouted with joy at finding his sight restored.

But he saw more. Instead of the old horse he had ridden into the lake he was bestride a noble steed, and as the steed swam to the bank the dwarf felt a change coming over himself, and an unknown vigour in his limbs.

When the steed touched the shore he galloped up the hillside, and on the top of the hill was a silver shield, bright as the sun, resting against a spear standing upright in the ground.

The dwarf jumped off, and, running towards the shield, he saw himself as in a looking-glass.

He was no longer a dwarf, but a gallant knight. At that moment his memory came back to him, and he knew he was Conal, one of the Knights of the Red Branch, and he remembered now that the spell of dumbness and deformity had been cast upon him by the Witch of the Palace of the Quicken Trees.

Slinging his shield upon his left arm, he plucked the spear from the ground and leaped on to his horse. With a light heart he swam back over the lake, and nowhere could he see the black Cormorants of the Western Seas, but three white swans floating abreast followed him to the bank. When he reached the bank he galloped down to the sea, and crossed to the shore.

Then he flung the reins upon his horse's neck, and swifter than the wind the gallant horse swept on and on, and it was not long until he was bounding over the enchanted moor. Wherever his hoofs struck the ground, grass and flowers sprang up, and great trees with leafy branches rose on every side.

At last the knight reached the little hut. Three times he struck the shield with the haft and three times with the blade of his spear. At the last blow the hut disappeared, and standing before him was the little princess.

The knight took her in his arms and kissed her; then he lifted her on to the horse, and, leaping up before her, he turned towards the north, to the palace of the Red Branch Knights, and as they rode on beneath the leafy trees from every tree the birds sang out, for the spell of silence over the lonely moor was broken for ever.

The House in the Lake

A LONG, LONG TIME AGO there lived in a little hut, in the midst of one of the inland lakes of Erin, an old fisherman and his son. The hut was built on stakes driven into the bed of the lake, and was so high above the waters that even when they were stirred into waves by the wind coming down from the mountains they did not reach the threshold of the door. Around, outside the hut, on a level with the floor, was a little wicker-work platform, and under the platform, close to the steps leading up to it from the water, the fisherman's curragh, made of willows, covered with skins, was moored, and it was only by means of the curragh that he and his son, Enda, could leave their lake dwelling.

On many a summer evening Enda lay stretched on the platform, watching the sunset fading from the mountain-tops, and the twilight creeping over the waters of the lake, and it chanced that once when he was so engaged he heard a rustle in a clump of sedge that grew close to one side of the hut. He turned to where the sound came from, and what should he see but an otter swimming towards him, with a little trout in his mouth. When the otter came up to where Enda was lying, he lifted his head and half his body from the water, and flung the trout on the platform, almost at Enda's feet, and then disappeared.

Enda took the little panting trout in his hand; but as he did so he heard, quite close to him, in the lake, a sound like that of water plashing upon water, and he saw the widening circles caused by a trout which had just risen to a fly; and he said to the little trout he held in his hand:

"I won't keep you, poor thing! Perhaps that was a little comrade come to look for you, and so I'll send you back to him."

And saying this, he dropped the little trout into the lake.

Well, when the next evening came, again Enda was lying stretched outside the hut, and once more he heard the rustle in the sedge, and once more the otter came and flung the little trout almost into his hands.

Enda, more surprised than ever, did not know what to do. He saw that it was the same little trout the otter had brought him the night before, and he said:

"Well, I gave you a chance last night. I'll give you another, if only to see what will come of it."

And he dropped the trout into the lake; but no sooner had it touched the waters than it was changed into a beautiful, milk-white swan. And Enda could hardly believe his eyes, as he saw it sailing across the lake, until it was lost in the sedges growing by the shore.

All that night he lay awake, thinking of what he had seen, and as soon as the morning stood on the hill-tops, and cast its shafts of golden light across the lake, Enda rose and got into his curragh.

He rowed all round the shores, beating the sedges with his oar, in pursuit of the swan; but all in vain; he could not catch a glimpse of her white plumage anywhere. Day after day he rowed about the lake in search of her, and every evening he lay outside the hut watching the waters. At long last, one night, when the full moon, rising above the mountains, flooded the whole lake with light, he saw the swan coming swiftly towards him, shining brighter than the moonbeams. The swan came on until it was almost within a boat's length of the hut; and what should Enda hear but the swan speaking to him in his own language:

"Get into your curragh, Enda, and follow me," said she, and, saying this, she turned round and sailed away.

Enda jumped into the curragh, and soon the water, dripping from his oar, was flashing like diamonds in the moonlight. And he rowed after the swan, who glided on before him, until she came to where the shadows of the mountains lay deepest on the lake. Then the swan rested, and when Enda came up to her:

"Enda," said she, "I have brought you where none may hear what I wish to say to you. I am Mave, the daughter of the king of Erin. By the magic arts of my cruel stepmother I was changed into a trout, and cast into this lake a year and a day before the evening when you restored me to the waters the second time. If you had not done so the first night the otter brought me to you I should have been changed into a hooting owl; if you had not done so the second night, I should have been changed into a croaking raven. But, thanks to you, Enda, I am now a snow-white swan, and for one hour on the first night of every full moon the power of speech is and will be given to me as long as I remain a swan. And a swan I must always remain, unless you are willing to break the spell of enchantment that is over me; and you alone can break it."

"I'll do anything I can for you, O princess!" said Enda. "But how can I break the spell?"

"You can do so," said the swan, "only by pouring upon my plumage the perfumed water that fills the golden bowl that is in the inmost room of the palace of the fairy queen, beneath the lake."

"And how can I get that?" said Enda.

"Well," said the swan, "you must dive beneath the lake, and walk along its bed, until you come to where the lake dragon guards the entrance of the fairy queen's dominions."

"I can dive like a fish," said Enda; "but how can I walk beneath the waters?"

"You can do it easily enough," said the swan, "if you get the water-dress of Brian, one of the three sons of Turenn, and his helmet of transparent crystal, by the aid of which he was able to walk under the green salt sea."

"And where shall I find them?"

"They are in the water-palace of Angus of the Boyne," said the swan; "but you should set out at once, for if the spell be not broken before the moon is full again, it cannot be broken for a year and a day."

"I'll set out in the first ray of the morning," said Enda.

"May luck and joy go with you," said the swan. "And now the hours of silence are coming upon me, and I have only time to warn you that dangers you little dream of will lie before you in your quest for the golden cup."

"I am willing to face all dangers for your sake, O princess," said Enda.

"Blessings be upon you, Enda," said the swan, and she sailed away from the shadow out into the light across the lake to the sedgy banks. And Enda saw her no more.

He rowed his curragh home, and he lay on his bed without taking off his clothes. And as the first faint glimmer of the morning came slanting down the mountains, he stepped into his curragh and pulled across the lake, and took the road towards the water-palace of Angus of the Boyne.

When he reached the banks of the glancing river a little woman, dressed in red, was standing there before him.

"You are welcome, Enda," said she. "And glad am I to see the day that brings you here to help the winsome Princess Mave. And now wait a second, and the water-dress and crystal helmet will be ready for you."

And, having said this, the little woman plucked a handful of wild grasses, and she breathed upon them three times and then flung them on the river, and a dozen fairy nymphs came springing up through the water, bearing the water-dress and crystal helmet and a shining spear. And they laid them down upon the bank at Enda's feet, and then disappeared.

"Now, Enda," said the fairy woman, "take these; by the aid of the dress and the helmet you can walk beneath the waters. You will need the spear to enable you to meet the dangers that lie before you. But with that spear, if you only have courage, you can overcome everything and everyone that may attempt to bar your way."

Having said this, she bid good-bye to Enda, and stepping off the bank, she floated out upon the river as lightly as a red poppy leaf. And when she came to the middle of the stream she disappeared beneath the waters.

Enda took the helmet, dress, and spear, and it was not long until he came to the sedgy banks where his little boat was waiting for him. As he stepped into the curragh the moon was rising above the mountains. He rowed on until he came to the hut, and having moored the boat to the door, he put on the water-dress and the crystal helmet, and taking the spear in his hand, he leaped over the side of the curragh, and sank down and down until he touched the bottom. Then he walked along without minding where he was going, and the only light he had was the shimmering moonlight, which descended as faintly through the waters as if it came through muffled glass. He had not gone very far when he heard a horrible hissing, and straight before him he saw what he thought were two flaming coals. After a few more steps he found himself face to face with the dragon of the lake, the guardian of the palace of the fairy queen. Before he had time to raise his spear, the dragon had wound its coils around him, and he heard its horrible teeth crunching against the side of his crystal helmet, and he felt the pressure of its coils around his side, and the breath almost left his body; but the dragon, unable to pierce the helmet, unwound his coils, and soon Enda's hands were free, and before the dragon could attempt to seize him again, he drove his spear through one of its fiery eyes, and, writhing with pain, the hissing dragon darted through a cave behind him. Enda, gaining courage from the dragon's flight, marched on until he came to a door of dull brass set in the rocks. He tried to push it in before him, but he might as well have tried to push away the rocks. While he was wondering what he should do, he heard again the fierce hissing of the dragon, and saw the red glare of his fiery eye dimly in the water.

Lifting his spear and hastily turning round to meet the furious monster, Enda accidently touched the door with the point of the spear, and the door flew open. Enda passed through, and the door closed behind him with a grating sound, and he marched along through a rocky pass which led to a sandy plain.

As he stepped from the pass into the plain the sands began to move, as if they were alive. In a second a thousand hideous serpents, almost the colour of the sand, rose hissing up, and with their forked tongues made a horrible, poisonous hedge in front of him. For

a second he stood dismayed, but then, levelling his spear, he rushed against the hedge of serpents, and they, shooting poison at him, sank beneath the sand. But the poison did not harm him, because of his water-dress and crystal helmet.

When he had passed over the sandy plain, he had to climb a great steep, jagged rock. When he got to the top of the rock he saw spread out before him a stony waste without a tuft or blade of grass. At some distance in front of him he noticed a large dark object, which he took to be a rock, but on looking at it more closely he saw that it was a huge, misshapen, swollen mass, apparently alive. And it was growing bigger and bigger every moment. Enda stood amazed at the sight, and before he knew where he was the loathsome creature rose from the ground, and sprang upon him before he could use his spear, and, catching him in its horrid grasp, flung him back over the rocks on to the sandy plain. Enda was almost stunned, but the hissing of the serpents rising from the sand around him brought him to himself, and, jumping to his feet, once more he drove them down beneath the surface. He then approached the jagged rock, on the top of which he saw the filthy monster glaring at him with bloodshot eyes. Enda poised his spear and hurled it against his enemy. It entered between the monster's eyes, and from the wound the blood flowed down like a black torrent and dyed the plain, and the shrunken carcass slipped down the front of the rocks and disappeared beneath the sand. Enda once more ascended the rock, and without meeting or seeing anything he passed over the stony waste, and at last he came to a leafy wood. He had not gone far in the wood until he heard the sound of fairy music, and walking on he came upon a mossy glade, and there he found the fairies dancing around their queen. They were so small, and were all

so brightly dressed, that they looked like a mass of waving flowers; but when he was seen by them they vanished like a glorious dream, and no one remained before him but the fairy queen. The queen blushed at finding herself alone, but on stamping her little foot three times upon the ground, the frightened fairies all crept back again.

"You are welcome, Enda," said the queen. "My little subjects have been alarmed by your strange dress and crystal helmet. I pray you take them off; you do not need them here."

Enda did as he was bidden, and he laid down his water-dress and helmet on the grass, and the little fairies, seeing him in his proper shape, got over their fright, and, unrestrained by the presence of the queen, they ran tumbling over one another to try and get a good look at the crystal helmet.

"I know what you have come for, Enda," said the queen. "The golden cup you shall have tomorrow; but tonight you must share our feast, so follow me to the palace."

Having said this, the queen beckoned her pages to her, and, attended by them and followed by Enda, she went on through the wood. When they had left it behind them Enda saw on a green hill before him the snow-white palace of the fairy queen.

As the queen approached the steps that led up to the open door, a band of tiny fairies, dressed in rose-coloured silk, came out, carrying baskets of flowers, which they flung down on the steps to make a fragrant carpet for her. They were followed by a band of harpers dressed in yellow silken robes, who ranged themselves on each side of the steps and played their sweetest music as the queen ascended.

When the queen, followed by Enda, entered the palace, they passed through a crystal hall that led to a banquet-room. The room was lighted by a single star, large as a battle-shield. It was fixed against the wall above a diamond throne.

The queen seated herself upon the throne, and the pages, advancing towards her, and bending low, as they approached the steps, handed her a golden wand.

The queen waved the wand three times, and a table laden with all kinds of delicacies appeared upon the floor. Then she beckoned Enda to her, and when he stood beside her the fairy table was no higher than his knee.

"I am afraid I must make you smaller, Enda," said the queen, "or you will never be able to seat yourself at my fairy table."

And having said this, she touched Enda with the golden wand, and at once he became as small as her tallest page. Then she struck the steps of her throne, and all the nobles of her court, headed by her bards, took their places at the festive board.

The feast went on right merrily, and when the tiny jewelled drinking-cups were placed upon the table, the queen ordered the harpers to play.

And the little harpers struck the chords, and as Enda listened to the music it seemed to him as if he was being slowly lifted from his seat, and when the music ended the fairies vanished, the shining star went out, and Enda was in perfect darkness.

The air blew keenly in his face, and he knew not where he was. At last he saw a faint grey light, and soon this light grew broader and brighter, and as the shadows fled before it, he could hardly believe his eyes when he found himself in his curragh on the lake, and the moonlight streaming down from the mountain-tops.

For a moment he thought he must have been dreaming; but there in the boat before him were the crystal helmet, and the water-dress, and the gleaming spear, and the golden bowl of perfumed water that was to remove the spell of enchantment from the white swan of the lake, and sailing towards him from the sedgy bank came the snow-white swan; and when she touched the boat, Enda put out his hands and lifted her in, and then over her plumage he poured the perfumed water from the golden bowl, and the Princess Mave in all her maiden beauty stood before him.

"Take your oar, Enda," she said, "and row to the southern bank."

Enda seized his oar, and the curragh sped across the waters swifter than a swallow in its flight. When the boat touched the shore Enda jumped out, and lifted the princess on to the bank.

"Send your boat adrift, Enda," she said; "but first take out your shining spear; the water-dress and the crystal helmet will take care of themselves."

Enda took out the spear, and then pushed the boat from the bank. It sped on towards the hut in the middle of the lake; but before it had reached halfway six nymphs sprang up from the water and, seizing the helmet and dress, sank with them beneath the tide, and the boat went on until it pushed its prow against the steps of the little hut, where it remained.

Then Enda and the princess turned towards the south, and it was not long until they came to a deep forest that was folding up its shadows and spreading out its mossy glades before the glancing footsteps of the morning. They had not gone far through the forest when they heard the music of hounds and the cries of huntsmen, and crashing towards them through the low branches they saw a fierce wild boar. Enda, gently pushing the princess behind him, levelled his spear, and when the boar came close to him he drove it into his throat. The brute fell dead at his feet, and the dogs rushing up began to tear it to pieces. The princess fainted at the sight, and while Enda was endeavouring to restore her, the king of Erin, followed by his huntsmen, appeared, and when the king saw the princess he started in amazement, as he recognised the features of his daughter Mave.

At that moment the princess came to herself, and her father, lifting her tenderly in his arms, kissed her again and again.

"I have mourned you as dead, my darling," said he, "and now you are restored to me more lovely than ever. I would gladly have given up my throne for this. But say who is the champion who has brought you hither, and who has slain the wild boar we have hunted so many years in vain?"

The princess blushed like a rose as she said:

"His name is Enda, father; it is he has brought me back to you."

Then the king embraced Enda and said:

"Forgive me, Enda, for asking any questions about you before you have shared the hospitality of my court. My palace lies beyond the forest, and we shall reach it soon."

Then the king ordered his huntsman to sound the bugle-horn, and all his nobles galloped up in answer to it, and when they saw the Princess Mave they were so dazzled by her beauty that they scarcely gave a thought to the death of the wild boar.

"It is my daughter, Mave, come back to me," said the king.

And all the nobles lowered their lances, and bowed in homage to the lady.

"And there stands the champion who has brought her home," said the king, pointing to Enda.

The nobles looked at Enda, and bowed courteously, but in their hearts they were jealous of the champion, for they saw he was already a favourite of the king's.

Then the pages came up, leading milk-white steeds with golden bridles, and the king, ordering Enda to mount one of them, lifted Mave on to his own, and mounted behind her. The pages, carrying the boar's head on a hollow shield, preceded by the huntsmen sounding their horns, set out towards the palace, and the royal party followed them.

As the procession approached the palace crowds came rushing out to see the trophies of the chase, and through the snow-white door the queen, Mave's cruel stepmother, attended by her maids-of-honour and the royal bards, came forth to greet the king. But when she saw seated before him the Princess Mave, who she thought was at the bottom of the lake under a spell of enchantment, she uttered a loud cry, and fell senseless to the ground.

The king jumped from his horse, and rushing to the queen, lifted her up and carried her in his arms to her apartments, for he had no suspicion of the wickedness of which she had been guilty.

And the court leeches were summoned to attend her, but she died that very night, and it was not until a green mound, worthy of a queen of Erin, had been raised over her grave that the Princess Mave told her father of the wickedness of her stepmother. And when she told him the whole story of how Enda had broken the spell of enchantment, and of the dangers which he had faced for her sake, the king summoned an assembly of all his nobles, and seated on his throne, wearing his golden helmet, the bards upon his right hand and the Druids upon his left, and the nobles in ranks before him with gleaming helmets and flashing spears, he told them the story of the princess, and of the service which Enda had rendered to her.

"And now," said the king, "if the princess is willing to take her deliverer for her husband, I am willing that she shall be his bride; and if you, my subjects, Bards and Druids and Nobles and Chiefs of Erin, have anything to say against this union, speak. But first, Mave," said the king, as he drew the blushing princess to him, "speak, darling, as becomes the daughter of a king – speak in the presence of the nobles of Erin, and say if it is your wish to become Enda's bride."

The princess flung her white arms around her father's neck, as she murmured:

"Father, it was Enda brought me back to you, and before all the princes and nobles of Erin I am willing to be his bride."

And she buried her head upon the king's breast, and as he stroked her silken hair falling to her feet, the bards struck their golden harps, but the sound of the joyous music could hardly drown the murmurs of the jealous nobles.

When the music ceased the king beckoned Enda to him, and was about to place his hand in Mave's when a Druid, whose white beard almost touched the ground, and who had been a favourite of the dead stepmother, and hated Mave for her sake, stepped forward and said:

"O King of Erin, never yet has the daughter of a king been freely given in marriage to any save a battle champion; and that stripling there has never struck his spear against a warrior's shield."

A murmur of approbation rose from the jealous princes, and Congal, the bravest of them all, stepped out from the ranks, and said:

"The Druid speaks the truth, O king! That stripling has never faced a battle champion yet, and, speaking for all the nobles of your land, I challenge him to fight any one of us; and as he is young and unused to arms, we are willing that the youngest and least experienced amongst us should be set against him."

When Congal had spoken, the nobles, in approval of his words, struck their shields with their swords, and the brazen sound ascended to the skies.

The face of the princess, blushing a moment before like a rose, became as white as a lily; but the colour returned to her cheeks when she heard Enda's voice ringing loud and clear.

"It is true, O king!" said he, "that I have never used my spear in battle yet. The Prince Congal has challenged me to meet the youngest and least experienced of the chiefs of Erin. I have risked my life already for your daughter's sake. I would face death a thousand times for the chance of winning her for my bride; but I would scorn to claim her hand if I dared not meet the boldest battle champion of the nobles of Erin, and here before you, O king, and bards, Druids, and nobles, and chiefs of Erin, and here, in the presence of the Lady Mave, I challenge the boldest of them all."

The king's eyes flashed with joy as he listened to the brave words of Enda.

"It is well," said the king; "the contest shall take place tomorrow on the lawn outside our palace gates; but before our assembly dissolves I call on you, nobles and chiefs of Erin, to name your boldest champion."

Loud cries of "Congal! Congal!" answered the king's speech.

"Are you willing, Congal?" asked the king.

"Willing, O king!" answered Congal.

"It is well," said the king. "We shall all meet again tonight in our banquet-hall."

And the king, with the Princess Mave on his arm, attended by his bards and Druids, entered the palace, and the chiefs and nobles went their several ways.

At the feast that night the princess sat beside the king, and Enda beside the princess, and the bards and Druids, nobles and chiefs, took their places in due order. And the bards sang songs of love and battle, and never merrier hours were spent than those which passed away that night in the banquet-hall of Erin's king.

When the feast was over Enda retired to his apartment to spend the night dreaming of the Princess Mave, and Congal went to his quarters; but not to sleep or dream, for the Druid who had provoked the contest came to him bringing his golden wand, and all night long the Druid was weaving spells to charm the shield and spear and helmet of Congal, to make them invulnerable in the battle of the morrow.

But while Enda lay dreaming of the Princess Mave, the little fairy woman who gave him the water-dress, and crystal helmet, and shining spear on the banks of the Boyne, slid into his room, and she placed beside his couch a silver helmet and a silver shield. And she rubbed the helmet, and the shield, and the blue blade and haft of his spear with the juice of the red rowan berries, and she let a drop fall upon his face and hands, and then she slid out as silently as she came.

When the morning broke, Enda sprang from his couch, and he could hardly believe his eyes when he saw the silver shield and helmet. At the sight of them he longed for the hour of battle, and he watched with eager gaze the sun climbing the sky; and, after hours of suspense, he heard the trumpet's sound and the clangour of the hollow shields, struck by the hard-pointed spears.

Putting on the helmet, and fastening the shield upon his left arm, and taking the spear in his right hand, he stepped out bravely to the fight. The edge of the lawn before the palace gates was ringed by the princes, nobles, and chiefs of Erin. And the palace walls were thronged by all the beauties of the Court and all the noble ladies of the land. And on his throne, surrounded by his Druids, his brehons, and his bards, was the king of Erin, and at his feet sat the lovely Lady Mave.

As Enda stepped out upon the lawn, he saw Congal advancing from the ranks of the nobles, and the two champions approached each other until they met right in front of the throne.

Then both turned towards the throne, and bowed to the king and the Princess Mave; and then facing each other again, they retired a space, and when their spears were poised, ready for battle, the king gave the signal, which was answered by the clang of stricken shields, and Congal and Enda launched their gleaming spears. They flashed like lightning in the sunlit air, and in a second Congal's had broken against Enda's shield; but Enda's, piercing Congal's helmet, hurled him senseless on the plain.

The nobles and chiefs could hardly realize that in that single second their boldest champion was overthrown; but when they saw him stretched motionless on the grassy sward, from out their ranks six warriors advanced to where the chieftain lay, and sadly they bore him away upon their battle-shields, and Enda remained victor upon the field.

And then the king's voice rang out clear as the sound of a trumpet in the still morning:

"Bards and brehons, princes and nobles, and chiefs of Erin, Enda has proved himself a battle champion, and who amongst you now will dare gainsay his right to claim my daughter for his bride?"

And no answer came.

But when he summoned Enda to his throne, and placed the lady's hand in his, a cheer arose from the great assembly, that proved that jealousy was extinguished in all hearts, and that all believed that Enda was worthy of the winsome bride; and never since that day, although a thousand years have passed, was there in all the world a brighter and gayer wedding than the wedding of Enda and the Princess Mave.

The Enchanted Cave

A LONG, LONG TIME AGO, Prince Cuglas, master of the hounds to the high King of Erin, set out from Tara to the chase. As he was leaving the palace the light mists were drifting away from the hill-tops, and the rays of the morning sun were falling aslant on the grinan or sunny bower of the Princess Ailinn. Glancing towards it the prince doffed his plumed and jewelled hunting-cap, and the princess answered his salute by a wave of her little hand, that was as white as a wild rose in the hedges in June, and leaning from her bower, she watched the huntsman until his tossing plumes were hidden by the green waving branches of the woods.

The Princess Ailinn was over head and ears in love with Cuglas, and Cuglas was over head and ears in love with the Princess Ailinn, and he believed that never was summer morning half as bright, or as sweet, or as fair as she. The glimpse which he had just caught of her filled his heart with delight, and almost put all thought of hunting out of his head, when suddenly the tuneful cries of the hounds, answered by a hundred echoes from the groves, broke upon his ear.

The dogs had started a dappled deer that bounded away through the forest. The prince, spurring his gallant steed, pushed on in eager pursuit.

On through the forest sped the deer, through soft, green, secret ways and flowery dells, then out from the forest, up heathery hills, and over long stretches of moorland, and across brown rushing streams, sometimes in view of the hounds, sometimes lost to sight, but always ahead of them.

All day long the chase continued, and at last, when the sun was sinking, the dogs were close upon the panting deer, and the prince believed he was about to secure his game, when the deer suddenly disappeared through the mouth of a cave which opened before him. The dogs followed at his heels, and the prince endeavoured to rein in his steed, but the impetuous animal bore him on, and soon was clattering over the stony floor of the cave in perfect darkness. Cuglas could hear ahead of him the cries of the hounds growing fainter and fainter, as they increased the distance between them and him. Then the cries ceased altogether, and the only sound the prince heard was the noise of his horse's hoofs sounding in the hollow cave. Once more he endeavoured to check his career, but the reins broke in his hands, and in that instant the prince felt the horse had taken a plunge into a gulf, and was sinking down and down, as a stone cast from the summit of a cliff sinks down to the sea. At last the horse struck the ground again, and the prince was almost thrown out of his saddle, but he succeeded in regaining his seat. Then on through the darkness galloped the steed, and when he came into the light the prince's eyes were for some time unable to bear it. But when he got used to the brightness he saw he was galloping over a grassy plain, and in the distance he perceived the hounds rushing towards a wood faintly visible through a luminous summer haze. The prince galloped on, and as he approached the wood he

saw coming towards him a comely champion, wearing a shining brown cloak, fastened by a bright bronze spear-like brooch, and bearing a white hazel wand in one hand, and a single-edged sword with a hilt made from the tooth of a sea-horse in the other; and the prince knew by the dress of the champion, and by his wand and sword, that he was a royal herald. As the herald came close to him the prince's steed stopped of his own accord.

"You are welcome, Cuglas," said the herald, "and I have been sent by the Princess Crede to greet you and to lead you to her court, where you have been so long expected."

"I know not how this may be," said Cuglas.

"How it has come about I shall tell you as we go along," said the herald. "The Princess Crede is the Queen of the Floating Island. And it chanced, once upon a day, when she was visiting her fairy kinsmen, who dwell in one of the pleasant hills that lie near Tara, she saw you with the high king and princes and nobles of Erin following the chase. And seeing you her heart went out to you, and wishing to bring you to her court, she sent one of her nymphs, in the form of a deer, to lure you on through the cave, which is the entrance to this land."

"I am deeply honoured by the preference shown me by the princess," said Cuglas, "but I may not tarry in her court; for above in Erin there is the Lady Ailinn, the loveliest of all the ladies who grace the royal palace, and before the princess and chiefs of Erin she has promised to be my bride."

"Of that I know not," said the herald; "but a true champion, like you, cannot, I know, refuse to come with me to the court of the Princess Crede."

As the herald had said these words the prince and he were on the verge of the wood, and they entered upon a mossy pathway that broadened out as they advanced until it was as wide as one of the great roads of Erin. Before they had gone very far the prince heard the tinkling of silver bells in the distance, and almost as soon as he heard them he saw coming up towards him a troop of warriors on coal black steeds. All the warriors wore helmets of shining silver, and cloaks of blue silk. And on the horses' breasts were crescents of silver, on which were hung tiny silver bells, shaking out music with the motion of the horses. As the prince approached the champions they lowered their spears, and dividing in two lines the prince and the herald passed between the ranks, and the champions, forming again, followed on behind the prince.

At last they passed through the wood, and they found themselves on a green plain, speckled with flowers, and they had not gone far when the prince saw coming towards him a hundred champions on snow-white steeds, and around the breasts of the steeds were crescents of gold, from which were hanging little golden bells. The warriors all wore golden helmets, and the shafts of their shining spears were of gold, and golden sandals on their feet, and yellow silken mantles fell down over their shoulders. And when the prince came near them they lowered their lances, and then they turned their horses' heads around and marched before him. And it was not long until above the pleasant jingle of the bells the prince heard the measured strains of music, and he saw coming towards him a band of harpers, dressed in green and gold, and when the harpers had saluted the prince they marched in front of the cavalcade, playing all the time, and it was not long until they came to a stream that ran like a blue riband around the foot of a green hill, on the top of which was a sparkling palace; the stream was crossed by a golden bridge, so narrow that the horsemen had to go two-by-two. The herald asked the prince to halt and to allow all the champions to go before him; and the cavalcade ascended the hill, the sunlight brightly glancing on helmet and on lance, and when it reached the palace the horsemen filed around the walls.

When at length the prince and herald crossed the bridge and began to climb the hill, the prince thought he felt the ground moving under them, and on looking back he could see no sign of the golden bridge, and the blue stream had already become as wide as a great river, and was becoming wider every second.

"You are on the floating island now," said the herald, "and before you is the palace of the Princess Crede."

At that moment the queen came out through the palace door, and the prince was so dazzled by her beauty, that only for the golden bracelet he wore upon his right arm, under the sleeve of his silken tunic, he might almost have forgotten the Princess Ailinn. This bracelet was made by the dwarfs who dwell in the heart of the Scandinavian Mountains, and was sent with other costly presents by the King of Scandinavia to the King of Erin, and he gave it to the princess, and it was the virtue of this bracelet, that whoever was wearing it could not forget the person who gave it to him, and it could never be loosened from the arm by any art or magic spell; but if the wearer, even for a single moment, liked anyone better than the person who gave it to him, that very moment the bracelet fell off from the arm and could never again be fastened on. And when the princess promised her hand in marriage to the Prince Cuglas, she closed the bracelet on his arm.

The fairy queen knew nothing about the bracelet, and she hoped that before the prince was long in the floating island he would forget all about the princess.

"You are welcome, Cuglas," said the queen, as she held out her hand, and, Cuglas having thanked her for her welcome, they entered the palace together.

"You must be weary after your long journey," said the queen. "My page will lead you to your apartments, where a bath of the cool blue waters of the lake has been made ready for you, and when you have taken your bath the pages will lead you to the banquet hall, where the feast is spread."

At the feast the prince was seated beside the queen, and she talked to him of all the pleasures that were in store for him in fairyland, where pain, and sickness, and sorrow, and old age, are unknown, and where every rosy hour that flies is brighter than the one that has fled before it. And when the feast was ended the queen opened the dance with the prince, and it was not until the moon was high above the floating island that the prince retired to rest.

He was so tired after his journey and the dancing that he fell into a sound sleep. When he awoke the next morning the sun was shining brightly, and he heard outside the palace the jingle of bells and the music of baying hounds, and his heart was stirred by memories of the many pleasant days on which he had led the chase over the plains and through the green woods of Tara.

He looked out through the window, and he saw all the fairy champions mounted on their steeds ready for the chase, and at their head the fairy queen. And at that moment the pages came to say the queen wished to know if he would join them, and the prince went out and found his steed ready saddled and bridled, and they spent the day hunting in the forest that stretched away for miles behind the palace, and the night in feasting and dancing.

When the prince awoke the following morning he was summoned by the pages to the presence of the queen. The prince found the queen on the lawn outside the palace surrounded by her court.

"We shall go on the lake today, Cuglas," said the queen, and taking his arm she led him along the water's edge, all the courtiers following.

When she was close to the water she waved her wand, and in a second a thousand boats, shining like glass, shot up from beneath the lake and set their bows against the bank. The queen and Cuglas stepped into one, and when they were seated two fairy harpers took their places in the prow. All the other boats were soon thronged by fairies, and then the queen waved her wand again, and an awning of purple silk rose over the boat, and silken awning of various colours over the others, and the royal boat moved off from the bank followed by all the rest, and in every boat sat a harper with a golden harp, and when the queen waved her wand for the third time, the harpers struck the trembling chords, and to the sound of the delightful music the boats glided over the sunlit lake. And on they went until they approached the mouth of a gentle river sliding down between banks clad with trees. Up the river, close to the bank and under the drooping trees, they sailed, and when they came to a bend in the river, from which the lake could be no longer seen, they pushed their prows in against the bank, and the queen and Cuglas, and all the party, left the boats and went on under the trees until they came to a mossy glade.

Then the queen waved her wand, and silken couches were spread under the trees, and she and Cuglas sat on one apart from the others, and the courtiers took their places in proper order.

And the queen waved her wand again, and wind shook the trees above them, and the most luscious fruit that was ever tasted fell down into their hands; and when the feast was over there was dancing in the glades to the music of the harps, and when they were tired dancing they set out for the boats, and the moon was rising above the trees as they sailed away over the lake, and it was not long until they reached the bank below the fairy palace.

Well, between hunting in the forest, and sailing over the lake, and dancing in the greenwood glade and in the banquet hall, the days passed, but all the time the prince was thinking of the Princess Ailinn, and one moonlit night, when he was lying awake on his couch thinking of her, a shadow was suddenly cast on the floor.

The prince looked towards the window, and what should he see sitting on the sill outside but a little woman tapping the pane with a golden bodkin.

The prince jumped from his couch and opened the window, and the little woman floated on the moonbeams into the room and sat down on the floor.

"You are thinking of the Princess Ailinn," said the little woman.

"I never think of anyone else," said the prince.

"I know that," said the little woman, "and it's because of your love for each other, and because her mother was a friend to me in the days gone by, that I have come here to try and help you; but there is not much time for talking, the night advances. At the bank below a boat awaits you. Step into it and it will lead you to the mainland, and when you reach it you will find before you a path that will take you to the green fields of Erin and the plains of Tara. I know you will have to face danger. I know not what kind of danger; but whatever it may be do not draw your sword before you tread upon the mainland, for if you do you shall never reach it, and the boat will come back again to the floating island; and now go and may luck go with you;" and saying this the little woman climbed up the moonbeams and disappeared.

The prince left the palace and descended to the lake, and there before him he saw a glistening boat; he stepped into it, and the boat went on and on beneath the moon, and at last he saw the mainland, and he could trace a winding pathway going away from the shore. The sight filled his heart with joy, but suddenly the milk-white moonshine died away, and looking up to the sky he saw the moon turning fiery red, and the waters of the lake, shining like silver a moment before, took a blood-red hue, and a wind arose that stirred the waters, and they leaped up against the little boat, tossing it from side to side. While Cuglas was wondering at the change, he heard a strange, unearthly noise ahead of him, and a bristling monster, lifting its claws above the water, in a moment was beside the boat and stuck one of his claws in the left arm of the prince, and pierced the flesh to the bone. Maddened by the pain the prince drew his sword and chopped off the monster's claw. The monster disappeared beneath the lake, and, as it did so, the colour of the water changed, and the silver moonlight shone down from the sky again, but the boat no longer went on towards the mainland, but sped back towards the floating island, while forth from the island came a fleet of fairy boats to meet it, led by the shallop of the fairy queen. The queen greeted the prince as if she knew not of his attempted flight, and to the music of the harps the fleet returned to the palace.

The next day passed and the night came, and again the prince was lying on the couch, thinking of the Princess Ailinn, and again he saw the shadow on the floor and heard the tapping against the window.

And when he opened it the little woman slid into the room.

"You failed last night," she said, "but I come to give you another chance. Tomorrow the queen must set out on a visit to her fairy kinsmen, who dwell in the green hill near the plain of Tara; she cannot take you with her, for if your feet once touched the green grass that grows in the fruitful fields of Erin, she could never bring you back again. And so, when you find she has left the palace, go at once into the banquet hall and look behind the throne, and you will see a small door let down into the ground. Pull this up and descend the steps which you will see. Where they lead to I cannot tell. What dangers may be before you I do not know; but this I know, if you accept anything, no matter what it is, from anyone you may meet on your way, you shall not set foot on the soil of Erin."

And having said this the little woman, rising from the floor, floated out through the window.

The prince returned to his couch, and the next morning, as soon as he heard the queen had left the palace, he hastened to the banquet hall. He discovered the door and descended the steps, and he found himself in a gloomy and lonesome valley. Jagged mountains, black as night, rose on either side, and huge rocks seemed ready to topple down upon him at every step. Through broken clouds a watery moon shed a faint, fitful light, that came and went as the clouds, driven by a moaning wind, passed over the valley.

Cuglas, nothing daunted, pushed on boldly until a bank of cloud shut out completely the struggling moon, and closing over the valley covered it like a pall, leaving him in perfect darkness. At the same moment the moaning wind died away, and with it died away all sound. The darkness and the death-like silence sent an icy chill to the heart of Cuglas. He held his hand close to his eyes, but he saw it not. He shouted that he might hear the sound of his own voice, but he heard it not. He stamped his foot on the rocky ground, but no sound was returned to him. He rattled his sword in its brazen scabbard, but it gave no answer back to him. His heart grew colder and colder, when suddenly the cloud above him was rent in a dozen places, and lightning flashed through the valley, and the thunder rolled over the echoing mountains. In the lurid glare of the lightning Cuglas saw a hundred ghostly forms sweeping towards him, uttering as they came nearer and nearer shrieks so terrible that the silence of death could more easily be borne. Cuglas turned to escape, but they hemmed him round, and pressed their clammy hands upon his face.

With a yell of horror he drew his sword and slashed about him, and that very moment the forms vanished, the thunder ceased, the dark cloud passed, and the sun shone out as bright as on a summer day, and then Cuglas knew the forms he had seen were those of the wild people of the glen.

With renewed courage he pursued his way through the valley, and after three or four windings it took him out upon a sandy desert. He had no sooner set foot upon the desert than he heard behind him a crashing sound louder than thunder. He looked around, and he saw that the walls of mountain through which he had just passed had fallen into the valley, and filled it up so that he could no longer tell where it had been.

The sun was beating fiercely on the desert, and the sands were almost as hot as burning cinders; and as Cuglas advanced over them his body became dried up, and his tongue clove to the roof of his mouth, and when his thirst was at its height a fountain of sparkling water sprang up in the burning plain a few paces in front of him; but when he came up quite close to it and stretched out his parched hands to cool them in the limped waters, the fountain vanished as suddenly as it appeared. With great pain, and almost choking with heat and thirst, he struggled on, and again the fountain sprang up in front of him and moved before him, almost within his reach. At last he came to the end of the desert, and he saw a green hill up which a pathway climbed; but as he came to the foot of the hill, there, sitting right in his way, was a beautiful fairy holding out towards him a crystal cup, over the rim of which flowed water as clear as crystal. Unable to resist the temptation, the prince seized the cold, bright goblet, and drank the water. When he did so his thirst vanished, but the fairy, and the green hill, and the burning desert disappeared, and he was standing in the forest behind the palace of the fairy queen.

That evening the queen returned, and at the feast she talked as gaily to the prince as if she knew not of his attempt to leave the Floating Island, and the prince spoke as gaily as he could to her, although in his heart there was sadness when he remembered that if he had only dashed away the crystal cup, he would be at that moment in the royal banquet hall of Tara, sitting beside the Princess Ailinn.

And he thought the feast would never end; but it was over at last, and the prince returned to his apartments. And that night, as he lay on his couch, he kept his eyes fixed upon the window; but hours passed, and there was no sign of anyone. At long last, and when he had given up all hope of seeing her, he heard a tapping at the window, and he got up and opened it, and the little woman came in.

"You failed again today," said she – "failed just at the very moment when you were about to step on the green hills of Erin. I can give you only one chance more. It will be your last. The queen will go hunting in the morning. Join the hunt, and when you are separated from the rest of the party in the wood throw your reins upon your horse's neck and he will lead you to the edge of the lake. Then cast this golden bodkin into the lake in the direction of the mainland, and a golden bridge will be thrown across, over which you can pass safely to the fields of Erin; but take care and do not draw your sword, for if you do your steed will bear you back again to the Floating Island, and here you must remain for ever." Then handing the bodkin to the prince, and saying goodbye, the little woman disappeared.

The next morning the queen and the prince and all the court went out to hunt, and a fleet white deer started out before them, and the royal party pressed after him in pursuit. The prince's steed outstripped the others, and when he was alone the prince flung the reins upon his horse's neck, and before long he came to the edge of the lake.

Then the prince cast the bodkin on to the water, and a golden bridge was thrown across to the mainland, and the horse galloped on to it, and when the prince was more than half-way he saw riding towards him a champion wearing a silver helmet, and carrying on his left arm a silver shield, and holding in his right hand a gleaming sword. As he came nearer he struck his shield with his sword and challenged the prince to battle. The prince's sword almost leaped out of its scabbard at the martial sound, and, like a true knight of Tara, he dashed against his foe, and swinging his sword above his head, with one blow he clove the silver helmet, and the strange warrior reeled from his horse and fell upon the golden bridge. The prince, content with this achievement, spurred his horse to pass the fallen champion, but the horse refused to stir, and the bridge broke in two almost at his feet, and the part of it between him and the mainland disappeared beneath the lake, carrying with it the horse and the body of the champion, and before the prince could recover from his surprise, his steed wheeled round and was galloping back, and when he reached the land he rushed through the forest, and the prince was not able to pull him up until he came to the palace door.

All that night the prince lay awake on his couch with his eyes fixed upon the window, but no shadow fell upon the floor, and there was no tapping at the pane, and with a heavy heart he joined the hunting party in the morning. And day followed day, and his heart was sadder and sadder, and found no pleasure in the joys and delights of fairyland. And when all in the palace were at rest he used to roam through the forest, always thinking of the Princess Ailinn, and hoping against hope that the little woman would come again to him, but at last he began to despair of ever seeing her. It chanced one night he rambled so far that he found himself on the verge of the lake, at the very spot from which the golden bridge had been thrown across the waters, and as he gazed wistfully upon them a boat shot up and came swiftly to the bank, and who should he see sitting in the stern but the little woman.

"Ah, Cuglas, Cuglas," she said, "I gave you three chances, and you failed in all of them."

"I should have borne the pain inflicted by the monster's claw," said Cuglas. "I should have borne the thirst on the sandy desert, and dashed the crystal cup untasted from the fairy's hand; but I could never have faced the nobles and chiefs of Erin if I had refused to meet the challenge of the battle champion on the golden bridge."

"And you would have been no true knight of Erin, and you would not have been worthy of the wee girl who loves you, the bonny Princess Ailinn, if you had refused to meet it," said the little woman; "but for all that you can never return to the fair hills of Erin. But cheer up, Cuglas, there are mossy ways and forest paths and nestling bowers in fairyland. Lonely they are, I know, in your eyes now," said the little woman; "but maybe," she added, with a laugh as musical as the ripple on a streamlet when summer is in the air, "maybe you won't always think them so lonely."

"You think I'll forget Ailinn for the fairy queen," said Cuglas, with a sigh.

"I don't think anything of the kind," said she.

"Then what do you mean?" said the prince.

"Oh, I mean what I mean," said the little woman. "But I can't stop here all night talking to you: and, indeed, it is in your bed you ought to be yourself. So now good night; and I have no more to say, except that perhaps, if you happen to be here this night week at this very hour, when the moon will be on the waters, you will see –. But no matter what you will see," said she; "I must be off."

And before the prince could say another word the boat sped away from the bank, and he was alone. He went back to the palace, and he fell asleep that night only to dream of the Princess Ailinn.

As for the princess, she was pining away in the palace of Tara, the colour had fled from her cheeks, and her eyes, which had been once so bright they would have lighted darkness like a star, lost nearly all their lustre, and the king's leeches could do nothing for her, and at last they gave up all hope, and the king and queen of Erin and the ladies of the court watched her couch by night and by day sadly waiting for her last hour.

At length one day, when the sun was shining brightly over Tara's plain, and its light, softened by the intervening curtains, was falling in the sick chamber, the royal watchers noticed a sweet change coming over the face of the princess; the bloom of love and youth were flushing on her cheeks, and from her eyes shone out the old, soft, tender light, and they began to hope she was about to be restored to them, when suddenly the room was in darkness as if the night had swept across the sky, and blotted out the sun. Then they heard the sound of fairy music, and over the couch where the princess lay they beheld a gleam of golden light, but only for a moment; and again there was perfect darkness, and the fairy music ceased. Then, as suddenly as it came the darkness vanished, the softened sunlight once more filled the chamber, and rested upon the couch; but the couch was empty, and the royal watchers, looking at each other, said in whispers: "The fairies have carried away the Princess Ailinn to fairyland."

Well, that very day the prince roamed by himself through the forest, counting the hours until the day would fade in the sky and the moon come climbing up, and at last, when it was shining full above the waters, he went down to the verge of the lake, and he looked out over the gleaming surface watching for the vision promised by the little woman. But he could see nothing, and was about to turn away when he heard the faint sound of fairy music. He listened and listened, and the sound came nearer and clearer, and away in the distance, like drops of glistening water breaking the level of the lake, he saw a fleet of fairy boats, and he thought it was the fairy queen sailing in the moonlight. And it was the fairy queen, and soon he was able to recognise the royal shallop leading the others, and as it came close to the bank he saw the little woman sitting in the prow between the little harpers, and at the stern was the fairy queen, and by her side the lady of his heart, the Princess Ailinn. In a second the boat was against the bank, and the princess in his arms. And he kissed her again and again.

"And have you never a kiss for me," said the little woman, tapping his hand with the little gold bodkin.

"A kiss and a dozen," said Cuglas, as he caught the little fairy up in his arms.

"Oh, fie, Cuglas," said the queen.

"Oh, the princess isn't one bit jealous," said the little woman. "Are you, Ailinn?"

"Indeed I am not," said Ailinn.

"And you should not be," said the fairy queen, "for never lady yet had truer knight than Cuglas. I loved him, and I love him dearly. I lured him here hoping that in the delights of fairyland he might forget you. It was all in vain. I know now that there is one thing no fairy power above or below the stars, or beneath the waters, can ever subdue, and that is love. And here together forever shall you and Cuglas dwell, where old age shall never come upon you, and where pain or sorrow or sickness are unknown."

And Cuglas never returned to the fair hills of Erin, and ages passed away since the morning he followed the hounds into the fatal cave, but his story was remembered by the firesides, and sometimes, even yet, the herdboy watching his cattle in the fields hears the tuneful cry of hounds, and follows it till it leads him to a darksome cave, and as fearfully he listens to the sound becoming fainter and fainter he hears the clatter of hoofs over the stony floor, and to this day the cave bears the name of the prince who entered it never to return.

The Little White Cat

A LONG, LONG TIME AGO, in a valley far away, the giant Trencoss lived in a great castle, surrounded by trees that were always green. The castle had a hundred doors, and every door was guarded by a huge, shaggy hound, with tongue of fire and claws of iron, who tore to pieces anyone who went to the castle without the giant's leave. Trencoss had made war on the King of the Torrents, and, having killed the king, and slain his people, and burned his palace, he carried off his only daughter, the Princess Eileen, to the castle in the valley. Here he provided her with beautiful rooms, and appointed a hundred dwarfs, dressed in blue and yellow satin, to wait upon her, and harpers to play sweet music for her, and he gave her diamonds without number, brighter than the sun; but he would not allow her to go outside the castle, and told her if she went one step beyond its doors, the hounds, with tongues of fire and claws of iron, would tear her to pieces. A week after her arrival, war broke out between the giant and the king of the islands, and before he set out for battle, the giant sent for the princess, and informed her that on his return he would make her his wife. When the princess heard this she began to cry, for she would rather die than marry the giant who had slain her father.

"Crying will only spoil your bright eyes, my little princess," said Trencoss, "and you will have to marry me whether you like it or no."

He then bade her go back to her room, and he ordered the dwarfs to give her everything she asked for while he was away, and the harpers to play the sweetest music for her. When the princess gained her room she cried as if her heart would break. The long day passed slowly, and the night came, but brought no sleep to Eileen, and in the grey light of the morning she rose and opened the window, and looked about in every direction to see if there were any chance of escape. But the window was ever so high above the ground, and below were the hungry and ever watchful hounds. With a heavy heart she was about to close the window when she thought she saw the branches of the tree that was nearest to it moving. She looked again, and she saw a little white cat creeping along one of the branches.

"Mew!" cried the cat.

"Poor little pussy," said the princess. "Come to me, pussy."

"Stand back from the window," said the cat, "and I will."

The princess stepped back, and the little white cat jumped into the room. The princess took the little cat on her lap and stroked him with her hand, and the cat raised up its back and began to purr.

"Where do you come from, and what is your name?" asked the princess.

"No matter where I come from or what's my name," said the cat, "I am a friend of yours, and I come to help you."

"I never wanted help worse," said the princess.

"I know that," said the cat; "and now listen to me. When the giant comes back from battle and asks you to marry him, say to him you will marry him."

"But I will never marry him," said the princess.

"Do what I tell you," said the cat. "When he asks you to marry him, say to him you will if his dwarfs will wind for you three balls from the fairy dew that lies on the bushes on a misty morning as big as these," said the cat, putting his right forefoot into his ear and taking out three balls – one yellow, one red, and one blue.

"They are very small," said the princess. "They are not much bigger than peas, and the dwarfs will not be long at their work."

"Won't they," said the cat. "It will take them a month and a day to make one, so that it will take three months and three days before the balls are wound; but the giant, like you, will think they can be made in a few days, and so he will readily promise to do what you ask. He will soon find out his mistake, but he will keep his word, and will not press you to marry him until the balls are wound."

"When will the giant come back?" asked Eileen.

"He will return tomorrow afternoon," said the cat.

"Will you stay with me until then?" said the princess. "I am very lonely."

"I cannot stay," said the cat. "I have to go away to my palace on the island on which no man ever placed his foot, and where no man but one shall ever come."

"And where is that island?" asked the princess, "and who is the man?"

"The island is in the far-off seas where vessel never sailed; the man you will see before many days are over; and if all goes well, he will one day slay the giant Trencoss, and free you from his power."

"Ah!" sighed the princess, "that can never be, for no weapon can wound the hundred hounds that guard the castle, and no sword can kill the giant Trencoss."

"There is a sword that will kill him," said the cat; "but I must go now. Remember what you are to say to the giant when he comes home, and every morning watch the tree on which you saw me, and if you see in the branches anyone you like better than yourself," said the cat, winking at the princess, "throw him these three balls and leave the rest to me; but take care not to speak a single word to him, for if you do all will be lost."

"Shall I ever see you again?" asked the princess.

"Time will tell," answered the cat, and, without saying so much as goodbye, he jumped through the window on to the tree, and in a second was out of sight.

The morrow afternoon came, and the giant Trencoss returned from battle. Eileen knew of his coming by the furious barking of the hounds, and her heart sank, for she knew that in a few moments she would be summoned to his presence. Indeed, he had hardly entered the castle when he sent for her, and told her to get ready for the wedding. The princess tried to look cheerful, as she answered:

"I will be ready as soon as you wish; but you must first promise me something."

"Ask anything you like, little princess," said Trencoss.

"Well, then," said Eileen, "before I marry you, you must make your dwarfs wind three balls as big as these from the fairy dew that lies on the bushes on a misty morning in summer."

"Is that all?" said Trencoss, laughing. "I shall give the dwarfs orders at once, and by this time tomorrow the balls will be wound, and our wedding can take place in the evening."

"And will you leave me to myself until then?"

"I will," said Trencoss.

"On your honour as a giant?" said Eileen.

"On my honour as a giant," replied Trencoss.

The princess returned to her rooms, and the giant summoned all his dwarfs, and he ordered them to go forth in the dawning of the morn and to gather all the fairy dew lying on the bushes, and to wind three balls – one yellow, one red, and one blue. The next morning, and the next, and the next, the dwarfs went out into the fields and searched all the hedgerows, but they could gather only as much fairy dew as would make a thread as long as a wee girl's eyelash; and so they had to go out morning after morning, and the giant fumed and threatened, but all to no purpose. He was very angry with the princess, and he was vexed with himself that she was so much cleverer than he was, and, moreover, he saw now that the wedding could not take place as soon as he expected.

When the little white cat went away from the castle he ran as fast as he could up hill and down dale, and never stopped until he came to the Prince of the Silver River. The prince was alone, and very sad and sorrowful he was, for he was thinking of the Princess Eileen, and wondering where she could be.

"Mew," said the cat, as he sprang softly into the room; but the prince did not heed him. "Mew," again said the cat; but again the prince did not heed him. "Mew," said the cat the third time, and he jumped up on the prince's knee.

"Where do you come from, and what do you want?" asked the prince.

"I come from where you would like to be," said the cat.

"And where is that?" said the prince.

"Oh, where is that, indeed! As if I didn't know what you are thinking of, and of whom you are thinking," said the cat; "and it would be far better for you to try and save her."

"I would give my life a thousand times over for her," said the prince.

"For whom?" said the cat, with a wink. "I named no name, your highness," said he.

"You know very well who she is," said the prince, "if you knew what I was thinking of; but do you know where she is?"

"She is in danger," said the cat. "She is in the castle of the giant Trencoss, in the valley beyond the mountains."

"I will set out there at once," said the prince "and I will challenge the giant to battle, and will slay him."

"Easier said than done," said the cat. "There is no sword made by the hands of man can kill him, and even if you could kill him, his hundred hounds, with tongues of fire and claws of iron, would tear you to pieces."

"Then, what am I to do?" asked the prince.

"Be said by me," said the cat. "Go to the wood that surrounds the giant's castle, and climb the high tree that's nearest to the window that looks towards the sunset, and shake the branches, and you will see what you will see. Then hold out your hat with the silver plumes, and three balls – one yellow, one red, and one blue – will be thrown into it. And then come back here as fast as you can; but speak no word, for if you utter a single word the hounds will hear you, and you shall be torn to pieces."

Well, the prince set off at once, and after two days' journey he came to the wood around the castle, and he climbed the tree that was nearest to the window that looked towards the sunset, and he shook the branches. As soon as he did so, the window opened and he saw the Princess Eileen, looking lovelier than ever. He was going to call out her name, but she placed her fingers on her lips, and he remembered what the cat had told him, that he was to speak no word. In silence he held out the hat with the silver plumes, and the princess threw into it the three balls, one after another, and, blowing him a kiss, she shut the window. And well it was she did so, for at that very moment she heard the voice of the giant, who was coming back from hunting.

The prince waited until the giant had entered the castle before he descended the tree. He set off as fast as he could. He went up hill and down dale, and never stopped until he arrived at his own palace, and there waiting for him was the little white cat.

"Have you brought the three balls?" said he.

"I have," said the prince.

"Then follow me," said the cat.

On they went until they left the palace far behind and came to the edge of the sea.

"Now," said the cat, "unravel a thread of the red ball, hold the thread in your right hand, drop the ball into the water, and you shall see what you shall see."

The prince did as he was told, and the ball floated out to sea, unravelling as it went, and it went on until it was out of sight.

"Pull now," said the cat.

The prince pulled, and, as he did, he saw far away something on the sea shining like silver. It came nearer and nearer, and he saw it was a little silver boat. At last it touched the strand.

"Now," said the cat, "step into this boat and it will bear you to the palace on the island on which no man has ever placed his foot – the island in the unknown seas that were never sailed by vessels made of human hands. In that palace there is a sword with a diamond hilt, and by that sword alone the giant Trencoss can be killed. There also are a hundred cakes, and it is only on eating these the hundred hounds can die. But mind what I say to you: if you eat or drink until you reach the palace of the little cat in the island in the unknown seas, you will forget the Princess Eileen."

"I will forget myself first," said the prince, as he stepped into the silver boat, which floated away so quickly that it was soon out of sight of land.

The day passed and the night fell, and the stars shone down upon the waters, but the boat never stopped. On she went for two whole days and nights, and on the third morning the prince saw an island in the distance, and very glad he was; for he thought it was his journey's end, and he was almost fainting with thirst and hunger. But the day passed and the island was still before him.

At long last, on the following day, he saw by the first light of the morning that he was quite close to it, and that trees laden with fruit of every kind were bending down over the water. The boat sailed round and round the island, going closer and closer every round, until, at last, the drooping branches almost touched it. The sight of the fruit within his reach made the prince hungrier and thirstier than he was before, and forgetting his promise to the little cat – not to eat anything until he entered the palace in the unknown seas – he caught one of the branches, and, in a moment, was in the tree eating the delicious fruit. While he was doing so the boat floated out to sea and soon was lost to sight; but the prince, having eaten, forgot all about it, and, worse still, forgot all about the princess in the giant's castle. When he had eaten enough he descended the tree, and, turning his back on the sea, set out straight before him. He had not gone far when he heard the sound of music, and soon after he saw a number of maidens playing on silver harps coming towards him. When they saw him they ceased playing, and cried out:

"Welcome! Welcome! Prince of the Silver River, welcome to the island of fruits and flowers. Our king and queen saw you coming over the sea, and they sent us to bring you to the palace."

The prince went with them, and at the palace gates the king and queen and their daughter Kathleen received him, and gave him welcome. He hardly saw the king and queen, for his eyes were fixed on the princess Kathleen, who looked more beautiful than a flower. He thought he had never seen anyone so lovely, for, of course, he had forgotten all about poor Eileen pining away in her castle prison in the lonely valley. When the king and queen had given welcome to the prince a great feast was spread, and all the lords and ladies of the court sat down to it, and the prince sat between the queen and the princess Kathleen, and long before the feast was finished he was over head and ears in love with her. When the feast was ended the queen ordered the ballroom to be made ready, and when night fell the dancing began, and was kept up until the morning star, and the prince danced all night with the princess, falling deeper and deeper in love with her every minute. Between dancing by night and feasting by day weeks went by. All the time poor Eileen in the giant's castle was counting the hours, and all this time the dwarfs were winding the balls, and a ball and a half were already wound. At last the prince asked the king and queen for their daughter in marriage, and they were delighted to be able to say yes, and the day was fixed for the wedding. But on the evening before the day on which it was to take place the prince was in his room, getting ready for a dance, when he felt something rubbing against his leg, and, looking down, who should he see but the little white cat. At the sight of him the prince remembered everything, and sad and sorry he was when he thought of Eileen watching and waiting and counting the days until he returned to save her. But he was very fond of the princess Kathleen, and so he did not know what to do.

"You can't do anything tonight," said the cat, for he knew what the prince was thinking of, "but when morning comes go down to the sea, and look not to the right or the left, and let no living thing touch you, for if you do you shall never leave the island. Drop the second ball into the water, as you did the first, and when the boat comes step in at once. Then you may look behind you, and you shall see what you shall see, and you'll know which you love best, the Princess Eileen or the Princess Kathleen, and you can either go or stay."

The prince didn't sleep a wink that night, and at the first glimpse of the morning he stole from the palace. When he reached the sea he threw out the ball, and when it had floated out of sight, he saw the little boat sparkling on the horizon like a newly-risen star. The prince had scarcely passed through the palace doors when he was missed, and the king and queen and the princess, and all the lords and ladies of the court, went in search of him, taking the quickest way to the sea. While the maidens with the silver harps played sweetest music, the princess, whose voice was sweeter than any music, called on the prince by his name, and so moved his heart that he was about to look behind, when he remembered how the cat had told him he should not do so until he was in the boat. Just as it touched the shore the princess put out her hand and almost caught the prince's arm, but he stepped into the boat in time to save himself, and it sped away like a receding wave. A loud scream caused the prince to look round suddenly, and when he did he saw no sign of king or queen, or princess, or lords or ladies, but only big green serpents, with red eyes and tongues, that hissed out fire and poison as they writhed in a hundred horrible coils.

The prince, having escaped from the enchanted island, sailed away for three days and three nights, and every night he hoped the coming morning would show him the island he was in search of. He was faint with hunger and beginning to despair, when on the fourth morning he saw in the distance an island that, in the first rays of the sun, gleamed like fire. On coming closer to it he saw that it was clad with trees, so covered with bright red berries that hardly a leaf was to be seen. Soon the boat was almost within a stone's cast of the island, and it began to sail round and round until it was well under the bending branches. The scent of the berries was so sweet that it sharpened the prince's hunger, and he longed to pluck them; but, remembering what had happened to him on the enchanted island, he was afraid to touch them. But the boat kept on sailing round and round, and at last a great wind rose from the sea and shook the branches, and the bright, sweet berries fell into the boat until it was filled with them, and they fell upon the prince's hands, and he took up some to look at them, and as he looked the desire to eat them grew stronger, and he said to himself it would be no harm to taste one; but when he tasted it the flavour was so delicious he swallowed it, and, of course, at once he forgot all about Eileen, and the boat drifted away from him and left him standing in the water.

He climbed on to the island, and having eaten enough of the berries, he set out to see what might be before him, and it was not long until he heard a great noise, and a huge iron ball knocked down one of the trees in front of him, and before he knew where he was a hundred giants came running after it. When they saw the prince they turned towards him, and one of them caught him up in his hand and held him up that all might see him. The prince was nearly squeezed to death, and seeing this the giant put him on the ground again.

"Who are you, my little man?" asked the giant.

"I am a prince," replied the prince.

"Oh, you are a prince, are you?" said the giant. "And what are you good for?" said he.

The prince did not know, for nobody had asked him that question before.

"I know what he's good for," said an old giantess, with one eye in her forehead and one in her chin. "I know what he's good for. He's good to eat."

When the giants heard this they laughed so loud that the prince was frightened almost to death.

"Why," said one, "he wouldn't make a mouthful."

"Oh, leave him to me," said the giantess, "and I'll fatten him up; and when he is cooked and dressed he will be a nice dainty dish for the king."

The giants, on this, gave the prince into the hands of the old giantess. She took him home with her to the kitchen, and fed him on sugar and spice and all things nice, so that he should be a sweet morsel for the king of the giants when he returned to the island. The poor prince would not eat anything at first, but the giantess held him over the fire until his feet were scorched, and then he said to himself it was better to eat than to be burnt alive.

Well, day after day passed, and the prince grew sadder and sadder, thinking that he would soon be cooked and dressed for the king; but sad as the prince was, he was not half as sad as the Princess Eileen in the giant's castle, watching and waiting for the prince to return and save her.

And the dwarfs had wound two balls, and were winding a third.

At last the prince heard from the old giantess that the king of the giants was to return on the following day, and she said to him:

"As this is the last night you have to live, tell me if you wish for anything, for if you do your wish will be granted."

"I don't wish for anything," said the prince, whose heart was dead within him.

"Well, I'll come back again," said the giantess, and she went away.

The prince sat down in a corner, thinking and thinking, until he heard close to his ear a sound like "purr, purr!" He looked around, and there before him was the little white cat.

"I ought not to come to you," said the cat; "but, indeed, it is not for your sake I come. I come for the sake of the Princess Eileen. Of course, you forgot all about her, and, of course, she is always thinking of you. It's always the way –

"Favoured lovers may forget,
Slighted lovers never yet."

The prince blushed with shame when he heard the name of the princess.

"'Tis you that ought to blush," said the cat; "but listen to me now, and remember, if you don't obey my directions this time you'll never see me again, and you'll never set your eyes on the Princess Eileen. When the old giantess comes back tell her you wish, when the morning comes, to go down to the sea to look at it for the last time. When you reach the sea you will know what to do. But I must go now, as I hear the giantess coming." And the cat jumped out of the window and disappeared.

"Well," said the giantess, when she came in, "is there anything you wish?"

"Is it true I must die tomorrow?" asked the prince.

"It is."

"Then," said he, "I should like to go down to the sea to look at it for the last time."

"You may do that," said the giantess, "if you get up early."

"I'll be up with the lark in the light of the morning," said the prince.

"Very well," said the giantess, and, saying "goodnight", she went away.

The prince thought the night would never pass, but at last it faded away before the grey light of the dawn, and he sped down to the sea. He threw out the third ball, and before long he saw the little boat coming towards him swifter than the wind. He threw himself into it the moment it touched the shore. Swifter than the wind it bore him out to sea, and before he had time to look behind him the island of the giantess was like a faint red speck in the distance. The day passed and the night fell, and the stars looked down, and the boat sailed on, and just as the sun rose above the sea it pushed its silver prow on the golden strand of an island greener than the leaves in summer. The prince jumped out, and went on and on until he entered a pleasant valley, at the head of which he saw a palace white as snow.

As he approached the central door it opened for him. On entering the hall he passed into several rooms without meeting with anyone; but, when he reached the principal apartment, he found himself in a circular room, in which were a thousand pillars, and every pillar was of marble, and on every pillar save one, which stood in the centre of the room, was a little white cat with black eyes. Ranged round the wall, from one door-jamb to the other, were three rows of precious jewels. The first was a row of brooches of gold and silver, with their pins fixed in the wall and their heads outwards; the second a row of torques of gold and silver; and the third a row of great swords, with hilts of gold and silver. And on many tables was food of all kinds, and drinking horns filled with foaming ale.

While the prince was looking about him the cats kept on jumping from pillar to pillar; but seeing that none of them jumped on to the pillar in the centre of the room, he began to wonder why this was so, when, all of a sudden, and before he could guess how it came about, there right before him on the centre pillar was the little white cat.

"Don't you know me?" said he.

"I do," said the prince.

"Ah, but you don't know who I am. This is the palace of the Little White Cat, and I am the King of the Cats. But you must be hungry, and the feast is spread."

Well, when the feast was ended, the king of the cats called for the sword that would kill the giant Trencoss, and the hundred cakes for the hundred watch-dogs.

The cats brought the sword and the cakes and laid them before the king.

"Now," said the king, "take these; you have no time to lose. Tomorrow the dwarfs will wind the last ball, and tomorrow the giant will claim the princess for his bride. So you should go at once; but before you go take this from me to your little girl."

And the king gave him a brooch lovelier than any on the palace walls.

The king and the prince, followed by the cats, went down to the strand, and when the prince stepped into the boat all the cats 'mewed' three times for good luck, and the prince waved his hat three times, and the little boat sped over the waters all through the night as brightly and as swiftly as a shooting star. In the first flush of the morning it touched the strand. The prince jumped out and went on and on, up hill and down dale, until he came to the giant's castle. When the hounds saw him they barked furiously, and bounded towards him to tear him to pieces. The prince flung the cakes to them, and as each hound swallowed his cake he fell dead. The prince then struck his shield three times with the sword which he had brought from the palace of the little white cat.

When the giant heard the sound he cried out: "Who comes to challenge me on my wedding day?"

The dwarfs went out to see, and, returning, told him it was a prince who challenged him to battle.

The giant, foaming with rage, seized his heaviest iron club, and rushed out to the fight. The fight lasted the whole day, and when the sun went down the giant said:

"We have had enough of fighting for the day. We can begin at sunrise tomorrow."

"Not so," said the prince. "Now or never; win or die."

"Then take this," cried the giant, as he aimed a blow with all his force at the prince's head; but the prince, darting forward like a flash of lightning, drove his sword into the giant's heart, and, with a groan, he fell over the bodies of the poisoned hounds.

When the dwarfs saw the giant dead they began to cry and tear their hair. But the prince told them they had nothing to fear, and he bade them go and tell the princess Eileen he wished to speak with her. But the princess had watched the battle from her window, and when she saw the giant fall she rushed out to greet the prince, and that very night he and she and all the dwarfs and harpers set out for the Palace of the Silver River, which they reached the next morning, and from that day to this there never has been a gayer wedding than the wedding of the Prince of the Silver River and the Princess Eileen; and though she had diamonds and pearls to spare, the only jewel she wore on her wedding day was the brooch which the prince had brought her from the Palace of the Little White Cat in the far-off seas.

The Lazy Beauty and Her Aunts

THERE WAS ONCE a poor widow woman, who had a daughter that was as handsome as the day, and as lazy as a pig, saving your presence. The poor mother was the most industrious person in the townland, and was a particularly good hand at the spinning-wheel. It was the wish of her heart that her daughter should be as handy as herself; but she'd get up late, eat her breakfast before she'd finish her prayers, and then go about dawdling, and anything she handled seemed to be burning her fingers. She drawled her words as if it was a great trouble to her to speak, or as if her tongue was as lazy as her body. Many a heart-scald her poor mother got with her, and still she was only improving like dead fowl in August.

Well, one morning that things were as bad as they could be, and the poor woman was giving tongue at the rate of a mill-clapper, who should be riding by but the king's son. "Oh dear, oh dear, good woman!" said he, "you must have a very bad child to make you scold so terribly. Sure it can't be this handsome girl that vexed you!"

"Oh, please your Majesty, not at all," says the old dissembler. "I was only checking her for working herself too much. Would your majesty believe it? She spins three pounds of flax in a day, weaves it into linen the next, and makes it all into shirts the day after."

"My gracious," says the prince, "she's the very lady that will just fill my mother's eye, and herself's the greatest spinner in the kingdom. Will you put on your daughter's bonnet and cloak, if you please, ma'am, and set her behind me? Why, my mother will be so delighted with her, that perhaps she'll make her her daughter-in-law in a week, that is, if the young woman herself is agreeable."

Well, between the confusion, and the joy, and the fear of being found out, the women didn't know what to do; and before they could make up their minds, young Anty (Anastasia) was set behind the prince, and away he and his attendants went, and a good heavy purse was left behind with the mother. She *pulillued* a long time after all was gone, in dread of something bad happening to the poor girl.

The prince couldn't judge of the girl's breeding or wit from the few answers he pulled out of her. The queen was struck in a heap when she saw a young country girl sitting behind her son, but when she saw her handsome face, and heard all she could do, she didn't think she could make too much of her. The prince took an opportunity of whispering her that if she didn't object to be his wife she must strive to please his mother.

Well, the evening went by, and the prince and Anty were getting fonder and fonder of one another, but the thought of the spinning used to send the cold to her heart every moment. When bedtime came, the old queen went along with her to a beautiful bedroom, and when she was bidding her goodnight, she pointed to a heap of fine flax, and said, "You may begin as soon as you like tomorrow morning, and I'll expect to see these three pounds in nice thread the morning after."

Little did the poor girl sleep that night. She kept crying and lamenting that she didn't mind her mother's advice better. When she was left alone next morning, she began with a heavy heart; and though she had a nice mahogany wheel and the finest flax you ever saw, the thread was breaking every moment. One while it was as fine as a cobweb, and the next as coarse as a little boy's whipcord. At last she pushed her chair back, let her hands fall in her lap, and burst out a-crying.

A small, old woman with surprising big feet appeared before her at the same moment, and said, "What ails you, you handsome colleen?"

"An' haven't I all that flax to spin before tomorrow morning, and I'll never be able to have even five yards of fine thread of it put together."

"An' would you think bad to ask poor *Colliagh Cushmōr* (Old woman Big-foot) to your wedding with the young prince? If you promise me that, all your three pounds will be made into the finest of thread while you're taking your sleep tonight."

"Indeed, you must be there and welcome, and I'll honour you all the days of your life."

"Very well; stay in your room till tea-time, and tell the queen she may come in for her thread as early as she likes tomorrow morning." It was all as she said; and the thread was finer and evener than the gut you see with fly-fishers. "My brave girl you were!" says the queen. "I'll get my own mahogany loom brought in to you, but you needn't do anything more today. Work and rest, work and rest, is my motto. Tomorrow you'll weave all this thread, and who knows what may happen?"

The poor girl was more frightened this time than the last, and she was so afraid to lose the prince. She didn't even know how to put the warp in the gears, nor how to use the shuttle, and she was sitting in the greatest grief, when a little woman, who was mighty well-shouldered about the hips, all at once appeared to her, told her her name was *Colliach Cromanmōr*, and made the same bargain with her as Colliach Cushmōr. Great was the queen's pleasure when she found early in the morning a web as fine and white as the finest paper you ever saw. "The darling you were!" says she. "Take your ease with the ladies and gentlemen today, and if your have all this made into nice shirts tomorrow you may present one of them to my son, and be married to him out of hand."

Oh, wouldn't you pity poor Anty the next day, she was now so near the prince, and, maybe, would be soon so far from him. But she waited as patiently as she could with scissors, needle, and thread in hand, till a minute after noon. Then she was rejoiced to see the third old woman appear. She had a big red nose, and informed Anty that people called her *Shron Mor Rua* on that account. She was up to her as good as the others, for a dozen fine shirts were lying on the table when the queen paid her an early visit.

Now there was nothing talked of but the wedding, and I needn't tell you it was grand. The poor mother was there along with the rest, and at the dinner the old queen could talk of nothing but the lovely shirts, and how happy herself and the bride would be after the honeymoon, spinning, and weaving, and sewing shirts and shifts without end. The bridegroom didn't like the discourse, and the bride liked it less, and he was going to say something, when the footman came up to the head of the table and said to the bride, "Your ladyship's aunt, Colliach Cushmōr, bade me ask might she come in."

The bride blushed and wished she was seven miles under the floor, but well became the prince. "Tell Mrs. Cushmōr," said he, "that any relation of my bride's will be always heartily welcome wherever she and I are."

In came the woman with the big foot, and got a seat near the prince. The old queen didn't like it much, and after a few words she asked rather spitefully, "Dear ma'am, what's the reason your foot is so big?"

"*Musha*, faith, your majesty, I was standing almost all my life at the spinning-wheel, and that's the reason."

"I declare to you, my darling," said the prince, "I'll never allow you to spend one hour at the same spinning-wheel." The same footman said again, "Your ladyship's aunt, Colliach Cromanmōr, wishes to come in, if the genteels and yourself have no objection." Very *sharoose* (displeased) was Princess Anty, but the prince sent her welcome, and she took her seat, and drank healths apiece to the company. "May I ask, ma'am?" says the old queen, "why you're so wide half-way between the head and the feet?"

"That, your majesty, is owing to sitting all my life at the loom."

"By my sceptre," says the prince, "my wife shall never sit there an hour." The footman again came up. "Your ladyship's aunt, Colliach Shron Mor Rua, is asking leave to come into the banquet." More blushing on the bride's face, but the bridegroom spoke out cordially, "Tell Mrs. Shron Mor Rua she's doing us an honour." In came the old woman, and great respect she got near the top of the table, but the people down low put up their tumblers and glasses to their noses to hide the grins. "Ma'am," says the old queen, "will you tell us, if you please, why your nose is so big and red?"

"Throth, your majesty, my head was bent down over the stitching all my life, and all the blood in my body ran into my nose."

"My darling," said the prince to Anty, "if ever I see a needle in your hand, I'll run a hundred miles from you."

"And in troth, girls and boys, though it's a diverting story, I don't think the moral is good; and if any of you *thuckeens* go about imitating Anty in her laziness, you'll find it won't thrive with you as it did with her. She was beautiful beyond compare, which none of you are, and she had three powerful fairies to help her besides. There's no fairies now, and no prince or lord to ride by, and catch you idling or working; and maybe, after all, the prince and herself were not so very happy when the cares of the world or old age came on them."

Thus was the tale ended by poor old *Shebale* (Sybilla), Father Murphy's housekeeper, in Coolbawn, Barony of Bantry, about half a century since.

The Twelve Wild Geese

THERE WAS ONCE a King and Queen that lived very happily together, and they had twelve sons and not a single daughter. We are always wishing for what we haven't, and don't care for what we have, and so it was with the Queen. One day in winter, when the bawn was covered with snow, she was looking out of the parlour window, and saw there a calf that was just killed by the butcher, and a raven standing near it.

"Oh," says she, "if I had only a daughter with her skin as white as that snow, her cheeks as red as that blood, and her hair as black as that raven, I'd give away every one of my twelve sons for her." The moment she said the word, she got a great fright, and a shiver went through her, and in an instant after, a severe-looking old woman stood before her. "That was a wicked wish you made," said she, "and to punish you it will be granted. You will have such a daughter as you desire, but the very day of her birth you will lose your other children." She vanished the moment she said the words.

And that very way it turned out. When she expected her delivery, she had her children all in a large room of the palace, with guards all round it, but the very hour her daughter came into the world, the guards inside and outside heard a great whirling and whistling, and the twelve princes were seen flying one after another out through the open window, and away like so many arrows over the woods. Well, the king was in great grief for the loss of his sons, and he would be very enraged with his wife if he only knew that she was so much to blame for it.

Everyone called the little princess Snow-white-and-Rose-red on account of her beautiful complexion. She was the most loving and lovable child that could be seen anywhere. When she was twelve years old she began to be very sad and lonely, and to torment her mother, asking her about her brothers that she thought were dead, for none up to that time ever told her the exact thing that happened to them. The secret was weighing very heavy on the Queen's conscience, and as the little girl persevered in her questions, at last she told her. "Well, mother," said she, "it was on my account my poor brothers were changed into wild geese, and are now suffering all sorts of hardship; before the world is a day older, I'll be off to seek them, and try to restore them to their own shapes."

The King and Queen had her well watched, but all was no use. Next night she was getting through the woods that surrounded the palace, and she went on and on that night, and till the evening of next day. She had a few cakes with her, and she got nuts, and *mugoreens* (fruit of the sweet briar), and some sweet crabs, as she went along. At last she came to a nice wooden house just at sunset. There was a fine garden round it, full of the handsomest flowers, and a gate in the hedge. She went in, and saw a table laid out with twelve plates, and twelve knives and forks, and twelve spoons, and there were cakes, and cold wild fowl, and fruit along with the plates, and there was a good fire, and in another long room there were twelve beds. Well, while she was looking about her she heard the gate opening, and footsteps along the walk, and in came twelve young men, and there was great grief and surprise on all their faces when they laid eyes on her. "Oh, what misfortune sent you here?" said the eldest. "For the sake of a girl we were obliged to leave our father's court, and be in the shape of wild geese all day. That's twelve years ago, and we took a solemn oath that we would kill the first young girl that came into our hands. It's a pity to put such an innocent and handsome girl as you are out of the world, but we must keep our oath."

"But," said she, "I'm your only sister, that never knew anything about this till yesterday; and I stole away from our father's and mother's palace last night to find you out and relieve you if I can." Every one of them clasped his hands, and looked down on the floor, and you could hear a pin fall till the eldest cried out, "A curse light on our oath! What shall we do?"

"I'll tell you that," said an old woman that appeared at the instant among them. "Break your wicked oath, which no one should keep. If you attempted to lay an uncivil finger on her I'd change you into twelve *booliaun buis* (stalks of ragweed), but I wish well to you as well as to her. She is appointed to be your deliverer in this way. She must spin and knit twelve shirts for you out of bog-down, to be gathered by her own hands on the moor just outside of the wood. It will take her five years to do it, and if she once speaks, or laughs, or cries the whole time, you will have to remain wild geese by day till you're called out of the world. So take care of your sister; it is worth your while." The fairy then vanished, and it was only a strife with the brothers to see who would be first to kiss and hug their sister.

So for three long years the poor young princess was occupied pulling bog-down, spinning it, and knitting it into shirts, and at the end of the three years she had eight made. During all that time, she never spoke a word, nor laughed, nor cried: the last was the hardest to refrain from. One fine day she was sitting in the garden spinning, when in sprung a fine greyhound and bounded up to her, and laid his paws on her shoulder, and licked her forehead and her hair. The next minute a beautiful young prince rode up to the little garden gate, took off his hat, and asked for leave to come in. She gave him a little nod, and in he walked. He made ever so many apologies for intruding, and asked her ever so many questions, but not a word could he get out of her. He loved her so much from the first moment, that he could not leave her till he told her he was king of a country just bordering on the forest, and he begged her to come home with him, and be his wife. She couldn't help loving him as much as he did her, and though she shook her head very often, and was very sorry to leave her brothers, at last she nodded her head, and put her hand in his. She knew well enough that the good fairy and her brothers would be able to find her out. Before she went she brought out a basket holding all her bog-down, and another holding the eight shirts. The attendants took charge of these, and the prince placed her before him on his horse. The only thing that disturbed him while riding along was the displeasure his stepmother would feel at what he had done. However, he was full master at home, and as soon as he arrived he sent for the bishop, got his bride nicely dressed, and the marriage was celebrated, the bride answering by signs. He knew by her manners she was of high birth, and no two could be fonder of each other.

The wicked stepmother did all she could to make mischief, saying she was sure she was only a woodman's daughter; but nothing could disturb the young king's opinion of his wife. In good time the young queen was delivered of a beautiful boy, and the king was so glad he hardly knew what to do for joy. All the grandeur of the christening and the happiness of the parents tormented the bad woman more than I can tell you, and she determined to put a stop to all their comfort. She got a sleeping posset given to the young mother, and while she was thinking and thinking how she could best make away with the child, she saw a wicked-looking wolf in the garden, looking up at her, and licking his chops. She lost no time, but snatched the child from the arms of the sleeping woman, and pitched it out. The beast caught it in his mouth, and was over the garden fence in a minute. The wicked woman then pricked her own fingers, and dabbled the blood round the mouth of the sleeping mother.

Well, the young king was just then coming into the big bawn from hunting, and as soon as he entered the house, she beckoned to him, shed a few crocodile tears, began to cry and wring her hands, and hurried him along the passage to the bedchamber.

Oh, wasn't the poor king frightened when he saw the queen's mouth bloody, and missed his child? It would take two hours to tell you the devilment of the old queen, the confusion and fright, and grief of the young king and queen, the bad opinion he began to feel of his wife, and the struggle she had to keep down her bitter sorrow, and not give way to it by speaking or lamenting. The young king would not allow anyone to be called, and ordered his stepmother to give out that the child fell from the mother's arms at the window, and that a wild beast ran off with it. The wicked woman pretended to do so, but she told underhand to everybody she spoke to what the king and herself saw in the bedchamber.

The young queen was the most unhappy woman in the three kingdoms for a long time, between sorrow for her child, and her husband's bad opinion; still she neither spoke nor cried, and she gathered bog-down and went on with the shirts. Often the twelve wild geese would be seen lighting on the trees in the park or on the smooth sod, and looking in at her windows. So she worked on to get the shirts finished, but another year was at an end, and she had the twelfth shirt finished except one arm, when she was obliged to take to her bed, and a beautiful girl was born.

Now the king was on his guard, and he would not let the mother and child be left alone for a minute; but the wicked woman bribed some of the attendants, set others asleep, gave the sleepy posset to the queen, and had a person watching to snatch the child away, and kill it. But what should she see but the same wolf in the garden looking up and licking his chops again? Out went the child, and away with it flew the wolf, and she smeared the sleeping mother's mouth and face with blood, and then roared, and bawled, and cried out to the king and to everybody she met, and the room was filled, and everyone was sure the young queen had just devoured her own babe.

The poor mother thought now her life would leave her. She was in such a state she could neither think nor pray, but she sat like a stone, and worked away at the arm of the twelfth shirt.

The king was for taking her to the house in the wood where he found her, but the stepmother, and the lords of the court, and the judges would not hear of it, and she was condemned to be burned in the big bawn at three o'clock the same day. When the hour drew near, the king went to the farthest part of his palace, and there was no more unhappy man in his kingdom at that hour.

When the executioners came and led her off, she took the pile of shirts in her arms. There was still a few stitches wanted, and while they were tying her to the stakes she still worked on. At the last stitch she seemed overcome and dropped a tear on her

work, but the moment after she sprang up, and shouted out, "I am innocent; call my husband!" The executioners stayed their hands, except one wicked-disposed creature, who set fire to the faggot next him, and while all were struck in amaze, there was a rushing of wings, and in a moment the twelve wild geese were standing around the pile. Before you could count twelve, she flung a shirt over each bird, and there in the twinkling of an eye were twelve of the finest young men that could be collected out of a thousand. While some were untying their sister, the eldest, taking a strong stake in his hand, struck the busy executioner such a blow that he never needed another.

While they were comforting the young queen, and the king was hurrying to the spot, a fine-looking woman appeared among them holding the babe on one arm and the little prince by the hand. There was nothing but crying for joy, and laughing for joy, and hugging and kissing, and when anyone had time to thank the good fairy, who in the shape of a wolf, carried the child away, she was not to be found. Never was such happiness enjoyed in any palace that ever was built, and if the wicked queen and her helpers were not torn by wild horses, they richly deserved it.

The Haughty Princess

THERE WAS ONCE a very worthy king, whose daughter was the greatest beauty that could be seen far or near, but she was as proud as Lucifer, and no king or prince would she agree to marry. Her father was tired out at last, and invited every king, and prince, and duke, and earl that he knew or didn't know to come to his court to give her one trial more. They all came, and next day after breakfast they stood in a row in the lawn, and the princess walked along in the front of them to make her choice. One was fat, and says she, "I won't have you, Beer-barrel!" One was tall and thin, and to him she said, "I won't have you, Ramrod!" To a white-faced man she said, "I won't have you, Pale Death"; and to a red-cheeked man she said, "I won't have you, Cockscomb!" She stopped a little before the last of all, for he was a fine man in face and form. She wanted to find some defect in him, but he had nothing remarkable but a ring of brown curling hair under his chin. She admired him a little, and then carried it off with, "I won't have you, Whiskers!"

So all went away, and the king was so vexed, he said to her, "Now to punish your *impudence*, I'll give you to the first beggarman or singing *sthronshuch* that calls"; and, as sure as the hearth-money, a fellow all over-rags, and hair that came to his shoulders, and a bushy red beard all over his face, came next morning, and began to sing before the parlour window.

When the song was over, the hall-door was opened, the singer asked in, the priest brought, and the princess married to Beardy. She roared and she bawled, but her father didn't mind her. "There," says he to the bridegroom, "is five guineas for you. Take your wife out of my sight, and never let me lay eyes on you or her again."

Off he led her, and dismal enough she was. The only thing that gave her relief was the tones of her husband's voice and his genteel manners. "Whose wood is this?" said she, as they were going through one. "It belongs to the king you called Whiskers yesterday." He gave her the same answer about meadows and corn-fields, and at last a fine city. "Ah, what a fool I was!" said she to herself. "He was a fine man, and I might have him for a husband." At last they were coming up to a poor cabin. "Why are you bringing me here?" says the poor lady. "This was my house," said he, "and now it's yours." She began to cry, but she was tired and hungry, and she went in with him.

Ovoch! There was neither a table laid out, nor a fire burning, and she was obliged to help her husband to light it, and boil their dinner, and clean up the place after; and next day he made her put on a stuff gown and a cotton handkerchief. When she had her house readied up, and no business to keep her employed, he brought home *sallies* (willows), peeled them, and showed her how to make baskets. But the hard twigs bruised her delicate fingers, and she began to cry. Well, then he asked her to mend their clothes, but the needle drew blood from her fingers, and she cried again. He couldn't bear to see her tears, so he bought a creel of earthenware, and sent her to the market to sell them. This was the hardest trial of all, but she looked so handsome and sorrowful, and had such a nice air about her, that all her pans, and jugs, and plates, and dishes were gone before noon, and the only mark of her old pride she showed was a slap she gave a buckeen across the face when he *axed* her to go in an' take share of a quart.

Well, her husband was so glad, he sent her with another creel the next day; but faith! Her luck was after deserting her. A drunken huntsman came up riding, and his beast got in among her ware, and made *brishe* of every mother's son of 'em. She went home cryin', and her husband wasn't at all pleased. "I see," said he, "you're not fit for business. Come along, I'll get you a kitchen-maid's place in the palace. I know the cook."

So the poor thing was obliged to stifle her pride once more. She was kept very busy, and the footman and the butler would be very impudent about looking for a kiss, but she let a screech out of her the first attempt was made, and the cook gave the fellow such a lambasting with the besom that he made no second offer. She went home to her husband every night, and she carried broken victuals wrapped in papers in her side pockets.

A week after she got service there was great bustle in the kitchen. The king was going to be married, but no one knew who the bride was to be. Well, in the evening the cook filled the princess's pockets with cold meat and puddings, and, says she, "Before you go, let us have a look at the great doings in the big parlour." So they came near the door to get a peep, and who should come out but the king himself, as handsome as you please, and no other but King Whiskers himself. "Your handsome helper must pay for her peeping," said he to the cook, "and dance a jig with me." Whether she would or no, he held her hand and brought her into the parlour. The fiddlers struck up, and away went *him* with *her*. But they hadn't danced two steps when the meat and the *puddens* flew out of her pockets. Everyone roared out, and she flew to the door, crying piteously. But she was soon caught by the king, and taken into the back parlour. "Don't you know me, my darling?" said he. "I'm both King Whiskers, your husband the ballad-singer, and the drunken huntsman. Your father knew me well enough when he gave you to me, and all was to drive your pride out of you." Well, she didn't know how she was with fright, and shame, and joy. Love was uppermost anyhow, for she laid her head on her husband's breast and cried like a child. The maids-of-honour soon had her away and dressed her as fine as hands and pins could do it; and there were her mother and father, too; and while the company were wondering what end of the handsome girl and the king, he and his queen, *who* they didn't know in her fine clothes, and the other king and queen, came in, and such rejoicings and fine doings as there was, none of us will ever see, any way.

The Fate of the Children of Lir

IT HAPPENED THAT the five Kings of Ireland met to determine who should have the head kingship over them, and King Lir of the Hill of the White Field expected surely he would be elected. When the nobles went into council together they chose for head king, Dearg, son of Daghda, because his father had been so great a Druid and he was the eldest of his father's sons. But Lir left the Assembly of the Kings and went home to the Hill of the White Field. The other kings would have followed after Lir to give him wounds of spear and wounds of sword for not yielding obedience to the man to whom they had given the over-lordship. But Dearg the king would not hear of it and said: "Rather let us bind him to us by the bonds of kinship, so that peace may dwell in the land. Send over to him for wife the choice of the three maidens of the fairest form and best repute in Erin, the three daughters of Oilell of Aran, my own three bosom-nurslings."

So the messengers brought word to Lir that Dearg the king would give him a foster-child of his foster-children. Lir thought well of it, and set out next day with fifty chariots from the Hill of the White Field. And he came to the Lake of the Red Eye near Killaloe. And when Lir saw the three daughters of Oilell, Dearg the king said to him: "Take thy choice of the maidens, Lir."

"I know not," said Lir, "which is the choicest of them all; but the eldest of them is the noblest, it is she I had best take."

"If so," said Dearg the king, "Ove is the eldest, and she shall be given to thee, if thou willest." So Lir and Ove were married and went back to the Hill of the White Field.

And after this there came to them twins, a son and a daughter, and they gave them for names Fingula and Aod. And two more sons came to them, Fiachra and Conn. When they came Ove died, and Lir mourned bitterly for her, and but for his great love for his children he would have died of his grief. And Dearg the king grieved for Lir and sent to him and said: "We grieve for Ove for thy sake; but, that our friendship may not be rent asunder, I will give unto thee her sister, Oifa, for a wife." So Lir agreed, and they were united, and he took her with him to his own house. And at first Oifa felt affection and honour for the children of Lir and her sister, and indeed everyone who saw the four children could not help giving them the love of his soul. Lir doted upon the children, and they always slept in beds in front of their father, who used to rise at early dawn every morning and lie down among his children. But thereupon the dart of jealousy passed into Oifa on account of this and she came to regard the children with hatred and enmity. One day her chariot was yoked for her and she took with her the four children of Lir in it. Fingula was not willing to go with her on the journey, for she had dreamed a dream in the night warning her against Oifa: but she was not to avoid her fate. And when the chariot came to the Lake of the Oaks, Oifa said to the people: "Kill the four children of Lir and I will give you your own reward of every kind in the world."

But they refused and told her it was an evil thought she had. Then she would have raised a sword herself to kill and destroy the children, but her own womanhood and her weakness prevented her; so she drove the children of Lir into the lake to bathe, and they did as Oifa told them. As soon as they were upon the lake she struck them with a Druid's wand of spells and wizardry and put them into the forms of four beautiful, perfectly white swans, and she sang this song over them:

> *"Out with you upon the wild waves, children of the king!*
> *Henceforth your cries shall be with the flocks of birds."*

And Fingula answered:

> *"Thou witch! We know thee by thy right name!*
> *Thou mayest drive us from wave to wave,*
> *But sometimes we shall rest on the headlands;*
> *We shall receive relief, but thou punishment.*
> *Though our bodies may be upon the lake,*
> *Our minds at least shall fly homewards."*

And again she spoke: "Assign an end for the ruin and woe which thou hast brought upon us."

Oifa laughed and said: "Never shall ye be free until the woman from the south be united to the man from the north, until Lairgnen of Connaught wed Deoch of Munster; nor shall any have power to bring you out of these forms. Nine hundred years shall you wander over the lakes and streams of Erin. This only I will grant unto you: that you retain your own speech, and there shall be no music in the world equal to yours, the plaintive music you shall sing." This she said because repentance seized her for the evil she had done.

And then she spake this lay:

> *"Away from me, ye children of Lir,*
> *Henceforth the sport of the wild winds*
> *Until Lairgnen and Deoch come together,*
> *Until ye are on the north-west of Red Erin.*
> *A sword of treachery is through the heart of Lir,*
> *Of Lir the mighty champion,*
> *Yet though I have driven a sword.*
> *My victory cuts me to the heart."*

Then she turned her steeds and went on to the Hall of Dearg the king. The nobles of the court asked her where were the children of Lir, and Oifa said: "Lir will not trust them to Dearg the king." But Dearg thought in his own mind that the woman had played some treachery upon them, and he accordingly sent messengers to the Hall of the White Field.

Lir asked the messengers: "Wherefore are ye come?"

"To fetch thy children, Lir," said they.

"Have they not reached you with Oifa?" said Lir.

"They have not," said the messengers; "and Oifa said it was you would not let the children go with her."

Then was Lir melancholy and sad at heart, hearing these things, for he knew that Oifa had done wrong upon his children, and he set out towards the Lake of the Red Eye. And when the children of Lir saw him coming Fingula sang the lay:

> "Welcome the cavalcade of steeds
> Approaching the Lake of the Red Eye,
> A company dread and magical
> Surely seek after us.
> Let us move to the shore, O Aod,
> Fiachra and comely Conn,
> No host under heaven can those horsemen be
> But King Lir with his mighty household."

Now as she said this King Lir had come to the shores of the lake and heard the swans speaking with human voices. And he spake to the swans and asked them who they were. Fingula answered and said: "We are thy own children, ruined by thy wife, sister of our own mother, through her ill mind and her jealousy."

"For how long is the spell to be upon you?" said Lir. "None can relieve us till the woman from the south and the man from the north come together, till Lairgnen of Connaught wed Deoch of Munster."

Then Lir and his people raised their shouts of grief, crying, and lamentation, and they stayed by the shore of the lake listening to the wild music of the swans until the swans flew away, and King Lir went on to the Hall of Dearg the king. He told Dearg the king what Oifa had done to his children. And Dearg put his power upon Oifa and bade her say what shape on earth she would think the worst of all. She said it would be in the form of an air-demon.

"It is into that form I shall put you," said Dearg the king, and he struck her with a Druid's wand of spells and wizardry and put her into the form of an air-demon. And she flew away at once, and she is still an air-demon, and shall be so for ever.

But the children of Lir continued to delight the Milesian clans with the very sweet fairy music of their songs, so that no delight was ever heard in Erin to compare with their music until the time came appointed for leaving the Lake of the Red Eye.

Then Fingula sang this parting lay:

> "Farewell to thee, Dearg the king,
> Master of all Druid's lore!
> Farewell to thee, our father dear,
> Lir of the Hill of the White Field!
> We go to pass the appointed time
> Away and apart from the haunts of men
> In the current of the Moyle,
> Our garb shall be bitter and briny,
> Until Deoch come to Lairgnen.
> So come, ye brothers of once ruddy cheeks;
> Let us depart from this Lake of the Red Eye,
> Let us separate in sorrow from the tribe that has loved us."

And after they took to flight, flying highly, lightly, aerially till they reached the Moyle, between Erin and Albain.

The men of Erin were grieved at their leaving, and it was proclaimed throughout Erin that henceforth no swan should be killed. Then they stayed all solitary, all alone, filled with cold and grief and regret, until a thick tempest came upon them and Fingula said: "Brothers, let us appoint a place to meet again if the power of the winds separate us." And they said: "Let us appoint to meet, O sister, at the Rock of the Seals." Then the waves rose up and the thunder roared, the lightnings flashed, the sweeping tempest passed over the sea, so that the children of Lir were scattered from each other over the great sea. There came, however, a placid calm after the great tempest and Fingula found herself alone, and she said this lay:

> *"Woe upon me that I am alive!*
> *My wings are frozen to my sides.*
> *O beloved three, O beloved three,*
> *Who hid under the shelter of my feathers,*
> *Until the dead come back to the living*
> *I and the three shall never meet again!"*

And she flew to the Lake of the Seals and soon saw Conn coming towards her with heavy step and drenched feathers, and Fiachra also, cold and wet and faint, and no word could they tell, so cold and faint were they: but she nestled them under her wings and said: "If Aod could come to us now our happiness would be complete." But soon they saw Aod coming towards them with dry head and preened feathers: Fingula put him under the feathers of her breast, and Fiachra under her right wing, and Conn under her left, and they made this lay:

> *"Bad was our stepmother with us,*
> *She played her magic on us,*
> *Sending us north on the sea*
> *In the shapes of magical swans.*
> *Our bath upon the shore's ridge*
> *Is the foam of the brine-crested tide,*
> *Our share of the ale feast*
> *Is the brine of the blue-crested sea."*

One day they saw a splendid cavalcade of pure white steeds coming towards them, and when they came near they were the two sons of Dearg the king who had been seeking for them to give them news of Dearg the king and Lir their father. "They are well," they said, "and live together happy in all except that ye are not with them, and for not knowing where ye have gone since the day ye left the Lake of the Red Eye."

"Happy are not we," said Fingula, and she sang this song:

> *"Happy this night the household of Lir,*
> *Abundant their meat and their wine.*
> *But the children of Lir – what is their lot?*
> *For bed-clothes we have our feathers,*
> *And as for our food and our wine –*

> *The white sand and the bitter brine,*
> *Fiachra's bed and Conn's place*
> *Under the cover of my wings on the Moyle,*
> *Aod has the shelter of my breast,*
> *And so side by side we rest."*

So the sons of Dearg the king came to the Hall of Lir and told the king the condition of his children.

Then the time came for the children of Lir to fulfil their lot, and they flew in the current of the Moyle to the Bay of Erris, and remained there till the time of their fate, and then they flew to the Hill of the White Field and found all desolate and empty, with nothing but unroofed green raths and forests of nettles – no house, no fire, no dwelling-place. The four came close together, and they raised three shouts of lamentation aloud, and Fingula sang this lay:

> *"Uchone! It is bitterness to my heart*
> *To see my father's place forlorn – No hounds, no packs of dogs,*
> *No women, and no valiant kings.*
> *No drinking-horns, no cups of wood,*
> *No drinking in its lightsome halls.*
> *Uchone! I see the state of this house*
> *That its lord our father lives no more.*
> *Much have we suffered in our wandering years*
> *By winds buffeted, by cold frozen;*
> *Now has come the greatest of our pain –*
> *here lives no man who knoweth us in the house*
> *where we were born."*

So the children of Lir flew away to the Glory Isle of Brandan the saint, and they settled upon the Lake of the Birds until the holy Patrick came to Erin and the holy Mac Howg came to Glory Isle.

And the first night he came to the island the children of Lir heard the voice of his bell ringing for matins, so that they started and leaped about in terror at hearing it; and her brothers left Fingula alone. "What is it, beloved brothers?" said she. "We know not what faint, fearful voice it is we have heard." Then Fingula recited this lay:

> *"Listen to the Cleric's bell,*
> *Poise your wings and raise*
> *Thanks to God for his coming,*
> *Be grateful that you hear him.*
> *He shall free you from pain,*
> *And bring you from the rocks and stones.*
> *Ye comely children of Lir*
> *Listen to the bell of the Cleric."*

And Mac Howg came down to the brink of the shore and said to them: "Are ye the children of Lir?"

"We are indeed," said they. "Thanks be to God!" said the saint; "it is for your sakes I have come to this Isle beyond every other island in Erin. Come ye to land now and put your trust in me." So they came to land, and he made for them chains of bright white silver, and put a chain between Aod and Fingula and a chain between Conn and Fiachra.

It happened at this time that Lairgnen was prince of Connaught and he was to wed Deoch the daughter of the king of Munster. She had heard the account of the birds and she became filled with love and affection for them, and she said she would not wed till she had the wondrous birds of Glory Isle. Lairgnen sent for them to the Saint Mac Howg. But the Saint would not give them, and both Lairgnen and Deoch went to Glory Isle. And Lairgnen went to seize the birds from the altar: but as soon as he had laid hands on them their feathery coats fell off, and the three sons of Lir became three withered bony old men, and Fingula, a lean withered old woman without blood or flesh. Lairgnen started at this and left the place hastily, but Fingula chanted this lay:

> *"Come and baptise us, O Cleric,*
> *Clear away our stains!*
> *This day I see our grave – Fiachra and Conn on each side,*
> *And in my lap, between my two arms,*
> *Place Aod, my beauteous brother."*

After this lay, the children of Lir were baptised. And they died, and were buried as Fingula had said, Fiachra and Conn on either side, and Aod before her face. A cairn was raised for them, and on it their names were written in runes. And that is the fate of the children of Lir.

Fair, Brown, and Trembling

KING HUGH CURUCHA lived in Tir Conal, and he had three daughters, whose names were Fair, Brown, and Trembling. Fair and Brown had new dresses, and went to church every Sunday. Trembling was kept at home to do the cooking and work. They would not let her go out of the house at all; for she was more beautiful than the other two, and they were in dread she might marry before themselves.

They carried on in this way for seven years. At the end of seven years the son of the king of Emania fell in love with the eldest sister.

One Sunday morning, after the other two had gone to church, the old henwife came into the kitchen to Trembling, and said: "It's at church you ought to be this day, instead of working here at home."

"How could I go?" said Trembling. "I have no clothes good enough to wear at church; and if my sisters were to see me there, they'd kill me for going out of the house."

"I'll give you," said the henwife, "a finer dress than either of them has ever seen. And now tell me what dress will you have?"

"I'll have," said Trembling, "a dress as white as snow, and green shoes for my feet."

Then the henwife put on the cloak of darkness, clipped a piece from the old clothes the young woman had on, and asked for the whitest robes in the world and the most beautiful that could be found, and a pair of green shoes.

That moment she had the robe and the shoes, and she brought them to Trembling, who put them on. When Trembling was dressed and ready, the henwife said: "I have a honey-bird here to sit on your right shoulder, and a honey-finger to put on your left. At the door stands a milk-white mare, with a golden saddle for you to sit on, and a golden bridle to hold in your hand."

Trembling sat on the golden saddle; and when she was ready to start, the henwife said: "You must not go inside the door of the church, and the minute the people rise up at the end of Mass, do you make off, and ride home as fast as the mare will carry you."

When Trembling came to the door of the church there was no one inside who could get a glimpse of her but was striving to know who she was; and when they saw her hurrying away at the end of Mass, they ran out to overtake her. But no use in their running; she was away before any man could come near her. From the minute she left the church till she got home, she overtook the wind before her, and outstripped the wind behind.

She came down at the door, went in, and found the henwife had dinner ready. She put off the white robes, and had on her old dress in a twinkling.

When the two sisters came home the henwife asked: "Have you any news today from the church?"

"We have great news," said they. "We saw a wonderful grand lady at the church-door. The like of the robes she had we have never seen on woman before. It's little that was thought of our dresses beside what she had on; and there wasn't a man at the church, from the king to the beggar, but was trying to look at her and know who she was."

The sisters would give no peace till they had two dresses like the robes of the strange lady; but honey-birds and honey-fingers were not to be found.

Next Sunday the two sisters went to church again, and left the youngest at home to cook the dinner.

After they had gone, the henwife came in and asked: "Will you go to church today?"

"I would go," said Trembling, "if I could get the going."

"What robe will you wear?" asked the henwife.

"The finest black satin that can be found, and red shoes for my feet."

"What colour do you want the mare to be?"

"I want her to be so black and so glossy that I can see myself in her body."

The henwife put on the cloak of darkness, and asked for the robes and the mare. That moment she had them. When Trembling was dressed, the henwife put the honey-bird on her right shoulder and the honey-finger on her left. The saddle on the mare was silver, and so was the bridle.

When Trembling sat in the saddle and was going away, the henwife ordered her strictly not to go inside the door of the church, but to rush away as soon as the people rose at the end of Mass, and hurry home on the mare before any man could stop her.

That Sunday, the people were more astonished than ever, and gazed at her more than the first time; and all they were thinking of was to know who she was. But they had no chance; for the moment the people rose at the end of Mass she slipped from the church, was in the silver saddle, and home before a man could stop her or talk to her.

The henwife had the dinner ready. Trembling took off her satin robe, and had on her old clothes before her sisters got home.

"What news have you today?" asked the henwife of the sisters when they came from the church.

"Oh, we saw the grand strange lady again! And it's little that any man could think of our dresses after looking at the robes of satin that she had on! And all at church, from high to low, had their mouths open, gazing at her, and no man was looking at us."

The two sisters gave neither rest nor peace till they got dresses as nearly like the strange lady's robes as they could find. Of course they were not so good; for the like of those robes could not be found in Erin.

When the third Sunday came, Fair and Brown went to church dressed in black satin. They left Trembling at home to work in the kitchen, and told her to be sure and have dinner ready when they came back.

After they had gone and were out of sight, the henwife came to the kitchen and said: "Well, my dear, are you for church today?"

"I would go if I had a new dress to wear."

"I'll get you any dress you ask for. What dress would you like?" asked the henwife.

"A dress red as a rose from the waist down, and white as snow from the waist up; a cape of green on my shoulders; and a hat on my head with a red, a white, and a green feather in it; and shoes for my feet with the toes red, the middle white, and the backs and heels green."

The henwife put on the cloak of darkness, wished for all these things, and had them. When Trembling was dressed, the henwife put the honey-bird on her right shoulder and the honey-finger on her left, and, placing the hat on her head, clipped a few hairs from one lock and a few from another with her scissors, and that moment the most beautiful golden hair was flowing down over the girl's shoulders. Then the henwife asked what kind of a mare she would ride. She said white, with blue and gold-coloured diamond-shaped spots all over her body, on her back a saddle of gold, and on her head a golden bridle.

The mare stood there before the door, and a bird sitting between her ears, which began to sing as soon as Trembling was in the saddle, and never stopped till she came home from the church.

The fame of the beautiful strange lady had gone out through the world, and all the princes and great men that were in it came to church that Sunday, each one hoping that it was himself would have her home with him after Mass.

The son of the king of Emania forgot all about the eldest sister, and remained outside the church, so as to catch the strange lady before she could hurry away.

The church was more crowded than ever before, and there were three times as many outside. There was such a throng before the church that Trembling could only come inside the gate.

As soon as the people were rising at the end of Mass, the lady slipped out through the gate, was in the golden saddle in an instant, and sweeping away ahead of the wind. But if she was, the prince of Emania was at her side, and, seizing her by the foot, he ran with the mare for thirty perches, and never let go of the beautiful lady till the shoe was pulled from her foot, and he was left behind with it in his hand. She came home as fast as the mare could carry her, and was thinking all the time that the henwife would kill her for losing the shoe.

Seeing her so vexed and so changed in the face, the old woman asked: "What's the trouble that's on you now?"

"Oh! I've lost one of the shoes off my feet," said Trembling.

"Don't mind that; don't be vexed," said the henwife; "maybe it's the best thing that ever happened to you."

Then Trembling gave up all the things she had to the henwife, put on her old clothes, and went to work in the kitchen. When the sisters came home, the henwife asked: "Have you any news from the church?"

"We have indeed," said they, "for we saw the grandest sight today. The strange lady came again, in grander array than before. On herself and the horse she rode were the finest colours of the world, and between the ears of the horse was a bird which never stopped singing from the time she came till she went away. The lady herself is the most beautiful woman ever seen by man in Erin."

After Trembling had disappeared from the church, the son of the king of Emania said to the other kings' sons: "I will have that lady for my own."

They all said: "You didn't win her just by taking the shoe off her foot; you'll have to win her by the point of the sword; you'll have to fight for her with us before you can call her your own."

"Well," said the son of the king of Emania, "when I find the lady that shoe will fit, I'll fight for her, never fear, before I leave her to any of you."

Then all the kings' sons were uneasy, and anxious to know who was she that lost the shoe; and they began to travel all over Erin to know could they find her. The prince of Emania and all the others went in a great company together, and made the round of Erin; they went everywhere – north, south, east, and west. They visited every place

where a woman was to be found, and left not a house in the kingdom they did not search, to know could they find the woman the shoe would fit, not caring whether she was rich or poor, of high or low degree.

The prince of Emania always kept the shoe; and when the young women saw it, they had great hopes, for it was of proper size, neither large nor small, and it would beat any man to know of what material it was made. One thought it would fit her if she cut a little from her great toe; and another, with too short a foot, put something in the tip of her stocking. But no use; they only spoiled their feet, and were curing them for months afterwards.

The two sisters, Fair and Brown, heard that the princes of the world were looking all over Erin for the woman that could wear the shoe, and every day they were talking of trying it on; and one day Trembling spoke up and said: "Maybe it's my foot that the shoe will fit."

"Oh, the breaking of the dog's foot on you! Why say so when you were at home every Sunday?"

They were that way waiting, and scolding the younger sister, till the princes were near the place. The day they were to come, the sisters put Trembling in a closet, and locked the door on her. When the company came to the house, the prince of Emania gave the shoe to the sisters. But though they tried and tried, it would fit neither of them.

"Is there any other young woman in the house?" asked the prince.

"There is," said Trembling, speaking up in the closet; "I'm here."

"Oh! We have her for nothing but to put out the ashes," said the sisters.

But the prince and the others wouldn't leave the house till they had seen her; so the two sisters had to open the door. When Trembling came out, the shoe was given to her, and it fitted exactly.

The prince of Emania looked at her and said: "You are the woman the shoe fits, and you are the woman I took the shoe from."

Then Trembling spoke up, and said: "Do you stay here till I return."

Then she went to the henwife's house. The old woman put on the cloak of darkness, got everything for her she had the first Sunday at church, and put her on the white mare in the same fashion. Then Trembling rode along the highway to the front of the house. All who saw her the first time said: "This is the lady we saw at church."

Then she went away a second time, and a second time came back on the black mare in the second dress which the henwife gave her. All who saw her the second Sunday said: "That is the lady we saw at church."

A third time she asked for a short absence, and soon came back on the third mare and in the third dress. All who saw her the third time said: "That is the lady we saw at church." Every man was satisfied, and knew that she was the woman.

Then all the princes and great men spoke up, and said to the son of the king of Emania: "You'll have to fight now for her before we let her go with you."

"I'm here before you, ready for combat," answered the prince.

Then the son of the king of Lochlin stepped forth. The struggle began, and a terrible struggle it was. They fought for nine hours; and then the son of the king of Lochlin stopped, gave up his claim, and left the field. Next day the son of the king of Spain fought six hours, and yielded his claim. On the third day the son of the king of Nyerfói fought eight hours, and stopped. The fourth day the son of the king of Greece fought six hours, and stopped. On the fifth day no more strange princes wanted to fight; and

all the sons of kings in Erin said they would not fight with a man of their own land, that the strangers had had their chance, and, as no others came to claim the woman, she belonged of right to the son of the king of Emania.

The marriage-day was fixed, and the invitations were sent out. The wedding lasted for a year and a day. When the wedding was over, the king's son brought home the bride, and when the time came a son was born. The young woman sent for her eldest sister, Fair, to be with her and care for her. One day, when Trembling was well, and when her husband was away hunting, the two sisters went out to walk; and when they came to the seaside, the eldest pushed the youngest sister in. A great whale came and swallowed her.

The eldest sister came home alone, and the husband asked, "Where is your sister?"

"She has gone home to her father in Ballyshannon; now that I am well, I don't need her."

"Well," said the husband, looking at her, "I'm in dread it's my wife that has gone."

"Oh! No," said she; "it's my sister Fair that's gone."

Since the sisters were very much alike, the prince was in doubt. That night he put his sword between them, and said: "If you are my wife, this sword will get warm; if not, it will stay cold."

In the morning when he rose up, the sword was as cold as when he put it there.

It happened, when the two sisters were walking by the seashore, that a little cowboy was down by the water minding cattle, and saw Fair push Trembling into the sea; and next day, when the tide came in, he saw the whale swim up and throw her out on the sand. When she was on the sand she said to the cowboy: "When you go home in the evening with the cows, tell the master that my sister Fair pushed me into the sea yesterday; that a whale swallowed me, and then threw me out, but will come again and swallow me with the coming of the next tide; then he'll go out with the tide, and come again with tomorrow's tide, and throw me again on the strand. The whale will cast me out three times. I'm under the enchantment of this whale, and cannot leave the beach or escape myself. Unless my husband saves me before I'm swallowed the fourth time, I shall be lost. He must come and shoot the whale with a silver bullet when he turns on the broad of his back. Under the breast-fin of the whale is a reddish-brown spot. My husband must hit him in that spot, for it is the only place in which he can be killed."

When the cowboy got home, the eldest sister gave him a draught of oblivion, and he did not tell.

Next day he went again to the sea. The whale came and cast Trembling on shore again. She asked the boy "Did you tell the master what I told you to tell him?"

"I did not," said he; "I forgot."

"How did you forget?" asked she.

"The woman of the house gave me a drink that made me forget."

"Well, don't forget telling him this night; and if she gives you a drink, don't take it from her."

As soon as the cowboy came home, the eldest sister offered him a drink. He refused to take it till he had delivered his message and told all to the master. The third day the prince went down with his gun and a silver bullet in it. He was not long down when the whale came and threw Trembling upon the beach as the two days before. She had no power to speak to her husband till he had killed the whale. Then the whale went out, turned over once on the broad of his back, and showed the spot for a moment only. That moment the prince fired. He had but the one chance, and a short one at that; but he took it, and hit the spot, and the whale, mad with pain, made the sea all around red with blood, and died.

That minute Trembling was able to speak, and went home with her husband, who sent word to her father what the eldest sister had done. The father came, and told him any death he chose to give her to give it. The prince told the father he would leave her life and death with himself. The father had her put out then on the sea in a barrel, with provisions in it for seven years.

In time Trembling had a second child, a daughter. The prince and she sent the cowboy to school, and trained him up as one of their own children, and said: "If the little girl that is born to us now lives, no other man in the world will get her but him."

The cowboy and the prince's daughter lived on till they were married. The mother said to her husband, "You could not have saved me from the whale but for the little cowboy; on that account I don't grudge him my daughter."

The son of the king of Emania and Trembling had fourteen children, and they lived happily till the two died of old age.

Murtough and the Witch Woman

IN THE DAYS when Murtough Mac Erca was in the High Kingship of Ireland, the country was divided between the old beliefs of paganism and the new doctrines of the Christian teaching. Part held with the old creed and part with the new, and the thought of the people was troubled between them, for they knew not which way to follow and which to forsake. The faith of their forefathers clung close around them, holding them by many fine and tender threads of memory and custom and tradition; yet still the new faith was making its way, and every day it spread wider and wider through the land.

The family of Murtough had joined itself to the Christian faith, and his three brothers were bishops and abbots of the Church, but Murtough himself remained a pagan, for he was a wild and lawless prince, and the peaceful teachings of the Christian doctrine, with its forgiveness of enemies, pleased him not at all. Fierce and cruel was his life, filled with dark deeds and bloody wars, and savage and tragic was his death, as we shall hear.

Now Murtough was in the sunny summer palace of Cletty, which Cormac, son of Art, had built for a pleasure house on the brink of the slow-flowing Boyne, near the Fairy Brugh of Angus the Ever Young, the God of Youth and Beauty. A day of summer was that day, and the King came forth to hunt on the borders of the Brugh, with all his boon companions around him. But when the high-noon came the sun grew hot, and the King sat down to rest upon the fairy mound, and the hunt passed on beyond him, and he was left alone.

There was a witch woman in that country whose name was 'Sigh, Sough, Storm, Rough Wind, Winter Night, Cry, Wail, and Groan'. Star-bright and beautiful was she in face and form, but inwardly she was cruel as her names. And she hated Murtough because he had scattered and destroyed the Ancient Peoples of the Fairy Tribes of Erin, her country and her fatherland, and because in the battle which he fought at Cerb on the Boyne her father and her mother and her sister had been slain. For in those days women went to battle side by side with men.

She knew, too, that with the coming of the new faith trouble would come upon the fairy folk, and their power and their great majesty would depart from them, and men would call them demons, and would drive them out with psalm-singing and with the saying of prayers, and with the sound of little tinkling bells. So trouble and anger wrought in the witch woman, and she waited the day to be revenged on Murtough, for he being yet a pagan, was still within her power to harm.

So when Sheen (for Sheen or 'Storm' was the name men gave to her) saw the King seated on the fairy mound and all his comrades parted from him, she arose softly, and combed her hair with her comb of silver adorned with little ribs of gold, and she washed her hands in a silver basin wherein were four golden birds sitting on the rim of the bowl, and little bright gems of carbuncle set round about the rim. And she donned her fairy mantle of flowing green, and her cloak, wide and hooded, with silvery fringes, and a brooch of fairest gold. On her head were tresses yellow like to gold, plaited in four locks, with a golden drop at the end of each long tress. The hue of her hair was like the flower of the iris in summer or like red gold after the burnishing thereof. And she wore on her breasts and at her shoulders marvellous clasps of gold, finely worked with the tracery of the skilled craftsman, and a golden twisted torque around her throat. And when she was decked she went softly and sat down beside Murtough on the turfy hunting mound. And after a space Murtough perceived her sitting there, and the sun shining upon her, so that the glittering of the gold and of her golden hair and the bright shining of the green silk of her garments, was like the yellow iris-beds upon the lake on a sunny summer's day. Wonder and terror seized on Murtough at her beauty, and he knew not if he loved her or if he hated her the most; for at one moment all his nature was filled with longing and with love of her, so that it seemed to him that he would give the whole of Ireland for the loan of one hour's space of dalliance with her; but after that he felt a dread of her, because he knew his fate was in her hands, and that she had come to work him ill. But he welcomed her as if she were known to him and he asked her wherefore she was come. "I am come," she said, "because I am beloved of Murtough, son of Erc, King of Erin, and I come to seek him here." Then Murtough was glad, and he said, "Dost thou not know me, maiden?"

"I do," she answered, "for all secret and mysterious things are known to me and thou and all the men of Erin are well known."

After he had conversed with her awhile, she appeared to him so fair that the King was ready to promise her anything in life she wished, so long as she would go with him to Cletty of the Boyne. "My wish," she said, "is that you take me to your house, and that you put out from it your wife and your children because they are of the new faith, and all the clerics that are in your house, and that neither your wife nor any cleric be permitted to enter the house while I am there."

"I will give you," said the King, "a hundred head of every herd of cattle that is within my kingdom, and a hundred drinking horns, and a hundred cups, and a hundred rings of gold, and a feast every other night in the summer palace of Cletty. But I pledge thee my word, oh, maiden, it were easier for me to give thee half of Ireland than to do this thing that thou hast asked." For Murtough feared that when those that were of the Christian faith were put out of his house, she would work her spells upon him, and no power would be left with him to resist those spells.

"I will not take thy gifts," said the damsel, "but only those things that I have asked; moreover, it is thus, that my name must never be uttered by thee, nor must any man or woman learn it."

"What is thy name," said Murtough, "that it may not come upon my lips to utter it?"

And she said, "Sigh, Sough, Storm, Rough Wind, Winter Night, Cry, Wail, Groan, this is my name, but men call me Sheen, for 'Storm' or Sheen is my chief name, and storms are with me where I come."

Nevertheless, Murtough was so fascinated by her that he brought her to his home, and drove out the clerics that were there, with his wife and children along with them, and drove out also the nobles of his own clan, the children of Niall, two great and gallant battalions. And Duivsech, his wife, went crying along the road with her children around her to seek Bishop Cairnech, the half-brother of her husband, and her own soul-friend, that she might obtain help and shelter from him.

But Sheen went gladly and light-heartedly into the House of Cletty, and when she saw the lovely lightsome house and the goodly nobles of the clan of Niall, and the feasting and banqueting and the playing of the minstrels and all the joyous noise of that kingly dwelling, her heart was lifted within her, and "Fair as a fairy palace is this house of Cletty," said she.

"Fair, indeed, it is," replied the King; "for neither the Kings of Leinster nor the Kings of mighty Ulster, nor the lords of the clans of Owen or of Niall, have such a house as this; nay, in Tara of the Kings itself, no house to equal this house of mine is found." And that night the King robed himself in all the splendour of his royal dignity, and on his right hand he seated Sheen, and a great banquet was made before them, and men said that never on earth was to be seen a woman more goodly of appearance than she. And the King was astonished at her, and he began to ask her questions, for it seemed to him that the power of a great goddess of the ancient time was in her; and he asked her whence she came, and what manner was the power that he saw in her. He asked her, too, did she believe in the God of the clerics, or was she herself some goddess of the older world? For he feared her, feeling that his fate was in her hands.

She laughed a careless and a cruel laugh, for she knew that the King was in their power, now that she was there alone with him, and the clerics and the Christian teachers gone.

"Fear me not, O Murtough," she cried; "I am, like thee, a daughter of the race of men of the ancient family of Adam and of Eve; fit and meet my comradeship with thee; therefore, fear not nor regret. And as to that true God of thine, worker of miracles and helper of His people, no miracle in all the world is there that I, by mine own unaided power, cannot work the like. I can create a sun and moon; the heavens I can sprinkle with radiant stars of night. I can call up to life men fiercely fighting in conflict, slaughtering one another. Wine I could make of the cold water of the Boyne, and sheep of lifeless stones, and swine of ferns. In the presence of the hosts I can make gold and silver, plenty and to spare; and hosts of famous fighting men I can produce from naught. Now, tell me, can thy God work the like?"

"Work for us," says the King, "some of these great wonders." Then Sheen went forth out of the house, and she set herself to work spells on Murtough, so that he knew not whether he was in his right mind or no. She took of the water of the Boyne and made a magic wine thereout, and she took ferns and spiked thistles and light puff-balls of the woods, and out of them she fashioned magic swine and sheep and goats, and with these she fed Murtough and the hosts. And when they had eaten, all their strength went from them, and the magic wine sent them into an uneasy sleep and restless slumbers. And out of stones and sods of earth she fashioned three battalions, and one of the battalions she placed at one side of the house, and the other at the further side beyond it, and one encircling the rest southward along the hollow windings of the glen. And thus were these battalions, one of them all made of men stark-naked and their colour blue, and the second with heads of goats with shaggy beards and horned; but the third, more terrible than they, for these were headless men, fighting like human beings, yet finished at the neck; and the sound of heavy shouting as of hosts and multitudes came from the first and the second battalion, but from the third no sound save only that they waved their arms and struck their weapons together, and smote the ground with their feet impatiently. And though terrible was the shout of the blue men and the bleating of the goats with human limbs, more horrible yet was the stamping and the rage of those headless men, finished at the neck.

And Murtough, in his sleep and in his dreams, heard the battle-shout, and he rose impetuously from off his bed, but the wine overcame him, and his strength departed from him, and he fell helplessly upon the floor. Then he heard the challenge a second time, and the stamping of the feet without, and he rose again, and madly, fiercely, he set on them, charging the hosts and scattering them before him, as he thought, as far as the fairy palace of the Brugh. But all his strength was lost in fighting phantoms, for they were but stones and sods and withered leaves of the forest that he took for fighting men.

Now Duivsech, Murtough's wife, knew what was going on. She called upon Cairnech to arise and to gather together the clans of the children of his people, the men of Owen and of Niall, and together they went to the fort; but Sheen guarded it well, so that they could by no means find an entrance. Then Cairnech was angry, and he cursed the place, and he dug a grave before the door, and he stood up upon the mound of the grave, and rang his bells and cursed the King and his house, and prophesied his downfall. But he blessed the clans of Owen and of Niall, and they returned to their own country.

Then Cairnech sent messengers to seek Murtough and to draw him away from the witch woman who sought his destruction, but because she was so lovely the King would believe no evil of her; and whenever he made any sign to go to Cairnech, she threw her spell upon the King, so that he could not break away. When he was so weak and faint that he had no power left, she cast a sleep upon him, and she went round the house, putting everything in readiness. She called upon her magic host of warriors, and set them round the fortress, with their spears and javelins pointed inwards towards the house, so that the King would not dare to go out amongst them. And that night was a night of Samhain-tide, the eve of Wednesday after All Souls' Day.

Then she went everywhere throughout the house, and took lighted brands and burning torches, and scattered them in every part of the dwelling. And she returned into the room wherein Murtough slept, and lay down by his side. And she caused a great wind to spring up, and it came soughing through the house from the north-west; and the King said, "This is the sigh of the winter night." And Sheen smiled, because, unwittingly, the King had spoken her name, for she knew by that that the hour of her revenge had come. "'Tis I myself that am Sigh and Winter Night," she said, "and I am Rough Wind and Storm, a daughter of fair nobles; and I am Cry and Wail, the maid of elfin birth, who brings ill-luck to men."

After that she caused a great snowstorm to come round the house; and like the noise of troops and the rage of battle was the storm, beating and pouring in on every side, so that drifts of deep snow were piled against the walls, blocking the doors and chilling the folk that were feasting within the house. But the King was lying in a heavy, unresting sleep, and Sheen was at his side. Suddenly he screamed out of his sleep and stirred himself, for he heard the crash of falling timbers and the noise of the magic hosts, and he smelled the strong smell of fire in the palace.

He sprang up. "It seems to me," he cried, "that hosts of demons are around the house, and that they are slaughtering my people, and that the house of Cletty is on fire."

"It was but a dream," the witch maiden said. Then he slept again, and he saw a vision, to wit, that he was tossing in a ship at sea, and the ship floundered, and above his head a griffin, with sharp beak and talons, sailed, her wings outspread and covering all the sun, so that it was dark as middle-night; and lo! As she rose on high, her plumes quivered for a moment in the air; then down she swooped and picked him from the waves, carrying him to her eyrie on the dismal cliff outhanging o'er the ocean; and the griffin began to pierce him and to prod him with her talons, and to pick out pieces of his flesh with her beak; and this went on awhile, and then a flame, that came he knew not whence, rose from the nest, and he and the griffin were enveloped in the flame. Then in her beak the griffin picked him up, and together they fell downward over the cliff's edge into the seething ocean; so that, half by fire and half by water, he died a miserable death.

When the King saw that vision, he rose screaming from his sleep, and donned his arms; and he made one plunge forward seeking for the magic hosts, but he found no man to answer him. The damsel went forth from the house, and Murtough made to follow her, but as he turned the flames leaped out, and all between him and the door was one vast sheet of flame. He saw no way of escape, save the vat of wine that stood in the banqueting hall, and into that he got; but the burning timbers of the roof fell upon his head and the hails of fiery sparks rained on him, so that half of him was burned and half was drowned, as he had seen in his dream.

The next day, amid the embers, the clerics found his corpse, and they took it up and washed it in the Boyne, and carried it to Tuilen to bury it. And they said, "Alas! That Mac Erca, High King of Erin, of the noble race of Conn and of the descendants of Ugaine the Great, should die fighting with sods and stones! Alas! That the Cross of Christ was not signed upon his face that he might have known the witchdoms of the maiden what they were."

As they went thus, bewailing the death of Murtough and bearing him to his grave, Duivsech, wife of Murtough, met them, and when she found her husband dead, she struck her hands together and she made a great and mournful lamentation; and because weakness came upon her she leaned her back against the ancient tree that is in Aenech Reil; and a burst of blood broke from her heart, and there she died, grieving for her husband. And the grave of Murtough was made wide and deep, and there they laid the Queen beside him, two in the one grave, near the north side of the little church that is in Tuilen.

Now, when the burial was finished, and the clerics were reciting over his grave the deeds of the King, and were making prayers for Murtough's soul that it might be brought out of hell, for Cairnech showed great care for this, they saw coming towards them across the sward a lonely woman, star-bright and beautiful, and a kirtle of priceless silk upon her, and a green mantle with its fringes of silver thread flowing to the ground. She reached the place where the clerics were, and saluted them, and they saluted her. And they marvelled at her beauty, but they perceived on her an appearance of sadness and of heavy grief. They asked of her, "Who art thou, maiden, and wherefore art thou come to the house of mourning? For a king lies buried here."

"A king lies buried here, indeed," said she, "and I it was who slew him, Murtough of the many deeds, of the race of Conn and Niall, High King of Ireland and of the West. And though it was I who wrought his death, I myself will die for grief of him."

And they said, "Tell us, maiden, why you brought him to his death, if so be that he was dear to thee?" And she said, "Murtough was dear to me, indeed, dearest of the men of the whole world; for I am Sheen, the daughter of Sige, the son of Dian, from whom Ath Sigi or the 'Ford of Sige' is called today. But Murtough slew my father, and my mother and sister were slain along with him, in the battle of Cerb upon the Boyne, and there was none of my house to avenge their death, save myself alone. Moreover, in his time the Ancient Peoples of the Fairy Tribes of Erin were scattered and destroyed, the folk of the underworld and of my fatherland; and to avenge the wrong and loss he wrought on them I slew the man I loved. I made poison for him; alas! I made for him magic drink and food which took his strength away, and out of the sods of earth and puff-balls that float down the wind, I wrought men and armies of headless, hideous folk, till all his senses were distraught. And, now, take me to thee, O Cairnech, in fervent and true repentance, and sign the Cross of Christ upon my brow, for the time of my death is come." Then she made penitence for the sin that she had sinned, and she died there upon the grave of grief and of sorrow after the King. And they digged a grave lengthways across the foot of the wide grave of Murtough and his spouse, and there they laid the maiden who had wrought them woe. And the clerics wondered at those things, and they wrote them and revised them in a book.

The Story of Deirdre

THERE WAS A MAN in Ireland once who was called Malcolm Harper. The man was a right good man, and he had a goodly share of this world's goods. He had a wife, but no family. What did Malcolm hear but that a soothsayer had come home to the place, and as the man was a right good man, he wished that the soothsayer might come near them. Whether it was that he was invited or that he came of himself, the soothsayer came to the house of Malcolm.

"Are you doing any soothsaying?" says Malcolm. "Yes, I am doing a little. Are you in need of soothsaying?"

"Well, I do not mind taking soothsaying from you, if you had soothsaying for me, and you would be willing to do it."

"Well, I will do soothsaying for you. What kind of soothsaying do you want?"

"Well, the soothsaying I wanted was that you would tell me my lot or what will happen to me, if you can give me knowledge of it."

"Well, I am going out, and when I return, I will tell you." And the soothsayer went forth out of the house and he was not long outside when he returned.

"Well," said the soothsayer, "I saw in my second sight that it is on account of a daughter of yours that the greatest amount of blood shall be shed that has ever been shed in Erin since time and race began. And the three most famous heroes that ever were found will lose their heads on her account."

After a time a daughter was born to Malcolm, he did not allow a living being to come to his house, only himself and the nurse. He asked this woman, "Will you yourself bring up the child to keep her in hiding far away where eye will not see a sight of her nor ear hear a word about her?"

The woman said she would, so Malcolm got three men, and he took them away to a large mountain, distant and far from reach, without the knowledge or notice of anyone. He caused there a hillock, round and green, to be dug out of the middle, and the hole thus made to be covered carefully over so that a little company could dwell there together. This was done.

Deirdre and her foster-mother dwelt in the bothy mid the hills without the knowledge or the suspicion of any living person about them and without anything occurring, until Deirdre was sixteen years of age. Deirdre grew like the white sapling, straight and trim as the rash on the moss. She was the creature of fairest form, of loveliest aspect, and of gentlest nature that existed between earth and heaven in all Ireland – whatever colour of hue she had before, there was nobody that looked into her face but she would blush fiery red over it.

The woman that had charge of her gave Deirdre every information and skill of which she herself had knowledge and skill. There was not a blade of grass growing from root, nor a bird singing in the wood, nor a star shining from heaven but Deirdre had a name for it. But one thing, she did not wish her to have either part or parley with any single living man of the rest of the world. But on a gloomy winter night, with black, scowling clouds, a hunter of game was wearily travelling the hills, and what happened but that he missed the trail of the hunt, and

lost his course and companions. A drowsiness came upon the man as he wearily wandered over the hills, and he lay down by the side of the beautiful green knoll in which Deirdre lived, and he slept. The man was faint from hunger and wandering, and benumbed with cold, and a deep sleep fell upon him. When he lay down beside the green hill where Deirdre was, a troubled dream came to the man, and he thought that he enjoyed the warmth of a fairy broch, the fairies being inside playing music. The hunter shouted out in his dream, if there was anyone in the broch, to let him in for the Holy One's sake. Deirdre heard the voice and said to her foster-mother: "O foster-mother, what cry is that?"

"It is nothing at all, Deirdre – merely the birds of the air astray and seeking each other. But let them go past to the bosky glade. There is no shelter or house for them here."

"Oh, foster-mother, the bird asked to get inside for the sake of the God of the Elements, and you yourself tell me that anything that is asked in His name we ought to do. If you will not allow the bird that is being benumbed with cold, and done to death with hunger, to be let in, I do not think much of your language or your faith. But since I give credence to your language and to your faith, which you taught me, I will myself let in the bird." And Deirdre arose and drew the bolt from the leaf of the door, and she let in the hunter. She placed a seat in the place for sitting, food in the place for eating, and drink in the place for drinking for the man who came to the house. "Oh, for this life and raiment, you man that came in, keep restraint on your tongue!" said the old woman. "It is not a great thing for you to keep your mouth shut and your tongue quiet when you get a home and shelter of a hearth on a gloomy winter's night."

"Well," said the hunter, "I may do that – keep my mouth shut and my tongue quiet, since I came to the house and received hospitality from you; but by the hand of thy father and grandfather, and by your own two hands, if some other of the people of the world saw this beauteous creature you have here hid away, they would not long leave her with you, I swear."

"What men are these you refer to?" said Deirdre.

"Well, I will tell you, young woman," said the hunter. "They are Naois, son of Uisnech, and Allen and Arden his two brothers."

"What like are these men when seen, if we were to see them?" said Deirdre.

"Why, the aspect and form of the men when seen are these," said the hunter: "they have the colour of the raven on their hair, their skin like swan on the wave in whiteness, and their cheeks as the blood of the brindled red calf, and their speed and their leap are those of the salmon of the torrent and the deer of the grey mountain side. And Naois is head and shoulders over the rest of the people of Erin."

However they are," said the nurse, "be you off from here and take another road. And, King of Light and Sun! In good sooth and certainty, little are my thanks for yourself or for her that let you in!"

The hunter went away, and went straight to the palace of King Connachar. He sent word in to the king that he wished to speak to him if he pleased. The king answered the message and came out to speak to the man. "What is the reason of your journey?" said the king to the hunter.

"I have only to tell you, O king," said the hunter, "that I saw the fairest creature that ever was born in Erin, and I came to tell you of it."

"Who is this beauty and where is she to be seen, when she was not seen before till you saw her, if you did see her?"

"Well, I did see her," said the hunter. "But, if I did, no man else can see her unless he get directions from me as to where she is dwelling."

"And will you direct me to where she dwells? And the reward of your directing me will be as good as the reward of your message," said the king.

"Well, I will direct you, O king, although it is likely that this will not be what they want," said the hunter.

Connachar, King of Ulster, sent for his nearest kinsmen, and he told them of his intent. Though early rose the song of the birds mid the rocky caves and the music of the birds in the grove, earlier than that did Connachar, King of Ulster, arise, with his little troop of dear friends, in the delightful twilight of the fresh and gentle May; the dew was heavy on each bush and flower and stem, as they went to bring Deirdre forth from the green knoll where she stayed. Many a youth was there who had a lithe leaping and lissom step when they started whose step was faint, failing, and faltering when they reached the bothy on account of the length of the way and roughness of the road.

"Yonder, now, down in the bottom of the glen is the bothy where the woman dwells, but I will not go nearer than this to the old woman," said the hunter.

Connachar with his band of kinsfolk went down to the green knoll where Deirdre dwelt and he knocked at the door of the bothy. The nurse replied, "No less than a king's command and a king's army could put me out of my bothy tonight. And I should be obliged to you, were you to tell who it is that wants me to open my bothy door."

"It is I, Connachar, King of Ulster." When the poor woman heard who was at the door, she rose with haste and let in the king and all that could get in of his retinue.

When the king saw the woman that was before him that he had been in quest of, he thought he never saw in the course of the day nor in the dream of night a creature so fair as Deirdre and he gave his full heart's weight of love to her. Deirdre was raised on the topmost of the heroes' shoulders and she and her foster-mother were brought to the Court of King Connachar of Ulster.

With the love that Connachar had for her, he wanted to marry Deirdre right off there and then, will she nill she marry him. But she said to him, "I would be obliged to you if you will give me the respite of a year and a day." He said "I will grant you that, hard though it is, if you will give me your unfailing promise that you will marry me at the year's end." And she gave the promise. Connachar got for her a woman-teacher and merry modest maidens fair that would lie down and rise with her, that would play and speak with her. Deirdre was clever in maidenly duties and wifely understanding, and Connachar thought he never saw with bodily eye a creature that pleased him more.

Deirdre and her women companions were one day out on the hillock behind the house enjoying the scene, and drinking in the sun's heat. What did they see coming but three men a-journeying. Deirdre was looking at the men that were coming, and wondering at them. When the men neared them, Deirdre remembered the language of the huntsman, and she said to herself that these were the three sons of Uisnech, and that this was Naois, he having what was above the bend of the two shoulders above the men of Erin all. The three brothers went past without taking any notice of them, without even glancing at the young girls on the hillock. What happened but that love for Naois struck the heart of Deirdre, so that she could not but follow after him. She girded up her raiment and went after the men that went past the base of the knoll, leaving her women attendants there. Allen and Arden had heard of the woman that Connachar, King of Ulster, had with him, and they thought that, if Naois, their brother, saw her, he would have her himself, more especially as she was not married to the King. They perceived the woman coming, and called on one another to hasten their step as they had a long distance to travel, and the dusk of night was coming on. They did so. She cried: "Naois, son of Uisnech, will you leave me?"

"What piercing, shrill cry is that – the most melodious my ear ever heard, and the shrillest that ever struck my heart of all the cries I ever heard?"

"It is anything else but the wail of the wave-swans of Connachar," said his brothers.

"No! Yonder is a woman's cry of distress," said Naois, and he swore he would not go further until he saw from whom the cry came, and Naois turned back. Naois and Deirdre met, and Deirdre kissed Naois three times, and a kiss each to his brothers. With the confusion that she was in, Deirdre went into a crimson blaze of fire, and her colour came and went as rapidly as the movement of the aspen by the stream side. Naois thought he never saw a fairer creature, and Naois gave Deirdre the love that he never gave to thing, to vision, or to creature but to herself. Then Naois placed Deirdre on the topmost height of his shoulder, and told his brothers to keep up their pace, and they kept up their pace. Naois thought that it would not be well for him to remain in Erin on account of the way in which Connachar, King of Ulster, his uncle's son, had gone against him because of the woman, though he had not married her; and he turned back to Alba, that is, Scotland. He reached the side of Loch-Ness and made his habitation there. He could kill the salmon of the torrent from out his own door, and the deer of the grey gorge from out his window. Naois and Deirdre and Allen and Arden dwelt in a tower, and they were happy so long a time as they were there.

By this time the end of the period came at which Deirdre had to marry Connachar, King of Ulster. Connachar made up his mind to take Deirdre away by the sword whether she was married to Naois or not. So he prepared a great and gleeful feast. He sent word far and wide through Erin all to his kinspeople to come to the feast. Connachar thought to himself that Naois would not come though he should bid him; and the scheme that arose in his mind was to send for his father's brother, Ferchar Mac Ro, and to send him on an embassy to Naois. He did so; and Connachar said to Ferchar, "Tell Naois, son of Uisnech, that I am setting forth a great and gleeful feast to my friends and kinspeople throughout the wide extent of Erin all, and that I shall not have rest by day nor sleep by night if he and Allen and Arden be not partakers of the feast."

Ferchar Mac Ro and his three sons went on their journey, and reached the tower where Naois was dwelling by the side of Loch Etive. The sons of Uisnech gave a cordial kindly welcome to Ferchar Mac Ro and his three sons, and asked of him the news of Erin. "The best news that I have for you," said the hardy hero, "is that Connachar, King of Ulster, is setting forth a great sumptuous feast to his friends and kinspeople throughout the wide extent of Erin all, and he has vowed by the earth beneath him, by the high heaven above him, and by the sun that wends to the west, that he will have no rest by day nor sleep by night if the sons of Uisnech, the sons of his own father's brother, will not come back to the land of their home and the soil of their nativity, and to the feast likewise, and he has sent us on embassy to invite you."

"We will go with you," said Naois.

"We will," said his brothers.

But Deirdre did not wish to go with Ferchar Mac Ro, and she tried every prayer to turn Naois from going with him – she said: "I saw a vision, Naois, and do you interpret it to me," – then she sang:

> O Naois, son of Uisnech, hear
> What was shown in a dream to me.
> There came three white doves out of the South

Flying over the sea,
And drops of honey were in their mouth
From the hive of the honey-bee.
O Naois, son of Uisnech, hear,
What was shown in a dream to me.
I saw three grey hawks out of the south
Come flying over the sea,
And the red red drops they bare in their mouth
They were dearer than life to me.

Said Naois: –

It is nought but the fear of woman's heart,
And a dream of the night, Deirdre.

"The day that Connachar sent the invitation to his feast will be unlucky for us if we don't go, O Deirdre."

"You will go there," said Ferchar Mac Ro; "and if Connachar show kindness to you, show ye kindness to him; and if he will display wrath towards you display ye wrath towards him, and I and my three sons will be with you."

"We will," said Daring Drop. "We will," said Hardy Holly. "We will," said Fiallan the Fair.

"I have three sons, and they are three heroes, and in any harm or danger that may befall you, they will be with you, and I myself will be along with them." And Ferchar Mac Ro gave his vow and his word in presence of his arms that, in any harm or danger that came in the way of the sons of Uisnech, he and his three sons would not leave head on live body in Erin, despite sword or helmet, spear or shield, blade or mail, be they ever so good.

Deirdre was unwilling to leave Alba, but she went with Naois. Deirdre wept tears in showers and she sang:

"Dear is the land, the land over there,
Alba full of woods and lakes;
Bitter to my heart is leaving thee,
But I go away with Naois."

Ferchar Mac Ro did not stop till he got the sons of Uisnech away with him, despite the suspicion of Deirdre.

The coracle was put to sea,
The sail was hoisted to it;
And the second morrow they arrived
On the white shores of Erin.

As soon as the sons of Uisnech landed in Erin, Ferchar Mac Ro sent word to Connachar, king of Ulster, that the men whom he wanted were come, and let him now show kindness to them. "Well," said Connachar, "I did not expect that the sons of Uisnech would come, though I sent for them, and I am not quite ready to receive them.

But there is a house down yonder where I keep strangers, and let them go down to it today, and my house will be ready before them tomorrow." But he that was up in the palace felt it long that he was not getting word as to how matters were going on for those down in the house of the strangers.

"Go you, Gelban Grednach, son of Lochlin's King, go you down and bring me information as to whether her former hue and complexion are on Deirdre. If they be, I will take her out with edge of blade and point of sword, and if not, let Naois, son of Uisnech, have her for himself," said Connachar.

Gelban, the cheering and charming son of Lochlin's King, went down to the place of the strangers, where the sons of Uisnech and Deirdre were staying. He looked in through the bicker-hole on the door-leaf. Now she that he gazed upon used to go into a crimson blaze of blushes when anyone looked at her. Naois looked at Deirdre and knew that someone was looking at her from the back of the door-leaf. He seized one of the dice on the table before him and fired it through the bicker-hole, and knocked the eye out of Gelban Grednach the Cheerful and Charming, right through the back of his head. Gelban returned back to the palace of King Connachar.

"You were cheerful, charming, going away, but you are cheerless, charmless, returning. What has happened to you, Gelban? But have you seen her, and are Deirdre's hue and complexion as before?" said Connachar.

"Well, I have seen Deirdre, and I saw her also truly, and while I was looking at her through the bicker-hole on the door, Naois, son of Uisnech, knocked out my eye with one of the dice in his hand. But of a truth and verity, although he put out even my eye, it were my desire still to remain looking at her with the other eye, were it not for the hurry you told me to be in," said Gelban.

"That is true," said Connachar; "let three hundred bravo heroes go down to the abode of the strangers, and let them bring hither to me Deirdre, and kill the rest." Connachar ordered three hundred active heroes to go down to the abode of the strangers and to take Deirdre up with them and kill the rest. "The pursuit is coming," said Deirdre.

"Yes, but I will myself go out and stop the pursuit," said Naois.

"It is not you, but we that will go," said Daring Drop, and Hardy Holly, and Fiallan the Fair; "it is to us that our father entrusted your defence from harm and danger when he himself left for home." And the gallant youths, full noble, full manly, full handsome, with beauteous brown locks, went forth girt with battle arms fit for fierce fight and clothed with combat dress for fierce contest fit, which was burnished, bright, brilliant, bladed, blazing, on which were many pictures of beasts and birds and creeping things, lions and lithe-limbed tigers, brown eagle and harrying hawk and adder fierce; and the young heroes laid low three-thirds of the company.

Connachar came out in haste and cried with wrath: "Who is there on the floor of fight, slaughtering my men?"

"We, the three sons of Ferchar Mac Ro."

"Well," said the king, "I will give a free bridge to your grandfather, a free bridge to your father, and a free bridge each to you three brothers, if you come over to my side tonight."

"Well, Connachar, we will not accept that offer from you nor thank you for it. Greater by far do we prefer to go home to our father and tell the deeds of heroism we have done, than accept anything on these terms from you. Naois, son of Uisnech, and Allen and Arden are as nearly related to yourself as they are to us, though you are so keen to shed their blood, and you would shed our blood also, Connachar." And the noble, manly, handsome youths with beauteous, brown locks returned inside. "We are now," said they, "going home to tell our father that you are now safe from the hands of the king." And the youths all fresh and tall and lithe and beautiful, went home to their father to tell that the sons of Uisnech were safe. This happened at the parting of the day and night in the morning twilight time, and Naois said they must go away, leave that house, and return to Alba.

Naois and Deirdre, Allan and Arden started to return to Alba. Word came to the king that the company he was in pursuit of were gone. The king then sent for Duanan Gacha Druid, the best magician he had, and he spoke to him as follows: – "Much wealth have I expended on you, Duanan Gacha Druid, to give schooling and learning and magic mystery to you, if these people get away from me today without care, without consideration or regard for me, without chance of overtaking them, and without power to stop them."

"Well, I will stop them," said the magician, "until the company you send in pursuit return." And the magician placed a wood before them through which no man could go, but the sons of Uisnech marched through the wood without halt or hesitation, and Deirdre held on to Naois's hand. "What is the good of that? That will not do yet," said Connachar. "They are off without bending of their feet or stopping of their step, without heed or respect to me, and I am without power to keep up to them or opportunity to turn them back this night."

"I will try another plan on them," said the druid; and he placed before them a grey sea instead of a green plain. The three heroes stripped and tied their clothes behind their heads, and Naois placed Deirdre on the top of his shoulder.

> They stretched their sides to the stream,
> And sea and land were to them the same,
> The rough grey ocean was the same
> As meadow-land green and plain.

"Though that be good, O Duanan, it will not make the heroes return," said Connachar; "they are gone without regard for me, and without honour to me, and without power on my part to pursue them or to force them to return this night."

"We shall try another method on them, since yon one did not stop them," said the druid. And the druid froze the grey ridged sea into hard rocky knobs, the sharpness of sword being on the one edge and the poison power of adders on the other. Then Arden cried that he was getting tired, and nearly giving over. "Come you, Arden, and sit on my right shoulder," said Naois. Arden came and sat, on Naois's shoulder. Arden was long in this posture when he died; but though he was dead Naois would not let him go.

Allen then cried out that he was getting faint and nigh-well giving up. When Naois heard his prayer, he gave forth the piercing sigh of death, and asked Allen to lay hold of him and he would bring him to land.

Allen was not long when the weakness of death came on him and his hold failed. Naois looked around, and when he saw his two well-beloved brothers dead, he cared not whether he lived or died, and he gave forth the bitter sigh of death, and his heart burst.

"They are gone," said Duanan Gacha Druid to the king, "and I have done what you desired me. The sons of Uisnech are dead and they will trouble you no more; and you have your wife hale and whole to yourself."

"Blessings for that upon you and may the good results accrue to me, Duanan. I count it no loss what I spent in the schooling and teaching of you. Now dry up the flood, and let me see if I can behold Deirdre," said Connachar. And Duanan Gacha Druid dried up the flood from the plain and the three sons of Uisnech were lying together dead, without breath of life, side by side on the green meadow plain and Deirdre bending above showering down her tears.

Then Deirdre said this lament: "Fair one, loved one, flower of beauty; beloved upright and strong; beloved noble and modest warrior. Fair one, blue-eyed, beloved of thy wife; lovely to me at the trysting-place came thy clear voice through the woods of Ireland. I cannot eat or smile henceforth. Break not today, my heart: soon enough shall I lie within my grave. Strong are the waves of sorrow, but stronger is sorrow's self, Connachar."

The people then gathered round the heroes' bodies and asked Connachar what was to be done with the bodies. The order that he gave was that they should dig a pit and put the three brothers in it side by side. Deirdre kept sitting on the brink of the grave, constantly asking the gravediggers to dig the pit wide and free. When the bodies of the brothers were put in the grave, Deirdre said: –

> *"Come over hither, Naois, my love,*
> *Let Arden close to Allen lie;*
> *If the dead had any sense to feel,*
> *Ye would have made a place for Deirdre."*

The men did as she told them. She jumped into the grave and lay down by Naois, and she was dead by his side.

The king ordered the body to be raised from out the grave and to be buried on the other side of the loch. It was done as the king bade, and the pit closed. Thereupon a fir shoot grew out of the grave of Deirdre and a fir shoot from the grave of Naois, and the two shoots united in a knot above the loch. The king ordered the shoots to be cut down, and this was done twice, until, at the third time, the wife whom the king had married caused him to stop this work of evil and his vengeance on the remains of the dead.

Heroes
&
Giants

Introduction

ANCIENT TALES of Celtic warriors and their fearsome opponents exist so strongly in the mind to this day due to the richness of the storytelling tradition. Fionn Mac Cumhail, legendary hero of the Fenian Cycle of stories, holds a firm place in this section, as does the great Cuchulain of the Ulster cycle. The latter's adventures are recounted most memorably in 'The Cattle-Raid of Cualnge', in a translation by L. Winifred Faraday here.

The Cattle-Raid of Cualnge, or, Táin Bó Cúailnge

Introduction

THE CATTLE-RAID of Cualnge (pronounced *Cooley*) is the chief story belonging to the heroic cycle of Ulster, which had its centre in the deeds of the Ulster king, Conchobar Mac Nessa, and his nephew and chief warrior, Cuchulainn Mac Sualtaim. Tradition places their date at the beginning of the Christian era.

The events leading up to this tale, the most famous of Irish mythical stories, may be shortly summarised here from the Book of Leinster introduction to the *Tain*, and from the other tales belonging to the Ulster cycle.

It is elsewhere narrated that the Dun Bull of Cualnge, for whose sake Ailill and Medb (pronounced *Maive*), the king and queen of Connaught, undertook this expedition, was one of two bulls in whom two rival swineherds, belonging to the supernatural race known as the people of the *Sid*, or fairy-mounds, were re-incarnated, after passing through various other forms. The other bull, Findbennach, the White-horned, was in the herd of Medb at Cruachan Ai, the Connaught capital, but left it to join Ailill's herd. This caused Ailill's possessions to exceed Medb's, and to equalise matters she determined to secure the great Dun Bull, who alone equalled the White-horned. An embassy to the owner of the Dun Bull failed, and Ailill and Medb therefore began preparations for an invasion of Ulster, in which province (then ruled by Conchobar Mac Nessa) Cualnge was situated. A number of smaller *Tana*, or cattle-raids, prefatory to the great *Tain Bo Cuailnge*, relate some of their efforts to procure allies and provisions.

Medb chose for the expedition the time when Conchobar and all the warriors of Ulster, except Cuchulainn and Sualtaim, were at their capital, Emain Macha, in a sickness which fell on them periodically, making them powerless for action; another story relates the cause of this sickness, the effect of a curse laid on them by a fairy woman. Ulster was therefore defended only by the seventeen-year-old Cuchulainn, for Sualtaim's appearance is only spasmodic. Cuchulainn (Culann's Hound) was the son of Dechtire, the king's sister, his father being, in different accounts, either Sualtaim, an Ulster warrior; Lug Mac Ethlend, one of the divine heroes from the *Sid*, or fairy-mound; or Conchobar himself. The two former both appear as Cuchulainn's father in the present narrative. Cuchulainn is accompanied, throughout the adventures here told, by his charioteer, Loeg Mac Riangabra.

In Medb's force were several Ulster heroes, including Cormac Condlongas, son of Conchobar, Conall Cernach, Dubthach Doeltenga, Fiacha Mac Firfebe, and Fergus Mac Roich. These were exiled from Ulster through a bitter quarrel with Conchobar, who had caused the betrayal and murder of the sons of Uisnech, when they had come to

Ulster under the sworn protection of Fergus, as told in the *Exile of the Sons of Uisnech*. The Ulster mischief-maker, Bricriu of the Poison-tongue, was also with the Connaught army. Though fighting for Connaught, the exiles have a friendly feeling for their former comrades, and a keen jealousy for the credit of Ulster. There is a constant interchange of courtesies between them and their old pupil, Cuchulainn, whom they do not scruple to exhort to fresh efforts for Ulster's honour. An equally half-hearted warrior is Lugaid Mac Nois, king of Munster, who was bound in friendship to the Ulstermen.

Other characters who play an important part in the story are Findabair, daughter of Ailill and Medb, who is held out as a bribe to various heroes to induce them to fight Cuchulainn, and is on one occasion offered to the latter in fraud on condition that he will give up his opposition to the host; and the war-goddess, variously styled the Nemain, the Badb (scald-crow), and the Morrigan (great queen), who takes part against Cuchulainn in one of his chief fights. Findabair is the bait which induces several old comrades of Cuchulainn's, who had been his fellow-pupils under the sorceress Scathach, to fight him in single combat.

The Cattle-Raid of Cualnge

Chapter I

A great hosting was brought together by the Connaughtmen, that is, by Ailill and Medb; and they sent to the three other provinces. And messengers were sent by Ailill to the seven sons of Magach: Ailill, Anluan, Mocorb, Cet, En, Bascall, and Doche; a cantred with each of them. And to Cormac Condlongas Mac Conchobair with his three hundred, who was billeted in Connaught. Then they all come to Cruachan Ai.

Now Cormac had three troops which came to Cruachan. The first troop had many-coloured cloaks folded round them; hair like a mantle; the tunic falling to the knee, and long shields; and a broad grey spearhead on a slender shaft in the hand of each man.

The second troop wore dark grey cloaks, and tunics with red ornamentation down to their calves, and long hair hanging behind from their heads, and white shields, and five-pronged spears were in their hands.

"This is not Cormac yet," said Medb.

Then comes the third troop; and they wore purple cloaks and hooded tunics with red ornamentation down to their feet, hair smooth to their shoulders, and round shields with engraved edges, and spears as large as the pillars of a palace in the hand of each man.

"This is Cormac now," said Medb.

Then the four provinces of Ireland were assembled, till they were in Cruachan Ai. And their poets and their druids did not let them go thence till the end of a fortnight, for waiting for a good omen. Medb said then to her charioteer the day that they set out:

"Everyone who parts here today from his love or his friend will curse me," said she, "for it is I who have gathered this hosting."

"Wait then," said the charioteer, "till I turn the chariot with the sun, and till there come the power of a good omen that we may come back again."

Then the charioteer turned the chariot, and they set forth. Then they saw a full-grown maiden before them. She had yellow hair, and a cloak of many colours, and a golden pin in it; and a hooded tunic with red embroidery. She wore two shoes with buckles of gold. Her face was narrow below and broad above. Very black were her two eyebrows; her black delicate eyelashes cast a shadow into the middle of her two cheeks. You would think it was with *partaing* her lips were adorned. You would think it was a shower of pearls that was in her mouth, that is, her teeth. She had three tresses: two tresses round her head above, and a tress behind, so that it struck her two thighs behind her. A shuttle (a beam used for making fringe) of white metal, with an inlaying of gold, was in her hand. Each of her two eyes had three pupils. The maiden was armed, and there were two black horses to her chariot.

"What is your name?" said Medb to the maiden.

"Fedelm, the prophetess of Connaught, is my name," said the maiden.

"Whence do you come?" said Medb.

"From Scotland, after learning the art of prophecy," said the maiden.

"Have you the inspiration which illumines?" said Medb.

"Yes, indeed," said the maiden.

"Look for me how it will be with my hosting," said Medb.

Then the maiden looked for it; and Medb said: "O Fedelm the prophetess, how seest thou the host?"

Fedelm answered and said: "I see very red, I see red."

"That is not true," said Medb; 'for Conchobar is in his sickness at Emain and the Ulstermen with him, with all the best of their warriors; and my messengers have come and brought me tidings thence.

"Fedelm the prophetess, how seest thou our host?" said Medb.

"I see red," said the maiden.

"That is not true," said Medb; "for Celtchar Mac Uithichair is in Dun Lethglaise, and a third of the Ulstermen with him; and Fergus, son of Roich, son of Eochaid, is here with us, in exile, and a cantred with him. Fedelm the prophetess, how seest thou our host?"

"I see very red, I see red," said the maiden.

"That matters not," said Medb; "for there are mutual angers, and quarrels, and wounds very red in every host and in every assembly of a great army. Look again for us then, and tell us the truth. Fedelm the prophetess, how seest thou our host?"

"I see very red, I see red," said Fedelm.

"I see a fair man who will make play
With a number of wounds on his girdle;
A hero's flame over his head,
His forehead a meeting-place of victory.

"There are seven gems of a hero of valour
In the middle of his two irises;
There is — on his cloak,
He wears a red clasped tunic.

"He has a face that is noble,
Which causes amazement to women.
A young man who is fair of hue
Comes —

"Like is the nature of his valour
To Cuchulainn of Murthemne.
I do not know whose is the Hound
Of Culann, whose fame is the fairest.
But I know that it is thus
That the host is very red from him.

"I see a great man on the plain
He gives battle to the hosts;
Four little swords of feats

There are in each of his two hands.

"Two Gae-bolga[1], he carries them,
Besides an ivory-hilted sword and spear;
— he wields to the host;
Different is the deed for which each arm goes from him.

"A man in a battle-girdle, of a red cloak,
He puts — every plain.
He smites them, over left chariot wheel;
The Riastartha[2] wounds them.
The form that appeared to me on him hitherto,
I see that his form has been changed.

"He has moved forward to the battle,
If heed is not taken of him it will be treachery.
I think it likely it is he who seeks you:
Cuchulainn Mac Sualtaim.

"He will strike on whole hosts,
He will make dense slaughters of you,
Ye will leave with him many thousands of heads.
The prophetess Fedelm conceals not.

"Blood will rain from warriors' wounds
At the hand of a warrior – 'twill be full harm.
He will slay warriors, men will wander
Of the descendants of Deda Mac Sin.
Corpses will be cut off, women will lament
Through the Hound of the Smith that I see."

The Monday after Samain ('summer-end', about the beginning of November) they set forth, and this is the way they took: south-east from Cruachan Ai, i.e. by Muicc Cruimb, by Teloch Teora Crich, by Tuaim Mona, by Cul Sibrinne, by Fid, by Bolga, by Coltain, by Glune-gabair, by Mag Trego, by North Tethba, by South Tethba, by Tiarthechta, by Ord, by Slais southwards, by Indiuind, by Carnd, by Ochtrach, by Midi, by Findglassa Assail, by Deilt, by Delind, by Sailig, by Slaibre, by Slechta Selgatar, by Cul Sibrinne, by Ochaind southwards, by Uatu northwards, by Dub, by Comur southwards, by Tromma, by Othromma eastwards, by Slane, by Gortslane, by Druim Licce southwards, by Ath Gabla, by Ard Achad, by Feraind northwards, by Findabair, by Assi southwards, by Druim Salfind, by Druim Cain, by Druim Mac n-Dega, by Eodond Mor, by Eodond Bec, by Methe Togmaill, by Methe Eoin, by Druim Caemtechta, by Scuaip, by Imscuaip, by Cend Ferna, by Baile, by Aile, by Bail Scena, by Dail Scena, by Fertse, by Ross Lochad, by Sale, by Lochmach, by Anmag, by Deind, by Deilt, by Dubglaiss, by Fid Mor, by Colbtha, by Cronn, to Cualnge.

From Findabair Cuailnge, it is thence the hosts of Ireland were divided over the province to seek the Bull. For it is past these places that they came, till they reached Findabair.

(Here ends the title; and the story begins as follows:)

This is the Story in Order

WHEN THEY HAD come on their first journey from Cruachan as far as Cul Sibrinne, Medb told her charioteer to get ready her nine chariots for her, that she might make a circuit in the camp, to see who disliked and who liked the expedition.

Now his tent was pitched for Ailill, and the furniture was arranged, both beds and coverings. Fergus Mac Roich in his tent was next to Ailill; Cormac Condlongas Mac Conchobair beside him; Conall Cernach by him; Fiacha Mac Fir-Febe, the son of Conchobar's daughter, by him. Medb, daughter of Eochaid Fedlech, was on Ailill's other side; next to her, Findabair, daughter of Ailill and Medb. That was besides servants and attendants.

Medb came, after looking at the host, and she said it were folly for the rest to go on the hosting, if the cantred of the Leinstermen went.

"Why do you blame the men?" said Ailill.

"We do not blame them," said Medb; "splendid are the warriors. When the rest were making their huts, they had finished thatching their huts and cooking their food; when the rest were at dinner, they had finished dinner, and their harpers were playing to them. It is folly for them to go," said Medb; "it is to their credit the victory of the hosts will be."

"It is for us they fight," said Ailill.

"They shall not come with us," said Medb.

"Let them stay then," said Ailill.

"They shall not stay," said Medb. "They will come on us after we have gone," said she, "and seize our land against us."

"What is to be done to them?" said Ailill; "will you have them neither stay nor go?"

"To kill them," said Medb.

"We will not hide that this is a woman's plan," said Ailill; "what you say is not good!"

"With this folk," said Fergus, "it shall not happen thus (for it is a folk bound by ties to us Ulstermen), unless we are all killed."

"Even that we could do," said Medb; "for I am here with my retinue of two cantreds." said she, "and there are the seven Manes, that is, my seven sons, with seven cantreds; their luck can protect them," said she; "that is Mane-Mathramail, and Mane-Athramail, and Mane-Morgor, and Mane-Mingor, and Mane-Moepert (and he is Mane-Milscothach), Mane-Andoe, and Mane-who-got-everything: he got the form of his mother and of his father, and the dignity of both."

"It would not be so," said Fergus. "There are seven kings of Munster here, and a cantred with each of them, in friendship with us Ulstermen. I will give battle to you," said Fergus, "in the middle of the host in which we are, with these seven cantreds, and with my own cantred, and with the cantred of the Leinstermen. But I will not urge that," said Fergus, "we will provide for the warriors otherwise, so that they shall not prevail over the host. Seventeen cantreds for us," said Fergus, "that is the number of our army, besides our rabble, and our women (for with each king there is his queen, in Medb's company), and besides our striplings. This is the eighteenth cantred, the cantred of the Leinstermen. Let them be distributed among the rest of the host."

"I do not care," said Medb, "provided they are not gathered as they are."

Then this was done; the Leinstermen were distributed among the host.

They set out next morning to Moin Choiltrae, where eight score deer fell in with them in one herd. They surrounded them and killed them then; wherever there was a man of the Leinstermen, it was he who got them, except five deer that all the rest of the host got. Then they came to Mag Trego, and stopped there and prepared their food. They say that it is there that Dubthach sang this song:

"Grant what you have not heard hitherto,
Listening to the fight of Dubthach.
A hosting very black is before you,
Against Findbend of the wife of Ailill[3].

"The man of expeditions will come
Who will defend Murthemne.
Ravens will drink milk of —
From the friendship of the swineherds.

"The turfy Cronn[4] *will resist them;*
He will not let them into Murthemne
Until the work of warriors is over
In Sliab Tuad Ochaine.

"'Quickly,' said Ailill to Cormac,
'Go that you may — your son.
The cattle do not come from the fields
That the din of the host may not terrify them.

"'This will be a battle in its time
For Medb with a third of the host.
There will be flesh of men therefrom
If the Riastartha comes to you.'"

Then the Nemain attacked them, and that was not the quietest of nights for them, with the uproar of the churl (i.e. Dubthach) through their sleep. The host started up at once, and a great number of the host were in confusion, till Medb came to reprove him.

Then they went and spent the night in Granard Tethba Tuascirt, after the host had been led astray over bogs and over streams. A warning was sent from Fergus to the Ulstermen here, for friendship. They were now in the weakness, except Cuchulainn and his father Sualtaim.

Cuchulainn and his father went, after the coming of the warning from Fergus, till they were in Iraird Cuillend, watching the host there.

"I think of the host tonight," said Cuchulainn to his father. "Go from us with a warning to the Ulstermen. I am forced to go to a tryst with Fedelm Noichride, from my own pledge that went out to her."

He made a spancel-withe[5] then before he went, and wrote an ogam on its — and threw it on the top of the pillar.

The leadership of the way before the army was given to Fergus. Then Fergus went far astray to the south, till Ulster should have completed the collection of an army; he did this for friendship. Ailill and Medb perceived it; it was then Medb said:

"O Fergus, this is strange,
What kind of way do we go?
Straying south or north
We go over every other folk.

"Ailill of Ai with his hosting
Fears that you will betray them.
You have not given your mind hitherto
To the leading of the way.

"If it is in friendship that you do it,
Do not lead the horses
Peradventure another may be found
To lead the way."

Fergus replied:

"O Medb, what troubles you?
This is not like treachery.
It belongs to the Ulstermen, O woman,
The land across which I am leading you.

"It is not for the disadvantage of the host
That I go on each wandering in its turn;
It is to avoid the great man
Who protects Mag Murthemne.

"Not that my mind is not distressed
On account of the straying on which I go,
But if perchance I may avoid even afterwards
Cuchulainn Mac Sualtaim."

Then they went till they were in Iraird Cuillend. Eirr and Indell, Foich and Foclam (their two charioteers), the four sons of Iraird Mac Anchinne, it is they who were before the host, to protect their brooches and their cushions and their cloaks, that the dust of the host might not soil them. They found the withe that Cuchulainn threw, and perceived the grazing that the horses had grazed. For Sualtaim's two horses had eaten the grass with its roots from the earth; Cuchulainn's two horses had licked the earth as far as the stones beneath the grass. They sit down then, until the host came, and the musicians play to them. They give the withe into the hands of Fergus Mac Roich; he read the ogam that was on it.

When Medb came, she asked, "Why are you waiting here?"

"We wait," said Fergus, "because of the withe yonder. There is an ogam on its —, and this is what is in it: 'Let no one go past till a man is found to throw a like withe with his one hand, and let it be one twig of which it is made; and I except my friend Fergus.' Truly," said Fergus, "Cuchulainn has thrown it, and they are his horses that grazed the plain."

And he put it in the hands of the druids; and Fergus sang this song:

"Here is a withe, what does the withe declare to us?
What is its mystery?
What number threw it?
Few or many?

"Will it cause injury to the host,
If they go a journey from it?
Find out, ye druids, something therefore
For what the withe has been left.

"— of heroes the hero who has thrown it,
Full misfortune on warriors;
A delay of princes, wrathful is the matter,
One man has thrown it with one hand.

"Is not the king's host at the will of him,
Unless it breaks fair play?
Until one man only of you
Throw it, as one man has thrown it.
I do not know anything save that
For which the withe should have been put.
Here is a withe."

Then Fergus said to them: "If you outrage this withe," said he, "or if you go past it, though he be in the custody of a man, or in a house under a lock, the — of the man who wrote the ogam on it will reach him, and will slay a goodly slaughter of you before morning, unless one of you throw a like withe."

"It does not please us, indeed, that one of us should be slain at once," said Ailill. "We will go by the neck of the great wood yonder, south of us, and we will not go over it at all."

The troops hewed down then the wood before the chariots. This is the name of that place, Slechta. It is there that Partraige is. (According to others, the conversation between Medb and Fedelm the prophetess took place there, as we told before; and then it is after the answer she gave to Medb that the wood was cut down; i.e. "Look for me," said Medb, "how my hosting will be." "It is difficult to me," said the maiden; "I cannot cast my eye over them in the wood." "It is ploughland there shall be," said Medb; "we will cut down the wood." Then this was done, so that Slechta was the name of the place.)

They spent the night then in Cul Sibrille; a great snowstorm fell on them, to the girdles of the men and the wheels of the chariots. The rising was early next morning. And it was not the most peaceful of nights for them, with the snow; and they had not prepared food that night. But it was not early when Cuchulainn came from his tryst; he waited to wash and bathe.

Then he came on the track of the host. "Would that we had not gone there," said Cuchulainn, "nor betrayed the Ulstermen; we have let the host go to them unawares. Make us an estimation of the host," said Cuchulainn to Loeg, "that we may know the number of the host."

Loeg did this, and said to Cuchulainn: "I am confused," said he, "I cannot attain this."

"It would not be confusion that I see, if only I come," said Cuchulainn.

"Get into the chariot then," said Loeg.

Cuchulainn got into the chariot, and put a reckoning over the host for a long time.

"Even you," said Loeg, "you do not find it easy."

"It is easier indeed to me than to you," said Cuchulainn; "for I have three gifts, the gifts of eye, and of mind, and of reckoning. I have put a reckoning on this," said he; "there are eighteen cantreds," said he, "for their number; only that the eighteenth cantred is distributed among all the host, so that their number is not clear; that is, the cantred of the Leinstermen."

Then Cuchulainn went round the host till he was at Ath Gabla. He cuts a fork (of a tree) there with one blow of his sword, and put it on the middle of the stream, so that a chariot could not pass it on this side or that. Eirr and Indell, Foich and Fochlam (their two charioteers) came upon him thereat. He strikes their four heads off, and throws them on to the four points of the fork. Hence is Ath Gabla.

Then the horses of the four went to meet the host, and their cushions very red on them. They supposed it was a battalion that was before them at the ford. A troop went from them to look at the ford; they saw nothing there but the track of one chariot and the fork with the four heads, and a name in ogam written on the side. All the host came then.

"Are the heads yonder from our people?" said Medb.

"They are from our people and from our choice warriors," said Ailill.

One of them read the ogam that was on the side of the fork; that is: "A man has thrown the fork with his one hand; and you shall not go past it till one of you, except Fergus, has thrown it with one hand."

"It is a marvel," said Ailill, "the quickness with which the four were struck."

"It was not that that was a marvel," said Fergus; "it was the striking of the fork from the trunk with one blow; and if the end was cut with one blow, it is the fairer for it, and that it was thrust in in this manner; for it is not a hole that has been dug for it, but it is from the back of the chariot it has been thrown with one hand."

"Avert this strait from us, O Fergus," said Medb.

"Bring me a chariot then," said Fergus, "that I may take it out, that you may see whether its end was hewn with one blow." Fergus broke then fourteen chariots of his chariots, so that it was from his own chariot that he took it out of the ground, and he saw that the end was hewn with one blow.

"Heed must be taken to the character of the tribe to which we are going," said Ailill. "Let each of you prepare his food; you had no rest last night for the snow. And something shall be told to us of the adventures and stories of the tribe to which we are going."

It is then that the adventures of Cuchulainn were related to them.

Ailill asked: "Is it Conchobar who has done this?"

"Not he," said Fergus; "he would not have come to the border of the country without the number of a battalion round him."

"Was it Celtchar Mac Uithidir?"

"Not he; he would not have come to the border of the country without the number of a battalion round him."

"Was it Eogan Mac Durtacht?"

"Not he," said Fergus; "he would not have come over the border of the country without thirty chariots two-pointed round him. This is the man who would have done the deed," said Fergus, "Cuchulainn; it is he who would have cut the tree at one blow from the trunk, and who would have killed the four yonder as quickly as they were killed, and who would have come to the boundary with his charioteer."

"What kind of man," said Ailill, "is this Hound of whom we have heard among the Ulstermen? What age is this youth who is famous?"

"An easy question, truly," said Fergus. "In his fifth year he went to the boys at Emain Macha to play; in his sixth year he went to learn arms and feats with Scathach. In his seventh year he took arms. He is now seventeen years old at this time."

"Is it he who is hardest to deal with among the Ulstermen?" said Medb.

"Over every one of them," said Fergus. "You will not find before you a warrior who is harder to deal with, nor a point that is sharper or keener or swifter, nor a hero who is fiercer, nor a raven that is more flesh-loving, nor a match of his age that can equal him as far as a third; nor a lion that is fiercer, nor a fence of battle, nor a hammer of destruction, nor a door of battle, nor judgment on hosts, nor preventing of a great host that is more worthy. You will not find there a man who would reach his age, and his growth, and his dress, and his terror, his speech, his splendour, his fame, his voice, his form, his power, his hardness, his accomplishment, his valour, his striking, his rage, his anger, his victory, his doom-giving, his violence, his estimation, his hero-triumph, his speed, his pride, his madness, with the feat of nine men on every point, like Cuchulainn!"

"I don't care for that," said Medb; "he is in one body; he endures wounding; he is not above capturing. Therewith his age is that of a grown-up girl, and his manly deeds have not come yet."

"Not so," said Fergus. "It would be no wonder if he were to do a good deed today; for even when he was younger his deeds were manly."

Here Are His Boyish Deeds

"HE WAS BROUGHT UP," said Fergus, "by his mother and father at the — in Mag Murthemne. The stories of the boys in Emain were related to him; for there are three fifties of boys there,' said Fergus, 'at play. It is thus that Conchobar enjoys his sovereignty: a third of the day watching the boys; another third playing chess; another third drinking beer till sleep seizes him therefrom. Although we are in exile, there is not in Ireland a warrior who is more wonderful," said Fergus.

"Cuchulainn asked his mother then to let him go to the boys.

"'You shall not go,' said his mother, 'until you have company of warriors.'

"'I deem it too long to wait for it,' said Cuchulainn. 'Show me on which side Emain is.'

"'Northwards so,' said his mother; 'and the journey is hard,' said she, 'Sliab Fuait is between you.'

"'I will find it out,' said Cuchulainn.

"He goes forth then, and his shield of lath with him, and his toy-spear, and his playing-club, and his ball. He kept throwing his staff before him, so that he took it by the point before the end fell on the ground.

"He goes then to the boys without binding them to protect him. For no one used to go to them in their play-field till his protection was guaranteed. He did not know this.

"'The boy insults us,' said Follomon Mac Conchobair, 'besides we know he is of the Ulstermen. Throw at him!'

"They throw their three fifties of toy-spears at him, and they all remained standing in his shield of lath. Then they throw all the balls at him; and he takes them, each single ball, in his bosom. Then they throw their three fifties of hurling-clubs at him; he warded them off so that they did not touch him, and he took a bundle of them on his back. Then contortion seized him. You would have thought that it was a hammering wherewith each little hair had been driven into his head, with the arising with which he arose. You would have thought there was a spark of fire on every single hair. He shut one of his eyes so that it was not wider than the eye of a needle. He opened the other so that it was as large as the mouth of a meadcup. He laid bare from his jawbone to his ear; he opened his mouth to his jaw so that his gullet was visible. The hero's light rose from his head. Then he strikes at the boys. He overthrows fifty of them before they reached the door of Emain. Nine of them came over me and Conchobar as we were playing chess. Then he springs over the chessboard after the nine. Conchobar caught his elbow.

"'The boys are not well treated,' said Conchobar.

"'Lawful for me, O friend Conchobar,' said he. 'I came to them from my home to play, from my mother and father; and they have not been good to me.'

"'What is your name?' said Conchobar.

"'Setanta Mac Sualtaim am I,' said he, 'and the son of Dechtere, your sister. It was not fitting to hurt me here.'

"'Why were the boys not bound to protect you?' said Conchobar.

"'I did not know this,' said Cuchulainn. 'Undertake my protection against them then.'

"'I recognise it,' said Conchobar.

"Then he turned aside on (to attack) the boys throughout the house.

"'What ails you at them now?' said Conchobar.

"'That I may be bound to protect them,' said Cuchulainn.

"'Undertake it,' said Conchobar.

"'I recognise it,' said Cuchulainn.

"Then they all went into the play-field, and those boys who had been struck down there arose. Their foster-mothers and foster-fathers helped them.

"Once," said Fergus, "when he was a youth, he used not to sleep in Emain Macha till morning.

"'Tell me,' said Conchobar to him, 'why you do not sleep?'

"'I do not do it,' said Cuchulainn, 'unless it is equally high at my head and my feet.'

"Then a stone pillar was put by Conchobar at his head, and another at his feet, and a bed was made for him separately between them.

"Another time a certain man went to awaken him, and he struck him with his fist in his forehead, so that it took the front of his forehead on to the brain, and so that he overthrew the pillar with his arm."

"It is known," said Ailill, "that it was the fist of a warrior and that it was the arm of a hero."

"From that time," said Fergus, "no one dared to waken him till he awoke of himself.

"Another time he was playing ball in the play-field east of Emain; he alone apart against the three fifties of boys; he used to defeat them in every game in this way always. The boys lay hold of him therewith, and he plied his fist upon them until fifty of them were killed. He took to flight then, till he was under the pillow of Conchobar's bed. All the Ulstermen rise round him, and I rise, and Conchobar himself. Then he rose under the bed, and put the bed from him, with the thirty heroes who were on it, till it was in the middle of the house. The Ulstermen sit round him in the house. We arrange and make peace then," said Fergus, "between the boys and him.

"There was contention between Ulster and Eogan Mac Durtacht. The Ulstermen went to the battle. He was left asleep. The Ulstermen were defeated. Conchobar was left on the field, and Cuscraid Mend Macha, and many more beside. Their lament awoke Cuchulainn. He stretched himself then, so that the two stones that were about him broke; in the presence of Bricriu yonder it was done," said Fergus. "Then he arose. I met him in the door of the fort, and I wounded.

"'Alas! God save you, friend Fergus,' said he, 'where is Conchobar?'

"'I do not know,' said I.

"Then he went forth. The night was dark. He made for the battlefield. He saw a man before him, with half his head on, and half of another man on his back.

"'Help me, O Cuchulainn,' said he; 'I have been wounded and I have brought half of my brother on my back. Carry it for me a while.'

"'I will not carry it,' said he.

"Then he throws the burden to him; he throws it from him; they wrestle; Cuchulainn was overthrown. I heard something, the Badb from the corpses: 'Ill the stuff of a hero that is under the feet of a phantom.' Then Cuchulainn rose against him, and strikes his head off with his playing-club, and begins to drive his ball before him across the plain.

"'Is my friend Conchobar in this battlefield?'

"He answered him. He goes to him, till he sees him in the trench, and there was the earth round him on every side to hide him.

"'Why have you come into the battlefield,' said Conchobar, 'that you may swoon there?'

"He lifts him out of the trench then; six of the strong men of Ulster with us would not have brought him out more bravely.

"'Go before us to the house yonder,' said Conchobar; 'if a roast pig came to me, I should live.'

"'I will go and bring it,' said Cuchulainn.

"He goes then, and saw a man at a cooking-hearth in the middle of the wood; one of his two hands had his weapons in it, the other was cooking the pig.

"The hideousness of the man was great; nevertheless he attacked him and took his head and his pig with him. Conchobar ate the pig then.

"'Let us go to our house,' said Conchobar.

"They met Cuscraid Mac Conchobair. There were sure wounds on him; Cuchulainn took him on his back. The three of them went then to Emain Macha.

"Another time the Ulstermen were in their weakness. There was not among us," said Fergus, "weakness on women and boys, nor on anyone who was outside the country of the Ulstermen, nor on Cuchulainn and his father. And so no one dared to shed their blood; for the suffering springs on him who wounds them.

"Three times nine men came to us from the Isles of Faiche. They went over our back court when we were in our weakness. The women screamed in the court. The boys were in the play-field; they come at the cries. When the boys saw the dark, black men, they all take to flight except Cuchulainn alone. He plies hand-stones and his playing-club on them. He kills nine of them, and they leave fifty wounds on him, and they go forth besides. A man who did these deeds when his five years were not full, it would be no wonder that he should have come to the edge of the boundary and that he should have cut off the heads of yonder four."

"We know him indeed, this boy," said Conall Cernach, "and we know him none the worse that he is a fosterling of ours. It was not long after the deed that Fergus has just related, when he did another deed. When Culann the smith served a feast to Conchobar, Culann said that it was not a multitude that should be brought to him, for the preparation which he had made was not from land or country, but from the fruit of his two hands and his pincers. Then Conchobar went, and fifty chariots with him, of those who were noblest and most eminent of the heroes. Now Conchobar visited then his play-field. It was always his custom to visit and revisit them at going and coming, to seek a greeting of the boys. He saw then Cuchulainn driving his ball against the three fifties of boys, and he gets the victory over them. When it was hole-driving that they did, he filled the hole with his balls and they could not ward him off. When they were all throwing into the hole, he warded them off alone, so that not a single ball would go in it. When it was wrestling they were doing, he overthrew the three fifties of boys by himself, and there did not meet round him a number that could overthrow him. When it was stripping that they did, he stripped them all so that they were quite naked, and they could not take from him even his brooch out of his cloak.

"Conchobar thought this wonderful. He said, 'Would he bring his deeds to completion, provided the age of manhood came to them?' Everyone said: 'He would bring them to completion.' Conchobar said to Cuchulainn: 'Come with me,' said he, 'to the feast to which we are going, because you are a guest.'

"'I have not had enough of play yet, O friend Conchobar,' said the boy; 'I will come after you.'

"When they had all come to the feast, Culann said to Conchobar: 'Do you expect anyone to follow you?' said he.

"'No,' said Conchobar. He did not remember the appointment with his foster-son who was following him.

"'I'll have a watch-dog,' said Culann; 'there are three chains on him, and three men to each chain. Let him be let slip because of our cattle and stock, and let the court be shut.'

"Then the boy comes. The dog attacks him. He went on with his play still: he threw his ball, and threw his club after it, so that it struck the ball. One stroke was not greater than another; and he threw his toy-spear after them, and he caught it before falling; and it did not hinder his play, though the dog was approaching him. Conchobar and his retinue — this, so that they could not move; they thought they would not find him alive when they came, even though the court were open. Now when the dog came to him, he threw away his ball and his club, and seized the dog with his two hands; that is, he put one of his hands to the apple of the dog's throat; and he put the other at its back; he struck it against the pillar that was beside him, so that every limb sprang apart. (According to another, it was his ball that he threw into its mouth, and brought out its entrails through it.)

"The Ulstermen went towards him, some over the wall, others over the doors of the court. They put him on Conchobar's knee. A great clamour arose among them, that the king's sister's son should have been almost killed. Then Culann comes into the house.

"'Welcome, boy, for the sake of your mother. Would that I had not prepared a feast! My life is a life lost, and my husbandry is a husbandry without, without my dog. He had kept honour and life for me,' said he, 'the man of my household who has been taken from me, that is, my dog. He was defence and protection to our property and our cattle; he was the protection of every beast to us, both field and house.'

"'It is not a great matter,' said the boy; 'a whelp of the same litter shall be raised for you by me, and I will be a dog for the defence of your cattle and for your own defence now, until that dog grows, and until he is capable of action; and I will defend Mag Murthemne, so that there shall not be taken away from me cattle nor herd, unless I have —.'

"'Then your name shall be Cu-chulainn,' said Cathbad.

"'I am content that it may be my name,' said Cuchulainn.

"A man who did this in his seventh year, it would be no wonder that he should have done a great deed now when his seventeen years are completed," said Conall Cernach.

"He did another exploit," said Fiacha Mac Fir-Febe. "Cathbad the Druid was with his son, Conchobar Mac Nessa. A hundred active men were with him, learning magic from him. That is the number that Cathbad used to teach. A certain one of his pupils asked of him for what this day would be good. Cathbad said a warrior should take arms therein whose name should be over Ireland for ever, for deed of valour, and his fame should continue for ever. Cuchulainn heard this. He comes to Conchobar to ask for arms. Conchobar said, 'Who has instructed you?'

"'My friend Cathbad,' said Cuchulainn.

"'We know indeed,' said Conchobar.

'He gave him spear and shield. He brandished them in the middle of the house, so that nothing remained of the fifteen sets of armour that were in store in Conchobar's household against the breaking of weapons or taking of arms by any one. Conchobar's own armour was given to him. That withstood him, and he brandished it, and blessed the king whose armour it was, and said, 'Blessing to the people and race to whom is king the man whose armour that is.'

"Then Cathbad came to them, and said: 'Has the boy taken arms?' said Cathbad.

"'Yes,' said Conchobar.

"'This is not lucky for the son of his mother,' said he.

"'What, is it not you advised it?' said Conchobar.

"'Not I, surely,' said Cathbad.

"'What advantage to you to deceive me, wild boy?' said Conchobar to Cuchulainn.

"'O king of heroes, it is no trick,' said Cuchulainn; 'it is he who taught it to his pupils this morning; and I heard him, south of Emain, and I came to you then.'

"'The day is good thus,' said Cathbad; 'it is certain he will be famous and renowned, who shall take arms therein; but he will be short-lived only.'

"'A wonder of might,' said Cuchulainn; 'provided I be famous, I am content though I were but one day in the world.'

"Another day a certain man asked the druids what it is for which that day was good.

"'Whoever shall go into a chariot therein,' said Cathbad, 'his name shall be over Ireland for ever.'

"Then Cuchulainn heard this; he comes to Conchobar and said to him: 'O friend Conchobar,' said he, 'give me a chariot.' He gave him a chariot. He put his hand between the two poles of the chariot, so that the chariot broke. He broke twelve chariots in this way. Then Conchobar's chariot was given to him. This withstood him. He goes then in the chariot, and Conchobar's charioteer with him. The charioteer (Ibor was his name) turned the chariot under him. 'Come out of the chariot now,' said the charioteer.

"'The horses are fine, and I am fine, their little lad,' said Cuchulainn. 'Go forward round Emain only, and you shall have a reward for it.'

"So the charioteer goes, and Cuchulainn forced him then that he should go on the road to greet the boys 'and that the boys might bless me'.

"He begged him to go on the way again. When they come, Cuchulainn said to the charioteer: 'Ply the goad on the horses,' said he.

"'In what direction?' said the charioteer.

"'As long as the road shall lead us,' said Cuchulainn.

"They come thence to Sliab Fuait, and find Conall Cernach there. It fell to Conall that day to guard the province; for every hero of Ulster was in Sliab Fuait in turn, to protect anyone who should come with poetry, or to fight against a man; so that it should be there that there should be some one to encounter him, that no one should go to Emain unperceived.

"'May that be for prosperity,' said Conall; 'may it be for victory and triumph.'

"'Go to the fort, O Conall, and leave me to watch here now,' said Cuchulainn.

"'It will be enough," said Conall, "if it is to protect any one with poetry; if it is to fight against a man, it is early for you yet.'

"'Perhaps it may not be necessary at all,' said Cuchulainn. 'Let us go meanwhile,' said Cuchulainn, 'to look upon the edge of Loch Echtra. Heroes are wont to abide there.'

"'I am content,' said Conall.

"Then they go thence. He throws a stone from his sling, so that a pole of Conall Cernach's chariot breaks.

"'Why have you thrown the stone, O boy?' said Conall.

"'To try my hand and the straightness of my throw,' said Cuchulainn; 'and it is the custom with you Ulstermen, that you do not travel beyond your peril. Go back to Emain, O friend Conall, and leave me here to watch.'

"'Content, then,' said Conall.

"Conall Cernach did not go past the place after that. Then Cuchulainn goes forth to Loch Echtra, and they found no one there before them. The charioteer said to Cuchulainn that they should go to Emain, that they might be in time for the drinking there.

"'No,' said Cuchulainn. 'What mountain is it yonder?' said Cuchulainn.

"'Sliab Monduirn,' said the charioteer.

"'Let us go and get there,' said Cuchulainn. They go then till they reach it. When they had reached the mountain, Cuchulainn asked: 'What is the white cairn yonder on the top of the mountain?'

"'Find Carn,' said the charioteer.

"'What plain is that over there?' said Cuchulainn.

"'Mag Breg,' said the charioteer. He tells him then the name of every chief fort between Temair and Cenandas. He tells him first their meadows and their fords, their famous places and their dwellings, their fortresses and their high hills. He shows him then the fort of the three sons of Nechta Scene; Foill, Fandall, and Tuachell were their names.

"'Is it they who say,' said Cuchulainn, 'that there are not more of the Ulstermen alive than they have slain of them?'

"'It is they indeed,' said the charioteer.

"'Let us go till we reach them,' said Cuchulainn.

"'Indeed it is peril to us,' said the charioteer.

"'Truly it is not to avoid it that we go,' said Cuchulainn.

"Then they go forth and unharness their horses at the meeting of the bog and the river, to the south above the fort of the others; and he threw the withe that was on the pillar as far as he could throw into the river and let it go with the stream, for this was a breach of *geis* to the sons of Nechta Scene. They perceive it then, and come to them. Cuchulainn goes to sleep by the pillar after throwing the withe at the stream; and he said to the charioteer: 'Do not waken me for few; but waken me for many.'

"Now the charioteer was very frightened, and he made ready their chariot and pulled its coverings and skins which were over Cuchulainn; for he dared not waken him, because Cuchulainn told him at first that he should not waken him for a few.

"Then come the sons of Nechta Scene.

"'Who is it who is there?' said one of them.

"'A little boy who has come today into the chariot for an expedition,' said the charioteer.

"'May it not be for his happiness,' said the champion; 'and may it not be for his prosperity, his first taking of arms. Let him not be in our land, and let the horses not graze there any more,' said the champion.

"'Their reins are in my hands,' said the charioteer.

"'It should not be yours to earn hatred,' said Ibar to the champion; 'and the boy is asleep.'

"'I am not a boy at all,' said Cuchulainn; 'but it is to seek battle with a man that the boy who is here has come.'

"'That pleases me well,' said the champion.

"'It will please you now in the ford yonder,' said Cuchulainn.

"'It befits you,' said the charioteer, 'take heed of the man who comes against you. Foill is his name,' said he; 'for unless you reach him in the first thrust, you will not reach him till evening.'

"'I swear by the god by whom my people swear, he will not ply his skill on the Ulstermen again, if the broad spear of my friend Conchobar should reach him from my hand. It will be an outlaw's hand to him.'

"Then he cast the spear at him, so that his back broke. He took with him his accoutrements and his head.

"'Take heed of another man,' said the charioteer, 'Fandall ('Swallow') is his name. Not more heavily does he traverse the water than swan or swallow."

"'I swear that he will not ply that feat again on the Ulstermen,' said Cuchulainn. 'You have seen,' said he, 'the way I travel the pool at Emain.'

"They meet then in the ford. Cuchulainn kills that man, and took his head and his arms.

"'Take heed of another man who comes towards you,' said the charioteer. 'Tuachell (i.e. 'Cunning') is his name. It is no misname for him, for he does not fall by arms at all.'

"'Here is the javelin for him to confuse him, so that it may make a red-sieve of him,' said Cuchulainn.

"He cast the spear at him, so that it reached him in his —. Then he went to him and cut off his head. Cuchulainn gave his head and his accoutrements to his own charioteer. He heard then the cry of their mother, Nechta Scene, behind them.

"He puts their spoils and the three heads in his chariot with him, and said: 'I will not leave my triumph,' said he, 'till I reach Emain Macha.'

"Then they set out with his triumph.

"Then Cuchulainn said to the charioteer: 'You promised us a good run,' said he, 'and we need it now because of the strife and the pursuit that is behind us.' They go on to Sliab Fuait; and such was the speed of the run that they made over Breg after the spurring of the charioteer, that the horses of the chariot overtook the wind and the birds in flight, and that Cuchulainn caught the throw that he sent from his sling before it reached the ground.

"When they reached Sliab Fuait, they found a herd of wild deer there before them.

"'What are those cattle yonder so active?' said Cuchulainn.

"'Wild deer,' said the charioteer.

"'Which would the Ulstermen think best,' said Cuchulainn, 'to bring them dead or alive?'

"'It is more wonderful alive,' said the charioteer; 'it is not everyone who can do it so. Dead, there is not one of them who cannot do it. You cannot do this, to carry off any of them alive,' said the charioteer.

"'I can indeed,' said Cuchulainn. 'Ply the goad on the horses into the bog.'

"The charioteer does this. The horses stick in the bog. Cuchulainn sprang down and seized the deer that was nearest, and that was the finest of them. He lashed the horses through the bog, and overcame the deer at once, and bound it between the two poles of the chariot.

"They saw something again before them, a flock of swans.

"'Which would the Ulstermen think best,' said Cuchulainn, 'to have them dead or alive?'

"'All the most vigorous and finest bring them alive,' said the charioteer.

"Then Cuchulainn aims a small stone at the birds, so that he struck eight of the birds. He threw again a large stone, so that he struck twelve of them. All that was done by his return stroke.

'Collect the birds for us,' said Cuchulainn to his charioteer. 'If it is I who go to take them,' said he, 'the wild deer will spring upon you.'

"'It is not easy for me to go to them,' said the charioteer. 'The horses have become wild so that I cannot go past them. I cannot go past the two iron tyres of the chariot, because of their sharpness; and I cannot go past the deer, for his horn has filled all the space between the two poles of the chariot.'

"'Step from its horn,' said Cuchulainn. 'I swear by the god by whom the Ulstermen swear, the bending with which I will bend my head on him, and the eye that I will make at him, he will not turn his head on you, and he will not dare to move.'

"That was done then. Cuchulainn made fast the reins, and the charioteer collects the birds. Then Cuchulainn bound the birds from the strings and thongs of the chariot; so that it was thus he went to Emain Macha: the wild deer behind his chariot, and the flock of swans flying over it, and the three heads in his chariot. Then they come to Emain.

'A man in a chariot is coming to you,' said the watchman in Emain Macha; 'he will shed the blood of every man who is in the court, unless heed is taken, and unless naked women go to him.'

"Then he turned the left side of his chariot towards Emain, and that was a *geis* (an insult) to it; and Cuchulainn said: "I swear by the god by whom the Ulstermen swear, unless a man is found to fight with me, I will shed the blood of everyone who is in the fort."

"'Naked women to meet him!' said Conchobar.

"Then the women of Emain go to meet him with Mugain, the wife of Conchobar Mac Nessa, and bare their breasts before him. 'These are the warriors who will meet you today,' said Mugain.

"He covers his face; then the heroes of Emain seize him and throw him into a vessel of cold water. That vessel bursts round him. The second vessel into which he was thrown boiled with bubbles as big as the fist therefrom. The third vessel into which he went, he warmed it so that its heat and its cold were rightly tempered. Then he comes out; and the queen, Mugain, puts a blue mantle on him, and a silver brooch therein, and a hooded tunic; and he sits at Conchobar's knee, and that was his couch always after that. The man who did this in his seventh year," said Fiacha Mac Fir-Febe, "it were not wonderful though he should rout an overwhelming force, and though he should exhaust an equal force, when his seventeen years are complete today."

(What follows is a separate version to the death of Orlam.)

"Let us go forth now," said Ailill.

Then they reached Mag Mucceda. Cuchulainn cut an oak before them there, and wrote an ogam in its side. It is this that was therein: that no one should go past it till a warrior should leap it with one chariot. They pitch their tents there, and come to leap over it in their chariots. There fall thereat thirty horses, and thirty chariots are broken. Belach n-Ane, that is the name of that place for ever.

The Death of Fraech

THEY ARE THERE till next morning; then Fraech is summoned to them. "Help us, O Fraech," said Medb. "Remove from us the strait that is on us. Go before Cuchulainn for us, if perchance you shall fight with him."

He set out early in the morning with nine men, till he reached Ath Fuait. He saw the warrior bathing in the river.

"Wait here," said Fraech to his retinue, "till I come to the man yonder; not good is the water," said he.

He took off his clothes, and goes into the water to him.

"Do not come to me," said Cuchulainn. "You will die from it, and I should be sorry to kill you."

"I shall come indeed," said Fraech, "that we may meet in the water; and let your play with me be fair."

"Settle it as you like," said Cuchulainn.

"The hand of each of us round the other," said Fraech.

They set to wrestling for a long time on the water, and Fraech was submerged. Cuchulainn lifted him up again.

"This time," said Cuchulainn, "will you yield and accept your life?"

"I will not suffer it," said Fraech.

Cuchulainn put him under it again, until Fraech was killed. He comes to land; his retinue carry his body to the camp. Ath Fraich, that was the name of that ford for ever. All the host lamented Fraech. They saw a troop of women in green tunics (Fraech was descended from the people of the Sid, his mother Bebind being a fairy woman. Her sister was Boinn (the river Boyne)) on the body of Fraech Mac Idaid; they drew him from them into the mound. Sid Fraich was the name of that mound afterwards.

Fergus springs over the oak in his chariot. They go till they reach Ath Taiten; Cuchulainn destroys six of them there: that is, the six Dungals of Irress.

Then they go on to Fornocht. Medb had a whelp named Baiscne. Cuchulainn throws a cast at him, and took his head off. Druim was the name of that place henceforth.

"Great is the mockery to you," said Medb, "not to hunt the deer of misfortune yonder that is killing you."

Then they start hunting him, till they broke the shafts of their chariots thereat.

The Death of Orlam

THEY GO FORTH then over Iraird Culend in the morning. Cuchulainn went forward; he overtook the charioteer of Orlam, son of Ailill and Medb, in Tamlacht Orlaim, a little to the north of Disert Lochait, cutting wood there. (According to another version, it is the shaft of Cuchulainn's chariot that had broken, and it is to cut a shaft that he had gone when he met Orlam's charioteer. It is the charioteer who cut the shafts according to this version.)

"It is over-bold what the Ulstermen are doing, if it is they who are yonder," said Cuchulainn, "while the host is behind them." He goes to the charioteer to reprove him; he thought that he was of Ulster, and he saw the man cutting wood, that is the chariot shaft.

"What are you doing here?" said Cuchulainn.

"Cutting chariot-shafts," said the charioteer. "We have broken our chariots hunting the wild deer Cuchulainn yonder. Help me," said the charioteer. "Look only whether you are to select the shafts, or to strip them."

"It will be to strip them indeed," said Cuchulainn.

Then Cuchulainn stripped the shafts through his fingers in the presence of the other, so that he cleared them both of bark and knots.

"This cannot be your proper work that I put on you," said the charioteer; he was greatly afraid.

"Whence are you?" said Cuchulainn.

"The charioteer of Orlam, son of Ailill and Medb," said he. "And you?" said the charioteer.

"My name is Cuchulainn," said he.

"Alas!" said the charioteer.

"Fear nothing," said Cuchulainn. "Where is your master?" said he.

"He is in the trench yonder," said the charioteer.

"Go forth then with me," said Cuchulainn, "for I do not kill charioteers at all."

Cuchulainn goes to Orlam, kills him, cuts his head off, and shakes his head before the host. Then he puts the head on the charioteer's back, and said to him:

"Take that with you," said Cuchulainn, "and go to the camp thus. If you do not go thus, a stone will come to you from my sling."

When he got near the camp, he took the head from his back, and told his adventures to Ailill and Medb.

"This is not like taking birds," said she.

And he said, "Unless I brought it on my back to the camp, he would break my head with a stone."

The Death of Meic Garach

THEN THE MEIC GARACH waited on their ford. These are their names: Lon and Ualu and Diliu; and Mes-Ler, and Mes-Laech, and Mes-Lethan were their three charioteers. They thought it too much what Cuchulainn had done: to slay two foster-sons of the king, and his son, and to shake the head before the host. They would slay Cuchulainn in return for him, and would themselves remove this annoyance from the host. They cut three aspen wands for their charioteers, that the six of them should pursue combat against him. He killed them all then, because they had broken fair-play towards him.

Orlam's charioteer was then between Ailill and Medb. Cuchulainn hurled a stone at him, so that his head broke, and his brains came over his ears; Fertedil was his name. (Thus it is not true that Cuchulainn did not kill charioteers; howbeit, he did not kill them without fault.)

The Death of the Squirrel

CUCHULAINN threatened in Methe, that wherever he should see Ailill or Medb afterwards he would throw a stone from his sling at them. He did this then: he threw a stone from his sling, so that he killed the squirrel that was on Medb's shoulder south of the ford: hence is Methe Togmaill. And he killed the bird that was on Ailill's shoulder north of the ford: hence is Methe n-Eoin. (Or it is on Medb's shoulder that both squirrel and bird were together, and it is their heads that were struck from them by the casts.) Reoin was drowned in his lake. Hence is Loch Reoin.

"That other is not far from you," said Ailill to the Manes.

They arose and looked round. When they sat down again, Cuchulainn struck one of them, so that his head broke.

"It was well that you went for that: your boasting was not fitting," said Maenen the fool. "I would have taken his head off."

Cuchulainn threw a stone at him, so that his head broke. It is thus then that these were killed: Orlam in the first place on his hill; the Meic Garach on their ford; Fertedil in his —; Maenan in his hill.

"I swear by the god by whom my people swear," said Ailill, "that man who shall make a mock of Cuchulainn here, I will make two halves of him."

"Go forth for us both day and night," said Ailill, "till we reach Cualnge. That man will kill two-thirds of the host in this way." It is there that the harpers of the *Cainbili* (a sort of wizard) from Ossory came to them to amuse them. They thought it was from the Ulstermen to spy on them. They set to hunting them, till they went before them in the forms of deer into the stones at Liac Mor on the north. For they were wizards with great cunning.

The Death of Lethan

LETHAN came on to his ford on the Nith in Conaille. He waited himself to meet Cuchulainn. It vexed him what Cuchulainn had done. Cuchulainn cuts off his head and left it, hence it is Ath Lethan on the Nith. And their chariots broke in the battle on the ford by him; hence it is Ath Carpat. Mulcha, Lethan's charioteer, fell on the shoulder of the hill that is between them; hence is Gulo Mulchai. While the hosts were going over Mag Breg, he struck their — still.

Yet that was the Morrigan in the form of a bird on the pillar in Temair Cuailnge; and she spoke to the Bull:

"Does the Black know," etc.

Then the Bull went, and fifty heifers with him, to Sliab Culind; and his keeper, Forgemen by name, went after him. He threw off the three fifties of boys who used always to play on him, and he killed two-thirds of his boys, and dug a trench in Tir Marcceni in Cualnge before he went.

The Death of Lochu

CUCHULAINN killed no one from the Saile ind Orthi in the Conaille territory, until they reached Cualnge. Cuchulainn was then in Cuince; he threatened then that when he saw Medb he would throw a stone at her head. This was not easy to him, for it is thus that Medb went and half the host about her, with their shelter of shields over her head.

Then a waiting-woman of Medb's, Lochu by name, went to get water, and a great troop of women with her. Cuchulainn thought it was Medb. He threw two stones from Cuince, so that he slew her in her plain. Hence is Ath Rede Locha in Cualnge.

From Findabair Cuailnge the hosts divided, and they set the country on fire. They collect all there were of women, and boys, and maidens; and cattle, in Cualnge together, so that they were all in Findabair.

"You have not gone well," said Medb; "I do not see the Bull with you."

"He is not in the province at all," said everyone.

Lothar the cowherd is summoned to Medb.

"Where is the Bull?" said she. "Have you an idea?"

"I have great fear to tell it," said the herd. "The night," said he, "when the Ulstermen went into their weakness, he went with three twenties of heifers with him, so that he is at the Black Corrie of Glenn Gatt."

"Go," said Medb, "and carry a withe between each two of you."

They do this: hence this glen is called Glenn Gatt. Then they bring the Bull to Findabair. The place where he saw the herd, Lothar, he attacked him, so that he brought his entrails out on his horns; and he attacked the camp with his three fifties of heifers, so that fifty warriors were killed. And that is the death of Lothar on the Foray.

Then the Bull went from them out of the camp, and they knew not where he had gone from them; and they were ashamed. Medb asked the herd if he had an idea where the Bull was.

"I think he would be in the secret places of Sliab Culind."

When they returned thus after ravaging Cualnge, and did not find the Bull there. The river Cronn rose against them to the tops of the trees; and they spent the night by it. And Medb told part of her following to go across.

A wonderful warrior went next day, Ualu his name. He took a great stone on his back to go across the water; the stream drove him backwards with the stone on his back. His grave and his stone are on the road at the stream: Lia Ualand is its name.

They went round the river Cronn to the source, and they would have gone between the source and the mountain, only that they could not get leave from Medb; she preferred to go across the mountain, that their track might remain there for ever, for an insult to the Ulstermen. They waited there three days and three nights, till they dug the earth in front of them, the Bernas Bo Cuailnge.

It is there that Cuchulainn killed Crond and Coemdele and —. A hundred warriors — died with Roan and Roae, the two historians of the Foray. A hundred and forty-four, kings died by him at the same stream. They came then over the Bernas Bo Cuailnge with the cattle and stock of Cualnge, and spent the night in Glenn Dail Imda in Cualnge. Botha is the name of this place, because they made huts over them there. They come next day to Colptha. They try to cross it through heedlessness. It rose against them then, and it carries a hundred charioteers of them to the sea; this is the name of the land in which they were drowned, Cluain Carptech.

They go round Colptha then to its source, to Belat Alioin, and spent the night at Liasa Liac; that is the name of this place, because they made sheds over their calves there between Cualnge and Conaille. They came over Glenn Gatlaig, and Glass Gatlaig rose against them. Sechaire was its name before; Glass Gatlaig thenceforth, because it was in withes they brought their calves; and they slept at Druim Fene in Conaille. (Those then are the wanderings from Cualnge to Machaire according to this version.)

This Is the Harrying of Cualnge

(OTHER AUTHORS and books make it that another way was taken on their journeyings from Findabair to Conaille, as follows:

Medb said after everyone had come with their booty, so that they were all in Findabair Cuailnge: "Let the host be divided," said Medb; "it will be impossible to bring this expedition by one way. Let Ailill go with half the expedition by Midluachair; Fergus and I will go by Bernas Ulad."

"It is not fine," said Fergus, "the half of the expedition that has fallen to us. It will be impossible to bring the cattle over the mountain without dividing it."

That was done then, so that it is from that there is Bernas Bo n-Ulad.)

It is there then that Ailill said to his charioteer Cuillius: "Find out for me today Medb and Fergus. I know not what has brought them to this union. I shall be pleased that a token should come to me by you."

Cuillius came when they were in Cluichre. The pair remained behind, and the warriors went on. Cuillius came to them, and they heard not the spy. Fergus' sword happened to be beside him. Cuillius drew it out of its sheath, and left the sheath empty. Cuillius came to Ailill.

"So?" said Ailill.

"So indeed," said Cuillius; "there is a token for you."

"It is well," said Ailill.

Each of them smiles at the other.

"As you thought," said Cuillius, "it is thus that I found them, in one another's arms."

"It is right for her," said Ailill; "it is for help on the Foray that she has done it. See that the sword is kept in good condition," said Ailill. "Put it under your seat in the chariot, and a cloth of linen around it."

Fergus got up for his sword after that.

"Alas!" said he.

"What is the matter with you?" said Medb.

"An ill deed have I done to Ailill," said he. "Wait here, while I go into the wood," said Fergus; "and do not wonder though it be long till I come."

It happened that Medb knew not the loss of the sword. He goes thence, and takes the sword of his charioteer with him in his hand. He makes a wooden sword in the wood. Hence there is Fid Mor Drualle in Ulster.

"Let us go on after our comrades," said Fergus. All their hosts meet in the plain. They pitch their tents. Fergus is summoned to Ailill to play chess. When Fergus went to the tent, Ailill began to laugh at him.

* * *

Cuchulainn came so that he was at Ath Cruinn before them.

"O friend Loeg," said he to his charioteer, "the hosts are at hand to us."

"I swear by the gods," said the charioteer, "I will do a mighty feat before warriors... on slender steeds with yokes of silver, with golden wheels..."

"Take heed, O Loeg," said Cuchulainn; "hold the reins for great victory of Macha...I beseech," said Cuchulainn, "the waters to help me. I beseech heaven and earth, and the Cronn in particular."

The (river) Cronn takes to fighting against them; it will not let them into Murthemne until the work of heroes be finished in Sliab Tuath Ochaine.

Therewith the water rose up till it was in the tops of the trees.

Mane, son of Ailill and Medb, went before the rest. Cuchulainn smites them on the ford, and thirty horsemen of Mane's retinue were drowned in the water. Cuchulainn overthrew two sixteens of warriors of them again by the water.

They pitch their tents at that ford. Lugaid Mac Nois, descendant of Lomarc Allchomach, came to speak to Cuchulainn, with thirty horsemen.

"Welcome, O Lugaid," said Cuchulainn. "If a flock of birds graze upon Mag Murthemne, you shall have a duck with half of another; if fish come to the estuaries, you shall have a salmon with half of another. You shall have the three sprigs, the sprig of watercress, and the sprig of marshwort, and the sprig of seaweed. You shall have a man in the ford in your place."

"I believe it," said Lugaid. "Excellence of people to the boy whom I desire."

"Your hosts are fine," said Cuchulainn.

"It would not be sad for you alone before them," said Lugaid.

"Fair-play and valour will support me," said Cuchulainn. "O friend Lugaid, do the hosts fear me?"

"I swear by God," said Lugaid, "one man nor two dare not go out of the camp, unless it be in twenties or thirties."

"It will be something extra for them," said Cuchulainn, "if I take to throwing from the sling. Fitting for you will be this fellow-vassal, O Lugaid, that you have among the

Ulstermen, if there come to me the force of every man. Say what you would have," said Cuchulainn.

"That I may have a truce with you towards my host."

"You shall have it, provided there be a token on it. And tell my friend Fergus that there be a token on his host. Tell the physicians, let there be a token on their host. And let them swear preservation of life to me, and let there come to me provision every night from them."

Then Lugaid goes from him. Fergus happened to be in the tent with Ailill. Lugaid called him out, and told him this. Something was heard, namely Ailill...(Ailill asks protection also).

"I swear by God I cannot do it," said Lugaid, "unless I ask the boy again."

"Help me, O Lugaid, go to him to see whether Ailill may come with a cantred into my troop. Take an ox with bacon to him and a jar of wine." said Fergus.

He goes to Cuchulainn then and tells him this.

"I do not mind though he go," said Cuchulainn.

Then their two troops join. They are there till night. Cuchulainn kills thirty men of them with the sling. (Or they would be twenty nights there, as some books say.)

"Your journeyings are bad," said Fergus. "The Ulstermen will come to you out of their weakness, and they will grind you to earth and gravel. 'The corner of battle' in which we are is bad."

He goes thence to Cul Airthir. It happened that Cuchulainn had gone that night to speak to the Ulstermen.

"Have you news?" said Conchobar.

"Women are captured," said Cuchulainn, "cattle are driven away, men are slain."

"Who carries them off? Who drives them away? Who kills them?"

"...Ailill Mac Matae carries them off, and Fergus Mac Roich very bold..."

"It is not great profit to you," said Conchobar, "today, our smiting has come to us all the same."

Cuchulainn goes thence from them; he saw the hosts going forth.

"Alas," said Ailill, "I see chariots..."

Cuchulainn kills thirty men of them on Ath Duirn. They could not reach Cul Airthir then till night. He slays thirty of them there, and they pitch their tents there. Ailill's charioteer, Cuillius, was washing the chariot tyres in the ford in the morning; Cuchulainn struck him with a stone and killed him. Hence is Ath Cuillne in Cul Airthir. They reach Druim Feine in Conaille and spent the night there, as we have said before.

Cuchulainn attacked them there; he slays a hundred men of them every night of the three nights that they were there; he took a sling to them from Ochaine near them.

"Our host will be short-lived through Cuchulainn in this way," said Ailill. "Let an agreement be carried from us to him: that he shall have the equal of Mag Murthemne from Mag Ai, and the best chariot that is in Ai, and the equipment of twelve men. Offer, if it pleases him better, the plain in which he was brought up, and three sevens of cumals The *cumal* (bondmaid) was a standard of value; and everything that has been destroyed of his household and cattle shall be made good, and he shall have full compensation, and let him go into my service; it is better for him than the service of a sub king."

"Who shall go for that?"

"Mac Roth yonder."

Mac Roth, the messenger of Ailill and Medb, went on that errand to Delga: it is he who encircles Ireland in one day. It is there that Fergus thought that Cuchulainn was, in Delga.

"I see a man coming towards us," said Loeg to Cuchulainn. "He has a yellow head of hair, and a linen emblem round it; a club of fury in his hand, an ivory-hilted sword at his waist; a hooded tunic with red ornamentation on him."

"Which of the warriors of the king is that?" said Cuchulainn.

Mac Roth asked Loeg whose man he was.

"Vassal to the man down yonder," said Loeg.

Cuchulainn was there in the snow up to his two thighs, without anything at all on him, examining his shirt.

Then Mac Roth asked Cuchulainn whose man he was.

"Vassal of Conchobar Mac Nessa," said Cuchulainn.

"Is there no clearer description?"

"That is enough," said Cuchulainn.

"Where then is Cuchulainn?" said Mac Roth.

"What would you say to him?" said Cuchulainn.

Mac Roth tells him then all the message, as we have told it.

"Though Cuchulainn were near, he would not do this; he will not barter the brother of his mother for another king."

He came to him again, and it was said to Cuchulainn that there should be given over to him the noblest of the women and the cows that were without milk, on condition that he should not ply his sling on them at night, even if he should kill them by day.

"I will not do it," said Cuchulainn; "if our slavewomen are taken from us, our noble women will be at the querns; and we shall be without milk if our milch-cows are taken from us."

He came to him again, and he was told that he should have the slave-women and the milch-cows.

"I will not do it," said Cuchulainn; "the Ulstermen will take their slave-women to their beds, and there will be born to them a servile offspring, and they will use their milch-cows for meat in the winter."

"Is there anything else then?" said the messenger.

"There is," said Cuchulainn; "and I will not tell it you. It shall be agreed to, if anyone tell it you."

"I know it," said Fergus; "I know what the man tried to suggest; and it is no advantage to you. And this is the agreement," said Fergus: "that the ford on which takes place his battle and combat with one man, the cattle shall not be taken thence a day and a night; if perchance there come to him the help of the Ulstermen. And it is a marvel to me," said Fergus, "that it is so long till they come out of their sufferings."

"It is indeed easier for us," said Ailill, "a man every day than a hundred every night."

The Death of Etarcomol

THEN FERGUS went on this errand; Etarcomol, son of Edan and Lethrinne, foster-son of Ailill and Medb, followed.

"I do not want you to go," said Fergus, "and it is not for hatred of you; but I do not like combat between you and Cuchulainn. Your pride and insolence, and the fierceness and hatred, pride and madness of the other, Cuchulainn: there will be no good from your meeting."

"Are you not able to protect me from him?" said Etarcomol.

"I can," said Fergus, "provided only that you do not treat his, sayings with disrespect."

They go thence in two chariots to Delga. Cuchulainn was then playing chess (*Buanfach*, like *fidchell*, is apparently a game something like chess or draughts) with Loeg; the back of his head was towards them, and Loeg's face.

"I see two chariots coming towards us," said Loeg; "a great dark man in the first chariot, with dark and bushy hair; a purple cloak round him, and a golden pin therein; a hooded tunic with gold embroidery on him; and a round shield with an engraved edge of white metal, and a broad spear-head, with rings from point to haft, in his hand. A sword as long as the rudder of a boat on his two thighs."

"It is empty, this great rudder that is brought by my friend Fergus," said Cuchulainn; "for there is no sword in its sheath except a sword of wood. It has been told to me," said Cuchulainn; "Ailill got a chance of them as they slept, he and Medb; and he took away his sword from Fergus, and gave it to his charioteer to take care of, and the sword of wood was put into its sheath."

Then Fergus comes up.

"Welcome, O friend Fergus," said Cuchulainn; "if a fish comes into the estuary, you shall have it with half of another; if a flock comes into the plain, you shall have a duck with half of another; a spray of cress or seaweed, a spray of marshwort; a drink from the sand; you shall have a going to the ford to meet a man, if it should happen to be your watch, till you have slept."

"I believe it," said Fergus; "it is not your provision that we have come for; we know your housekeeping here."

Then Cuchulainn receives the message from Fergus; anti Fergus goes away. Etarcomol remains looking at Cuchulainn.

"What are you looking at?" said Cuchulainn.

"You," said Etarcomol.

"The eye soon compasses it indeed," said Cuchulainn.

"That is what I see," said Etarcomol. "I do not know at all why you should be feared by anyone. I do not see terror or fearfulness, or overwhelming of a host, in you; you are merely a fair youth with arms of wood, and with fine feats."

"Though you speak ill of me," said Cuchulainn, "I will not kill you for the sake of Fergus. But for your protection, it would have been your entrails drawn and your quarters scattered, that would have gone from me to the camp behind your chariot."

"Threaten me not thus," said Etarcomol. "The wonderful agreement that he has bound, that is, the single combat, it is I who will first meet you of the men of Ireland tomorrow."

Then he goes away. He turned back from Methe and Cethe and said to his charioteer:

"I have boasted," said he, "before Fergus combat with Cuchulainn tomorrow. It is not possible for us to wait for it; turn the horses back again from the hill."

Loeg sees this and says to Cuchulainn: 'There is the chariot back again, and it has put its left board (an insult) towards us."

"It is not a 'debt of refusal'," said Cuchulainn. "I do not wish," said Cuchulainn, "what you demand of me."

"This is obligatory to you," said Etarcomol.

Cuchulainn strikes the sod under his feet, so that he fell prostrate, and the sod behind him.

"Go from me," said Cuchulainn. "I am loath to cleanse my hands in you. I would have divided you into many parts long since but for Fergus."

"We will not part thus," said Etarcomol, "till I have taken your head, or left my head with you."

"It is that indeed that will be there," said Cuchulainn.

Cuchulainn strikes him with his sword in his two armpits, so that his clothes fell from him, and it did not wound his skin.

"Go then," said Cuchulainn.

"No," said Etarcomol.

Then Cuchulainn attacked him with the edge of his sword, and took his hair off as if it was shaved with a razor; he did not put even a scratch on the surface. When the churl was troublesome then and stuck to him, he struck him on the hard part of his crown, so that he divided him down to the navel.

Fergus saw the chariot go past him, and the one man therein. He turned to quarrel with Cuchulainn.

"Ill done of you, O wild boy!" said he, "to insult me. You would think my club short," said he.

"Be not angry with me, O friend Fergus," said Cuchulainn..."Reproach me not, O friend Fergus."

He stoops down, so that Fergus's chariot went past him thrice.

He asked his charioteer: "Is it I who have caused it?"

"It is not you at all," said his charioteer.

"He said," said Cuchulainn, "he would not go till he took my head, or till he left his head with me. Which would you think easier to bear, O friend Fergus?" said Cuchulainn.

"I think what has been done the easier truly," said Fergus, "for it is he who was insolent."

Then Fergus put a spancel-withe through Etarcomol's two heels and took him behind his own chariot to the camp. When they went over rocks, one-half would separate from the other; when it was smooth, they came together again.

Medb saw him. "Not pleasing is that treatment of a tender whelp, O Fergus," said Medb.

"The dark churl should not have made fight," said Fergus, "against the great Hound whom he could not contend with."

His grave is dug then and his stone planted; his name is written in ogam; his lament is celebrated. Cuchulainn did not molest them that night with his sling; and the women and maidens and half the cattle are taken to him; and provision continued to be brought to him by day.

The Death of Nadcrantail

WHAT MAN have you to meet Cuchulainn tomorrow?" said Lugaid.

"They will give it to you tomorrow," said Mane, son of Ailill.

"We can find no one to meet him," said Medb. "Let us have peace with him till a man be sought for him."

They get that then.

"Whither will you send," said Ailill, "to seek that man to meet Cuchulainn?"

"There is no one in Ireland who could be got for him," said Medb, "unless Curoi Mac Dare can be brought, or Nadcrantail the warrior."

There was one of Curoi's followers in the tent. "Curoi will not come," said he; "he thinks enough of his household has come. Let a message be sent to Nadcrantail."

Mane Andoi goes to him, and they tell their tale to him.

"Come with us for the sake of the honour of Connaught."

"I will not go," said he, "unless Findabair be given to me."

He comes with them then. They bring his armour in a chariot, from the east of Connaught till it was in the camp.

"You shall have Findabair," said Medb, "for going against that man yonder."

"I will do it," said he.

Lugaid comes to Cuchulainn that night.

"Nadcrantail is coming to meet you tomorrow; it is unlucky for you: you will not withstand him."

"That does not matter," said Cuchulainn.

Nadcrantail goes next morning from the camp, and he takes nine spits of holly, sharpened and burned. Now Cuchulainn was there catching birds, and his chariot near him. Nadcrantail throws a spear at Cuchulainn; Cuchulainn performed a feat on to the point of that spear, and it did not hinder him from catching the birds. The same with the eight other spears. When he throws the ninth spear, the flock flies from Cuchulainn, and he went after the flock. He goes on the points of the spears like a bird, from each spear to the next, pursuing the birds that they should not escape. It seemed to everyone, however, that it was in flight that Cuchulainn went before Nadcrantail.

"Your Cuchulainn yonder," said he, "has gone in flight before me."

"That is of course," said Medb; "if good warriors should come to him, the wild boy would not resist —."

This vexed Fergus and the Ulstermen; Fiacha Mac Fir-Febe comes from them to remonstrate with Cuchulainn.

"Tell him," said Fergus, "it was noble to be before the warriors while he did brave deeds. It is more noble for him," said Fergus, "to hide himself when he flees before one man, for it were not greater shame to him than to the rest of Ulster."

"Who has boasted that?" said Cuchulainn.

"Nadcrantail," said Fiacha.

"Though it were that that he should boast, the feat that I have done before him, it was no more shame to me," said Cuchulainn. "He would by no means have boasted it had there been a weapon in his hand. You know full well that I kill no one unarmed. Let him come tomorrow," said Cuchulainn, "till he is between Ochaine and the sea, and however early he comes, he will find me there, and I shall not flee before him."

Cuchulainn came then to his appointed meeting-place, and he threw the hem of his cloak round him after his night-watch, and he did not perceive the pillar that was near him, of equal size with himself. He embraced it under his cloak, and placed it near him.

Therewith Nadcrantail came; his arms were brought with him in a wagon.

"Where is Cuchulainn?" said he.

"There he is yonder," said Fergus.

"It was not thus he appeared to me yesterday," said Nadcrantail.

"Are you Cuchulainn?"

"And if I am then?" said Cuchulainn.

"If you are indeed," said Nadcrantail, "I cannot bring the head of a little lamb to camp; I will not take the head of a beardless boy."

"It is not I at all," said Cuchulainn. "Go to him round the hill."

Cuchulainn comes to Loeg: "Smear a false beard on me," said he; "I cannot get the warrior to fight me without a beard." It was done for him. He goes to meet him on the hill. "I think that more fitting," said he.

"Take the right way of fighting with me," said Nadcrantail.

"You shall have it if only we know it," said Cuchulainn.

"I will throw a cast at you," said Nadcrantail, "and do not avoid it."

"I will not avoid it except on high," said Cuchulainn.

Nadcrantail throws a cast at him; Cuchulainn leaps on high before it.

"You do ill to avoid my cast," said Nadcrantail.

"Avoid my throw then on high," said Cuchulainn.

Cuchulainn throws the spear at him, but it was on high, so that from above it alighted in his crown, and it went through him to the ground.

"Alas! It is you are the best warrior in Ireland!" said Nadcrantail. "I have twenty-four sons in the camp. I will go and tell them what hidden treasures I have, and I will come that you may behead me, for I shall die if the spear is taken out of my head."

"Good," said Cuchulainn. "You will come back."

Nadcrantail goes to the camp then. Everyone comes to meet him.

"Where is the madman's head?" said everyone.

"Wait, O heroes, till I tell my tale to my sons, and go back that I may fight with Cuchulainn."

He goes thence to seek Cuchulainn, and throws his sword at Cuchulainn. Cuchulainn leaps on high, so that it struck the pillar, and the sword broke in two. Then Cuchulainn went mad as he had done against the boys in Emain, and he springs on his shield therewith, and struck his head off. He strikes him again on the neck down to the navel. His four quarters fall to the ground. Then Cuchulainn said this:

"If Nadcrantail has fallen,
It will be an increase to the strife.
Alas! That I cannot fight at this time
With Medb with a third of the host."

Here is the Finding of the Bull According to This Version

IT IS THEN that Medb went with a third of the host with her to Cuib to seek the Bull; and Cuchulainn went after her. Now on the road of Midluachair she had gone to harry Ulster and Cruthne as far as Dun Sobairche. Cuchulainn saw something: Bude Mac Bain from Sliab Culinn with the Bull, and fifteen heifers round him; and his force was sixty men of Ailill's household, with a cloak folded round every man. Cuchulainn comes to them.

"Whence have you brought the cattle?" said Cuchulainn.

"From the mountain yonder," said the man.'

"Where are their cow-herds?" said Cuchulainn.

"He is as we found him," said the man.

Cuchulainn made three leaps after them to seek speech with them as far as the ford. It is there he said to the leader:

"What is your name?" said he.

"One who fears you not and loves you not; Bude Mac Bain," said he.

"This spear at Bude!" said Cuchulainn. He hurls at him the javelin, so that it went through his armpits, and one of the livers broke in two before the spear. He kills him on his ford; hence is Ath Bude. The Bull is brought into the camp then. They considered then that it would not be difficult to deal with Cuchulainn, provided his javelin were got from him.

The Death of Redg the Satirist

IT IS THEN that Redg, Ailill's satirist, went to him on an errand to seek the javelin, that is, Cuchulainn's spear.

"Give me your spear," said the satirist.

"Not so," said Cuchulainn; "but I will give you treasure."

"I will not take it," said the satirist.

Then Cuchulainn wounded the satirist, because he would not accept from him what he offered him, and the satirist said he would take away his honour unless he got the javelin. Then Cuchulainn threw the javelin at him, and it went right through his head.

"This gift is overpowering," said the satirist. Hence is Ath Tolam Set.

There was now a ford east of it, where the copper of the javelin rested; Humarrith, then, is the name of that ford. It is there that Cuchulainn killed all those that we have mentioned in Cuib; i.e. Nathcoirpthe at his trees; Cruthen on his ford; the sons of the Herd at their cairn; Marc on his hill; Meille on his hill; Bodb in his tower; Bogaine in his marsh.

Cuchulainn turned back to Mag Murthemne; he liked better to defend his own home. After he went, he killed the men of Crocen (or Cronech), i.e. Focherd; twenty men of Focherd. He overtook them taking camp: ten cup-bearers and ten fighting-men.

Medb turned back from the north when she had remained a fortnight ravaging the province, and when she had fought a battle against Findmor, wife of Celtchar Mac Uthidir. And after taking Dun Sobairche upon her, she brought fifty women into the province of Dalriada. Wherever Medb placed a horse-switch in Cuib its name is Bile Medba; every ford and every hill by which she slept, its name is Ath Medba and Dindgna Medba.

They all meet then at Focherd, both Ailill and Medb and the troop that drove the Bull. But their herd took their Bull from them, and they drove him across into a narrow gap with their spear-shafts on their shields. So that the feet of the cattle drove him through the ground. Forgemen was the herd's name. He is there afterwards, so that that is the name of the hill, Forgemen. There was no annoyance to them that night, provided a man were got toward off Cuchulainn on the ford.

"Let a sword-truce be asked by us from Cuchulainn," said Ailill.

"Let Lugaid go for it," said everyone.

Lugaid goes then to speak to him.

"How am I now with the host?" said Cuchulainn.

"Great indeed is the mockery that you asked of them," said Lugaid, "that is, your women and your maidens and half your cattle. And they think it heavier than anything to be killed and to provide you with food."

A man fell there by Cuchulainn every day to the end of a week. Fair-play is broken with Cuchulainn: twenty are sent to attack him at one time; and he killed them all.

"Go to him, O Fergus," said Ailill, "that he may allow us a change of place."

They go then to Cronech. This is what fell by him in single combat at this place: two Roths, two Luans, two female horse messengers, ten fools, ten cup-bearers, ten Ferguses, six Fedelms, six Fiachras. These then were all killed by him in single combat. When they pitched their tents in Cronech, they considered what they should do against Cuchulainn.

"I know," said Medb, "what is good in this case: let a message be sent from us to ask him that we may have a sword-truce from him towards the host, and he shall have half the cattle that are here."

This message is taken to him.

"I will do this," said Cuchulainn, "provided the compact is not broken by you."

The Meeting of Cuchulainn and Findabair

"LET AN OFFER go to him," said Ailill, "that Findabair will be given to him on condition that he keeps away from the hosts."

Mane Athramail goes to him. He goes first to Loeg.

"Whose man are you?" said he.

Loeg does not speak to him. Mane spoke to him thrice in this way.

"Cuchulainn's man," said he, "and do not disturb me, lest I strike your head off."

"This man is fierce," said Mane, turning from him. He goes then to speak to Cuchulainn. Now Cuchulainn had taken off his tunic, and the snow was round him up to his waist as he sat, and the snow melted round him a cubit for the greatness of the heat of the hero.

Mane said to him in the same way thrice, "Whose man was he?"

"Conchobar's man, and do not disturb me. If you disturb me any longer, I will strike your head from you as the head is taken from a blackbird."

"It is not easy," said Mane, "to speak to these two."

Mane goes from them then and tells his tale to Ailill and Medb.

"Let Lugaid go to him," said Ailill, "and offer to him the maiden."

Lugaid goes then and tells Cuchulainn that.

"O friend Lugaid," said Cuchulainn, "this is a snare."

"It is the king's word that has said it," said Lugaid; "there will be no snare therefrom."

"Let it be done so," said Cuchulainn.

Lugaid went from him therewith, and tells Ailill and Medb that answer.

"Let the fool go in my form," said Ailill, "and a king's crown on his head, and let him stand at a distance from Cuchulainn lest he recognise him, and let the maiden go with him, and let him betroth her to him, and let them depart quickly in this way; and it is likely that you will play a trick on him thus, so that he will not hinder you, till he comes with the Ulstermen to the battle."

Then the fool goes to him, and the maiden also; and it was from a distance he spoke to Cuchulainn. Cuchulainn goes to meet them. It happened that he recognised by the man's speech that he was a fool. He threw a sling stone that was in his hand at him, so that it sprang into his head and brought his brains out. Then he comes to the maiden, cuts her two tresses off, and thrusts a stone through her mantle and through her tunic, and thrusts a stone pillar through the middle of the fool. There are their two pillars there: the pillar of Findabair, and the fool's pillar.

Cuchulainn left them thus. A party was sent from Ailill and Medb to seek out their folk, for they thought they were long; they were seen in this position. All this was heard throughout the camp. There was no truce for them with Cuchulainn afterwards.

The Combat of Munremar and Curoi

WHEN THE HOSTS were there in the evening; they saw that one stone lighted on them from the east, and another from the west to meet it. They met in the air, and kept falling between Fergus's camp, and Ailill's, and Era's. This sport and play went on from that hour to the same hour next day; and the hosts were sitting down, and their shields were over their heads to protect them against the masses of stones, till the plain was full of the stones. Hence is Mag Clochair. It happened that Curoi Mac Daire did this; he had come to help his comrades, and he was in Cotal over against Munremar Mac Gerrcind. He had come from Emain Macha to help Cuchulainn, and he was in Ard Roich. Curoi knew that there was no man in the host who could withstand Munremar. So it was these two who had made this sport between them. They were asked by the host to be quiet; then Munremar and Curoi make peace, and Curoi goes to his house and Munremar to Emain Macha. And Munremar did not come till the day of the battle; Curoi did not come till the combat with Fer Diad.

"Speak to Cuchulainn," said Medb and Ailill, "that he allow us change of place."

It is granted to them then, and they change the place. The weakness of the Ulstermen was over then. For when they awoke from their suffering, some of them kept coming on the host, that they might take to slaying them again.

The Death of the Boys

THEN THE BOYS of Ulster had consulted in Emain Macha.

"Wretched indeed," said they, "for our friend Cuchulainn to be without help."

"A question indeed," said Fiachna Fulech Mac Fir-Febe, own brother to Fiacha Fialdama Mac Fir-Febe, "shall I have a troop among you, and go to take help to him therefrom?"

Three fifties of boys go with their playing-clubs, and that was a third of the boys of Ulster. The host saw them coming towards them across the plain.

"A great host is at hand to us over the plain," said Ailill.

Fergus goes to look at them. "Some of the boys of Ulster that,' said he; 'and they come to Cuchulainn's help."

"Let a troop go against them," said Ailill, "without Cuchulainn's knowledge; for if they meet him, you will not withstand them."

Three fifties of warriors go to meet them. They fell by one another so that no one escaped alive of the abundance of the boys at Lia Toll. Hence it is the Stone of Fiachra Mac Fir-Febe; for it is there he fell.

"Make a plan," said Ailill.

"Ask Cuchulainn about letting you go out of this place, for you will not come beyond him by force, because his flame of valour has sprung."

For it was customary with him, when his flame of valour sprang in him, that his feet would go round behind him, and his hams before; and the balls of his calves on his shins, and one eye in his head and the other out of his head; a man's head could have gone into his mouth. Every hair on him was as sharp as a thorn of hawthorn, and a drop of blood on each hair. He would not recognise comrades or friends. He would strike alike before and behind. It is from this that the men of Connaught gave Cuchulainn the name Riastartha.

The Woman-Fight of Rochad

CUCHULAINN sent his charioteer to Rochad Mac Fatheman of Ulster, that he should come to his help. Now it happened that Findabair loved Rochad, for he was the fairest of the warriors among the Ulstermen at that time. The man goes to Rochad and told him to come to help Cuchulainn if he had come out of his weakness; that they should deceive the host, to get at some of them to slay them. Rochad comes from the north with a hundred men.

"Look at the plain for us today," said Ailill.

"I see a troop coming over the plain," said the watchman, "and a warrior of tender years among them; the men only reach up to his shoulders."

"Who is it yonder, O Fergus?" said Ailill.

"Rochad Mac Fatheman," said he, "and it is to help Cuchulainn he comes."

"I know what you had better do with him," said Fergus. "Let a hundred men go from you with the maiden yonder to the middle of the plain, and let the maiden go before them; and let a horseman go to speak to him, that he come alone to speak with the maiden, and let hands be laid on him, and this will keep off the attack of his army from us."

This is done then. Rochad goes to meet the horseman.

"I have come from Findabair to meet you, that you come to speak with her."

He goes then to speak with her alone. The host rushes about him from every side. He is taken, and hands are laid on him. His force breaks into flight. He is let go then, and he is bound over not to go against the host till he should come together with all Ulster. It was promised to him that Findabair should be given to him, and he returned from them then. So that that is Rochad's Woman-fight.

The Death of the Princes

"LET A SWORD-TRUCE be asked of Cuchulainn for us,' said Ailill and Medb.

Lugaid goes on that errand, and Cuchulainn grants the truce.

"Put a man on the ford for me tomorrow," said Cuchulainn.

There were with Medb six princes, i.e. six king's heirs of the Clanna Dedad, the three Blacks of Imlech, and the three Reds of Sruthair.

"Why should we not go against Cuchulainn?" said they.

They go next day, and Cuchulainn slew the six of them.

The Death of Cur

THEN Cur Mac Dalath is besought to go against Cuchulainn. He from whom he shed blood, he is dead before the ninth day.

"If he slay him," said Medb, "it is victory; and though it be he who is slain, it is removing a load from the host: for it is not easy to be with him in regard to eating and sleeping."

Then he goes forth. He did not think it good to go against a beardless wild boy.

"Not so indeed," said he, "right is the honour that you give us! If I had known that it was against this man that I was sent, I would not have bestirred myself to seek him; it were enough in my opinion for a boy of his own age from my troop to go against him."

"Not so," said Cormac Condlongas; "it were a marvel for us if you yourself were to drive him off."

"Howbeit," said he, "since it is on myself that it is laid you shall go forth tomorrow morning; it will not delay me to kill the young deer yonder."

He goes then early in the morning to meet him; and he tells the host to get ready to take the road before them, for it was a clear road that he would make by going against Cuchulainn.

This Is the Number of the Feats

HE WENT on that errand then. Cuchulainn was practising feats at that time, i.e. the apple-feat, the edge-feat, the supine-feat, the javelin-feat, the ropefeat, the — feat, the cat-feat, the hero's salmon-leap, the cast —, the leap over —, the noble champion's turn, the *gae bolga*, the — of swiftness, the wheel-feat, the —, the feat on breath, the mouth-rage, the champion's shout, the stroke with proper adjustment, the back-stroke, the climbing a javelin with stretching of the body on its point, with the binding of a noble warrior.

Cur was plying his weapons against him in a fence of his shield till a third of the day; and not a stroke of the blow reached Cuchulainn for the madness of the feats, and he did not know that a man was trying to strike him, till Fiacha Mac Fir-Febe said to him: "Beware of the man who is attacking you."

Cuchulainn looked at him; he threw the feat-apple that remained in his hand, so that it went between the rim and the body of the shield, and went back through the head of the churl. It would be in Imslige Glendanach that Cur fell according to another version.

Fergus returned to the army. "If your security hold you," said he, "wait here till tomorrow."

"It would not be there," said Ailill; "we shall go back to our camp."

Then Lath Mac Dabro is asked to go against Cuchulainn, as Cur had been asked. He himself fell then also. Fergus returns again to put his security on them. They remained there until there were slain there Cur Mac Dalath, and Lath Mac Dabro, and Foirc, son of the three Swifts, and Srubgaile Mac Eobith. They were all slain there in single combat.

The Death of Ferbaeth

"GO TO THE CAMP for us, O friend Loeg," said Cuchulainn, "and consult Lugaid Mac Nois, descendant of Lomarc, to know who is coming against me tomorrow. Let it be asked diligently, and give him my greeting."

Then Loeg went.

"Welcome," said Lugaid; "it is unlucky for Cuchulainn, the trouble in which he is, alone against the men of Ireland. It is a comrade of us both, Ferbaeth (ill-luck to his arms!), who goes against him tomorrow. Findabair is given to him for it, and the kingdom of his race."

Loeg turns back to where Cuchulainn is.

"He is not very joyful over his answer, my friend Loeg," said Cuchulainn.

Loeg tells him all that. Ferbaeth had been summoned into the tent to Ailill and Medb, and he is told to sit by Findabair, and that she should be given to him, for he was her choice for fighting with Cuchulainn. He was the man they thought worthy of them, for they had both learned the same arts with Scathach. Then wine is given to him, till he was intoxicated, and he is told, "They thought that wine fine, and there had only been brought the load of fifty wagons. And it was the maiden who used to put hand to his portion therefrom."

"I do not wish it," said Ferbaeth; "Cuchulainn is my foster-brother, and a man of perpetual covenant with me. Nevertheless I will go against him tomorrow and cut off his head."

"It will be you who would do it," said Medb.

Cuchulainn told Loeg to go to meet Lugaid, that he should come and speak with him. Lugaid comes to him.

"So Ferbaeth is coming against me tomorrow," said Cuchulainn.

"He indeed," said Lugaid.

"An evil day!" said Cuchulainn; "I shall not be alive therefrom. Two of equal age we, two of equal deftness, two equal when we meet. O Lugaid, greet him for me; tell him that it is not true valour to come against me; tell him to come to meet me tonight, to speak with me."

Lugaid tells him this. When Ferbaeth did not avoid it, he went that night to renounce his friendship with Cuchulainn, and Fiacha Mac Fir-Febe with him. Cuchulainn appealed to him by his foster-brotherhood, and Scathach, the foster-mother of them both.

"I must," said Ferbaeth. "I have promised it."

"Take back your bond of friendship then," said Cuchulainn.

Cuchulainn went from him in anger. A spear of holly was driven into Cuchulainn's foot in the glen, and appeared up by his knee. He draws it out.

"Go not, O Ferbaeth, till you have seen the find that I have found."

"Throw it," said Ferbaeth.

Cuchulainn threw the spear then after Ferbaeth so that it hit the hollow of his poll, and came out at his mouth in front, so that he fell back into the glen.

"That is a throw indeed," said Ferbaeth. Hence is Focherd Murthemne. (Or it is Fiacha who had said, "Your throw is vigorous today, O Cuchulainn," said he; so that Focherd Murthemne is from that.)

Ferbaeth died at once in the glen. Hence is Glenn Firbaith.

Something was heard: Fergus, who said:

> *"O Ferbaeth, foolish is thy expedition*
> *In the place in which thy grave is.*
> *Ruin reached thee…*
> *In Croen Corand.*

> *"The hill is named Fithi for ever;*
> *Croenech in Murthemne,*
> *From today Focherd will be the name*
> *Of the place in which thou didst fall, O Ferbaeth.*
> *O Ferbaeth," etc.*

"Your comrade has fallen," said Fergus. "Say will you pay for this man on the morrow?"

"I will pay indeed," said Cuchulainn.

Cuchulainn sends Loeg again for news, to know how they are in the camp, and whether Ferbaeth lived. Lugaid said: "Ferbaeth is dead," and Cuchulainn comes in turn to talk with them.

The Combat of Larine Mac Nois

"ONE OF YOU tomorrow to go readily against the other," said Lugaid.

"He will not be found at all," said Ailill, "unless you practise trickery therein. Any man who comes to you, give him wine, so that his mind may be glad, and it shall be said to him that that is all the wine that has been brought from Cruachan. It grieves us that you should be on water in the camp. And Findabair shall be put at his right hand, and it shall be said: 'She shall come to you, if you bring us the head of the Riastartha.'"

A messenger used to be sent to every hero on his night, and that used to be told to him; he continued to kill every man of them in. turn. No one could be got by them to meet him at last. Larine Mac Nois, brother to Lugaid, King of Munster, was summoned to them the next day. Great was his pride. Wine is given to him, and Findabair is put at his right hand.

Medb looked at the two. "It pleases me, yonder pair," said she; "a match between them would be fitting."

"I will not stand in your way," said Ailill; "he shall have her if he brings me the head of the Riastartha."

"I will bring it," said Larine.

Then Lugaid comes. "What man have you for the ford tomorrow?" said he.

'Larine goes,' said Ailill.

Then Lugaid comes to speak with Cuchulainn. They meet in Glenn Firbaith. Each gives the other welcome.

"It is for this I have come to speak to you," said Lugaid: "there is a churl here, a fool and proud," said he, "a brother of mine named Larine; he is befooled about the same maiden. On your friendship then, do not kill him, lest you should leave me without a brother. For it is for this that he is being sent to you, so that we two might quarrel. I should be content, however, that you should give him a sound drubbing, for it is in my despite that he comes."

Larine goes next day to meet Cuchulainn, and the maiden near him to encourage him. Cuchulainn attacks him without arms. He takes Larine's arms from him perforce. He takes him then between his two hands, and grinds and shakes him...and threw him till he was between Lugaid's two hands... nevertheless, he is the only man who escaped even a bad escape from him, of all who met him on the Tain.

The Conversation of the Morrigan with Cuchulainn

CUCHULAINN saw a young woman coming towards him, with a dress of every colour on, and her form very excellent.

"Who are you?" said Cuchulainn.

"Daughter of Buan the king," said she. "I have come to you; I have loved you for your reputation, and I have brought my treasures and my cattle with me."

"The time at which you have come to us is not good. For our condition is evil, through hunger. It is not easy to me to meet a woman, while I am in this strife."

"I will be a help to you...I shall be more troublesome to you," said she, "when I come against you when you are in combat against the men. I will come in the form of an eel about your feet in the ford, so that you shall fall."

"I think that likelier than the daughter of a king. I will take you," said he, "between my toes, till your ribs are broken, and you will be in this condition till a doom of blessing comes on you."

"I will drive the cattle on the ford to you, in the form of a grey she-wolf."

"I will throw a stone at you from my sling, so that it shall break your eye in your head; and you will be in that state till a doom of blessing comes on you."

"I will come to you in the form of a hornless red heifer before the cattle. They will rush on you on the plains, and on the fords, and on the pools, and you will not see me before you."

"I will throw a stone at you," said he, "so that your leg shall break under you, and you will be in this state till a doom of blessing comes on you."

Therewith she goes from him.

So he was a week on Ath Grencha, and a man used to fall every day by him in Ath Grencha, i.e. in Ath Darteisc.

The Death of Loch Mac Emonis

THEN Loch Mac Emonis was asked like the others, and there was promised to him a piece of the arable land of Mag Ai equal in size to Mag Murthemne, and the equipment of twelve warriors and a chariot worth seven cumals (a measure of value); and he did not think combat with a youth worthy.

He had a brother, Long Mac Emonis himself.

The same price was given to him, both maiden and raiment and chariots and land. He goes to meet Cuchulainn. Cuchulainn slays him, and he was brought dead before his brother, Loch.

This latter said that if he only knew that it was a bearded man who slew him, he would kill him for it.

"Take a battle-force to him," said Medb to her household, "across the ford from the west, that you may go-across; and let fair-play be broken on him."

Then the seven Manes, warriors, go first, so that they saw him on the edge of the ford westward. He puts his feast-dress on that day. It is then that the women kept climbing on the men to look at him.

"I am sorry," said Medb; "I cannot see the boy about whom they go there."

"Your mind will not be the gladder for it," said Lethrend, Ailill's squire, "if you could see him."

He comes to the ford then as he was.

"What man is it yonder, O Fergus?" said Medb.

"A boy who wards off," etc.… "if it is Culann's Hound.'

Medb climbed on the men then to look at him.

It is then that the women said to Cuchulainn 'that he was laughed at in the camp because he had no beard, and no good warriors would go against him, only wild men; "it were easier to make a false beard." So this is what he did, in order to seek combat with a man; i.e. with Loch. Cuchulainn took a handful of grass, and said a spell over it, so that everyone thought he had a beard.

"True," said the troop of women, "Cuchulainn has a beard. It is fitting for a warrior to fight with him."

They had done this on urging Loch.

"I will not make combat against him till the end of seven days from today," said Loch.

"It is not fitting for us to have no attack on the man for this space," said Medb. "Let us put a hero to hunt him every night, if perchance we may get a chance at him."

This is done then. A hero used to come every night to hunt him, and he used to kill them all. These are the names of the men who fell there: seven Conalls, seven Oenguses, seven Uarguses, seven Celtris, eight Fiacs, ten Ailills, ten Delbaths, ten Tasachs. These are his deeds of this week in Ath Grencha.

Medb asked advice, to know what she should do to Cuchulainn, for what had been killed of their hosts by him distressed her greatly. This is the plan she arrived at, to put brave, high-spirited men to attack him all at once when he should come to an appointed meeting to speak with Medb. For she had an appointment the next day with Cuchulainn to make a peace in fraud with him, to get hold of him. She sent messengers forth to seek him that he should come to meet her; and it was thus he should come, and he unarmed: "for she would come only with her troop of women to meet him."

The messenger, Traigtren, went to the place where Cuchulainn was, and tells him Medb's message. Cuchulainn promised that he would do so.

"In what manner does it please you to go to meet Medb tomorrow, O Cuchulainn?" said Loeg.

"As Medb has asked me," said Cuchulainn.

"Great are Medb's deeds," said the charioteer; "I fear a hand behind the back with her."

"How is it to be done then?" said he.

"Your sword at your waist," said the charioteer, "that you may not be taken at an unfair advantage. For the warrior is not entitled to his honour-price if he is without arms; and it is the coward's law that he deserves in that way."

"Let it be done so then," said Cuchulainn.

The meeting-place was in Ard Aignech, which is called Fochaird today. Now Medb came to the meeting-place and set in ambush fourteen men of her own special following, of those who were of most prowess, ready for him. These are they: two Glassines, the two sons of Bucchridi; two Ardans, the two sons of Licce; two Glasogmas, the two sons of Crund; Drucht and Delt and Dathen; Tea and Tascra and Tualang; Taur and Glese.

Then Cuchulainn comes to meet her. The men rise to attack him. Fourteen spears are thrown at him at once. Cuchulainn guards himself so that his skin or his — is not touched. Then he turns on them and kills them, the fourteen of them. So that they are the fourteen men of Focherd, and they are the men of Cronech, for it is in Cronech at Focherd that they were killed. Hence Cuchulainn said: "Good is my feat of heroism."

So it is from this that the name Focherd stuck to the place; that is, *focherd*, i.e. 'good is the feat of arms' that happened to Cuchulainn there.

So Cuchulainn came, and overtook them taking camp, and there were slain two Daigris and two Anlis and four Dungais of Imlech. Then Medb began to urge Loch there.

"Great is the mockery of you," said she, "for the man who has killed your brother to be destroying our host, and you do not go to battle with him! For we deem it certain that the wild man, great and fierce, the like of him yonder, will not be able to withstand the rage and fury of a hero like you. For it is by one foster-mother and instructress that an art was built up for you both."

Then Loch came against Cuchulainn, to avenge his brother on him, for it was shown to him that Cuchulainn had a beard.

"Come to the upper ford," said Loch; "it would not be in the polluted ford that we shall meet, where Long fell."

When he came then to seek the ford, the men drove the cattle across.

"It will be across your water here today," said Gabran the poet. Hence is Ath Darteisc, and Tir Mor Darteisc from that time on this place.

When the men met then on the ford, and when they began to fight and to strike each other there, and when each of them began to strike the other, the eel threw three folds round Cuchulainn's feet, till he lay on his back athwart the ford. Loch attacked him with the sword, till the ford was blood-red with his blood.

"Ill indeed," said Fergus, "is this deed before the enemy. Let each of you taunt the man, O men," said he to his following, "that he may not fall for nothing."

Bricriu Poison-tongue Mac Carbatha rose and began inciting Cuchulainn.

"Your strength is gone," said he, "when it is a little salmon that overthrows you when the Ulstermen are at hand coming to you out of their sickness yonder. Grievous for you to undertake a hero's deed in the presence of the men of Ireland and to ward off a formidable warrior in arms thus!"

Therewith Cuchulainn arises and strikes the eel so that its ribs broke in it, and the cattle were driven over the hosts eastwards by force, so that they took the tents on their horns, with the thunder-feat that the two heroes had made in the ford.

The she-wolf attacked him, and drove the cattle on him westwards. He throws a stone from his sling, so that her eye broke in her head. She goes in the form of a hornless red heifer; she rushes before the cows upon the pools and fords. It is then he said: "I cannot see the fords for water." He throws a stone at the hornless red heifer, so that her leg breaks under her. Then he sang a song:

"I am all alone before flocks;
I get them not, I let them not go;

I am alone at cold hours
Before many peoples.

"Let some one say to Conchobar
Though he should come to me it were not too soon;
Magu's sons have carried off their kine
And divided them among them.

"There may be strife about one head
Only that one tree blazes not;
If there were two or three
Their brands would blaze.

"The men have almost worn me out
By reason of the number of single combats;
I cannot work the slaughter of glorious warriors
As I am all alone.
I am all alone."

* * *

It is there then that Cuchulainn did to the Morrigan the three things that he had promised her in the *Tain Bo Regamna* (one of the introductory stories to the *Tain Bo Cuailnge*); and he fights Loch in the ford with the gae-bolga, which the charioteer threw him along the stream. He attacked him with it, so that it went into his body's armour, for Loch had a horn-skin in fighting with a man.

"Give way to me," said Loch. Cuchulainn gave way, so that it was on the other side that Loch fell. Hence is Ath Traiged in Tir Mor. Cuchulainn cut off his head then.

Then fair-play was broken with him that day when five men came against him at one time; i.e. two Cruaids, two Calads, Derothor; Cuchulainn killed them by himself. Hence is Coicsius Focherda, and Coicer Oengoirt; or it is fifteen days that Cuchulainn was in Focherd, and hence is Coicsius Focherda in the Foray.

Cuchulainn hurled at them from Delga, so that not a living thing, man or beast, could put its head past him southwards between Delga and the sea.

The Healing of the Morrigan

WHEN CUCHULAINN was in this great weariness, the Morrigan met him in the form of an old hag, and she blind and lame, milking a cow with three teats, and he asked her for a drink. She gave him milk from a teat.

"He will be whole who has brought it," said Cuchulainn; "the blessings of gods and non-gods on you," said he. (Gods with them were the Mighty Folk (i.e. the dwellers in the Sid); non-gods the people of husbandry.)

Then her head was healed so that it was whole.

She gave the milk of the second teat, and her eye was whole; and gave the milk of the third teat, and her leg was whole. So that this was what he said about each thing of them, "A doom of blessing on you," said he.

"You told me," said the Morrigan, "I should not have healing from you for ever."

"If I had known it was you," said Cuchulainn, "I would not have healed you ever."

So that formerly Cuchulainn's throng on Tarthesc was the name of this story in the Foray.

It is there that Fergus claimed of his securities that faith should not be broken with Cuchulainn; and it is there that Cuchulainn...i.e. Delga Murthemne at that time.

Then Cuchulainn killed Fota in his field; Bomailce on his ford; Salach in his village; Muine in his hill; Luair in Leth-bera; Fer-Toithle in Toithle; these are the names of these lands for ever, every place in which each man of them fell. Cuchulainn killed also Traig and Dornu and Dernu, Col and Mebul and Eraise on this side of Ath Tire Moir, at Methe and Cethe: these were three druids and their three wives.

Then Medb sent a hundred men of her special retinue to kill Cuchulainn. He killed them all on Ath Ceit-Chule. Then Medb said:

"It is *cuillend* (a crime) to us, the slaying of our people." Hence is Glass Chrau and Cuillend Cind Duin and Ath Ceit-Chule.

Then the four provinces of Ireland took camp and fortified post in the Breslech Mor in Mag Murthemne, and send part of their cattle and booty beyond them to the south into Clithar Bo Ulad. Cuchulainn took his post at the mound in Lerga near them, and his charioteer Loeg Mac Riangabra kindled a fire for him on the evening of that night. He saw the fiery sheen of the bright golden arms over the heads of the four provinces of Ireland at the setting of the clouds of evening. Fury and great rage came over him at sight of the host, at the multitude of his enemies, the abundance of his foes. He took his two spears and his shield and his sword; he shook his shield and brandished his spears and waved his sword; and he uttered his hero's shout from his throat, so that goblins and sprites and spectres of the glen and demons of the air answered, for the terror of the shout which they uttered on high. So that the Nemain produced confusion on the host. The four provinces of Ireland came into a tumult of weapons about the points of their own spears and weapons, so that a hundred warriors of them died of terror and of heart-burst in the middle of the camp and of the position that night.

When Loeg was there, he saw something: a single man who came straight across the camp of the men of Ireland from the north-east straight towards him.

"A single man is coming to us now, O Little Hound!" said Loeg.

"What kind of man is there?" said Cuchulainn.

"An easy question: a man fair and tall is he, with hair cut broad, waving yellow hair; a green mantle folded round him; a brooch of white silver in the mantle on his breast; a tunic of royal silk, with red ornamentation of red gold against the white skin, to his knees. A black shield with a hard boss of white metal; a five pointed spear in his hand; a forked javelin beside it. Wonderful is the play and sport and exercise that he makes; but no one attacks him, and he attacks no one, as if no one saw him."

"It is true, O fosterling," said he; "which of my friends from the *sid* is that who comes to have pity on me, because they know the sore distress in which I am, alone against the four great provinces of Ireland, on the Cattle-Foray of Cualnge at this time?"

That was true for Cuchulainn. When the warrior had reached the place where Cuchulainn was, he spoke to him, and had pity on him for it.

"This is manly, O Cuchulainn," said he.

"It is not much at all," said Cuchulainn.

"I will help you," said the man.

"Who are you at all?" said Cuchulainn.

"It is I, your father from the *síd*, Lug Mac Ethlend."

"My wounds are heavy, it were high time that I should be healed."

"Sleep a little, O Cuchulainn," said the warrior; "your heavy swoon of sleep at the mound of Lerga till the end of three days and three nights, and I will fight against the hosts for that space."

Then he sings the *ferdord* to him, and he sleeps from it. Lug looked at each wound that it was clean. Then Lug said:

"Arise, O great son of the Ulstermen, whole of thy wounds.... Go into thy chariot secure. Arise, arise!"

For three days and three nights Cuchulainn was asleep. It were right indeed though his sleep equalled his weariness. From the Monday after the end of summer exactly to the Wednesday after Candlemas, for this space Cuchulainn had not slept, except when he slept a little while against his spear after midday, with his head on his clenched fist, and his clenched fist on his spear, and his spear on his knee; but he was striking and cutting and attacking and slaying the four great provinces of Ireland for that space.

It is then that the warrior of the síd cast herbs and grasses of curing and charms of healing into the hurts and wounds and into the injuries and into the many wounds of Cuchulainn, so that Cuchulainn recovered in his sleep without his perceiving it at all.

Now it was at this time that the boys came south from Emain Macha: Folloman Mac Conchobair with three fifties of kings' sons of Ulster, and they gave battle thrice to the hosts, so that three times their own number fell, and all the boys fell except Folloman Mac Conchobair. Folloman boasted that he would not go back to Emain for ever and ever, until he should take the head of Ailill with him, with the golden crown that was above it. This was not easy to him; for the two sons of Bethe Mac Bain, the two sons of Ailill's foster-mother and foster-father, came on him, and wounded him so that he fell by them. So that that is the death of the boys of Ulster and of Folloman Mac Conchobair.

Cuchulainn for his part was in his deep sleep till the end of three days and three nights at the mound in Lerga. Cuchulainn arose then from his sleep, and put his hand over his face, and made a purple wheelbeam from head to foot, and his mind was strong in him, and he would have gone to an assembly, or a march, or a tryst, or a beer-house, or to one of the chief assemblies of Ireland.

"How long have I been in this sleep now, O warrior?" said Cuchulainn.

"Three days and three nights," said the warrior.

"Alas for that!" said Cuchulainn.

"What is the matter?" said the warrior.

"The hosts without attack for this space," said Cuchulainn.

"They are not that at all indeed," said the warrior.

"Who has come upon them?" said Cuchulainn.

"The boys came from the north from Emain Macha; Folloman Mac Conchobair with three fifties of boys of the kings' sons of Ulster; and they gave three battles to the hosts for the space of the three days and the three nights in which you have been in your sleep now. And three times their own number fell, and the boys fell, except Folloman Mac Conchobair. Folloman boasted that he would take Ailill's head, and that was not easy to him, for he was killed."

"Pity for that, that I was not in my strength! For if I had been in my strength, the boys would not have fallen as they have fallen, and Folloman Mac Conchobair would not have fallen."

"Strive further, O Little Hound, it is no reproach to thy honour and no disgrace to thy valour."

"Stay here for us tonight, O warrior," said Cuchulainn, "that we may together avenge the boys on the hosts."

"I will not stay indeed," said the warrior, "for however great the contests of valour and deeds of arms any one does near thee, it is not on him there will be the renown of it or the fame or the reputation, but it is on thee; therefore I will not stay. But ply thy deed of arms thyself alone on the hosts, for not with them is there power over thy life this time."

"The scythe-chariot, O my friend Loeg!" said Cuchulainn; "Can you yoke it? And is its equipment here? If you can yoke it, and if you have its equipment, yoke it; and if you have not its equipment, do not yoke it at all."

It is then that the charioteer arose, and he put on his hero's dress of charioteering. This was his hero's dress of charioteering that he put on: his soft tunic of skin, light and airy, well-turned ('kneaded'), made of skin, sewn, of deer-skin, so that it did not restrain the movement of his hands outside. He put on his black upper-cloak over it outside: Simon Magus had made it for Darius, King of the Romans, so that Darius gave it to Conchobar, and Conchobar gave it to Cuchulainn, and Cuchulainn gave it to his charioteer. The charioteer took first then his helm, ridged, like a board, four-cornered, with much of every colour and every form, over the middle of his shoulders. This was well-measured to him, and it was not an overweight. His hand brought the circlet of red-yellow, as though it were a plate of red-gold, of refined gold smelted over the edge of an anvil, to his brow, as a sign of his charioteering, in distinction to his master.

He took the goads of his horses, and his whip inlaid in his right hand. He took the reins to hold back his horses in his left hand. Then he put the iron inlaid breastplates on the horses, so that they were covered from forehead to forefoot with spears and points and lances and hard points, so that every motion in this chariot was spear-near, so that every corner and every point and every end and every front of this chariot was a way of tearing. It is then that he cast a spell of covering over his horses and over his companion, so that he was not visible to anyone in the camp, and so that everyone in the camp was visible to them. It was proper that he should cast this, because there were the three gifts of charioteering on the charioteer that day, the leap over —, and the straight —, and the —.

Then the hero and the champion and he who made the fold of the Badb (The Badb (scald-crow) was a war-goddess. This is an expressive term for the piled-up bodies of the slain.) of the men of the earth, Cuchulainn Mac Sualtaim, took his battle-array of battle and contest and strife. This was his battle-array of battle and contest and strife: he put on twenty-seven skin tunics, waxed, like board, equally thick, which used to be under strings and chains and thongs, against his white skin, that he might not lose his mind nor his understanding when his rage should come. He put on his hero's battle-girdle over it outside, of hard-leather, hard, tanned, of the choice of seven ox-hides of a heifer, so that it covered him from the thin part of his sides to the thick part of his arm-pit; it used to be on him to repel spears, and points, and darts, and lances, and arrows. For they were cast from him just as if it was stone or rock or horn that they struck. Then he put on his apron, skin like, silken, with its edge of white gold variegated, against the soft lower part of his body. He put on his dark apron of dark leather, well tanned, of the choice of four ox-hides of a heifer, with his battle-girdle of cows' skins about it over his silken skin-like apron. Then the royal hero took his battle-arms of battle and contest and strife. These then were his battle-arms of battle: he took his ivory-hilted, bright-faced weapon, with his eight little swords; he took his five-pointed spear, with his eight little spears; he took his spear of battle, with his eight little darts; he took his javelin with his eight little javelins; his eight shields of feats, with his round shield, dark red, in which a boar that would be shown at a feast would go into the boss, with its edge sharp, keen, very sharp, round about it, so that it would cut hairs against the stream for sharpness and keenness and great sharpness; when the warrior did the edge-feat with it, he would cut equally with his shield, and with his spear, and with his sword.

Then he put on his head a ridged-helmet of battle and contest and strife, from which there was uttered the shout of a hundred warriors, with a long cry from every corner and every angle of it. For there used to cry from it equally goblins and sprites and ghosts of the glen and demons of the air, before and above and around, wherever he used to go before shedding the blood of warriors and enemies. There was cast over him his dress of concealment by the garment of the Land of Promise that was given by his foster-father in wizardry.

It is then came the first contortion on Cuchulainn, so that it made him horrible, many-shaped, wonderful, strange. His shanks shook like a tree before the stream, or like a rush against the stream, every limb and every joint and every end and every member, of him from head to foot. He made a — of rage of his body inside his skin. His feet and his shins and his knees came so that they were behind him; his heels and his calves and his hams came so that they were in front. The front-sinews of his calves came so that they were on the front of his shins, so that every huge knot of them was as great as a warrior's clenched fist. The temple-sinews of his head were stretched, so that they were on the hollow of his neck, so that every round lump of them, very great, innumerable, not to be equalled, measureless, was as great as the head of a month old child.

Then he made a red bowl of his face and of his visage on him; he swallowed one of his two eyes into his head, so that from his cheek a wild crane could hardly have reached it to drag it from the back of his skull. The other sprang out till it was on his cheek outside. His lips were marvellously contorted. Tie drew the cheek from the jawbone, so that his gullet was visible. His lungs and his lights came so that they were flying in his mouth and in his throat. He struck a blow of the — of a lion with his upper palate on the roof of his skull, so that every flake of fire that came into his mouth from his throat was as large as a wether's skin. His heart was heard light-striking against his ribs· like the roaring of a bloodhound at its food, or like a lion going through bears. There were seen the palls of the Badb, and the rain-clouds of poison, and the sparks of fire very red in clouds and in vapours over his head with the boiling of fierce rage, that rose over him.

His hair curled round his head like the red branches of a thorn in the gap of Atalta. Though a royal apple-tree under royal fruit had been shaken about it, hardly would an apple have reached the ground through it, but an apple would have fixed on every single hair there, for the twisting of the rage that rose from his hair above him.

The hero's light rose from his forehead, so that it was as long, and as thick, as a warrior's whet-stone, so that it was equally long with the nose, till he went mad in playing with the shields, in pressing on the charioteer, in — the hosts. As high, as thick, as strong, as powerful, as long, as the mast of a great ship, was the straight stream of dark blood that rose straight up from the very top of his head, so that it made a dark smoke of wizardry like the smoke of a palace when the king comes to equip himself in the evening of a wintry day.

After that contortion wherewith Cuchulainn was contorted, then the hero of valour sprang into his scythed battle-chariot, with its iron points, with its thin edges, with its hooks, and with its hard points, with its sharp points of a hero, with their pricking goads, with its nails of sharpness that were on shafts and thongs and cross-pieces and ropes of that chariot.

It was thus the chariot was, with its body thin-framed, dry-framed, feat-high, straight-shouldered, of a champion, on which there would have been room for eight weapons fit for a lord, with the speed of swallow or of wind or of deer across the level of the plain. The chariot was placed on two horses, swift, vehement, furious, small-headed, small-round, small-end, pointed, red-breasted, easy to recognise, well-yoked…. One of these two horses was supple, swift-leaping, great of strength, great of curve, great of foot, great of length,—. The other horse was flowing-maned, slender-footed, thin-footed, slender-heeled, —.

It is then that he threw the thunder-feat of a hundred, and the thunder-feat of four hundred, and he stopped at the thunder-feat of five hundred, for he did not think it too much for this equal number to fall by him in his first attack, and in his first contest of battle on the four provinces of Ireland; and he came forth in this way to attack his enemies, and he took his chariot in a great circuit about the four great provinces of Ireland, and he put the attack of an enemy among enemies on them. And a heavy course was put on his chariot, and the iron wheels of the chariot went into the ground, so that it was enough for fort and fortress, the way the iron wheels of the chariot went into the ground; for there arose alike turfs and stones and rocks and flagstones and gravel of the ground as high as the iron wheels of the chariot.

The reason why he cast the circle of war round about the four great provinces of Ireland, was that they might not flee from him, and that they might not scatter, that he might make sure of them, to avenge the boys on them; and he comes into the battle thus in the middle, and overthrew great fences of his enemies' corpses round about the host thrice, and puts the attack of an enemy among enemies on them, so that they fell sole to sole, and neck to neck; such was the density of the slaughter.

He went round again thrice thus, so that he left a layer of six round them in the great circuit; i.e. soles of three to necks of three in the course of a circuit round the camp. So that its name in the Foray is Sesrech Breslige, and it is one of the three not to be numbered in the Foray; i.e. Sesrech Breslige and Imslige Glendamnach and the battle on Garach and Irgarach, except that it was alike dog and horse and man there.

This is what others say, that Lug Mac Ethlend fought along with Cuchulainn the Sesrech Breslige. Their number is not known, and it is impossible to count what number fell there of the rabble. But the chief only have been counted. These are the names of the princes and chiefs: two Cruads, two Calads, two Cirs, two Ciars, two Ecells, three Croms, three Caurs, three Combirge, four Feochars, four Furachars, four Cass, four Fotas, five Caurs, five Cermans, five Cobthachs, six Saxans, six Dachs, six

Dares, seven Rochads, seven Ronans, seven Rurthechs, eight Roclads, eight Rochtads, eight Rindachs, eight Corpres, eight Mulachs, nine Daigs, nine Dares, nine Damachs, ten Fiachs, ten Fiachas, ten Fedelmids.

Ten kings over seven fifties did Cuchulainn slay in Breslech Mor in Mag Murthemne; and an innumerable number besides of dogs and horses and women and boys and people of no consequence and rabble. For there did not escape one man out of three of the men of Ireland without a thigh-bone or half his head or one eye broken, or without being marked for ever. And he came from them after giving them battle without wound or blood-stain on himself or on his servant or on either of his horses.

Cuchulainn came next day to survey the host and to show his soft fair form to the women and the troops of women and the girls and the maidens and the poets and the bards, for he did not hold in honour or dignity that haughty form of wizardry that had appeared to them on him the night before. Therefore he came to show his soft fair form that day.

Fair indeed the boy who came then to show his form to the hosts, that is, Cuchulainn Mac Sualtaim. The appearance of three heads of hair on him, dark against the skin of his head, blood-red in the middle, a crown gold-yellow which covers them. A fair arrangement of this hair so that it makes three circles round the hollow of the back of his head, so that each hair —, dishevelled, very golden, excellent, in long curls, distinguished, fair-coloured, over his shoulders, was like gold thread.

A hundred ringlets, bright purple, of red-gold, gold-flaming, round his neck; a hundred threads with mixed carbuncle round his head. Four dimples in each of his two cheeks; that is, a yellow dimple, and a green dimple, and a blue dimple, and a purple dimple. Seven gems of brilliance of an eye, in each of his two royal eyes. Seven toes on each of his two feet, seven fingers on each of his two hands, with the grasp of a hawk's claws, with the seizure of a griffin's claws on each of them separately.

Then he puts on his feast-dress that day. This was his raiment on him: a fair tunic, proper; bright-purple, with a border with five folds. A white brooch of white silver with adorned gold inlaid over his white breast, as if it was a lantern full of light, that the eyes of men could not look at for its splendour and its brightness. A silken tunic of silk against his skin so that it covered him to the top of his dark apron of dark-red, soldierly, royal, silken.

A dark shield; dark red, dark purple, with five chains of gold, with a rim of white metal on it. A sword gold-hilted, inlaid with ivory hilt of red-gold raised high on his girdle. A spear, long, grey-edged, with a spear-head sharp, attacking, with rivets of gold, gold-flaming by him in the chariot. Nine heads in one of his two hands, and ten heads in the other hand. He shook them from him towards the hosts. So that this is the contest of a night to Cuchulainn. Then the women of Connaught raised themselves on the hosts, and the women were climbing on the men to look at Cuchulainn's form. Medb hid her face and dare not show her face, but was under the shield-shelter for fear of Cuchulainn. So that it is hence Dubthach Doeltenga of Ulster said:

"If it is the Riastartha, there will be corpses of men therefrom" etc.

Fiacha Fialdana from Imraith came to speak with the son of his mother's sister, Mane Andoe his name. Docha Mac Magach went with Mane Andoe: Dubthach Doeltenga of Ulster came with Fiacha Fialdana from Imraith. Docha threw a spear at Fiacha, so that it went into Dubthach. Then Dubthach threw a spear at Mane, so that it went into Docha. The mothers of Dubthach and Docha were two sisters. Hence is Imroll Belaig Euin. (i.e. the Random Throw of Belach Euin.)

(Or Imroll Belaig Euin is from this: the hosts go to Belach Euin, their two troops wait there. Diarmait Mac Conchobair comes from the north from Ulster.

"Let a horseman go from you," said Diarmait, "that Mane may come to speak with me with one man, and I will come with one man to meet him." They meet then.

"I have come," said Diarmait, "from Conchobar, who says to Medb and Ailill, that they let the cows go, and make whole all that they have done there, and bring the Bull (i.e. bring Findbennach to meet the Dun of Cualnge) from the west hither to the Bull, that they may meet, because Medb has promised it."

"I will go and tell them," said Mane. He tells this then to Medb and Ailill.

"This cannot be got of Medb," said Mane.

"Let us exchange arms then," said Diarmait, "if you think it better."

"I am content," said Mane. Each of them throws his spear at the other, so that the two of them die, and so that the name of this place is Imroll Belaig Euin.)

Their forces rush at each other: there fall three twenties of them in each of the forces. Hence is Ard-in-Dirma (The Height of the Troop).

Ailill's folk put his king's crown on Tamun the fool; Ailill dare not have it on himself. Cuchulainn threw a stone at him at Ath Tamuin, so that his head broke thereby. Hence is Ath Tamuin and Tuga-im-Tamun (i.e. Covering about Tamun).

Then Oengus, son of Oenlam the Fair, a bold warrior of Ulster, turned all the host at Moda Loga (that is the same as Lugmod) as far as Ath Da Ferta: He did not let them go past, and he pelted them with stones, and the learned say — before till they should go under the sword at Emain Macha, if it had been in single combat that they had come against him. Fair-play was broken on him, and they slew him in an unequal fight.

"Let someone come from you against me," said Cuchulainn at Ath Da Ferta.

"It will not be I, it will not be I," said every one from his place. "A scapegoat is not owed from my race, and if it were owed, it would not be I whom they would give in his stead for a scapegoat."

Then Fergus Mac Roich was asked to go against him. He refuses to go against his foster-son Cuchulainn. Wine was given to him, and he was greatly intoxicated, and he was asked about going to the combat. He goes forth then since they were urgently imploring him.

Then Cuchulainn said: "It is with my security that you come against me, O friend Fergus," said he, "with no sword in its place." For Ailill had stolen it, as we said before.

"I do not care at all," said Fergus; "though there were a sword there, it would not be plied on you. Give way to me, O Cuchulainn," said Fergus.

"You will give way to me in return then," said Cuchulainn.

"Even so," said Fergus.

Then Cuchulainn fled back before Fergus as far as Grellach Doluid, that Fergus might give way to him on the day of the battle. Then Cuchulainn sprang in to Grellach Doluid.

"Have you his head, O Fergus?" said everyone.

"No," said Fergus, "it is not like a tryst. He who is there is too lively for me. Till my turn comes round again, I will not go."

Then they go past him, and take camp at Crich Ross. Then Ferchu, an exile, who was in exile against Ailill, hears them. He comes to meet Cuchulainn. Thirteen men was his number. Cuchulainn kills Ferchu's warriors. Their thirteen stones are there.

Medb sent Mand of Muresc, son of Daire, of the Domnandach, to fight Cuchulainn. Own brothers were lie and Fer Diad, and two sons of one father. This Mand was a man fierce and excessive in eating and sleeping, a man ill-tongued, foul-mouthed, like Dubthach Doeltenga of Ulster. He was a man strong, active, with strength of limb like Munremar Mac Gerrcind; a fiery warrior like Triscod Trenfer of Conchobar's house.

"I will go, and I unarmed, and I will grind him between my hands, for I deem it no honour or dignity to ply weapons on a beardless wild boy such as he."

He went then to seek Cuchulainn. He and his charioteer were there on the plain watching the host.

"One man coming towards us," said Loeg to Cuchulainn.

"What kind of man?" said Cuchulainn.

"A man black, dark, strong, bull-like, and he unarmed."

"Let him come past you," said Cuchulainn.

He came to them therewith.

"To fight against you have I come," said Mand.

Then they begin to wrestle for a long time, and Mand overthrows Cuchulainn thrice, so that the charioteer urged him.

"If you had a strife for the hero's portion in Emain," said he, "you would be mighty over the warriors of Emain!"

His hero's rage comes, and his warrior's fury rises, so that he overthrew Mand against the pillar, so that he falls in pieces. Hence is Mag Mand Achta, that is, Mand Echta, that is, Mand's death there.

* * *

On the morrow Medb sent twenty-seven men to Cuchulainn's bog. Fuilcarnn is the name of the bog, on this side of Fer Diad's Ford. They threw their twenty-nine spears at him at once; i.e. Gaile-dana with his twenty-seven sons and his sister's son, Glas Mac Delgna. When then they all stretched out their hands to their swords, Fiacha Mac Fir-Febe came after them out of the camp. He gave a leap from his chariot when he saw all their hands against Cuchulainn, and he strikes off the arms of the twenty-nine of them.

Then Cuchulainn said: "What you have done I deem help at the nick of time."

"This little," said Fiacha, "is a breach of compact for us Ulstermen. If any of them reaches the camp, we will go with our cantred under the point of the sword."

"I swear, etc., since I have emitted my breath," said Cuchulainn, "not a man of them shall reach it alive."

Cuchulainn slew then the twenty-nine men and the two sons of Ficce with them, two bold warriors of Ulster who came to ply their might on the host. This is that deed on the Foray, when they went to the battle with Cuchulainn.

This Is the Combat of Fer Diad and Cuchulainn

THEN THEY considered what man among them would be fit to ward off Cuchulainn. The four provinces of Ireland spoke, and confirmed, and discussed, whom it would be fitting to send to the ford against Cuchulainn. All said that it was the Horn-skin from

Irrus Domnand, the weight that is not supported, the battle-stone of doom, his own dear and ardent foster-brother. For Cuchulainn had not a feat that he did not possess, except it were the Gae Bolga alone; and they thought he could avoid it, and defend himself against it, because of the horn about him, so that neither arms nor many edges pierced it.

Medb sent messengers to bring Fer Diad. Fer Diad did not come with those messengers. Medb sent poets and bards and satirists (*aes glantha gemaidi*, the folk who brought blotches on the cheeks (i.e. by their lampoons)) to him, that they might satirise him and mock him and put him to ridicule, that he might not find a place for his head in the world, until he should come to the tent of Medb and Ailill on the Foray. Fer Diad came with those messengers, for the fear of their bringing shame on him.

Findabair, the daughter of Medb and Ailill, was put on one side of him: it is Findabair who put her hand on every goblet and on every cup of Fer Diad; it is she who gave him three kisses at every cup of them; it is she who distributed apples right frequent over the bosom of his tunic. This is what she said: that he, Fer Diad, was her darling and her chosen wooer of the men of the world.

When Fer Diad was satisfied and happy and very joyful, Medb said:

"Alé! O Fer Diad, do you know why you have been summoned into this tent?"

"I do not know indeed," said Fer Diad; "except that the nobles of the men of Ireland are there. What is there less fitting for me to be there than for any other good warrior?"

"It is not that indeed," said Medb; "but to give you a chariot worth three sevens of cumals and the equipment of twelve men, and the equal of Mag Murthemne from the arable land of Mag Ai; and that you should be in Cruachan always, and wine to be poured for you there; and freedom of your descendants and of your race for ever without tribute or tax; my leaf-shaped brooch of gold to be given to you, in which there are ten score ounces and ten score half-ounces, and ten score *crosach* and ten score quarters; Findabair, my daughter and Ailill's daughter, for your one wife, and you shall get my love if you need it over and above."

"He does not need it," said everyone: "great are the rewards and gifts."

"That is true," said Fer Diad, "they are great; and though they are great, O Medb, it is with you yourself they will be left, rather than that I should go against my foster-brother to battle."

"O men," said she, said Medb (through the right way of division and setting by the ears), "true is the word that Cuchulainn spoke," as if she had not heard Fer Diad at all.

"What word is this, O Medb?" said Fer Diad.

"He said indeed," said she, "that he would not think it too much that you should fall by him as the first fruits of his prowess in the province to which he should come."

"To say that was not fitting for him. For it is not weariness or cowardice that he has ever known in me, day nor night. I swear by the god by whom my people swear that I will be the first man who will come tomorrow morning to the ford of combat."

"May victory and blessing come to you," said Medb. "And I think it better that weariness or cowardice be found with you, because of friendship beyond my own men. Why is it more fitting for him to seek the good of Ulster because his mother was of them, than for you to seek the good of the province of Connaught, because you are the son of a king of Connaught?"

It is thus they were binding their covenants and their compact, and they made a song there:

"Thou shalt have a reward," etc.

There was a wonderful warrior of Ulster who witnessed that bargaining, and that was Fergus Mac Roich. Fergus came to his tent.

"Woe is me! The deed that is done tomorrow morning!" said Fergus.

"What deed is that?" said the folk in the tent.

"My good fosterling Cuchulainn to be slain."

"Good lack! Who makes that boast?"

"An easy question: his own dear ardent foster-brother, Fer Diad Mac Damain. Why do ye not win my blessing?" said Fergus; "and let one of you go with a warning and with compassion to Cuchulainn, if perchance he would leave the ford tomorrow morning."

"On our conscience," said they, "though it were you yourself who were on the ford of combat, we would not come as far as to seek you."

"Good, my lad," said Fergus; "get our horses for us and yoke the chariot."

The lad arose and got the horses and yoked the chariot. They came forth to the ford of combat where Cuchulainn was.

"One chariot coming hither towards us, O Cuchulainn!" said Loeg. For it is thus the lad was, with his back towards his lord. He used to win every other game of *brandub* (a game; probably of the nature of chess or draughts) and of chess-playing from his master: the sentinel and watchman on the four quarters of Ireland over and above that.

"What kind of chariot then?" said Cuchulainn.

"A chariot like a huge royal fort, with its yolcs strong golden, with its great panel of copper, with its shafts of bronze, with its body thin-framed, dry-framed, feat-high, scythed, sword-fair, of a champion, on two horses, swift, stout, well-yoked, —. One royal warrior, wide-eyed, was the combatant of the chariot. A beard curly, forked, on him, so that it reached over the soft lower part of his soft shirt, so that it would shelter fifty warriors to be under the heavy — of the warrior's beard, on a day of storm and rain. A round shield, white, variegated, many-coloured on him, with three chains —, so that there would be room from front to back for four troops of ten men behind the leather of the shield which is upon the — of the warrior. A sword, long, hard-edged, red-broad in the sheath, woven and twisted of white silver, over the skin of the bold-in-battle. A spear, strong, three-ridged, with a winding and with bands of white silver all white by him across the chariot."

"Not hard the recognition," said Cuchulainn; "my friend Fergus comes there, with a warning and with compassion to me before all the four provinces."

Fergus reached them and sprang from his chariot and Cuchulainn greeted him.

"Welcome your coming, O my friend, O Fergus," said Cuchulainn.

"I believe your welcome," said Fergus.

"You may believe it," said Cuchulainn; "if a flock of birds come to the plain, you shall have a duck with half of another; if fish come to the estuaries, you shall have a salmon with half of another; a sprig of watercress, and a sprig of marshwort, and a sprig of seaweed, and a drink of cold sandy water after it."

"That portion is that of an outlaw," said Fergus.

"That is true, it is an outlaw's portion that I have," said Cuchulainn, "for I have been from the Monday after Samain to this time, and I have not gone for a night's entertainment, through strongly obstructing the men of Ireland on the Cattle-Foray of Cualnge at this time."

"If it were for this we came," said Fergus, "we should have thought it the better to leave it; and it is not for this that we have come."

"Why else have you come to me?" said Cuchulainn.

"To tell you the warrior who comes against you in battle and combat tomorrow morning," said he.

"Let us find it out and let us hear it from you then," said Cuchulainn.

"Your own foster-brother, Fer Diad Mac Damain."

"On our word, we think it not best that it should be he we come to meet," said Cuchulainn, "and it is not for fear of him but for the greatness of our love for him."

"It is fitting to fear him," said Fergus, "for he has a skin of horn in battle against a man, so that neither weapon nor edge will pierce it."

"Do not say that at all," said Cuchulainn, "for I swear the oath that my people swear, that every joint and every limb of him will be as pliant as a pliant rush in the midst of a stream under the point of my sword, if he shows himself once to me on the ford."

It is thus they were speaking, and they made a song:

"O Cuchulainn, a bright meeting," etc.

After that, "Why have you come, O my friend, O Fergus?" said Cuchulainn.

"That is my purpose," said Fergus.

"Good luck and profit," said Cuchulainn, "that no other of the men of Ireland has come for this purpose, unless the four provinces of Ireland all met at one time. I think nothing of a warning before a single warrior."

Then Fergus went to his tent.

As regards the charioteer and Cuchulainn:

"What shall you do tonight?" said Loeg.

"What indeed?" said Cuchulainn.

"It is thus that Fer Diad will come to seek you, with new beauty of plaiting and haircutting, and washing and bathing, and the four provinces of Ireland with him to look at the fight. It would please me if you went to the place where you will get the same adorning for yourself, to the place where is Emer of the Beautiful Hair, to Cairthend of Cluan Da Dam in Sliab Fuait."

So Cuchulainn went thither that night, and spent the night with his own wife. His adventures from this time are not discussed here now. As to Fer Diad, he came to his tent; it was gloomy and weary that Fer Diad's tent-servants were that night. They thought it certain that where the two pillars of the battle of the world should meet, that both would fall; or the issue of it would be, that it would be their own lord who would fall there. For it was not easy to fight with Cuchulainn on the Foray.

There were great cares on Fer Diad's mind that night, so that they did not let him sleep. One of his great anxieties was that he should let pass from him all the treasures that had been offered to him, and the maiden, by reason of combat with one man. If he did not fight with that one man, he must fight with the six warriors on the morrow. His care that was greater than this was that if he should show himself once on the ford to Cuchulainn, he was certain that he himself would not have power of his head or life thereafter; and Fer Diad arose early on the morrow.

"Good, my lad," said he, "get our horses for us, and harness the chariot."

"On our word," said the servant, "we think it not greater praise to go this journey than not to go it."

He was talking with his charioteer, and he made this little song, inciting his charioteer:

"Let us go to this meeting," etc.

The servant got the horses and yoked the chariot, and they went forth from the camp.

"My lad," said Fer Diad, "it is not fitting that we make our journey without farewell to the men of Ireland. Turn the horses and the chariot for us towards the men of Ireland."

The servant turned the horses and the chariot thrice towards the men of Ireland. ...

"Does Ailill sleep now?" said Medb.

"Not at all," said Ailill.

"Do you hear your new son-in-law greeting you?"

"Is that what he is doing?" said Ailill.

"It is indeed," said Medb, "and I swear by what my people swear, the man who makes the greeting yonder will not come back to you on the same feet."

"Nevertheless we have profited by the good marriage connection with him," said Ailill; "provided Cuchulainn fell by him, I should not care though they both fell. But we should think it better for Fer Diad to escape."

Fer Diad came to the ford of combat.

"Look, my lad," said Fer Diad; "is Cuchulainn on the ford?"

"He is not, indeed," said the servant.

"Look well for us," said Fer Diad.

"Cuchulainn is not a little speck in hiding where he would be," said the lad.

"It is true, O boy, until today Cuchulainn has not heard of the coming of a good warrior (or a good man) against him on the Cattle Foray of Cualnge, and when he has heard of it he has left the ford."

"A great pity to slander Cuchulainn in his absence! For do you remember how when you gave battle to German Garbglas above the edge-borders of the Tyrrhene Sea, you left your sword with the hosts, and it was Cuchulainn who killed a hundred warriors in reaching it, and he brought it to you; and do you remember where we were that night?" said the lad.

"I do not know it," said Fer Diad.

"At the house of Scathach's steward," said the lad, "and you went — and haughtily before us into the house first. The churl gave you a blow with the three-pointed flesh-hook in the small of your back, so that it threw you out over the door like a shot. Cuchulainn came into the house and gave the churl a blow with his sword, so that it made two pieces of him. It was I who was steward for you while you were in that place. If only for that day, you should not say that you are a better warrior than Cuchulainn."

"What you have done is wrong," said Fer Diad, "for I would not have come to seek the combat if you had said it to me at first. Why do you not pull the cushions of the chariot under my side and my skin-cover under my head, so that I might sleep now?"

"Alas!" said the lad, "it is the sleep of a fey man before deer and hounds here."

"What, O lad, are you not fit to keep watch and ward for me?"

"I am fit," said the lad; "unless men come in clouds or in mist to seek you, they will not come at all from east or west to seek you without warning and observation."

The cushions of his chariot were pulled under his side and the skin under his head. And yet he could not sleep a little.

As to Cuchulainn it is set forth:

"Good, O my friend, O Loeg, take the horses and yoke the chariot; if Fer Diad is waiting for us, he is thinking it long."

The boy rose and took the horses and yoked the chariot.

Cuchulainn stepped into his chariot and they came on to the ford. As to Fer Diad's servant, he had not long to watch till he heard the creaking of the chariot coming towards them. He took to waking his master, and made a song:

"I hear a chariot," etc.

(This is the description of Cuchulainn's chariot: one of the three chief chariots of the narration on the Cattle Foray of Cualnge.)

"How do you see Cuchulainn?" said he, said Fer Diad, to his charioteer.

"I see," said he, "the chariot broad above, fine, of white crystal, with a yoke of gold with —, with great panels of copper, with shafts of bronze, with tyres of white metal, with its body thin-framed dry-framed, feat-high, sword-fair, of a champion, on which there would be room for seven arms fit for a lord. A fair seat for its lord; so that this chariot, Cuchulainn's chariot, would reach with the speed of a swallow or of a wild deer, over the level land of Mag Slebe. That is the speed and — which they attain, for it is towards us they go. This chariot is at hand on two horses small-headed, small-round, small-end, pointed, —, red-breasted, —, easy to recognise, well-yoked…. One of the two horses is supple, swift-leaping, great of strength, great of foot, great of length, —. The other horse is curly-maned, slender-footed, narrow-footed, heeled, —. Two wheels dark, black. A pole of metal adorned with red enamel, of a fair colour. Two bridles golden, inlaid. There is a man with fair curly hair, broad cut, in the front of this chariot. There is round him a blue mantle, red-purple. A spear with wings, and it red, furious; in his clenched fist, red-flaming. The appearance of three heads of hair on him, i.e. dark hair against the skin of his head, hair blood-red in the middle, a crown of gold covers the third hair.

"A fair arrangement of the hair so that it makes three circles round about his shoulders down behind. I think it like gold thread, after its colour has been made over the edge of the anvil; or like the yellow of bees on which the sun shines in a summer day, is the shining of each single hair of his hair. Seven toes on each of his feet, and seven fingers on each of his hands, and the shining of a very great fire round his eye, — and the hoofs of his horses; a hero's — in his hands.

"The charioteer of the chariot is worthy of him in his presence: curly hair very black has he, broad-cut along his head. A cowl-dress is on him open; two very fine golden leaf-shaped switches in his hand, and a light grey mantle round him, and a goad of white silver in his hand, plying the goad on the horses, whichever way the champion of great deeds goes who was at hand in the chariot.

"He is veteran of his land: he and his servant think little of Ireland."

"Go, O fellow,' said he, said Fer Diad; "you praise too much altogether; and prepare the arms in the ford against his coming."

"If I turned my face backwards, it seems to me the chariot would come through the back of my neck."

"O fellow," said he, "too greatly do you praise Cuchulainn, for it is not a reward for praising he has given you"; and it is thus he was giving his description, and he said:

"The help is timely," etc.

It is not long afterwards that they met in the middle of the ford, and Fer Diad said to Cuchulainn:

"Whence come you, O Cua?" said he (for *cua* was the name of squinting in old Gaelic; and there were seven pupils in Cuchulainn's royal eye, and two of these pupils were squinting, and the ugliness of it is no greater than its beauty on him; and if there had been a greater blemish on Cuchulainn, it is that with which he reproached him; and he was proclaiming it); and he made a song, and Cuchulainn answered:

"Whence art thou come, O Hound," etc.

Then Cuchulainn said to his charioteer that he was to taunt him when he was overcome, and that he was to praise him when he was victorious, in the combat against Fer Diad. Then the charioteer said to him:

"The man goes over thee as the tail over a cat; he washes thee as foam is washed in water, he squeezes thee as a loving mother her son."

Then they took to the ford-play. Scathach's — came to them both. Fer Diad and Cuchulainn performed marvellous feats. Cuchulainn went and leapt into Fer Diad's shield; Fer Diad hurled him from him thrice into the ford; so that the charioteer taunted him again — and he swelled like breath in a bag.

His size increased till he was greater than Fer Diad.

"Give heed to the *Gae bolga*," said the charioteer; he sent it to him along the stream. Cuchulainn seized it between his toes, and wielded it on Fer Diad, into his body's armour. It advances like one spear, so that it became twenty-four points. Then Fer Diad turned the shield below. Cuchulainn thrust at him with the spear over the shield, so that it broke the shaft of his ribs and went through Fer Diad's heart.

[*Fer Diad*:] "Strong is the ash from thy right hand! The — rib breaks, my heart is blood. Well hast thou given battle! I fall, O Hound."

[*Cuchulainn*:] "Alas, O golden brooch, O Fer Diad! —, O fair strong striker! Thy hand was victorious; our dear foster brotherhood, O delight of the eyes! Thy shield with the rim of gold, thy sword was dear. Thy ring of white silver round thy noble arm. Thy chess-playing was worthy of a great man. Thy cheek fair-purple; thy yellow curling hair was great, it was a fair treasure. Thy soft folded girdle which used to be about thy side. That thou shouldst fall at Cuchulainn's hands was sad, O Calf! Thy shield did not suffice which used to be for service. Our combat with thee is not fitting, our horses and our tumult. Fair was the great hero! Every host used to be defeated and put under foot. Alas, O golden brooch, O Fer Diad!"

This Is the Long Warning of Sualtaim

WHILE THE THINGS that we have related were done, Suallaith heard from Rath Sualtaim in Mag Murthemne the vexing of his son Cuchulainn against twelve sons of Gaile Dana and his sister's son.

It is then that Sualtaim said:

"Is it heaven that bursts, or the sea over its boundaries, or earth that is destroyed, or the shout of my son against odds?"

Then he comes to his son. Cuchulainn was displeased that he should come to him.

"Though he were slain, I should not have strength to avenge him. Go to the Ulstermen," says Cuchulainn, "and let them give battle to the warriors at once; if they do not give it, they will not be avenged for ever."

When his father saw him, there was not in his chariot as much as the point of a rush would cover that was not pierced. His left hand which the shield protected, twenty wounds were in it.

Sualtaim came over to Emain and shouted to the Ulstermen:

"Men are being slain, women carried off, cows driven away!"

His first shout was from the side of the court; his second from the side of the fortress; the third shout was on the mound of the hostages in Emain. No one answered; it was the practice of the Ulstermen that none of them should speak except to Conchobar; and Conchobar did not speak before the three druids.

"Who takes them, who steals them, who carries them off?" said the druid.

"Ailill Mac Mata carries them off and steals them and takes them, through the guidance of Fergus Mac Roich," said Sualtaim. "Your people have been enslaved as far as Dun Sobairce; their cows and their women and their cattle have been taken. Cuchulainn did not let them into Mag Murthemne and into Crich Rois; three months of winter then, bent branches of hazel held together his dress upon him. Dry wisps are on his wounds. He has been wounded so that he has been parted joint from joint."

"Fitting," said the druid, "were the death of the man who has spurred on the king."

"It is fitting for him," said Conchobar.

"It is fitting for him," said the Ulstermen.

"True is what Sualtaim says," said Conchobar; "from the Monday night of Samain to the Monday night of Candlemas he has been in this foray."

Sualtaim gave a leap out thereupon. He did not think sufficient the answer that he had. He falls on his shield, so that the engraved edge of the shield cut his head off. His head is brought back into Emain into the house on the shield, and the head says the same word (though some say that he was asleep on the stone, and that he fell thence on to his shield in awaking).

"Too great was this shout," said Conchobar. "The sea before them, the heaven over their tops, the earth under their feet. I will bring every cow into its milking-yard, and every woman and every boy from their house, after the victory in battle."

Then Conchobar struck his hand on his son, Findchad Fer m-Bend.

Hence he is so called because there were horns of silver on him.

The Muster of the Ulstermen

"ARISE, O Findchad, I will send thee to Deda," etc.

It was not difficult for Findchad to take his message, for they were, the whole province of Conchobar, every chief of them, awaiting Conchobar; every one was then east and north and west of Emain. When they were there, they all came till they were at Emain Macha. When they were there, they heard the uprising of Conchobar in Emain. They went past Emain southwards after the host. Their first march then was from Emain to Irard Cuillend.

"What are you waiting for here?' said Conchobar.

"Waiting for your sons," said the host. "They have gone with thirty with them to Temair to seek Eirc, son of Coirpre Niafer and Fedelm Noicride. Till their two cantreds should come to us, we will not go from this place."

"I will not remain indeed," said Conchobar, "till the men of Ireland know that I have awaked from the sickness in which I was."

Conchobar and Celtchar went with three fifties of chariots, and they brought eight twenties of heads from Ath Airthir Midi; hence is Ath Fene. They were there watching the host. And eight twenties of women, that was their share of the spoil. Their heads were brought there, and Conchobar and Celtchar sent them to the camp. It is there that Celtchar said to Conchobar...

(Or it was Cuscraid, the Stammerer of Macha, son of Conchobar, sang this song the night before the battle, after the song which Loegaire Buadach had sung, to wit, "Arise, kings of Macha," etc., and it would be in the camp it was sung.)

It was in this night that the vision happened to Dubthach Doeltenga of Ulster, when the hosts were on Garach and Irgarach. It is there that he said in his sleep…

The Vision of Dubthach

"A WONDER of a morning, a wonder of a time, when hosts will be confused, kings will be turned, necks will break, the sun will grow red, three hosts will be routed by the track of a host about Conchobar. They will strive for their women, they will chase their flocks in fight on the morning, heroes will be smitten, dogs will be checked, horses will be pressed, — will drip, from the assemblies of great peoples."

Therewith they awoke through their sleep. The Nemain threw the host into confusion there; a hundred men of them died. There is silence there then; when they heard Cormac Condlongas again (or it is Ailill Mac Matae in the camp who sang this):

"The time of Ailill. Great his truce, the truce of Cuillend," etc.

The March of the Companies

WHILE THESE THINGS were being done, the Connaughtman determined to send messengers by the counsel of Ailill and Medb and Fergus, to look at the Ulstermen, to see whether they had reached the plain. It is there that Ailill said:

"Go, O Mac Roth," said Ailill, "and look for us whether the men are all in the plain of Meath in which we are. If they have not come, I have carried off their spoil and their cows; let them give battle to me, if it suits them. I will not await them here any longer."

Then Mac Roth went to look at and to watch the plain. He came back to Ailill and Medb and Fergus The first time then that Mac Roth looked from the circuit of Sliab Fuait, he saw that all the wild beast came out of the wood, so that they were all in the plain.

"The second time," said Mac Roth, "that I surveyed the plain, I saw a heavy mist that filled the glens and the valleys, so that it made the hills between them like islands in lakes. Then there appeared to me sparks of fire out of this great mist: there appeared to me a variegation of every different colour in the world. I saw then lightning and din and thunder and a great wind that almost took my hair from my head, and threw me on my back; and yet the wind of the day was not great."

"What is it yonder, O Fergus?" said Ailill. "Say what it means."

"That is not hard; this is what it means," said Fergus: "This is the Ulstermen after coming out of their sickness. It is they who have come into the wood. The throng and the greatness and the violence of the heroes, it is that which has shaken the wood; it is before them that the wild beasts have fled into the plain. The heavy mist that you saw, which filled the valleys, was the breath of those warriors, which filled the glens so that it made the hills between them like islands in lakes. The lightning and the sparks of fire and the many colours that you saw, O Mac Roth," said Fergus, "are the eyes of the warriors from their heads which have shone to you like sparks of fire. The thunder and the din and the noise that you heard, was the whistling of the swords and of the ivory-hilted weapons, the clatter of arms, the creaking of the chariots, the beating of the hoofs of the horses, the strength of the warriors, the roar of the fighting-men, the noise of the soldiers, the great rage and anger and fierceness of the heroes going in madness to the battle, for the greatness of the rage and of the fury. They would think they would not reach it at all," said Fergus.

"We will await them," said Ailill; "we have warriors for them."

"You will need that," said Fergus, "for there will not be found in all Ireland, nor in the west of the world, from Greece and Scythia westward to the Orkneys and to the Pillars of Hercules and to the Tower of Bregon and to the island of Gades, anyone who shall endure the Ulstermen in their fury and in their rage," said Fergus.

Then Mac Roth went again to look at the march of the men of Ulster, so that he was in their camp at Slemon Midi, and Fergus; and he told them certain tidings, and Mac Roth said in describing them:

"A great company has come, of great fury, mighty, fierce, to the hill at Slemon Midi," said Mac Roth. "I think there is a cantred therein; they took off their clothing at once, and dug a mound of sods under their leader's seat. A warrior fair and tall and long and high, beautiful, the fairest of kings his form, in the front of the company. Hair white-yellow has he, and it curly, neat, bushy, ridged, reaching to the hollow of his shoulders. A tunic curly, purple, folded round him; a brooch excellent, of red-gold, in his cloak on his breast; eyes very grey, very fair, in his head; a face proper, purple, has he, and it narrow below and broad above: a beard forked, very curly, gold-yellow he has; a shirt white, hooded, with red ornamentation, round about him; a sword gold-hilted on his shoulders; a white shield with rivets of gold; abroad grey spear-head on a slender shaft in his hand. The fairest of the princes of the world his march, both in host and rage and form and dress, both in face and terror and battle and triumph, both in prowess and horror and dignity.

"Another company has come there," said Mac Roth; "it is next to the other in number and quarrelling and dress and terror and horror. A fair warrior, heroic, is in the front of this company. A green cloak folded round him; a brooch of gold over his arm; hair curly and yellow: an ivory-hilted sword with a hilt of ivory at his left. A shirt with — to his knee; a wound-giving shield with engraved edge; the candle of a palace (i.e. spear) in his hand; a ring of silver about it, and it runs round along the shaft forward to the point, and again it runs to the grip. And that troop sat down on the left hand of the leader of the first troop, and it is thus they sat down, with their knees to the ground, and the rims of their shields against their chins. And I thought there was stammering in the speech of the great fierce warrior who is the leader of that company.

"Another company has come there," said Mac Roth; "its appearance is vaster than a cantred; a man brave, difficult, fair, with broad head, before it. Hair dark and curly on him; a beard long, with slender points, forked, has he; a cloak dark-grey, —, folded round him; a leaf-shaped brooch of white metal over his breast; a white, hooded shirt to his knees; a hero's shield with rivets on him; a sword of white silver about his waist; a five-pointed spear in his hand. He sat down in front of the leader of the first troop."

"Who is that, O Fergus?" said Ailill.

"I know indeed," said Fergus, "those companies. Conchobar, king of a province of Ireland, it is he who has sat down on the mound of sods. Sencha Mac Aililla, the orator of Ulster, it is he who has sat down before him. Cuscraid, the Stammerer of Macha, son of Conchobar, it is he who has sat down at his father's side. It is the custom for the spear that is in his hand in sport yonder before victory — before or after. That is a goodly folk for wounding, for essaying every conflict, that has come," said Fergus.

"They will find men to speak with them here," said Medb.

"I swear by the god by whom my people swear," said Fergus, "there has not been born in Ireland hitherto a man who would check the host of Ulster."

"Another company has come there," said Mac Roth. "Greater than a cantred its number. A great warrior, brave, with horror and terror, and he mighty, fiery-faced, before it. Hair dark, greyish on him, and it smooth-thin on his forehead. Around shield with engraved edge on him, a spear five-pointed in his hand, a forked javelin beside him; a hard sword on the back of his head; a purple cloak folded round him; a brooch of gold on his arm; a shirt, white, hooded, to his knee."

"Who is that, O Fergus?" said Ailill.

"He is the putting of a hand on strife; he is a battle champion for fight; he is judgment against enemies who has come there; that is, Eogan Mac Durthacht, King of Fermoy is that," said Fergus.

"Another company has come, great, fierce, to the hill at Slemon Midi," said Mac Roth. "They have put their clothing behind them. Truly, it is strong, dark, they have come to the hill; heavy is the terror and great the horror which they have put upon themselves; terrible the clash of arms that they made in marching. A man thick of head, brave, like a champion, before it; and he horrible, hideous; hair light, grey on him; eyes yellow, great, in his head; a cloak yellow, with white — round about him. A shield, wound-giving, with engraved edge, on him, without; a broad spear, a javelin with a drop of blood along the shaft; and a spear its match with the blood of enemies along its edge in his hand; a great wound-giving sword on his shoulders."

"Who is that, O Fergus?" said Ailill.

"The man who has so come does not avoid battle or combat or strife: that is, Loegaire the Victorious, Mac Connaid Meic Ilech, from Immail from the north," said Fergus.

"Another great company has come to Slemon Midi to the hill," said Mac Roth. "A warrior thick-necked, fleshy, fair, before that company. Hair black and curly on him, and he purple, blue-faced; eyes grey, shining, in his head; a cloak grey, lordly, about him; a brooch of white silver therein; a black shield with a boss of bronze on it; a spear, covered with eyes, with —, in his hand; a shirt, braided, with red ornamentation, about him; a sword with a hilt of ivory over his dress outside."

"Who is that, O Fergus?" said Ailill.

"He is the putting of a hand on a skirmish; he is the wave of a great sea that drowns little streams; he is a man of three shouts; he is the judgment of — of enemies, who so comes," said Fergus; "that is, Munremar Mac Gerrcind, from Moduirn in the north."

"Another great company has come there to the hill to Slemon Midi," said Mac Roth. "A company very fair, very beautiful, both in number and strife and raiment. It is fiercely that they make for the hill; the clatter of arms which they raised in going on their course shook the host. A warrior fair, excellent, before the company. Most beautiful of men his form, both in hair and eyes and fear, both in raiment and form and voice and whiteness, both in dignity and size and beauty, both in weapons and knowledge and adornment, both in equipment and armour and fitness, both in honour and wisdom and race."

"This is his description," said Fergus; "he is the brightness of fire, the fair man, Fedlimid, who so comes there; he is fierceness of warriors, he is the wave of a storm that drowns, he is might that is not endured, with triumphs out of other territories after destruction of his foes; that is Fedlimid — there."

"Another company has come there to the hill to Slemon Midi," said Mac Roth, "which is not fewer than a warlike cantred. A warrior great, brave, grey, proper, —, in front of it. Hair black, curly, on him; round eyes, grey, very high, in his head. A man bull-like, strong, rough; a grey cloak about him, with a brooch of silver on his arm; a shirt white, hooded, round him; a sword at his side; a red shield with a hard boss of silver on it. A spear with three rivets, broad, in his hand."

"Who is that, O Fergus?" said Ailill.

"He is the fierce glow of wrath, he is a shaft of every battle; he is the victory of every combat, who has so come there, Connad Mac Mornai from Callann," said Fergus.

"Another company has come to the hill at Slemon Midi," said Mac Roth. "It is the march of an army for greatness. The leader who is in front of that company, not common is a warrior fairer both in form and attire and equipment. Hair bushy, red-yellow, on him; a face proper, purple, well-proportioned; a face narrow below, broad above; lips red, thin; teeth shining, pearly; a voice clear, ringing; a face fair, purple, shapely; most beautiful of the forms of men; a purple cloak folded round him; a brooch with full adornment of gold, over his white breast; a bent shield with many-coloured rivets, with a boss of silver, at his left; a long spear, grey-edged, with a sharp javelin for attack in his hand; a sword gold-hilted, of gold, on his back; a hooded shirt with red ornamentation about him."

"Who is that, O Fergus?" said Ailill.

"We know, indeed," said Fergus. "He is half of a combat truly," said he, "who so comes there; he is a fence of battle, he is fierce rage of a bloodhound; Rochad Mac Fathemain from Bridamae, your son-in-law, is that, who wedded your daughter yonder, that is, Findabair."

"Another company has come to the hill, to Slemon Midi," said Mac Roth. "A warrior with great calves, stout, with great thighs, big, in front of that company. Each of his limbs is almost as thick as a man. Truly, he is a man down to the ground," said he. "Hair black on him; a face full of wounds, purple, has he; an eye parti-coloured, very high, in his head; a man glorious, dexterous, thus, with horror and terror, who has a wonderful apparel, both raiment and weapons and appearance and splendour and dress; he raises himself with the prowess of a warrior, with achievements of —, with the pride of wilfulness, with a going through battle to rout overwhelming numbers, with wrath upon foes, with a marching on many hostile countries without protection. In truth, mightily have they come on their course into Slemon Midi."

"He was — of valour and of prowess, in sooth," said Fergus; "he was of — pride and of haughtiness, he was — of strength and dignity, — then of armies and hosts of my own foster-brother, Fergus Mac Leiti, King of Line, point of battle of the north of Ireland."

"Another company, great, fierce, has come to the hill, to Slemon Midi," said Mac Roth. "Strife before it, strange dresses on them. A warrior fair, beautiful, before it; gift of every form, both hair and eye and whiteness, both size and strife and fitness; five chains of gold on him; a green cloak folded about him; a brooch of gold in the cloak over his arm; a shirt white, hooded, about him; the tower of a palace in his hand; a sword gold-hilted on his shoulders."

"Fiery is the bearing of the champion of combat who has so come there," said Fergus. "Amorgene, son of Eccet Salach the smith, from Buais in the north is that."

"Another company has come there, to the hill, to Slemon Midi," said Mac Roth. It is a drowning for size, it is a fire for splendour, it is a pin for sharpness, it is a battalion for number, it is a rock for greatness, it is — for might, it is a judgment for its —, it is thunder for pride. A warrior rough-visaged, terrible, in front of this company, and he great-bellied, large-lipped; rough hair, a grey beard on him; and he great-nosed, red-limbed; a dark cloak about him, an iron spike on his cloak; a round shield with an engraved edge on him; a rough shirt, braided, about him; a great grey spear in his hand, and thirty rivets therein; a sword of seven charges of metal on his shoulders. All the host rose before him, and he overthrew multitudes of the battalion about him in going to the hill."

"He is a head of strife who has so come," said Fergus; "he is a half of battle, he is a warrior for valour, he is a wave of a storm which drowns, he is a sea over boundaries; that is, Celtchar Mac Uithechair from Dunlethglaisi in the north."

"Another company has come there to the hill, to Slemon Midi," said Mac Roth. "A warrior of one whiteness in front of it, all white, both hair and eyelashes and beard and equipment; a shield with a boss of gold on him, and a sword with a hilt of ivory, and a broad spear with rings in his hand. Very heroic has his march come."

"Dear is the bear, strong-striking, who has so come," said Fergus; "the bear of great deeds against enemies, who breaks men, Feradach Find Fechtnach from the grove of Sliab Fuait in the north is that."

"Another company has come there to the hill, to Slemon Midi," said Mac Roth. 'A hideous warrior in front of it, and he great-bellied, large-lipped; his lips as big as the lips of a horse; hair dark, curly, on him, and he himself —, broad-headed, long-handed; a cloak black, hairy, about him; a chain of copper over it, a dark grey buckler over his left hand; a spear with chains in his right hand; a long sword on his shoulders."

"He is a lion red-handed, fierce of —, who so comes," said Fergus. 'He is high of deeds, great in battle, rough; he is a raging on the land who is unendurable, Eirrgi Horse-lipped from Bri Eirge in the north," said Fergus.

"Another company has come there to the hill, to Slemon Midi," said Mac Roth. "Two warriors, fair, both alike, in front of it; yellow hair on them; two white shields with rivets of silver; they are of equal age. They lift up their feet and set them down together; it is not their manner for either of them to lift up his feet without the other. Two heroes, two splendid flames, two points of battle, two warriors, two pillars of fight, two dragons, two fires, two battle-soldiers, two champions of combat, two rods, two bold ones, two pets of Ulster about the king."

"Who are those, O Fergus?" said Ailill.

"Fiachna and Fiacha, two sons of Conchobar Mac Nessa, two darlings of the north of Ireland," said Fergus.

"Another company has come to the hill, to Slemon Midi," said Mac Roth. 'Three warriors, fiery, noble, blue-faced, before it. Three heads of hair very yellow have they; three cloaks of one colour in folds about them; three brooches of gold over their arms, three shirts — with red ornamentation round about them; three shields alike have they; three swords gold-hilted on their shoulders; three spears, broad-grey, in their right hands. They are of equal age."

"Three glorious champions of Coba, three of great deeds of Midluachair, three princes of Roth, three veterans of the east of Sliab Fuait," said Fergus; "the three sons of Fiachna are these, after the Bull; that is, Rus and Dairi and Imchath," said Fergus.

"Another company has come there to the hill, to Slemon Midi," said Mac Roth. "A man lively, fiery, before it; eyes very red, of a champion, in his head; a many-coloured cloak about him; a chain of silver thereon; a grey shield on his left; a sword with a hilt of silver at his side; a spear, excellent with a striking of cruelty in his vengeful right hand;

a shirt white, hooded, to his knee. A company very red, with wounds, about him, and he himself wounded and bleeding."

"That," said Fergus, "is the bold one, unsparing; that is the tearing; it is the boar (a beast that wounds or gores) of combat, it is the mad bull; it is the victorious one of Baile; it is the warlike one of the gap; it is the champion of Colptha, the door of war of the north of Ireland: that is, Menn Mac Salchalca from Corann. To avenge his wounds upon you has that man come," said Fergus.

"Another company has come there to the hill, to Slemon Midi," said Mac Roth, "and they very heroic, mutually willing. A warrior grey, great, broad, tall, before it. Hair dark, curly, on him; a cloak red, woollen, about him; a shirt excellent; a brooch of gold over his arms in his cloak; a sword, excellent, with hilt of white silver on his left; a red shield has he; a spear-head broad-grey on a fair shaft of ash in his hand."

"A man of three strong blows who has so come," said Fergus; "a man of three roads, a man of three highways, a man of three gifts, a man of three shouts, who breaks battles on enemies in another province: Fergrae Mac Findchoime from Corann is that."

"Another company has come there to the hill, to Slemon Midi," said Mac Roth. "Its appearance is greater than a cantred. A warrior white-breasted, very fair, before it; like to Ailill yonder in size and beauty and equipment and raiment. A crown of gold above his head; a cloak excellent folded about him; a brooch of gold in the cloak on his breast; a shirt with red ornamentation round about him; a shield wound-giving with rims of gold; the pillar of a palace in his hand; a sword gold-hilted on his shoulders."

"It is a sea over rivers who has so come, truly," said Fergus; "it is a fierce glow of fire; his rage towards foes is insupportable: Furbaidi Ferbend is that," said Fergus.

"Another company has come there to the hill, to Slemon Midi," said Mac Roth. "Very heroic, innumerable," said Mac Roth; "strange garments, various, about them, different from other companies. Famously have they come, both in arms and raiment and dress. A great host and fierce is that company. A lad flame red before it; the most beautiful of the forms of men his form; ...a shield with white boss in his hand, the shield of gold and a rim of gold round it; a spear sharp, light, with in his hand; a cloak purple, fringed, folded about him; a brooch of silver in the cloak, on his breast; a shirt white, hooded, with red ornamentation, about him; a sword gold-hilted over his dress outside."

Therewith Fergus is silent.

"I do not know indeed," said Fergus, "the like of this lad in Ulster, except that I think it is the men of Temair about a lad proper, wonderful, noble: with Erc, son of Coirpre Niafer and of Conchobar's daughter. They love not one another; — without his father's leave has that man come, to help his grandfather. It is through the combat of that lad," said Fergus, "that you will be defeated in the battle. That lad knows not terror nor fear at coming to you among them into the midst of your battalion. It would be like men that the warriors of the men of Ulster will roar in saving the calf their heart, in striking the battle. There will come to them a feeling of kinship at seeing that lad in the great battle, striking the battle before them. There will be heard the rumble of Conchobar's sword like the barking of a watch-dog in saving the lad. He will throw three walls of men about the battle in seeking the lad. It will be with the affection of kinsmen that the warriors of Ulster will attack the countless host," said Fergus.

"I think it long," said Mac Roth, "to be recounting all that I have seen, but I have come meanwhile with tidings to you."

"You have brought it," said Fergus.

"Conall Cernach has not come with his great company," said Mac Roth; "the three sons of Conchobar with their three cantreds have not come; Cuchulainn too has not come there after his wounding in combat against odds. Unless it is a warrior with one chariot," said Mac Roth, "I think it would be he who has come there. Two horses... under his chariot; they are long-tailed, broad-hoofed, broad above, narrow beneath, high-headed, great of curve, thin-mouthed, with distended nostrils. Two wheels black, —, with tyres even, smooth-running; the body very high, clattering; the tent...therein; the pillars carved. The warrior in that chariot four-square, purple-faced; hair cropped short on the top, curly, very black has he, down to his shoulders; ...a cloak red about him; four thirties of feat-poles in each of his two arms. A sword gold-hilted on his left; shield and spear has he, and twenty-four javelins about him on strings and thongs. The charioteer in front of him; the back of the charioteer's head towards the horses, the reins grasped by his toes before him; the chessboard spread between them, half the men of yellow gold, the others of white metal; the *buanfach* (a game; probably in the nature of chess or draughts) under their thighs. Nine feats were performed by him on high."

"Who is that, O Fergus?" said Ailill.

"An easy question," said Fergus. "Cuchulainn Mac Sualtaim from the *Sid* (Cuchulainn was of fairy birth), and Loeg Mac Riangabra his charioteer. Cuchulainn is that," said Fergus.

"Many hundreds and thousands," said Mac Roth, "have reached the camp of Ulster. Many heroes and champions and fighting-men have come with a race to the assembly. Many companies," said Mac Roth, "were reaching the same camp, of those who had not reached or come to the camp when I came; only," said Mac Roth, "my eye did not rest on hill or height of all that my eye reached from Fer Diad's Ford to Slemon Midi, but upon horse and man."

"You saw the household of a man truly," said Fergus.

Then Conchobar went with his hosts and took camp near the others. Conchobar asked for a truce till sunrise on the morrow from Ailill, and Ailill ratified it for the men of Ireland and for the exiles, and Conchobar ratified it for the Ulstermen; and then Conchobar's tents are pitched. The ground between them is a space, —, bare, and the Ulstermen came to it before sunset. Then said the Morrigan in the twilight between the two camps...

* * *

Now Cuchulainn was at Fedan Chollna near them. Food was brought to him by the hospitallers that night; and they used to come to speak to him by day.

He did not kill any of them to the left of Fer Diad's Ford.

"Here is a small herd from the camp from the west to the camp to the east," said the charioteer to Cuchulainn. "Here is a troop of lads to meet them."

"Those lads shall come," said Cuchulainn. "The little herd shall come over the plain. He who will not — shall come to help the lads."

This was done then as Cuchulainn had said.

"How do the lads of Ulster fight the battle?"

"Like men," said the charioteer.

"It would be a vow for them, to fall in rescuing their herds," said Cuchulainn. "And now?"

"The beardless striplings are fighting now," said the charioteer.

"Has a bright cloud come over the sun yet?"

"Not so," said the charioteer.

"Alas, that I had not strength to go to them!' said Cuchulainn.

"There will be contest without that today," said the charioteer, "at sunrise; haughty folk fight the battle now," said the charioteer, "save that there are not kings there, for they are still asleep."

Then Fachna said when the sun rose (or it is Conchobar who sang in his sleep):

"Arise, Kings of Macha, of mighty deeds, noble household, grind your weapons, fight the battle," etc.

"Who has sung this?" said everyone.

"Conchobar Mac Nessa," said they; "or Fachtna sang it," said they.

"Sleep, sleep, save your sentinels."

Loegaire the Victorious was heard: "Arise, Kings of Macha," etc.

"Who has sung that?" said everyone.

"Loegaire the Victorious, son of Connad Buide Mac Ilech. Sleep, sleep, except your sentinels."

"Wait for it still," said Conchobar, "till sunrise...in the glens and heights of Ireland."

When Cuchulainn saw the kings from the east taking their crowns on their heads and marshalling the companies, Cuchulainn said to his charioteer that he should awaken the Ulstermen; and the charioteer said (or it is Amairgen, son of Eccet the poet, who said):

"Arise, Kings of Macha," etc.

"I have awakened them," said the charioteer. "Thus have they come to the battle, quite naked, except for their arms only. He, the door of whose tent is east, has come out through it west."

"It is a 'goodly help of necessity'," said Cuchulainn.

The adventures of the Ulstermen are not followed up here now. As for the men of Ireland, Badb and Net's wife and Nemain (the wife of Net, the war-god, according to Cormac) called upon them that night on Garach and Irgarach, so that a hundred warriors of them died for terror; that was not the most peaceful of nights for them.

The Muster of the Men of Ireland Here

AILILL MAC MATAE sang that night before the battle, and said:

"Arise, arise," etc

As for Cuchulainn, this is what is told here now.

"Look for us, O my friend, O Loeg, how the Ulstermen are fighting the battle now."

"Like men," said the charioteer.

"Though I were to go with my chariot, and Oen the charioteer of Conall Cernach with his chariot, so that we should go from one wing to the other along the dense mass, neither hoofs nor tyres shall go through it."

"That is the stuff for a great battle," said Cuchulainn. "Nothing must be done in the battle," said Cuchulainn to his charioteer, "that we shall not know from you."

"That will be true, so far as I can," said the charioteer. "The place where the warriors are now from the west,' said the charioteer, 'they make a breach in the battle eastwards. Their first defence from the east, they make a breach in the battle westwards."

"Alas! That I am not whole!" said Cuchulainn; "my breach would be manifest like the rest."

Then came the men of the bodyguard to the ford of the hosting. Fine the way in which the fightingmen came to the battle on Garach and Irgarach. Then came the nine chariot-men of the champions of Iruath, three before them on foot. Not more slowly did they come than the chariot-men. Medb did not let them into the battle, for dragging Ailill out of the battle if it is him they should defeat, or for killing Conchobar if it is he who should be defeated.

Then his charioteer told Cuchulainn that Ailill and Medb were asking Fergus to go into the battle; and they said to him that it was only right for him to do it, for they had done him much kindness on his exile.

"If I had my sword indeed," said Fergus, "the heads of men over shields would be more numerous with me than hailstones in the mire to which come the horses of a king after they have broken into the land."

Then Fergus made this oath: 'I swear, etc., there would be broken by me cheeks of men from their necks, necks of men with their (lower) arms, arms of men with their elbows, elbows of men with their arms, arms of men with their fists, fists of men with their fingers, fingers of men with their nails, nails of men with their skull-roofs, skull-roofs of men with their middle, middle of men with their thighs, thighs of men with their knees, knees of men with their calves, calves of men with their feet, feet of men with their toes, toes of men with their nails. I would make their necks whizz — as a bee would move to and fro on a day of beauty."

Then Ailill said to his charioteer: "Let there come to me the sword which destroys skin. I swear by the god by whom my people swear, if you have its bloom worse today than on the day on which I gave it to you in the hillside in the boundary of Ulster, though the men of Ireland were protecting you from me, they should not protect you."

Then his sword was brought to Fergus, and Ailill said: "Take thy sword," etc.

"A pity for thee to fall on the field of battle, thick with slain," said Fergus to Ailill.

The Badb and Net's wife and the Nemain called on them that night on Garach and Irgarach; so that a hundred warriors of them died for terror. That was not the quietest of nights for them.

Then Fergus takes his arms and turns into the battle, and clears a gap of a hundred in the battle with his sword in his two hands. Then Medb took the arms of Fergus and rushed into the battle, and she was victorious thrice, so that she was driven back by force of arms.

"I do not know," said Conchobar to his retinue who were round him, "before whom has the battle been broken against us from the north. Do you maintain the fight here, that I may go against him."

"We will hold the place in which we are," said the warriors, "unless the earth bursts beneath us, or the heaven upon us from above, so that we shall break therefrom."

Then Conchobar came against Fergus. He lifts his shield against him, i.e. Conchobar's shield Ochan, with three horns of gold on it, and four — of gold over it. Fergus strikes three blows on it, so that even the rim of his shield over his head did not touch him.

"Who of the Ulstermen holds the shield?" said Fergus.

"A man who is better than you," said Conchobar; "and he has brought you into exile into the dwellings of wolves and foxes, and he will repel you today in combat in the presence of the men of Ireland."

Fergus aimed on him a blow of vengeance with his two hands on Conchobar, so that the point of the sword touched the ground behind him.

Cormac Condlongas put his hands upon him, and closed his two hands about his arm.

"—, O my friend, O Fergus," said Cormac. "...Hostile is the friendship; right is your enmity; your compact has been destroyed; evil are the blows that you strike, O friend, O Fergus," said Cormac.

"Whom shall I smite?" said Fergus.

"Smite the three hills...in some other direction over them; turn your hand; smite about you on every side, and have no consideration for them. Take thought for the honour of Ulster: what has not been lost shall not be lost, if it be not lost through you today.

"Go in some other direction, O Conchobar," said Cormac to his father; "this man will not put out his rage on the Ulstermen any more here."

Fergus turned away. He slew a hundred warriors of Ulster in the first combat with the sword. He met Conall Cernach.

"Too great rage is that," said Conall Cernach, "on people and race, for a wanton."

"What shall I do, O warriors?" said he.

"Smite the hills across them and the champions round them," said Conall Cernach.

Fergus smote the hills then, so that he struck the three Maela (flat-topped hills) of Meath with his three blows.

Cuchulainn heard the blows then that Fergus gave on the hills or on the shield of Conchobar himself.

"Who strikes the three strong blows, great and distant?" said Cuchulainn.

...Then Loeg answered and said: "The choice of men, Fergus Mac Roich the very bold, smites them."

Then Cuchulainn said: "Unloose quickly the hazeltwigs; blood covers men, play of swords will be made, men will be spent therefrom."

Then his dry wisps spring from him on high, as far as — goes; and his hazel-twigs spring off, till they were in Mag Tuag in Connaught...and he smote the head of each of the two handmaidens against the other, so that each of them was grey from the brain of the other. They came from Medb for pretended lamentation over him, that his wounds might burst forth on him; and to say that the Ulstermen had been defeated, and that Fergus had fallen in opposing the battle, since Cuchulainn's coming into the battle had been prevented. The contortion came on him, and twenty-seven skin-tunics were given to him, that used to be about him under strings and thongs when he went into battle; and he takes his chariot on his back with its body and its two tyres, and he made for Fergus round about the battle.

"Turn hither, O friend Fergus," said Cuchulainn; and he did not answer till the third time. "I swear by the god by whom the Ulstermen swear," said he, "I will wash thee as foam is washed in a pool, I will go over thee as the tail goes over a cat, I will smite thee as a fond mother smites her son."

"Which of the men of Ireland speaks thus to me?" said Fergus.

"Cuchulainn Mac Sualtaim, sister's son to Conchobar," said Cuchulainn; "and avoid me," said he.

"I have promised even that," said Fergus.

"Your promise falls due, then," said Cuchulainn.

"Good," said Fergus, "you avoided me, when you are pierced with wounds."

Then Fergus went away with his cantred; the Leinstermen go and the Munstermen; and they left in the battle nine cantreds of Medb's and Ailill's and their seven sons.

In the middle of the day it is that Cuchulainn came into the battle; when the sun came into the leaves of the wood, it is then that he defeated the last company, so that there remained of the chariot only a handful of the ribs about the body, and a handful of the shafts about the wheel.

Cuchulainn overtook Medb then when he went into the battle.

"Protect me," said Medb.

"Though I should slay thee with a slaying, it were lawful for me," said Cuchulainn.

Then he protected her, because he used not to slay women. He convoyed them westward, till they passed Ath Luain. Then he stopped. He struck three blows with his sword on the stone in Ath Luain. Their name is the Maelana (flat-topped hills) of Ath Luain.

When the battle was broken, then said Medb to Fergus: "Faults and meet here today, O Fergus," said she.

"It is customary," said Fergus, "to every herd which a mare precedes; ...after a woman who has ill consulted their interest."

They take away the Bull then in that morning of the battle, so that he met the White-horned at Tarbga in Mag Ai; i.e. Tarbguba or Tarbgleo, 'Bull-Sorrow or Bull-Fight'. The first name of that hill was Roi Dedond. Every one who escaped in the fight was intent on nothing but beholding the two Bulls fighting.

Bricriu Poison-tongue was in the west in his sadness after Fergus had broken his head with his draughtmen (this story is told in the *Echtra Nerai*). He came with the rest then to see the combat of the Bulls. The two Bulls went in fighting over Bricriu, so that he died therefrom. That is the Death of Bricriu.

The foot of the Dun of Cualnge lighted on the horn of the other.

For a day and a night he did not draw his foot towards him, till Fergus incited him and plied a rod along his body.

"'Twere no good luck," said Fergus, "that this conbative old calf which has been brought here should leave the honour of clan and race; and on both sides men have been left dead through you." Therewith he drew his foot to him so that his leg was broken, and the horn sprang from the other and was in the mountain by him. It was Sliab n-Adarca (Mountain of the Horn) afterwards.

He carried them then a journey of a day and a night, till he lighted in the loch which is by Cruachan, and he came to Cruachan out of it with the loin and the shoulder-blade and the liver of the other on his horns. Then the hosts came to kill him. Fergus did not allow it, but that he should go where he pleased. He came then to his land and drank a draught in Findlethe on coming. It is there that he left the shoulderblade of the other. Findlethe afterwards was the name of the land. He drank another draught in Ath Luain; he left the loin of the other there: hence is Ath Luain. He gave forth his roar on Iraird Chuillend; it was heard through all the province. He drank a draught in Tromma. There the liver of the other fell from his horns; hence is Tromma. He came to Etan Tairb (The Bull's Forehead). He put his forehead against the hill at Ath Da Ferta; hence is Etan Tairb in Mag Murthemne. Then he went on the road of Midluachair in Cuib. There he used to be with the milkless cow of Dairi, and he made a trench there. Hence is Gort Buraig. (The Field of the Trench). Then he went till he died between Ulster and Iveagh at Druim Tairb. Druim Tairb is the name of that place.

Ailill and Medb made peace with the Ulstermen and with Cuchulainn. For seven years after there was no wounding of men between them. Findabair stayed with Cuchulainn, and the Connaughtmen went to their country, and the Ulstermen to Emain Macha with their great triumph. Finit, amen.

Footnotes for *The Cattle-Raid of Cualnge*

1. The Gae-bolga was a special kind of spear, which only Cuchulainn could use.
2. The Riastartha ('distorted one') was a name given to Cuchulainn because of the contortion, described later, which came over him.
3. Findbennach, the Whitehorned; i.e. the other of the two bulls in whom the rival swineherds were reincarnated.
4. The river Cronn.
5. A twig twisted in the form of two rings, joined by one straight piece, as used for hobbling horses and cattle.

The Knighting of Cuculain

ONE NIGHT in the month of the fires of Bel, Cathvah, the Druid and star-gazer, was observing the heavens through his astrological instruments. Beside him was Cuculain, just then completing his sixteenth year. Since the exile of Fergus MacRoy, Cuculain had attached himself most to the Ard-Druid, and delighted to be along with him in his studies and observations. Suddenly the old man put aside his instruments and meditated a long time in silence.

"Setanta," said he at length, "art thou yet sixteen years of age?"

"No, father," replied the boy.

"It will then be difficult to persuade the king to knight thee and enrol thee among his knights," said Cathvah. "Yet this must be done tomorrow, for it has been revealed to me that he whom Concobar MacNessa shall present with arms tomorrow will be renowned to the most distant ages, and to the ends of the earth. Thou shalt be presented with arms tomorrow, and after that thou mayest retire for a season among thy comrades, nor go out among the warriors until thy strength is mature."

The next day Cathvah procured the king's consent to the knighting of Cuculain. Now on the same morning, one of his grooms came to Concobar MacNessa and said: "O chief of the Red Branch, thou knowest how no horse has eaten barley, or ever occupied the stall where stood the divine steed which, with another of mortal breed, in the days of Kimbay MacFiontann, was accustomed to bear forth to the battle the great war-queen, Macha Monga-Rue; but ever since that stall has been empty, and no mortal steed hath profaned the stall in which the deathless Lia Macha was wont to stand. Yet, O Concobar, as I passed into the great stables on the east side of the courtyard, wherein are the steeds of thy own ambus, and in which is that spot since held sacred, I saw in the empty stall a mare, gray almost to whiteness, and of a size and beauty such as I have never seen, who turned to look upon me as I entered the stable, having very gentle eyes, but such as terrified me, so that I let fall the vessel in which I was bearing curds for the steed of Konaul Clareena; and she approached me, and laid her head upon my shoulder, making a strange noise."

Now as the groom was thus speaking, Cowshra Mend Macha, a younger son of Concobar, came before the king, and said: "Thou knowest, O my father, that house in which is preserved the chariot of Kimbay MacFiontann, wherein he and she, whose name I bear, the great queen that protects our nation, rode forth to the wars in the ancient days, and how it has been preserved ever since, and that it is under my care to keep bright and clean. Now this day at sunrise I approached the house, as is my custom, and approaching, I heard dire voices, clamorous and terrible, that came from within, and noises like the noise of battle, and shouts as of warriors in the agony of the conflict, that raise their voices with short intense cries as they ply their weapons, avoiding or inflicting death. Then I went back terrified, but there met me Minrowar, son of Gerkin, for he came but last night from Moharne, in the east, and he went to look at his own steeds; but together we opened the gate of the chariot-house, and the bronze of the chariot burned like glowing fire, and the voices cried out in acclaim, when we stood in the doorway, and the light streamed into the dark chamber. Doubtless, a great warrior will appear amongst the Red Branch, for men say that not for a hundred years have these voices been heard, and I know not for whom Macha sends these portents, if it be not for the son of Sualtam, though he is not yet of an age to bear arms."

Thus was Concobar prepared for the knighting of Cuculain.

Then in the presence of his court, and his warriors, and the youths who were the comrades and companions of Cuculain, Concobar presented the young hero with his weapons of war, after he had taken the vows of the Red Branch, and having also bound himself by certain gæsa. But Cuculain looked narrowly upon the weapons, and he struck the spears together and clashed the sword upon the shield, and he brake the spears in pieces, and the sword, and made chasms in the shield.

"These are not good weapons, O my King," said the boy.

Then the king presented him with others that were larger and stronger, and these too the boy brake into little pieces.

"These are still worse, O son of Nessa," said the boy, "and it is not seemly, O chief of the Red Branch, that on the day that I am to receive my arms I should be made a laughing-stock before the Clanna Rury, being yet but a boy."

But Concobar MacNessa exulted exceedingly when he beheld the amazing strength and the waywardness of the boy, and beneath delicate brows his eyes glittered like gleaming swords as he glanced rapidly round on the crowd of martial men that surrounded him; but amongst them all he seemed himself a bright torch of valour and war, more pure and clear than polished steel. But he beckoned to one of his knights, who hastened away and returned, bringing Concobar's own shield and spears and the sword out of the Tayta Brac, where they were kept, an equipment in reserve. And Cuculain shook them and bent them, and clashed them together, but they held firm.

"These are good arms, O son of Nessa," said Cuculain.

Then there were led forward a pair of noble steeds and a war-car, and the king conferred them on Cuculain. Then Cuculain sprang into the chariot, and standing with legs apart, he stamped from side to side, and shook and shook, and jolted the car until the axle brake and the car itself was broken in pieces.

"This is not a good chariot, O my King," said the boy.

Then there were led forward three chariots, and all these he brake in succession.

"These are not good chariots, O chief of the Red Branch," said Cuculain. "No brave warrior would enter the battle or fight from such rotten foothold."

Then the king called to his son Cowshra Mead Macha and bade him take Læg, and harness to the war-chariot, of which he had the care, the wondrous gray steed, and that one which had been given him by Kelkar, the son of Uther, and to give Læg a charioteering equipment, to be charioteers of Cuculain. For now it was apparent to all the nobles and to the king that a lion of war had appeared amongst them, and that it was for him Macha had sent these omens.

Then Cuculain's heart leaped in his breast when he heard the thunder of the great war-car and the mad whinnying of the horses that smelt the battle afar. Soon he beheld them with his eyes, and the charioteer with the golden fillet of his office, erect in the car, struggling to subdue their fury. A gray, long-maned steed, whale-bellied, broad-chested, behind one yoke; a black, ugly-maned steed behind the other.

Like a hawk swooping along the face of a cliff when the wind is high, or like the rush of the March wind over the plain, or like the fleetness of the stag roused from his lair by the hounds and covering his first field, was the rush of those steeds when they had broken through the restraint of the charioteer, as though they galloped over fiery flags, so that the earth shook and trembled with the velocity of their motion, and all the time the great car brayed and shrieked as the wheels of solid and glittering bronze went round, for there were demons that had their abode in that car.

The charioteer restrained the steeds before the assembly, but nay-the-less a deep pur, like the pur of a tiger, proceeded from the axle. Then the whole assembly lifted up their voices and shouted for Cuculain, and he himself, Cuculain the son of Sualtam, sprang into his chariot, all armed, with a cry as of a warrior springing into his chariot in the battle, and he stood erect and brandished his spears, and the war-sprites of the Gæil shouted along with them, to the Bocanahs and Bananahs and the Genitii Glindi, the wild people of the glens, and the demons of the air, roared around him, when first the great warrior of the Gæil, his battle-arms in his hands, stood equipped for war in his chariot before all the warriors of his tribe, the kings of the Clanna Rury, and the people of Emain Macha.

The Leeching of Kayn's Leg

THERE WERE FIVE HUNDRED blind men, and five hundred deaf men, and five hundred limping men, and five hundred dumb men, and five hundred cripple men. The five hundred deaf men had five hundred wives, and the five hundred limping men had five hundred wives, and the five hundred dumb men had five hundred wives, and the five hundred cripple men had five hundred wives. Each five hundred of these had five hundred children and five hundred dogs. They were in the habit of going about in one band, and were called the Sturdy Strolling Beggarly Brotherhood.

There was a knight in Erin called O'Cronicert, with whom they spent a day and a year; and they ate up all that he had, and made a poor man of him, till he had nothing left but an old tumble-down black house, and an old lame white horse.

There was a king in Erin called Brian Boru; and O'Cronicert went to him for help. He cut a cudgel of grey oak on the outskirts of the wood, mounted the old lame white horse, and set off at speed through wood and over moss and rugged ground, till he reached the king's house. When he arrived he went on his knees to the king; and the king said to him, "What is your news, O'Cronicert?"

"I have but poor news for you, king."

"What poor news have you?" said the king.

"That I have had the Sturdy Strolling Beggarly Brotherhood for a day and a year, and they have eaten all that I had, and made a poor man of me," said he.

"Well!" said the king, "I am sorry for you; what do you want?"

"I want help," said O'Cronicert; "anything that you may be willing to give me."

The king promised him a hundred cows. He went to the queen, and made his complaint to her, and she gave him another hundred. He went to the king's son, Murdoch Mac Brian, and he got another hundred from him. He got food and drink at the king's; and when he was going away he said, "Now I am very much obliged to you. This will set me very well on my feet. After all that I have got there is another thing that I want."

"What is it?" said the king.

"It is the lap-dog that is in and out after the queen that I wish for."

"Ha!" said the king, "it is your mightiness and pride that has caused the loss of your means; but if you become a good man you shall get this along with the rest."

O'Cronicert bade the king goodbye, took the lap-dog, leapt on the back of the old lame white horse, and went off at speed through wood, and over moss and rugged ground. After he had gone some distance through the wood a roebuck leapt up and the lap-dog went after it. In a moment the deer started up as a woman behind O'Cronicert, the handsomest that eye had ever seen from the beginning of the universe till the end of eternity. She said to him, "Call your dog off me."

"I will do so if you promise to marry me," said O'Cronicert.

"If you keep three vows that I shall lay upon you I will marry you," said she.

"What vows are they?" said he.

"The first is that you do not go to ask your worldly king to a feast or a dinner without first letting me know," said she.

"Hoch!" said O'Cronicert, "do you think that I cannot keep that vow? I would never go to invite my worldly king without informing you that I was going to do so. It is easy to keep that vow."

"You are likely to keep it!" said she.

"The second vow is," said she, "that you do not cast up to me in any company or meeting in which we shall be together, that you found me in the form of a deer."

"Hoo!" said O'Cronicert, "you need not to lay that vow upon me. I would keep it at any rate."

"You are likely to keep it!" said she.

"The third vow is," said she, "that you do not leave me in the company of only one man while you go out." It was agreed between them that she should marry him.

They reached the old tumble-down black house. Grass they cut in the clefts and ledges of the rocks; a bed they made and laid down. O'Cronicert's wakening from sleep was the lowing of cattle and the bleating of sheep and the neighing of mares, while he himself was in a bed of gold on wheels of silver, going from end to end of the Tower of Castle Town.

"I am sure that you are surprised," said she.

"I am indeed," said he.

"You are in your own room," said she.

"In my own room," said he. "I never had such a room."

"I know well that you never had," said she; "but you have it now. So long as you keep me you shall keep the room."

He then rose, and put on his clothes, and went out. He took a look at the house when he went out; and it was a palace, the like of which he had never seen, and the king himself did not possess. He then took a walk round the farm; and he never saw so many cattle, sheep, and horses as were on it. He returned to the house, and said to his wife that the farm was being ruined by other people's cattle and sheep. "It is not," said she: "your own cattle and sheep are on it."

"I never had so many cattle and sheep," said he.

"I know that," said she; "but so long as you keep me you shall keep them. There is no good wife whose tocher does not follow her."

He was now in good circumstances, indeed wealthy. He had gold and silver, as well as cattle and sheep. He went about with his gun and dogs hunting every day, and was a great man. It occurred to him one day that he would go to invite the King of Erin to dinner, but he did not tell his wife that he was going. His first vow was now broken. He sped away to the King of Erin, and invited him and his great court to dinner. The King of Erin said to him, "Do you intend to take away the cattle that I promised you?"

"Oh! No, King of Erin," said O'Cronicert; "I could give you as many today."

"Ah!" said the king, "how well you have got on since I saw you last!"

"I have indeed," said O'Cronicert! "I have fallen in with a rich wife who has plenty of gold and silver, and of cattle and sheep."

"I am glad of that," said the King of Erin.

O'Cronicert said, "I shall feel much obliged if you will go with me to dinner, yourself and your great court."

"We will do so willingly," said the king.

They went with him on that same day. It did not occur to O'Cronicert how a dinner could be prepared for the king without his wife knowing that he was coming. When they were going on, and had reached the place where O'Cronicert had met the deer, he remembered that his vow was broken, and he said to the king, "Excuse me; I am going on before to the house to tell that you are coming."

The king said, "We will send off one of the lads."

"You will not," said O'Cronicert; "no lad will serve the purpose so well as myself."

He set off to the house; and when he arrived his wife was diligently preparing dinner. He told her what he had done, and asked her pardon. "I pardon you this time," said she: "I know what you have done as well as you do yourself. The first of your vows is broken."

The king and his great court came to O'Cronicert's house; and the wife had everything ready for them as befitted a king and great people; every kind of drink and food. They spent two or three days and nights at dinner, eating and drinking. They were praising the dinner highly, and O'Cronicert himself was praising it; but his wife was not. O'Cronicert was angry that she was not praising it and he went and struck her in the mouth with his fist and knocked out two of her teeth. "Why are you not praising the dinner like the others, you contemptible deer?" said he.

"I am not," said she: "I have seen my father's big dogs having a better dinner than you are giving tonight to the King of Erin and his court."

O'Cronicert got into such a rage that he went outside of the door. He was not long standing there when a man came riding on a black horse, who in passing caught O'Cronicert by the collar of his coat, and took him up behind him: and they set off. The rider did not say a word to O'Cronicert. The horse was going so swiftly that O'Cronicert thought the wind would drive his head off. They arrived at a big, big palace, and came off the black horse. A stableman came out, and caught the horse, and took it in. It was with wine that he was cleaning the horse's feet. The rider of the black horse said to O'Cronicert, "Taste the wine to see if it is better than the wine that you are giving to Brian Boru and his court tonight."

O'Cronicert tasted the wine, and said, "This is better wine."

The rider of the black horse said, "How unjust was the fist a little ago! The wind from your fist carried the two teeth to me."

He then took him into that big, handsome, and noble house, and into a room that was full of gentlemen eating and drinking, and he seated him at the head of the table, and gave him wine to drink, and said to him, "Taste that wine to see if it is better than the wine that you are giving to the King of Erin and his court tonight."

"This is better wine," said O'Cronicert.

"How unjust was the fist a little ago!" said the rider of the black horse.

When all was over the rider of the black horse said, "Are you willing to return home now?"

"Yes," said O'Cronicert, "very willing."

They then rose, and went to the stable: and the black horse was taken out; and they leaped on its back, and went away. The rider of the black horse said to O'Cronicert, after they had set off, "Do you know who I am?"

"I do not," said O'Cronicert.

"I am a brother-in-law of yours," said the rider of the black horse; "and though my sister is married to you there is not a king or knight in Erin who is a match for her. Two of your vows are now broken; and if you break the other vow you shall lose your wife and all that you possess."

They arrived at O'Cronicert's house; and O'Cronicert said, "I am ashamed to go in, as they do not know where I have been since night came."

"Hoo!" said the rider, "they have not missed you at all. There is so much conviviality among them, that they have not suspected that you have been anywhere. Here are the two teeth that you knocked out of the front of your wife's mouth. Put them in their place, and they will be as strong as ever."

"Come in with me," said O'Cronicert to the rider of the black horse.

"I will not: I disdain to go in," said the rider of the black horse.

The rider of the black horse bade O'Cronicert goodbye, and went away.

O'Cronicert went in; and his wife met him as she was busy waiting on the gentlemen. He asked her pardon, and put the two teeth in the front of her mouth, and they were as strong as ever. She said, "Two of your vows are now broken." No one took notice of him when he went in, or said "Where have you been?" They spent the night in eating and drinking, and the whole of the next day.

In the evening the king said, "I think that it is time for us to be going"; and all said that it was. O'Cronicert said, "You will not go tonight. I am going to get up a dance. You will go tomorrow."

"Let them go," said his wife.

"I will not," said he.

The dance was set a-going that night. They were playing away at dancing and music till they became warm and hot with perspiration. They were going out one after another to cool themselves at the side of the house. They all went out except O'Cronicert and his wife, and a man called Kayn Mac Loy. O'Cronicert himself went out, and left his wife and Kayn Mac Loy in the house, and when she saw that he had broken his third vow she gave a spring through a room, and became a big filly, and gave Kayn Mac Loy a kick with her foot, and broke his thigh in two. She gave another spring, and smashed the door and went away, and was seen no more. She took with her the Tower of Castle Town as an armful on her shoulder and a light burden on her back, and she left Kayn Mac Loy in the old tumble-down black house in a pool of rain-drip on the floor.

At daybreak next day poor O'Cronicert could only see the old house that he had before. Neither cattle nor sheep, nor any of the fine things that he had was to be seen. One awoke in the morning beside a bush, another beside a dyke, and another beside a ditch. The king only had the honour of having O'Cronicert's little hut over his head. As they were leaving, Murdoch Mac Brian remembered that he had left his own foster-brother Kayn Mac Loy behind, and said there should be no separation in life between them and that he would go back for him. He found Kayn in the old tumble-down black house, in the middle of the floor, in a pool of rain-water, with his leg broken; and he said the earth should make a nest in his sole and the sky a nest in his head if he did not find a man to cure Kayn's leg.

They told him that on the Isle of Innisturk was a herb that would heal him.

So Kayn Mac Loy was then borne away, and sent to the island, and he was supplied with as much food as would keep him for a month, and with two crutches on which he would be going out and in as he might desire. At last the food was spent, and he was destitute, and he had not found the herb. He was in the habit of going down to the shore, and gathering shell-fish, and eating it.

As he was one day on the shore, he saw a big, big man landing on the island, and he could see the earth and the sky between his legs. He set off with the crutches to try if he could get into the hut before the big man would come upon him. Despite his efforts, the big man was between him and the door, and said to him, "Unless you deceive me, you are Kayn Mac Loy."

Kayn Mac Loy said, "I have never deceived a man: I am he."

The big man said to him:

"Stretch out your leg, Kayn, till I put a salve of herbs and healing to it. Salve and binding herb and the poultice are cooling; the worm is channering. Pressure and haste hard bind me, for I must hear Mass in the great church at Rome, and be in Norway before I sleep."

Kayn Mac Loy said:

"May it be no foot to Kayn or a foot to any one after one, or I be Kayn son of Loy, if I stretch out my foot for you to put a salve of herbs and healing on it, till you tell me why you have no church of your own in Norway, so as, as now, to be going to the great church of Rome to Rome tomorrow. Unless you deceive me you are Machkan-an-Athar, the son of the King of Lochlann."

The big man said, "I have never deceived any man: I am he. I am now going to tell you why we have not a church in Lochlann. Seven masons came to build a church, and they and my father were bargaining about the building of it. The agreement that the masons wanted was that my mother and sister would go to see the interior of the church when it would be finished. My father was glad to get the church built so cheaply. They agreed accordingly; and the masons went in the morning to the place where the church was to be built. My father pointed out the spot for the foundation. They began to build in the morning, and the church was finished before the evening. When it was finished they requested my mother and sister to go to see its interior. They had no sooner entered than the doors were shut; and the church went away into the skies in the form of a tuft of mist.

"Stretch out your leg, Kayn, till I put a salve of herbs and healing to it. Salve and binding herb and the poultice are cooling; the worm is channering. Pressure and haste hard bind me, for I must hear Mass in the great church at Rome, and be in Norway before I sleep."

Kayn Mac Loy said:

"May it be no foot to Kayn or a foot to anyone after one, or I be Kayn son of Loy, if I stretch out my foot for you to put a salve of herbs and healing on it, till you tell me if you heard what befell your mother and sister."

"Ah!" said the big man, "the mischief is upon you; that tale is long to tell; but I will tell you a short tale about the matter. On the day on which they were working at the church I was away in the hill hunting game; and when I came home in the evening my brother told me what had happened, namely, that my mother and sister had gone away in the form of a tuft of mist. I became so cross and angry that I resolved to destroy the world till I should find out where my mother and sister were. My brother said to me that I was a fool to think of such a thing. 'I'll tell you,' said he, 'what you'll do. You will first go to try to find out where they are. When you find out where they are you will demand them peaceably, and if you do not get them peaceably you will fight for them.'

"I took my brother's advice, and prepared a ship to set off with. I set off alone, and embraced the ocean. I was overtaken by a great mist, and I came upon an island, and there was a large number of ships at anchor near it; I went in amongst them, and went ashore. I saw there a big, big woman reaping rushes; and when she would raise her head she would throw her right breast over her shoulder and when she would bend it would fall down between her legs. I came once behind her, and caught the breast with my mouth, and said to her, 'You are yourself witness, woman, that I am the foster-son of your right breast.' 'I perceive that, great hero,' said the old woman, 'but my advice to you is to leave this island as fast as you can.' 'Why?' said I. 'There is a big giant in the cave up there,' said she, 'and every one of the ships that you see he has taken in from the ocean with his breath, and he has killed and eaten the men. He is asleep at present, and when he wakens he will have you in a similar manner. A large iron door and an oak door are on the cave. When the giant draws in his breath the doors open, and when he emits his breath the doors shut; and they are shut as fast as though seven small bars, and seven large bars, and seven locks were on them. So fast are they that seven crowbars could not force them open.' I said to the old woman, 'Is there any way of destroying him?' 'I'll tell you,' said she, 'how it can be done. He has a weapon above the door that is called the short spear: and if you succeed in taking off his head with the first blow it will be well; but if you do not, the case will be worse than it was at first.'

"I set off, and reached the cave, the two doors of which opened. The giant's breath drew me into the cave; and stools, chairs, and pots were by its action dashing against each other, and like to break my legs. The door shut when I went in, and was shut as fast as though seven small bars, and seven large bars, and seven locks were on it; and seven crowbars could not force it open; and I was a prisoner in the cave. The giant drew in his breath again, and the doors opened. I gave a look upwards, and saw the short spear, and laid hold of it. I drew the short spear, and I warrant you that I dealt him such a blow with it as did not require to be repeated; I swept the head off him. I took the head down to the old woman, who was reaping the rushes, and said to her, 'There is the giant's head for you.' The old woman said, 'Brave man! I knew that you were a hero. This island had need of your coming to it today. Unless you deceive me, you are Mac Connachar son of the King of Lochlann.' 'I have never deceived a man. I am he,' said I. 'I am a soothsayer,' said she, 'and know the object of your journey. You are going in quest of your mother and sister.' 'Well,' said I, 'I am so far on the way if

I only knew where to go for them.' 'I'll tell you where they are,' said she; 'they are in the kingdom of the Red Shield, and the King of the Red Shield is resolved to marry your mother, and his son is resolved to marry your sister. I'll tell you how the town is situated. A canal of seven times seven paces breadth surrounds it. On the canal there is a drawbridge, which is guarded during the day by two creatures that no weapon can pierce, as they are covered all over with scales, except two spots below the neck in which their death-wounds lie. Their names are Roar and Rustle. When night comes the bridge is raised, and the monsters sleep. A very high and big wall surrounds the king's palace.'

"Stretch out your leg, Kayn, till I put a salve of herbs and healing to it. Salve and binding herb and the poultice are cooling; the worm is channering. Pressure and haste hard bind me, for I must hear Mass in the great church at Rome, and be in Norway before I sleep."

Kayn Mac Loy said:

"May it be no foot to Kayn or a foot to anyone after one, or I be Kayn son of Loy, if I stretch out my foot for you to put a salve of herbs and healing on it, till you tell me if you went farther in search of your mother and sister, or if you returned home, or what befell you."

"Ah!" said the big man, "the mischief is upon you; that tale is long to tell; but I will tell you another tale. I set off, and reached the big town of the Red Shield; and it was surrounded by a canal, as the old woman told me; and there was a drawbridge on the canal. It was night when I arrived, and the bridge was raised, and the monsters were asleep. I measured two feet before me and a foot behind me of the ground on which I was standing, and I sprang on the end of my spear and on my tiptoes, and reached the place where the monsters were asleep; and I drew the short spear, and I warrant you that I dealt them such a blow below the neck as did not require to be repeated. I took up the heads and hung them on one of the posts of the bridge. I then went on to the wall that surrounded the king's palace. This wall was so high that it was not easy for me to spring over it; and I set to work with the short spear, and dug a hole through it, and got in. I went to the door of the palace and knocked; and the doorkeeper called out, 'Who is there?' 'It is I,' said I. My mother and sister recognised my speech; and my mother called, 'Oh! It is my son; let him in.' I then got in, and they rose to meet me with great joy. I was supplied with food, drink, and a good bed. In the morning breakfast was set before us; and after it I said to my mother and sister that they had better make ready, and go with me. The King of the Red Shield said, 'It shall not be so. I am resolved to marry your mother, and my son is resolved to marry your sister.' 'If you wish to marry my mother, and if your son wishes to marry my sister, let both of you accompany me to my home, and you shall get them there.' The King of the Red Shield said, 'So be it.'

"We then set off, and came to where my ship was, went on board of it, and sailed home. When we were passing a place where a great battle was going on, I asked the King of the Red Shield what battle it was, and the cause of it. 'Don't you know at all?' said the King of the Red Shield. 'I do not,' said I. The King of the Red Shield said, 'That is the battle for the daughter of the King of the Great Universe, the most beautiful woman in the world; and whoever wins her by his heroism shall get her in marriage. Do you see yonder castle?' 'I do,' said I. 'She is on the top of that castle, and sees from it the hero that wins her,' said the King of the Red Shield. I requested to be put on shore, that I might win her by my swiftness and strength. They put me on shore; and I got a sight of her on the top of the castle. Having measured two feet behind me and a foot before me, I sprang on the end of my spear and on my tiptoes, and reached the top of the castle; and I caught the daughter of the King of the Universe in my arms and flung her over the castle. I was with her and intercepted her before she reached the ground, and I took her away on my shoulder, and set off to the shore as fast as I could, and delivered her to the King of the Red Shield to be put on board the ship. 'Am I not the best warrior that ever sought you?' said I. 'You can jump well' said she, 'but I have not seen any of your prowess.' I turned back to meet the warriors, and attacked them with the short spear, and did not leave a head on a neck of any of them. I then returned, and called to the King of the Red Shield to come in to the shore for me. Pretending not to hear me, he set the sails in order to return home with the daughter of the King of the Great Universe, and marry her. I measured two feet behind me and a foot before me, and sprang on the end of my spear and on my tiptoes and got on board the ship. I then said to the King of the Red Shield, 'What were you going to do? Why did you not wait for me?' 'Oh!' said the king, 'I was only making the ship ready and setting the sails to her before going on shore for you. Do you know what I am thinking of?' 'I do not,' said I. 'It is,' said the King, 'that I will return home with the daughter of the King of the Great Universe, and that you shall go home with your mother and sister.' 'That is not to be the way of it,' said I. 'She whom I have won by my prowess neither you nor any other shall get.'

"The king had a red shield, and if he should get it on, no weapon could make an impression on him. He began to put on the red shield, and I struck him with the short spear in the middle of his body, and cut him in two, and threw him overboard. I then struck the son, and swept his head off, and threw him overboard.

"Stretch out your leg, Kayn, till I put a salve of herbs and healing to it. Salve and binding herb and the poultice are cooling; the worm is channering. Pressure and haste hard bind me, for I must hear Mass in the great church at Rome, and be in Norway before I sleep."

Kayn Mac Loy said:

"May it be no foot to Kayn or a foot to anyone after one, or I be Kayn son of Loy, if I stretch out my foot for you to put a salve of herbs and healing on it, till you tell me whether any search was made for the daughter of the King of the Universe."

"Ah! The mischief is upon you," said the big man; "I will tell you another short tale. I came home with my mother and sister, and the daughter of the King of the Universe, and I married the daughter of the King of the Universe. The first son I had I named Machkan-na-skaya-jayrika (son of the red shield). Not long after this a hostile force came to enforce compensation for the King of the Red Shield, and a hostile force came from the King of the Universe to enforce compensation for the daughter of the King of the Universe. I took the daughter of the King of the Universe with me on the one shoulder and Machkan-na-skaya-jayrika on the other, and I went on board the ship and set the sails to her, and I placed the ensign of the King of the Great Universe on the one mast, and that of the King of the Red Shield on the other, and I blew a trumpet, and passed through the midst of them, and I said to them that here was the man, and that if they were going to enforce their claims, this was the time. All the ships that were there chased me; and we set out on the expanse of ocean. My ship would be equalled in speed by but few. One day a thick dark mist came on, and they lost sight of me. It happened that I came to an island called The Wet Mantle. I built a hut there; and another son was born to me, and I called him Son of the Wet Mantle.

"I was a long time in that island; but there was enough of fruit, fish, and birds in it. My two sons had grown to be somewhat big. As I was one day out killing birds, I saw a big, big man coming towards the island, and I ran to try if I could get into the house before him. He met me, and caught me, and put me into a bog up to the armpits, and he went into the house, and took out on his shoulder the daughter of the King of the Universe, and passed close to me in order to irritate me the more. The saddest look that I ever gave or ever shall give was that I gave when I saw the daughter of the King of the Universe on the shoulder of another, and could not take her from him. The boys came out where I was; and I bade them bring me the short spear from the house. They dragged the short spear after them, and brought it to me; and I cut the ground around me with it till I got out.

"I was a long time in the Wet Mantle, even till my two sons grew to be big lads. They asked me one day if I had any thought of going to seek their mother. I told them that I was waiting till they were stronger, and that they should then go with me. They said that they were ready to go with me at any time. I said to them that we had better get the ship ready, and go. They said, 'Let each of us have a ship to himself.' We arranged accordingly; and each went his own way.

"As I happened one day to be passing close to land I saw a great battle going on. Being under vows never to pass a battle without helping the weaker side, I went on shore, and set to work with the weaker side, and I knocked the head off every one with the short spear. Being tired, I lay myself down among the bodies and fell asleep.

"Stretch out your leg, Kayn, till I put a salve of herbs and healing to it. Salve and binding herb and the poultice are cooling; the worm is channering. Pressure and haste hard bind me, for I must hear Mass in the great church at Rome, and be in Norway before I sleep."

Kayn Mac Loy said:

"May it be no foot to Kayn or a foot to anyone after one, or I be Kayn son of Loy, if I stretch out my foot for you to put a salve of herbs and healing on it, till you tell me if you found the daughter of the King of the Universe, or if you went home, or what happened to you."

"The mischief is upon you," said the big man; "that tale is long to tell, but I will tell another short tale. When I awoke out of sleep I saw a ship making for the place where I was lying, and a big giant with only one eye dragging it after him: and the ocean reached no higher than his knees. He had a big fishing-rod with a big strong line hanging from it on which was a very big hook. He was throwing the line ashore, and fixing the hook in a body, and lifting it on board, and he continued this work till the ship was loaded with bodies. He fixed the hook once in my clothes; but I was so heavy that the rod could not carry me on board. He had to go on shore himself, and carry me on board in his arms. I was then in a worse plight than I ever was in. The giant set off with the ship, which he dragged after him, and reached a big, precipitous rock, in the face of which he had a large cave: and a damsel as beautiful as I ever saw came out, and stood in the door of the cave. He was handing the bodies to her, and she was taking hold of them and putting them into the cave.

As she took hold of each body she said, 'Are you alive?' At last the giant took hold of me, and handed me in to her, and said, 'Keep him apart; he is a large body, and I will have him to breakfast the first day that I go from home.' My best time was not when I heard the giant's sentence upon me. When he had eaten enough of the bodies, his dinner and supper, he lay down to sleep. When he began to snore the damsel came to speak to me; and she told me that she was a king's daughter the giant had stolen away and that she had no way of getting away from him. 'I am now,' she said, 'seven years except two days with him, and there is a drawn sword between us. He dared not come nearer me than that till the seven years should expire.' I said to her, 'Is there no way of killing him?' 'It is not easy to kill him, but we will devise an expedient for killing him,' said she. 'Look at that pointed bar that he uses for roasting the bodies. At dead of night gather the embers of the fire together, and put the bar in the fire till it be red. Go, then, and thrust it into his eye with all your strength, and take care that he does not get hold of you, for if he does he will mince you as small as midges.' I then went and gathered the embers together, and put the bar in the fire, and made it red, and thrust it into his eye; and from the cry that he gave I thought that the rock had split. The giant sprang to his feet and chased me through the cave in order to catch me; and I picked up a stone that lay on the floor of the cave, and pitched it into the sea; and it made a plumping noise. The bar was sticking in his eye all the time. Thinking it was I that had sprung into the sea, he rushed to the mouth of the cave, and the bar struck against the doorpost of the cave, and knocked off his brain-cap. The giant fell down cold and

dead, and the damsel and I were seven years and seven days throwing him into the sea in pieces.

"I wedded the damsel, and a boy was born to us. After seven years I started forth again.

"I gave her a gold ring, with my name on it, for the boy, and when he was old enough he was sent out to seek me.

"I then set off to the place where I fought the battle, and found the short spear where I left it; and I was very pleased that I found it, and that the ship was safe. I sailed a day's distance from that place, and entered a pretty bay that was there, hauled my ship up above the shore, and erected a hut there, in which I slept at night. When I rose next day I saw a ship making straight for the place where I was. When it struck the ground, a big, strong champion came out of it, and hauled it up; and if it did not surpass my ship it was not a whit inferior to it; and I said to him, 'What impertinent fellow are you that has dared to haul up your ship alongside of my ship?' 'I am Machkan-na-skaya-jayrika,' said the champion, 'going to seek the daughter of the King of the Universe for Mac Connachar, son of the King of Lochlann.' I saluted and welcomed him, and said to him, 'I am your father: it is well that you have come.' We passed the night cheerily in the hut.

"When I arose on the following day I saw another ship making straight for the place where I was; and a big, strong hero came out of it, and hauled it up alongside of our ships; and if it did not surpass them it was not a whit inferior to them. 'What impertinent fellow are you that has dared to haul up your ship alongside of our ships?' said I. 'I am,' said he, 'the Son of the Wet Mantle, going to seek the daughter of the King of the Universe for Mac Connachar, son of the King of Lochlann.' 'I am your father, and this is your brother: it is well that you have come,' said I. We passed the night together in the hut, my two sons and I.

"When I rose next day I saw another ship coming, and making straight for the place where I was. A big, strong champion sprang out of it, and hauled it up alongside of our ships; and if it was not higher than they, it was not lower. I went down where he was, and said to him, 'What impertinent fellow are you that has dared to haul up your ship alongside of our ships?' 'I am the Son of the Wet Mantle,' said he, 'going to seek the daughter of the King of the Universe for Mac Connachar, son of the King of Lochlann. 'Have you any token in proof of that?' said I. 'I have,' said he: 'here is a ring that my mother gave me at my father's request.' I took hold of the ring, and saw my name on it: and the matter was beyond doubt. I said to him, 'I am your father, and here are two half-brothers of yours. We are now stronger for going in quest of the daughter of the King of the Universe. Four piles are stronger than three piles.' We spent that night cheerily and comfortably together in the hut.

"On the morrow we met a soothsayer, and he spoke to us: 'You are going in quest of the daughter of the King of the Universe. I will tell you where she is: she is with the Son of the Blackbird.'

"Machkan-na-skaya-jayrika then went and called for combat with a hundred fully trained heroes, or the sending out to him of the daughter of the King of the Universe. The hundred went out; and he and they began on each other, and he killed every one of them. The Son of the Wet Mantle called for combat with another hundred, or the sending out of the daughter of the King of the Universe. He killed that hundred with the short spear. The Son of Secret called for combat with another hundred, or the daughter of the King of the Universe. He killed every one of these with the short spear. I then went out to the field, and sounded a challenge on the shield, and made the town tremble. The Son of the Blackbird had not a man to send out: he had to come out himself; and he and I began on each other, and I drew the short spear, and swept his head off. I then went into the castle, and took out the daughter of the King of the Universe. It was thus that it fared with me.

"Stretch out your leg, Kayn, till I put a salve of herbs and healing to it. Salve and binding herb and the poultice are cooling; the worm is channering. Pressure and haste hard bind me, for I must hear Mass in the great church at Rome, and be in Norway before I sleep."

Kayn Mac Loy stretched his leg; and the big man applied to it leaves of herbs and healing; and it was healed. The big man took him ashore from the island, and allowed him to go home to the king.

Thus did O'Cronicert win and lose a wife, and thus befell the Leeching of the leg of Kayn, son of Loy.

The Boyhood of Finn Mac Cumhal

IN IRELAND LONG AGO, centuries before the English appeared in that country, there were kings and chiefs, lawyers and merchants, men of the sword and men of the book, men who tilled their own ground and men who tilled the ground of others, just as there are now. But there was also, as ancient poets and historians tell us, a great company or brotherhood of men who were bound to no fixed calling, unless it was to fight for the High King of Ireland whenever foes threatened him from within the kingdom or without it. This company was called the Fianna of Erinn. They were mighty hunters and warriors, and though they had great possessions in land, and rich robes, and gold ornaments, and weapons wrought with beautiful chasing and with coloured enamels, they lived mostly a free outdoor life in the light hunting-booths which they made in the woods where the deer and the wolf ranged. There were then vast forests in Ireland, which are all gone now, and there were also, as there still are, many great and beautiful lakes and rivers, swarming with fish and water-fowl. In the forests and on the mountain sides roamed the wild boar and the wolf, and great herds of deer, some of giant size, whose enormous antlers are sometimes found when bogs are being drained. The Fianna chased these and the wolves with great dogs, whose courage and strength and beauty were famous throughout Europe, and which they prized and loved above all things. To the present day in Ireland there still remain some of this breed of Irish hounds, but the giant deer and the wolf are gone, and the Fianna of Erinn live only in the ancient books that were written of them, and in the tales that are still told of them in the winter evenings by the Irish peasant's fireside.

The Fianna were under the rule of one great captain or chief, and at the time I tell of his name was Cumhal, son of Trenmor. Now a tribe or family of the Fianna named the Clan Morna, or Sons of Morna, rose in rebellion against Cumhal, for they were jealous and greedy of his power and glory, and sought to have the captaincy for themselves. They defeated and slew him at the battle of Cnucha, which is now called Castleknock, near the City of the Hurdle Ford, which is the name that Dublin still bears in the Irish tongue. Goll, son of Morna, slew Cumhal, and they spoiled him of the Treasure Bag of the Fianna, which was a bag made of a crane's skin and having in it jewels of great price, and magic weapons, and strange things that had come down from far-off days when the Fairy Folk and mortal men battled for the lordship of Ireland. The Bag with its treasures was given to Lia, the chief of Luachar in Connacht, who had the keeping of it before, for he was the treasurer of Cumhal, and he was the first man who had wounded Cumhal in the battle when he fell.

Cumhal's wife was named Murna, and she bore him two sons. The elder was named Tulcha, and he fled from the country for fear of Goll and took service with the King of Scotland. The younger was born after Cumhal's death, and his name was called Demna. And because his mother feared that the sons of Morna would find him out and kill him, she gave him to a Druidess and another wise woman of Cumhal's household, and bade them

take him away and rear him as best they could. So they took him into the wild woods on the Slieve Bloom Mountains, and there they trained him to hunt and fish and to throw the spear, and he grew strong, and as beautiful as a child of the Fairy Folk. If he were in the same field with a hare he could run so that the hare could never leave the field, for Demna was always before it. He could run down and slay a stag with no dogs to help him, and he could kill a wild duck on the wing with a stone from his sling. And the Druidess taught him the learning of the time, and also the story of his race and nation, and told him of his right to be captain of the Fianna of Erinn when his day of destiny should come.

One day, while still a boy, he was roaming through the woods when he came to the mansion of a great lord, where many boys, sons of the chief men of Ireland, were being trained in manly arts and exercises. He found them playing at hurling, and they invited him to join them. He did so, but the side he was on won too easily, so they divided again, and yet again, giving fewer and fewer to Demna's side, till at last he alone drove the ball to the goal through them all, flashing among them as a salmon among a shoal of minnows. And then their anger and jealousy rose and grew bitter against the stranger, and instead of honouring him as gallant lads of gentle blood should have done they fell upon him with their hurling clubs and sought to kill him. But Demna felled seven of them to the ground and put the rest to flight, and then went his way home. When the boys told what had happened the chief asked them who it was that had defeated and routed them single-handed. They said, "It was a tall shapely lad, and very fair (*finn*)." So the name of Finn, the Fair One, clung to him thenceforth, and by that name he is known to this day.

By and by Finn gathered round him a band of youths who loved him for his strength and valour and for his generous heart, and with them he went hunting in the forests. And Goll, and the sons of Morna, who were now captains of the Fianna under the High King, began to hear tales of him and his exploits, and they sent trackers to inquire about him, for they had an inkling of who this wonderful fair-haired youth might be. Finn's foster mothers heard of this. "You must leave this place," they said to him, "and see our faces no more, for if Goll's men find you here they will slay you. We have cherished the blood of Cumhal," they said, "and now our work is done. Go, and may blessing and victory go with you." So Finn departed with naught but his weapons and his hunting gear, very sorrowful at leaving the wise and loving friends who had fostered his childhood; but deep in his heart was a wild and fierce delight at the thought of the trackless ways he would travel, and the wonders he would see; and all the future looked to him as beautiful and dim as the mists that fill a mountain glen under the morning sun.

Now after the death of Cumhal, his brother Crimmal and a few others of the aged warriors of the Fianna, who had not fallen in the fight at Cnucha, fled away into Connacht, and lived there in the deepest recesses of a great forest, where they hoped the conquerors might never find them. Here they built themselves a poor dwelling of tree branches, plastered with mud and roofed with reeds from the lake, and here they lived on what game they could kill or snare in the wild wood; and harder and harder it grew, as age and feebleness crept on them, to find enough to eat, or to hew wood for their fire. In this retreat, never having seen the friendly face of man, they were one day startled to hear voices and the baying of hounds approaching them through the wood, and they thought that the sons of Morna were upon them at last, and that their hour of doom was at hand. Soon they perceived a company of youths coming towards their hut, with one in front who seemed to be their leader. Taller he was by a head than the rest, broad-shouldered, and with masses of bright hair clustering round his forehead, and he carried in his hand a large bag made of some delicate skin and stained in patterns of red and blue. The old men thought when they saw him of a saying there was about the mighty Lugh, who was brother to the wife of Cumhal, that when he came among his army as they mustered for battle, men felt as though they beheld the rising of the sun. As they came near, the young men halted and looked upon the elders with pity, for their clothing of skins was ragged and the weapons they strove to hold were rusted and blunt, and except for their proud bearing and the fire in their old eyes they looked more like aged and worthless slaves in the household of a niggardly lord than men who had once been the flower of the fighting men of Erinn.

But the tall youth stepped in front of his band and cried aloud –

"Which of ye is Crimmal, son of Trenmor?" And one of the elders said, "I am Crimmal." Then tears filled the eyes of the youth, and he knelt down before the old man and put his hands in his.

"My lord and chief," he said, "I am Finn, son of Cumhal, and the day of deliverance is come."

And that night there was feasting and joy in the lonely hut
And that night there was feasting and joy in the lonely hut

So the youths brought in the spoils of their hunting, and yet other spoils than these; and that night there was feasting and joy in the lonely hut. And Crimmal said –

"It was foretold to us that one day the blood of Cumhal should be avenged, and the race of Cumhal should rule the Fianna again. This was the sign that the coming champion should give of his birth and destiny; he was to bear with him the Treasure Bag of Cumhal and the sacred things that were therein."

Finn said, "Ye know the Bag and its treasures, tell us if these be they." And he laid his skin bag on the knees of Crimmal.

Crimmal opened it, and he took out the jewels of sovranty, the magic spear-head made by the smiths of the Fairy Folk, and he said, "These be the treasures of Cumhal; truly the ripeness of the time is come."

And Finn then told the story of how he had won these things.

"But yesterday morning," he said, "we met on our way a woman of noble aspect, and she knelt over the body of a slain youth. When she lifted her head as we drew near, tears of blood ran down her cheeks, and she cried to me, 'Whoever thou art, I bind thee by the bonds of the sacred ordinances of the Gael that thou avenge my wrong. This was my son Glonda,' she said, 'my only son, and he was slain today wantonly by the Lord of Luachar and his men.' So we went, my company and I, to the Dún of the Lord of Luachar, and found an earthen rampart with a fosse before it, and on the top of the rampart was a fence of oaken posts interlaced with wattles, and over this we saw the many-coloured thatch of a great dwelling-house, and its white walls painted with bright colours under the broad eaves. So I stood forth and called to the Lord of Luachar and bade him make ready to pay an eric to the mother of Glonda, whatsoever she should demand. But he laughed at us and cursed us and bade us begone. Then we withdrew into the forest, but returned with a great pile of dry brushwood, and while some of us shot stones and arrows at whoever should appear above the palisade, others rushed up with bundles of brushwood and laid it against the palisade and set it on fire, and the Immortal Ones sent a blast of wind that set the brushwood and palisade quickly in a blaze, and through that fiery gap we charged in shouting. And half of the men of Luachar we killed and the rest fled, and the Lord of Luachar I slew in the doorway of his palace. We took a great spoil then, O Crimmal – these vessels of bronze and silver, and spears and bows, smoked bacon and skins of Greek wine; and in a great chest of yewwood we found this bag. All these things shall now remain with you, and my company shall also remain to hunt for you and protect you, for ye shall know want and fear no longer while ye live."

And Finn said, "I would fain know if my mother Murna still lives, or if she died by the sons of Morna."

Crimmal said, "After thy father's death, Finn, she was wedded to Gleor, Lord of Lamrigh, in the south, and she still lives in honour with him, and the sons of Morna have let her be. Didst thou never see her since she gave thee, an infant, to the wise women on the day of Cnucha?"

"I remember," said Finn, "when I was, as they tell me, but six years old, there came one day to our shieling in the woods of Slieve Bloom a chariot with bronze-shod wheels and a bronze wolf's head at the end of the pole, and two horsemen riding with it, besides him who drove. A lady was in it, with a gold frontlet on her brow and her cloak was fastened with a broad golden brooch. She came into our hut and spoke long with my foster-mothers, and me she clasped in her arms and kissed many times, and I felt her tears on my face. And they told me afterwards that this was Murna of the White Neck, and my mother. If she have suffered no harm at the hands of the sons of Morna, so much the less is the debt that they shall one day pay."

Now it is to be told what happened to Finn at the house of Finegas the Bard. Finn did not deem that the time had come for him to seize the captaincy of the Fianna until he had perfected himself in wisdom and learning. So on leaving the shelter of the old men in the wood he went to learn wisdom and the art of poetry from Finegas, who dwelt by the River Boyne, near to where is now the village of Slane. It was a belief among the poets of Ireland that the place of the revealing of poetry is always by the margin of water. But Finegas had another reason for the place where he made his dwelling, for there was an old prophecy that whoever should first eat of the Salmon of Knowledge that lived in the River Boyne, should become the wisest of men. Now this salmon was called Finntan in ancient times and was one of the Immortals, and he might be eaten and yet live. But in the time of Finegas he was called the Salmon of the Pool of Fec, which is the place where the fair river broadens out into a great still pool, with green banks softly sloping upward from the clear brown water. Seven years was Finegas watching the pool, but not until after Finn had come to be his disciple was the salmon caught. Then Finegas gave it to Finn to cook, and bade him eat none of it. But when Finegas saw him coming with the fish, he knew that something had chanced to the lad, for he had been used to have the eye of a young man but now he had the eye of a sage. Finegas said, "Hast thou eaten of the salmon?"

"Nay," said Finn, "but it burnt me as I turned it upon the spit and I put my thumb in my mouth" And Finegas smote his hands together and was silent for a while. Then he said to the lad who stood by obediently, "Take the salmon and eat it, Finn, son of Cumhal, for to thee the prophecy is come. And now go hence, for I can teach thee no more, and blessing and victory be thine."

With Finegas, Finn learned the three things that make a poet, and they are Fire of Song, and Light of Knowledge, and the Art of Extempore Recitation. Before he departed he made this lay to prove his art, and it is called 'The Song of Finn in Praise of May':

May Day! Delightful day!
Bright colours play the vales along.
Now wakes at morning's slender ray,
Wild and gay, the blackbird's song.

Now comes the bird of dusty hue,
The loud cuckoo, the summer-lover;
Branching trees are thick with leaves;
The bitter, evil time is over.

Swift horses gather nigh
Where half dry the river goes;
Tufted heather crowns the height;
Weak and white the bogdown blows.

Corncrake sings from eve till morn,
Deep in corn, a strenuous bard!
Sings the virgin waterfall,
White and tall, her one sweet word.

Loaded bees of little power
Goodly flower-harvest win;
Cattle roam with muddy flanks;
Busy ants go out and in.

Through, the wild harp of the wood
Making music roars the gale –
Now it slumbers without motion,
On the ocean sleeps the sail.

Men grow mighty in the May,
Proud and gay the maidens grow;
Fair is every wooded height;
Fair and bright the plain below.

A bright shaft has smit the streams,
With gold gleams the water-flag;
Leaps the fish, and on the hills
Ardour thrills the flying stag.

Carols loud the lark on high,
Small and shy, his tireless lay,
Singing in wildest, merriest mood
Of delicate-hued, delightful May.

How Fin Went to the Kingdom of the Big Men

FIN AND HIS MEN were in the Harbour of the Hill of Howth on a hillock, behind the wind and in front of the sun, where they could see every person, and nobody could see them, when they saw a speck coming from the west. They thought at first it was the blackness of a shower; but when it came nearer, they saw it was a boat. It did not lower sail till it entered the harbour. There were three men in it; one for guide in the bow, one for steering in the stern, and one for the tackle in the centre. They came ashore, and drew it up seven times its own length in dry grey grass, where the scholars of the city could not make it stock for derision or ridicule.

They then went up to a lovely green spot, and the first lifted a handful of round pebbles or shingle, and commanded them to become a beautiful house, that no better could be found in Ireland; and this was done. The second one lifted a slab of slate, and commanded it to be slate on the top of the house, that there was not better in Ireland; and this was done. The third one caught a bunch of shavings and commanded them to be pine-wood and timber in the house, that there was not in Ireland better; and this was done.

This caused much wonder to Fin, who went down where the men were, and made inquiries of them, and they answered him. He asked whence they were, or whither they were going. They said, "We are three Heroes whom the King of the Big Men has sent to ask combat of the Fians." He then asked, "What was the reason for doing this?" They said they did not know, but they heard that they were strong men, and they came to ask combat of Heroes from them. "Is Fin at Home?"

"He is not." (Great is a man's leaning towards his own life.) Fin then put them under crosses and under enchantments, that they were not to move from the place where they were till they saw him again.

He went away and made ready his coracle, gave its stern to land and prow to sea, hoisted the spotted towering sails against the long, tough, lance-shaped mast, cleaving the billows in the embrace of the wind in whirls, with a soft gentle breeze from the height of the sea-coast, and from the rapid tide of the red rocks, that would take willom from the hill, foliage from the tree, and heather from its stock and roots. Fin was guide in her prow, helm in her stern, and tackle in her middle; and stopping of head or foot he did not make till he reached the Kingdom of the Big Men. He went ashore and drew up his coracle in grey grass. He went up, and a Big Wayfarer met him. Fin asked who he was.

"I am," he said, "the Red-haired Coward of the King of the Big Men; and," said he to Fin, "you are the one I am in quest of. Great is my esteem and respect towards you; you are the best maiden I have ever seen; you will yourself make a dwarf for the King, and your dog (this was Bran) a lapdog. It is long since the King has been in want of a dwarf and a lapdog." He took with him Fin; but another Big Man came, and was going to take Fin from him. The two fought; but when they had torn each other's clothes, they left it to Fin to judge. He chose the first one. He took Fin with him to the palace of the King, whose worthies and high nobles assembled to see the little man. The king lifted him upon the palm of his hand, and went three times round the town with Fin upon one palm and Bran upon the other. He made a sleeping-place for him at the end of his own bed. Fin was waiting, watching, and observing everything that was going on about the house. He observed that the King, as soon as night came, rose and went out, and returned no more till morning. This caused him much wonder, and at last he asked the King why he went away every night and left the Queen by herself. "Why," said the King, "do you ask?"

"For satisfaction to myself," said Fin; "for it is causing me much wonder." Now the King had a great liking for Fin; he never saw anything that gave him more pleasure than he did; and at last he told him. "There is," he said, "a great Monster who wants my daughter in marriage, and to have half my kingdom to himself; and there is not another man in the kingdom who can meet him but myself; and I must go every night to hold combat with him."

"Is there," said Fin, "no man to combat with him but yourself?"

"There is not," said the King, "one who will war with him for a single night."

"It is a pity," said Fin, "that this should be called the Kingdom of the Big Men. Is he bigger than yourself?"

"Never you mind," said the King.

"I will mind," said Fin; "take your rest and sleep tonight, and I shall go to meet him."

"Is it you?" said the King; "you would not keep half a stroke against him."

When night came, and all men went to rest, the King was for going away as usual; but Fin at last prevailed upon him to allow himself to go. "I shall combat him," said he, "or else he knows a trick."

"I think much," said the King, "of allowing you to go, seeing he gives myself enough to do."

"Sleep you soundly tonight," said Fin, "and let me go; if he comes too violently upon me, I shall hasten home."

Fin went and reached the place where the combat was to be. He saw no one before him, and he began to pace backwards and forwards. At last he saw the sea coming in kilns of fire and as a darting serpent, till it came down below where he was. A Huge Monster came up and looked towards him, and from him. "What little speck do I see there?" he said.

"It is I," said Fin. "What are you doing here?"

"I am a messenger from the King of the Big Men; he is under much sorrow and distress; the Queen has just died, and I have come to ask if you will be so good as to go home tonight without giving trouble to the kingdom."

"I shall do that," said he; and he went away with the rough humming of a song in his mouth.

Fin went home when the time came, and lay down in his own bed, at the foot of the King's bed. When the King awoke, he cried out in great anxiety, "My kingdom is lost, and my dwarf and my lapdog are killed!"

"They are not," said Fin; "I am here yet; and you have got your sleep, a thing you were saying it was rare for you to get."

"How," said the King, "did you escape, when you are so little, while he is enough for myself, though I am so big."

"Though you," said Fin, "are so big and strong, I am quick and active."

Next night the King was for going; but Fin told him to take his sleep tonight again. "I shall stand myself in your place, or else a better hero than yonder one must come."

"He will kill you," said the King. "I shall take my chance," said Fin.

He went, and as happened the night before, he saw no one; and he began to pace backwards and forwards. He saw the sea coming in fiery kilns and as a darting serpent; and that Huge Man came up. "Are you here tonight again?" said he. "I am, and this is my errand: when the Queen was being put in the coffin, and the King heard the coffin being nailed, and the joiner's stroke, he broke his heart with pain and grief; and the Parliament has sent me to ask you to go home tonight till they get the King buried." The Monster went this night also, roughly humming a song; and Fin went home when the time came.

In the morning the King awoke in great anxiety, and called out, "My kingdom is lost, and my dwarf and my lapdog are killed!" and he greatly rejoiced that Fin and Bran were alive, and that he himself got rest, after being so long without sleep.

Fin went the third night, and things happened as before. There was no one before him, and he took to pacing to and fro. He saw the sea coming till it came down below him: the Big Monster came up; he saw the little black speck, and asked who was there, and what he wanted. "I have come to combat you," said Fin.

Fin and Bran began the combat. Fin was going backwards, and the Huge Man was following. Fin called to Bran, "Are you going to let him kill me?" Bran had a venomous shoe; and he leaped and struck the Huge Man with the venomous shoe on the breast-bone, and took the heart and lungs out of him. Fin drew his sword, Mac-a-Luin, cut off his head, put it on a hempen rope, and went with it to the Palace of the King. He took it into the Kitchen, and put it behind the door. In the morning the servant could not turn it, nor open the door. The King went down; he saw the Huge Mass, caught it by the top of the head, and lifted it, and knew it was the head of the Man who was for so long a time asking combat from him, and keeping him from sleep. "How at all," said he, "has this head come here? Surely it is not my dwarf that has done it."

"Why," said Fin, "should he not?"

Next night the King wanted to go himself to the place of combat; "because," said he, "a bigger one than the former will come tonight, and the kingdom will be destroyed, and you yourself killed; and I shall lose the pleasure I take in having you with me." But Fin went, and that Big Man came, asking vengeance for his son, and to have the kingdom for himself, or equal combat. He and Fin fought; and Fin was going backwards. He spoke to Bran, "Are you going to allow him to kill me?" Bran whined, and went and sat down on the beach. Fin was ever being driven back, and he called out again to Bran. Then Bran jumped and struck the Big Man with the venomous shoe, and took the heart and the lungs out of him. Fin cut the head off, and took it with him, and left it in front of the house. The King awoke in great terror, and cried out, "My kingdom is lost, and my dwarf and my lapdog are killed!" Fin raised himself up and said, "They are not"; and the King's joy was not small when he went out and saw the head that was in front of the house.

The next night a Big Hag came ashore, and the tooth in the door of her mouth would make a distaff. She sounded a challenge on her shield: "You killed," she said, "my husband and my son."

"I did kill them," said Fin. They fought; and it was worse for Fin to guard himself from the tooth than from the hand of the Big Hag. When she had nearly done for him Bran struck her with the venomous shoe, and killed her as he had done to the rest. Fin took with him the head, and left it in front of the house. The King awoke in great anxiety, and called out, "My kingdom is lost, and my dwarf and my lapdog are killed!"

"They are not," said Fin, answering him; and when they went out and saw the head, the King said, "I and my kingdom will have peace ever after this. The mother herself of the brood is killed; but tell me who you are. It was foretold for me that it would be Fin-mac-Coul that would give me relief, and he is only now eighteen years of age. Who are you, then, or what is your name?"

"There never stood," said Fin, "on hide of cow or horse, one to whom I would deny my name. I am Fin, the Son of Coul, son of Looach, son of Trein, son of Fin, son of Art, son of the young High King of Erin; and it is time for me now to go home. It has been with much wandering out of my way that I have come to your kingdom; and this is the reason why I have come, that I might find out what injury I have done to you, or the reason why you sent the three heroes to ask combat from me, and bring destruction on my Men."

"You never did any injury to me," said the King; "and I ask a thousand pardons. I did not send the heroes to you. It is not the truth they told. They were three men who were courting three fairy women, and these gave them their shirts; and when they have on their shirts, the combat of a hundred men is upon the hand of every one of them. But they must put off the shirts every night, and put them on the backs of chairs; and if the shirts were taken from them they would be next day as weak as other people."

Fin got every honour, and all that the King could give him, and when he went away, the King and the Queen and the people went down to the shore to give him their blessing.

Fin now went away in his coracle, and was sailing close by the side of the shore, when he saw a young man running and calling out to him. Fin came in close to land with his coracle, and asked what he wanted.

"I am," said the young man, "a good servant wanting a master."

"What work can you do?" said Fin.

"I am," said he, "the best soothsayer that there is."

"Jump into the boat then." The soothsayer jumped in, and they went forward.

They did not go far when another youth came running. "I am," he said, "a good servant wanting a master."

"What work can you do?" said Fin.

"I am as good a thief as there is."

"Jump into the boat, then"; and Fin took with him this one also. They saw then a third young man running and calling out. They came close to land. "What man are you?" said Fin.

"I am," said he, "the best climber that there is. I will take up a hundred pounds on my back in a place where a fly could not stand on a calm summer day."

"Jump in"; and this one came in also. "I have my pick of servants now," said Fin; "it cannot be but these will suffice."

They went; and stop of head or foot they did not make till they reached the Harbour of the Hill of Howth. He asked the soothsayer what the three Big Men were doing. "They are," he said, "after their supper, and making ready for going to bed."

He asked a second time. "They are," he said, "after going to bed; and their shirts are spread on the back of chairs."

After a while, Fin asked him again, "What are the Big Men doing now?"

"They are," said the soothsayer, "sound asleep."

"It would be a good thing if there was now a thief to go and steal the shirts."

"I would do that," said the thief, "but the doors are locked, and I cannot get in."

"Come," said the climber, "on my back, and I shall put you in." He took him up upon his back to the top of the chimney, and let him down, and he stole the shirts.

Fin went where the Fian band was; and in the morning they came to the house where the three Big Men were. They sounded a challenge upon their shields, and asked them to come out to combat.

They came out. "Many a day," said they, "have we been better for combat than we are today," and they confessed to Fin everything as it was. "You were," said Fin, "impertinent, but I will forgive you"; and he made them swear that they would be faithful to himself ever after, and ready in every enterprise he would place before them.

The Birth of Oisín

ONE DAY as Finn and his companions and dogs were returning from the chase to their Dún on the Hill of Allen, a beautiful fawn started up on their path and the chase swept after her, she taking the way which led to their home. Soon, all the pursuers were left far behind save only Finn himself and his two hounds Bran and Sceolaun. Now these hounds were of strange breed, for Tyren, sister to Murna, the mother of Finn, had been changed into a hound by the enchantment of a woman of the Fairy Folk, who loved Tyren's husband Ullan; and the two hounds of Finn were the children of Tyren, born to her in that shape. Of all hounds in Ireland they were the best, and Finn loved them much, so that it was said he wept but twice in his life, and once was for the death of Bran.

At last, as the chase went on down a valley side, Finn saw the fawn stop and lie down, while the two hounds began to play round her and to lick her face and limbs. So he gave commandment that none should hurt her, and she followed them to the Dún of Allen, playing with the hounds as she went.

The same night Finn awoke and saw standing by his bed the fairest woman his eyes had ever beheld.

"I am Saba, O Finn," she said, "and I was the fawn ye chased today. Because I would not give my love to the Druid of the Fairy Folk, who is named the Dark, he put that shape upon me by his sorceries, and I have borne it these three years. But a slave of his, pitying me, once revealed to me that if I could win to thy great Dún of Allen, O Finn, I should be safe from all enchantments and my natural shape would come to me again. But I feared to be torn in pieces by thy dogs, or wounded by thy hunters, till at last I let myself be overtaken by thee alone and by Bran and Sceolaun, who have the nature of man and would do me no hurt."

"Have no fear, maiden," said Finn, "we the Fianna, are free and our guest-friends are free; there is none who shall put compulsion on you here."

So Saba dwelt with Finn, and he made her his wife; and so deep was his love for her that neither the battle nor the chase had any delight for him, and for months he never left her side. She also loved him as deeply, and their joy in each other was like that of the Immortals in the Land of Youth. But at last word came to Finn that the warships of the Northmen were in the bay of Dublin, and he summoned his heroes to the fight, "for," said he to Saba, "the men of Erinn give us tribute and hospitality to defend them from the foreigner, and it were shame to take it from them and not to give that to which we, on our side, are pledged." And he called to mind that great saying of Goll mac Morna when they were once sore bested by a mighty host – "a man," said Goll, "lives after his life but not after his honour."

Seven days was Finn absent, and he drove the Northmen from the shores of Erinn. But on the eighth day he returned, and when he entered his Dún he saw trouble in

the eyes of his men and of their fair womenfolk, and Saba was not on the rampart expecting his return. So he bade them tell him what had chanced, and they said –

"Whilst thou, our father and lord, wert afar off smiting the foreigner, and Saba looking ever down the pass for thy return, we saw one day as it were the likeness of thee approaching, and Bran and Sceolaun at thy heels. And we seemed also to hear the notes of the Fian hunting call blown on the wind. Then Saba hastened to the great gate, and we could not stay her, so eager was she to rush to the phantom. But when she came near, she halted and gave a loud and bitter cry, and the shape of thee smote her with a hazel wand, and lo, there was no woman there anymore, but a deer. Then those hounds chased it, and ever as it strove to reach again the gate of the Dún they turned it back. We all now seized what arms we could and ran out to drive away the enchanter, but when we reached the place there was nothing to be seen, only still we heard the rushing of flying feet and the baying of dogs, and one thought it came from here, and another from there, till at last the uproar died away and all was still. What we could do, O Finn, we did; Saba is gone."

Finn then struck his hand on his breast but spoke no word, and he went to his own chamber. No man saw him for the rest of that day, nor for the day after. Then he came forth, and ordered the matters of the Fianna as of old, but for seven years thereafter he went searching for Saba through every remote glen and dark forest and cavern of Ireland, and he would take no hounds with him save Bran and Sceolaun. But at last he renounced all hope of finding her again, and went hunting as of old. One day as he was following the chase on Ben Gulban in Sligo, he heard the musical bay of the dogs change of a sudden to a fierce growling and yelping as though they were in combat with some beast, and running hastily up he and his men beheld, under a great tree, a naked boy with long hair, and around him the hounds struggling to seize him, but Bran and Sceolaun fighting with them and keeping them off. And the lad was tall and shapely, and as the heroes gathered round he gazed undauntedly on them, never heeding the rout of dogs at his feet. The Fians beat off the dogs and brought the lad home with them, and Finn was very silent and continually searched the lad's countenance with his eyes. In time, the use of speech came to him, and the story that he told was this:

He had known no father, and no mother save a gentle hind with whom he lived in a most green and pleasant valley shut in on every side by towering cliffs that could not be scaled, or by deep chasms in the earth. In the summer he lived on fruits and such-like, and in the winter, store of provisions was laid for him in a cave. And there came to them sometimes a tall dark-visaged man, who spoke to his mother, now tenderly, and now in loud menace, but she always shrunk away in fear, and the man departed in anger. At last there came a day when the Dark Man spoke very long with his mother in all tones of entreaty and of tenderness and of rage, but she would still keep aloof and give no sign save of fear and abhorrence. Then at length the Dark Man drew near and smote her with a hazel wand; and with that he turned and went his way, but she, this time, followed him, still looking back at her son and piteously complaining. And he, when he strove to follow, found himself unable to move a limb; and crying out with rage and desolation he fell to the earth and his senses left him. When he came to himself he was on the mountain side, on Ben Gulban, where he remained some days, searching for that green and hidden valley, which he never found again. And after a while the dogs found him; but of the hind his mother and of the Dark Druid, there is no man knows the end.

Finn called his name Oisín, and he became a warrior of fame, but far more famous for the songs and tales that he made; so that of all things to this day that are told of the Fianna of Erinn, men are wont to say, "So sang the bard, Oisín, son of Finn."

The Lad with the Goat-Skin

LONG AGO, a poor widow woman lived down near the iron forge, by Enniscorth, and she was so poor she had no clothes to put on her son; so she used to fix him in the ash-hole, near the fire, and pile the warm ashes about him; and according as he grew up, she sunk the pit deeper. At last, by hook or by crook, she got a goat-skin, and fastened it round his waist, and he felt quite grand, and took a walk down the street. So says she to him next morning, "Tom, you thief, you never done any good yet, and you six foot high, and past nineteen – take that rope and bring me a faggot from the wood."

"Never say't twice, mother," says Tom – "here goes."

When he had it gathered and tied, what should come up but a big giant, nine foot high, and made a lick of a club at him. Well become Tom, he jumped a-one side, and picked up a ram-pike; and the first crack he gave the big fellow, he made him kiss the clod.

"If you have e'er a prayer," says Tom, "now's the time to say it, before I make fragments of you."

"I have no prayers," says the giant; "but if you spare my life I'll give you that club; and as long as you keep from sin, you'll win every battle you ever fight with it."

Tom made no bones about letting him off; and as soon as he got the club in his hands, he sat down on the bresna, and gave it a tap with the kippeen, and says, "Faggot, I had great trouble gathering you, and run the risk of my life for you, the least you can do is to carry me home." And sure enough, the wind o' the word was all it wanted. It went off through the wood, groaning and crackling, till it came to the widow's door.

Well, when the sticks were all burned, Tom was sent off again to pick more; and this time he had to fight with a giant that had two heads on him. Tom had a little more trouble with him – that's all; and the prayers he said, was to give Tom a fife; that nobody could help dancing when he was playing it. Begonies, he made the big faggot dance home, with himself sitting on it. The next giant was a beautiful boy with three heads on him. He had neither prayers nor catechism no more nor the others; and so he gave Tom a bottle of green ointment, that wouldn't let you be burned, nor scalded, nor wounded. "And now," says he, "there's no more of us. You may come and gather sticks here till little Lunacy Day in Harvest, without giant or fairy-man to disturb you."

Well, now, Tom was prouder nor ten paycocks, and used to take a walk down street in the heel of the evening; but some o' the little boys had no more manners than if they were Dublin jackeens, and put out their tongues at Tom's club and Tom's goat-skin. He didn't like that at all, and it would be mean to give one of them a clout. At last, what should come through the town but a kind of a bellman, only it's a big bugle he had, and a huntsman's cap on his head, and a kind of a painted shirt. So this – he wasn't a bellman, and I don't know what to call him – bugleman, maybe, proclaimed that the King of Dublin's daughter was so melancholy that she didn't give a laugh for seven years, and that her father would grant her in marriage to whoever could make her laugh three times.

"That's the very thing for me to try," says Tom; and so, without burning any more daylight, he kissed his mother, curled his club at the little boys, and off he set along the yalla highroad to the town of Dublin.

At last Tom came to one of the city gates, and the guards laughed and cursed at him instead of letting him in. Tom stood it all for a little time, but at last one of them – out of fun, as he said – drove his bayonet half an inch or so into his side. Tom done nothing but take the fellow by the scruff o' the neck and the waistband of his corduroys, and fling him into the canal. Some run to pull the fellow out, and others to let manners into the vulgarian with their swords and daggers; but a tap from his club sent them headlong into the moat or down on the stones, and they were soon begging him to stay his hands.

So at last one of them was glad enough to show Tom the way to the palace-yard; and there was the king, and the queen, and the princess, in a gallery, looking at all sorts of wrestling, and sword-playing, and long-dances, and mumming, all to please the princess; but not a smile came over her handsome face.

Well, they all stopped when they seen the young giant, with his boy's face, and long black hair, and his short curly beard – for his poor mother couldn't afford to buy razors – and his great strong arms, and bare legs, and no covering but the goat-skin that reached from his waist to his knees. But an envious wizened bit of a fellow, with a red head, that wished to be married to the princess, and didn't like how she opened her eyes at Tom, came forward, and asked his business very snappishly.

"My business," says Tom, says he, "is to make the beautiful princess, God bless her, laugh three times."

"Do you see all them merry fellows and skilful swordsmen," says the other, "that could eat you up with a grain of salt, and not a mother's soul of 'em ever got a laugh from her these seven years?"

So the fellows gathered round Tom, and the bad man aggravated him till he told them he didn't care a pinch o' snuff for the whole bilin' of 'em; let 'em come on, six at a time, and try what they could do.

The king, who was too far off to hear what they were saying, asked what did the stranger want.

"He wants," says the red-headed fellow, "to make hares of your best men."

"Oh!" says the king, "if that's the way, let one of 'em turn out and try his mettle."

So one stood forward, with sword and pot-lid, and made a cut at Tom. He struck the fellow's elbow with the club, and up over their heads flew the sword, and down went the owner of it on the gravel from a thump he got on the helmet. Another took his place, and another, and another, and then half a dozen at once, and Tom sent swords, helmets, shields, and bodies, rolling over and over, and themselves bawling out that they were kilt, and disabled, and damaged, and rubbing their poor elbows and hips, and limping away. Tom contrived not to kill anyone; and the princess was so amused, that she let a great sweet laugh out of her that was heard over all the yard.

"King of Dublin," says Tom, "I've quarter your daughter."

And the king didn't know whether he was glad or sorry, and all the blood in the princess's heart run into her cheeks.

So there was no more fighting that day, and Tom was invited to dine with the royal family. Next day, Redhead told Tom of a wolf, the size of a yearling heifer, that used to

be serenading about the walls, and eating people and cattle; and said what a pleasure it would give the king to have it killed.

"With all my heart," says Tom; "send a jackeen to show me where he lives, and we'll see how he behaves to a stranger."

The princess was not well pleased, for Tom looked a different person with fine clothes and a nice green birredh over his long curly hair; and besides, he'd got one laugh out of her. However, the king gave his consent; and in an hour and a half the horrible wolf was walking into the palace-yard, and Tom a step or two behind, with his club on his shoulder, just as a shepherd would be walking after a pet lamb.

The king and queen and princess were safe up in their gallery, but the officers and people of the court that wor padrowling about the great bawn, when they saw the big baste coming in, gave themselves up, and began to make for doors and gates; and the wolf licked his chops, as if he was saying, "Wouldn't I enjoy a breakfast off a couple of yez!"

The king shouted out, "O Tom with the Goat-skin, take away that terrible wolf, and you must have all my daughter."

But Tom didn't mind him a bit. He pulled out his flute and began to play like vengeance; and dickens a man or boy in the yard but began shovelling away heel and toe, and the wolf himself was obliged to get on his hind legs and dance 'Tatther Jack Walsh', along with the rest. A good deal of the people got inside, and shut the doors, the way the hairy fellow wouldn't pin them; but Tom kept playing, and the outsiders kept dancing and shouting, and the wolf kept dancing and roaring with the pain his legs were giving him; and all the time he had his eyes on Redhead, who was shut out along with the rest. Wherever Redhead went, the wolf followed, and kept one eye on him and the other on Tom, to see if he would give him leave to eat him. But Tom shook his head, and never stopped the tune, and Redhead never stopped dancing and bawling, and the wolf dancing and roaring, one leg up and the other down, and he ready to drop out of his standing from fair tiresomeness.

When the princess seen that there was no fear of anyone being kilt, she was so divarted by the stew that Redhead was in, that she gave another great laugh; and well become Tom, out he cried, "King of Dublin, I have two halves of your daughter."

"Oh, halves or alls," says the king, "put away that divel of a wolf, and we'll see about it."

So Tom put his flute in his pocket, and says he to the baste that was sittin' on his currabingo ready to faint, "Walk off to your mountain, my fine fellow, and live like a respectable baste; and if ever I find you come within seven miles of any town, I'll –"

He said no more, but spit in his fist, and gave a flourish of his club. It was all the poor divel of a wolf wanted: he put his tail between his legs, and took to his pumps without looking at man or mortal, and neither sun, moon, or stars ever saw him in sight of Dublin again.

At dinner everyone laughed but the foxy fellow; and sure enough he was laying out how he'd settle poor Tom next day.

"Well, to be sure!" says he, "King of Dublin, you are in luck. There's the Danes moidhering us to no end. Deuce run to Lusk wid 'em! and if anyone can save us from 'em, it is this gentleman with the goat-skin. There is a flail hangin' on the collar-beam, in hell, and neither Dane nor devil can stand before it."

"So," says Tom to the king, "will you let me have the other half of the princess if I bring you the flail?"

"No, no," says the princess; "I'd rather never be your wife than see you in that danger."

But Redhead whispered and nudged Tom about how shabby it would look to reneague the adventure. So he asked which way he was to go, and Redhead directed him.

Well, he travelled and travelled, till he came in sight of the walls of hell; and, bedad, before he knocked at the gates, he rubbed himself over with the greenish ointment. When he knocked, a hundred little imps popped their heads out through the bars, and axed him what he wanted.

"I want to speak to the big divel of all," says Tom: "open the gate."

It wasn't long till the gate was thrune open, and the Ould Boy received Tom with bows and scrapes, and axed his business.

"My business isn't much," says Tom. "I only came for the loan of that flail that I see hanging on the collar-beam, for the king of Dublin to give a thrashing to the Danes."

"Well," says the other, "the Danes is much better customers to me; but since you walked so far I won't refuse. Hand that flail," says he to a young imp; and he winked the far-off eye at the same time. So, while some were barring the gates, the young devil climbed up, and took down the flail that had the handstaff and booltheen both made out of red-hot iron. The little vagabond was grinning to think how it would burn the hands o' Tom, but the dickens a burn it made on him, no more nor if it was a good oak sapling.

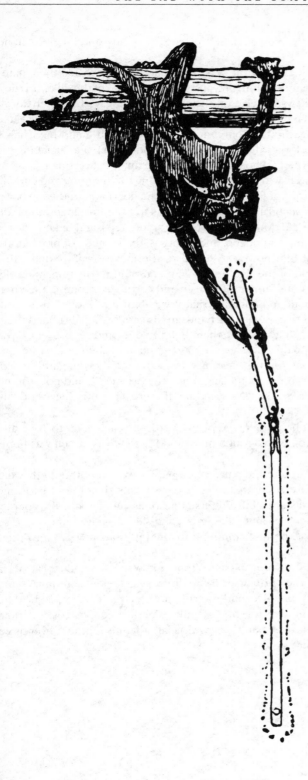

"Thankee," says Tom. "Now would you open the gate for a body, and I'll give you no more trouble."

"Oh, tramp!" says Ould Nick; "is that the way? It is easier getting inside them gates than getting out again. Take that tool from him, and give him a dose of the oil of stirrup."

So one fellow put out his claws to seize on the flail, but Tom gave him such a welt of it on the side of the head that he broke off one of his horns, and made him roar like a devil as he was. Well, they rushed at Tom, but he gave them, little and big, such a thrashing as they didn't forget for a while. At last says the ould thief of all, rubbing his elbow, "Let the fool out; and woe to whoever lets him in again, great or small."

So out marched Tom, and away with him, without minding the shouting and cursing they kept up at him from the tops of the walls; and when he got home to the big bawn of the palace, there never was such running and racing as to see himself and the flail. When he had his story told, he laid down the flail on the stone steps, and bid no one for their lives to touch it. If the king, and queen, and princess, made much of him before, they made ten times more of him now; but Redhead, the mean scruff-hound, stole over, and thought to catch hold of the flail to make an end of him. His fingers hardly touched it, when he let a roar out of him as if heaven and earth were coming together, and kept flinging his arms about and dancing, that it was pitiful to look at him. Tom run at him as soon as he could rise, caught his hands in his own two, and rubbed them this way and that, and the burning pain left them before you could reckon one. Well the poor fellow, between the pain that was only just gone, and the comfort he was in, had the comicalest face that you ever see, it was such a mixtherum-gatherum of laughing and crying. Everybody burst out a laughing – the princess could not stop no more than the rest; and then says Tom, "Now, ma'am, if there were fifty halves of you, I hope you'll give me them all."

Well, the princess looked at her father, and by my word, she came over to Tom, and put her two delicate hands into his two rough ones, and I wish it was myself was in his shoes that day!

Tom would not bring the flail into the palace. You may be sure no other body went near it; and when the early risers were passing next morning, they found two long clefts in the stone, where it was after burning itself an opening downwards, nobody could tell how far. But a messenger came in at noon, and said that the Danes were so frightened when they heard of the flail coming into Dublin, that they got into their ships, and sailed away.

Well, I suppose, before they were married, Tom got some man, like Pat Mara of Tomenine, to learn him the 'principles of politeness', fluxions, gunnery, and fortification, decimal fractions, practice, and the rule of three direct, the way he'd be able to keep up a conversation with the royal family. Whether he ever lost his time learning them sciences, I'm not sure, but it's as sure as fate that his mother never more saw any want till the end of her days.

A Legend of Knockmany

WHAT IRISH MAN, woman, or child has not heard of our renowned Hibernian Hercules, the great and glorious Fin M'Coul? Not one, from Cape Clear to the Giant's Causeway, nor from that back again to Cape Clear. And, by-the-way, speaking of the Giant's Causeway brings me at once to the beginning of my story. Well, it so happened that Fin and his men were all working at the Causeway, in order to make a bridge across to Scotland; when Fin, who was very fond of his wife Oonagh, took it into his head that he would go home and see how the poor woman got on in his absence. So, accordingly, he pulled up a fir-tree, and, after lopping off the roots and branches, made a walking-stick of it, and set out on his way to Oonagh.

Oonagh, or rather Fin, lived at this time on the very tip-top of Knockmany Hill, which faces a cousin of its own called Cullamore, that rises up, half-hill, half-mountain, on the opposite side.

There was at that time another giant, named Cucullin – some say he was Irish, and some say he was Scotch – but whether Scotch or Irish, sorrow doubt of it but he was a targer. No other giant of the day could stand before him; and such was his strength, that, when well vexed, he could give a stamp that shook the country about him. The fame and name of him went far and near; and nothing in the shape of a man, it was said, had any chance with him in a fight. By one blow of his fists he flattened a thunderbolt and kept it in his pocket, in the shape of a pancake, to show to all his enemies, when they were about to fight him. Undoubtedly he had given every giant in Ireland a considerable beating, barring Fin M'Coul himself; and he swore that he would never rest, night or day, winter or summer, till he would serve Fin with the same sauce, if he could catch him. However, the short and long of it was, with reverence be it spoken, that Fin heard Cucullin was coming to the Causeway to have a trial of strength with him; and he was seized with a very warm and sudden fit of affection for his wife, poor woman, leading a very lonely, uncomfortable life of it in his absence. He accordingly pulled up the fir-tree, as I said before, and having snedded it into a walking-stick, set out on his travels to see his darling Oonagh on the top of Knockmany, by the way.

In truth, the people wondered very much why it was that Fin selected such a windy spot for his dwelling-house, and they even went so far as to tell him as much.

"What can you mane, Mr. M'Coul," said they, "by pitching your tent upon the top of Knockmany, where you never are without a breeze, day or night, winter or summer, and where you're often forced to take your nightcap without either going to bed or turning up your little finger; ay, an' where, besides this, there's the sorrow's own want of water?"

"Why," said Fin, "ever since I was the height of a round tower, I was known to be fond of having a good prospect of my own; and where the dickens, neighbours, could I find a better spot for a good prospect than the top of Knockmany? As for water, I am sinking a pump, and, plase goodness, as soon as the Causeway's made, I intend to finish it."

Now, this was more of Fin's philosophy; for the real state of the case was, that he pitched upon the top of Knockmany in order that he might be able to see Cucullin coming towards the house. All we have to say is, that if he wanted a spot from which to keep a sharp look-out – and, between ourselves, he did want it grievously – barring Slieve Croob, or Slieve Donard, or its own cousin, Cullamore, he could not find a neater or more convenient situation for it in the sweet and sagacious province of Ulster.

"God save all here!" said Fin, good-humouredly, on putting his honest face into his own door.

"Musha, Fin, avick, an' you're welcome home to your own Oonagh, you darlin' bully." Here followed a smack that is said to have made the waters of the lake at the bottom of the hill curl, as it were, with kindness and sympathy.

Fin spent two or three happy days with Oonagh, and felt himself very comfortable, considering the dread he had of Cucullin. This, however, grew upon him so much that his wife could not but perceive something lay on his mind which he kept altogether to himself. Let a woman alone, in the meantime, for ferreting or wheedling a secret out of her good man, when she wishes. Fin was a proof of this.

"It's this Cucullin," said he, "that's troubling me. When the fellow gets angry, and begins to stamp, he'll shake you a whole townland; and it's well known that he can stop a thunderbolt, for he always carries one about him in the shape of a pancake, to show to anyone that might misdoubt it."

As he spoke, he clapped his thumb in his mouth, which he always did when he wanted to prophesy, or to know anything that happened in his absence; and the wife asked him what he did it for.

"He's coming," said Fin; "I see him below Dungannon."

"Thank goodness, dear! An' who is it, avick? Glory be to God!"

"That baste, Cucullin," replied Fin; "and how to manage I don't know. If I run away, I am disgraced; and I know that sooner or later I must meet him, for my thumb tells me so."

"When will he be here?" said she.

"Tomorrow, about two o'clock," replied Fin, with a groan.

"Well, my bully, don't be cast down," said Oonagh; "depend on me, and maybe I'll bring you better out of this scrape than ever you could bring yourself, by your rule o' thumb."

She then made a high smoke on the top of the hill, after which she put her finger in her mouth, and gave three whistles, and by that Cucullin knew he was invited to Cullamore – for this was the way that the Irish long ago gave a sign to all strangers and travellers, to let them know they were welcome to come and take share of whatever was going.

In the meantime, Fin was very melancholy, and did not know what to do, or how to act at all. Cucullin was an ugly customer to meet with; and, the idea of the 'cake' aforesaid flattened the very heart within him. What chance could he have, strong and brave though he was, with a man who could, when put in a passion, walk the country into earthquakes and knock thunderbolts into pancakes? Fin knew not on what hand to turn him. Right or left – backward or forward – where to go he could form no guess whatsoever.

"Oonagh," said he, "can you do nothing for me? Where's all your invention? Am I to be skivered like a rabbit before your eyes, and to have my name disgraced for ever in the sight of all my tribe, and me the best man among them? How am I to fight this man-mountain – this huge cross between an earthquake and a thunderbolt? – with a pancake in his pocket that was once – "

"Be easy, Fin," replied Oonagh; "troth, I'm ashamed of you. Keep your toe in your pump, will you? Talking of pancakes, maybe, we'll give him as good as any he brings with him – thunderbolt or otherwise. If I don't treat him to as smart feeding as he's got this many a day, never trust Oonagh again. Leave him to me, and do just as I bid you."

This relieved Fin very much; for, after all, he had great confidence in his wife, knowing, as he did, that she had got him out of many a quandary before. Oonagh then drew the nine woollen threads of different colours, which she always did to find out the best way of succeeding in anything of importance she went about. She then platted them into three plats with three colours in each, putting one on her right arm, one round her heart, and the third round her right ankle, for then she knew that nothing could fail with her that she undertook.

Having everything now prepared, she sent round to the neighbours and borrowed one-and-twenty iron griddles, which she took and kneaded into the hearts of one-and-twenty cakes of bread, and these she baked on the fire in the usual way, setting them aside in the cupboard according as they were done. She then put down a large pot of new milk, which she made into curds and whey. Having done all this, she sat down quite contented, waiting for his arrival on the next day about two o'clock, that being the hour at which he was expected – for Fin knew as much by the sucking of his thumb. Now this was a curious property that Fin's thumb had. In this very thing, moreover, he was very much resembled by his great foe, Cucullin; for it was well known that the huge strength he possessed all lay in the middle finger of his right hand, and that, if he happened by any mischance to lose it, he was no more, for all his bulk, than a common man.

At length, the next day, Cucullin was seen coming across the valley, and Oonagh knew that it was time to commence operations. She immediately brought the cradle, and made Fin to lie down in it, and cover himself up with the clothes.

"You must pass for your own child," said she; "so just lie there snug, and say nothing, but be guided by me."

About two o'clock, as he had been expected, Cucullin came in. "God save all here!" said he; "is this where the great Fin M'Coul lives?"

"Indeed it is, honest man," replied Oonagh; "God save you kindly – won't you be sitting?"

"Thank you, ma'am," says he, sitting down; "you're Mrs. M'Coul, I suppose?"

"I am," said she; "and I have no reason, I hope, to be ashamed of my husband."

"No," said the other, "he has the name of being the strongest and bravest man in Ireland; but for all that, there's a man not far from you that's very desirous of taking a shake with him. Is he at home?"

"Why, then, no," she replied; "and if ever a man left his house in a fury, he did. It appears that someone told him of a big basthoon of a – giant called Cucullin being down at the Causeway to look for him, and so he set out there to try if he could catch him. Troth, I hope, for the poor giant's sake, he won't meet with him, for if he does, Fin will make paste of him at once."

"Well," said the other, "I am Cucullin, and I have been seeking him these twelve months, but he always kept clear of me; and I will never rest night or day till I lay my hands on him."

At this Oonagh set up a loud laugh, of great contempt, by-the-way, and looked at him as if he was only a mere handful of a man.

"Did you ever see Fin?" said she, changing her manner all at once.

"How could I?" said he; "he always took care to keep his distance."

"I thought so," she replied; "I judged as much; and if you take my advice, you poor-looking creature, you'll pray night and day that you may never see him, for I tell you it will be a black day for you when you do. But, in the meantime, you perceive that the wind's on the door, and as Fin himself is from home, maybe you'd be civil enough to turn the house, for it's always what Fin does when he's here."

This was a startler even to Cucullin; but he got up, however, and after pulling the middle finger of his right hand until it cracked three times, he went outside, and getting his arms about the house, turned it as she had wished. When Fin saw this, he felt the sweat of fear oozing out through every pore of his skin; but Oonagh, depending upon her woman's wit, felt not a whit daunted.

"Arrah, then," said she, "as you are so civil, maybe you'd do another obliging turn for us, as Fin's not here to do it himself. You see, after this long stretch of dry weather we've had, we feel very badly off for want of water. Now, Fin says there's a fine spring-well somewhere under the rocks behind the hill here below, and it was his intention to pull them asunder; but having heard of you, he left the place in such a fury, that he never thought of it. Now, if you try to find it, troth I'd feel it a kindness."

She then brought Cucullin down to see the place, which was then all one solid rock; and, after looking at it for some time, he cracked his right middle finger nine times, and, stooping down, tore a cleft about four hundred feet deep, and a quarter of a mile in length, which has since been christened by the name of Lumford's Glen.

"You'll now come in," said she, "and eat a bit of such humble fare as we can give you. Fin, even although he and you are enemies, would scorn not to treat you kindly in his own house; and, indeed, if I didn't do it even in his absence, he would not be pleased with me."

She accordingly brought him in, and placing half-a-dozen of the cakes we spoke of before him, together with a can or two of butter, a side of boiled bacon, and a stack of cabbage, she desired him to help himself – for this, be it known, was long before the invention of potatoes. Cucullin put one of the cakes in his mouth to take a huge whack out of it, when he made a thundering noise, something between a growl and a yell. "Blood and fury!" he shouted; "how is this? Here are two of my teeth out! What kind of bread this is you gave me."

"What's the matter?" said Oonagh coolly.

"Matter!" shouted the other again; "why, here are the two best teeth in my head gone."

"Why," said she, "that's Fin's bread – the only bread he ever eats when at home; but, indeed, I forgot to tell you that nobody can eat it but himself, and that child in the cradle there. I thought, however, that, as you were reported to be rather a stout little fellow of your size, you might be able to manage it, and I did not wish to affront a man that thinks himself able to fight Fin. Here's another cake – maybe it's not so hard as that."

Cucullin at the moment was not only hungry, but ravenous, so he accordingly made a fresh set at the second cake, and immediately another yell was heard twice as loud as the first. "Thunder and gibbets!" he roared, "take your bread out of this, or I will not have a tooth in my head; there's another pair of them gone!"

"Well, honest man," replied Oonagh, "if you're not able to eat the bread, say so quietly, and don't be wakening the child in the cradle there. There, now, he's awake upon me."

Fin now gave a skirl that startled the giant, as coming from such a youngster as he was supposed to be.

"Mother," said he, "I'm hungry – get me something to eat." Oonagh went over, and putting into his hand a cake that had no griddle in it, Fin, whose appetite in the meantime had been sharpened by seeing eating going forward, soon swallowed it. Cucullin was thunderstruck, and secretly thanked his stars that he had the good fortune to miss meeting Fin, for, as he said to himself, "I'd have no chance with a man who could eat such bread as that, which even his son that's but in his cradle can munch before my eyes."

"I'd like to take a glimpse at the lad in the cradle," said he to Oonagh; "for I can tell you that the infant who can manage that nutriment is no joke to look at, or to feed of a scarce summer."

"With all the veins of my heart," replied Oonagh; "get up, acushla, and show this decent little man something that won't be unworthy of your father, Fin M'Coul."

Fin, who was dressed for the occasion as much like a boy as possible, got up, and bringing Cucullin out, "Are you strong?" said he.

"Thunder an' ounds!" exclaimed the other, "what a voice in so small a chap!"

"Are you strong?" said Fin again; "are you able to squeeze water out of that white stone?" he asked, putting one into Cucullin's hand. The latter squeezed and squeezed the stone, but in vain.

"Ah, you're a poor creature!" said Fin. "You a giant! Give me the stone here, and when I'll show what Fin's little son can do, you may then judge of what my daddy himself is."

Fin then took the stone, and exchanging it for the curds, he squeezed the latter until the whey, as clear as water, oozed out in a little shower from his hand.

"I'll now go in," said he, "to my cradle; for I scorn to lose my time with anyone that's not able to eat my daddy's bread, or squeeze water out of a stone. Bedad, you had better be off out of this before he comes back; for if he catches you, it's in flummery he'd have you in two minutes."

Cucullin, seeing what he had seen, was of the same opinion himself; his knees knocked together with the terror of Fin's return, and he accordingly hastened to bid Oonagh farewell, and to assure her, that from that day out, he never wished to hear of, much less to see, her husband. "I admit fairly that I'm not a match for him," said he, "strong as I am; tell him I will avoid him as I would the plague, and that I will make myself scarce in this part of the country while I live."

Fin, in the meantime, had gone into the cradle, where he lay very quietly, his heart at his mouth with delight that Cucullin was about to take his departure, without discovering the tricks that had been played off on him.

"It's well for you," said Oonagh, "that he doesn't happen to be here, for it's nothing but hawk's meat he'd make of you."

"I know that," says Cucullin; "divil a thing else he'd make of me; but before I go, will you let me feel what kind of teeth Fin's lad has got that can eat griddle-bread like that?"

"With all pleasure in life," said she; "only, as they're far back in his head, you must put your finger a good way in."

Cucullin was surprised to find such a powerful set of grinders in one so young; but he was still much more so on finding, when he took his hand from Fin's mouth, that he had left the very finger upon which his whole strength depended, behind him. He gave one loud groan, and fell down at once with terror and weakness. This was all Fin wanted, who now knew that his most powerful and bitterest enemy was at his mercy. He started out of the cradle, and in a few minutes the great Cucullin, that was for such a length of time the terror of him and all his followers, lay a corpse before him. Thus did Fin, through the wit and invention of Oonagh, his wife, succeed in overcoming his enemy by cunning, which he never could have done by force.

The Story of Conn-Eda
or, The Golden Apples of Lough Erne

IT WAS LONG BEFORE the time the western districts of *Innis Fodhla* had any settled name, but were indiscriminately called after the person who took possession of them, and whose name they retained only as long as his sway lasted, that a powerful king reigned over this part of the sacred island. He was a puissant warrior, and no individual was found able to compete with him either on land or sea, or question his right to his conquest. The great king of the west held uncontrolled sway from the island of Rathlin to the mouth of the Shannon by sea, and far as the glittering length by land. The ancient king of the west, whose name was Conn, was good as well as great, and passionately loved by his people. His queen was a *Breaton* (British) princess, and was equally beloved and esteemed, because she was the great counterpart of the king in every respect; for whatever good qualification was wanting in the one, the other was certain to indemnify the omission. It was plainly manifest that heaven approved of the career in life of the virtuous couple; for during their reign the earth produced exuberant crops, the trees fruit ninefold commensurate with their usual bearing, the rivers, lakes, and surrounding sea teemed with abundance of choice fish, while herds and flocks were unusually prolific, and kine and sheep yielded such abundance of rich milk that they shed it in torrents upon the pastures; and furrows and cavities were always filled with the pure lacteal produce of the dairy. All these were blessings heaped by heaven upon the western districts of *Innis Fodhla*, over which the benignant and just Conn swayed his sceptre, in approbation of the course of government he had marked out for his own guidance. It is needless to state that the people who owned the authority of this great and good sovereign were the happiest on the face of the wide expanse of earth. It was during his reign, and that of his son and successor, that Ireland acquired the title of the 'happy isle of the west' among foreign nations. Con Mór and his good Queen Eda reigned in great glory during many years; they were blessed with an only son, whom they named Conn-eda, after both his parents, because the Druids foretold at his birth that he would inherit the good qualities of both. According as the young prince grew in years, his amiable and benignant qualities of mind, as well as his great strength of body and manly bearing, became more manifest. He was the idol of his parents, and the boast of his people; he was beloved and respected to that degree that neither prince, lord, nor plebeian swore an oath by the sun, moon, stars, or elements, except by the head of Conn-eda. This career of glory, however, was doomed to meet a powerful but temporary impediment, for the good Queen Eda took a sudden and severe illness, of which she died in a few days, thus plunging her spouse, her son, and all her people into a depth of grief and sorrow from which it was found difficult to relieve them.

The good king and his subjects mourned the loss of Queen Eda for a year and a day, and at the expiration of that time Conn Mór reluctantly yielded to the advice of his Druids and counsellors, and took to wife the daughter of his Arch-Druid. The new queen appeared to walk in the footsteps of the good Eda for several years, and gave great satisfaction to her subjects. But, in course of time, having had several children, and perceiving that Conn-eda was the favourite son of the king and the darling of the people, she clearly foresaw that he would become successor to the throne after the demise of his father, and that her son would certainly be excluded. This excited the hatred and inflamed the jealousy of the Druid's daughter against her step-son to such an extent, that she resolved in her own mind to leave nothing in her power undone to secure his death, or even exile from the kingdom. She began by circulating evil reports of the prince; but, as he was above suspicion, the king only laughed at the weakness of the queen; and the great princes and chieftains, supported by the people in general, gave an unqualified contradiction; while the prince himself bore all his trials with the utmost patience, and always repaid her bad and malicious acts towards him with good and benevolent ones. The enmity of the queen towards Conn-eda knew no bounds when she saw that the false reports she circulated could not injure him. As a last resource, to carry out her wicked projects, she determined to consult her *Cailleach-chearc* (hen-wife), who was a reputed enchantress.

Pursuant to her resolution, by the early dawn of morning she hied to the cabin of the *Cailleach-chearc*, and divulged to her the cause of her trouble.

"I cannot render you any help," said the *Cailleach*, "until you name the *duais*" (reward).

"What *duais* do you require?" asked the queen, impatiently.

"My *duais*," replied the enchantress, "is to fill the cavity of my arm with wool, and the hole I shall bore with my distaff with red wheat."

"Your *duais* is granted, and shall be immediately given you," said the queen. The enchantress thereupon stood in the door of her hut, and bending her arm into a circle with her side, directed the royal attendants to thrust the wool into her house through her arm, and she never permitted them to cease until all the available space within was filled with wool. She then got on the roof of her brother's house, and, having made a hole through it with her distaff, caused red wheat to be spilled through it, until that was filled up to the roof with red wheat, so that there was no room for another grain within. "Now," said the queen, "since you have received your *duais*, tell me how I can accomplish my purpose."

"Take this chess-board and chess, and invite the prince to play with you; you shall win the first game. The condition you shall make is, that whoever wins a game shall be at liberty to impose whatever *geasa* (conditions) the winner pleases on the loser. When you win, you must bid the prince, under the penalty either to go into *ionarbadh* (exile), or procure for you, within the space of a year and a day, the three golden apples that grew in the garden, the *each dubh* (black steed), and *coileen con na mbuadh* (hound of supernatural powers), called Samer, which are in the possession of the king of the Firbolg race, who resides in Lough Erne. Those two things are so precious, and so well guarded, that he can never attain them by his own power; and, if he would rashly attempt to seek them, he should lose his life."

The queen was greatly pleased at the advice, and lost no time in inviting Conn-eda to play a game at chess, under the conditions she had been instructed to arrange by the enchantress. The queen won the game, as the enchantress foretold, but so great was her anxiety to have the prince completely in her power, that she was tempted to challenge him to play a second game, which Conn-eda, to her astonishment, and no less mortification, easily won.

"Now," said the prince, "since you won the first game, it is your duty to impose your *geis* first."

"My *geis*" said the queen, "which I impose upon you, is to procure me the three golden apples that grow in the garden, the *each dubh* (black steed), and *cuileen con na mbuadh* (hound of supernatural powers), which are in the keeping of the king of the Firbolgs, in Lough Erne, within the space of a year and a day; or, in case you fail, to go into *ionarbadh* (exile), and never return, except you surrender yourself to lose your head and *comhead beatha* (preservation of life)."

"Well, then," said the prince, "the *geis* which I bind you by, is to sit upon the pinnacle of yonder tower until my return, and to take neither food nor nourishment of any description, except what red-wheat you can pick up with the point of your bodkin; but if I do not return, you are at perfect liberty to come down at the expiration of the year and a day."

In consequence of the severe *geis* imposed upon him, Conn-eda was very much troubled in mind; and, well knowing he had a long journey to make before he would reach his destination, immediately prepared to set out on his way, not, however, before he had the satisfaction of witnessing the ascent of the queen to the place where she was obliged to remain exposed to the scorching sun of the summer and the blasting storms of winter, for the space of one year and a day, at least. Conn-eda being ignorant of what steps he should take to procure the *each dubh* and *cuileen con na mbuadh*, though he was well aware that human energy would prove unavailing, thought proper to consult the great Druid, Fionn Dadhna, of Sleabh Badhna, who was a friend of his before he ventured to proceed to Lough Erne. When he arrived at the bruighean of the Druid, he was received with cordial friendship, and the *failte* (welcome), as usual, was poured out before him, and when he was seated, warm water was fetched, and his feet bathed, so that the fatigue he felt after his journey was greatly relieved. The Druid, after he had partaken of refreshments, consisting of the newest of food and oldest of liquors, asked him the reason for paying the visit, and more particularly the cause of his sorrow; for the prince appeared exceedingly depressed in spirit. Conn-eda told his friend the whole history of the transaction with his stepmother from the beginning to end.

"Can you not assist me?" asked the Prince, with downcast countenance.

"I cannot, indeed, assist you at present," replied the Druid; "but I will retire to my *grianan* (green place) at sun-rising on the morrow, and learn by virtue of my Druidism what can be done to assist you."

The Druid, accordingly, as the sun rose on the following morning, retired to his *grianan*, and consulted the god he adored, through the power of his *draoidheacht*. When he returned, he called Conn-eda aside on the plain, and addressed him thus:

"My dear son, I find you have been under a severe – an almost impossible – *geis* intended for your destruction; no person on earth could have advised the queen to impose it except the Cailleach of Lough Corrib, who is the greatest Druidess now in Ireland, and sister to the Firbolg, King of Lough Erne. It is not in my power, nor in that of the Deity I adore, to interfere in your behalf; but go directly to Sliabh Mis, and consult *Eánchinn-duine* (the bird of the human head), and if there be any possibility of relieving you, that bird can do it, for there is not a bird in the western world so celebrated as that bird, because it knows all things that are past, all things that are present and exist, and all things that shall hereafter exist. It is difficult to find access to his place of concealment, and more difficult still to obtain an answer from him; but I will endeavour to regulate that matter for you; and that is all I can do for you at present."

The Arch-Druid then instructed him thus: – "Take," said he, "yonder little shaggy steed, and mount him immediately, for in three days the bird will make himself visible, and the little shaggy steed will conduct you to his place of abode. But lest the bird should refuse to reply to your queries, take this precious stone (*leag lorgmhar*), and present it to him, and then little danger and doubt exist but that he will give you a ready answer." The prince returned heartfelt thanks to the Druid, and, having saddled and mounted the little shaggy horse without much delay, received the precious stone from the Druid, and, after having taken his leave of him, set out on his journey. He suffered the reins to fall loose upon the neck of the horse according as he had been instructed, so that the animal took whatever road he chose.

It would be tedious to relate the numerous adventures he had with the little shaggy horse, which had the extraordinary gift of speech, and was a *draoidheacht* horse during his journey.

The Prince having reached the hiding-place of the strange bird at the appointed time, and having presented him with the *leag lorgmhar*, according to Fionn Badhna's instructions, and proposed his questions relative to the manner he could best arrange for the fulfilment of his *geis*, the bird took up in his mouth the jewel from the stone on which it was placed, and flew to an inaccessible rock at some distance, and, when there perched, he thus addressed the prince, "Conn-eda, son of the King of Cruachan," said he, in a loud, croaking human voice, "remove the stone just under your right foot, and take the ball of iron and *corna* (cup) you shall find under it; then mount your horse, cast the ball before you, and having so done, your horse will tell you all the other things necessary to be done." The bird, having said this, immediately flew out of sight.

Conn-eda took great care to do everything according to the instructions of the bird. He found the iron ball and *corna* in the place which had been pointed out. He took them up, mounted his horse, and cast the ball before him. The ball rolled on at a regular gait, while the little shaggy horse followed on the way it led until they reached the margin of Lough Erne. Here the ball rolled in the water and became invisible.

"Alight now," said the *draoidheacht* pony, "and put your hand into mine ear; take from thence the small bottle of *íce* (all-heal) and the little wicker basket which you will find there, and remount with speed, for just now your great dangers and difficulties commence."

Conn-eda, ever faithful to the kind advice of his *draoidheacht* pony, did what he had been advised. Having taken the basket and bottle of *íce* from the animal's ear, he remounted and proceeded on his journey, while the water of the lake appeared only like an atmosphere above his head. When he entered the lake the ball again appeared, and rolled along until it came to the margin, across which was a causeway, guarded by three frightful serpents; the hissings of the monsters was heard at a great distance, while, on a nearer approach, their yawning mouths and formidable fangs were quite sufficient to terrify the stoutest heart.

"Now," said the horse, "open the basket and cast a piece of the meat you find in it into the mouth of each serpent; when you have done this, secure yourself in your seat in the best manner you can, so that we may make all due arrangements to pass those *draoidheacht peists*. If you cast the pieces of meat into the mouth of each *peist* unerringly, we shall pass them safely, otherwise we are lost." Conn-eda flung the pieces of meat into the jaws of the serpents with unerring aim.

"Bare a benison and victory," said the *draoidheacht* steed, "for you are a youth that will win and prosper." And, on saying these words, he sprang aloft, and cleared in his leap the river and ford, guarded by the serpents, seven measures beyond the margin.

"Are you still mounted, prince Conn-eda?" said the steed.

"It has taken only half my exertion to remain so," replied Conn-eda.

"I find," said the pony, "that you are a young prince that deserves to succeed; one danger is now over, but two others remain."

They proceeded onwards after the ball until they came in view of a great mountain flaming with fire. "Hold yourself in readiness for another dangerous leap," said the horse. The trembling prince had no answer to make, but seated himself as securely as the magnitude of the danger before him would permit. The horse in the next instant sprang from the earth, and flew like an arrow over the burning mountain.

"Are you still alive, Conn-eda, son of Conn-mór?" inquired the faithful horse.

"I'm just alive, and no more, for I'm greatly scorched," answered the prince.

"Since you are yet alive, I feel assured that you are a young man destined to meet supernatural success and benisons," said the Druidic steed. "Our greatest dangers are over," added he, "and there is hope that we shall overcome the next and last danger."

After they had proceeded a short distance, his faithful steed, addressing Conn-eda, said, "Alight, now, and apply a portion of the little bottle of *ice* to your wounds." The prince immediately followed the advice of his monitor, and, as soon as he rubbed the *ice* (all-heal) to his wounds, he became as whole and fresh as ever he had been before. After having done this, Conn-eda remounted, and following the track of the ball, soon came in sight of a great city surrounded by high walls. The only gate that was visible was not defended by armed men, but by two great towers that emitted flames that could be seen at a great distance.

"Alight on this plain," said the steed, "and take a small knife from my other ear; and with this knife you shall kill and flay me. When you have done this, envelop yourself in my hide, and you can pass the gate unscathed and unmolested. When you get inside you can come out at pleasure; because when once you enter there is no danger, and you can pass and repass whenever you wish; and let me tell you that all I have to ask of you in return is that you, when once inside the gates, will immediately return and drive away the birds of prey that may be fluttering round to feed on my carcass; and more, that you will pour any drop of that powerful *ice*, if such still remain in the bottle, upon my flesh, to preserve it from corruption. When you do this in memory of me, if it be not too troublesome, dig a pit, and cast my remains into it."

"Well," said Conn-eda, "my noblest steed, because you have been so faithful to me hitherto, and because you still would have rendered me further service, I consider such a proposal insulting to my feelings as a man, and totally in variance with the spirit which can feel the value of gratitude, not to speak of my feelings as a prince. But as a prince I am able to say, come what may – come death itself in its most hideous forms and terrors – I never will sacrifice private friendship to personal interest. Hence, I am, I swear by my arms of valour, prepared to meet the worst – even death itself – sooner than violate the principles of humanity, honour, and friendship! What a sacrifice do you propose!"

"Pshaw, man! Heed not that; do what I advise you, and prosper."

"Never! never!" exclaimed the prince.

"Well, then, son of the great western monarch," said the horse, with a tone of sorrow, "if you do not follow my advice on this occasion, I tell you that both you and I shall perish, and shall never meet again; but, if you act as I have instructed you, matters shall assume a happier and more pleasing aspect than you may imagine. I have not misled you heretofore, and, if I have not, what need have you to doubt the most important portion of my counsel? Do exactly as I have directed you, else you will cause a worse fate than death to befall me. And, moreover, I can tell you that, if you persist in your resolution, I have done with you for ever."

When the prince found that his noble steed could not be persuaded from his purpose, he took the knife out of his ear with reluctance, and with a faltering and trembling hand essayed experimentally to point the weapon at his throat. Conn-eda's eyes were bathed in tears; but no sooner had he pointed the Druidic *scian* to the throat of his good steed, than the dagger, as if impelled by some Druidic power, stuck in his neck, and in an instant the work of death was done, and the noble animal fell dead at his feet. When the prince saw his noble steed fall dead by his hand, he cast himself on the ground, and cried aloud until his consciousness was gone. When he recovered, he perceived that the steed was quite dead; and, as he thought there was no hope of resuscitating him, he considered it the most prudent course he could adopt to act according to the advice he had given him. After many misgivings of mind and abundant showers of tears, he essayed the task of flaying him, which was only that of a few minutes. When he found he had the hide separated from the body, he, in the derangement of the moment, enveloped himself in it, and proceeding towards the magnificent city in rather a demented state of mind, entered it without any molestation or opposition. It was a surprisingly populous city, and an extremely wealthy place; but its beauty, magnificence, and wealth had no charms for Conn-eda, because the thoughts of the loss he sustained in his dear steed were paramount to those of all other earthly considerations.

He had scarcely proceeded more than fifty paces from the gate, when the last request of his beloved *draoidheacht* steed forced itself upon his mind, and compelled him to return to perform the last solemn injunctions upon him. When he came to the spot upon which the remains of his beloved *draoidheacht* steed lay, an appalling sight presented itself; ravens and other carnivorous birds of prey were tearing and devouring the flesh of his dear steed. It was but short work to put them to flight; and having uncorked his little jar of *íce*, he deemed it a labour of love to embalm the now mangled remains with the precious ointment. The potent *íce* had scarcely touched the inanimate flesh, when, to the surprise of Conn-eda, it commenced to undergo some strange change, and in a few minutes, to his unspeakable astonishment and joy, it assumed the form of one of the handsomest and noblest young men imaginable, and in the twinkling of an eye the prince was locked in his embrace, smothering him with kisses, and drowning him with tears of joy. When one recovered from his ecstasy of joy, the other from his surprise, the strange youth thus addressed the prince:

"Most noble and puissant prince, you are the best sight I ever saw with my eyes, and I am the most fortunate being in existence for having met you! Behold in my person, changed to the natural shape, your little shaggy *draoidheacht* steed! I am brother of the king of the city; and it was the wicked Druid, Fionn Badhna, who kept me so long in bondage; but he was forced to give me up when you came to *consult* him, for my *geis* was then broken; yet I could not recover my pristine shape and appearance unless you had acted as you have kindly done. It was my own sister that urged the queen, your stepmother, to send you in quest of the steed and powerful puppy hound, which my brother has now in keeping. My sister, rest assured, had no thought of doing you the least injury, but much good, as you will find hereafter; because, if she were maliciously inclined towards you, she could have accomplished her end without any trouble. In short, she only wanted to free you from all future danger and disaster, and recover me from my relentless enemies through your instrumentality. Come with me, my friend and deliverer, and the steed and the puppy-hound of extraordinary powers, and the golden apples, shall be yours, and a cordial welcome shall greet you in my brother's abode; for you will deserve all this and much more."

The exciting joy felt on the occasion was mutual, and they lost no time in idle congratulations, but proceeded on to the royal residence of the King of Lough Erne. Here they were both received with demonstrations of joy by the king and his chieftains; and, when the purpose of Conn-eda's visit became known to the king, he gave a free consent to bestow on Conn-eda the black steed, the *coileen con-na-mbuadh*, called Samer, and the three apples of health that were growing in his garden, under the special condition, however, that he would consent to remain as his guest until he could set out on his journey in proper time, to fulfil his *geis*. Conn-eda, at the earnest solicitation of his friends, consented, and remained in the royal residence of the Firbolg, King of Lough Erne, in the enjoyment of the most delicious and fascinating pleasures during that period.

When the time of his departure came, the three golden apples were plucked from the crystal tree in the midst of the pleasure-garden, and deposited in his bosom; the puppy-hound, Samer, was leashed, and the leash put into his hand; and the black steed, richly harnessed, was got in readiness for him to mount. The king himself helped him on horseback, and both he and his brother assured him that he might not fear burning mountains or hissing serpents, because none would impede him, as his steed was always a passport to and from his subaqueous kingdom. And both he and his brother extorted a promise from Conn-eda, that he would visit them once every year at least.

Conn-eda took leave of his dear friend, and the king his brother. The parting was a tender one, soured by regret on both sides. He proceeded on his way without meeting anything to obstruct him, and in due time came in sight of the *dún* of his father, where the queen had been placed on the pinnacle of the tower, in full hope that, as it was the last day of her imprisonment there, the prince would not make his appearance, and thereby forfeit all pretensions and right to the crown of his father for ever. But her hopes were doomed to meet a disappointment, for when it had been announced to her by her couriers, who had been posted to watch the arrival of the prince, that he approached, she was incredulous; but when she saw him mounted on a foaming black steed, richly harnessed, and leading a strange kind of animal by a silver chain, she at once knew he was returning in triumph, and that her schemes laid for his destruction were frustrated. In the excess of grief at her disappointment, she cast herself from the top of the tower, and was instantly dashed to pieces. Conn-eda met a welcome reception from his father, who mourned him as lost to him for ever, during his absence; and, when the base conduct of the queen became known, the king and his chieftains ordered her remains to be consumed to ashes for her perfidy and wickedness.

Conn-eda planted the three golden apples in his garden, and instantly a great tree, bearing similar fruit, sprang up. This tree caused all the district to produce an exuberance of crops and fruits, so that it became as fertile and plentiful as the dominions of the Firbolgs, in consequence of the extraordinary powers possessed by the golden fruit. The hound Samer and the steed were of the utmost utility to him; and his reign was long and prosperous, and celebrated among the old people for the great abundance of corn, fruit, milk, fowl, and fish that prevailed during this happy reign. It was after the name Conn-eda the province of Connaucht, or *Conneda*, or *Connacht*, was so called.

The Henpecked Giant

NO LOCALITY of Ireland is fuller of strange bits of fanciful legend than the neighborhood of the Giant's Causeway. For miles along the coast the geological strata resemble that of the Causeway, and the gradual disintegration of the stone has wrought many peculiar and picturesque effects among the basaltic pillars, while each natural novelty has woven round it a tissue of traditions and legends, some appropriate, others forced, others ridiculous misapplications of commonplace tales. Here, a long straight row of columns is known as the 'Giant's Organ', and tradition pictures the scene when the giants of old, with their gigantic families, sat on the Causeway and listened to the music; there, a group of isolated pillars is called the 'Giant's Chimneys', since they once furnished an exit for the smoke of the gigantic kitchen. A solitary pillar, surrounded by the crumbling remains of others, bears a distant resemblance to a seated female figure, the 'Giant's Bride', who slew her husband and attempted to flee, but was overtaken by the power of a magician, who changed her into stone as she was seated by the shore, waiting for the boat that was to carry her away. Further on, a cluster of columns forms the 'Giant's Pulpit', where a presumably outspoken gigantic preacher denounced the sins of a gigantic audience. The Causeway itself, according to legend, formerly extended to Scotland, being originally constructed by Finn Maccool and his friends, this notable giant having invited Benandoner, a Scotch giant of much celebrity, to come over and fight him. The invitation was accepted, and Maccool, out of politeness, built the Causeway the whole distance, the big Scotchman thus walking over dryshod to receive his beating.

Some distance from the mainland is found the Ladies' Wishing Chair, composed of blocks in the Great Causeway, wishes made while seated here being certain of realization. To the west of the Wishing Chair a solitary pillar rises from the sea, the 'Gray Man's Love'. Look to the mainland, and the mountain presents a deep, narrow cleft, with perpendicular sides, the 'Gray Man's Path'. Out in the sea, but unfortunately not often in sight, is the 'Gray Man's Isle', at present inhabited only by the Gray Man himself. As the island, however, appears but once in seventeen years, and the Gray Man is never seen save on the eve of some awful calamity, visitors to the Causeway have a very slight chance of seeing either island or man. There can be no doubt though of the existence of both, for everybody knows he was one of the greatest of the giants during his natural lifetime, nor could any better evidence be asked than the facts that his sweet-heart, turned into stone, still stands in sight of the Causeway; the precipice, from which she flung herself into the sea, is still known by the name of the 'Lovers' Leap'; and the path he made through the mountain is still used by him when he leaves his island and comes on shore.

It is not surprising that so important a personage as the Gray Man should be the central figure of many legends, and indeed over him the story-makers seem to have had vigorous competition, for thirty or forty narratives are current in the neighborhood

concerning him and the principal events of his life. So great a collection of legendary lore on one topic rendered the choice of a single tradition which should fairly cover the subject a matter of no little difficulty. As sometimes happens in grave undertakings, the issue was determined by accident. A chance boat excursion led to the acquaintance of Mr. Barney O'Toole, a fisherman, and conversation developed the fact that this gentleman was thoroughly posted in the local legends, and was also the possessor of a critical faculty which enabled him to differentiate between the probable and the improbable, and thus to settle the historical value of a tradition. In his way, he was also a philosopher, having evidently given much thought to social issues, and expressing his conclusions thereupon with the ease and freedom of a master mind.

Upon being informed of the variety and amount of legendary material collected about the Gray Man and his doings, Barney unhesitatingly pronounced the entire assortment worthless, and condemned all the gathered treasures as the creations of petty intellects, which could not get out of the beaten track, but sought in the supernatural a reason for and explanation of every fact that seemed at variance with the routine of daily experience. In his opinion, the Gray Man is never seen at all in our day and generation, having been gathered to his fathers ages ago; nor is there any enchanted island; to use his own language, "all thim shtories bein' made be thim blaggârd guides that set up av a night shtringin' out laigends for to enthertain the quol'ty."

"Now, av yer Anner wants to hear it, I can tell ye the thrue shtory av the Gray Man, no more is there anny thing wondherful in it, but it's just as I had it from me grandfather, that towld it to the childher for to entertain thim.

"It's very well beknownst that in thim owld days there were gionts in plinty hereabouts, but they didn't make the Causeway at all, for that's a work o' nacher, axceptin' the Gray Man's Path, that I'm goin' to tell ye av. But ivery wan knows that there were gionts, bekase if there wasn't, how cud we know o' thim at all, but wan thing's sartain, they were just like us, axceptin' in the matther o' size, for wan ov thim 'ud make a dozen like the men that live now.

"Among the gionts that lived about the Causeway there was wan, a young giont named Finn O'Goolighan, that was the biggest av his kind, an' none o' thim cud hide in a kish. So Finn, for the size av him, was a livin' terror. His little finger was the size av yer Anner's arrum, an' his wrist as big as yer leg, an' so he wint, bigger an' bigger. Whin he walked he carried an oak-tree for a shtick, ye cud crawl into wan av his shoes, an' his caubeen 'ud cover a boat. But he was a good-humored young felly wid a laugh that 'ud deefen ye, an' a plazin' word for all he met, so as if ye run across him in the road, he'd give ye 'good morrow kindly', so as ye'd feel the betther av it all day. He'd work an' he'd play an' do aither wid all the might that was in him. Av a week day you'd see him in the field or on the shore from sun to sun as busy as a hen wid a dozen chicks; an' av a fair-day or av a Sunday, there he'd be, palatherin' at the girls, an' dancin' jigs that he done wid extrame nateness, or havin' a bout wid a shtick on some other felly's head, an' indade, at that he was so clever that it was a delight for to see him, for he'd crack a giont's shkull that was as hard as a pot wid wan blow an' all the pleasure in life. So he got to be four or five an' twinty an' not his betther in the County Antrim.

"Wan fine day, his father, Bryan O'Goolighan, that was as big a giont as himself, says to him, says he, 'Finn, me Laddybuck, I'm thinkin' ye'll want to be gettin' marr'd.'

"'Not me,' says Finn.

"'An' why not?' says his father.

"'I've no consate av it,' says Finn.

"'Ye'd be the betther av it,' says his father.

"'Faix, I'm not sure o' that,' says Finn; 'gettin' marr'd is like turnin' a corner, ye don't know phat ye're goin' to see,' says he.

"'Thrue for ye,' says owld Bryan, for he'd had axpayrience himself, 'but if ye'd a purty woman to make the stirabout for ye av a mornin' wid her own white hands, an' to watch out o' the dure for ye in the avenin,' an' put on a sod o' turf whin she sees ye comin', ye'd be a betther man,' says he.

"'Bedad, it's not aisey for to conthravene that same,' says Finn, 'barrin' I mightn't git wan like that. Wimmin is like angels,' says he. 'There's two kinds av 'em, an' the wan that shmiles like a dhrame o' heaven afore she's marr'd, is the wan that gits to be a tarin' divil afther her market's made an' she's got a husband.'

"Ye see Finn was a mighty smart young felly, if he was a giont, but his father didn't give up hope av gettin' him marr'd, for owld folks that's been through a dale o' throuble that-a-way always thries to get the young wans into the same thrap, beways, says they, av taichin' thim to larn something. But Bryan was a wise owld giont, an' knewn, as the Bible says, there's time enough for all things. So he quit him, an' that night he spake wid the owld woman an' left it wid her, as knowin' that whin it's a matther o' marryin', a woman is more knowledgable an' can do more to bring on that sort o' mis'ry in wan day than a man can in all the years God gives him.

"Now, in ordher that ye see the pint, I'm undher the need-cessity av axplainin' to yer Anner that Finn didn't be no manes have the hathred at wimmin that he purtinded, for indade he liked thim purty well, but he thought he undhershtood thim well enough to know that the more ye talk swate to thim, the more they don't like it, barrin' they're fools, that sometimes happens. So whin he talked wid 'em or about thim, he spake o' thim shuperskillious, lettin' on to despize the lasht wan o' thim, that was a takin' way he had, for wimmin love thimselves a dale betther than ye'd think, unless yer Anner's marr'd an' knows, an' that Finn knew, so he always said o' thim the manest things he cud get out av his head, an' that made thim think av him, that was phat he wanted. They purtinded to hate him for it, but he didn't mind that, for he knewn it was only talk, an' there wasn't wan o' thim that wouldn't give the lasht tooth out av her jaw to have him for a husband.

"Well, as I was sayin', afther owld Bryan give Finn up, his mother tuk him in hand, throwin' a hint at him wanst in a while, sighin' to him how glad she'd be to have a young lady giont for a dawther, an' dhroppin' a word about phat an iligant girl Burthey O'Ghallaghy was, that was the dawther av wan o' the naburs, that she got Finn, unbeknownst to himself, to be thinkin' about Burthey. She was a fine young lady giont, about tin feet high, as broad as a cassel dure, but she was good size for Finn, as ye know be phat I said av him. So when Finn's mother see him takin' her home from church afther benediction, an' the nabers towld her how they obsarved him lanin' on O'Ghallaghy's wall an' Burthey lightin' his pipe wid a coal, she thought to herself, 'fair an' aisey goes far in a day,' an' made her mind up that Finn 'ud marry Burthey. An' so, belike, he'd a' done, if he hadn't gone over, wan onlucky day, to the village beyant, where the common people like you an' me lived.

"When he got there, in he wint to the inn to get him his dhrink, for it's a mishtake to think that thim gionts were all blood-suckin' blaggârds as the Causeway guides say, but, barrin' they were in dhrink, were as paceable as rabbits. So when Finn wint in, he says, 'God save ye,' to thim settin', an' gev the table a big crack wid his shillaylah as for to say he wanted his glass. But instead o' the owld granny that used for to fetch him his potheen, out shteps a nate little woman wid hair an' eyes as black as a crow an' two lips on her as red as a cherry an' a quick sharp way like a cat in a hurry.

"'An' who are you, me Dear?' says Finn, lookin' up.

"'I'm the new barmaid, Sorr, av it's plazin' to ye,' says she, makin' a curchey, an' lookin' shtrait in his face.

"'It is plazin',' says Finn. ''Tis I that's glad to be sarved be wan like you. Only,' says he, 'I know be the look o' yer eye ye 've a timper.'

"'Dade I have,' says she, talkin' back at him, 'an' ye'd betther not wake it.'

"Finn had more to say an' so did she, that I won't throuble yer Anner wid, but when he got his fill av dhrink an' said all he'd in his head, an' she kep' aven wid him at ivery

pint, he wint away mightily plazed. The next Sunday but wan he was back agin, an' the Sunday afther, an' afther that agin. By an' by, he'd come over in the avenin' afther the work was done, an' lane on the bar or set on the table, talkin' wid the barmaid, for she was as sharp as a thornbush, an' sorra a word Finn 'ud say to her in impidince or anny other way, but she'd give him his answer afore he cud get his mouth shut.

"Now, be this time, Finn's mother had made up her mind that Finn 'ud marry Burthey, an' so she sent for the match-maker, an' they talked it all over, an' Finn's father seen Burthey's father, an' they settled phat Burthey 'ud get an' phat Finn was to have, an' were come to an agraymint about the match, onbeknownst to Finn, bekase it was in thim days like it is now, the matches bein' made be the owld people, an' all the young wans did was to go an' be marr'd an' make the best av it. Afther all, maybe that's as good a way as anny, for whin ye've got all the throuble on yer back ye can stagger undher, there's not a haporth o' differ whether ye got undher it yerself or whether it was put on ye, an' so it is wid gettin' marr'd, at laste so I'm towld.

"Annyhow, Finn's mother was busy wid preparin' for the weddin' whin she heard how Finn was afther puttin' in his time at the village.

"'Sure that won't do,' she says to herself; 'he ought to know betther than to be spendin' ivery rap he's got in dhrink an' gostherin' at that black-eyed huzzy, an' he to be marr'd to the best girl in the county.' So that night, when Finn come in, she spake fair an' soft to him that he'd give up goin' to the inn, an' get ready for to be marr'd at wanst. An' that did well enough till she got to the marryin', when Finn riz up aff his sate, an' shut his taith so hard he bruk his pipestem to smithereens.

"'Say no more, mother,' he says to her. 'Burthey's good enough, but I wouldn't marry her if she was made av goold. Begob, she's too big. I want no hogs'ead av a girl like her,' says he. 'If I'm to be marr'd, I want a little woman. They're betther o' their size, an' it don't take so much to buy gowns for thim, naither do they ate so much,' says he.

"'A-a-ah, baithershin,' says his mother to him; 'phat d'ye mane be talkin' that-a-way, an' me workin' me fingers to the bone clanin' the house for ye, an' relavin' ye av all the coortin' so as ye'd not be bothered in the laste wid it.'

"'Shmall thanks to ye,' says Finn, 'sure isn't the coortin' the best share o' the job?'

"'Don't ye mane to marry her?' says his mother.

"'Divil a toe will I go wid her,' says Finn.

"'Out, ye onmannerly young blaggârd, I'd tell ye to go to the divil, but ye're on the way fast enough, an' bad luck to the fut I'll shtir to halt ye. Only I'm sorry for Burthey,' says she, 'wid her new gown made. When her brother comes back, begob 'tis he that'll be the death av ye immejitly afther he dhrops his two eyes on ye.'

"'Aisey now,' says Finn, 'if he opens his big mouth at me, I'll make him wondher why he wasn't born deaf an' dumb,' says he, an' so he would, for all that he was so paceable.

"Afther that, phat was his mother to do but lave aff an' go to bed, that she done, givin' Finn all the talk in her head an' a million curses besides, for she was mightily vexed at bein' bate that way an' was in a divil av a timper along o' the house-clanin', that always puts wimmin into a shtate av mind.

"So the next day the news was towld, an' Finn got to be a holy show for the nabers, bekase av not marryin' Burthey an' wantin' the barmaid. They were afeared to say annything to himself about it, for he'd an arm on him the thick o' yer waist, an' no wan wanted to see how well he cud use it, but they'd whisper afther him, an' whin he wint along the road, they'd pint afther him, an' by an' by a giont like himself, an uncle av him, towld him he'd betther lave the counthry, an' so he thought he'd do an' made ready for to shtart.

"But poor Burthey pined wid shame an' grief at the loss av him, for she loved him wid all the heart she had, an' that was purty big. So she fell aff her weight, till from the size av a hogs'ead she got no bigger round than a barrel an' was like to die. But all the time she kept on hopin' that he'd come to her, but whin she heard for sartain he was goin' to lave the counthry she let go an' jumped aff that clift into the say an' committed shooicide an' drownded herself. She wasn't turned into a pillar at all, that's wan o' thim guides' lies; she just drownded like annybody that fell into the wather would, an' was found afther an' berrid be the fishermen, an' a hard job av it they had, for she weighed a ton. But they called the place the Lovers' Lape, bekase she jumped from it, an' lovin' Finn the way she did, the lape she tuk made the place be called afther her an' that's razon enough.

"Finn was showbogher enough afore, but afther that he seen it was no use thryin' for to live in Ireland at all, so he got the barmaid, that was aiquel to goin' wid him, the more that ivery wan was agin him, that's beway o' the conthrariness av wimmin, that are always ready for to do annything ye don't want thim to do, an' wint to Scotland an' wasn't heard av for a long time.

"About twelve years afther, there was a great talk that Finn had got back from Scotland wid his wife an' had taken the farm over be the village, the first on the left as ye go down the mountain. At first there was no end av the fuss that was, for Burthey's frinds hadn't forgotten, but it all come to talk, so Finn settled down quite enough an' wint to work. But he was an althered man. His hair an' beard were gray as a badger, so they called him the Gray Man, an' he'd a look on him like a shape-stalin' dog. Everybody wondhered, but they didn't wondher long, for it was aisely persaived he had cause enough, for the tongue o' Missis Finn wint like a stame-ingine, kapin' so far ahead av her branes that she'd have to shtop an' say 'an'-uh, an'-uh', to give the latther time for to ketch up. Jagers, but she was the woman for to talk an' schold an' clack away till ye'd want to die to be rid av her. When she was young she was a purty nice girl, but as she got owlder her nose got sharp, her lips were as thin as the aidge av a sickle, an' her chin was as pinted as the bow av a boat. The way she managed Finn was beautiful to see, for he was that afeared av her tongue that he darn't say his sowl belonged to him when she was by.

"When he got up airly in the mornin', she'd ax, 'Now phat are ye raisin' up so soon for, an' me just closin' me eyes in slape?' An' if he'd lay abed, she'd tell him to 'get along out o' that now, ye big gossoon; if it wasn't for me ye'd do nothin' at all but slape like a pig.' If he'd go out, she'd gosther him about where he was goin' an' phat he meant to do when he got there; if he shtayed at home, she'd raymark that he done nothin' but set in the cabin like a boss o' shtraw. When he thried for to plaze her, she'd grumble at him bekase he didn't thry sooner; when he let her be, she'd fall into a fury an' shtorm till his hair shtud up like it was bewitched it was.

"She'd more thricks than a showman's dog. If scholdin' didn't do for Finn, she'd cry at him, an' had tin childher that she larned to cry at him too, an' when she begun, the tin o' thim 'ud set up a yell that 'ud deefen a thrumpeter, so Finn 'ud give in.

"She cud fall ill on tin minnits notice, an' if Finn was obsthreperous in that degray that she cudn't do him no other way, she'd let on her head ached fit to shplit, so she'd go to bed an' shtay there till she'd got him undher her thumb agin. So she knew just where to find him whin she wanted him; that wimmin undhershtand, for there's more divilmint in wan woman's head about gettin' phat she wants than in tin men's bodies.

"Sure, if iver annybody had raison to remimber the ould song, 'When I was single', it was Finn.

"So, ye see, Finn, the Gray Man, was afther havin' the divil's own time, an' that was beways av a mishtake he made about marryin'. He thought it was wan o' thim goold bands the quol'ty ladies wear on their arrums, but he found it was a handcuff it was. Sure wimmin are quare craythers. Ye think life wid wan o' thim is like a sunshiny day an' it's nothing but drizzle an' fog from dawn to dark, an' it's my belafe that Misther O'Day wasn't far wrong when he said wimmin are like the owld gun he had in the house an' that wint aff an the shly wan day an' killed the footman. 'Sure it looked innycent enough,' says he, 'but it was loaded all the same, an' only waitin' for an axcuse to go aff at some wan, an' that's like a woman, so it is,' he'd say, an' ivery wan 'ud laugh when he towld that joke, for he was the landlord, 'that's like a woman, for she's not to be thrusted avin when she's dead.'

"But it's me own belafe that the most sarious mishtake av Finn's was in marryin' a little woman. There's thim that says all wimmin is a mishtake be nacher, but there's a big differ bechuxt a little woman an' a big wan, the little wans have sowls too big for their bodies, so are always lookin' out for a big man to marry, an' the bigger he is, the betther they like him, as knowin' they can manage him all the aisier. So it was wid Finn an' his little wife, for be hook an' be crook she rejuiced him in that obejince that if she towld him for to go an' shtand on his head in the corner, he'd do it wid the risk av his life, bekase he'd wanted to die an' go to heaven as he heard the priest say there was no marryin' there, an' though he didn't dare to hint it, he belaved in his sowl that the rayzon was the wimmin didn't get that far.

"Afther they'd been living here about a year, Finn thought he'd fish a bit an' so help along, considherin' he'd a big family an' none o' the childher owld enough for to work. So he got a boat an' did purty well an' his wife used to come acrass the hill to the shore to help him wid the catch. But it was far up an' down agin an' she'd get tired wid climbin' the hill an' jawing at Finn on the way.

"So wan day as they were comin' home, they passed a cabin an' there was the man that lived there, that was only a ditcher, a workin' away on the side av the hill down the path to the shpring wid a crowbar, movin' a big shtone, an' the shweat rollin' in shtrames aff his face.

"'God save ye,' says Finn to him.

"'God save ye kindly,' says he to Finn.

"'It's a bizzy man ye are,' says Finn.

"'Thrue for ye,' says the ditcher. 'It's along o' the owld woman. "The way to the shpring is too stape an' shtoney," says she to me, an' sure, I'm afther makin' it aisey for her.'

"'Ye're the kind av a man to have,' says Missis Finn, shpakin' up. 'Sure all wimmin isn't blessed like your wife,' says she, lookin' at Finn, who let on to laugh when he wanted to shwear. They had some more discoorse, thin Finn an' his wife wint on, but it put a big notion into her head. If the bogthrotter, that was only a little ottommy, 'ud go to work like that an' make an aisey path for his owld woman to the shpring, phat's the rayzon Finn cudn't fall to an' dig a path through the mountains, so she cud go to the say an' to the church on the shore widout breakin' her back climbin' up an' then agin climbin' down. 'T was the biggest consate iver in the head av her, an' she wasn't wan o' thim that 'ud let it cool aff for the want o' talkin' about it, so she up an' towld it to Finn, an' got afther him to do it. Finn wasn't aiger for to thry, bekase it was Satan's own job, so he held out agin all her scholdin' an' beggin' an' cryin'. Then she got sick on him, wid her headache, an' wint to bed, an' whin Finn was about she'd wondher out loud phat she was iver born for an' why she cudn't die. Then she'd pray, so as Finn 'ud hear her, to all the saints to watch over her big gossoon av a husband an' not forget him just bekase he was a baste, an' if Finn 'ud thry to quiet her, she'd pray all the louder, an' tell him it didn't matther, she was dyin' an' 'ud soon be rid av him an' his brutal ways, so as Finn got half crazy wid her an' was ready to do annything in the worruld for to get her quiet.

"Afther about a week av this thratemint, Finn give in an' wint to work wid a pick an' shpade on the Gray Man's Path. But thim that says he made it in wan night is ignerant, for I belave it tuk him a month at laste; if not more. So that's the thrue shtory av the Gray Man's Path, as me grandfather towld it, an' shows that a giont's size isn't a taste av help to him in a contist wid a woman's jaw.

"But to be fair wid her, I belave the onliest fault Finn's wife had was, she was possist be the divil, an' there's thim that thinks that's enough. I mind me av a young felly wan time that was in love, an' so to be axcused, that wished he'd a hunderd tongues so to do justice to his swateheart. So afther that he marr'd her, an' whin they'd been marr'd a while an' she'd got him undher her fisht, says they to him, 'An' how about yer hunderd tongues?' 'Begorra,' says he to thim agin, 'wid a hunderd I'd get along betther av coorse than wid wan, but to be ayquel to the waggin' av her jaw I'd nade a hunderd t'ousand.'

"So it's a consate I have that Missis Finn was not a haporth worse nor the rest o' thim, an' that's phat me grandfather said too, that had been marr'd twict, an' so knewn phat he was talkin' about. An' whin he towld the shtory av the Gray Man, he'd always end it wid a bit av poethry:

"'*The first rib did bring in ruin*
As the rest have since been doin';
Some be wan way, some another,
Woman shtill is mischief's mother.

"'*Be she good or be she avil,*
Be she saint or be she divil,
Shtill unaisey is his life
That is marr'd wid a wife.'"

The Shee An Gannon and the Gruagach Gaire

THE SHEE AN GANNON was born in the morning, named at noon, and went in the evening to ask his daughter of the king of Erin.

"I will give you my daughter in marriage," said the king of Erin; "you won't get her, though, unless you go and bring me back the tidings that I want, and tell me what it is that put a stop to the laughing of the Gruagach Gaire, who before this laughed always, and laughed so loud that the whole world heard him. There are twelve iron spikes out here in the garden behind my castle. On eleven of the spikes are the heads of kings' sons who came seeking my daughter in marriage, and all of them went away to get the knowledge I wanted. Not one was able to get it and tell me what stopped the Gruagach Gaire from laughing. I took the heads off them all when they came back without the tidings for which they went, and I'm greatly in dread that your head'll be on the twelfth spike, for I'll do the same to you that I did to the eleven kings' sons unless you tell what put a stop to the laughing of the Gruagach."

The Shee an Gannon made no answer, but left the king and pushed away to know could he find why the Gruagach was silent.

He took a glen at a step, a hill at a leap, and travelled all day till evening. Then he came to a house. The master of the house asked him what sort was he, and he said: "A young man looking for hire."

"Well," said the master of the house, "I was going tomorrow to look for a man to mind my cows. If you'll work for me, you'll have a good place, the best food a man could have to eat in this world, and a soft bed to lie on."

The Shee an Gannon took service, and ate his supper. Then the master of the house said: "I am the Gruagach Gaire; now that you are my man and have eaten your supper, you'll have a bed of silk to sleep on."

Next morning after breakfast the Gruagach said to the Shee an Gannon: "Go out now and loosen my five golden cows and my bull without horns, and drive them to pasture; but when you have them out on the grass, be careful you don't let them go near the land of the giant."

The new cowboy drove the cattle to pasture, and when near the land of the giant, he saw it was covered with woods and surrounded by a high wall. He went up, put his back against the wall, and threw in a great stretch of it; then he went inside and threw out another great stretch of the wall, and put the five golden cows and the bull without horns on the land of the giant.

Then he climbed a tree, ate the sweet apples himself, and threw the sour ones down to the cattle of the Gruagach Gaire.

Soon a great crashing was heard in the woods, – the noise of young trees bending, and old trees breaking. The cowboy looked around and saw a five-headed giant pushing through the trees; and soon he was before him.

"Poor miserable creature!" said the giant; "but weren't you impudent to come to my land and trouble me in this way? You're too big for one bite, and too small for two. I don't know what to do but tear you to pieces."

"You nasty brute," said the cowboy, coming down to him from the tree, "'tis little I care for you"; and then they went at each other. So great was the noise between them that there was nothing in the world but what was looking on and listening to the combat.

They fought till late in the afternoon, when the giant was getting the upper hand; and then the cowboy thought that if the giant should kill him, his father and mother would never find him or set eyes on him again, and he would never get the daughter of the king of Erin. The heart in his body grew strong at this thought. He sprang on the giant, and with the first squeeze and thrust he put him to his knees in the hard ground, with the second thrust to his waist, and with the third to his shoulders.

"I have you at last; you're done for now!", said the cowboy. Then he took out his knife, cut the five heads off the giant, and when he had them off he cut out the tongues and threw the heads over the wall.

Then he put the tongues in his pocket and drove home the cattle. That evening the Gruagach couldn't find vessels enough in all his place to hold the milk of the five golden cows.

But when the cowboy was on the way home with the cattle, the son of the king of Tisean came and took the giant's heads and claimed the princess in marriage when the Gruagach Gaire should laugh.

After supper the cowboy would give no talk to his master, but kept his mind to himself, and went to the bed of silk to sleep.

On the morning the cowboy rose before his master, and the first words he said to the Gruagach were:

"What keeps you from laughing, you who used to laugh so loud that the whole world heard you?"

"I'm sorry," said the Gruagach, "that the daughter of the king of Erin sent you here."

"If you don't tell me of your own will, I'll make you tell me," said the cowboy; and he put a face on himself that was terrible to look at, and running through the house like a madman, could find nothing that would give pain enough to the Gruagach but some ropes made of untanned sheepskin hanging on the wall.

He took these down, caught the Gruagach, fastened him by the three smalls, and tied him so that his little toes were whispering to his ears. When he was in this state the Gruagach said: "I'll tell you what stopped my laughing if you set me free."

So the cowboy unbound him, the two sat down together, and the Gruagach said:

"I lived in this castle here with my twelve sons. We ate, drank, played cards, and enjoyed ourselves, till one day when my sons and I were playing, a slender brown hare came rushing in, jumped on to the hearth, tossed up the ashes to the rafters and ran away.

"On another day he came again; but if he did, we were ready for him, my twelve sons and myself. As soon as he tossed up the ashes and ran off, we made after him, and followed him till nightfall, when he went into a glen. We saw a light before us. I ran on, and came to a house with a great apartment, where there was a man named Yellow Face with twelve daughters, and the hare was tied to the side of the room near the women.

"There was a large pot over the fire in the room, and a great stork boiling in the pot. The man of the house said to me: 'There are bundles of rushes at the end of the room, go there and sit down with your men!'

"He went into the next room and brought out two pikes, one of wood, the other of iron, and asked me which of the pikes would I take. I said, 'I'll take the iron one'; for I thought in my heart that if an attack should come on me, I could defend myself better with the iron than the wooden pike.

"Yellow Face gave me the iron pike, and the first chance of taking what I could out of the pot on the point of the pike. I got but a small piece of the stork, and the man of the house took all the rest on his wooden pike. We had to fast that night; and when the man and his twelve daughters ate the flesh of the stork, they hurled the bare bones in the faces of my sons and myself. We had to stop all night that way, beaten on the faces by the bones of the stork.

"Next morning, when we were going away, the man of the house asked me to stay a while; and going into the next room, he brought out twelve loops of iron and one of wood, and said to me: 'Put the heads of your twelve sons into the iron loops, or your own head into the wooden one'; and I said: 'I'll put the twelve heads of my sons in the iron loops, and keep my own out of the wooden one.'

"He put the iron loops on the necks of my twelve sons, and put the wooden one on his own neck. Then he snapped the loops one after another, till he took the heads off my twelve sons and threw the heads and bodies out of the house; but he did nothing to hurt his own neck.

"When he had killed my sons he took hold of me and stripped the skin and flesh from the small of my back down, and when he had done that he took the skin of a black sheep that had been hanging on the wall for seven years and clapped it on my body in place of my own flesh and skin; and the sheepskin grew on me, and every year since then I shear myself, and every bit of wool I use for the stockings that I wear I clip off my own back."

When he had said this, the Gruagach showed the cowboy his back covered with thick black wool.

After what he had seen and heard, the cowboy said: "I know now why you don't laugh, and small blame to you. But does that hare come here still?"

"He does indeed," said the Gruagach.

Both went to the table to play, and they were not long playing cards when the hare ran in; and before they could stop him he was out again.

But the cowboy made after the hare, and the Gruagach after the cowboy, and they ran as fast as ever their legs could carry them till nightfall; and when the hare was entering the castle where the twelve sons of the Gruagach were killed, the cowboy caught him by the two hind legs and dashed out his brains against the wall; and the skull of the hare was knocked into the chief room of the castle, and fell at the feet of the master of the place.

"Who has dared to interfere with my fighting pet?" screamed Yellow Face.

"I," said the cowboy; "and if your pet had had manners, he might be alive now."

The cowboy and the Gruagach stood by the fire. A stork was boiling in the pot, as when the Gruagach came the first time. The master of the house went into the next room and brought out an iron and a wooden pike, and asked the cowboy which would he choose.

"I'll take the wooden one," said the cowboy; "and you may keep the iron one for yourself."

So he took the wooden one; and going to the pot, brought out on the pike all the stork except a small bite, and he and the Gruagach fell to eating, and they were eating

the flesh of the stork all night. The cowboy and the Gruagach were at home in the place that time.

In the morning the master of the house went into the next room, took down the twelve iron loops with a wooden one, brought them out, and asked the cowboy which would he take, the twelve iron or the one wooden loop.

"What could I do with the twelve iron ones for myself or my master? I'll take the wooden one."

He put it on, and taking the twelve iron loops, put them on the necks of the twelve daughters of the house, then snapped the twelve heads off them, and turning to their father, said: "I'll do the same thing to you unless you bring the twelve sons of my master to life, and make them as well and strong as when you took their heads."

The master of the house went out and brought the twelve to life again; and when the Gruagach saw all his sons alive and as well as ever, he let a laugh out of himself, and all the Eastern world heard the laugh.

Then the cowboy said to the Gruagach: "It's a bad thing you have done to me, for the daughter of the king of Erin will be married the day after your laugh is heard."

"Oh! Then we must be there in time," said the Gruagach; and they all made away from the place as fast as ever they could, the cowboy, the Gruagach, and his twelve sons.

They hurried on; and when within three miles of the king's castle there was such a throng of people that no one could go a step ahead. "We must clear a road through this," said the cowboy.

"We must indeed," said the Gruagach; and at it they went, threw the people some on one side and some on the other, and soon they had an opening for themselves to the king's castle.

As they went in, the daughter of the king of Erin and the son of the king of Tisean were on their knees just going to be married. The cowboy drew his hand on the bridegroom, and gave a blow that sent him spinning till he stopped under a table at the other side of the room.

"What scoundrel struck that blow?" asked the king of Erin.

"It was I," said the cowboy.

"What reason had you to strike the man who won my daughter?"

"It was I who won your daughter, not he; and if you don't believe me, the Gruagach Gaire is here himself. He'll tell you the whole story from beginning to end, and show you the tongues of the giant."

So the Gruagach came up and told the king the whole story, how the Shee an Gannon had become his cowboy, had guarded the five golden cows and the bull without horns, cut off the heads of the five-headed giant, killed the wizard hare, and brought his own twelve sons to life. "And then," said the Gruagach, "he is the only man in the whole world I have ever told why I stopped laughing, and the only one who has ever seen my fleece of wool."

When the king of Erin heard what the Gruagach said, and saw the tongues of the giant fitted in the head, he made the Shee an Gannon kneel down by his daughter, and they were married on the spot.

Then the son of the king of Tisean was thrown into prison, and the next day they put down a great fire, and the deceiver was burned to ashes.

The wedding lasted nine days, and the last day was better than the first.

The Black Thief and Knight of the Glen

IN TIMES of yore there was a King and a Queen in the south of Ireland who had three sons, all beautiful children; but the Queen, their mother, sickened unto death when they were yet very young, which caused great grief throughout the Court, particularly to the King, her husband, who could in no wise be comforted. Seeing that death was drawing near her, she called the King to her and spoke as follows:

"I am now going to leave you, and as you are young and in your prime, of course after my death you will marry again. Now all the request I ask of you is that you will build a tower in an island in the sea, wherein you will keep your three sons until they are come of age and fit to do for themselves; so that they may not be under the power or jurisdiction of any other woman. Neglect not to give them education suitable to their birth, and let them be trained up to every exercise and pastime requisite for king's sons to learn. This is all I have to say, so farewell."

The King had scarce time, with tears in his eyes, to assure her she should be obeyed in everything, when she, turning herself in her bed, with a smile gave up the ghost. Never was greater mourning seen than was throughout the Court and the whole kingdom; for a better woman than the Queen, to rich and poor, was not to be found in the world. She was interred with great pomp and magnificence, and the King, her husband, became in a manner inconsolable for the loss of her. However, he caused the tower to be built and his sons placed in it, under proper guardians, according to his promise.

In process of time the lords and knights of the kingdom counselled the King (as he was young) to live no longer as he had done, but to take a wife; which counsel prevailing, they chose him a rich and beautiful princess to be his consort – a neighbouring King's daughter, of whom he was very fond. Not long after, the Queen had a fine son, which caused great feasting and rejoicing at the Court, insomuch that the late Queen, in a manner, was entirely forgotten. That fared well, and King and Queen lived happy together for several years.

At length the Queen, having some business with the hen-wife, went herself to her, and, after a long conference passed, was taking leave of her, when the hen-wife prayed that if ever she should come back to her again she might break her neck. The Queen, greatly incensed at such a daring insult from one of her meanest subjects, demanded immediately the reason, or she would have her put to death.

"It was worth your while, madam," says the hen-wife, "to pay me well for it, for the reason I prayed so on you concerns you much."

"What must I pay you?" asked the Queen.

"You must give me," says she, "the full of a pack of wool, and I have an ancient crock which you must fill with butter, likewise a barrel which you must fill for me full of wheat."

"How much wool will it take to the pack?" says the Queen.

"It will take seven herds of sheep," said she, "and their increase for seven years."

"How much butter will it take to fill your crock?"

"Seven dairies," said she, "and their increase for seven years."

"And how much will it take to fill the barrel you have?" says the Queen.

"It will take the increase of seven barrels of wheat for seven years."

"That is a great quantity," says the Queen; "but the reason must be extraordinary, and before I want it, I will give you all you demand."

"Well," says the hen-wife, "it is because you are so stupid that you don't observe or find out those affairs that are so dangerous and hurtful to yourself and your child."

"What is that?" says the Queen.

"Why," says she, "the King your husband has three fine sons he had by the late Queen, whom he keeps shut up in a tower until they come of age, intending to divide the kingdom between them, and let your son push his fortune; now, if you don't find some means of destroying them; your child and perhaps yourself will be left desolate in the end."

"And what would you advise me to do?" said she; "I am wholly at a loss in what manner to act in this affair."

"You must make known to the King," says the hen-wife, "that you heard of his sons, and wonder greatly that he concealed them all this time from you; tell him you wish to see them, and that it is full time for them to be liberated, and that you would be desirous he would bring them to the Court. The King will then do so, and there will be a great feast prepared on that account, and also diversions of every sort to amuse the people; and in these sports," said she, "ask the King's sons to play a game at cards with you, which they will not refuse. Now," says the hen-wife, "you must make a bargain, that if you win they must do whatever you command them, and if they win, that you must do whatever they command you to do; this bargain must be made before the assembly, and here is a pack of cards," says she, "that I am thinking you will not lose by."

The Queen immediately took the cards, and, after returning the hen-wife thanks for her kind instruction, went back to the palace, where she was quite uneasy until she got speaking to the King in regard of his children; at last she broke it off to him in a very polite and engaging manner, so that he could see no muster or design in it. He readily consented to her desire, and his sons were sent for to the tower, who gladly came to Court, rejoicing that they were freed from such confinement. They were all very handsome, and very expert in all arts and exercises, so that they gained the love and esteem of all that had seen them.

The Queen, more jealous with them than ever, thought it an age until all the feasting and rejoicing was over, that she might get making her proposal, depending greatly on the power of the hen-wife's cards. At length this royal assembly began to sport and play at all kinds of diversions, and the Queen very cunningly challenged the three Princes to play at cards with her, making bargain with them as she had been instructed.

They accepted the challenge, and the eldest son and she played the first game, which she won; then the second son played, and she won that game likewise; the third son and she then played the last game, and he won it, which sorely grieved her that she had not him in her power as well as the rest, being by far the handsomest and most beloved of the three.

However, everyone was anxious to hear the Queen's commands in regard to the two Princes, not thinking that she had any ill design in her head against them. Whether it was the hen-wife instructed her, or whether it was from her own knowledge, I cannot tell; but she gave out they must go and bring her the Knight of the Glen's wild Steed of Bells, or they should lose their heads.

The young Princes were not in the least concerned, not knowing what they had to do; but the whole Court was amazed at her demand, knowing very well that it was impossible for them ever to get the steed, as all that ever sought him perished in the attempt. However, they could not retract the bargain, and the youngest Prince was desired to tell what demand he had on the Queen, as he had won his game.

"My brothers," says he, "are now going to travel, and, as I understand, a perilous journey wherein they know not what road to take or what may happen them. I am resolved, therefore, not to stay here, but to go with them, let what will betide; and I request and command, according to my bargain, that the Queen shall stand on the highest tower of the palace until we come back (or find out that we are certainly dead), with nothing but sheaf corn for her food and cold water for her drink, if it should be for seven years and longer."

All things being now fixed, the three princes departed the Court in search of the Knight of the Glen's palace, and travelling along the road they came up with a man who was a little lame, and seemed to be somewhat advanced in years; they soon fell into discourse, and the youngest of the princes asked the stranger his name, or what was the reason he wore so remarkable a black cap as he saw on him.

"I am called," said he, "the Thief of Sloan, and sometimes the Black Thief from my cap"; and so telling the prince the most of his adventures, he asked him again where they were bound for, or what they were about.

The prince, willing to gratify his request, told him their affairs from the beginning to the end. "And now," said he, "we are travelling, and do not know whether we are on the right road or not."

"Ah! My brave fellows," says the Black Thief, "you little know the danger you run. I am after that steed myself these seven years, and can never steal him on account of a silk covering he has on him in the stable, with sixty bells fixed to it, and whenever you approach the place he quickly observes it and shakes himself; which, by the sound of the bells, not only alarms the prince and his guards, but the whole country round, so that it is impossible ever to get him, and those that are so unfortunate as to be taken by the Knight of the Glen are boiled in a red-hot fiery furnace."

"Bless me," says the young prince, "what will we do? If we return without the steed we will lose our heads, so I see we are ill fixed on both sides."

"Well," says the Thief of Sloan, "if it were my case I would rather die by the Knight than by the wicked Queen; besides, I will go with you myself and show you the road, and whatever fortune you will have, I will take chance of the same."

They returned him sincere thanks for his kindness, and he, being well acquainted with the road, in a short time brought them within view of the knight's castle.

"Now," says he, "we must stay here till night comes; for I know all the ways of the place, and if there be any chance for it, it is when they are all at rest; for the steed is all the watch the knight keeps there."

Accordingly, in the dead hour of the night, the King's three sons and the Thief of Sloan attempted the Steed of Bells in order to carry him away, but before they could reach the stables the steed neighed most terribly and shook himself so, and the bells rung with such noise, that the knight and all his men were up in a moment.

The Black Thief and the King's sons thought to make their escape, but they were suddenly surrounded by the knight's guards and taken prisoners; where they were brought into that dismal part of the palace where the knight kept a furnace always boiling, in which he threw all offenders that ever came in his way, which in a few moments would entirely consume them.

"Audacious villains!" says the Knight of the Glen, "how dare you attempt so bold an action as to steal my steed? See, now, the reward of your folly; for your greater punishment I will not boil you all together, but one after the other, so that he that survives may witness the dire afflictions of his unfortunate companions."

So saying he ordered his servants to stir up the fire: "We will boil the eldest-looking of these young men first," said he, "and so on to the last, which will be this old champion with the black cap. He seems to be the captain, and looks as if he had come through many toils."

"I was as near death once as the prince is yet," says the Black Thief, "and escaped; and so will he too."

"No, you never were," said the knight; "for he is within two or three minutes of his latter end."

"But," says the Black Thief, "I was within one moment of my death, and I am here yet."

"How was that?" says the knight; "I would be glad to hear it, for it seems impossible."

"If you think, sir knight," says the Black Thief, "that the danger I was in surpasses that of this young man, will you pardon him his crime?"

"I will," says the knight, "so go on with your story."

"I was, sir," says he, "a very wild boy in my youth, and came through many distresses; once in particular, as I was on my rambling, I was benighted and could find no lodging. At length I came to an old kiln, and being much fatigued I went up and lay on the ribs. I had not been long there when I saw three witches coming in with three bags of gold. Each put their bags of gold under their heads, as if to sleep. I heard one of them say to the other that if the Black Thief came on them while they slept, he would not leave them a penny. I found by their discourse that everybody had got my name into their mouth, though I kept silent as death during their discourse. At length they fell fast asleep, and then I stole softly down, and seeing some turf convenient, I placed one under each of their heads, and off I went, with their gold, as fast as I could.

"I had not gone far," continued the Thief of Sloan, "until I saw a grey-hound, a hare, and a hawk in pursuit of me, and began to think it must be the witches that had taken the shapes in order that I might not escape them unseen either by land or water. Seeing they did not appear in any formidable shape, I was more than once resolved to attack them, thinking that with my broad sword I could easily destroy them. But considering again that it was perhaps still in their power to become alive again, I gave over the attempt and climbed with difficulty up a tree, bringing my sword in my hand and all the gold along with me. However, when they came to the tree they found what I had done, and making further use of their hellish art, one of them was changed into a smith's anvil and another into a piece of iron, of which the third soon made a hatchet. Having the hatchet made, she fell to cutting down the tree, and in the course of an hour it began to shake with me. At length it began to bend, and I found that one or two blows at the most would put it down. I then began to think that my death was inevitable, considering that those who were capable of doing so much would soon end my life; but just as she had the stroke drawn that would terminate my fate, the cock crew, and the witches disappeared, having resumed their natural shapes for fear of being known, and I got safe off with my bags of gold.

"Now, sir," says he to the Knight of the Glen, "if that be not as great an adventure as ever you heard, to be within one blow of a hatchet of my end, and that blow even drawn, and after all to escape, I leave it to yourself."

"Well, I cannot say but it is very extraordinary," says the Knight of the Glen, "and on that account pardon this young man his crime; so stir up the fire, till I boil this second one."

"Indeed," says the Black Thief, "I would fain think he would not die this time either."

"How so?" says the knight; "it is impossible for him to escape."

"I escaped death more wonderfully myself," says the Thief of Sloan, "than if you had him ready to throw into the furnace, and I hope it will be the case with him likewise."

"Why, have you been in another great danger?" says the knight. "I would be glad to hear the story too, and if it be as wonderful as the last, I will pardon this young man as I did the other."

"My way of living, sir," says the Black Thief, "was not good, as I told you before; and being at a certain time fairly run out of cash, and meeting with no enterprise worthy of notice, I was reduced to great straits. At length a rich bishop died in the neighbourhood I was then in, and I heard he was interred with a great deal of jewels and rich robes upon him, all which I intended in a short time to be master of. Accordingly that very night I set about it, and coming to the place, I understood he was placed at the further end of a long dark vault, which I slowly entered. I had not gone in far until I heard a foot coming towards me with a quick pace, and although naturally bold and daring, yet, thinking of the deceased bishop and the crime I was engaged in, I lost courage, and ran towards the entrance of the vault. I had retreated but a few paces when I observed, between me and the light, the figure of a tall black man standing in the entrance. Being in great fear and not knowing how to pass, I fired a pistol at him, and he immediately fell across the entrance. Perceiving he still retained the figure of a mortal man, I began to imagine that it could not be the bishop's ghost; recovering myself therefore from the fear I was in, I ventured to the upper end of the vault, where I found a large bundle, and upon further examination I found that the corpse was already rifled, and that which I had taken to be a ghost was no more than one of his own clergy. I was then very sorry that I had the misfortune to kill him, but it then could not be helped. I took up the bundle that contained everything belonging to the corpse that was valuable, intending to take my departure from this melancholy abode; but just as I came to the mouth of the entrance I saw the guards of the place coming towards me, and distinctly heard them saying that they would look in the vault, for that the Black Thief would think little of robbing the corpse if he was anywhere in the place. I did not then know in what manner to act, for if I was seen I would surely lose my life, as everybody had a look-out at that time, and because there was no person bold enough to come in on me. I knew very well on the first sight of me that could be got, I would be shot like a dog. However, I had not time to lose. I took and raised up the man which I had killed, as if he was standing on his feet, and I, crouching behind him, bore him up as well as I could, so that the guards readily saw him as they came up to the vault. Seeing the man in black, one of the men cried that was the Black Thief, and, presenting his piece, fired at the man, at which I let him fall, and crept into a little dark corner myself, that was at the entrance of the place. When they saw the man fall, they ran all into the vault, and never stopped until they were at the end of it, for fear, as I thought, that there might be some others along with him that was killed. But while they were busy inspecting the corpse and the vault to see what they could miss, I slipped out, and, once away, and still away; but they never had the Black Thief in their power since."

"Well, my brave fellow," says the Knight of the Glen, "I see you have come through many dangers: you have freed these two princes by your stories; but I am sorry myself that this young prince has to suffer for all. Now, if you could tell me something as wonderful as you have told already, I would pardon him likewise; I pity this youth and do not want to put him to death if I could help it."

"That happens well," says the Thief of Sloan, "for I like him best myself, and have reserved the most curious passage for the last on his account."

"Well, then," says the knight, "let us hear it."

"I was one day on my travels," says the Black Thief, "and I came into a large forest, where I wandered a long time, and could not get out of it. At length I came to a large castle, and fatigue obliged me to call in the same, where I found a young woman and a child sitting on her knee, and she crying. I asked her what made her cry, and where the lord of the castle was, for I wondered greatly that I saw no stir of servants or any person about the place.

"'It is well for you,' says the young woman, 'that the lord of this castle is not at home at present; for he is a monstrous giant, with but one eye on his forehead, who lives on human flesh. He brought me this child,' says she, 'I do not know where he got it, and ordered me to make it into a pie, and I cannot help crying at the command.'

"I told her that if she knew of any place convenient that I could leave the child safely I would do it, rather than it should be killed by such a monster.

"She told me of a house a distance off where I would get a woman who would take care of it. 'But what will I do in regard of the pie?'

"'Cut a finger off it,' said I, 'and I will bring you in a young wild pig out of the forest, which you may dress as if it was the child, and put the finger in a certain place, that if the giant doubts anything about it you may know where to turn it over at the first, and when he sees it he will be fully satisfied that the pie is made of the child.'

"She agreed to the scheme I proposed, and, cutting off the child's finger, by her direction I soon had it at the house she told me of, and brought her the little pig in the place of it. She then made ready the pie, and after eating and drinking heartily myself, I was just taking my leave of the young woman when we observed the giant coming through the castle gates.

"'Bless me,' said she, 'what will you do now? Run away and lie down among the dead bodies that he has in the room (showing me the place), and strip off your clothes that he may not know you from the rest if he has occasion to go that way.'

"I took her advice, and laid myself down among the rest, as if dead, to see how he would behave. The first thing I heard was him calling for his pie. When she set it down before him he swore it smelled like swine's flesh, but knowing where to find the finger, she immediately turned it up, which fairly convinced him of the contrary. The pie only served to sharpen his appetite, and I heard him sharpening his knife and saying he must have a collop or two, for he was not near satisfied. But what was my terror when I heard the giant groping among the bodies, and, fancying myself, cut the half of my hip off, and took it with him to be roasted. You may be certain I was in great pain, but the fear of being killed prevented me from making any complaint. However, when he had eaten all he began to drink hot liquors in great abundance, so that in a short time he could not hold up his head, but threw himself on a large creel he had made for the purpose, and fell fast asleep. When I heard him snoring, as I was I went up and caused the woman to bind my wound with a handkerchief; and, taking the giant's spit, reddened it in the fire, and ran it through the eye, but was not able to kill him.

"However, I left the spit sticking in his head, and took to my heels; but I soon found he was in pursuit of me, although blind; and having an enchanted ring he threw it at me, and it fell on my big toe and remained fastened to it.

"The giant then called to the ring, where it was, and to my great surprise it made him answer on my foot; and he, guided by the same, made a leap at me which I had the good luck to observe, and fortunately escaped the danger. However, I found running was of no use in saving me, as long as I had the ring on my foot; so I took my sword and cut off the toe it was fastened on, and threw both into a large fish-pond that was convenient. The giant called again to the ring, which by the power of enchantment always made him answer; but he, not knowing what I had done, imagined it was still on some part of me, and made a violent leap to seize me, when he went into the pond, over head and ears, and was drowned. Now, sir knight," says the Thief of Sloan, "you see what dangers I came through and always escaped; but, indeed, I am lame for the want of my toe ever since."

"My lord and master," says an old woman that was listening all the time, "that story is but too true, as I well know, for I am the very woman that was in the giant's castle, and you, my lord, the child that I was to make into a pie; and this is the very man that saved your life, which you may know by the want of your finger that was taken off, as you have heard, to deceive the giant."

The Knight of the Glen, greatly surprised at what he had heard the old woman tell, and knowing he wanted his finger from his childhood, began to understand that the story was true enough.

"And is this my deliverer?" says he. "O brave fellow, I not only pardon you all, but will keep you with myself while you live, where you shall feast like princes, and have every attendance that I have myself."

They all returned thanks on their knees, and the Black Thief told him the reason they attempted to steal the Steed of Bells, and the necessity they were under in going home.

"Well," says the Knight of the Glen, "if that's the case I bestow you my steed rather than this brave fellow should die; so you may go when you please, only remember to call and see me betimes, that we may know each other well."

They promised they would, and with great joy they set off for the King their father's palace, and the Black Thief along with them.

The wicked Queen was standing all this time on the tower, and, hearing the bells ringing at a great distance off, knew very well it was the princes coming home, and the steed with them, and through spite and vexation precipitated herself from the tower and was shattered to pieces.

The three princes lived happy and well during their father's reign, and always keeping the Black Thief along with them; but how they did after the old King's death is not known.

Lawn Dyarrig and the Knight of Terrible Valley

THERE WAS A KING in his own time in Erin, and he went hunting one day. The King met a man whose head was out through his cap, whose elbows and knees were out through his clothing, and whose toes were out through his shoes. The man went up to the King, gave him a blow on the face, and drove three teeth from his mouth. The same blow put the King's head in the dirt. When he rose from the earth, the King went back to his castle, and lay down sick and sorrowful.

The King had three sons, and their names were Ur, Arthur, and Lawn Dyarrig. The three were at school that day, and came home in the evening. The father sighed when the sons were coming in.

"What is wrong with our father?" asked the eldest.

"Your father is sick on his bed," said the mother.

The three sons went to their father and asked what was on him.

"A strong man that I met today gave me a blow in the face, put my head in the dirt, and knocked three teeth from my mouth. What would you do to him if you met him?" asked the father of the eldest son.

"If I met that man," replied Ur, "I would make four parts of him between four horses."

You are my son," said the King. "What would you do if you met him?" asked he then as he turned to the second son.

"If I had a grip on that man I would burn him between four fires."

"You, too, are my son. What would you do?" asked the King of Lawn Dyarrig.

"If I met that man, I would do my best against him, and he might not stand long before me."

"You are not my son. I would not lose lands or property on you," said the father. "You must go from me, and leave this tomorrow."

On the following morning the three brothers rose with the dawn; the order was given Lawn Dyarrig to leave the castle and make his own way for himself. The other two brothers were going to travel the world to know could they find the man who had injured their father. Lawn Dyarrig lingered outside till he saw the two, and they going off by themselves.

"It is a strange thing," said he, "for two men of high degree to go travelling without a servant."

"We need no one," said Ur.

"Company wouldn't harm us," said Arthur.

The two let Lawn Dyarrig go with them as a serving-boy, and set out to find the man who had struck down their father. They spent all that day walking, and came late to a house where one woman was living. She shook hands with Ur and Arthur, and greeted them. Lawn Dyarrig she kissed and welcomed; called him son of the King of Erin.

"It is a strange thing to shake hands with the elder, and kiss the younger," said Ur.

"This is a story to tell," said the woman, "the same as if your death were in it."

They made three parts of that night. The first part they spent in conversation, the second in telling tales, the third in eating and drinking, with sound sleep and sweet slumber. As early as the day dawned next morning the old woman was up, and had food for the young men. When the three had eaten, she spoke to Ur, and this is what she asked of him: "What was it that drove you from home, and what brought you to this place?"

"A champion met my father, and took three teeth from him and put his head in the dirt. I am looking for that man, to find him alive or dead."

"That was the Green Knight from Terrible Valley. He is the man who took the three teeth from your father. I am three hundred years living in this place, and there is not a year of the three hundred in which three hundred heroes, fresh, young, and noble, have not passed on the way to Terrible Valley, and never have I seen one coming back, and each of them had the look of a man better than you. And now where are you going, Arthur?"

"I am on the same journey with my brother."

"Where are you going, Lawn Dyarrig?"

"I am going with these as a servant," said Lawn Dyarrig.

God's help to you, it's bad clothing that's on your body," said the woman. "And now I will speak to Ur. A day and a year since a champion passed this way. He wore a suit as good as was ever above ground. I had a daughter sewing there in the open window. He came outside, put a finger under her girdle, and took her with him. Her father followed straightway to save her, but I have never seen daughter nor father from that day to this. That man was the Green Knight of Terrible Valley. He is better than all the men that could stand on a field a mile in length and a mile in breadth. If you take my advice you'll turn back and go home to your father."

'Tis how she vexed Ur with this talk, and he made a vow to himself to go on. When Ur did not agree to turn home, the woman said to Lawn Dyarrig, "Go back to my chamber; you'll find in it the apparel of a hero."

He went back, and there was not a bit of the apparel he did not go into with a spring.

"You may be able to do something now," said the woman, when Lawn Dyarrig came to the front. "Go back to my chamber and search through all the old swords. You will find one at the bottom. Take that."

He found the old sword, and at the first shake that he gave he knocked seven barrels of rust out of it; after the second shake it was as bright as when made.

"You may be able to do well with that," said the woman. "Go out, now, to that stable abroad, and take the slim white steed that is in it. That one will never stop nor halt in any place till he brings you to the Eastern World. If you like, take these two men behind you; if not, let them walk. But I think it is useless for you to have them at all with you."

Lawn Dyarrig went out to the stable, took the slim white steed, mounted, rode to the front, and catching the two brothers, planted them on the horse behind him.

"Now, Lawn Dyarrig," said the woman, "this horse will never stop till he stands on the little white meadow in the Eastern World. When he stops, you'll come down, and cut the turf under his beautiful right front foot."

The horse started from the door, and at every leap he crossed seven hills and valleys, seven castles with villages, acres, roods, and odd perches. He could overtake the whirlwind before him seven hundred times before the whirlwind behind him could overtake him once. Early in the afternoon of the next day he was in the Eastern World.

When he dismounted, Lawn Dyarrig cut the sod from under the foot of the slim white steed, in the name of the Father, Son, and Holy Ghost, and Terrible Valley was down under him there. What he did next was to tighten the reins on the neck of the steed and let him go home.

"Now," said Lawn Dyarrig to his brothers, "which would you rather be doing – making a basket or twisting gads (withes)?"

"We would rather be making a basket; our help is among ourselves," answered they.

Ur and Arthur went at the basket and Lawn Dyarrig at twisting the gads. When Lawn Dyarrig came to the opening with the gads all twisted and made into one, they hadn't the ribs of the basket in the ground yet.

"Oh, then, haven't ye anything done but that?"

"Stop your mouth," said Ur, "or we'll make a mortar of your head on the next stone."

"To be kind to one another is the best for us," said Lawn Dyarrig. "I'll make the basket."

While they'd be putting one rod in the basket he had the basket finished.

"Oh, brother," said they, "you are a quick workman."

They had not called him brother since they left home till that moment.

"Who will go in the basket now?" said Lawn Dyarrig when it was finished and the gad tied to it.

"Who but me?" said Ur. "I am sure, brothers, if I see anything to frighten me you'll draw me up."

"We will," said the other two.

He went in, but had not gone far when he cried to pull him up again.

"By my father, and the tooth of my father, and by all that is in Erin, dead or alive, I would not give one other sight on Terrible Valley!" he cried, when he stepped out of the basket.

"Who will go now?" said Lawn Dyarrig.

"Who will go but me?" answered Arthur.

Whatever length Ur went, Arthur didn't go the half of it.

"By my father, and the tooth of my father, I wouldn't give another look at Terrible Valley for all that's in Erin, dead or alive!"

"I will go now," said Lawn Dyarrig, "and as I put no foul play on you, I hope ye'll not put foul play on me."

"We will not, indeed," said they.

Whatever length the other two went, Lawn Dyarrig didn't go the half of it, till he stepped out of the basket and went down on his own feet. It was not far he had travelled in Terrible Valley when he met seven hundred heroes guarding the country.

"In what place here has the Green King his castle?" asked he of the seven hundred.

"What sort of a sprisawn goat or sheep from Erin are you?" asked they.

"If we had a hold of you, the two arms of me, that's a question you would not put a second time; but if we haven't you, we'll not be so long."

They faced Lawn Dyarrig then and attacked him; but he went through them like a hawk or a raven through small birds. He made a heap of their feet, a heap of their heads, and a castle of their arms.

After that he went his way walking, and had not gone far when he came to a spring. "I'll have a drink before I go further," thought he. With that he stooped down and took a drink of the water. When he had drunk he lay on the ground and fell asleep.

Now, there wasn't a morning that the lady in the Green Knight's castle didn't wash in the water of that spring, and she sent a maid for the water each time. Whatever part of the day it was when Lawn Dyarrig fell asleep, he was sleeping in the morning when the girl came. She thought it was dead the man was, and she was so in dread of him that she would not come near the spring for a long time. At last she saw he was asleep, and then she took the water. Her mistress was complaining of her for being so long.

"Do not blame me," said the maid.

"I am sure that if it was yourself that was in my place you'd not come back so soon."

"How so?" asked the lady.

"The finest hero that ever a woman laid eyes on is sleeping at the spring."

"That's a thing that cannot be till Lawn Dyarrig comes to the age of a hero. When that time comes he'll be sleeping at the spring."

"He is in it now," said the girl.

The lady did not stop to get any drop of the water on herself, but ran quickly from the castle. When she came to the spring she roused Lawn Dyarrig. If she found him lying, she left him standing. She smothered him with kisses, drowned him with tears, dried him with garments of fine silk and with her own hair. Herself and himself locked arms and walked into the castle of the Green Knight. After that they were inviting each other with the best food and entertainment till the middle of the following day. Then the lady said:

"When the Green Knight bore me away from my father and mother he brought me straight to this castle, but I put him under bonds not to marry me for seven years and a day, and he cannot; still, I must serve him. When he goes fowling he spends three days away and the next three days at home. This is the day for him to come back, and for me to prepare his dinner. There is no stir that you or I have made here today but that brass head beyond there will tell of it."

"It is equal to you what it tells," said Lawn Dyarrig, "only make ready a clean long chamber for me."

She did so, and he went back into it. Herself rose up then to prepare dinner for the Green Knight. When he came, she welcomed him as every day. She left down his food before him, and he sat to take his dinner. He was sitting with knife and fork in hand when the brass head spoke. "I thought when I saw you taking food and drink with your wife that you had the blood of a man in you. If you could see that sprisawn of a goat or sheep out of Erin taking meat and drink with her all day, what would you do?"

"Oh, my suffering and sorrow!" cried the knight. "I'll never take another bite or sup till I eat some of his liver and heart. Let three hundred heroes, fresh and young, go back and bring his heart to me, with the liver and lights, till I eat them."

The three hundred heroes went, and hardly were they behind in the chamber when Lawn Dyarrig had them all dead in one heap.

"He must have some exercise to delay my men, they are so long away," said the knight. "Let three hundred more heroes go for his heart, with the liver and lights, and bring them here to me."

The second three hundred went, and as they were entering the chamber Lawn Dyarrig was making a heap of them, till the last one was inside, where there were two heaps.

"He has some way of coaxing my men to delay," said the knight. "Do you go now, three hundred of my savage hirelings, and bring him." The three hundred savage hirelings went, and Lawn Dyarrig let every man of them enter before he raised a hand, then he caught the bulkiest of them all by the two ankles, and began to wallop the others with him, and he walloped them till he drove the life out of the two hundred and ninety-nine. The bulkiest one was worn to the shin-bones that Lawn Dyarrig held in his two hands. The Green Knight, who thought Lawn Dyarrig was coaxing the men, called out then, "Come down, my men, and take dinner."

"I'll be with you," said Lawn Dyarrig, "and have the best food in the house, and I'll have the best bed in the house. God not be good to you for it, either."

He went down to the Green Knight, and took the food from before him and put it before himself. Then he took the lady, set her on his own knee, and he and she went on eating. After dinner he put his finger under her girdle, took her to the best chamber in the castle, and stood on guard upon it till morning. Before dawn the lady said to Lawn Dyarrig:

"If the Green Knight strikes the pole of combat first, he'll win the day; if you strike first, you'll win if you do what I tell you. The Green Knight has so much enchantment that if he sees it is going against him the battle is, he'll rise like a fog in the air, come down in the same form, strike you, and make a green stone of you. When yourself and himself are going out to fight in the morning, cut a sod a perch long, in the name of the Father, Son, and Holy Ghost; you'll leave the sod on the next little hillock you meet. When the Green Knight is coming down and is ready to strike, give him a blow with the sod. You'll make a green stone of him."

As early as the dawn Lawn Dyarrig rose and struck the pole of combat. The blow that he gave did not leave calf, foal, lamb, kid, or child waiting for birth, without turning them five times to the left and five times to the right.

"What do you want?" asked the knight.

"All that's in your kingdom to be against me the first quarter of the day, and yourself the second quarter.

"You have not left in the kingdom now but myself, and it is early enough for you that I'll be at you."

The knight faced him, and they went at each other, and fought till late in the day. The battle was strong against Lawn Dyarrig, when the lady stood in the door of the castle.

"Increase on your blows and increase on your courage," cried she. "There is no woman here but myself to wail over you, or to stretch you before burial."

When the knight heard the voice he rose in the air like a lump of fog. As he was coming down Lawn Dyarrig struck him with the sod on the right side of his breast, and made a green stone of him.

The lady rushed out then, and whatever welcome she had for Lawn Dyarrig the first time, she had twice as much now. Herself and himself went into the castle, and spent that night very comfortably. In the morning they rose early, and collected all the gold, utensils, and treasures. Lawn Dyarrig found the three teeth of his father in a pocket of the Green Knight, and took them. He and the lady brought all the riches to where the basket was. "If I send up this beautiful lady," thought Lawn Dyarrig, "she may be taken from me by my brothers; if I remain below with her, she may be taken from me by people here." He put her in the basket, and she gave him a ring so that they might know each other if they met. He shook the gad, and she rose in the basket.

When Ur saw the basket, he thought, "What's above let it be above, and what's below let it stay where it is."

"I'll have you as wife for ever for myself," said he to the lady.

"I put you under bonds," says she, "not to lay a hand on me for a day and three years."

"That itself would not be long even if twice the time," said Ur.

The two brothers started home with the lady; on the way Ur found the head of an old horse with teeth in it, and took them, saying, "These will be my father's three teeth."

They travelled on, and reached home at last. Ur would not have left a tooth in his father's mouth, trying to put in the three that he had brought; but the father stopped him.

Lawn Dyarrig, left in Terrible Valley, began to walk around for himself. He had been walking but one day when whom should he meet but the lad Short-clothes, and he saluted him. "By what way can I leave Terrible Valley?" asked Lawn Dyarrig.

"If I had a grip on you that's what you wouldn't ask me a second time," said Short-clothes.

"If you haven't touched me, you will before you are much older."

"If you do, you will not treat me as you did all my people and my master."

"I'll do worse to you than I did to them," said Lawn Dyarrig.

They caught each other then, one grip under the arm and one on the shoulder. 'Tis not long they were wrestling when Lawn Dyarrig had Short-clothes on the earth, and he gave him the five thin tyings dear and tight.

"You are the best hero I have ever met," said Short-clothes; "give me quarter for my soul – spare me. When I did not tell you of my own will, I must tell in spite of myself."

"It is as easy for me to loosen you as to tie you," said Lawn Dyarrig, and he freed him.

"Since you are not dead now," said Short-clothes, "there is no death allotted to you. I'll find a way for you to leave Terrible Valley. Go and take that old bridle hanging there beyond and shake it; whatever beast comes and puts its head into the bridle will carry you."

Lawn Dyarrig shook the bridle, and a dirty, shaggy little foal came and put its head in the bridle. Lawn Dyarrig mounted, dropped the reins on the foal's neck, and let him take his own choice of roads. The foal brought Lawn Dyarrig out by another way to the upper world, and took him to Erin. Lawn Dyarrig stopped some distance from his father's castle, and knocked at the house of an old weaver.

"Who are you?" asked the old man.

"I am a weaver," said Lawn Dyarrig.

"What can you do?"

"I can spin for twelve and twist for twelve."

"This is a very good man," said the old weaver to his sons, "let us try him."

The work they had been doing for a year he had done in one hour. When dinner was over the old man began to wash and shave, and his two sons began to do the same.

"Why is this?" asked Lawn Dyarrig.

"Haven't you heard that Ur, son of the King, is to marry tonight the woman that he took from the Green Knight of Terrible Valley?"

"I have not," said Lawn Dyarrig; "as all are going to the wedding, I suppose I may go without offence?"

"Oh, you may," said the weaver; "there will be a hundred thousand welcomes before you."

"Are there any linen sheets within?"

"There are," said the weaver.

"It is well to have bags ready for yourself and two sons."

The weaver made bags for the three very quickly. They went to the wedding. Lawn Dyarrig put what dinner was on the first table into the weaver's bag, and sent the old man home with it. The food of the second table he put in the eldest son's bag, filled the second son's bag from the third table, and sent the two home.

The complaint went to Ur that an impudent stranger was taking all the food.

"It is not right to turn any man away," said the bridegroom, "but if that stranger does not mind he will be thrown out of the castle."

"Let me look at the face of the disturber," said the bride.

"Go and bring the fellow who is troubling the guests," said Ur to the servants.

Lawn Dyarrig was brought right away, and stood before the bride, who filled a glass with wine and gave it to him. Lawn Dyarrig drank half the wine, and dropped in the ring which the lady had given him in Terrible Valley.

When the bride took the glass again the ring went of itself with one leap on to her finger. She knew then who was standing before her.

"This is the man who conquered the Green Knight and saved me from Terrible Valley," said she to the King of Erin; "this is Lawn Dyarrig, your son."

Lawn Dyarrig took out the three teeth and put them in his father's mouth. They fitted there perfectly, and grew into their old place. The King was satisfied, and as the lady would marry no man but Lawn Dyarrig, he was the bridegroom.

"I must give you a present," said the bride to the Queen. "Here is a beautiful scarf which you are to wear as a girdle this evening."

The Queen put the scarf round her waist.

"Tell me now," said the bride to the Queen, "who was Ur's father."

"What father could he have but his own father, the King of Erin?"

"Tighten, scarf," said the bride.

That moment the Queen thought that her head was in the sky and the lower half of her body down deep in the earth.

"Oh, my grief and my woe!" cried the Queen.

"Answer my question in truth, and the scarf will stop squeezing you. Who was Ur's father?"

"The gardener," said the Queen.

"Whose son is Arthur?"

"The King's son."

"Tighten, scarf," said the bride.

If the Queen suffered before, she suffered twice as much this time, and screamed for help.

"Answer me truly, and you'll be without pain; if not, death will be on you this minute. Whose son is Arthur?"

"The swineherd's."

"Who is the King's son?"

"The King has no son but Lawn Dyarrig."

"Tighten, scarf."

The scarf did not tighten, and if the Queen had been commanding it a day and a year it would not have tightened, for the Queen told the truth that time. When the wedding was over, the King gave Lawn Dyarrig half his kingdom, and made Ur and Arthur his servants.

Fairies
&
Sea-Folk

Introduction

IN HIS BOOKS on fairies, Yeats tell us that the Irish word for fairy is sheehogue (*sidheóg*), a diminutive of 'shee' in banshee, and that fairies are deenee shee (*daoine sidh* – fairy people). This section covers both of what Yeats defines as 'trooping fairies' and 'solitary fairies', along with their often mischievous and fickle ways. Towards the end of the chapter we also turn to the watery depths of the sea, with classic Irish stories of sea-people, mermaids and selkies.

The Golden Spears

ONCE UPON A TIME there lived in a little house under a hill a little old woman and her two children, whose names were Connla and Nora. Right in front of the door of the little house lay a pleasant meadow, and beyond the meadow rose up to the skies a mountain whose top was sharp-pointed like a spear. For more than half-way up it was clad with heather, and when the heather was in bloom it looked like a purple robe falling from the shoulders of the mountain down to its feet. Above the heather it was bare and grey, but when the sun was sinking in the sea, its last rays rested on the bare mountain top and made it gleam like a spear of gold, and so the children always called it the 'Golden Spear'.

In summer days they gambolled in the meadow, plucking the sweet wild grasses – and often and often they clambered up the mountain side, knee deep in the heather, searching for frechans and wild honey, and sometimes they found a bird's nest – but they only peeped into it, they never touched the eggs or allowed their breath to fall upon them, for next to their little mother they loved the mountain, and next to the mountain they loved the wild birds who made the spring and summer weather musical with their songs.

Sometimes the soft white mist would steal through the glen, and creeping up the mountain would cover it with a veil so dense that the children could not see it, and then they would say to each other: "Our mountain is gone away from us." But when the mist would lift and float off into the skies, the children would clap their hands, and say: "Oh, there's our mountain back again."

In the long nights of winter they babbled of the spring and summertime to come, when the birds would once more sing for them, and never a day passed that they didn't fling crumbs outside their door, and on the borders of the wood that stretched away towards the glen.

When the spring days came they awoke with the first light of the morning, and they knew the very minute when the lark would begin to sing, and when the thrush and the blackbird would pour out their liquid notes, and when the robin would make the soft, green, tender leaves tremulous at his song.

It chanced one day that when they were resting in the noontide heat, under the perfumed shade of a hawthorn in bloom, they saw on the edge of the meadow, spread out before them, a speckled thrush cowering in the grass.

"Oh, Connla! Connla! Look at the thrush – and, look, look up in the sky, there is a hawk!" cried Nora.

Connla looked up, and he saw the hawk with quivering wings, and he knew that in a second it would pounce down on the frightened thrush. He jumped to his feet, fixed a stone in his sling, and before the whirr of the stone shooting through the air was silent, the stricken hawk tumbled headlong in the grass.

The thrush, shaking its wings, rose joyously in the air, and perching upon an elm-tree in sight of the children, he sang a song so sweet that they left the hawthorn shade and

walked along together until they stood under the branches of the elm; and they listened and listened to the thrush's song, and at last Nora said:

"Oh, Connla! Did you ever hear a song so sweet as this?"

"No," said Connla, "and I do believe sweeter music was never heard before."

"Ah," said the thrush, "that's because you never heard the nine little pipers playing. And now, Connla and Nora, you saved my life today."

"It was Nora saved it," said Connla, "for she pointed you out to me, and also pointed out the hawk which was about to pounce on you."

"It was Connla saved you," said Nora, "for he slew the hawk with his sling."

"I owe my life to both of you," said the thrush. "You like my song, and you say you have never heard anything so sweet; but wait till you hear the nine little pipers playing."

"And when shall we hear them?" said the children.

"Well," said the thrush, "sit outside your door tomorrow evening, and wait and watch until the shadows have crept up the heather, and then, when the mountain top is gleaming like a golden spear, look at the line where the shadow on the heather meets the sunshine, and you shall see what you shall see."

And having said this, the thrush sang another song sweeter than the first, and then saying "goodbye", he flew away into the woods.

The children went home, and all night long they were dreaming of the thrush and the nine little pipers; and when the birds sang in the morning, they got up and went out into the meadow to watch the mountain.

The sun was shining in a cloudless sky, and no shadows lay on the mountain, and all day long they watched and waited, and at last, when the birds were singing their farewell song to the evening star, the children saw the shadows marching from the glen, trooping up the mountainside and dimming the purple of the heather.

And when the mountain top gleamed like a golden spear, they fixed their eyes on the line between the shadow and the sunshine.

"Now," said Connla, "the time has come."

"Oh, look! Look!" said Nora, and as she spoke, just above the line of shadow a door opened out, and through its portals came a little piper dressed in green and gold. He stepped down, followed by another and another, until they were nine in all, and then the door slung back again. Down through the heather marched the pipers in single file, and all the time they played a music so sweet that the birds, who had gone to sleep in their nests, came out upon the branches to listen to them and then they crossed the meadow, and they went on and on until they disappeared in the leafy woods.

While they were passing the children were spell-bound, and couldn't speak, but when the music had died away in the woods, they said:

"The thrush is right, that is the sweetest music that was ever heard in all the world."

And when the children went to bed that night the fairy music came to them in their dreams. But when the morning broke, and they looked out upon their mountain and could see no trace of the door above the heather, they asked each other whether they had really seen the little pipers, or only dreamt of them.

That day they went out into the woods, and they sat beside a stream that pattered along beneath the trees, and through the leaves tossing in the breeze the sun flashed down upon the streamlet, and shadow and sunshine danced upon it. As the children watched the water sparkling where the sunlight fell, Nora said:

"Oh, Connla, did you ever see anything so bright and clear and glancing as that?"

"No," said Connla, "I never did."

"That's because you never saw the crystal hall of the fairy of the mountains," said a voice above the heads of the children.

And when they looked up, who should they see perched on a branch but the thrush.

"And where is the crystal hall of the fairy?" said Connla.

"Oh, it is where it always was, and where it always will be," said the thrush. "And you can see it if you like."

"We would like to see it," said the children.

"Well, then," said the thrush, "if you would, all you have to do is to follow the nine little pipers when they come down through the heather, and cross the meadow tomorrow evening."

And the thrush having said this, flew away.

Connla and Nora went home, and that night they fell asleep talking of the thrush and the fairy and the crystal hall.

All the next day they counted the minutes, until they saw the shadows thronging from the glen and scaling the mountain side. And, at last, they saw the door springing open, and the nine little pipers marching down.

They waited until the pipers had crossed the meadow and were about to enter the wood. And then they followed them, the pipers marching on before them and playing all the time. It was not long until they had passed through the wood, and then, what should the children see rising up before them but another mountain, smaller than their own, but, like their own, clad more than half-way up with purple heather, and whose top was bare and sharp-pointed, and gleaming like a golden spear.

Up through the heather climbed the pipers, up through the heather the children clambered after them, and the moment the pipers passed the heather a door opened and they marched in, the children following, and the door closed behind them.

Connla and Nora were so dazzled by the light that hit their eyes, when they had crossed the threshold, that they had to shade them with their hands; but, after a moment or two, they became able to bear the splendour, and when they looked around they saw that they were in a noble hall, whose crystal roof was supported by two rows of crystal pillars rising from a crystal floor; and the walls were of crystal, and along the walls were crystal couches, with coverings and cushions of sapphire silk with silver tassels.

Over the crystal floor the little pipers marched; over the crystal floor the children followed, and when a door at the end of the hall was opened to let the pipers pass, a crowd of colours came rushing in, and floor, and ceiling, and stately pillars, and glancing couches, and shining walls, were stained with a thousand dazzling hues.

Out through the door the pipers marched; out through the door the children followed, and when they crossed the threshold they were treading on clouds of amber, of purple, and of gold.

"Oh, Connla," said Nora, "we have walked into the sunset!"

And around and about them everywhere were soft, fleecy clouds, and over their heads was the glowing sky, and the stars were shining through it, as a lady's eyes shine through a veil of gossamer. And the sky and stars seemed so near that Connla thought he could almost touch them with his hand.

When they had gone some distance, the pipers disappeared, and when Connla and Nora came up to the spot where they had seen the last of them, they found themselves at the head of a ladder, all the steps of which were formed of purple and amber clouds that descended to what appeared to be a vast and shining plain, streaked with purple and gold. In the spaces between the streaks of gold and purple they saw soft, milk-white stars. And the children thought that the great plain, so far below them, also belonged to cloudland.

They could not see the little pipers, but up the steps was borne by the cool, sweet air the fairy music; and lured on by it step by step they travelled down the fleecy stairway. When they were little more than half-way down there came mingled with the music a sound almost as sweet – the sound of waters toying in the still air with pebbles on a shelving beach, and with the sound came the odorous brine of the ocean. And then the children knew that what they thought was a plain in the realms of cloudland was the sleeping sea unstirred by wind or tide, dreaming of the purple clouds and stars of the sunset sky above it.

When Connla and Nora reached the strand they saw the nine little pipers marching out towards the sea, and they wondered where they were going to. And they could hardly believe their eyes when they saw them stepping out upon the level ocean as if they were walking upon the land; and away the nine little pipers marched, treading the golden line cast upon the waters by the setting sun. And as the music became fainter and fainter as the pipers passed into the glowing distance, the children began to wonder what was to become of themselves. Just at that very moment they saw coming towards them from the sinking sun a little white horse, with flowing mane and tail and golden hoofs. On the horse's back was a little man dressed in shining green silk. When the horse galloped on to the strand the little man doffed his hat, and said to the children:

"Would you like to follow the nine little pipers?" The children said, "Yes."

"Well, then," said the little man, "come up here behind me; you, Nora, first, and Connla after."

Connla helped up Nora, and then climbed on to the little steed himself; and as soon as they were properly seated the little man said "swish", and away went the steed, galloping over the sea without wetting hair or hoof. But fast as he galloped the nine little pipers were always ahead of him, although they seemed to be going only at a walking pace. When at last he came up rather close to the hindmost of them the nine little pipers disappeared, but the children heard the music playing beneath the waters. The white steed pulled up suddenly, and wouldn't move a step further.

"Now," said the little man to the children, "clasp me tight, Nora, and do you, Connla, cling on to Nora, and both of you shut your eyes."

The children did as they were bidden, and the little man cried:

"Swish! Swash!"

And the steed went down and down until at last his feet struck the bottom.

"Now open your eyes," said the little man.

And when the children did so they saw beneath the horse's feet a golden strand, and above their heads the sea like a transparent cloud between them and the sky. And once more they heard the fairy music, and marching on the strand before them were the nine little pipers.

"You must get off now," said the little man, "I can go no farther with you."

The children scrambled down, and the little man cried "swish", and himself and the steed shot up through the sea, and they saw him no more. Then they set out after the nine little pipers, and it wasn't long until they saw rising up from the golden strand and pushing their heads up into the sea above, a mass of dark grey rocks. And as they were gazing at them they saw the rocks opening, and the nine little pipers disappearing through them.

The children hurried on, and when they came up close to the rocks they saw sitting on a flat and polished stone a mermaid combing her golden hair, and singing a strange sweet song that brought the tears to their eyes, and by the mermaid's side was a little sleek brown otter.

When the mermaid saw them she flung her golden tresses back over her snow-white shoulders, and she beckoned the children to her. Her large eyes were full of sadness; but there was a look so tender upon her face that the children moved towards her without any fear.

"Come to me, little one," she said to Nora, "come and kiss me," and in a second her arms were around the child. The mermaid kissed her again and again, as the tears rushed to her eyes, she said:

"Oh, Nora, avourneen, your breath is as sweet as the wild rose that blooms in the green fields of Erin, and happy are you, my children, who have come so lately from the pleasant land. Oh, Connla! Connla! I get the scent of the dew of the Irish grasses and of the purple heather from your feet. And you both can soon return to Erin of the Streams, but I shall not see it till three hundred years have passed away, for I am Liban the Mermaid, daughter of a line of kings. But I may not keep you here. The Fairy Queen is waiting for you in her snow-white palace and her fragrant bowers. And now kiss me once more, Nora, and kiss me, Connla. May luck and joy go with you, and all gentleness be upon you both."

Then the children said good-bye to the mermaid, and the rocks opened for them and they passed through, and soon they found themselves in a meadow starred with flowers, and through the meadow sped a sunlit stream. They followed the stream until it led them into a garden of roses, and beyond the garden, standing on a gentle hill, was a palace white as snow. Before the palace was a crowd of fairy maidens pelting each other with rose-leaves. But when they saw the children they gave over their play, and came trooping towards them.

"Our queen is waiting for you," they said; and then they led the children to the palace door. The children entered, and after passing through a long corridor they found themselves in a crystal hall so like the one they had seen in the mountain of the golden spear that they thought it was the same. But on all the crystal couches fairies, dressed in silken robes of many colours, were sitting, and at the end of the hall, on a crystal throne, was seated the fairy queen, looking lovelier than the evening star. The queen descended from her throne to meet the children, and taking them by the hands, she led them up the shining steps. Then, sitting down, she made them sit beside her, Connla on her right hand and Nora on her left.

Then she ordered the nine little pipers to come before her, and she said to them:

"So far you have done your duty faithfully, and now play one more sweet air and your task is done."

And the little pipers played, and from the couches at the first sound of the music all the fairies rose, and forming partners, they danced over the crystal floor as lightly as the young leaves dancing in the wind.

Listening to the fairy music, and watching the wavy motion of the dancing fairies, the children fell asleep. When they awoke next morning and rose from their silken beds they were no longer children. Nora was a graceful and stately maiden, and Connla a handsome and gallant youth. They looked at each other for a moment in surprise, and then Connla said:

"Oh, Nora, how tall and beautiful you are!"

"Oh, not so tall and handsome as you are, Connla," said Nora, as she flung her white arms round his neck and kissed her brother's lips.

Then they drew back to get a better look of each other, and who should step between them but the fairy queen.

"Oh, Nora, Nora," said she, "I am not as high as your knee, and as for you, Connla, you look as straight and as tall as one of the round towers of Erin."

"And how did we grow so tall in one night?" said Connla.

"In one night!" said the fairy queen. "One night, indeed! Why, you have been fast asleep, the two of you, for the last seven years!"

"And where was the little mother all that time?" said Connla and Nora together.

"Oh, the little mother was all right. She knew where you were; but she is expecting you today, and so you must go off to see her, although I would like to keep you – if I had my way – all to myself here in the fairyland under the sea. And you will see her today; but before you go here is a necklace for you, Nora; it is formed out of the drops of the ocean spray, sparkling in the sunshine. They were caught by my fairy nymph, for you, as they skimmed the sunlit billows under the shape of sea-birds, and no queen or princess in the world can match their lustre with the diamonds won with toil from the caves of earth. As for you, Connla, see here's a helmet of shining gold fit for a king of Erin – and a king of Erin you will be yet; and here's a spear that will pierce any shield, and here's a shield that no spear can pierce and no sword can cleave as long as you fasten your warrior cloak with this brooch of gold."

And as she spoke she flung round Connla's shoulders a flowing mantle of yellow silk, and pinned it at his neck with a red gold brooch.

"And now, my children, you must go away from me. You, Nora, will be a warrior's bride in Erin of the Streams. And you, Connla, will be king yet over the loveliest province in all the land of Erin; but you will have to fight for your crown, and days of battle are before you. They will not come for a long time after you have left the fairyland under the sea, and until they come lay aside your helmet, shield, and spear, and warrior's cloak and golden brooch. But when the time comes when you will be called to battle, enter not upon it without the golden brooch I give you fastened in your cloak, for if you do harm will come to you. Now, kiss me, children; your little mother is waiting for you at the foot of the golden spear, but do not forget to say goodbye to Liban the Mermaid, exiled from the land she loves, and pining in sadness beneath the sea."

Connla and Nora kissed the fairy queen, and Connla, wearing his golden helmet and silken cloak, and carrying his shield and spear, led Nora with him. They passed from the palace through the garden of roses, through the flowery meadow, through the dark grey rocks, until they reached the golden strand; and there, sitting and singing the strange, sweet song, was Liban the Mermaid.

"And so you are going up to Erin," she said, "up through the covering waters. Kiss me, children, once again; and when you are in Erin of the Streams, sometimes think of the exile from Erin beneath the sea."

And the children kissed the mermaid, and with sad hearts, bidding her goodbye, they walked along the golden strand. When they had gone what seemed to them a long way, they began to feel weary; and just then they saw coming towards them a little man in a red jacket leading a coal-black steed.

When they met the little man, he said: "Connla, put Nora up on this steed; then jump up before her."

Connla did as he was told, and when both of them were mounted –

"Now, Connla," said the little man, "catch the bridle in your hands, and you, Nora, clasp Connla round the waist, and close your eyes."

They did as they were bidden, and then the little man said, "Swash, swish!" and the steed shot up from the strand like a lark from the grass, and pierced the covering sea, and went bounding on over the level waters; and when his hoofs struck the hard ground, Connla and Nora opened their eyes, and they saw that they were galloping towards a shady wood.

On went the steed, and soon he was galloping beneath the branches that almost touched Connla's head. And on they went until they had passed through the wood, and then they saw rising up before them the 'Golden Spear'.

"Oh, Connla," said Nora, "we are at home at last."

"Yes," said Connla, "but where is the little house under the hill?"

And no little house was there; but in its stead was standing a lime-white mansion.

"What can this mean?" said Nora.

But before Connla could reply, the steed had galloped up to the door of the mansion, and, in the twinkling of an eye, Connla and Nora were standing on the ground outside the door, and the steed had vanished.

Before they could recover from their surprise the little mother came rushing out to them, and flung her arms around their necks, and kissed them both again and again.

"Oh, children! Children! You are welcome home to me; for though I knew it was all for the best, my heart was lonely without you."

And Connla and Nora caught up the little mother in their arms, and they carried her into the hall and set her down on the floor.

"Oh, Nora!" said the little mother, "you are a head over me; and as for you, Connla, you look almost as tall as one of the round towers of Erin."

"That's what the fairy queen said, mother," said Nora.

"Blessings on the fairy queen," said the little mother. "Turn round, Connla, till I look at you."

Connla turned round, and the little mother said:

"Oh, Connla, with your golden helmet and your spear, and your glancing shield, and your silken cloak, you look like a king. But take them off, my boy, beautiful as they are. Your little mother would like to see you, her own brave boy, without any fairy finery."

And Connla laid aside his spear and shield, and took off his golden helmet and his silken cloak. Then he caught the little mother and kissed her, and lifted her up until she was as high as his head. And said he:

"Don't you know, little mother, I'd rather have you than all the world."

And that night, when they were sitting down by the fire together, you may be sure that in the whole world no people were half as happy as Nora, Connla, and the little mother.

The Young Piper

THERE LIVED not long since, on the borders of the county Tipperary, a decent honest couple, whose names were Mick Flannigan and Judy Muldoon. These poor people were blessed, as the saying is, with four children, all boys: three of them were as fine, stout, healthy, good-looking children as ever the sun shone upon; and it was enough to make any Irishman proud of the breed of his countrymen to see them about one o'clock on a fine summer's day standing at their father's cabin door, with their beautiful flaxen hair hanging in curls about their head, and their cheeks like two rosy apples, and a big laughing potato smoking in their hand.

A proud man was Mick of these fine children, and a proud woman, too, was Judy; and reason enough they had to be so. But it was far otherwise with the remaining one, which was the third eldest: he was the most miserable, ugly, ill-conditioned brat that ever God put life into; he was so ill-thriven that he never was able to stand alone, or to leave his cradle; he had long, shaggy, matted, curled hair, as black as the soot; his face was of a greenish-yellow colour; his eyes were like two burning coals, and were forever moving in his head, as if they had the perpetual motion. Before he was a twelvemonth old he had a mouth full of great teeth; his hands were like kites' claws, and his legs were no thicker than the handle of a whip, and about as straight as a reaping-hook: to make the matter worse, he had the appetite of a cormorant, and the whinge, and the yelp, and the screech, and the yowl, was never out of his mouth.

The neighbours all suspected that he was something not right, particularly as it was observed, when people, as they do in the country, got about the fire, and began to talk of religion and good things, the brat, as he lay in the cradle, which his mother generally put near the fireplace that he might be snug, used to sit up, as they were in the middle of their talk, and begin to bellow as if the devil was in him in right earnest; this, as I said, led the neighbours to think that all was not right, and there was a general consultation held one day about what would be best to do with him. Some advised to put him out on the shovel, but Judy's pride was up at that. A pretty thing indeed, that a child of hers should be put on a shovel and flung out on the dunghill just like a dead kitten or a poisoned rat; no, no, she would not hear to that at all. One old woman, who was considered very skilful and knowing in fairy matters, strongly recommended her to put the tongs in the fire, and heat them red hot, and to take his nose in them, and that would beyond all manner of doubt make him tell what he was and where he came from (for the general suspicion was, that he had been changed by the good people); but Judy was too softhearted, and too fond of the imp, so she would not give in to this plan, though everybody said she was wrong, and maybe she was, but it's hard to blame a mother. Well, some advised one thing, and some another; at last one spoke of sending for the priest, who was a very holy and a very learned man, to see it. To this Judy of course had no objection; but one thing or other always prevented her doing so, and the upshot of the business was that the priest never saw him.

Things went on in the old way for some time longer. The brat continued yelping and yowling, and eating more than his three brothers put together, and playing all sorts of unlucky tricks, for he was mighty mischievously inclined, till it happened one day that Tim Carrol, the blind piper, going his rounds, called in and sat down by the fire to have a bit of chat with the woman of the house. So after some time Tim, who was no churl of his music, yoked on the pipes, and began to bellows away in high style; when the instant he began, the young fellow, who had been lying as still as a mouse in his cradle, sat up, began to grin and twist his ugly face, to swing about his long tawny arms, and to kick out his crooked legs, and to show signs of great glee at the music. At last nothing would serve him but he should get the pipes into his own hands, and to humour him his mother asked Tim to lend them to the child for a minute. Tim, who was kind to children, readily consented; and as Tim had not his sight, Judy herself brought them to the cradle, and went to put them on him; but she had no occasion, for the youth seemed quite up to the business. He buckled on the pipes, set the bellows under one arm, and the bag under the other, worked them both as knowingly as if he had been twenty years at the business, and lilted up 'Sheela na guira' in the finest style imaginable.

All were in astonishment: the poor woman crossed herself. Tim, who, as I said before, was *dark*, and did not well know who was playing, was in great delight; and when he heard that it was a little *prechan* not five years old, that had never seen a set of pipes in his life, he wished the mother joy of her son; offered to take him off her hands if she would part with him, swore he was a *born* piper, a natural *genus*, and declared that in a little time more, with the help of a little good instruction from himself, there would not be his match in the whole country. The poor woman was greatly delighted to hear all this, particularly as what Tim said about natural *genus* quieted some misgivings that were rising in her mind, lest what the neighbours said about his not being right might be too true; and it gratified her moreover to think that her dear child (for she really loved the whelp) would not be forced to turn out and beg, but might earn decent bread for himself. So when Mick came home in the evening from his work, she up and told him all that had happened, and all that Tim Carrol had said; and Mick, as was natural, was very glad to hear it, for the helpless condition of the poor creature was a great trouble to him. So next day he took the pig to the fair, and with what it brought set off to Clonmel, and bespoke a bran-new set of pipes, of the proper size for him.

In about a fortnight the pipes came home, and the moment the chap in his cradle laid eyes on them he squealed with delight and threw up his pretty legs, and bumped himself in his cradle, and went on with a great many comical tricks; till at last, to quiet him, they gave him the pipes, and he immediately set to and pulled away at 'Jig Polthog', to the admiration of all who heard him.

The fame of his skill on the pipes soon spread far and near, for there was not a piper in the six next counties could come at all near him, in 'Old Moderagh rue', or 'The Hare in the Corn', or 'The Fox-hunter's Jig', or 'The Rakes of Cashel', or 'The Piper's Maggot', or any of the fine Irish jigs which make people dance whether they will or no: and it was surprising to hear him rattle away 'The Fox-hunt'; you'd really think you heard the hounds giving tongue, and the terriers yelping always behind, and the huntsman and the whippers-in cheering or correcting the dogs; it was, in short, the very next thing to seeing the hunt itself.

The best of him was, he was noways stingy of his music, and many a merry dance the boys and girls of the neighbourhood used to have in his father's cabin; and he would play up music for them, that they said used as it were to put quicksilver in their feet; and they all declared they never moved so light and so airy to any piper's playing that ever they danced to.

But besides all his fine Irish music, he had one queer tune of his own, the oddest that ever was heard; for the moment he began to play it everything in the house seemed disposed to dance; the plates and porringers used to jingle on the dresser, the pots and pot-hooks used to rattle in the chimney, and people used even to fancy they felt the stools moving from under them; but, however it might be with the stools, it is certain that no one could keep long sitting on them, for both old and young always fell to capering as hard as ever they could. The girls complained that when he began this tune it always threw them out in their dancing, and that they never could handle their feet rightly, for they felt the floor like ice under them, and themselves every moment ready to come sprawling on their backs or their faces. The young bachelors who wished to show off their dancing and their new pumps, and their bright red or green and yellow garters, swore that it confused them so that they never could go rightly through the *heel and toe* or *cover the buckle*, or any of their best steps, but felt themselves always all bedizzied and bewildered, and then old and young would go jostling and knocking together in a frightful manner; and when the unlucky brat had them all in this way, whirligigging about the floor, he'd grin and chuckle and chatter, for all the world like Jacko the monkey when he has played off some of his roguery.

The older he grew the worse he grew, and by the time he was six years old there was no standing the house for him; he was always making his brothers burn or scald themselves, or break their shins over the pots and stools. One time, in harvest, he was left at home by himself, and when his mother came in she found the cat a-horseback on the dog, with her face to the tail, and her legs tied round him, and the urchin playing his queer tune to them; so that the dog went barking and jumping about, and puss was mewing for the dear life, and slapping her tail backwards and forwards, which, as it would hit against the dog's chaps, he'd snap at and bite, and then there was the philliloo. Another time, the farmer with whom Mick worked, a very decent, respectable man, happened to call in, and Judy wiped a stool with her apron, and invited him to sit down and rest himself after his walk. He was sitting with his back to the cradle, and behind him was a pan of blood, for Judy was making pig's puddings. The lad lay quite still in his nest, and watched his opportunity till he got ready a hook at the end of a piece of twine, which he contrived to fling so handily that it caught in the bob of the man's nice new wig, and soused it in the pan of blood. Another time his mother was coming in from milking the cow, with the pail on her head: the minute he saw her he lilted up his infernal tune, and the poor woman, letting go the pail, clapped her hands aside, and began to dance a jig, and tumbled the milk all a-top of her husband, who was bringing in some turf to boil the supper. In short, there would be no end to telling all his pranks, and all the mischievous tricks he played.

Soon after, some mischances began to happen to the farmer's cattle. A horse took the staggers, a fine veal calf died of the black-leg, and some of his sheep of the red-water; the cows began to grow vicious, and to kick down the milk-pails, and the roof of one end of the barn fell in; and the farmer took it into his head that Mick Flannigan's unlucky child was the cause of all the mischief. So one day he called Mick aside, and said to him, "Mick, you see things are not going on with me as they ought, and to be plain with you, Mick, I think that child of yours is the cause of it. I am really falling away to nothing with fretting, and I can hardly sleep on my bed at night for thinking of what may happen before the morning. So I'd be glad if you'd look out for work somewhere else; you're as good a man as any in the country, and there's no fear but you'll have your choice of work." To this Mick replied, "that he was sorry for his losses, and still sorrier that he or his should be thought to be the cause of them; that for his own part he was not quite easy in his mind about that child, but he had him and so must keep him"; and he promised to look out for another place immediately.

Accordingly, next Sunday at chapel Mick gave out that he was about leaving the work at John Riordan's, and immediately a farmer who lived a couple of miles off, and who wanted a ploughman (the last one having just left him), came up to Mick, and offered him a house and garden, and work all the year round. Mick, who knew him to be a good employer, immediately closed with him; so it was agreed that the farmer should send a car to take his little bit of furniture, and that he should remove on the following Thursday.

When Thursday came, the car came according to promise, and Mick loaded it, and put the cradle with the child and his pipes on the top, and Judy sat beside it to take care of him, lest he should tumble out and be killed. They drove the cow before them, the dog followed, but the cat was of course left behind; and the other three children went along the road picking skeehories (haws) and blackberries, for it was a fine day towards the latter end of harvest.

They had to cross a river, but as it ran through a bottom between two high banks, you did not see it till you were close on it. The young fellow was lying pretty quiet in the bottom of the cradle, till they came to the head of the bridge, when hearing the roaring of the water (for there was a great flood in the river, as it had rained heavily for the last two or three days), he sat up in his cradle and looked about him; and the instant he got a sight of the water, and found they were going to take him across it, oh, how he did bellow and how he did squeal! No rat caught in a snap-trap ever sang out equal to him.

"Whist! A lanna," said Judy, "there's no fear of you; sure it's only over the stone bridge we're going."

"Bad luck to you, you old rip!" cried he, "what a pretty trick you've played me to bring me here!" and still went on yelling, and the farther they got on the bridge the louder he yelled; till at last Mick could hold out no longer, so giving him a great skelp of the whip he had in his hand, "Devil choke you, you brat!" said he, "will you never stop bawling? A body can't hear their ears for you." The moment he felt the thong of the whip he leaped up in the cradle, clapped the pipes under his arm, gave a most wicked grin at Mick, and jumped clean over the battlements of the bridge down into the water. "Oh, my child, my child!" shouted Judy, "he's gone for ever from me."

Mick and the rest of the children ran to the other side of the bridge, and looking over, they saw him coming out from under the arch of the bridge, sitting cross-legged on the top of a white-headed wave, and playing away on the pipes as merrily as if nothing had happened. The river was running very rapidly, so he was whirled away at a great rate; but he played as fast, ay, and faster, than the river ran; and though they set off as hard as they could along the bank, yet, as the river made a sudden turn round the hill, about a hundred yards below the bridge, by the time they got there he was out of sight, and no one ever laid eyes on him more; but the general opinion was that he went home with the pipes to his own relations, the good people, to make music for them.

The Brewery of Egg-Shells

MRS. SULLIVAN fancied that her youngest child had been exchanged by 'fairies theft', and certainly appearances warranted such a conclusion; for in one night her healthy, blue-eyed boy had become shrivelled up into almost nothing, and never ceased squalling and crying. This naturally made poor Mrs. Sullivan very unhappy; and all the neighbours, by way of comforting her, said that her own child was, beyond any kind of doubt, with the good people, and that one of themselves was put in his place.

Mrs. Sullivan of course could not disbelieve what every one told her, but she did not wish to hurt the thing; for although its face was so withered, and its body wasted away to a mere skeleton, it had still a strong resemblance to her own boy. She, therefore, could not find it in her heart to roast it alive on the griddle, or to burn its nose off with the red-hot tongs, or to throw it out in the snow on the road-side, notwithstanding these, and several like proceedings, were strongly recommended to her for the recovery of her child.

One day who should Mrs. Sullivan meet but a cunning woman, well known about the country by the name of Ellen Leah (or Grey Ellen). She had the gift, however she got it, of telling where the dead were, and what was good for the rest of their souls; and could charm away warts and wens, and do a great many wonderful things of the same nature.

"You're in grief this morning, Mrs. Sullivan," were the first words of Ellen Leah to her.

"You may say that, Ellen," said Mrs. Sullivan, "and good cause I have to be in grief, for there was my own fine child whipped of from me out of his cradle, without as much as 'by your leave' or 'ask your pardon', and an ugly dony bit of a shrivelled-up fairy put in his place; no wonder, then, that you see me in grief, Ellen."

"Small blame to you, Mrs. Sullivan," said Ellen Leah, "but are you sure 'tis a fairy?"

"Sure!" echoed Mrs. Sullivan, "sure enough I am to my sorrow, and can I doubt my own two eyes? Every mother's soul must feel for me!"

"Will you take an old woman's advice?" said Ellen Leah, fixing her wild and mysterious gaze upon the unhappy mother; and, after a pause, she added, "but maybe you'll call it foolish?"

"Can you get me back my child, my own child, Ellen?" said Mrs. Sullivan with great energy.

"If you do as I bid you," returned Ellen Leah, "you'll know." Mrs. Sullivan was silent in expectation, and Ellen continued, "Put down the big pot, full of water, on the fire, and make it boil like mad; then get a dozen new-laid eggs, break them, and keep the shells, but throw away the rest; when that is done, put the shells in the pot of boiling water, and you will soon know whether it is your own boy or a fairy. If you find that it is a fairy in the cradle, take the red-hot poker and cram it down his ugly throat, and you will not have much trouble with him after that, I promise you."

Home went Mrs. Sullivan, and did as Ellen Leah desired. She put the pot on the fire, and plenty of turf under it, and set the water boiling at such a rate, that if ever water was red-hot, it surely was.

The child was lying, for a wonder, quite easy and quiet in the cradle, every now and then cocking his eye, that would twinkle as keen as a star in a frosty night, over at the great fire, and the big pot upon it; and he looked on with great attention at Mrs. Sullivan breaking the eggs and putting down the egg-shells to boil. At last he asked, with the voice of a very old man, "What are you doing, mammy?"

Mrs. Sullivan's heart, as she said herself, was up in her mouth ready to choke her, at hearing the child speak. But she contrived to put the poker in the fire, and to answer, without making any wonder at the words, "I'm brewing, *a vick* (my son)".

"And what are you brewing, mammy?" said the little imp, whose supernatural gift of speech now proved beyond question that he was a fairy substitute.

"I wish the poker was red," thought Mrs. Sullivan; but it was a large one, and took a long time heating; so she determined to keep him in talk until the poker was in a proper state to thrust down his throat, and therefore repeated the question.

"Is it what I'm brewing, *a vick*," said she, "you want to know?"

"Yes, mammy: what are you brewing?" returned the fairy.

"Egg-shells, *a vick*," said Mrs. Sullivan.

"Oh!" shrieked the imp, starting up in the cradle, and clapping his hands together, "I'm fifteen hundred years in the world, and I never saw a brewery of egg-shells before!" The poker was by this time quite red, and Mrs. Sullivan, seizing it, ran furiously towards the cradle; but somehow or other her foot slipped, and she fell flat on the floor, and the poker flew out of her hand to the other end of the house. However, she got up without much loss of time and went to the cradle, intending to pitch the wicked thing that was in it into the pot of boiling water, when there she saw her own child in a sweet sleep, one of his soft round arms rested upon the pillow – his features were as placid as if their repose had never been disturbed, save the rosy mouth, which moved with a gentle and regular breathing.

Frank Martin and the Fairies

MARTIN WAS a thin pale man, when I saw him, of a sickly look, and a constitution naturally feeble. His hair was a light auburn, his beard mostly unshaven, and his hands of a singular delicacy and whiteness, owing, I dare say, as much to the soft and easy nature of his employment as to his infirm health. In everything else he was as sensible, sober, and rational as any other man; but on the topic of fairies, the man's mania was peculiarly strong and immovable. Indeed, I remember that the expression of his eyes was singularly wild and hollow, and his long narrow temples sallow and emaciated.

Now, this man did not lead an unhappy life, nor did the malady he laboured under seem to be productive of either pain or terror to him, although one might be apt to imagine otherwise. On the contrary, he and the fairies maintained the most friendly intimacy, and their dialogues – which I fear were wofully one-sided ones – must have been a source of great pleasure to him, for they were conducted with much mirth and laughter, on his part at least.

"Well, Frank, when did you see the fairies?"

"Whist! There's two dozen of them in the shop (the weaving shop) this minute. There's a little ould fellow sittin' on the top of the sleys, an' all to be rocked while I'm weavin'. The sorrow's in them, but they're the greatest little skamers alive, so they are. See, there's another of them at my dressin' noggin. Go out o' that, you *shingawn*; or, bad cess to me, if you don't, but I'll lave you a mark. Ha! cut, you thief you!"

"Frank, arn't you afeard o' them?"

"Is it me! Arra, what 'ud I be afeard o' them for? Sure they have no power over me."

"And why haven't they, Frank?"

"Because I was baptized against them."

"What do you mean by that?"

"Why, the priest that christened me was tould by my father, to put in the proper prayer against the fairies – an' a priest can't refuse it when he's asked – an' he did so. Begorra, it's well for me that he did – (let the tallow alone, you little glutton – see, there's a weeny thief o' them aitin' my tallow) – becaise, you see, it was their intention to make me king o' the fairies."

"Is it possible?"

"Devil a lie in it. Sure you may ax them, an' they'll tell you."

"What size are they, Frank?"

"Oh, little wee fellows, with green coats, an' the purtiest little shoes ever you seen. There's two of them – both ould acquaintances o' mine – runnin' along the yarn-beam. That ould fellow with the bob-wig is called Jim Jam, an' the other chap, with the three-cocked hat, is called Nickey Nick. Nickey plays the pipes. Nickey, give us a tune, or I'll malivogue you – come now, 'Lough Erne Shore'. Whist, now – listen!"

The poor fellow, though weaving as fast as he could all the time, yet bestowed every possible mark of attention to the music, and seemed to enjoy it as much as if it had been real.

But who can tell whether that which we look upon as a privation may not after all be a fountain of increased happiness, greater, perhaps, than any which we ourselves enjoy? I forget who the poet is who says –

> *"Mysterious are thy laws;*
> *The vision's finer than the view;*
> *Her landscape Nature never drew*
> *So fair as Fancy draws."*

Many a time, when a mere child, not more than six or seven years of age, have I gone as far as Frank's weaving-shop, in order, with a heart divided between curiosity and fear, to listen to his conversation with the good people. From morning till night his tongue was going almost as incessantly as his shuttle; and it was well known that at night, whenever he awoke out of his sleep, the first thing he did was to put out his hand, and push them, as it were, off his bed.

"Go out o' this, you thieves, you – go out o' this now, an' let me alone. Nickey, is this any time to be playing the pipes, and me wants to sleep? Go off, now – troth if yez do, you'll see what I'll give yez tomorrow. Sure I'll be makin' new dressin's; and if yez behave decently, maybe I'll lave yez the scrapin' o' the pot. There now. Och! Poor things, they're dacent crathurs. Sure they're all gone, barrin' poor Red-cap, that doesn't like to lave me." And then the harmless monomaniac would fall back into what we trust was an innocent slumber.

About this time there was said to have occurred a very remarkable circumstance, which gave poor Frank a vast deal of importance among the neighbours. A man named Frank Thomas, the same in whose house Mickey M'Rorey held the first dance at which I ever saw him, as detailed in a former sketch; this man, I say, had a child sick, but of what complaint I cannot now remember, nor is it of any importance. One of the gables of Thomas's house was built against, or rather into, a Forth or Rath, called Towny, or properly Tonagh Forth. It was said to be haunted by the fairies, and what gave it a character peculiarly wild in my eyes was, that there were on the southern side of it two or three little green mounds, which were said to be the graves of unchristened children, over which it was considered dangerous and unlucky to pass. At all events, the season was mid-summer; and one evening about dusk, during the illness of the child, the noise of a hand-saw was heard upon the Forth. This was considered rather strange, and, after a little time, a few of those who were assembled at Frank Thomas's went to see who it could be that was sawing in such a place, or what they could be sawing at so late an hour, for everyone knew that nobody in the whole country about them would dare to cut down the few white-thorns that grew upon the Forth. On going to examine, however, judge of their surprise, when, after surrounding and searching the whole place, they could discover no trace of either saw or sawyer. In fact, with the exception of themselves, there was no one, either natural or supernatural, visible. They then returned to the house, and had scarcely sat down, when it was heard again within ten yards of them. Another examination of the premises took place, but with equal success. Now, however, while standing on the Forth, they heard the sawing in a little

hollow, about a hundred and fifty yards below them, which was completely exposed to their view, but they could see nobody. A party of them immediately went down to ascertain, if possible, what this singular noise and invisible labour could mean; but on arriving at the spot, they heard the sawing, to which were now added hammering, and the driving of nails upon the Forth above, whilst those who stood on the Forth continued to hear it in the hollow. On comparing notes, they resolved to send down to Billy Nelson's for Frank Martin, a distance of only about eighty or ninety yards. He was soon on the spot, and without a moment's hesitation solved the enigma.

"'Tis the fairies," said he. "I see them, and busy crathurs they are."

"But what are they sawing, Frank?"

"They are makin' a child's coffin," he replied; "they have the body already made, an' they're now nailin' the lid together."

That night the child died, and the story goes that on the second evening afterwards, the carpenter who was called upon to make the coffin brought a table out from Thomas's house to the Forth, as a temporary bench; and, it is said, that the sawing and hammering necessary for the completion of his task were precisely the same which had been heard the evening but one before – neither more nor less. I remember the death of the child myself, and the making of its coffin, but I think the story of the supernatural carpenter was not heard in the village for some months after its interment.

Frank had every appearance of a hypochondriac about him. At the time I saw him, he might be about thirty-four years of age, but I do not think, from the debility of his frame and infirm health, that he has been alive for several years. He was an object of considerable interest and curiosity, and often have I been present when he was pointed out to strangers as 'the man that could see the good people'.

The Fairy Tree of Dooros

ONCE UPON A TIME the fairies of the west, going home from a hurling-match with the fairies of the lakes, rested in Dooros Wood for three days and three nights. They spent the days feasting and the nights dancing in the light of the moon, and they danced so hard that they wore the shoes off their feet, and for a whole week after the leprechauns, the fairies' shoemakers, were working night and day making new ones, and the rip, rap, tap, tap of their little hammers were heard in all the hedgerows.

The food on which the fairies feasted were little red berries, and were so like those that grow on the rowan tree that if you only looked at them you might mistake one for the other; but the fairy berries grow only in fairyland, and are sweeter than any fruit that grows here in this world, and if an old man, bent and grey, ate one of them, he became young and active and strong again; and if an old woman, withered and wrinkled, ate one of them, she became young and bright and fair; and if a little maiden who was not handsome ate of them, she became lovelier than the flower of beauty.

The fairies guarded the berries as carefully as a miser guards his gold, and whenever they were about to leave fairyland they had to promise in the presence of the king and queen that they would not give a single berry to mortal man, nor allow one to fall upon the earth; for if a single berry fell upon the earth a slender tree of many branches, bearing clusters of berries, would at once spring up, and mortal men might eat of them.

But it chanced that this time they were in Dooros Wood they kept up the feasting and dancing so long, and were so full of joy because of their victory over the lake fairies, that one little, weeny fairy, not much bigger than my finger, lost his head, and dropped a berry in the wood.

When the feast was ended the fairies went back to fairyland, and were at home for more than a week before they knew of the little fellow's fault, and this is how they came to know of it.

A great wedding was about to come off, and the queen of the fairies sent six of her pages to Dooros Wood to catch fifty butterflies with golden spots on their purple wings, and fifty white without speck or spot, and fifty golden, yellow as the cowslip, to make a dress for herself, and a hundred white, without speck or spot, to make dresses for the bride and bridesmaids.

When the pages came near the wood they heard the most wonderful music, and the sky above them became quite dark, as if a cloud had shut out the sun. They looked up, and saw that the cloud was formed of bees, who in a great swarm were flying towards the wood and humming as they flew. Seeing this they were sore afraid until they saw the bees settling on a single tree, and on looking closely at the tree they saw it was covered with fairy berries.

The bees took no notice of the fairies, and so they were no longer afraid, and they hunted the butterflies until they had captured the full number of various colours. Then they returned to fairyland, and they told the queen about the bees and the berries, and the queen told the king.

The king was very angry, and he sent his heralds to the four corners of fairyland to summon all his subjects to his presence that he might find out without delay who was the culprit.

They all came except the little weeny fellow who dropped the berry, and of course everyone said that it was fear that kept him away, and that he must be guilty.

The heralds were at once sent in search of him, and after a while they found him hiding in a cluster of ferns, and brought him before the king.

The poor little fellow was so frightened that at first he could scarcely speak a word, but after a time he told how he never missed the berry until he had returned to fairyland, and that he was afraid to say anything to anyone about it.

The king, who would hear of no excuse, sentenced the little culprit to be banished into the land of giants beyond the mountains, to stay there for ever and a day unless he could find a giant willing to go to Dooros Wood and guard the fairy tree. When the king had pronounced sentence everyone was very sorry, because the little fellow was a favourite with them all. No fairy harper upon his harp, or piper upon his pipe, or fiddler upon his fiddle, could play half so sweetly as he could play upon an ivy leaf; and when they remembered all the pleasant moonlit nights on which they had danced to his music, and thought that they should never hear or dance to it any more, their little hearts were filled with sorrow. The queen was as sad as any of her subjects, but the king's word should be obeyed.

When the time came for the little fellow to set out into exile the queen sent her head page to him with a handful of berries. These the queen said he was to offer to the giants, and say at the same time that the giant who was willing to guard the tree could feast on berries just as sweet from morn till night.

As the little fellow went on his way nearly all the fairies followed him to the borders of the land, and when they saw him go up the mountain towards the land of the giants, they all took off their little red caps and waved them until he was out of sight.

On he went walking all day and night, and when the sun rose on the morrow he was on the top of the mountain, and he could see the land of the giants in the valley stretched far below him. Before beginning his descent he turned round for a last glimpse of fairyland; but he could see nothing, for a thick, dark cloud shut it out from view. He was very sad, and tired, and footsore, and as he struggled down the rough mountain side, he could not help thinking of the soft, green woods and mossy pathways of the pleasant land he had left behind him.

When he awoke the ground was trembling, and a noise that sounded like thunder fell on his ears. He looked up and saw coming towards him a terrible giant, with one eye that burned like a live coal in the middle of his forehead, his mouth stretched from ear to ear, his teeth were long and crooked, the skin of his face was as black as night, and his arms and chest were all covered with black, shaggy hair; round his body was an iron band, and hanging from this by a chain was a great club with iron spikes. With one blow of this club he could break a rock into splinters, and fire could not burn him, and water could not drown him, and weapons could not wound him, and there was no way to kill him but by giving him three blows of his own club. And he was so bad-tempered that the other giants called him Sharvan the Surly. When the giant spied the red cap of the little fairy he gave the shout that sounded like thunder. The poor fairy was shaking from head to foot.

"What brought you here?" said the giant.

"Please, Mr. Giant," said the fairy, "the king of the fairies banished me here, and here I must stay for ever and a day, unless you come and guard the fairy tree in Dooros Wood."

"Unless what?" roared the giant, and he gave the fairy a touch of his foot that sent the little fellow rolling down head over heels.

The poor fairy lay as if he were dead, and then the giant, feeling sorry for what he had done, took him up gently between his finger and thumb.

"Don't be frightened, little man," said he, "and now, tell me all about the tree."

"It is the tree of the fairy berry that grows in the Wood of Dooros," said the fairy, "and I have some of the berries with me."

"Oh, you have, have you?" said the giant. "Let me see them."

The fairy took three berries from the pocket of his little green coat, and gave them to the giant.

The giant looked at them for a second. He then swallowed the three together, and when he had done so, he felt so happy that he began to shout and dance for joy.

"More, you little thief!" said he. "More, you little – what's your name?" said the giant.

"Pinkeen, please, Mr. Giant," said the fairy, as he gave up all the berries.

The giant shouted louder than before, and his shouts were heard by all the other giants, who came running towards him.

When Sharvan saw them coming, he caught up Pinkeen, and put him in his pocket, that they shouldn't see him.

"What were you shouting for?" said the giants.

"Because," said Sharvan, "that rock there fell down on my big toe."

"You did not shout like a man that was hurt," said they.

"What is it to you what way I shouted?" said he.

"You might give a civil answer to a civil question," said they; "but sure you were always Sharvan the Surly"; and they went away.

When the giants were out of sight, Sharvan took Pinkeen out of his wallet.

"Some more berries, you little thief – I mean little Pinkeen," said he.

"I have not any more," said Pinkeen; "but if you will guard the tree in Dooros Wood you can feast on them from morn till night."

"I'll guard every tree in the wood, if I may do that," said the giant.

"You'll have to guard only one," said Pinkeen.

"How am I to get to it?" said Sharvan.

"You must first come with me towards fairyland," said the fairy.

"Very well," said Sharvan; "let us go." And he took up the fairy and put him into his wallet, and before very long they were on the top of the mountain. Then the giant looked around towards the giant's land; but a black cloud shut it out from view, while the sun was shining on the valley that lay before him, and he could see away in the distance the green woods and shining waters of fairyland.

It was not long until he reached its borders, but when he tried to cross them his feet stuck to the ground and he could not move a step. Sharvan gave three loud shouts that were heard all over fairyland, and made the trees in the woods tremble, as if the wind of a storm was sweeping over them.

"Oh, please, Mr. Giant, let me out," said Pinkeen. Sharvan took out the little fellow, who, as soon as he saw he was on the borders of fairyland ran as fast as his legs could carry him, and before he had gone very far he met all the little fairies who, hearing the shouts of the giant, came trooping out from the ferns to see what was the matter. Pinkeen told them it was the giant who was to guard the tree, shouting because he was stuck fast on the borders, and they need have no fear of him. The fairies were so delighted to have Pinkeen back again, that they took him up on their shoulders and carried him to the king's palace, and all the harpers and pipers and fiddlers marched before him playing the most jocund music that was ever heard. The king and queen were on the lawn in front of the palace when the gay procession came up and halted before them. The queen's eyes glistened with pleasure when she saw the little favourite, and the king was also glad at heart, but he looked very grave as he said:

"Why have you returned, sirrah?"

Then Pinkeen told his majesty that he had brought with him a giant who was willing to guard the fairy tree.

"And who is he and where is he?" asked the king.

"The other giants called him Sharvan the Surly," said Pinkeen, "and he is stuck fast outside the borders of fairyland."

"It is well," said the king, "you are pardoned."

When the fairies heard this they tossed their little red caps in the air, and cheered so loudly that a bee who was clinging to a rose-bud fell senseless to the ground.

Then the king ordered one of his pages to take a handful of berries, and to go to Sharvan and show him the way to Dooros Wood. The page, taking the berries with him, went off to Sharvan, whose roaring nearly frightened the poor little fellow to death. But as soon as the giant tasted the berries he got into good humour, and he asked the page if he could remove the spell of enchantment from him.

"I can," said the page, "and I will if you promise me that you will not try to cross the borders of fairyland."

"I promise that, with all my heart," said the giant. "But hurry on, my little man, for there are pins and needles in my legs."

The page plucked a cowslip, and picking out the five little crimson spots in the cup of it, he flung one to the north, and one to the south, and one to the east, and one to the west, and one up into the sky, and the spell was broken, and the giant's limbs were free. Then Sharvan and the fairy page set off for Dooros Wood, and it was not long until they came within view of the fairy tree. When Sharvan saw the berries glistening in the sun, he gave a shout so loud and strong that the wind of it blew the little fairy back to fairyland. But he had to return to the wood to tell the giant that he was to stay all day at the foot of the tree ready to do battle with anyone who might come to steal the berries, and that during the night he was to sleep amongst the branches.

"All right," said the giant, who could scarcely speak, as his mouth was full of berries.

Well, the fame of the fairy-tree spread far and wide, and every day some adventurer came to try if he could carry away some of the berries; but the giant, true to his word, was always on the watch, and not a single day passed on which he did not fight and slay a daring champion, and the giant never received a wound, for fire could not burn him, nor water drown him, nor weapon wound him.

Now, at this time, when Sharvan was keeping watch and ward over the tree, a cruel king was reigning over the lands that looked towards the rising sun. He had slain the rightful king by foul means, and his subjects, loving their murdered sovereign, hated the usurper; but much as they hated him they feared him more, for he was brave and masterful, and he was armed with a helmet and shield which no weapon made by mortal hands could pierce, and he carried always with him two javelins that never missed their mark, and were so fatal that they were called 'the shafts of death'. The murdered king had two children – a boy, whose name was Niall, and a girl, who was called Rosaleen – that is, little Rose; but no rose that ever bloomed was half as sweet or fresh or fair as she. Cruel as the tyrant king was, he was afraid of the people to kill the children. He sent the boy adrift on the sea in an open boat, hoping the waves would swallow it; and he got an old witch to cast the spell of deformity over Rosaleen, and under the spell her beauty faded, until at last she became so ugly and wasted that scarcely anyone would speak to her. And, shunned by everyone, she spent her days in the out-houses with the cattle, and every night she cried herself to sleep.

One day, when she was very lonely, a little robin came to pick the crumbs that had fallen about her feet. He appeared so tame that she offered him the bread from her hand, and when he took it she cried with joy at finding that there was one living thing that did not shun her. After this the robin came every day, and he sang so sweetly for her that she almost forgot her loneliness and misery. But once while the robin was with her the tyrant king's daughter, who was very beautiful, passed with her maids of honour, and, seeing Rosaleen, the princess said:

"Oh, there is that horrid ugly thing."

The maids laughed and giggled, and said they had never seen such a fright.

Poor Rosaleen felt as if her heart would break, and when the princess and her maids were out of sight she almost cried her eyes out. When the robin saw her crying he perched on her shoulder and rubbed his little head against her neck and chirruped softly in her ear, and Rosaleen was comforted, for she felt she had at least one friend in the world, although it was only a little robin. But the robin could do more for her than she could dream of. He heard the remark made by the princess, and he saw Rosaleen's tears, and he knew now why she was shunned by everybody, and why she was so unhappy. And that very evening he flew off to Dooros Wood, and called on a cousin of his and told him all about Rosaleen.

"And you want some of the fairy berries, I suppose," said his cousin, Robin of the Wood.

"I do," said Rosaleen's little friend.

"Ah," said Robin of the Wood, "times have changed since you were here last. The tree is guarded now all the day long by a surly giant. He sleeps in the branches during the night, and he breathes upon them and around them every morning, and his breath is poison to bird and bee. There is only one chance open, and if you try that it may cost you your life."

"Then tell me what it is, for I would give a hundred lives for Rosaleen," said her own little robin.

"Well," said Robin of the Wood, "every day a champion comes to battle with the giant, and the giant, before he begins the fight, puts a branch of berries in the iron belt that's around his waist, so that when he feels tired or thirsty he can refresh himself, and there is just a bare chance, while he is fighting, of picking one of the berries from the branch; but if his breath fall on you it is certain death."

"I will take the chance," said Rosaleen's robin.

"Very well," said the other. And the two birds flew through the wood until they came within sight of the fairy tree. The giant was lying stretched at the foot of it, eating the berries; but it was not long until a warrior came, who challenged him to battle. The giant jumped up, and plucking a branch from the tree stuck it in his belt, and swinging his iron club above his head strode towards the warrior, and the fight began. The robin perched on a tree behind the giant, and watched and waited for his chance; but it was a long time coming, for the berries were in front of the giant's belt. At last the giant, with one great blow, struck the warrior down, but as he did so he stumbled and fell upon him, and before he had time to recover himself the little robin darted towards him like a flash and picked off one of the berries, and then, as fast as wings could carry him, he flew towards home, and on his way he passed over a troop of warriors on snow-white steeds. All the horsemen except one wore silver helmets and shining mantles of green silk, fastened by brooches of red gold, but the chief, who rode at the head of the troop, wore a golden helmet, and his mantle was of yellow silk, and he looked by far the noblest of them all. When the robin had left the horsemen far behind him he spied Rosaleen sitting outside the palace gates bemoaning her fate. The robin perched upon her shoulder, and almost before she knew he was there he put the berry between her lips, and the taste was so delicious that Rosaleen ate it at once, and that very moment the witch's withering spell passed away from her, and she became as lovely as the flower of beauty. Just then the warriors on the snow-white steeds came up, and the chief with the mantle of yellow silk and the golden helmet leaped from his horse, and bending his knee before her, said:

"Fairest of all fair maidens, you are surely the daughter of the king of these realms, even though you are without the palace gates, unattended, and wear not royal robes. I am the Prince of the Sunny Valleys."

"Daughter of a king I am," said Rosaleen, "but not of the king who rules these realms."

And saying this she fled, leaving the prince wondering who she could be. The prince then ordered his trumpeters to give notice of his presence outside the palace, and in a few moments the king and all his nobles came out to greet the prince and his warriors, and give them welcome. That night a great feast was spread in the banquet-hall, and the Prince of the Sunny Valleys sat by the king, and beside the prince sat the king's beautiful daughter, and then in due order sat the nobles of the court and the warriors who had come with the prince, and on the wall behind each noble and warrior his shield and helmet were suspended, flashing radiance through the room. During the feast the prince spoke most graciously to the lovely lady at his side, but all the time he was thinking of the unknown beauty he had met outside the palace gates, and his heart longed for another glimpse of her. When the feast was ended, and the jewelled drinking-cups had gone merrily around the table, the bards sang, to the accompaniment of harps, the 'Courtship of the Lady Eimer', and as they pictured her radiant beauty outshining that of all her maidens, the prince thought that fair as Lady Eimer was there was one still fairer.

When the feast was ended the king asked the prince what brought him into his realms.

"I come," said the prince, "to look for a bride, for it was foretold to me in my own country that here only I should find the lady who is destined to share my throne, and fame reported that in your kingdom are to be found the loveliest maidens in all the world, and I can well believe that," added the prince, "after what I have seen today."

When the king's daughter heard this she hung down her head and blushed like a rose, for, of course, she thought the prince was alluding only to herself, as she did not know that he had seen Rosaleen, and she had not heard of the restoration of her beauty.

Before another word could be spoken a great noise and the clang of arms were heard outside the palace. The king and his guests started from their seats and drew their swords, and the bards raised the song of battle; but their voices were stilled and their harps silenced when they saw at the threshold of the banquet hall a battle champion, in whose face they recognised the features of their murdered king.

"'Tis Niall come back to claim his father's throne," said the chief bard. "Long live Niall!"

"Long live Niall!" answered all the others.

The king, white with rage and amazement, turned to the chiefs and nobles of his court, and cried out:

"Is there none loyal enough to drive that intruder from the banquet hall?"

But no one stirred, and no answer was given. Then the king rushed forward alone, but before he could reach the spot where Niall was standing he was seized by a dozen chiefs and at once disarmed.

During this scene the king's daughter had fled frightened; but Rosaleen, attracted by the noise, and hearing her brother's name and the cheers which greeted it, had entered the banquet hall unperceived by anyone. But when her presence was discovered every eye was dazzled with her beauty. Niall looked at her for a second, wondering if the radiant maiden before him could be the little sister he had been separated from for so many years. In another second she was clasped in his arms.

Then the feast was spread again, and Niall told the story of his adventures; and when the Prince of the Sunny Valley asked for the hand of Rosaleen, Niall told his lovely sister to speak for herself. With downcast eyes and smiling lips she said, "Yes," and that very day was the gayest and brightest wedding that ever took place, and Rosaleen became the prince's bride.

In her happiness she did not forget the little robin, who was her friend in sorrow. She took him home with her to Sunny Valleys, and every day she fed him with her own hands, and every day he sang for her the sweetest songs that were ever heard in lady's bower.

The Fairy Nurse

THERE WAS ONCE a little farmer and his wife living near Coolgarrow. They had three children, and my story happened while the youngest was a baby. The wife was a good wife enough, but her mind was all on her family and her farm, and she hardly ever went to her knees without falling asleep, and she thought the time spent in the chapel was twice as long as it need be. So, friends, she let her man and her two children go before her one day to Mass, while she called to consult a fairy man about a disorder one of her cows had. She was late at the chapel, and was sorry all the day after, for her husband was in grief about it, and she was very fond of him.

Late that night he was wakened up by the cries of his children calling out "Mother! Mother!" When he sat up and rubbed his eyes, there was no wife by his side, and when he asked the little ones what was become of their mother, they said they saw the room full of nice little men and women, dressed in white and red and green, and their mother in the middle of them, going out by the door as if she was walking in her sleep. Out he ran, and searched everywhere round the house but, neither tale nor tidings did he get of her for many a day.

Well, the poor man was miserable enough, for he was as fond of his woman as she was of him. It used to bring the salt tears down his cheeks to see his poor children neglected and dirty, as they often were, and they'd be bad enough only for a kind neighbour that used to look in whenever she could spare time. The infant was away with a nurse.

About six weeks after – just as he was going out to his work one morning – a neighbour, that used to mind women when they were ill, came up to him, and kept step by step with him to the field, and this is what she told him.

"Just as I was falling asleep last night, I heard a horse's tramp on the grass and a knock at the door, and there, when I came out, was a fine-looking dark man, mounted on a black horse, and he told me to get ready in all haste, for a lady was in great want of me. As soon as I put on my cloak and things, he took me by the hand, and I was sitting behind him before I felt myself stirring. "Where are we going, sir?" says I. "You'll soon know," says he; and he drew his fingers across my eyes, and not a ray could I see. I kept a tight grip of him, and I little knew whether he was going backwards or forwards, or how long we were about it, till my hand was taken again, and I felt the ground under me. The fingers went the other way across my eyes, and there we were before a castle door, and in we went through a big hall and great rooms all painted in fine green colours, with red and gold bands and ornaments, and the finest carpets and chairs and tables and window curtains, and grand ladies and gentlemen walking about. At last we came to a bedroom, with a beautiful lady in bed, with a fine bouncing boy beside her. The lady clapped her hands, and in came the Dark Man and kissed her and the baby, and praised me, and gave me a bottle of green ointment to rub the child all over.

"Well, the child I rubbed, sure enough; but my right eye began to smart, and I put up my finger and gave it a rub, and then stared, for never in all my life was I so frightened. The beautiful room was a big, rough cave, with water oozing over the edges of the stones and through the clay; and the lady, and the lord, and the child weazened, poverty-bitten creatures – nothing but skin and bone – and the rich dresses were old rags. I didn't let on that I found any difference, and after a bit says the Dark Man, 'Go before me to the hall door, and I will be with you in a few moments, and see you safe home.' Well, just as I turned into the outside cave, who should I see watching near the door but poor Molly. She looked round all terrified, and says she to me in a whisper, 'I'm brought here to nurse the child of the king and queen of the fairies; but there is one chance of saving me. All the court will pass the cross near Templeshambo next Friday night, on a visit to the fairies of Old Ross. If John can catch me by the hand or cloak when I ride by, and has courage not to let go his grip, I'll be safe. Here's the king. Don't open your mouth to answer. I saw what happened with the ointment.'

"The Dark Man didn't once cast his eye towards Molly, and he seemed to have no suspicion of me. When we came out I looked about me, and where do you think we were but in the dyke of the Rath of Cromogue. I was on the horse again, which was nothing but a big rag-weed, and I was in dread every minute I'd fall off; but nothing happened till I found myself in my own cabin. The king slipped five guineas into my hand as soon as I was on the ground, and thanked me, and bade me good night. I hope I'll never see his face again. I got into bed, and couldn't sleep for a long time; and when I examined my five guineas this morning, that I left in the table drawer the last thing, I found five withered leaves of oak – bad luck to the giver!"

Well, you may all think the fright, and the joy, and the grief the poor man was in when the woman finished her story. They talked and they talked, but we needn't mind what they said till Friday night came, when both were standing where the mountain road crosses the one going to Ross.

There they stood, looking towards the bridge of Thuar, in the dead of the night, with a little moonlight shining from over Kilachdiarmid. At last she gave a start, and "By this and by that," says she, "here they come, bridles jingling and feathers tossing!" He looked, but could see nothing; and she stood trembling and her eyes wide open, looking down the way to the ford of Ballinacoola. "I see your wife," says she, "riding on the outside just so as to rub against us. We'll walk on quietly, as if we suspected nothing, and when we are passing I'll give you a shove. If you don't do *your* duty then, woe be with you!"

Well, they walked on easy, and the poor hearts beating in both their breasts; and though he could see nothing, he heard a faint jingle and trampling and rustling, and at last he got the push that she promised. He spread out his arms, and there was his wife's waist within them, and he could see her plain; but such a hullabulloo rose as if there was an earthquake, and he found himself surrounded by horrible-looking things, roaring at him and striving to pull his wife away. But he made the sign of the cross and bid them begone in God's name, and held his wife as if it was iron his arms were made of. Bedad, in one moment everything was as silent as the grave, and the poor woman lying in a faint in the arms of her husband and her good neighbour.

Well, all in good time she was minding her family and her business again; and I'll go bail, after the fright she got, she spent more time on her knees, and avoided fairy men all the days of the week, and particularly on Sunday.

It is hard to have anything to do with the good people without getting a mark from them. My brave nurse didn't escape no more than another. She was one Thursday at the market of Enniscorthy, when what did she see walking among the tubs of butter but the Dark Man, very hungry-looking, and taking a scoop out of one tub and out of another. "Oh, sir," says she, very foolish, "I hope your lady is well, and the baby."

"Pretty well, thank you," says he, rather frightened like. "How do I look in this new suit?" says he, getting to one side of her.

"I can't see you plain at all, sir," says she.

"Well, now?" says he, getting round her back to the other side.

"Musha, indeed, sir, your coat looks no better than a withered dock-leaf."

"Maybe, then," says he, "it will be different now," and he struck the eye next him with a switch. Friends, she never saw a glimmer after with that one till the day of her death.

Connla and the Fairy Maiden

CONNLA OF THE FIERY HAIR was son of Conn of the Hundred Fights. One day as he stood by the side of his father on the height of Usna, he saw a maiden clad in strange attire coming towards him.

"Whence comest thou, maiden?" said Connla.

"I come from the Plains of the Ever Living," she said, "there where there is neither death nor sin. There we keep holiday always, nor need we help from any in our joy. And in all our pleasure we have no strife. And because we have our homes in the round green hills, men call us the Hill Folk."

The king and all with him wondered much to hear a voice when they saw no one. For save Connla alone, none saw the Fairy Maiden.

"To whom art thou talking, my son?" said Conn the king.

Then the maiden answered, "Connla speaks to a young, fair maid, whom neither death nor old age awaits. I love Connla, and now I call him away to the Plain of Pleasure, Moy Mell, where Boadag is king for aye, nor has there been complaint or sorrow in that land since he has held the kingship. Oh, come with me, Connla of the Fiery Hair, ruddy as the dawn with thy tawny skin. A fairy crown awaits thee to grace thy comely face and royal form. Come, and never shall thy comeliness fade, nor thy youth, till the last awful day of judgment."

The king in fear at what the maiden said, which he heard though he could not see her, called aloud to his Druid, Coran by name.

"Oh, Coran of the many spells," he said, "and of the cunning magic, I call upon thy aid. A task is upon me too great for all my skill and wit, greater than any laid upon me since I seized the kingship. A maiden unseen has met us, and by her power would take from me my dear, my comely son. If thou help not, he will be taken from thy king by woman's wiles and witchery."

Then Coran the Druid stood forth and chanted his spells towards the spot where the maiden's voice had been heard. And none heard her voice again, nor could Connla see her longer. Only as she vanished before the Druid's mighty spell, she threw an apple to Connla.

For a whole month from that day Connla would take nothing, either to eat or to drink, save only from that apple. But as he ate it grew again and always kept whole. And all the while there grew within him a mighty yearning and longing after the maiden he had seen.

But when the last day of the month of waiting came, Connla stood by the side of the king his father on the Plain of Arcomin, and again he saw the maiden come towards him, and again she spoke to him.

"'Tis a glorious place, forsooth, that Connla holds among short-lived mortals awaiting the day of death. But now the folk of life, the ever-living ones, beg and bid thee come

to Moy Mell, the Plain of Pleasure, for they have learnt to know thee, seeing thee in thy home among thy dear ones."

When Conn the king heard the maiden's voice he called to his men aloud and said:

"Summon swift my Druid Coran, for I see she has again this day the power of speech."

Then the maiden said: "Oh, mighty Conn, fighter of a hundred fights, the Druid's power is little loved; it has little honour in the mighty land, peopled with so many of the upright. When the Law will come, it will do away with the Druid's magic spells that come from the lips of the false black demon."

Then Conn the king observed that since the maiden came, Connla his son spoke to none that spake to him. So Conn of the hundred fights said to him, "Is it to thy mind what the woman says, my son?"

"'Tis hard upon me," then said Connla; "I love my own folk above all things; but yet, but yet a longing seizes me for the maiden."

When the maiden heard this, she answered and said "The ocean is not so strong as the waves of thy longing. Come with me in my curragh, the gleaming, straight-gliding crystal canoe. Soon we can reach Boadag's realm. I see the bright sun sink, yet far as it is, we can reach it before dark. There is, too, another land worthy of thy journey, a land joyous to all that seek it. Only wives and maidens dwell there. If thou wilt, we can seek it and live there alone together in joy."

When the maiden ceased to speak, Connla of the Fiery Hair rushed away from them and sprang into the curragh, the gleaming, straight-gliding crystal canoe. And then they all, king and court, saw it glide away over the bright sea towards the setting sun. Away and away, till eye could see it no longer, and Connla and the Fairy Maiden went their way on the sea, and were no more seen, nor did any know where they came.

How Cormac Mac Art Went to Faery

CORMAC, SON OF ART, son of Conn of the Hundred Battles, was high King of Ireland, and held his Court at Tara. One day he saw a youth upon the green having in his hand a glittering fairy branch with nine apples of red. And whensoever the branch was shaken, wounded men and women enfeebled by illness would be lulled to sleep by the sound of the very sweet fairy music which those apples uttered, nor could anyone upon earth bear in mind any want, woe, or weariness of soul when that branch was shaken for him.

"Is that branch thy own?" said Cormac.

"It is indeed mine."

"Wouldst thou sell it? And what wouldst thou require for it?"

"Will you give me what I ask?" said the youth.

The king promised, and the youth then claimed his wife, his daughter, and his son. Sorrowful of heart was the king, heaviness of heart filled his wife and children when they learned that they must part from him. But Cormac shook the branch amongst them, and when they heard the soft sweet music of the branch they forgot all care and sorrow and went forth to meet the youth, and he and they took their departure and were seen no more. Loud cries of weeping and mourning were made throughout Erin when this was known: but Cormac shook the branch so that there was no longer any grief or heaviness of heart upon anyone.

After a year Cormac said: "It is a year today since my wife, my son, and my daughter were taken from me. I will follow them by the same path that they took."

Cormac went off, and a dark magical mist rose about him, and he chanced to come upon a wonderful marvellous plain. Many horsemen were there, busy thatching a house with the feathers of foreign birds; when one side was thatched they would go and seek more, and when they returned not a feather was on the roof. Cormac gazed at them for a while and then went forward.

Again, he saw a youth dragging up trees to make a fire; but before he could find a second tree the first one would be burnt, and it seemed to Cormac that his labour would never end.

Cormac journeyed onwards until he saw three immense wells on the border of the plain, and on each well was a head. From out the mouth of the first head there flowed two streams, into it there flowed one; the second head had a stream flowing out of and another stream into its mouth, whilst three streams were flowing from the mouth of the third head. Great wonder seized Cormac, and he said: "I will stay and gaze upon these wells, for I should find no man to tell me your story." With that he set onwards till he came to a house in the middle of a field. He entered and greeted the inmates.

There sat within a tall couple clad in many-hued garments, and they greeted the king, and bade him welcome for the night.

Then the wife bade her husband seek food, and he arose and returned with a huge wild boar upon his back and a log in his hand. He cast down the swine and the log upon the floor, and said: "There is meat; cook it for yourselves."

"How can I do that?" said Cormac.

"I will teach you," said the youth. "Split this great log, make four pieces of it, and make four quarters of the hog; put a log under each quarter; tell a true story, and the meat will be cooked."

"Tell the first story yourself," said Cormac.

"Seven pigs I have of the same kind as the one I brought, and I could feed the world with them. For if a pig is killed I have but to put its bones into the stye again, and it will be found alive the next morning."

The story was true, and a quarter of the pig was cooked.

Then Cormac begged the woman of the house to tell a story.

"I have seven white cows, and they fill seven cauldrons with milk every day, and I give my word that they yield as much milk as would satisfy the men of the whole world if they were out on yonder plain drinking it."

That story was true, and a second quarter of the pig was cooked.

Cormac was bidden now to tell a story for his quarter, and he told how he was upon a search for his wife, his son and his daughter that had been borne away from him a year before by a youth with a fairy branch.

"If what thou sayest be true," said the man of the house, "thou art indeed Cormac, son of Art, son of Conn of the Hundred Battles."

"Truly I am," quoth Cormac.

That story was true, and a quarter of the pig was cooked.

"Eat thy meal now," said the man of the house.

"I never ate before," said Cormac, "having only two people in my company."

"Wouldst thou eat it with three others?"

"If they were dear to me, I would," said Cormac.

Then the door opened, and there entered the wife and children of Cormac: great was his joy and his exultation.

Then Manannan mac Lir, lord of the fairy Cavalcade, appeared before him in his own true form, and said thus:

"I it was, Cormac, who bore away these three from thee. I it was who gave thee this branch, all that I might bring thee here. Eat now and drink."

"I would do so," said Cormac, "could I learn the meaning of the wonders I saw today."

"Thou shalt learn them," said Manannan. "The horsemen thatching the roof with feathers are a likeness of people who go forth into the world to seek riches and fortune; when they return their houses are bare, and so they go on for ever. The young man dragging up the trees to make a fire is a likeness of those who labour for others: much trouble they have, but they never warm themselves at the fire. The three heads in the wells are three kinds of men. Some there are who give freely when they get freely; some who give freely though they get little; some who get much and give little, and they are the worst of the three, Cormac," said Manannan.

After that Cormac and his wife and his children sat down, and a table-cloth was spread before them.

"That is a very precious thing before thee," said Manannan, "there is no food however delicate that shall be asked of it but it shall be had without doubt."

"That is well," quoth Cormac.

After that Manannan thrust his hand into his girdle and brought out a goblet and set it upon his palm. "This cup has this virtue," said he, "that when a false story is told before it, it makes four pieces of it, and when a true story is related it is made whole again."

"Those are very precious things you have, Manannan," said the king.

"They shall all be thine," said Manannan, "the goblet, the branch and the tablecloth."

Then they ate their meal, and that meal was good, for they could not think of any meat but they got it upon the table-cloth, nor of any drink but they got it in the cup. Great thanks did they give to Manannan.

When they had eaten their meal a couch was prepared for them and they laid down to slumber and sweet sleep.

Where they rose on the morrow morn was in Tara of the kings, and by their side were tablecloth, cup, and branch.

Thus did Cormac fare at the Court of Manannan, and this is how he got the fairy branch.

The Legend of Knockgrafton

THERE WAS ONCE a poor man who lived in the fertile glen of Aherlow, at the foot of the gloomy Galtee mountains, and he had a great hump on his back: he looked just as if his body had been rolled up and placed upon his shoulders; and his head was pressed down with the weight so much that his chin, when he was sitting, used to rest upon his knees for support. The country people were rather shy of meeting him in any lonesome place, for though, poor creature, he was as harmless and as inoffensive as a new-born infant, yet his deformity was so great that he scarcely appeared to be a human creature, and some ill-minded persons had set strange stories about him afloat. He was said to have a great knowledge of herbs and charms; but certain it was that he had a mighty skilful hand in plaiting straw and rushes into hats and baskets, which was the way he made his livelihood.

Lusmore, for that was the nickname put upon him by reason of his always wearing a sprig of the fairy cap, or lusmore (the foxglove), in his little straw hat, would ever get a higher penny for his plaited work than anyone else, and perhaps that was the reason why someone, out of envy, had circulated the strange stories about him.

Be that as it may, it happened that he was returning one evening from the pretty town of Cahir towards Cappagh, and as little Lusmore walked very slowly, on account of the great hump upon his back, it was quite dark when he came to the old moat of Knockgrafton, which stood on the right-hand side of his road. Tired and weary was he, and noways comfortable in his own mind at thinking how much farther he had to travel, and that he should be walking all the night; so he sat down under the moat to rest himself, and began looking mournfully enough upon the moon.

Presently there rose a wild strain of unearthly melody upon the ear of little Lusmore; he listened, and he thought that he had never heard such ravishing music before. It was like the sound of many voices, each mingling and blending with the other so strangely that they seemed to be one, though all singing different strains, and the words of the song were these – *Da Luan, Da Mort, Da Luan, Da Mort, Da Luan, Da Mort*; when there would be a moment's pause, and then the round of melody went on again.

Lusmore listened attentively, scarcely drawing his breath lest he might lose the slightest note. He now plainly perceived that the singing was within the moat; and though at first it had charmed him so much, he began to get tired of hearing the same round sung over and over so often without any change; so availing himself of the pause when the *Da Luan, Da Mort*, had been sung three times, he took up the tune, and raised it with the words *augus Da Cadine*, and then went on singing with the voices inside of the moat, *Da Luan, Da Mort*, finishing the melody, when the pause again came, with *augus Da Cadine*.

The fairies within Knockgrafton, for the song was a fairy melody, when they heard this addition to the tune, were so much delighted that, with instant resolve, it was determined to bring the mortal among them, whose musical skill so far exceeded theirs, and little Lusmore was conveyed into their company with the eddying speed of a whirlwind.

Glorious to behold was the sight that burst upon him as he came down through the moat, twirling round and round, with the lightness of a straw, to the sweetest music that kept time to his motion. The greatest honour was then paid him, for he was put above all the musicians, and he had servants tending upon him, and everything to his heart's content, and a hearty welcome to all; and, in short, he was made as much of as if he had been the first man in the land.

Presently Lusmore saw a great consultation going forward among the fairies, and, notwithstanding all their civility, he felt very much frightened, until one stepping out from the rest came up to him and said –

> *"Lusmore! Lusmore!*
> *Doubt not, nor deplore,*
> *For the hump which you bore*
> *On your back is no more;*
> *Look down on the floor,*
> *And view it, Lusmore!"*

When these words were said, poor little Lusmore felt himself so light, and so happy, that he thought he could have bounded at one jump over the moon, like the cow in the history of the cat and the fiddle; and he saw, with inexpressible pleasure, his hump tumble down upon the ground from his shoulders. He then tried to lift up his head, and he did so with becoming caution, fearing that he might knock it against the ceiling of the grand hall, where he was; he looked round and round again with greatest wonder and delight upon everything, which appeared more and more beautiful; and, overpowered at beholding such a resplendent scene, his head grew dizzy, and his eyesight became dim. At last he fell into a sound sleep, and when he awoke he found that it was broad daylight, the sun shining brightly, and the birds singing sweetly; and that he was lying just at the foot of the moat of Knockgrafton, with the cows and sheep grazing peacefully round about him. The first thing Lusmore did, after saying his prayers, was to put his hand behind to feel for his hump, but no sign of one was there on his back, and he looked at himself with great pride, for he had now become a well-shaped dapper little fellow, and more than that, found himself in a full suit of new clothes, which he concluded the fairies had made for him.

Towards Cappagh he went, stepping out as lightly, and springing up at every step as if he had been all his life a dancing-master. Not a creature who met Lusmore knew him without his hump, and he had a great work to persuade everyone that he was the same man – in truth he was not, so far as outward appearance went.

Of course it was not long before the story of Lusmore's hump got about, and a great wonder was made of it. Through the country, for miles round, it was the talk of every one, high and low.

One morning, as Lusmore was sitting contented enough, at his cabin door, up came an old woman to him, and asked him if he could direct her to Cappagh.

"I need give you no directions, my good woman," said Lusmore, "for this is Cappagh; and whom may you want here?"

"I have come," said the woman, "out of Decie's country, in the county of Waterford looking after one Lusmore, who, I have heard tell, had his hump taken off by the fairies; for there is a son of a gossip of mine who has got a hump on him that will be his death; and maybe if he could use the same charm as Lusmore, the hump may be taken off him. And now I have told you the reason of my coming so far: 'tis to find out about this charm, if I can."

Lusmore, who was ever a good-natured little fellow, told the woman all the particulars, how he had raised the tune for the fairies at Knockgrafton, how his hump had been removed from his shoulders, and how he had got a new suit of clothes into the bargain.

The woman thanked him very much, and then went away quite happy and easy in her own mind. When she came back to her gossip's house, in the county of Waterford, she told her everything that Lusmore had said, and they put the little hump-backed man, who was a peevish and cunning creature from his birth, upon a car, and took him all the way across the country. It was a long journey, but they did not care for that, so the hump was taken from off him; and they brought him, just at nightfall, and left him under the old moat of Knockgrafton.

Jack Madden, for that was the humpy man's name, had not been sitting there long when he heard the tune going on within the moat much sweeter than before; for the fairies were singing it the way Lusmore had settled their music for them, and the song was going on; *Da Luan, Da Mort, Da Luan, Da Mort, Da Luan, Da Mort, augus Da Cadine*, without ever stopping. Jack Madden, who was in a great hurry to get quit of his hump, never thought of waiting until the fairies had done, or watching for a fit opportunity to raise the tune higher again than Lusmore had; so having heard them sing it over seven times without stopping, out he bawls, never minding the time or the humour of the tune, or how he could bring his words in properly, *augus Da Cadine, augus Da Hena*, thinking that if one day was good, two were better; and that if Lusmore had one new suit of clothes given him, he should have two.

No sooner had the words passed his lips than he was taken up and whisked into the moat with prodigious force; and the fairies came crowding round about him with great anger, screeching, and screaming, and roaring out, "Who spoiled our tune? Who spoiled our tune?" and one stepped up to him, above all the rest and said:

> *"Jack Madden! Jack Madden!*
> *Your words came so bad in*
> *The tune we felt glad in; –*
> *This castle you're had in,*
> *That your life we may sadden;*
> *Here's two humps for Jack Madden!"*

And twenty of the strongest fairies brought Lusmore's hump and put it down upon poor Jack's back, over his own, where it became fixed as firmly as if it was nailed on with twelve-penny nails, by the best carpenter that ever drove one. Out of their castle they then kicked him; and, in the morning, when Jack Madden's mother and her gossip came to look after their little man, they found him half dead, lying at the foot of the moat, with the other hump upon his back. Well to be sure, how they did look at each other! But they were afraid to say anything, lest a hump might be put upon their own shoulders. Home they brought the unlucky Jack Madden with them, as downcast in their hearts and their looks as ever two gossips were; and what through the weight of his other hump, and the long journey, he died soon after, leaving they say his heavy curse to anyone who would go to listen to fairy tunes again.

The Leprechawn

EVERY MYTHOLOGY has its good and evil spirits which are objects of adoration and subjects of terror, and often both classes are worshipped from opposite motives; the good, that the worshipper may receive benefit; the evil, that he may escape harm. Sometimes good deities are so benevolent that they are neglected, superstitious fear directing all devotion towards the evil spirits to propitiate them and avert the calamities they are ever ready to bring upon the human race; sometimes the malevolent deities have so little power that the prayer of the pious is offered up to the good spirits that they may pour out still further favors, for man is a worshipping being, and will prostrate himself with equal fervor before the altar whether the deity be good or bad.

Midway, however, between the good and evil beings of all mythologies there is often one whose qualities are mixed; not wholly good nor entirely evil, but balanced between the two, sometimes doing a generous action, then descending to a petty meanness, but never rising to nobility of character nor sinking to the depths of depravity; good from whim, and mischievous from caprice.

Such a being is the Leprechawn of Ireland, a relic of the pagan mythology of that country. By birth the Leprechawn is of low descent, his father being an evil spirit and his mother a degenerate fairy; by nature he is a mischief-maker, the Puck of the Emerald Isle. He is of diminutive size, about three feet high, and is dressed in a little red jacket or roundabout, with red breeches buckled at the knee, gray or black stockings, and a hat, cocked in the style of a century ago, over a little, old, withered face. Round his neck is an Elizabethan ruff, and frills of lace are at his wrists. On the wild west coast, where the Atlantic winds bring almost constant rains, he dispenses with ruff and frills and wears a frieze overcoat over his pretty red suit, so that, unless on the lookout for the cocked hat, "ye might pass a Leprechawn on the road and never know it's himself that's in it at all."

In Clare and Galway, the favorite amusement of the Leprechawn is riding a sheep or goat, or even a dog, when the other animals are not available, and if the sheep look weary in the morning or the dog is muddy and worn out with fatigue, the peasant understands that the local Leprechawn has been going on some errand that lay at a greater distance than he cared to travel on foot. Aside from riding the sheep and dogs almost to death, the Leprechawn is credited with much small mischief about the house. Sometimes he will make the pot boil over and put out the fire, then again he will make it impossible for the pot to boil at all. He will steal the bacon-flitch, or empty the potato-kish, or fling the baby down on the floor, or occasionally will throw the few poor articles of furniture about the room with a strength and vigor altogether disproportioned to his diminutive size. But his mischievous pranks seldom go further than to drink up all the milk or despoil the proprietor's bottle of its poteen,

sometimes, in sportiveness, filling the bottle with water, or, when very angry, leading the fire up to the thatch, and then startling the in-mates of the cabin with his laugh as they rise, frightened, to put out the flames.

To offset these troublesome attributes, the Leprechawn is very domestic, and sometimes attaches himself to a family, always of the "rale owld shtock", accompanying its representatives from the castle to the cabin and never deserting them unless driven away by some act of insolence or negligence, "for, though he likes good atin', he wants phat he gets to come wid an open hand, an' 'ud laver take the half av a pratee that's freely given than the whole av a quail that's begrudged him."

But what he eats must be specially intended for him, an instance being cited by a Clare peasant of a Leprechawn that deserted an Irish family, because, on one occasion, the dog having left a portion of his food, it was set by for the Leprechawn. "Jakers, 't was as mad as a little wasp he was, an' all that night they heard him workin' away in the cellar as busy as a nailer, an' a sound like a catheract av wather goin' widout saycin'. In the mornin' they wint to see phat he'd been at, but he was gone, an' whin they come to thry for the wine, bad loock to the dhrop he'd left, but all was gone from ivery cask an' bottle, and they were filled wid say-wather, beways av rayvinge o' phat they done him."

In different country districts the Leprechawn has different names. In the northern counties he is the Logheryman; in Tipperary, he is the Lurigadawne; in Kerry, the

Luricawne; in Monaghan, the Cluricawne. The dress also varies. The Logheryman wears the uniform of some British infantry regiments, a red coat and white breeches, but instead of a cap, he wears a broad-brimmed, high, pointed hat, and after doing some trick more than usually mischievous, his favorite position is to poise himself on the extreme point of his hat, standing at the top of a wall or on a house, feet in the air, then laugh heartily and disappear. The Lurigadawne wears an antique slashed jacket of red, with peaks all round and a jockey cap, also sporting a sword, which he uses as a magic wand. The Luricawne is a fat, pursy little fellow whose jolly round face rivals in redness the cut-a-way jacket he wears, that always has seven rows of seven buttons in each row, though what use they are has never been determined, since his jacket is never buttoned, nor, indeed, can it be, but falls away from a shirt invariably white as the snow. When in full dress he wears a helmet several sizes too large for him, but, in general, prudently discards this article of headgear as having a tendency to render him conspicuous in a country where helmets are obsolete, and wraps his head in a handkerchief that he ties over his ears.

The Cluricawne of Monaghan is a little dandy, being gorgeously arrayed in a swallow-tailed evening coat of red with green vest, white breeches, black stockings, and shoes that "fur the shine av 'em 'ud shame a lookin'-glass." His hat is a long cone without a brim, and is usually set jauntily on one side of his curly head. When greatly provoked, he will sometimes take vengeance by suddenly ducking and poking the sharp point of his hat into the eye of the offender. Such conduct is, however, exceptional, as he commonly contents himself with soundly abusing those at whom he has taken offence, the objects of his anger hearing his voice but seeing nothing of his person.

One of the most marked peculiarities of the Leprechawn family is their intense hatred of schools and schoolmasters, arising, perhaps, from the ridicule of them by teachers, who affect to disbelieve in the existence of the Leprechawn and thus insult him, for "it's very well beknownst, that onless ye belave in him an' thrate him well, he'll lave an' come back no more." He does not even like to remain in the neighborhood where a national school has been established, and as such schools are now numerous in Ireland, the Leprechawns are becoming scarce. "Wan gineration of taichers is enough for thim, bekase the families where the little fellys live forgit to set thim out the bit an' sup, an' so they lave." The few that remain must have a hard time keeping soul and body together for nowhere do they now receive any attention at meal-times, nor is the anxiety to see one by any means so great as in the childhood of men still living. Then, to catch a Leprechawn was certain fortune to him who had the wit to hold the mischief-maker a captive until demands for wealth were complied with.

"Mind ye," said a Kerry peasant, "the onliest time ye can ketch the little vagabone is whin he's settin' down, an' he niver sets down axceptin' whin his brogues want mendin'. He runs about so much he wears thim out, an' whin he feels his feet on the ground, down he sets undher a hidge or behind a wall, or in the grass, an' takes thim aff an' mends thim. Thin comes you by, as quiet as a cat an' sees him there, that ye can aisily, be his red coat, an' you shlippin' up on him, catches him in yer arrums.

"'Give up yer goold,' says you.

"'Begob, I've no goold,' says he.

"'Then outs wid yer magic purse,' says you.

"But it's like pullin' a hat full av taith to get aither purse or goold av him. He's got goold be the ton, an' can tell ye where ye can put yer finger on it, but he wont, till ye make him, an' that ye must do be no aisey manes. Some cuts aff his wind be chokin' him, an' some bates him, but don't for the life o' ye take yer eyes aff him, fur if ye do, he's aff like a flash an' the same man niver sees him agin, an' that's how it was wid Michael O'Dougherty.

"He was afther lookin' for wan nigh a year, fur he wanted to get married an' hadn't anny money, so he thought the aisiest was to ketch a Luricawne. So he was lookin' an' watchin' an' the fellys makin' fun av him all the time. Wan night he was comin' back afore day from a wake he'd been at, an' on the way home he laid undher the hidge an' shlept awhile, thin riz an' walked on. So as he was walkin', he seen a Luricawne in the grass be the road a-mendin' his brogues. So he shlipped up an' got him fast enough, an' thin made him tell him where was his goold. The Luricawne tuk him to nigh the place in the break o' the hills an' was goin' fur to show him, when all at wanst Mike heard the most outprobrious scraich over the head av him that 'ud make the hairs av ye shtand up like a mad cat's tail.

"'The saints defind me,' says he, 'phat's that?' an' he looked up from the Luricawne that he was carryin' in his arrums. That minnit the little attomy wint out av his sight, fur he looked away from it an' it was gone, but he heard it laugh when it wint an' he niver got the goold but died poor, as me father knows, an' he a boy when it happened."

Although the Leprechawns are skilful in evading curious eyes, and, when taken, are shrewd in escaping from their captors, their tricks are sometimes all in vain, and after resorting to every device in their power, they are occasionally compelled to yield up their hidden stores, one instance of which was narrated by a Galway peasant.

"It was Paddy Donnelly av Connemara. He was always hard at work as far as anny wan seen, an' bad luck to the day he'd miss, barrin' Sundays. When all 'ud go to the fair, sorra a fut he'd shtir to go near it, no more did a dhrop av dhrink crass his lips. When they'd ax him why he didn't take divarshun, he'd laugh an' tell thim his field was divarshun enough fur him, an' by an' by he got rich, so they knewn that when they were at the fair or wakes or shports, it was lookin' fur a Leprechawn he was an' not workin', an' he got wan too, fur how else cud he get rich at all."

And so it must have been, in spite of the denials of Paddy Donnelly, though, to do him justice, he stoutly affirmed that his small property was acquired by industry, economy, and temperance. But according to the opinions of his neighbors, "bad scran to him 't was as greedy as a pig he was, fur he knewn where the goold was, an' wanted it all fur himself, an' so lied about it like the Leprechawns, that's known to be the biggest liars in the world."

The Leprechawn is an old bachelor elf who successfully resists all efforts of scheming fairy mammas to marry him to young and beautiful fairies, persisting in single blessedness even in exile from his kind, being driven off as a punishment for his heterodoxy on matrimonial subjects. This is one explanation of the fact that Leprechawns are always seen alone, though other authorities make the Leprechawn solitary by preference, he having learned the hollowness of fairy friendship and the deceitfulness of fairy femininity, and left the society of his kind in disgust at its lack of sincerity.

It must be admitted that the latter explanation seems the more reasonable, since whenever the Leprechawn has been captured and forced to engage in conversation with his captor he displayed conversational powers that showed an ability to please, and as woman kind, even among fairy circles, are, according to an Irish proverb, "aisily caught be an oily tongue", the presumption is against the expulsion of the Leprechawn and in favor of his voluntary retirement.

However this may be, one thing is certain to the minds of all wise women and fairy-men, that he is the "thrickiest little divil that iver wore a brogue", whereof abundant proof is given. There was Tim O'Donovan, of Kerry, who captured a Leprechawn and forced him to disclose the spot where the "pot o' goold" was concealed. Tim was going to make the little rogue dig up the money for him, but, on the Leprechawn advancing the plea that he had no spade, released him, marking the spot by driving a stick into the ground and placing his hat on it. Returning the next morning with a spade, the spot pointed out by the "little ottomy av a desaver" being in the centre of a large bog, he found, to his unutterable disgust, that the Leprechawn was too smart for him, for in every direction innumerable sticks rose out of the bog, each bearing aloft an old "caubeen" so closely resembling his own that poor Tim, after long search, was forced to admit himself baffled and give up the gold that, on the evening before, had been fairly within his grasp, if "he'd only had the brains in his shkull to make the Leprechawn dig it for him, shpade or no shpade."

Even when caught, therefore, the captor must outwit the captive, and the wily little rascal, having a thousand devices, generally gets away without giving up a penny, and sometimes succeeds in bringing the eager fortune-hunter to grief, a notable instance of which was the case of Dennis O'Bryan, of Tipperary, as narrated by an old woman of Crusheen.

"It's well beknownst that the Leprechawn has a purse that's got the charmed shillin'. Only wan shillin', but the wondher av the purse is this: No matther how often ye take out a shillin' from it, the purse is niver empty at all, but whin ye put yer finger in agin, ye always find wan there, fur the purse fills up when ye take wan from it, so ye may shtand all day countin' out the shillin's an' they comin', that's a thrick av the good peoples an' be magic.

"Now Dinnis was a young blaggârd that was always afther peepin' about undher the hidge fur to ketch a Leprechawn, though they do say that thim that doesn't sarch afther thim sees thim oftener than thim that does, but Dinnis made his mind up that if there was wan in the counthry, he'd have him, fur he hated work worse than sin, an' did be settin' in a shebeen day in an' out till you'd think he'd grow on the sate. So wan day he was comin' home, an' he seen something red over in the corner o' the field, an' in he goes, as quiet as a mouse, an' up on the Leprechawn an' grips him be the collar an' down's him on the ground.

"'Arrah, now, ye ugly little vagabone,' says he, 'I've got ye at last. Now give up yer goold, or by jakers I'll choke the life out av yer pin-squazin' carkidge, ye owld cobbler, ye,' says he, shakin' him fit to make his head dhrop aff.

"The Leprechawn begged, and scritched, an' cried, an' said he wasn't a rale Leprechawn that was in it, but a young wan that hadn't anny goold, but Dinnis wouldn't let go av him, an' at last the Leprechawn said he'd take him to the pot ov goold that was hid be the say, in a glen in Clare. Dinnis didn't want to go so far, bein' afeared the Leprechawn 'ud get away, an' he thought the divilish baste was afther lyin' to him, bekase he knewn there was goold closter than that, an' so he was chokin' him that his eyes stood out till ye cud knock 'em aff wid a shtick, an' the Leprechawn axed him would he lave go if he'd give him the magic purse. Dinnis thought he'd betther do it, fur he was mortially afeared the oudacious little villin 'ud do him some thrick an' get away, so he tuk the purse, afther lookin' at it to make sure it was red shilk, an' had the shillin' in it, but the minnit he tuk his two eyes aff the Leprechawn, away wint the rogue wid a laugh that Dinnis didn't like at all.

"But he was feelin' very comfortable be razon av gettin' the purse, an' says to himself, 'Begorra, 'tis mesilf that'll ate the full av me waistband fur wan time, an' dhrink till a stame-ingine can't squaze wan dhrop more down me neck,' says he, and aff he goes like a quarther-horse fur Miss Clooney's sheebeen, that's where he used fur to go. In he goes, an' there was Paddy Grogan, an' Tim O'Donovan, an' Mike Conathey, an' Bryan Flaherty, an' a shtring more av 'em settin' on the table, an' he pulls up a sate an' down he sets, a-callin' to Miss Clooney to bring her best.

"'Where's yer money?' says she to him, fur he didn't use to have none barrin' a tuppence or so.

"'Do you have no fear,' says he, 'fur the money,' says he, 'ye pinny-schrapin' owld shkeleton,' this was beways av a shot at her, fur it was the size av a load o' hay she was, an' weighed a ton. 'Do you bring yer best,' says he. 'I'm a gintleman av forchune, bad loock to the job o' work I'll do till the life laves me. Come, jintlemin, dhrink at my axpinse.' An' so they did an' more than wanst, an' afther four or five guns apace, Dinnis ordhered dinner fur thim all, but Miss Clooney towld him sorra the bit or sup more 'ud crass the lips av him till he paid fur that he had. So out he pulls the magic purse fur to pay, an' to show it thim an' towld thim phat it was an' where he got it.

"'And was it the Leprechawn gev it ye?' says they.

"'It was,' says Dinnis, 'an' the varchew av this purse is sich, that if ye take shillin's out av it be the handful all day long, they'll be comin' in a shtrame like whishkey out av a jug,' says he, pullin' out wan.

"And thin, me jewel, he put in his fingers afther another, but it wasn't there, for the Leprechawn made a ijit av him, an' instid o' givin' him the right purse, gev him wan just like it, so as onless ye looked clost, ye cudn't make out the differ betune thim. But the face on Dinnis was a holy show when he seen the Leprechawn had done him, an' he wid only a shillin', an' half a crown av dhrink down the troats av thim.

"'To the divil wid you an' yer Leprechawns, an' purses, an' magic shillin's,' schreamed Miss Clooney, belavin', an' small blame to her that's, that it was lyin' to her he was. 'Ye're a thafe, so ye are, dhrinkin' up me dhrink, wid a lie on yer lips about the purse, an' insultin' me into the bargain,' says she, thinkin' how he called her a shkeleton, an' her a load fur a waggin. 'Yer impidince bates owld Nick, so it does,' says she; so she up an' hits him a power av a crack on the head wid a bottle; an' the other felly's, a-thinkin' sure that it was a lie he was afther tellin' them, an' he laving thim to pay fur the dhrink he'd had, got on him an' belted him out av the face till it was nigh onto dead he was. Then a consthable comes along an' hears the phillaloo they did be makin' an' comes in.

"'Tatther an' agers,' says he, 'lave aff. I command the pace. Phat's the matther here?'

"So they towld him an' he consayved that Dinnis shtole the purse an' tuk him be the collar.

"'Lave go,' says Dinnis. 'Sure phat's the harrum o' getting the purse av a Leprechawn?'

"'None at all,' says the polisman, 'av ye projuice the Leprechawn an' make him teshtify he gev it ye an' that ye haven't been burglarious an' sarcumvinted another man's money,' says he.

"But Dinnis cudn't do it, so the cunsthable tumbled him into the jail. From that he wint to coort an' got thirty days at hard labor, that he niver done in his life afore, an' afther he got out, he said he'd left lookin' for Leprechawns, fur they were too shmart fur him entirely, an' it's thrue fur him, bekase I belave they were."

The Field of Boliauns

ONE FINE DAY IN HARVEST – it was indeed Lady-day in harvest, that everybody knows to be one of the greatest holidays in the year – Tom Fitzpatrick was taking a ramble through the ground, and went along the sunny side of a hedge; when all of a sudden he heard a clacking sort of noise a little before him in the hedge. "Dear me," said Tom, "but isn't it surprising to hear the stonechatters singing so late in the season?" So Tom stole on, going on the tops of his toes to try if he could get a sight of what was making the noise, to see if he was right in his guess. The noise stopped; but as Tom looked sharply through the bushes, what should he see in a nook of the hedge but a brown pitcher, that might hold about a gallon and a half of liquor; and by-and-by a little wee teeny tiny bit of an old man, with a little motty of a cocked hat stuck upon the top of his head, a deeshy daushy leather apron hanging before him, pulled out a little wooden stool, and stood up upon it, and dipped a little piggin into the pitcher, and took out the full of it, and put it beside the stool, and then sat down under the pitcher, and began to work at putting a heel-piece on a bit of a brogue just fit for himself. "Well, by the powers," said Tom to himself, "I often heard tell of the Leprechauns, and, to tell God's truth, I never rightly believed in them – but here's one of them in real earnest. If I go knowingly to work, I'm a made man. They say a body must never take their eyes off them, or they'll escape."

Tom now stole on a little further, with his eye fixed on the little man just as a cat does with a mouse. So when he got up quite close to him, "God bless your work, neighbour," said Tom.

The little man raised up his head, and "Thank you kindly," said he.

"I wonder you'd be working on the holiday!" said Tom.

"That's my own business, not yours," was the reply.

"Well, maybe you'd be civil enough to tell us what you've got in the pitcher there?" said Tom.

"That I will, with pleasure," said he; "it's good beer."

"Beer!" said Tom. "Thunder and fire! Where did you get it?"

"Where did I get it, is it? Why, I made it. And what do you think I made it of?"

"Devil a one of me knows," said Tom; "but of malt, I suppose, what else?"

"There you're out. I made it of heath."

"Of heath!" said Tom, bursting out laughing; "sure you don't think me to be such a fool as to believe that?"

"Do as you please," said he, "but what I tell you is the truth. Did you never hear tell of the Danes?"

"Well, what about *them*?" said Tom.

"Why, all the about them there is, is that when they were here they taught us to make beer out of the heath, and the secret's in my family ever since."

"Will you give a body a taste of your beer?" said Tom.

"I'll tell you what it is, young man, it would be fitter for you to be looking after your father's property than to be bothering decent quiet people with your foolish questions. There now, while you're idling away your time here, there's the cows have broke into the oats, and are knocking the corn all about."

Tom was taken so by surprise with this that he was just on the very point of turning round when he recollected himself; so, afraid that the like might happen again, he made a grab at the Leprechaun, and caught him up in his hand; but in his hurry he overset the pitcher, and spilt all the beer, so that he could not get a taste of it to tell what sort it was. He then swore that he would kill him if he did not show him where his money was. Tom looked so wicked and so bloody-minded that the little man was quite frightened; so says he, "Come along with me a couple of fields off, and I'll show you a crock of gold."

So they went, and Tom held the Leprechaun fast in his hand, and never took his eyes from off him, though they had to cross hedges and ditches, and a crooked bit of bog, till at last they came to a great field all full of boliauns, and the Leprechaun pointed to a big boliaun, and says he, "Dig under that boliaun, and you'll get the great crock all full of guineas."

Tom in his hurry had never thought of bringing a spade with him, so he made up his mind to run home and fetch one; and that he might know the place again he took off one of his red garters, and tied it round the boliaun.

Then he said to the Leprechaun, "Swear ye'll not take that garter away from that boliaun." And the Leprechaun swore right away not to touch it.

"I suppose," said the Leprechaun, very civilly, "you have no further occasion for me?"

"No," says Tom; "you may go away now, if you please, and God speed you, and may good luck attend you wherever you go."

"Well, goodbye to you, Tom Fitzpatrick," said the Leprechaun; "and much good may it do you when you get it."

So Tom ran for dear life, till he came home and got a spade, and then away with him, as hard as he could go, back to the field of boliauns; but when he got there, lo and behold! Not a boliaun in the field but had a red garter, the very model of his own, tied about it; and as to digging up the whole field, that was all nonsense, for there were more than forty good Irish acres in it. So Tom came home again with his spade on his shoulder, a little cooler than he went, and many's the hearty curse he gave the Leprechaun every time he thought of the neat turn he had served him.

Master and Man

BILLY MAC DANIEL was once as likely a young man as ever shook his brogue at a patron, emptied a quart, or handled a shillelagh; fearing for nothing but the want of drink; caring for nothing but who should pay for it; and thinking of nothing but how to make fun over it; drunk or sober, a word and a blow was ever the way with Billy Mac Daniel; and a mighty easy way it is of either getting into or of ending a dispute. More is the pity that, through the means of his thinking, and fearing, and caring for nothing, this same Billy Mac Daniel fell into bad company; for surely the good people are the worst of all company anyone could come across.

It so happened that Billy was going home one clear frosty night not long after Christmas; the moon was round and bright; but although it was as fine a night as heart could wish for, he felt pinched with cold. "By my word," chattered Billy, "a drop of good liquor would be no bad thing to keep a man's soul from freezing in him; and I wish I had a full measure of the best."

"Never wish it twice, Billy," said a little man in a three-cornered hat, bound all about with gold lace, and with great silver buckles in his shoes, so big that it was a wonder how he could carry them, and he held out a glass as big as himself, filled with as good liquor as ever eye looked on or lip tasted.

"Success, my little fellow," said Billy Mac Daniel, nothing daunted, though well he knew the little man to belong to the *good people*; "here's your health, anyway, and thank you kindly; no matter who pays for the drink;" and he took the glass and drained it to the very bottom without ever taking a second breath to it.

"Success," said the little man; "and you're heartily welcome, Billy; but don't think to cheat me as you have done others – out with your purse and pay me like a gentleman."

"Is it I pay you?" said Billy; "could I not just take you up and put you in my pocket as easily as a blackberry?"

"Billy Mac Daniel," said the little man, getting very angry, "you shall be my servant for seven years and a day, and that is the way I will be paid; so make ready to follow me."

When Billy heard this, he began to be very sorry for having used such bold words towards the little man; and he felt himself, yet could not tell how, obliged to follow the little man the live-long night about the country, up and down, and over hedge and ditch, and through bog and brake, without any rest.

When morning began to dawn, the little man turned round to him and said, "You may now go home, Billy, but on your peril don't fail to meet me in the Fort-field tonight; or if you do it may be the worse for you in the long run. If I find you a good servant, you will find me an indulgent master."

Home went Billy Mac Daniel; and though he was tired and weary enough, never a wink of sleep could he get for thinking of the little man; but he was afraid not to do his bidding, so up he got in the evening, and away he went to the Fort-field. He was not long there before the little man came towards him and said, "Billy, I want to go a long journey tonight; so saddle one of my horses, and you may saddle another for yourself, as you are to go along with me, and may be tired after your walk last night."

Billy thought this very considerate of his master, and thanked him accordingly: "But," said he, "if I may be so bold, sir, I would ask which is the way to your stable, for never a thing do I see but the fort here, and the old thorn tree in the corner of the field, and the stream running at the bottom of the hill, with the bit of bog over against us."

"Ask no questions, Billy," said the little man, "but go over to that bit of bog, and bring me two of the strongest rushes you can find."

Billy did accordingly, wondering what the little man would be at; and he picked two of the stoutest rushes he could find, with a little bunch of brown blossom stuck at the side of each, and brought them back to his master.

"Get up, Billy," said the little man, taking one of the rushes from him and striding across it.

"Where shall I get up, please your honour?" said Billy.

"Why, upon horseback, like me, to be sure," said the little man.

"Is it after making a fool of me you'd be," said Billy, "bidding me get a horseback upon that bit of a rush? May be you want to persuade me that the rush I pulled but a while ago out of the bog over there is a horse?"

"Up! Up! And no words," said the little man, looking very angry; "the best horse you ever rode was but a fool to it." So Billy, thinking all this was in joke, and fearing to vex his master, straddled across the rush. "Borram! Borram! Borram!" cried the little man three times (which, in English, means to become great), and Billy did the same after him; presently the rushes swelled up into fine horses, and away they went full speed; but Billy, who had put the rush between his legs, without much minding how he did it, found himself sitting on horseback the wrong way, which was rather awkward, with his face to the horse's tail; and so quickly had his steed started off with him that he had no power to turn round, and there was therefore nothing for it but to hold on by the tail.

At last they came to their journey's end, and stopped at the gate of a fine house. "Now, Billy," said the little man, "do as you see me do, and follow me close; but as you did not know your horse's head from his tail, mind that your own head does not spin round until you can't tell whether you are standing on it or on your heels: for remember that old liquor, though able to make a cat speak, can make a man dumb."

The little man then said some queer kind of words, out of which Billy could make no meaning; but he contrived to say them after him for all that; and in they both went through the key-hole of the door, and through one key-hole after another, until they got into the wine-cellar, which was well stored with all kinds of wine.

The little man fell to drinking as hard as he could, and Billy, no way disliking the example, did the same. "The best of masters are you, surely," said Billy to him; "no matter who is the next; and well pleased will I be with your service if you continue to give me plenty to drink."

"I have made no bargain with you," said the little man, "and will make none; but up and follow me." Away they went, through key-hole after key-hole; and each mounting upon the rush which he left at the hall door, scampered off, kicking the clouds before them like snow-balls, as soon as the words, "Borram, Borram, Borram," had passed their lips.

When they came back to the Fort-field the little man dismissed Billy, bidding him to be there the next night at the same hour. Thus did they go on, night after night, shaping their course one night here, and another night there; sometimes north, and sometimes east, and sometimes south, until there was not a gentleman's wine-cellar in all Ireland they had not visited, and could tell the flavour of every wine in it as well, ay, better than the butler himself.

One night when Billy Mac Daniel met the little man as usual in the Fort-field, and was going to the bog to fetch the horses for their journey, his master said to him, "Billy, I shall want another horse tonight, for may be we may bring back more company than we take." So Billy, who now knew better than to question any order given to him by his master, brought a third rush, much wondering who it might be that would travel back in their company, and whether he was about to have a fellow-servant. "If I have," thought Billy, "he shall go and fetch the horses from the bog every night; for I don't see why I am not, every inch of me, as good a gentleman as my master."

Well, away they went, Billy leading the third horse, and never stopped until they came to a snug farmer's house, in the county Limerick, close under the old castle of Carrigogunniel, that was built, they say, by the great Brian Boru. Within the house there was great carousing going forward, and the little man stopped outside for some time to listen; then turning round all of a sudden, said, "Billy, I will be a thousand years old tomorrow!"

"God bless us, sir," said Billy; "will you?"

"Don't say these words again, Billy," said the little old man, "or you will be my ruin for ever. Now Billy, as I will be a thousand years in the world tomorrow, I think it is full time for me to get married."

"I think so too, without any kind of doubt at all," said Billy, "if ever you mean to marry."

"And to that purpose," said the little man, "have I come all the way to Carrigogunniel; for in this house, this very night, is young Darby Riley going to be married to Bridget Rooney; and as she is a tall and comely girl, and has come of decent people, I think of marrying her myself, and taking her off with me."

"And what will Darby Riley say to that?" said Billy.

"Silence!" said the little man, putting on a mighty severe look; "I did not bring you here with me to ask questions;" and without holding further argument, he began saying the queer words which had the power of passing him through the key-hole as free as air, and which Billy thought himself mighty clever to be able to say after him.

In they both went; and for the better viewing the company, the little man perched himself up as nimbly as a cocksparrow upon one of the big beams which went across the house over all their heads, and Billy did the same upon another facing him; but not being much accustomed to roosting in such a place, his legs hung down as untidy as may be, and it was quite clear he had not taken pattern after the way in which the little man had bundled himself up together. If the little man had been a tailor all his life he could not have sat more contentedly upon his haunches.

There they were, both master and man, looking down upon the fun that was going forward; and under them were the priest and piper, and the father of Darby Riley, with Darby's two brothers and his uncle's son; and there were both the father and the mother of Bridget Rooney, and proud enough the old couple were that night of their daughter, as good right they had; and her four sisters, with bran new ribbons in their caps, and her three brothers all looking as clean and as clever as any three boys in Munster, and there were uncles and aunts, and gossips and cousins enough besides to make a full house of it; and plenty was there to eat and drink on the table for every one of them, if they had been double the number.

Now it happened, just as Mrs. Rooney had helped his reverence to the first cut of the pig's head which was placed before her, beautifully bolstered up with white savoys, that the bride gave a sneeze, which made everyone at table start, but not a soul said 'God bless us'. All thinking that the priest would have done so, as he ought if he had done his duty, no one wished to take the word out of his mouth, which, unfortunately, was preoccupied with pig's head and greens. And after a moment's pause the fun and merriment of the bridal feast went on without the pious benediction.

Of this circumstance both Billy and his master were no inattentive spectators from their exalted stations. "Ha!" exclaimed the little man, throwing one leg from under him with a joyous flourish, and his eye twinkled with a strange light, whilst his eyebrows became elevated into the curvature of Gothic arches; "Ha!" said he, leering down at the bride, and then up at Billy, "I have half of her now, surely. Let her sneeze but twice more, and she is mine, in spite of priest, mass-book, and Darby Riley."

Again the fair Bridget sneezed; but it was so gently, and she blushed so much, that few except the little man took, or seemed to take, any notice; and no one thought of saying 'God bless us'.

Billy all this time regarded the poor girl with a most rueful expression of countenance; for he could not help thinking what a terrible thing it was for a nice young girl of nineteen, with large blue eyes, transparent skin, and dimpled cheeks, suffused with health and joy, to be obliged to marry an ugly little bit of a man, who was a thousand years old, barring a day.

At this critical moment the bride gave a third sneeze, and Billy roared out with all his might, "God save us!" Whether this exclamation resulted from his soliloquy, or from the mere force of habit, he never could tell exactly himself; but no sooner was it uttered than the little man, his face glowing with rage and disappointment, sprung from the beam on which he had perched himself, and shrieking out in the shrill voice of a cracked bagpipe, "I discharge you from my service, Billy Mac Daniel – take that for your wages," gave poor Billy a most furious kick in the back, which sent his unfortunate servant sprawling upon his face and hands right in the middle of the supper-table.

If Billy was astonished, how much more so was everyone of the company into which he was thrown with so little ceremony. But when they heard his story, Father Cooney laid down his knife and fork, and married the young couple out of hand with all speed; and Billy Mac Daniel danced the Rinka at their wedding, and plenty he did drink at it too, which was what he thought more of than dancing.

Taming the Pooka

THE WEST AND NORTHWEST coast of Ireland shows many remarkable geological formations, but, excepting the Giant's Causeway, no more striking spectacle is presented than that to the south of Galway Bay. From the sea, the mountains rise in terraces like gigantic stairs, the layers of stone being apparently harder and denser on the upper surfaces than beneath, so the lower portion of each layer, disintegrating first, is washed away by the rains and a clearly defined step is formed. These terraces are generally about twenty feet high, and of a breadth, varying with the situation and exposure, of from ten to fifty feet.

The highway from Ennis to Ballyvaughn, a fishing village opposite Galway, winds, by a circuitous course, through these freaks of nature, and, on the long descent from the high land to the sea level, passes the most conspicuous of the neighboring mountains, the Corkscrew Hill. The general shape of the mountain is conical, the terraces composing it are of wonderful regularity from the base to the peak, and the strata being sharply upturned from the horizontal, the impression given is that of a broad road carved out of the sides of the mountain and winding by an easy ascent to the summit.

"'Tis the Pooka's Path they call it," said the car-man. "Phat's the Pooka? Well, that's not aisy to say. It's an avil sper't that does be always in mischief, but sure it niver does sarious harrum axceptin' to thim that desarves it, or thim that shpakes av it disrespictful. I never seen it, Glory be to God, but there's thim that has, and be the same token, they do say that it looks like the finest black horse that iver wore shoes. But it isn't a horse at all at all, for no horse 'ud have eyes av fire, or be breathin' flames av blue wid a shmell o' sulfur, savin' yer presince, or a shnort like thunder, and no mortial horse 'ud take the lapes it does, or go as fur widout gettin' tired. Sure when it give Tim O'Bryan the ride it give him, it wint from Gort to Athlone wid wan jump, an' the next it tuk he was in Mullingyar, an' the next was in Dublin, and back agin be way av Kilkenny an' Limerick, an' niver turned a hair. How far is that? Faith I dunno, but it's a power av distance, an' clane acrost Ireland an' back. He knew it was the Pooka bekase it shpake to him like a Christian mortial, only it isn't agrayble in its language an' 'ull niver give ye a dacint word afther ye're on its back, an' sometimes not before aither.

"Sure Dennis O'Rourke was afther comin' home wan night, it was only a boy I was, but I mind him tellin' the shtory, an' it was at a fair in Galway he'd been. He'd been havin' a sup, some says more, but whin he come to the rath, and jist beyant where the fairies dance and ferninst the wall where the polisman was shot last winther, he fell in the ditch, quite spint and tired complately. It wasn't the length as much as the wideness av the road was in it, fur he was goin' from wan side to the other an' it was too much fur him entirely. So he laid shtill fur a bit and thin thried fur to get up, but his legs wor light and his head was heavy, an' whin he attempted to get his feet an the road 'twas his head that was an it, bekase his legs cudn't balance it. Well, he laid there and was bet entirely, an' while he was studyin' how he'd raise, he heard the throttin' av a horse on the road. "'Tis meself 'ull get the lift now,' says he, and laid waitin', and up comes the Pooka. Whin Dennis seen him, begob, he kivered his face wid his hands and turned on the breast av him, and roared wid fright like a bull.

"'Arrah thin, ye snakin' blaggârd,' says the Pooka, mighty short, 'lave aff yer bawlin' or I'll kick ye to the ind av next week,' says he to him.

"But Dennis was scairt, an' bellered louder than afore, so the Pooka, wid his hoof, give him a crack on the back that knocked the wind out av him.

"'Will ye lave aff,' says the Pooka, 'or will I give ye another, ye roarin' dough-face?'

"Dennis left aff blubberin' so the Pooka got his timper back.

"'Shtand up, ye guzzlin' sarpint,' says the Pooka, 'I'll give ye a ride.'

"'Plaze yer Honor,' says Dennis, 'I can't. Sure I've not been afther drinkin' at all, but shmokin' too much an' atin', an' it's sick I am, and not ontoxicated.'

"'Och, ye dhrunken buzzard,' says the Pooka, 'Don't offer fur to desave me,' liftin' up his hoof agin, an' givin' his tail a swish that sounded like the noise av a catheract, 'Didn't I thrack ye for two miles be yer breath,' says he, 'An' you shmellin' like a potheen fact'ry,' says he, 'An' the nose on yer face as red as a turkey-cock's. Get up, or I'll lift ye,' says he, jumpin' up an' cracking his hind fut like he was doin' a jig.

"Dennis did his best, an' the Pooka helped him wid a grip o' the teeth on his collar.

"'Pick up yer caubeen,' says the Pooka, 'an' climb up. I'll give ye such a ride as ye niver dhramed av.'

"'Ef it's plazin' to yer Honor,' says Dennis, 'I'd laver walk. Ridin' makes me dizzy,' says he.

"'Tis not plazin',' says the Pooka, 'will ye get up or will I kick the shtuffin' out av yer cowardly carkidge,' says he, turnin' round an' flourishin' his heels in Dennis' face.

"Poor Dennis thried, but he cudn't, so the Pooka tuk him to the wall an' give him a lift an it, an' whin Dennis was mounted, an' had a tight howld on the mane, the first lep he give was down the rock there, a thousand feet into the field ye see, thin up agin, an' over the mountain, an' into the say, an' out agin, from the top av the waves to the top av the mountain, an' afther the poor soggarth av a ditcher was nigh onto dead, the Pooka come back here wid him an' dhropped him in the ditch where he found him, an' blowed in his face to put him to slape, so lavin' him. An' they found Dennis in the mornin' an' carried him home, no more cud he walk for a fortnight be razon av the wakeness av his bones fur the ride he'd had.

"But sure, the Pooka's a different baste entirely to phat he was afore King Bryan-Boru tamed him. Niver heard av him? Well, he was the king av Munster an' all Ireland an' tamed the Pooka wanst fur all on the Corkschrew Hill forninst ye.

"Ye see, in the owld days, the counthry was full av avil sper'ts, an' fairies an' witches, an' divils entirely, and the harrum they done was onsaycin', for they wor always comin' an' goin', like Mulligan's blanket, an' widout so much as sayin', by yer lave. The fairies 'ud be dancin' on the grass every night be the light av the moon, an' stalin' away the childhre, an' many's the wan they tuk that niver come back. The owld rath on the hill beyant was full av the dead, an' afther nightfall they'd come from their graves an' walk in a long line wan afther another to the owld church in the valley where they'd go in an' stay till cock-crow, thin they'd come out agin an' back to the rath. Sorra a parish widout a witch, an' some nights they'd have a great enthertainmint on the Corkschrew Hill, an' you'd see thim, wid shnakes on their arrums an' necks an' ears, be way av jewels, an' the eyes av dead men in their hair, comin' for miles an' miles, some ridin' through the air on shticks an' bats an' owls, an' some walkin', an' more on Pookas an' horses wid wings that 'ud come up in line to the top av the hill, like the cabs at the dure o' the theayter, an' lave thim there an' hurry aff to bring more.

"Sometimes the Owld Inimy, Satan himself, 'ud be there at the enthertainmint, comin' an a monsthrous draggin, wid grane shcales an' eyes like the lightnin' in the heavens, an' a roarin' fiery mouth like a lime-kiln. It was the great day thin, for they do say all the witches brought their rayports at thim saysons fur to show him phat they done.

"Some 'ud tell how they shtopped the wather in a spring, an' inconvanienced the nabers, more 'ud show how they dhried the cow's milk, an' made her kick the pail, an' they'd all laugh like to shplit. Some had blighted the corn, more had brought the rains on the harvest. Some towld how their enchantmints made the childhre fall ill, some said how they set the thatch on fire, more towld how they shtole the eggs, or spiled the crame in the churn, or bewitched the butther so it 'udn't come, or led the shape into the bog. But that wasn't all.

"Wan 'ud have the head av a man murthered be her manes, an' wid it the hand av him hung fur the murther; wan 'ud bring the knife she'd scuttled a boat wid an' pint in the say to where the corpses laid av the fishermen she'd dhrownded; wan 'ud carry on her breast the child she'd shtolen an' meant to bring up in avil, an' another wan 'ud show the little white body av a babby she'd smothered in its slape. And the corpse-candles 'ud tell how they desaved the thraveller, bringin' him to the river, an' the avil sper'ts 'ud say how they dhrew him in an' down to the bottom in his sins an' thin to the pit wid him. An' owld Belzebub 'ud listen to all av thim, wid a rayporther, like thim that's afther takin' down the spaches at a Lague meetin', be his side, a-writing phat they said, so as whin they come to be paid, it 'udn't be forgotten.

"Thim wor the times fur the Pookas too, fur they had power over thim that wint forth afther night, axceptin' it was on an arriant av marcy they were. But sorra a sinner that hadn't been to his juty reglar 'ud iver see the light av day agin afther meetin' a Pooka thin, for the baste 'ud aither kick him to shmithereens where he stud, or lift him on his back wid his teeth an' jump into the say wid him, thin dive, lavin' him to dhrownd, or shpring over a clift wid him an' tumble him to the bottom a bleedin' corpse. But wasn't there the howls av joy whin a Pooka 'ud catch a sinner unbeknownst, an' fetch him on the Corkscrew wan o' the nights Satan was there. Och, God defind us, phat a sight it was. They made a ring wid the corpse-candles, while the witches tore him limb from limb, an' the fiends drunk his blood in red-hot iron noggins wid shrieks o' laughter to smother his schreams, an' the Pookas jumped on his body an' thrampled it into the ground, an' the timpest 'ud whishle a chune, an' the mountains about 'ud kape time, an' the Pookas, an' witches, an' sper'ts av avil, an' corpse-candles, an' bodies o' the dead, an' divils, 'ud all jig together round the rock where owld Belzebub 'ud set shmilin', as fur to say he'd ax no betther divarshun. God's presince be wid us, it makes me crape to think av it.

"Well, as I was afther sayin', in the time av King Bryan, the Pookas done a dale o' harrum, but as thim that they murthered wor dhrunken bastes that wor in the shebeens in the day an' in the ditch be night, an' wasn't missed whin the Pookas tuk them, the King paid no attintion, an' small blame to him that 's.

"But wan night, the queen's babby fell ill, an' the king says to his man, says he, 'Here, Riley, get you up an' on the white mare an' go fur the docther.'

"'Musha thin,' says Riley, an' the king's counthry house was in the break o' the hills, so Riley 'ud pass the rath an' the Corkschrew on the way afther the docther; 'Musha thin,' says he, aisey and on the quiet, 'it's mesilf that doesn't want that same job.'

"So he says to the king, 'Won't it do in the mornin'?'

"'It will not,' says the king to him. 'Up, ye lazy beggar, atin' me bread, an' the life lavin' me child.'

"So he wint, wid great shlowness, tuk the white mare, an' aff, an' that was the last seen o' him or the mare aither, fur the Pooka tuk 'em. Sorra a taste av a lie's in it, for thim that said they seen him in Cork two days afther, thrading aff the white mare, was desaved be the sper'ts, that made it seem to be him whin it wasn't that they've a thrick o' doin'.

"Well, the babby got well agin, bekase the docther didn't get there, so the king left botherin' afther it and begun to wondher about Riley an' the white mare, and sarched fur thim but didn't find thim. An' thin he knewn that they was gone entirely, bekase, ye see, the Pooka didn't lave as much as a hair o' the mare's tail.

"'Wurra thin,' says he, 'is it horses that the Pooka 'ull be stalin'? Bad cess to its impidince! This 'ull niver do. Sure we'll be ruinated entirely,' says he.

"Mind ye now, it's my consate from phat he said, that the king wasn't consarned much about Riley, fur he knewn that he cud get more Irishmen whin he wanted thim, but phat he meant to say was that if the Pooka tuk to horse-stalin', he'd be ruinated entirely, so he would, for where 'ud he get another white mare? So it was a mighty sarious question an' he retired widin himself in the coort wid a big book that he had that towld saycrets. He'd a sight av larnin', had the king, aquel to a school-masther, an' a head that 'ud sarcumvint a fox.

"So he read an' read as fast as he cud, an' afther readin' widout shtoppin', barrin' fur the bit an' sup, fur siven days an' nights, he come out, an' whin they axed him cud he bate the Pooka now, he said niver a word, axceptin' a wink wid his eye, as fur to say he had him.

"So that day he was in the fields an' along be the hedges an' ditches from sunrise to sunset, collectin' the matarials av a dose fur the Pooka, but phat he got, faith, I dunno, no more does anywan, fur he never said, but kep the saycret to himself an' didn't say it aven to the quane, fur he knewn that saycrets run through a woman like wather in a ditch. But there was wan thing about it that he cudn't help tellin', fur he wanted it but cudn't get it widout help, an' that was three hairs from the Pooka's tail, axceptin' which the charm 'udn't work. So he towld a man he had, he'd give him no end av goold if he'd get thim fur him, but the felly pulled aff his caubeen an' scrotched his head an' says, 'Faix, yer Honor, I dunno phat'll be the good to me av the goold if the Pooka gets a crack at me carkidge wid his hind heels,' an' he wudn't undhertake the job on no wages, so the king begun to be afeared that his loaf was dough.

"But it happen'd av the Friday, this bein' av a Chewsday, that the Pooka caught a sailor that hadn't been on land only long enough to get bilin' dhrunk, an' got him on his back, so jumped over the clift wid him lavin' him dead enough, I go bail. Whin they come to sarch the sailor to see phat he had in his pockets, they found three long hairs round the third button av his top-coat. So they tuk thim to the king tellin' him where they got thim, an' he was greatly rejiced, bekase now he belaved he had the Pooka sure enough, so he ended his inchantmint.

"But as the avenin' come, he riz a doubt in the mind av him thish-a-way. Ev the three hairs wor out av the Pooka's tail, the charm 'ud be good enough, but if they wasn't, an' was from his mane inshtead, or from a horse inshtead av a Pooka, the charm 'udn't work an' the Pooka 'ud get atop av him wid all the feet he had at wanst an' be the death av him immejitly. So this nate and outprobrious argymint shtruck the king wid great force an' fur a bit, he was onaisey. But wid a little sarcumvintion, he got round it, for he confist an' had absolution so as he'd be ready, thin he towld wan av the sarvints to come in an' tell him afther supper, that there was a poor widdy in the boreen beyant the Corkschrew that wanted help that night, that it 'ud be an arriant av marcy he'd be on, an' so safe agin the Pooka if the charm didn't howld.

"'Sure, phat'll be the good o' that?' says the man, 'It 'ull be a lie, an' won't work.'

"'Do you be aisey in yer mind,' says the king to him agin, 'do as yer towld an' don't argy, for that's a pint av mettyfisics,' says he, faix it was a dale av deep larnin' he had, 'that's a pint av mettyfisics an' the more ye argy on thim subjics, the less ye know,' says he, an' it's thrue fur him. 'Besides, aven if it's a lie, it'll desave the Pooka, that's no mettyfishian, an' it's my belafe that the end is good enough for the manes,' says he, a-thinking av the white mare.

"So, afther supper, as the king was settin' afore the fire, an' had the charm in his pocket, the sarvint come in and towld him about the widdy.

"'Begob,' says the king, like he was surprised, so as to desave the Pooka complately, 'Ev that's thrue, I must go relave her at wanst.' So he riz an' put on sojer boots, wid shpurs on 'em a fut acrost, an' tuk a long whip in his hand, for fear, he said, the widdy 'ud have dogs, thin wint to his chist an' tuk his owld stockin' an' got a suv'rin out av it, – Och, 'twas the shly wan he was, to do everything so well – an' wint out wid his right fut first, an' the shpurs a-rattlin' as he walked.

"He come across the yard, an' up the hill beyant yon an' round the corner, but seen nothin' at all. Thin up the fut path round the Corkscrew an' met niver a sowl but a dog that he cast a shtone at. But he didn't go out av the road to the widdy's, for he was afeared that if he met the Pooka an' he caught him in a lie, not bein' in the road to where he said he was goin', it 'ud be all over wid him. So he walked up an' down bechuxt the owld church below there an' the rath on the hill, an' jist as the clock was shtrikin' fur twelve, he heard a horse in front av him, as he was walkin' down, so he turned an' wint the other way, gettin' his charm ready, an' the Pooka come up afther him.

"'The top o' the mornin' to yer Honor,' says the Pooka, as perlite as a Frinchman, for he seen be his close that the king wasn't a common blaggârd like us, but was wan o' the rale quolity.

"'Me sarvice to ye,' says the king to him agin, as bowld as a ram, an' whin the Pooka heard him shpake, he got perliter than iver, an' made a low bow an' shcrape wid his fut, thin they wint on together an' fell into discoorse.

"''Tis a black night for thravelin',' says the Pooka.

"'Indade it is,' says the king, 'it's not me that 'ud be out in it, if it wasn't a case o' needcessity. I'm on an arriant av charity,' says he.

"'That's rale good o' ye,' says the Pooka to him, 'and if I may make bowld to ax, phat's the needcessity?'

"''Tis to relave a widdy-woman,' says the king.

"'Oho,' says the Pooka, a-throwin' back his head laughin' wid great plazin'ness an' nudgin' the king wid his leg on the arrum, beways that it was a joke it was bekase the king said it was to relave a widdy he was goin'. 'Oho,' says the Pooka, ''tis mesilf that's glad to be in the comp'ny av an iligint jintleman that's on so plazin' an arriant av marcy,' says he. 'An' how owld is the widdy-woman?' says he, bustin' wid the horrid laugh he had.

"'Musha thin,' says the king, gettin' red in the face an' not likin' the joke the laste bit, for jist betune us, they do say that afore he married the quane, he was the laddy-buck wid the wimmin, an' the quane's maid towld the cook, that towld the footman, that said to the gârdener, that towld the nabers that many's the night the poor king was as wide awake as a hare from sun to sun wid the quane a-gostherin' at him about that same. More betoken, there was a widdy in it, that was as sharp as a rat-thrap an' surrounded him whin he was young an' hadn't as much sinse as a goose, an' was like to marry him at wanst in shpite av all his relations, as widdys undhershtand how to do. So it's my consate that it wasn't dacint for the Pooka to be after laughin' that-a-way, an' shows

that avil sper'ts is dirthy blaggârds that can't talk wid jintlemin. 'Musha,' thin, says the king, bekase the Pooka's laughin' wasn't agrayble to listen to, 'I don't know that same, fur I niver seen her, but, be jagers, I belave she's a hundherd, an' as ugly as Belzebub, an' whin her owld man was alive, they tell me she had a timper like a gandher, an' was as aisey to manage as an armful o' cats,' says he. 'But she's in want, an' I'm afther bringin' her a suv'rin,' says he.

"Well, the Pooka sayced his laughin', fur he seen the king was very vexed, an' says to him, 'And if it's plazin', where does she live?'

"'At the ind o' the boreen beyant the Corkschrew,' says the king, very short.

"'Begob, that's a good bit,' says the Pooka.

"'Faix, it's thrue for ye,' says the king, 'more betoken, it's up hill ivery fut o' the way, an' me back is bruk entirely wid the stapeness,' says he, be way av a hint he'd like a ride.

"'Will yer Honor get upon me back,' says the Pooka. 'Sure I'm afther goin' that-a-way, an' you don't mind gettin' a lift?' says he, a-fallin' like the stupid baste he was, into the thrap the king had made fur him.

"'Thanks,' says the king, 'I b'lave not. I've no bridle nor saddle,' says he, 'besides, it's the shpring o' the year, an' I'm afeared ye're sheddin', an' yer hair 'ull come aff an' spile me new britches,' says he, lettin' on to make axcuse.

"'Have no fear,' says the Pooka. 'Sure I niver drop me hair. It's no ordhinary garron av a horse I am, but a most oncommon baste that's used to the quolity,' says he.

"'Yer spache shows that,' says the king, the clever man that he was, to be perlite that-a-way to a Pooka, that's known to be a divil out-en-out, 'but ye must exqueeze me this avenin', bekase, d'ye mind, the road's full o' shtones an' monsthrous stape, an' ye look so young, I'm afeared ye'll shtumble an' give me a fall,' says he.

"'Arrah thin,' says the Pooka, 'it's thrue fur yer Honor, I do look young,' an' he begun to prance on the road givin' himself airs like an owld widdy man afther wantin' a young woman, 'but me age is owlder than ye'd suppoge. How owld 'ud ye say I was,' says he, shmilin'.

"'Begorra, divil a bit know I,' says the king, 'but if it's agrayble to ye, I'll look in yer mouth an' give ye an answer,' says he.

"So the Pooka come up to him fair an' soft an' stratched his mouth like as he thought the king was wantin' fur to climb in, an' the king put his hand on his jaw like as he was goin' to see the teeth he had: and thin, that minnit he shlipped the three hairs round the Pooka's jaw, an' whin he done that, he dhrew thim tight, an' said the charm crossin' himself the while, an' immejitly the hairs wor cords av stale, an' held the Pooka tight, be way av a bridle.

"'Arra-a-a-h, now, ye bloody baste av a murtherin' divil ye,' says the king, pullin' out his big whip that he had consaled in his top-coat, an' giving the Pooka a crack wid it undher his stummick, 'I'll give ye a ride ye won't forgit in a hurry,' says he, 'ye black Turk av a four-legged nagur an' you shtaling me white mare,' says he, hittin' him agin.

"'Oh my,' says the Pooka, as he felt the grip av the iron on his jaw an' knewn he was undher an inchantmint, 'Oh my, phat's this at all,' rubbin' his breast wid his hind heel, where the whip had hit him, an' thin jumpin' wid his fore feet out to cotch the air an' thryin' fur to break away. 'Sure I'm ruined, I am, so I am,' says he.

"'It's thrue fur ye,' says the king, 'begob it's the wan thrue thing ye iver said,' says he, a-jumpin' on his back, an' givin' him the whip an' the two shpurs wid all his might.

"Now I forgot to tell ye that whin the king made his inchantmint, it was good fur siven miles round, and the Pooka knewn that same as well as the king an' so he shtarted like a cunshtable was afther him, but the king was afeared to let him go far, thinkin' he'd do the siven miles in a jiffy, an' the inchantmint 'ud be broken like a rotten shtring, so he turned him up the Corkschrew.

"'I'll give ye all the axercise ye want,' says he, 'in thravellin' round this hill,' an' round an' round they wint, the king shtickin' the big shpurs in him every jump an' crackin' him wid the whip till his sides run blood in shtrames like a mill race, an' his schreams av pain wor heard all over the worruld so that the king av France opened his windy and axed the polisman why he didn't shtop the fightin' in the shtrate. Round an' round an' about the Corkschrew wint the king, a-lashin' the Pooka, till his feet made the path ye see on the hill bekase he wint so often.

"And whin mornin' come, the Pooka axed the king phat he'd let him go fur, an' the king was gettin' tired an' towld him that he must niver shtale another horse, an' never kill another man, barrin' furrin blaggârds that wasn't Irish, an' whin he give a man a ride, he must bring him back to the shpot where he got him an' lave him there. So the Pooka consinted, Glory be to God, an' got aff, an' that's the way he was tamed, an' axplains how it was that Dennis O'Rourke was left be the Pooka in the ditch jist where he found him."

"More betoken, the Pooka's an althered baste every way, fur now he dhrops his hair like a common horse, and it's often found shtickin' to the hedges where he jumped over, an' they do say he doesn't shmell half as shtrong o' sulfur as he used, nor the fire out o' his nose isn't so bright. But all the king did fur him 'ud n't taiche him to be civil in his spache, an' whin he meets ye in the way, he spakes just as much like a blaggârd as ever. An' it's out av divilmint entirely he does it, bekase he can be perlite as ye know be phat I towld ye av him sayin' to the king, an' that proves phat I said to ye that avil sper'ts can't larn rale good manners, no matther how hard they thry.

"But the fright he got never left him, an' so he kapes out av the highways an' thravels be the futpaths, an' so isn't often seen. An' it's my belafe that he can do no harrum at all to thim that fears God, an' there's thim that says he niver shows himself nor meddles wid man nor mortial barrin' they're in dhrink, an' mebbe there's something in that too, fur it doesn't take much dhrink to make a man see a good dale."

The Kildare Pooka

MR. H— R—, when he was alive, used to live a good deal in Dublin, and he was once a great while out of the country on account of the 'ninety-eight' business. But the servants kept on in the big house at Rath— all the same as if the family was at home. Well, they used to be frightened out of their lives after going to their beds with the banging of the kitchen-door, and the clattering of fire-irons, and the pots and plates and dishes. One evening they sat up ever so long, keeping one another in heart with telling stories about ghosts and fetches, and that when – what would you have of it? – the little scullery boy that used to be sleeping over the horses, and could not get room at the fire, crept into the hot hearth, and when he got tired listening to the stories, sorra fear him, but he fell dead asleep.

Well and good, after they were all gone and the kitchen fire raked up, he was woke with the noise of the kitchen door opening, and the trampling of an ass on the kitchen floor. He peeped out, and what should he see but a big ass, sure enough, sitting on his curabingo and yawning before the fire. After a little he looked about him, and began scratching his ears as if he was quite tired, and says he, "I may as well begin first as last." The poor boy's teeth began to chatter in his head, for says he, "Now he's goin' to ate me"; but the fellow with the long ears and tail on him had something else to do. He stirred the fire, and then he brought in a pail of water from the pump, and filled a big pot that he put on the fire before he went out. He then put in his hand – foot, I mean – into the hot hearth, and pulled out the little boy. He let a roar out of him with the fright, but the pooka only looked at him, and thrust out his lower lip to show how little he valued him, and then he pitched him into his pew again.

Well, he then lay down before the fire till he heard the boil coming on the water, and maybe there wasn't a plate, or a dish, or a spoon on the dresser that he didn't fetch and put into the pot, and wash and dry the whole bilin' of 'em as well as e'er a kitchen-maid from that to Dublin town. He then put all of them up on their places on the shelves; and if he didn't give a good sweepin' to the kitchen, leave it till again. Then he comes and sits foment the boy, let down one of his ears, and cocked up the other, and gave a grin. The poor fellow strove to roar out, but not a dheeg 'ud come out of his throat. The last thing the pooka done was to rake up the fire, and walk out, giving such a slap o' the door, that the boy thought the house couldn't help tumbling down.

Well, to be sure if there wasn't a hullabulло next morning when the poor fellow told his story! They could talk of nothing else the whole day. One said one thing, another said another, but a fat, lazy scullery girl said the wittiest thing of all. "Musha!" says she, "if the pooka does be cleaning up everything that way when we are asleep, what should we be slaving ourselves for doing his work?"

"*Shu gu dheine*," says another; "them's the wisest words you ever said, Kauth; it's meeself won't contradict you."

So said, so done. Not a bit of a plate or dish saw a drop of water that evening, and not a besom was laid on the floor, and everyone went to bed soon after sundown. Next morning everything was as fine as fine in the kitchen, and the lord mayor might eat his dinner off the flags. It was great ease to the lazy servants, you may depend, and everything went on well till a foolhardy gag of a boy said he would stay up one night and have a chat with the pooka.

He was a little daunted when the door was thrown open and the ass marched up to the fire.

"An then, sir," says he, at last, picking up courage, "if it isn't taking a liberty, might I ax who you are, and why you are so kind as to do half of the day's work for the girls every night?"

"No liberty at all," says the pooka, says he: "I'll tell you, and welcome. I was a servant in the time of Squire R.'s father, and was the laziest rogue that ever was clothed and fed, and done nothing for it. When my time came for the other world, this is the punishment was laid on me – to come here and do all this labour every night, and then go out in the cold. It isn't so bad in the fine weather; but if you only knew what it is to stand with your head between your legs, facing the storm, from midnight to sunrise, on a bleak winter night."

"And could we do anything for your comfort, my poor fellow?" says the boy.

"Musha, I don't know," says the pooka; "but I think a good quilted frieze coat would help to keep the life in me them long nights."

"Why then, in troth, we'd be the ungratefullest of people if we didn't feel for you."

To make a long story short, the next night but two the boy was there again; and if he didn't delight the poor pooka, holding up a fine warm coat before him, it's no mather! Betune the pooka and the man, his legs was got into the four arms of it, and it was buttoned down the breast and the belly, and he was so pleazed he walked up to the glass to see how he looked. "Well," says he, "it's a long lane that has no turning. I am much obliged to you and your fellow-servants. You have made me happy at last. Good-night to you."

So he was walking out, but the other cried, "Och! Sure your going too soon. What about the washing and sweeping?"

"Ah, you may tell the girls that they must now get their turn. My punishment was to last till I was thought worthy of a reward for the way I done my duty. You'll see me no more." And no more they did, and right sorry they were for having been in such a hurry to reward the ungrateful pooka.

Daniel O'Rourke

PEOPLE MAY HAVE HEARD of the renowned adventures of Daniel O'Rourke, but how few are there who know that the cause of all his perils, above and below, was neither more nor less than his having slept under the walls of the Pooka's tower. I knew the man well. He lived at the bottom of Hungry Hill, just at the right-hand side of the road as you go towards Bantry. An old man was he, at the time he told me the story, with grey hair and a red nose; and it was on the 25th of June 1813 that I heard it from his own lips, as he sat smoking his pipe under the old poplar tree, on as fine an evening as ever shone from the sky. I was going to visit the caves in Dursey Island, having spent the morning at Glengariff.

"I am often *axed* to tell it, sir," said he, "so that this is not the first time. The master's son, you see, had come from beyond foreign parts in France and Spain, as young gentlemen used to go before Buonaparte or any such was heard of; and sure enough there was a dinner given to all the people on the ground, gentle and simple, high and low, rich and poor. The *ould* gentlemen were the gentlemen after all, saving your honour's presence. They'd swear at a body a little, to be sure, and, maybe, give one a cut of a whip now and then, but we were no losers by it in the end; and they were so easy and civil, and kept such rattling houses, and thousands of welcomes; and there was no grinding for rent, and there was hardly a tenant on the estate that did not taste of his landlord's bounty often and often in a year; but now it's another thing. No matter for that, sir, for I'd better be telling you my story.

"Well, we had everything of the best, and plenty of it; and we ate, and we drank, and we danced, and the young master by the same token danced with Peggy Barry, from the Bohereen – a lovely young couple they were, though they are both low enough now. To make a long story short, I got, as a body may say, the same thing as tipsy almost, for I can't remember ever at all, no ways, how it was I left the place; only I did leave it, that's certain. Well, I thought, for all that, in myself, I'd just step to Molly Cronohan's, the fairy woman, to speak a word about the bracket heifer that was bewitched; and so as I was crossing the stepping-stones of the ford of Ballyashenogh, and was looking up at the stars and blessing myself – for why? it was Lady-day – I missed my foot, and souse I fell into the water. 'Death alive!' thought I, 'I'll be drowned now!' However, I began swimming, swimming, swimming away for the dear life, till at last I got ashore, somehow or other, but never the one of me can tell how, upon a *dissolute* island.

"I wandered and wandered about there, without knowing where I wandered, until at last I got into a big bog. The moon was shining as bright as day, or your fair lady's eyes, sir (with your pardon for mentioning her), and I looked east and west, and north and south, and every way, and nothing did I see but bog, bog, bog – I could never find out how I got into it; and my heart grew cold with fear, for sure and

certain I was that it would be my *berrin* place. So I sat down upon a stone which, as good luck would have it, was close by me, and I began to scratch my head, and sing the *Ullagone* – when all of a sudden the moon grew black, and I looked up, and saw something for all the world as if it was moving down between me and it, and I could not tell what it was. Down it came with a pounce, and looked at me full in the face; and what was it but an eagle? As fine a one as ever flew from the kingdom of Kerry. So he looked at me in the face, and says he to me, 'Daniel O'Rourke,' says he, 'how do you do?' 'Very well, I thank you, sir,' says I; 'I hope you're well'; wondering out of my senses all the time how an eagle came to speak like a Christian. 'What brings you here, Dan,' says he. 'Nothing at all, sir,' says I; 'only I wish I was safe home again.' 'Is it out of the island you want to go, Dan?' says he. ''Tis, sir,' says I: so I up and told him how I had taken a drop too much, and fell into the water; how I swam to the island; and how I got into the bog and did not know my way out of it. 'Dan,' says he, after a minute's thought, 'though it is very improper for you to get drunk on Lady-day, yet as you are a decent sober man, who 'tends mass well, and never fling stones at me or mine, nor cries out after us in the fields – my life for yours,' says he; 'so get up on my back, and grip me well for fear you'd fall off, and I'll fly you out of the bog.' 'I am afraid,' says I, 'your honour's making game of me; for who ever heard of riding a horseback on an eagle before?' ''Pon the honour of a gentleman,' says he, putting his right foot on his breast, 'I am quite in earnest: and so now either take my offer or starve in the bog – besides, I see that your weight is sinking the stone.'

"It was true enough as he said, for I found the stone every minute going from under me. I had no choice; so thinks I to myself, faint heart never won fair lady, and this is fair persuadance. 'I thank your honour,' says I, 'for the loan of your civility; and I'll take your kind offer.' I therefore mounted upon the back of the eagle, and held him tight enough by the throat, and up he flew in the air like a lark. Little I knew the trick he was going to serve me. Up – up – up, God knows how far up he flew. 'Why then,' said I to him – thinking he did not know the right road home – very civilly, because why? I was in his power entirely; 'sir,' says I, 'please your honour's glory, and with humble submission to your better judgment, if you'd fly down a bit, you're now just over my cabin, and I could be put down there, and many thanks to your worship.'

"'*Arrah*, Dan,' said he, 'do you think me a fool? Look down in the next field, and don't you see two men and a gun? By my word it would be no joke to be shot this way, to oblige a drunken blackguard that I picked up off of a *could* stone in a bog.' 'Bother you,' said I to myself, but I did not speak out, for where was the use? Well, sir, up he kept, flying, flying, and I asking him every minute to fly down, and all to no use. 'Where in the world are you going, sir?' says I to him. 'Hold your tongue, Dan,' says he: 'mind your own business, and don't be interfering with the business of other people.' 'Faith, this is my business, I think,' says I. 'Be quiet, Dan,' says he: so I said no more.

"At last where should we come to, but to the moon itself. Now you can't see it from this, but there is, or there was in my time, a reaping-hook sticking out of the side of the moon, this way (drawing the figure on the ground with the end of his stick).

"'Dan,' said the eagle, 'I'm tired with this long fly; I had no notion 'twas so far.' 'And my lord, sir,' said I, 'who in the world *axed* you to fly so far – was it I? Did not

I beg and pray and beseech you to stop half an hour ago?' 'There's no use talking, Dan,' said he; 'I'm tired bad enough, so you must get off, and sit down on the moon until I rest myself.' 'Is it sit down on the moon?' said I; 'is it upon that little round thing, then? Why, then, sure I'd fall off in a minute, and be *kilt* and spilt, and smashed all to bits; you are a vile deceiver – so you are.' 'Not at all, Dan,' said he; 'you can catch fast hold of the reaping-hook that's sticking out of the side of the moon, and 'twill keep you up.' 'I won't then,' said I. 'Maybe not,' said he, quite quiet. 'If you don't, my man, I shall just give you a shake, and one slap of my wing, and send you down to the ground, where every bone in your body will be smashed as small as a drop of dew on a cabbage-leaf in the morning.' 'Why, then, I'm in a fine way,' said I to myself, 'ever to have come along with the likes of you;' and so giving him a hearty curse in Irish, for fear he'd know what I said, I got off his back with a heavy heart, took hold of the reaping-hook, and sat down upon the moon, and a mighty cold seat it was, I can tell you that.

"When he had me there fairly landed, he turned about on me, and said, 'Good morning to you, Daniel O'Rourke,' said he; 'I think I've nicked you fairly now. You robbed my nest last year' ('twas true enough for him, but how he found it out is hard to say), 'and in return you are freely welcome to cool your heels dangling upon the moon like a cockthrow.'

"'Is that all, and is this the way you leave me, you brute, you,' says I. 'You ugly unnatural *baste*, and is this the way you serve me at last? Bad luck to yourself, with your hook'd nose, and to all your breed, you blackguard.' 'Twas all to no manner of use; he spread out his great big wings, burst out a laughing, and flew away like lightning. I bawled after him to stop; but I might have called and bawled forever, without his minding me. Away he went, and I never saw him from that day to this – sorrow fly away with him! You may be sure I was in a disconsolate condition, and kept roaring out for the bare grief, when all at once a door opened right in the middle of the moon, creaking on its hinges as if it had not been opened for a month before, I suppose they never thought of greasing 'em, and out there walks – who do you think, but the man in the moon himself? I knew him by his bush.

"'Good morrow to you, Daniel O'Rourke,' said he; 'how do you do?' 'Very well, thank your honour,' said I. 'I hope your honour's well.' 'What brought you here, Dan?' said he. So I told him how I was a little overtaken in liquor at the master's, and how I was cast on a *dissolute* island, and how I lost my way in the bog, and how the thief of an eagle promised to fly me out of it, and how, instead of that, he had fled me up to the moon.

"'Dan,' said the man in the moon, taking a pinch of snuff when I was done, 'you must not stay here.' 'Indeed, sir,' says I, ''tis much against my will I'm here at all; but how am I to go back?' 'That's your business,' said he; 'Dan, mine is to tell you that here you must not stay; so be off in less than no time.' 'I'm doing no harm,' says I, 'only holding on hard by the reaping-hook, lest I fall off.' 'That's what you must not do, Dan,' says he. 'Pray, sir,' says I, 'may I ask how many you are in family, that you would not give a poor traveller lodging: I'm sure 'tis not so often you're troubled with strangers coming to see you, for 'tis a long way.' 'I'm by myself, Dan,' says he; 'but you'd better let go the reaping-hook.' 'Faith, and with your leave,' says I, 'I'll not let go the grip, and the more you bids me, the more I won't let go – so I will.' 'You had better, Dan,' says he again. 'Why, then, my little fellow,' says I, taking the whole weight of him with my eye from head to foot, 'there are two words to that bargain; and I'll not budge, but you may if you like.' 'We'll see how that is to be,' says he; and back he went, giving the door such a great bang after him (for it was plain he was huffed) that I thought the moon and all would fall down with it.

"Well, I was preparing myself to try strength with him, when back again he comes, with the kitchen cleaver in his hand, and, without saying a word, he gives two bangs to the handle of the reaping-hook that was keeping me up, and *whap!* it came in two. 'Good morning to you, Dan,' says the spiteful little old blackguard, when he saw me cleanly falling down with a bit of the handle in my hand; 'I thank you for your visit, and fair weather after you, Daniel.' I had not time to make any answer to him, for I was tumbling over and over, and rolling and rolling, at the rate of a fox-hunt. 'God help me!' says I, 'but this is a pretty pickle for a decent man to be seen in at this time of night: I am now sold fairly.' The word was not out of my mouth when, *whiz!* what should fly by close to my ear but a flock of wild geese, all the way from my own bog of Ballyasheenogh, else how should they know *me*? The *ould* gander, who was their general, turning about his head, cried out to me, 'Is that you, Dan?' 'The same,' said I, not a bit daunted now at what he said, for I was by this time used to all kinds of *bedevilment*, and, besides, I knew him of *ould*. 'Good morrow to you,' says he, 'Daniel O'Rourke; how are you in health this morning?' 'Very well, sir,' says I, 'I thank you kindly,' drawing my breath, for I was mightily in want of some. 'I hope your honour's the same.' 'I think 'tis falling you are, Daniel,' says he. 'You may say that, sir,' says I. 'And where are you going all the way so fast?' said the gander. So I told him how I had taken the drop, and how I came on the island, and how I lost my way in the bog, and how the thief of an eagle flew me up to the moon, and how the man in the moon turned me out. 'Dan,' said he, 'I'll save you: put out your hand and catch me by the leg, and I'll fly you home.' 'Sweet is your hand in a pitcher of honey, my jewel,' says I, though all the time I thought within myself that I don't much trust you; but there was no help, so I caught the gander by the leg, and away I and the other geese flew after him as fast as hops.

"We flew, and we flew, and we flew, until we came right over the wide ocean. I knew it well, for I saw Cape Clear to my right hand, sticking up out of the water. 'Ah, my lord,' said I to the goose, for I thought it best to keep a civil tongue in my head any way, 'fly to land if you please.' 'It is impossible, you see, Dan,' said he, 'for a while, because you see we are going to Arabia.' 'To Arabia!' said I; 'that's surely some place in foreign parts, far away. Oh! Mr. Goose: why then, to be sure, I'm a man to be pitied among you.' 'Whist, whist, you fool,' said he, 'hold your tongue; I tell you Arabia is a very decent sort of place, as like West Carbery as one egg is like another, only there is a little more sand there.'

"Just as we were talking, a ship hove in sight, scudding so beautiful before the wind. 'Ah! then, sir,' said I, 'will you drop me on the ship, if you please?' 'We are not fair over it,' said he; 'if I dropped you now you would go splash into the sea.' 'I would not,' says I; 'I know better than that, for it is just clean under us, so let me drop now at once.'

"'If you must, you must,' said he; 'there, take your own way;' and he opened his claw, and faith he was right – sure enough I came down plump into the very bottom of the salt sea! Down to the very bottom I went, and I gave myself up then for ever, when a whale walked up to me, scratching himself after his night's sleep, and looked me full in the face, and never the word did he say, but lifting up his tail, he splashed me all over again with the cold salt water till there wasn't a dry stitch upon my whole carcass! And I heard somebody saying – 'twas a voice I knew, too – 'Get up, you drunken brute, off o' that;' and with that I woke up, and there was Judy with a tub full of water, which she was splashing all over me – for, rest her soul! Though she was a good wife, she never could bear to see me in drink, and had a bitter hand of her own.

"'Get up,' said she again: 'and of all places in the parish would no place *sarve* your turn to lie down upon but under the *ould* walls of Carrigapooka? Uneasy resting I am sure you had of it.' And sure enough I had: for I was fairly bothered out of my senses with eagles, and men of the moons, and flying ganders, and whales, driving me through bogs, and up to the moon, and down to the bottom of the green ocean. If I was in drink ten times over, long would it be before I'd lie down in the same spot again, I know that."

The Huntsman's Son

A LONG, LONG TIME AGO there lived in a little hut on the borders of a great forest a huntsman and his wife and son. From his earliest years the boy, whose name was Fergus, used to hunt with his father in the forest, and he grew up strong and active, sure and swift-footed as a deer, and as free and fearless as the wind. He was tall and handsome; as supple as a mountain ash, his lips were as red as its berries; his eyes were as blue as the skies in spring; and his hair fell down over his shoulders like a shower of gold. His heart was as light as a bird's, and no bird was fonder of green woods and waving branches. He had lived since his birth in the hut in the forest, and had never wished to leave it, until one winter night a wandering minstrel sought shelter there, and paid for his night's lodging with songs of love and battle. Ever since that night Fergus pined for another life. He no longer found joy in the music of the hounds or in the cries of the huntsmen in forest glades. He yearned for the chance of battle, and the clang of shields, and the fierce shouts of fighting warriors, and he spent all his spare hours practising on the harp and learning the use of arms, for in those days the bravest warriors were also bards. In this way the spring and summer and autumn passed; and when the winter came again it chanced that on a stormy night, when thunder was rattling through the forest, smiting the huge oaks and hurling them crashing to the earth, Fergus lay awake thinking of his present lot, and wondering what the future might have in store for him. The lightning was playing around the hut, and every now and then a flash brightened up the interior.

After a peal, louder than any which had preceded it, Fergus heard three loud knocks at the door. He called out to his parents that someone was knocking.

"If that is so," said his father, "open at once; this is no night to keep a poor wanderer outside our door."

Fergus did as he was bidden, and as he opened the door a flash of lightning showed him, standing at the threshold, a little wizened old man with a small harp under his arm.

"Come in, and welcome," said Fergus, and the little man stepped into the room.

"It is a wild night, neighbours," said he.

"It is, indeed, a wild night," said the huntsman and his wife, who had got up and dressed themselves; "and sorry we are we have no better shelter or better fare to offer you, but we give you the best we have."

"A king cannot do more than his best," said the little man.

The huntsman's wife lit the fire, and soon the pine logs flashed up into a blaze, and made the hut bright and warm. She then brought forth a peggin of milk and a cake of barley-bread.

"You must be hungry, sir," she said.

"Hungry I am," said he; "but I wouldn't ask for better fare than this if I were in the king's palace."

"Thank you kindly, sir," said she, "and I hope you will eat enough, and that it will do you good."

"And while you are eating your supper," said the huntsman, "I'll make you a bed of fresh rushes."

"Don't put yourself to that trouble," said the little man. "When I have done my supper I'll lie down here by the fire, if it is pleasing to you, and I'll sleep like a top until morning. And now go back to your beds and leave me to myself, and maybe some time when you won't be expecting it I'll do a good turn for your kindness to the poor wayfarer."

"Oh, it's no kindness at all," said the huntsman's wife. "It would be a queer thing if an Irish cabin would not give shelter and welcome in a wild night like this. So goodnight, now, and we hope you will sleep well."

"Goodnight," said the little man, "and may you and yours never sup sorrow until your dying day."

The huntsman and his wife and Fergus then went back to their beds, and the little man, having finished his supper, curled himself up by the fire, and was soon fast asleep.

About an hour after a loud clap of thunder awakened Fergus, and before it had died away he heard three knocks at the door. He aroused his parents and told them.

"Get up at once," said his mother, "this is no night to keep a stranger outside our door."

Fergus rose and opened the door, and a flash of lightning showed him a little old woman, with a shuttle in her hand, standing outside.

"Come in, and welcome," said he, and the little old woman stepped into the room.

"Blessings be on them who give welcome to a wanderer on a wild night like this," said the old woman.

"And who wouldn't give welcome on a night like this?" said the huntsman's wife, coming forward with a peggin of milk and a barley cake in her hand, "and sorry we are we have not better fare to offer you."

"Enough is as good as a feast," said the little woman, "and now go back to your beds and leave me to myself."

"Not till I shake down a bed of rushes for you," said the huntsman's wife.

"Don't mind the rushes," said the little woman; "go back to your beds. I'll sleep here by the fire."

The huntsman's wife went to bed, and the little old woman, having eaten her supper, lay down by the fire, and was soon fast asleep.

About an hour later another clap of thunder startled Fergus. Again he heard three knocks at the door. He roused his parents, but he did not wait for orders from them. He opened the door, and a flash of lightning showed him outside the threshold a low-sized, shaggy, wild-looking horse. And Fergus knew it was the Pooka, the wild horse of the mountains. Bold as Fergus was, his heart beat quickly as he saw fire issuing from the Pooka's nostrils. But, banishing fear, he cried out:

"Come in, and welcome."

"Welcome you are," said the huntsman, "and sorry we are that we have not better shelter or fare to offer you."

"I couldn't wish a better welcome," said the Pooka, as he came over near the fire and sat down on his haunches.

"Maybe you would like a little bit of this, Master Pooka," said the huntsman's wife, as she offered him a barley cake.

"I never tasted anything sweeter in my life," said the Pooka, crunching it between his teeth, "and now if you can give me a sup of milk, I'll want for nothing."

The huntsman's wife brought him a peggin of milk. When he had drunk it, "Now," says the Pooka, "go back to your beds, and I'll curl myself up by the fire and sleep like a top till morning."

And soon everybody in the hut was fast asleep.

When the morning came the storm had gone, and the sun was shining through the windows of the hut. At the song of the lark Fergus got up, and no one in the world was ever more surprised than he when he saw no sign of the little old man, or the little old woman, or the wild horse of the mountains. His parents were also surprised, and they all thought that they must have been dreaming until they saw the empty peggins around the fire and some pieces of broken bread; and they did not know what to think of it all.

From that day forward the desire grew stronger in the heart of Fergus for a change of life; and one day he told his parents that he was resolved to seek his fortune. He said he wished to be a soldier, and that he would set out for the king's palace, and try to join the ranks of the Feni.

About a week afterwards he took leave of his parents, and having received their blessing he struck out for the road that led to the palace of the High King of Erin. He arrived there just at the time when the great captain of the Fenian host was recruiting his battalions, which had been thinned in recent battle.

The manly figure of Fergus, his gallant bearing, and handsome face, all told in his favour. But before he could be received into the Fenian ranks he had to prove that he could play the harp like a bard, that he could contend with staff and shield against nine Fenian warriors, that he could run with plaited hair through the tangled forest without loosening a single hair, and that in his course he could jump over trees as high as his head, and stoop under trees as low as his knee, and that he could run so lightly that the rotten twigs should not break under his feet. Fergus proved equal to all the tests, thanks to the wandering minstrel who taught him the use of the harp, to his own brave heart, and to his forest training. He was enrolled in the second battalion of the Feni, and before long he was its bravest and ablest champion.

At that very time it happened that the niece of the High King of Erin was staying with the king and queen in their palace at Tara. The princess was the loveliest lady in all the land. She was as proud as she was beautiful. The princes and chieftains of Erin in vain sought her hand in marriage. From Alba and Spain, and the far-off isles of Greece, kings came to woo her. From the northern lands came vikings in stately galleys with brazen prows, whose oarsmen tore the white foam from the emerald seas as they swept towards the Irish coasts. But the lady had vowed she would wed with no one except a battle champion who could excel in music the chief bard of the High King of Erin; who could outstrip on his steed in the great race of Tara the white steed of the plains; and who could give her as a wedding robe a garment of all the colours of the rainbow, so finely spun that when folded up it would fit in the palm of her small white hand. To fulfil these three conditions was impossible for all her suitors, and it seemed as if the loveliest lady of the land should go unmarried to her grave.

It chanced that once, on a day when the Fenian battalions were engaged in a hurling-match, Fergus beheld the lady watching the match from her sunny bower. He no sooner saw her than he fell over head and ears in love with her, and he thought of her by night, and he thought of her by day, and believing that his love was hopeless, he often wished he had never left his forest-home.

The great fair of Tara was coming on, and all the Feni were busy from morning till night practising feats of arms and games, in order to take part in the contests to be held during the fair. And Fergus, knowing that the princess would be present, determined to do his best to win the prizes which were to be contended for before the ladies' eyes.

The fair began on the 1st of August, but for a whole week before the five great roads of Erin were thronged with people of all sorts. Princes and warriors on their steeds, battle champions in their chariots, harpers in hundreds, smiths with gleaming spears and shields and harness for battle steeds and chariots; troops of men and boys leading racehorses; jewellers with gold drinking-horns, and brooches, and pins, and earrings, and costly gems of all kinds, and chess-boards of silver and gold, and golden and silver chessmen in bags of woven brass; dyers with their many-coloured fabrics; bands of jugglers; drovers goading on herds of cattle; shepherds driving their sheep; huntsmen with spoils of the chase; dwellers in the lakes or by the fish-abounding rivers with salmon and speckled trout; and countless numbers of peasants on horseback and on foot, all wending their way to the great meeting-place by the mound, which a thousand years before had been raised over the grave of the great queen. For there the fair was to be held.

On the opening day the High King, attended by the four kings of Erin, set out from the palace, and with them went the queen and the ladies of the court in sparkling chariots. The princess rode in the chariot with the high queen, under an awning made of the wings of birds, to protect them from the rays of the sun. Following the queen were the court ladies in other chariots, under awnings of purple or of yellow silk. Then came the brehons, the great judges of the land, and the chief bards of the high court of Tara, and the Druids, crowned with oak leaves, and carrying wands of divination in their hands.

When the royal party reached the ground it took its place in enclosures right up against the monumental mound. The High King sat with the four kings of Erin, all wearing their golden helmets, for they wore their diadems in battle only. In an enclosure next to the king's sat the queen and the princess and all the ladies of the court. At either side of the royal pavilions were others for the dames and ladies and nobles and chiefs of different degrees, forming part of a circle on the plain, and the stands and benches for the people were so arranged as to complete the circle, and in the round green space within it, so that all might hear and see, the contests were to take place.

At a signal from the king, who was greeted with a thunderous cheer, the heralds rode round the circle, and having struck their sounding shields three times with their swords, they made a solemn proclamation of peace. Then was sung by all the assembled bards, to the accompaniment of their harps, the chant in honour of the mighty dead. When this was ended, again the heralds struck their shields, and the contests began. The first contest was the contest of spear-throwing between the champions of the seven battalions of the Feni. When the seven champions took their places in front of the royal enclosure, everyone, even the proud princess, was struck by the manly beauty and noble bearing of Fergus.

The champions poised their spears, and at a stroke from the heralds upon their shields the seven spears sped flashing through the air. They all struck the ground, shafts up, and it was seen that two were standing side by side in advance of the rest, one belonged to Fergus, the other to the great chief, Oscar. The contest for the prize then lay between Oscar and Fergus, and when they stood in front of the king, holding their spears aloft, every heart was throbbing with excitement. Once more the heralds struck their shields, and, swifter than the lightning's flash, forth went the spears, and when Fergus's spear was seen shivering in the ground a full length ahead of the great chief Oscar's, the air was shaken by a wild cheer that was heard far beyond the plains of Tara. And as Fergus approached the high king to receive the prize the cheers were renewed. But Fergus thought more of the winsome glance of the princess than he did of the prize or the sounding cheers. And Princess Maureen was almost sorry for her vow, for her heart was touched by the beauty of the Fenian champion.

Other contests followed, and the day passed, and the night fell, and while the Fenian warriors were revelling in their camps the heart of Fergus, victor as he was, was sad and low. He escaped from his companions, and stole away to his native forest, for –

> "When the heart is sick and sorest,
> There is balsam in the forest –
> There is balsam in the forest
> For its pain."

And as he lay under the spreading branches, watching the stars glancing through the leaves, and listening to the slumb'rous murmur of the waters, a strange peace came over him.

But in the camp which he had left, and in the vast multitude on the plains of Tara, there was stir and revelry, and babbling speculation as to the contest of tomorrow – the contest which was to decide whether the chief bard of Erin was to hold his own against all comers, or yield the palm. For rumour said that a great Skald had come from the northern lands to compete with the Irish bard.

At last, over the Fenian camp, and over the great plain and the multitude that thronged it, sleep fell, clothing them with a silence as deep as that which dwelt in the forest, where, dreaming of the princess, Fergus lay. He awoke at the first notes of the birds, but though he felt he ought to go back to his companions and be witness of the contest which might determine whether the princess was to be another's bride, his great love and his utter despair of winning her so oppressed him that he lay as motionless as a broken reed. He scarcely heard the music of the birds, and paid no heed to the murmur of the brook rushing by his feet. The crackling of branches near him barely disturbed him, but when a shadow fell across his eyes he looked up gloomily, and saw, or thought he saw, someone standing before him. He started up, and who should he see but the little wizened old man who found shelter in his father's hut on the stormy night.

"This is a nice place for a battle champion to be. This is a nice place for *you* to be on the day which is to decide who will be the successful suitor of the princess."

"What is it to me," said Fergus, "who is to win her since I cannot."

"I told you," said the little man, "the night you opened the door for me, that the time might come when I might be able to do a good turn for you and yours. The time has come. Take this harp, and my luck go with you, and in the contest of the bards today you'll reap the reward of the kindness you did when you opened your door to the poor old wayfarer in the midnight storm."

The little man handed his harp to Fergus and disappeared as swiftly as the wind that passes through the leaves.

Fergus, concealing the harp under his silken cloak, reached the camp before his comrades had aroused themselves from sleep.

At length the hour arrived when the great contest was to take place.

The king gave the signal, and as the chief bard of Erin was seen ascending the mound in front of the royal enclosures he was greeted with a roar of cheers, but at the first note of his harp silence like that of night fell on the mighty gathering.

As he moved his fingers softly over the strings every heart was hushed, filled with a sense of balmy rest. The lark soaring and singing above his head paused mute and motionless in the still air, and no sound was heard over the spacious plain save the dreamy music. Then the bard struck another key, and a gentle sorrow possessed the hearts of his hearers, and unbidden tears gathered to their eyes. Then, with bolder hand, he swept his fingers across his lyre, and all hearts were moved to joy and pleasant laughter, and eyes that had been dimmed by tears sparkled as brightly as running waters dancing in the sun. When the last notes had died away a cheer arose, loud as the voice of the storm in the glen when the live thunder is revelling on the mountain tops. As soon as the bard had descended the mound the Skald from the northern lands took his place, greeted by cries of welcome from a hundred thousand throats. He touched his harp, and in the perfect silence was heard the strains of the mermaid's song, and through it the pleasant ripple of summer waters on the pebbly beach. Then the theme was changed, and on the air was borne the measured sweep of countless oars and the swish of waters around the prows of contending galleys, and the breezy voices of the sailors and the sea-bird's cry. Then his theme was changed to the mirth and laughter of the banquet-hall, the clang of meeting drinking-horns, and songs of battle. When the last strain ended, from the mighty host a great shout went up, loud as the roar of winter billows breaking in the hollows of the shore; and men knew not whom to declare the victor, the chief bard of Erin or the Skald of the northern lands.

In the height of the debate the cry arose that another competitor had ascended the mound, and there standing in view of all was Fergus, the huntsman's son. All eyes were fastened upon him, but no one looked so eagerly as the princess.

He touched his harp with gentle fingers, and a sound low and soft as a faint summer breeze passing through forest trees stole out, and then was heard the rustle of birds through the branches, and the dreamy murmur of waters lost in deepest woods, and all the fairy echoes whispering when the leaves are motionless in the noonday heat; then followed notes cool and soft as the drip of summer showers on the parched grass, and then the song of the blackbird, sounding as clearly as it sounds in long silent spaces of the evening, and then in one sweet jocund burst the multitudinous voices that hail the breaking of the morn. And the lark, singing and soaring above the minstrel, sank mute and motionless upon his shoulder, and from all the leafy woods the birds came thronging out and formed a fluttering canopy above his head.

When the bard ceased playing no shout arose from the mighty multitude, for the strains of his harp, long after its chords were stilled, held their hearts spell-bound.

And when he had passed away from the mound of contest all knew there was no need to declare the victor. And all were glad the comely Fenian champion had maintained the supremacy of the bards of Erin. But there was one heart sad, the heart of the princess; and now she wished more than ever that she had never made her hateful vow.

Other contests went on, but Fergus took no interest in them; and once more he stole away to the forest glade. His heart was sorrowful, for he thought of the great race of the morning, and he knew that he could not hope to compete with the rider of the white steed of the plains. And as he lay beneath the spreading branches during the whole night long his thoughts were not of the victory he had won, but of the princess, who was as far away from him as ever. He passed the night without sleep, and when the morning came he rose and walked aimlessly through the woods.

A deer starting from a thicket reminded him of the happy days of his boyhood, and once more the wish came back to him that he had never left his forest home. As his eyes followed the deer wistfully, suddenly he started in amazement. The deer vanished from view, and in his stead was the wild horse of the mountains.

"I told you I'd do you a good turn," said the Pooka, "for the kindness you and yours did me on that wild winter's night. The day is passing. You have no time to lose. The white steed of the plains is coming to the starting-post. Jump on my back, and remember, 'Faint heart never won fair lady.'"

In half a second Fergus was bestride the Pooka, whose coat of shaggy hair became at once as glossy as silk, and just at the very moment when the king was about to declare there was no steed to compete with the white steed of the plains, the Pooka with Fergus upon his back, galloped up in front of the royal enclosure. When the people saw the champion a thunderous shout rose up that startled the birds in the skies, and sent them flying to the groves.

And in the ladies' enclosure was a rustle of many-coloured scarves waving in the air. At the striking of the shields the contending steeds rushed from the post with the swiftness of a swallow's flight. But before the white steed of the plains had gone half-way round, Fergus and the wild horse of the mountains had passed the winning post, greeted by such cheers as had never before been heard on the plains of Tara.

Fergus heard the cheers, but scarcely heeded them, for his heart went out through his eyes that were fastened on the princess, and a wild hope stirred him that his glance was not ungrateful to the loveliest lady of the land.

And the princess was sad and sorry for her vow, for she believed that it was beyond the power of Fergus to bring her a robe of all the colours of the rainbow, so subtly woven as to fit in the palm of her soft, white hand.

That night also Fergus went to the forest, not too sad, because there was a vague hope in his heart that had never been there before. He lay down under the branches, with his feet towards the rustling waters, and the smiles of the princess gilded his slumbers, as the rays of the rising sun gild the glades of the forest; and when the morning came he was scarcely surprised when before him appeared the little old woman with the shuttle he had welcomed on the winter's night.

"You think you have won her already," said the little woman. "And so you have, too; her heart is all your own, and I'm half inclined to think that my trouble will be thrown away, for if you had never a wedding robe to give her, she'd rather have you this minute than all the kings of Erin, or than all the other princes and kings and chieftains in the whole world. But you and your father and mother were kind to me on a wild winter's night, and I'd never see your mother's son without a wedding robe fit for the greatest princess that ever set nations to battle for her beauty. So go and pluck me a handful of wild forest flowers, and I'll weave out of them a wedding robe with all the colours of the rainbow, and one that will be as sweet and as fragrant as the ripe, red lips of the princess herself."

Fergus, with joyous heart, culled the flowers, and brought them to the little old woman.

In the twinkling of an eye she wove with her little shuttle a wedding robe, with all the colours of the rainbow, as light as the fairy dew, as soft as the hand of the princess, as fragrant as her little red mouth, and so small that it would pass through the eye of a needle.

"Go now, Fergus," said she, "and may luck go with you; but, in the days of your greatness and of the glory which will come to you when you are wedded to the princess, be as kind, and have as open a heart and as open a door for the poor as you had when you were only a poor huntsman's son."

Fergus took the robe and went towards Tara. It was the last day of the fair, and all the contests were over, and the bards were about to chant the farewell strains to the memory of the great queen. But before the chief bard could ascend the mound, Fergus, attended by a troop of Fenian warriors on their steeds, galloped into the enclosure, and rode up in front of the queen's pavilion. Holding up the glancing and many-coloured robe, he said:

"O Queen and King of Erin! I claim the princess for my bride. You, O king, have decided that I have won the prize in the contest of the bards; that I have won the prize in the race against the white steed of the plains; it is for the princess to say if the robe which I give her will fit in the hollow of her small white hand."

"Yes," said the king. "You are victor in the contests; let the princess declare if you have fulfilled the last condition."

The princess took the robe from Fergus, closed her fingers over it, so that no vestige of it was seen.

"Yes, O king!" said she, "he has fulfilled the last condition; but before ever he had fulfilled a single one of them, my heart went out to the comely champion of the Feni. I was willing then, I am ready now, to become the bride of the huntsman's son."

Guleesh

THERE WAS ONCE A BOY in the County Mayo; Guleesh was his name. There was the finest rath a little way off from the gable of the house, and he was often in the habit of seating himself on the fine grass bank that was running round it. One night he stood, half leaning against the gable of the house, and looking up into the sky, and watching the beautiful white moon over his head. After he had been standing that way for a couple of hours, he said to himself: "My bitter grief that I am not gone away out of this place altogether. I'd sooner be any place in the world than here. Och, it's well for you, white moon," says he, "that's turning round, turning round, as you please yourself, and no man can put you back. I wish I was the same as you."

Hardly was the word out of his mouth when he heard a great noise coming like the sound of many people running together, and talking, and laughing, and making sport, and the sound went by him like a whirl of wind, and he was listening to it going into the rath. "Musha, by my soul," says he, "but ye're merry enough, and I'll follow ye."

What was in it but the fairy host, though he did not know at first that it was they who were in it, but he followed them into the rath. It's there he heard the fulparnee, and the folpornee, the rap-lay-hoota, and the roolya-boolya, that they had there, and every man of them crying out as loud as he could: "My horse, and bridle, and saddle! My horse, and bridle, and saddle!"

"By my hand," said Guleesh, "my boy, that's not bad. I'll imitate ye," and he cried out as well as they: "My horse, and bridle, and saddle! My horse, and bridle, and saddle!" And on the moment there was a fine horse with a bridle of gold, and a saddle of silver, standing before him. He leaped up on it, and the moment he was on its back he saw clearly that the rath was full of horses, and of little people going riding on them.

Said a man of them to him: "Are you coming with us tonight, Guleesh?"

"I am surely," said Guleesh.

"If you are, come along," said the little man, and out they went all together, riding like the wind, faster than the fastest horse ever you saw a-hunting, and faster than the fox and the hounds at his tail.

The cold winter's wind that was before them, they overtook her, and the cold winter's wind that was behind them, she did not overtake them. And stop nor stay of that full race, did they make none, until they came to the brink of the sea.

Then every one of them said: "Hie over cap! Hie over cap!" and that moment they were up in the air, and before Guleesh had time to remember where he was, they were down on dry land again, and were going like the wind.

At last they stood still, and a man of them said to Guleesh: "Guleesh, do you know where you are now?"

"Not a know," says Guleesh.

"You're in France, Guleesh," said he. "The daughter of the king of France is to be married tonight, the handsomest woman that the sun ever saw, and we must do our best to bring her with us; if we're only able to carry her off; and you must come with us that we may be able to put the young girl up behind you on the horse, when we'll be bringing her away, for it's not lawful for us to put her sitting behind ourselves. But you're flesh and blood, and she can take a good grip of you, so that she won't fall off the horse. Are you satisfied, Guleesh, and will you do what we're telling you?"

"Why shouldn't I be satisfied?" said Guleesh. "I'm satisfied, surely, and anything that ye will tell me to do I'll do it without doubt."

They got off their horses there, and a man of them said a word that Guleesh did not understand, and on the moment they were lifted up, and Guleesh found himself and his companions in the palace. There was a great feast going on there, and there was not a nobleman or a gentleman in the kingdom but was gathered there, dressed in silk and satin, and gold and silver, and the night was as bright as the day with all the lamps and candles that were lit, and Guleesh had to shut his two eyes at the brightness. When he opened them again and looked from him, he thought he never saw anything as fine as all he saw there. There were a hundred tables spread out, and their full of meat and drink on each table of them, flesh-meat, and cakes and sweetmeats, and wine and ale, and every drink that ever a man saw. The musicians were at the two ends of the hall, and they were playing the sweetest music that ever a man's ear heard, and there were young women and fine youths in the middle of the hall, dancing and turning, and going round so quickly and so lightly, that it put a soorawn in Guleesh's head to be looking at them. There were more there playing tricks, and more making fun and laughing, for such a feast as there was that day had not been in France for twenty years, because the old king had no children alive but only the one daughter, and she was to be married to the son of another king that night. Three days the feast was going on, and the third night she was to be married, and that was the night that Guleesh and the sheehogues came, hoping, if they could, to carry off with them the king's young daughter.

Guleesh and his companions were standing together at the head of the hall, where there was a fine altar dressed up, and two bishops behind it waiting to marry the girl, as soon as the right time should come. Now nobody could see the sheehogues, for they said a word as they came in, that made them all invisible, as if they had not been in it at all.

"Tell me which of them is the king's daughter," said Guleesh, when he was becoming a little used to the noise and the light.

"Don't you see her there away from you?" said the little man that he was talking to.

Guleesh looked where the little man was pointing with his finger, and there he saw the loveliest woman that was, he thought, upon the ridge of the world. The rose and the lily were fighting together in her face, and one could not tell which of them got the victory. Her arms and hands were like the lime, her mouth as red as a strawberry when it is ripe, her foot was as small and as light as another one's hand, her form was smooth and slender, and her hair was falling down from her head in buckles of gold. Her garments and dress were woven with gold and silver, and the bright stone that was in the ring on her hand was as shining as the sun.

Guleesh was nearly blinded with all the loveliness and beauty that was in her; but when he looked again, he saw that she was crying, and that there was the trace of tears in her eyes. "It can't be," said Guleesh, "that there's grief on her, when everybody round her is so full of sport and merriment."

"Musha, then, she is grieved," said the little man; "for it's against her own will she's marrying, and she has no love for the husband she is to marry. The king was going to give her to him three years ago, when she was only fifteen, but she said she was too young, and requested him to leave her as she was yet. The king gave her a year's grace, and when that year was up he gave her another year's grace, and then another; but a week or a day he would not give her longer, and she is eighteen years old tonight, and it's time for her to marry; but, indeed," says he, and he crooked his mouth in an ugly way – "indeed, it's no king's son she'll marry, if I can help it."

Guleesh pitied the handsome young lady greatly when he heard that, and he was heart-broken to think that it would be necessary for her to marry a man she did not like, or, what was worse, to take a nasty sheehogue for a husband. However, he did not say a word, though he could not help giving many a curse to the ill-luck that was laid out for himself, to be helping the people that were to snatch her away from her home and from her father.

He began thinking, then, what it was he ought to do to save her, but he could think of nothing. "Oh! If I could only give her some help and relief," said he, "I wouldn't care whether I were alive or dead; but I see nothing that I can do for her."

He was looking on when the king's son came up to her and asked her for a kiss, but she turned her head away from him. Guleesh had double pity for her then, when he saw the lad taking her by the soft white hand, and drawing her out to dance. They went round in the dance near where Guleesh was, and he could plainly see that there were tears in her eyes.

When the dancing was over, the old king, her father, and her mother the queen, came up and said that this was the right time to marry her, that the bishop was ready, and it was time to put the wedding-ring on her and give her to her husband.

The king took the youth by the hand, and the queen took her daughter, and they went up together to the altar, with the lords and great people following them.

When they came near the altar, and were no more than about four yards from it, the little sheehogue stretched out his foot before the girl, and she fell. Before she was able to rise again he threw something that was in his hand upon her, said a couple of words, and upon the moment the maiden was gone from amongst them. Nobody could see her, for that word made her invisible. The little man*een* seized her and raised her up behind Guleesh, and the king nor no one else saw them, but out with them through the hall till they came to the door.

Oro! Dear Mary! It's there the pity was, and the trouble, and the crying, and the wonder, and the searching, and the rookawn, when that lady disappeared from their eyes, and without their seeing what did it. Out of the door of the palace they went, without being stopped or hindered, for nobody saw them, and, "My horse, my bridle, and saddle!" says every man of them. "My horse, my bridle, and saddle!" says Guleesh; and on the moment the horse was standing ready caparisoned before him. "Now, jump up, Guleesh," said the little man, "and put the lady behind you, and we will be going; the morning is not far off from us now."

Guleesh raised her up on the horse's back, and leaped up himself before her, and, "Rise, horse," said he; and his horse, and the other horses with him, went in a full race until they came to the sea.

"Hie over cap!" said every man of them.

"Hie over cap!" said Guleesh; and on the moment the horse rose under him, and cut a leap in the clouds, and came down in Erin.

They did not stop there, but went of a race to the place where was Guleesh's house and the rath. And when they came as far as that, Guleesh turned and caught the young girl in his two arms, and leaped off the horse.

"I call and cross you to myself, in the name of God!" said he; and on the spot, before the word was out of his mouth, the horse fell down, and what was in it but the beam of a plough, of which they had made a horse; and every other horse they had, it was that way they made it. Some of them were riding on an old besom, and some on a broken stick, and more on a bohalawn or a hemlock-stalk.

The good people called out together when they heard what Guleesh said:

"Oh! Guleesh, you clown, you thief, that no good may happen you, why did you play that trick on us?"

But they had no power at all to carry off the girl, after Guleesh had consecrated her to himself.

"Oh! Guleesh, isn't that a nice turn you did us, and we so kind to you? What good have we now out of our journey to France. Never mind yet, you clown, but you'll pay us another time for this. Believe us, you'll repent it."

"He'll have no good to get out of the young girl," said the little man that was talking to him in the palace before that, and as he said the word he moved over to her and struck her a slap on the side of the head. "Now," says he, "she'll be without talk any more; now, Guleesh, what good will she be to you when she'll be dumb? It's time for us to go – but you'll remember us, Guleesh!"

When he said that he stretched out his two hands, and before Guleesh was able to give an answer, he and the rest of them were gone into the rath out of his sight, and he saw them no more.

He turned to the young woman and said to her: "Thanks be to God, they're gone. Would you not sooner stay with me than with them?" She gave him no answer.

"There's trouble and grief on her yet," said Guleesh in his own mind, and he spoke to her again: "I am afraid that you must spend this night in my father's house, lady, and if there is anything that I can do for you, tell me, and I'll be your servant."

The beautiful girl remained silent, but there were tears in her eyes, and her face was white and red after each other.

"Lady," said Guleesh, "tell me what you would like me to do now. I never belonged at all to that lot of sheehogues who carried you away with them. I am the son of an honest farmer, and I went with them without knowing it. If I'll be able to send you back to your father I'll do it, and I pray you make any use of me now that you may wish."

He looked into her face, and he saw the mouth moving as if she was going to speak, but there came no word from it.

"It cannot be," said Guleesh, "that you are dumb. Did I not hear you speaking to the king's son in the palace tonight? Or has that devil made you really dumb, when he struck his nasty hand on your jaw?"

The girl raised her white smooth hand, and laid her finger on her tongue, to show him that she had lost her voice and power of speech, and the tears ran out of her two eyes like streams, and Guleesh's own eyes were not dry, for as rough as he was on the outside he had a soft heart, and could not stand the sight of the young girl, and she in that unhappy plight.

He began thinking with himself what he ought to do, and he did not like to bring her home with himself to his father's house, for he knew well that they would not believe him, that he had been in France and brought back with him the king of France's daughter, and he was afraid they might make a mock of the young lady or insult her.

As he was doubting what he ought to do, and hesitating, he chanced to remember the priest. "Glory be to God," said he, "I know now what I'll do; I'll bring her to the priest's house, and he won't refuse me to keep the lady and care for her." He turned to the lady again and told her that he was loth to take her to his father's house, but that there was an excellent priest very friendly to himself, who would take good care of her, if she wished to remain in his house; but that if there was any other place she would rather go, he said he would bring her to it.

She bent her head, to show him she was obliged, and gave him to understand that she was ready to follow him any place he was going. "We will go to the priest's house, then," said he; "he is under an obligation to me, and will do anything I ask him."

They went together accordingly to the priest's house, and the sun was just rising when they came to the door. Guleesh beat it hard, and as early as it was the priest was up, and opened the door himself. He wondered when he saw Guleesh and the girl, for he was certain that it was coming wanting to be married they were.

"Guleesh, Guleesh, isn't it the nice boy you are that you can't wait till ten o'clock or till twelve, but that you must be coming to me at this hour, looking for marriage, you and your sweetheart? You ought to know that I can't marry you at such a time, or, at all events, can't marry you lawfully. But ubbubboo!" said he, suddenly, as he looked again at the young girl, "in the name of God, who have you here? Who is she, or how did you get her?"

"Father," said Guleesh, "you can marry me, or anybody else, if you wish; but it's not looking for marriage I came to you now, but to ask you, if you please, to give a lodging in your house to this young lady."

The priest looked at him as though he had ten heads on him; but without putting any other question to him, he desired him to come in, himself and the maiden, and when they came in, he shut the door, brought them into the parlour, and put them sitting.

"Now, Guleesh," said he, "tell me truly who is this young lady, and whether you're out of your senses really, or are only making a joke of me."

"I'm not telling a word of lie, nor making a joke of you," said Guleesh; "but it was from the palace of the king of France I carried off this lady, and she is the daughter of the king of France."

He began his story then, and told the whole to the priest, and the priest was so much surprised that he could not help calling out at times, or clapping his hands together.

When Guleesh said from what he saw he thought the girl was not satisfied with the marriage that was going to take place in the palace before he and the sheehogues broke it up, there came a red blush into the girl's cheek, and he was more certain than ever that she had sooner be as she was – badly as she was – than be the married wife of the man she hated. When Guleesh said that he would be very thankful to the priest if he would keep her in his own house, the kind man said he would do that as long as Guleesh pleased, but that he did not know what they ought to do with her, because they had no means of sending her back to her father again.

Guleesh answered that he was uneasy about the same thing, and that he saw nothing to do but to keep quiet until they should find some opportunity of doing something better. They made it up then between themselves that the priest should let on that it was his brother's daughter he had, who was come on a visit to him from another county, and that he should tell everybody that she was dumb, and do his best to keep everyone away from her. They told the young girl what it was they intended to do, and she showed by her eyes that she was obliged to them.

Guleesh went home then, and when his people asked him where he had been, he said that he had been asleep at the foot of the ditch, and had passed the night there.

There was great wonderment on the priest's neighbours at the girl who came so suddenly to his house without anyone knowing where she was from, or what business she had there. Some of the people said that everything was not as it ought to be, and others, that Guleesh was not like the same man that was in it before, and that it was a great story, how he was drawing every day to the priest's house, and that the priest had a wish and a respect for him, a thing they could not clear up at all.

That was true for them, indeed, for it was seldom the day went by but Guleesh would go to the priest's house, and have a talk with him, and as often as he would come he used to hope to find the young lady well again, and with leave to speak; but, alas! She remained dumb and silent, without relief or cure. Since she had no other means of talking, she carried on a sort of conversation between herself and himself, by moving her hand and fingers, winking her eyes, opening and shutting her mouth, laughing or smiling, and a thousand other signs, so that it was not long until they understood each other very well. Guleesh was always thinking how he should send her back to her father; but there was no one to go with her, and he himself did not know what road to go, for he had never been out of his own country before the night he brought her away with him. Nor had the priest any better knowledge than he; but when Guleesh asked him, he wrote three or four letters to the king of France, and gave them to buyers and sellers of wares, who used to be going from place to place across the sea; but they all went astray, and never a one came to the king's hand.

This was the way they were for many months, and Guleesh was falling deeper and deeper in love with her every day, and it was plain to himself and the priest that she liked him. The boy feared greatly at last, lest the king should really hear where his daughter was, and take her back from himself, and he besought the priest to write no more, but to leave the matter to God.

So they passed the time for a year, until there came a day when Guleesh was lying by himself, on the grass, on the last day of the last month in autumn, and he was thinking over again in his own mind of everything that happened to him from the day that he went with the sheehogues across the sea. He remembered then, suddenly, that it was one November night that he was standing at the gable of the house, when the whirlwind came, and the sheehogues in it, and he said to himself: "We have November night again today, and I'll stand in the same place I was last year, until I see if the good people come again. Perhaps I might see or hear something that would be useful to me, and might bring back her talk again to Mary" – that was the name himself and the priest called the king's daughter, for neither of them knew her right name. He told his intention to the priest, and the priest gave him his blessing.

Guleesh accordingly went to the old rath when the night was darkening, and he stood with his bent elbow leaning on a grey old flag, waiting till the middle of the night should come. The moon rose slowly; and it was like a knob of fire behind him; and there was a white fog which was raised up over the fields of grass and all damp places, through the coolness of the night after a great heat in the day. The night was calm as is a lake when there is not a breath of wind to move a wave on it, and there was no sound to be heard but the cronawn of the insects that would go by from time to time, or the hoarse sudden scream of the wild-geese, as they passed from lake to lake, half a mile up in the air over his head; or the sharp whistle of the golden and green plover, rising and lying, lying and rising, as they do on a calm night. There were a thousand thousand bright stars shining over his head, and there was a little frost out, which left the grass under his foot white and crisp.

He stood there for an hour, for two hours, for three hours, and the frost increased greatly, so that he heard the breaking of the traneens under his foot as often as he moved. He was thinking, in his own mind, at last, that the sheehogues would not come that night, and that it was as good for him to return back again, when he heard a sound far away from him, coming towards him, and he recognised what it was at the first moment. The sound increased, and at first it was like the beating of waves on a stony shore, and then it was like the falling of a great waterfall, and at last it was like a loud storm in the tops of the trees, and then the whirlwind burst into the rath of one rout, and the sheehogues were in it.

It all went by him so suddenly that he lost his breath with it, but he came to himself on the spot, and put an ear on himself, listening to what they would say.

Scarcely had they gathered into the rath till they all began shouting, and screaming, and talking amongst themselves; and then each one of them cried out: "My horse, and bridle, and saddle! My horse, and bridle, and saddle!" and Guleesh took courage, and called out as loudly as any of them: "My horse, and bridle, and saddle! My horse, and bridle, and saddle!" But before the word was well out of his mouth, another man cried out: "Ora! Guleesh, my boy, are you here with us again? How are you getting on with your woman? There's no use in your calling for your horse tonight. I'll go bail you won't play such a trick on us again. It was a good trick you played on us last year?"

"It was," said another man; "he won't do it again."

"Isn't he a prime lad, the same lad! To take a woman with him that never said as much to him as, 'How do you do?' since this time last year!" says the third man.

"Perhaps be likes to be looking at her," said another voice.

"And if the omadawn only knew that there's a herb growing up by his own door, and if he were to boil it and give it to her, she'd be well," said another voice.

"That's true for you."

"He is an omadawn."

"Don't bother your head with him; we'll be going."

"We'll leave the bodach as he is."

And with that they rose up into the air, and out with them with one roolya-boolya the way they came; and they left poor Guleesh standing where they found him, and the two eyes going out of his head, looking after them and wondering.

He did not stand long till he returned back, and he thinking in his own mind on all he saw and heard, and wondering whether there was really a herb at his own door that would bring back the talk to the king's daughter.

"It can't be," says he to himself, "that they would tell it to me, if there was any virtue in it; but perhaps the sheehogue didn't observe himself when he let the word slip out of his mouth. I'll search well as soon as the sun rises, whether there's any plant growing beside the house except thistles and dockings."

He went home, and as tired as he was he did not sleep a wink until the sun rose on the morrow. He got up then, and it was the first thing he did to go out and search well through the grass round about the house, trying could he get any herb that he did not recognise. And, indeed, he was not long searching till he observed a large strange herb that was growing up just by the gable of the house.

He went over to it, and observed it closely, and saw that there were seven little branches coming out of the stalk, and seven leaves growing on every branch of them; and that there was a white sap in the leaves. "It's very wonderful," said he to himself, "that I never noticed this herb before. If there's any virtue in an herb at all, it ought to be in such a strange one as this."

He drew out his knife, cut the plant, and carried it into his own house; stripped the leaves off it and cut up the stalk; and there came a thick, white juice out of it, as there comes out of the sow-thistle when it is bruised, except that the juice was more like oil.

He put it in a little pot and a little water in it, and laid it on the fire until the water was boiling, and then he took a cup, filled it half up with the juice, and put it to his own mouth. It came into his head then that perhaps it was poison that was in it, and that the good people were only tempting him that he might kill himself with that trick, or put the girl to death without meaning it. He put down the cup again, raised a couple of drops on the top of his finger, and put it to his mouth. It was not bitter, and, indeed, had a sweet, agreeable taste. He grew bolder then, and drank the full of a thimble of it, and then as much again, and he never stopped till he had half the cup drunk. He fell asleep after that, and did not wake till it was night, and there was great hunger and great thirst on him.

He had to wait, then, till the day rose; but he determined, as soon as he should wake in the morning, that he would go to the king's daughter and give her a drink of the juice of the herb.

As soon as he got up in the morning, he went over to the priest's house with the drink in his hand, and he never felt himself so bold and valiant, and spirited and light, as he was that day, and he was quite certain that it was the drink he drank which made him so hearty.

When he came to the house, he found the priest and the young lady within, and they were wondering greatly why he had not visited them for two days.

He told them all his news, and said that he was certain that there was great power in that herb, and that it would do the lady no hurt, for he tried it himself and got good from it, and then he made her taste it, for he vowed and swore that there was no harm in it.

Guleesh handed her the cup, and she drank half of it, and then fell back on her bed and a heavy sleep came on her, and she never woke out of that sleep till the day on the morrow.

Guleesh and the priest sat up the entire night with her, waiting till she should awake, and they between hope and unhope, between expectation of saving her and fear of hurting her.

She awoke at last when the sun had gone half its way through the heavens. She rubbed her eyes and looked like a person who did not know where she was. She was like one astonished when she saw Guleesh and the priest in the same room with her, and she sat up doing her best to collect her thoughts.

The two men were in great anxiety waiting to see would she speak, or would she not speak, and when they remained silent for a couple of minutes, the priest said to her: "Did you sleep well, Mary?"

And she answered him: "I slept, thank you."

No sooner did Guleesh hear her talking than he put a shout of joy out of him, and ran over to her and fell on his two knees, and said: "A thousand thanks to God, who has given you back the talk; lady of my heart, speak again to me."

The lady answered him that she understood it was he who boiled that drink for her, and gave it to her; that she was obliged to him from her heart for all the kindness he showed her since the day she first came to Ireland, and that he might be certain that she never would forget it.

Guleesh was ready to die with satisfaction and delight. Then they brought her food, and she ate with a good appetite, and was merry and joyous, and never left off talking with the priest while she was eating.

After that Guleesh went home to his house, and stretched himself on the bed and fell asleep again, for the force of the herb was not all spent, and he passed another day and a night sleeping. When he woke up he went back to the priest's house, and found that the young lady was in the same state, and that she was asleep almost since the time that he left the house.

He went into her chamber with the priest, and they remained watching beside her till she awoke the second time, and she had her talk as well as ever, and Guleesh was greatly rejoiced. The priest put food on the table again, and they ate together, and Guleesh used after that to come to the house from day to day, and the friendship that was between him and the king's daughter increased, because she had no one to speak to except Guleesh and the priest, and she liked Guleesh best.

So they married one another, and that was the fine wedding they had, and if I were to be there then, I would not be here now; but I heard it from a birdeen that there was neither cark nor care, sickness nor sorrow, mishap nor misfortune on them till the hour of their death, and may the same be with me, and with us all!

The Banshee

ALTHOUGH THE IRISH have the reputation of being grossly superstitious, they are not a whit more so than the peasantry of England, France, or Germany, nor scarcely as much addicted to superstitious beliefs and fancies as the lower class of Scottish Highlanders. The Irish imagination is, however, so lively as to endow the legends of the Emerald Isle with an individuality not possessed by those of most other nations, while the Irish command of language presents the creatures of Hibernian fancy in a garb so vividly real and yet so fantastically original as to make an impression sometimes exceedingly startling.

Of the creations of the Irish imagination, some are humorous, some grotesque, and some awe-inspiring even to sublimity, and chief among the last class is 'the weird-wailing Banshee, that sings by night her mournful cry', giving notice to the family she attends that one of its members is soon to be called to the spirit-world. The name of this dreaded attendant is variously pronounced, as Banshee, Banshi, and Benshee, being translated by different scholars, the Female Fairy, the Woman of Peace, the Lady of Death, the Angel of Death, the White Lady of Sorrow, the Nymph of the Air, and the Spirit of the Air. The Banshee is quite distinct from the Fearshee or Shifra, the Man of Peace, the latter bringing good tidings and singing a joyful lay near the house when unexpected good fortune is to befall any or all its inmates. The Banshee is really a disembodied soul, that of one who, in life, was strongly attached to the family, or who had good reason to hate all its members. Thus, in different instances, the Banshee's song may be inspired by opposite motives. When the Banshee loves those whom she calls, the song is a low, soft chant, giving notice, indeed, of the close proximity of the angel of death, but with a tenderness of tone that reassures the one destined to die and comforts the survivors; rather a welcome than a warning, and having in its tones a thrill of exultation, as though the messenger spirit were bringing glad tidings to him summoned to join the waiting throng of his ancestors. If, during her lifetime, the Banshee was an enemy of the family, the cry is the scream of a fiend, howling with demoniac delight over the coming death-agony of another of her foes.

In some parts of Ireland there exists a belief that the spirits of the dead are not taken from earth, nor do they lose all their former interest in earthly affairs, but enjoy the happiness of the saved, or suffer the punishment imposed for their sins, in the neighborhood of the scenes among which they lived while clothed in flesh and blood. At particular crises in the affairs of mortals, these disenthralled spirits sometimes display joy or grief in such a manner as to attract the attention of living men and women. At weddings they are frequently unseen guests; at funerals they are always present; and sometimes, at both weddings and funerals, their presence is recognised by aerial voices or mysterious music known to be of unearthly origin. The spirits of the good wander with the living as guardian angels, but the spirits of the bad are restrained in their action, and compelled to do penance at or near the places where their crimes were committed. Some are chained at the bottoms of the lakes, others buried under ground, others confined in mountain gorges; some hang on the sides of precipices, others are transfixed on the tree-tops, while others haunt the homes of their ancestors, all waiting till the penance has been endured and the hour of release arrives. The Castle of Dunseverick, in Antrim, is believed to be still inhabited by the spirit of a chief, who there atones for a horrid crime, while the castles of Dunluce, of Magrath, and many others are similarly peopled by the wicked dead. In the Abbey of Clare, the ghost of a sinful abbot walks and will continue to do so until his sin has been atoned for by the prayers he unceasingly mutters in his tireless march up and down the aisles of the ruined nave.

The Banshee is of the spirits who look with interested eyes on earthly doings; and, deeply attached to the old families, or, on the contrary, regarding all their members with a hatred beyond that known to mortals, lingers about their dwellings to soften or to aggravate the sorrow of the approaching death. The Banshee attends only the old families, and though their descendants, through misfortune, may be brought down from high estate to the ranks of peasant-tenants, she never leaves nor forgets them till the last member has been gathered to his fathers in the churchyard. The MacCarthys, Magraths, O'Neills, O'Rileys, O'Sullivans, O'Reardons, O'Flahertys, and almost all other old families of Ireland, have Banshees, though many representatives of these names are in abject poverty.

The song of the Banshee is commonly heard a day or two before the death of which it gives notice, though instances are cited of the song at the beginning of a course of conduct or line of undertaking that resulted fatally. Thus, in Kerry, a young girl engaged herself to a youth, and at the moment her promise of marriage was given, both heard the low, sad wail above their heads. The young man deserted her, she died of a broken heart, and the night before her death, the Banshee's song, loud and clear, was heard outside the window of her mother's cottage. One of the O'Flahertys, of Galway, marched out of his castle with his men on a foray, and, as his troops filed through the gateway, the Banshee was heard high above the towers of the fortress. The next night she sang again, and was heard no more for a month, when his wife heard the wail under her window, and on the following day his followers brought back his corpse. One of the O'Neills of Shane Castle, in Antrim, heard the Banshee as he started on a journey before daybreak, and was accidentally killed some time after, but while on the same journey.

The wail most frequently comes at night, although cases are cited of Banshees singing during the daytime, and the song is often inaudible to all save the one for whom the warning is intended. This, however, is not general, the death notice being for the family rather than for the doomed individual. The spirit is generally alone, though rarely several are heard singing in chorus. A lady of the O'Flaherty family, greatly beloved for her social qualities, benevolence, and piety, was, some years ago, taken ill at the family mansion near Galway, though no uneasiness was felt on her account, as her ailment seemed nothing more than a slight cold. After she had remained indoors for a day or two several of her acquaintances came to her room to enliven her imprisonment, and while the little party were merrily chatting, strange sounds were heard, and all trembled and turned pale as they recognised the singing of a chorus of Banshees. The lady's ailment developed into pleurisy, and she died in a few days, the chorus being

again heard in a sweet, plaintive requiem as the spirit was leaving her body. The honor of being warned by more than one Banshee is, however, very great, and comes only to the purest of the pure.

The 'hateful Banshee' is much dreaded by members of a family against which she has enmity. A noble Irish family, whose name is still familiar in Mayo, is attended by a Banshee of this description. This Banshee is the spirit of a young girl deceived and afterwards murdered by a former head of the family. With her dying breath she cursed her murderer, and promised she would attend him and his forever. Many years passed, the chieftain reformed his ways, and his youthful crime was almost forgotten even by himself, when, one night, he and his family were seated by the fire, and suddenly the most horrid shrieks were heard outside the castle walls. All ran out, but saw nothing. During the night the screams continued as though the castle were besieged by demons, and the unhappy man recognised, in the cry of the Banshee, the voice of the young girl he had murdered. The next night he was assassinated by one of his followers, when again the wild, unearthly screams of the spirit were heard, exulting over his fate. Since that night, the 'hateful Banshee' has never failed to notify the family, with shrill cries of revengeful gladness, when the time of one of their number had arrived.

Banshees are not often seen, but those that have made themselves visible differ as much in personal appearance as in the character of their cries. The 'friendly Banshee' is a young and beautiful female spirit, with pale face, regular, well-formed features, hair sometimes coal-black, sometimes golden; eyes blue, brown, or black. Her long, white drapery falls below her feet as she floats in the air, chanting her weird warning, lifting her hands as if in pitying tenderness bestowing a benediction on the soul she summons to the invisible world. The 'hateful Banshee' is a horrible hag, with angry, distorted features; maledictions are written in every line of her wrinkled face, and her outstretched arms call down curses on the doomed member of the hated race. Though generally the only intimation of the presence of the Banshee is her cry, a notable instance of the contrary exists in the family of the O'Reardons, to the doomed member of which the Banshee always appears in the shape of an exceedingly beautiful woman, who sings a song so sweetly solemn as to reconcile him to his approaching fate.

The prophetic spirit does not follow members of a family who go to a foreign land, but should death overtake them abroad, she gives notice of the misfortune to those at home. When the Duke of Wellington died, the Banshee was heard wailing round the house of his ancestors, and during the Napoleonic campaigns, she frequently notified Irish families of the death in battle of Irish officers and soldiers. The night before the battle of the Boyne several Banshees were heard singing in the air over the Irish camp, the truth of their prophecy being verified by the death-roll of the next day.

How the Banshee is able to obtain early and accurate information from foreign parts of the death in battle of Irish soldiers is yet undecided in Hibernian mystical circles. Some believe that there are, in addition to the two kinds already mentioned, 'silent Banshees', who act as attendants to the members of old families, one to each member; that these silent spirits follow and observe, bringing back intelligence to the family Banshee at home, who then, at the proper seasons, sings her dolorous strain. A partial confirmation of this theory is seen in the fact that the Banshee has given notice at the family seat in Ireland of deaths in battles fought in every part of the world. From North America, the West Indies, Africa, Australia, India, China; from every point to which Irish regiments have followed the roll of the British drums, news of the prospective shedding of Irish blood has been brought home, and the slaughter preceded by a Banshee wail outside the ancestral windows. But it is due to the reader to state, that this silent Banshee theory is by no means well or generally received, the burden of evidence going to show that there are only two kinds of Banshees, and that, in a supernatural way, they know the immediate future of those in whom they are interested, not being obliged to leave Ireland for the purpose of obtaining their information.

Such is the wild Banshee, once to be heard in every part of Ireland, and formerly believed in so devoutly that to express a doubt of her existence was little less than blasphemy. Now, however, as she attends only the old families and does not change to the new, with the disappearance of many noble Irish names during the last half century have gone also their Banshees, until in only a few retired districts of the west coast is the dreaded spirit still found, while in most parts of the island she has become only a superstition, and from the majesty of a death-boding angel, is rapidly sinking to a level with the Fairy, the Leprechawn and the Pooka; the subject for tales to amuse the idle and terrify the young.

How Thomas Connolly Met the Banshee

"AW, THE BANSHEE, sir? Well, sir, as I was striving to tell ye, I was going home from work one day, from Mr. Cassidy's that I tould ye of, in the dusk o' the evening. I had more nor a mile – aye, it was nearer two mile – to thrack to, where I was lodgin' with a dacent widdy woman I knew, Biddy Maguire be name, so as to be near me work.

"It was the first week in November, an' a lonesome road I had to travel, an' dark enough, wid threes above it; an' about half-ways there was a bit of a brudge I had to cross, over one o' them little sthrames that runs into the Doddher. I walked on in the middle iv the road, for there was no toe-path at that time, Misther Harry, nor for many a long day afther that; but, as I was sayin', I walked along till I come nigh upon the brudge, where the road was a bit open, an' there, right enough, I seen the hog's back o' the ould-fashioned brudge that used to be there till it was pulled down, an' a white mist steamin' up out o' the wather all around it.

"Well, now, Misther Harry, often as I'd passed by the place before, that night it seemed sthrange to me, an' like a place ye might see in a dhrame; an' as I come up to it I began to feel a could wind blowin' through the hollow o' me heart. 'Musha Thomas,' sez I to meself, 'is it yerself that's in it?' sez I; 'or, if it is, what's the matter wid ye at all, at all?' sez I; so I put a bould face on it, an' I made a sthruggle to set one leg afore the other, ontil I came to the rise o' the brudge. And there, God be good to us! In a cantle o' the wall I seen an ould woman, as I thought, sittin' on her hunkers, all crouched together, an' her head bowed down, seemin'ly in the greatest affliction.

"Well, sir, I pitied the ould craythur, an' thought I wasn't worth a thraneen, for the mortial fright I was in, I up an' sez to her, 'That's a cowld lodgin' for ye, ma'am.' Well, the sorra ha'porth she sez to that, nor tuk no more notice o' me than if I hadn't let a word out o' me, but kep' rockin' herself to an' fro, as if her heart was breakin'; so I sez to her again, 'Eh, ma'am, is there anythin' the matther wid ye?' An' I made for to touch her on the shoulder, on'y somethin' stopt me, for as I looked closer at her I saw she was no more an ould woman nor she was an ould cat. The first thing I tuk notice to, Misther Harry, was her hair, that was sthreelin' down over his showldhers, an' a good yard on the ground on aich side of her. O, be the hoky farmer, but that was the hair! The likes of it I never seen on mortial woman, young or ould, before nor sense. It grew as sthrong out of her as out of e'er a young slip of a girl ye could see; but the colour of it was a misthery to describe. The first squint I got of it I thought it was silvery grey, like an ould crone's; but when I got up beside her I saw, be the glance o' the sky, it was a soart iv an Iscariot colour, an' a shine out of it like floss silk. It ran over her showldhers and the two shapely arms she was lanin' her head on, for all the world like Mary Magdalen's in a picther; and then I persaved that the grey cloak and the green gownd undhernaith it was made of no earthly matarial I ever laid eyes on. Now, I needn't tell ye, sir, that I seen all this in the twinkle of a bed-post – long as I take to make the narration of it. So I made a step back from her, an' 'The Lord be betune us an' harm!' sez I, out loud, an' wid that I blessed meself. Well, Misther Harry, the word wasn't out o' me mouth afore she turned her face on me. Aw, Misther Harry, but 'twas that was the awfullest apparation ever I seen, the face of her as she looked up at me! God forgive me for sayin' it, but 'twas more like the face of the 'Axy Homo' beyand in Marlboro' Sthreet Chapel nor like any face I could mintion – as pale as a corpse, an' a most o' freckles on it, like the freckles on a turkey's egg; an' the two eyes sewn in wid red thread, from the terrible power o' crying the' had to do; an' such a pair iv eyes as the' wor, Misther Harry, as blue as two forget-me-nots, an' as cowld as the moon in a bog-hole of a frosty night, an' a dead-an'-live look in them that sent a cowld shiver through the marra o' me bones. Be the mortial! Ye could ha' rung a tay cupful o' cowld paspiration out o' the hair o' me head that minute, so ye could. Well, I thought the life 'ud lave me intirely when she riz up from her hunkers, till, bedad! She looked mostly as tall as Nelson's Pillar; an' wid the two eyes gazin' back at me, an' her two arms stretched out before hor, an' a keine out of her that riz the hair o' me scalp till it was as stiff as the hog's bristles in a new hearth broom, away she glides – glides round the angle o' the brudge, an' down with her into the sthrame that ran undhernaith it. 'Twas then I began to suspect what she was. 'Wisha, Thomas!' says I to meself, sez I; an' I made a great struggle to get me two legs into a throt, in spite o' the spavin o' fright the pair o' them wor in; an' how I brought meself home that same night the Lord in heaven only knows, for I never could tell; but I must ha' tumbled agin the door, and shot in head foremost into the middle o' the flure, where I lay in a dead swoon for mostly an hour; and the first I knew was Mrs. Maguire stannin' over me with a jorum o' punch she was pourin' down me throath (throat), to bring back the life into me, an' me head in a pool of cowld wather she dashed over me in her first fright. 'Arrah, Mister Connolly,' shashee, 'what ails ye?' shashee, 'to put the scare on a lone woman like that?' shashee. 'Am I in this world or the next?' sez I. 'Musha! Where else would ye be on'y here in my kitchen?' shashee. 'O, glory be to God!' sez I, 'but I thought I was in Purgathory at the laste, not to mintion an uglier place,' sez I, 'only it's too cowld I find meself, an' not too hot,' sez I. 'Faix, an' maybe ye wor more nor half-ways there, on'y for me,' shashee; 'but what's come to you at all, at all? Is it your fetch ye seen, Mister Connolly?' – 'Aw, naboclish!' sez I. 'Never mind what I seen,' sez I. So be degrees I began to come to a little; an' that's the way I met the banshee, Misther Harry!"

"But how did you know it really was the banshee after all, Thomas?"

"Begor, sir, I knew the apparation of her well enough; but 'twas confirmed by a sarcumstance that occurred the same time. There was a Misther O'Nales was come on a visit, ye must know, to a place in the neighbourhood – one o' the ould O'Nales iv the county Tyrone, a rale ould Irish family – an' the banshee was heard keening round the house that same night, be more then one that was in it; an' sure enough, Misther Harry, he was found dead in his bed the next mornin'. So if it wasn't the banshee I seen that time, I'd like to know what else it could a' been."

The Banshee of the Mac Carthys

CHARLES MAC CARTHY was, in the year 1749, the only surviving son of a very numerous family. His father died when he was little more than twenty, leaving him the Mac Carthy estate, not much encumbered, considering that it was an Irish one. Charles was gay, handsome, unfettered either by poverty, a father, or guardians, and therefore was not, at the age of one-and-twenty, a pattern of regularity and virtue. In plain terms, he was an exceedingly dissipated – I fear I may say debauched, young man. His companions were, as may be supposed, of the higher classes of the youth in his neighbourhood, and, in general, of those whose fortunes were larger than his own, whose dispositions to pleasure were, therefore, under still less restrictions, and in whose example he found at once an incentive and an apology for his irregularities. Besides, Ireland, a place to this day not very remarkable for the coolness and steadiness of its youth, was then one of the cheapest countries in the world in most of those articles which money supplies for the indulgence of the passions. The odious exciseman – with his portentous book in one hand, his unrelenting pen held in the other, or stuck beneath his hat-band, and the ink-bottle ('black emblem of the informer') dangling from his waistcoat-button – went not then from ale-house to ale-house, denouncing all those patriotic dealers in spirits, who preferred selling whiskey, which had nothing to do with English laws (but to elude them), to retailing that poisonous liquor, which derived its name from the British 'Parliament' that compelled its circulation among a reluctant people. Or if the gauger – recording angel of the law – wrote down the peccadillo of a publican, he dropped a tear upon the word, and blotted it out forever! For, welcome to the tables of their hospitable neighbours, the guardians of the excise, where they existed at all, scrupled to abridge those luxuries which they freely shared; and thus the competition in the market between the smuggler, who incurred little hazard, and the personage who was named fair trader, who enjoyed little protection, made Ireland a land flowing, not merely with milk and honey, but with whiskey and wine. In the enjoyments supplied by these, and in the many kindred pleasures to which frail youth is but too prone, Charles Mac Carthy indulged to such a degree, that just about the time when he had completed his four-and-twentieth year, after a week of great excesses, he was seized with a violent fever, which, from its malignity, and the weakness of his frame, left scarcely a hope of his recovery. His mother, who had at first made many efforts to check his vices, and at last had been obliged to look on at his rapid progress to ruin in silent despair, watched day and night at his pillow. The anguish of parental feeling was blended with that still deeper misery which those only know who have striven hard to rear in virtue and piety a beloved and favourite child; have found him grow up all that their hearts could desire, until he reached manhood; and then, when their pride was highest, and their hopes almost ended in the fulfilment of their fondest expectations, have seen this idol of their affections plunge headlong into a course of reckless profligacy, and, after a rapid career of vice, hang upon the verge of eternity, without the leisure or the power of repentance. Fervently she prayed that, if his life could not be spared, at least the delirium, which continued with increasing violence from the first few hours of his disorder, might vanish before death, and leave enough of light and of calm for making his peace with offended Heaven. After several days, however, nature seemed quite exhausted, and he sunk into a state too like death to be mistaken for the repose of sleep. His face had that pale, glossy, marble look, which is in general so sure a symptom that life has left its tenement of clay. His eyes were closed and sunk; the lids having that compressed and stiffened appearance which seemed to indicate that some friendly hand had done its last office. The lips, half closed and perfectly ashy, discovered just so much of the teeth as to give to the features of death their most ghastly, but most impressive look. He lay upon his back, with his hands stretched beside him, quite motionless; and his distracted mother, after repeated trials, could discover not the least symptom of animation. The medical man who attended, having tried the usual modes for ascertaining the presence of life, declared at last his opinion that it was flown, and prepared to depart from the house of mourning. His horse was seen to come to the door. A crowd of people who were collected before the windows, or scattered in groups on the lawn in front, gathered around when the door opened. These were tenants, fosterers, and poor relations of the family, with others attracted by affection, or by that interest which partakes of curiosity, but is something more, and which collects the lower ranks round a house where a human being is in his passage to another world. They saw the professional man come out from the hall door and approach his horse; and while slowly, and with a melancholy air, he prepared to mount, they clustered round him with inquiring and wistful looks. Not a word was spoken, but their meaning could not be misunderstood; and the physician, when he had got into his saddle, and while the servant was still holding the bridle as if to delay him, and was looking anxiously at his face as if expecting that he would relieve the general suspense, shook his head, and said in a low voice, "It's all over, James"; and moved slowly away. The moment he had spoken, the women present, who were very numerous, uttered a shrill cry, which, having been sustained for about half a minute, fell suddenly into a full, loud, continued, and discordant but plaintive wailing, above which occasionally were heard the deep sounds of a man's voice, sometimes in deep sobs, sometimes in more distinct exclamations of sorrow. This was Charles's foster-brother, who moved about the crowd, now clapping his hands, now rubbing them together in an agony of grief. The poor fellow had been Charles's playmate and companion when a boy, and afterwards his servant; had always been distinguished by his peculiar regard, and loved his young master as much, at least, as he did his own life.

When Mrs. Mac Carthy became convinced that the blow was indeed struck, and that her beloved son was sent to his last account, even in the blossoms of his sin, she remained for some time gazing with fixedness upon his cold features; then, as if something had suddenly touched the string of her tenderest affections, tear after tear trickled down her cheeks, pale with anxiety and watching. Still she continued looking at her son, apparently unconscious that she was weeping, without once lifting her handkerchief to her eyes, until reminded of the sad duties which the custom of the country imposed upon her, by the crowd of females belonging to the better class of the peasantry, who now, crying audibly, nearly filled the apartment. She then withdrew, to give directions for the ceremony of waking, and for supplying the numerous visitors of all ranks with the refreshments usual on these melancholy occasions. Though her voice was scarcely heard, and though no one saw her but the servants and one or two old followers of the family, who assisted her in the necessary arrangements, everything was conducted with the greatest regularity; and though she made no effort to check her sorrows they never once suspended her attention, now more than ever required to preserve order in her household, which, in this season of calamity, but for her would have been all confusion.

The night was pretty far advanced; the boisterous lamentations which had prevailed during part of the day in and about the house had given place to a solemn and mournful stillness; and Mrs. Mac Carthy, whose heart, notwithstanding her long fatigue and watching, was yet too sore for sleep, was kneeling in fervent prayer in a chamber adjoining that of her son. Suddenly her devotions were disturbed by an unusual noise, proceeding from the persons who were watching round the body. First there was a low murmur, then all was silent, as if the movements of those in the chamber were checked by a sudden panic, and then a loud cry of terror burst from all within. The door of the chamber was thrown open, and all who were not overturned in the press rushed wildly into the passage which led to the stairs, and into which Mrs. Mac Carthy's room opened. Mrs. Mac Carthy made her way through the crowd into her son's chamber, where she found him sitting up in the bed, and looking vacantly around, like one risen from the grave. The glare thrown upon his sunk features and thin lathy frame gave an unearthly horror to his whole aspect. Mrs. Mac Carthy was a woman of some firmness; but she was a woman, and not quite free from the superstitions of her country. She dropped on her knees, and, clasping her hands, began to pray aloud. The form before her moved only its lips, and barely uttered "Mother"; but though the pale lips moved, as if there was a design to finish the sentence, the tongue refused its office. Mrs. Mac Carthy sprung forward, and catching the arm of her son, exclaimed, "Speak! In the name of God and His saints, speak! Are you alive?"

He turned to her slowly, and said, speaking still with apparent difficulty, "Yes, my mother, alive, and – but sit down and collect yourself; I have that to tell which will astonish you still more than what you have seen." He leaned back upon his pillow, and while his mother remained kneeling by the bedside, holding one of his hands clasped in hers, and gazing on him with the look of one who distrusted all her senses, he proceeded: "Do not interrupt me until I have done. I wish to speak while the excitement of returning life is upon me, as I know I shall soon need much repose. Of the commencement of my illness I have only a confused recollection; but within the last twelve hours I have been before the judgment-seat of God. Do not stare incredulously on me – 'tis as true as have been my crimes, and as, I trust, shall be repentance. I saw the awful Judge arrayed in all the terrors which invest him when mercy gives place to justice. The dreadful pomp of offended omnipotence, I saw – I remember. It is fixed here; printed on my brain in characters indelible; but it passeth human language. What I *can* describe I *will* – I may speak it briefly. It is enough to say, I was weighed in the balance, and found wanting. The irrevocable sentence was upon the point of being pronounced; the eye of my Almighty Judge, which had already glanced upon me, half spoke my doom; when I observed the guardian saint, to whom you so often directed my prayers when I was a child, looking at me with an expression of benevolence and compassion. I stretched forth my hands to him, and besought his intercession. I implored that one year, one month, might be given to me on earth to do penance and atonement for my transgressions. He threw himself at the feet of my Judge, and supplicated for mercy. Oh! Never – not if I should pass through ten thousand successive states of being – never, for eternity, shall I forget the horrors of that moment, when my fate hung suspended – when an instant was to decide whether torments unutterable were to be my portion for endless ages! But Justice suspended its decree, and Mercy spoke in accents of firmness, but mildness, 'Return to that world in which thou hast lived but to outrage the laws of Him who made that world and thee. Three years are given thee for repentance; when these are ended, thou shalt again stand here, to be saved or lost for ever.' I heard no more; I saw no more, until I awoke to life, the moment before you entered."

Charles's strength continued just long enough to finish these last words, and on uttering them he closed his eyes, and lay quite exhausted. His mother, though, as was before said, somewhat disposed to give credit to supernatural visitations, yet hesitated whether or not she should believe that, although awakened from a swoon which might have been the crisis of his disease, he was still under the influence of delirium. Repose, however, was at all events necessary, and she took immediate measures that he should enjoy it undisturbed. After some hours' sleep, he awoke refreshed, and thenceforward gradually but steadily recovered.

Still he persisted in his account of the vision, as he had at first related it; and his persuasion of its reality had an obvious and decided influence on his habits and conduct. He did not altogether abandon the society of his former associates, for his temper was not soured by his reformation; but he never joined in their excesses, and often endeavoured to reclaim them. How his pious exertions succeeded, I have never learnt; but of himself it is recorded that he was religious without ostentation, and temperate without austerity; giving a practical proof that vice may be exchanged for virtue, without the loss of respectability, popularity, or happiness.

Time rolled on, and long before the three years were ended the story of his vision was forgotten, or, when spoken of, was usually mentioned as an instance proving the folly of believing in such things. Charles's health, from the temperance and regularity of his habits, became more robust than ever. His friends, indeed, had often occasion to rally him upon a seriousness and abstractedness of demeanour, which grew upon him as he approached the completion of his seven-and-twentieth year, but for the most part his manner exhibited the same animation and cheerfulness for which he had always been remarkable. In company he evaded every endeavour to draw from him a distinct opinion on the subject of the supposed prediction; but among his own family it was well known that he still firmly believed it. However, when the day had nearly arrived on which the prophecy was, if at all, to be fulfilled, his whole appearance gave such promise of a long and healthy life, that he was persuaded by his friends to ask a large party to an entertainment at Spring House, to celebrate his birthday. But the occasion of this party, and the circumstances which attended it, will be best learned from a perusal of the following letters, which have been carefully preserved by some relations of his family. The first is from Mrs. Mac Carthy to a lady, a very near connection and valued friend of her's, who lived in the county of Cork, at about fifty miles' distance from Spring House.

To Mrs. Barry, Castle Barry.
Spring House, Tuesday morning,
October 15th, 1752.
My Dearest Mary,

I am afraid I am going to put your affection for your old friend and kinswoman to a severe trial. A two days' journey at this season, over bad roads and through a troubled country, it will indeed require friendship such as yours to persuade a sober woman to encounter. But the truth is, I have, or fancy I have, more than usual cause for wishing you near me. You know my son's story. I can't tell you how it is, but as next Sunday approaches, when the prediction of his dream, or vision, will be proved false or true, I feel a sickening of the heart, which I cannot suppress, but which your presence, my dear Mary, will soften, as it has done so many of my sorrows. My nephew, James Ryan, is to be married to Jane Osborne (who, you know, is my son's ward), and the bridal entertainment will take place here on Sunday next, though Charles pleaded hard to have it postponed for a day or two longer. Would to God – but no more of this till we meet. Do prevail upon yourself to leave your good man for one week, if his farming concerns will not admit of his accompanying you; and come to us, with the girls, as soon before Sunday as you can.

Ever my dear Mary's attached cousin and friend,
Ann Mac Carthy.

Although this letter reached Castle Barry early on Wednesday, the messenger having travelled on foot over bog and moor, by paths impassable to horse or carriage, Mrs. Barry, who at once determined on going, had so many arrangements to make for the regulation of her domestic affairs (which, in Ireland, among the middle orders of the gentry, fall soon into confusion when the mistress of the family is away), that she and her two young daughters were unable to leave until late on the morning of Friday. The eldest daughter remained to keep her father company, and superintend the concerns of the household. As the travellers were to journey in an open one-horse vehicle, called a jaunting-car (still used in Ireland), and as the roads, bad at all times, were rendered still worse by the heavy rains, it was their design to make two easy stages – to stop about midway the first night, and reach Spring House early on Saturday evening. This arrangement was now altered, as they found that from the lateness of their departure they could proceed, at the utmost, no farther than twenty miles on the first day; and they, therefore, purposed sleeping at the house of a Mr. Bourke, a friend of theirs, who lived at somewhat less than that distance from Castle Barry. They reached Mr. Bourke's in safety after a rather disagreeable ride. What befell them on their journey the next day to Spring House, and after their arrival there, is fully recounted in a letter from the second Miss Barry to her eldest sister.

Spring House, Sunday evening,
20th October 1752.
Dear Ellen,

As my mother's letter, which encloses this, will announce to you briefly the sad intelligence which I shall here relate more fully, I think it better to go regularly through the recital of the extraordinary events of the last two days.

The Bourkes kept us up so late on Friday night that yesterday was pretty far advanced before we could begin our journey, and the day closed when we were nearly fifteen miles distant from this place. The roads were excessively deep, from the heavy rains of the last week, and we proceeded so slowly that, at last, my mother resolved on passing the night at the house of Mr. Bourke's brother (who lives about a quarter-of-a-mile off the road), and coming here to breakfast in the morning. The day had been windy and showery, and the sky looked fitful, gloomy, and uncertain. The moon was full, and at times shone clear and bright; at others it was wholly concealed behind the thick, black, and rugged masses of clouds that rolled rapidly along, and were every moment becoming larger, and collecting together as if gathering strength for a coming storm. The wind, which blew in our faces, whistled bleakly along the low hedges of the narrow road, on which we proceeded with difficulty from the number of deep sloughs, and which afforded not the least shelter, no plantation being within some miles of us. My mother, therefore, asked Leary, who drove the jaunting-car, how far we were from Mr. Bourke's? "'Tis about ten spades from this to the cross, and we have then only to turn to the left into the avenue, ma'am." "Very well, Leary; turn up to Mr. Bourke's as soon as you reach the cross roads." My mother had scarcely spoken these words, when a shriek, that made us thrill as if our very hearts were pierced by it, burst from the hedge to the right of our way. If it resembled anything earthly it seemed the cry of a female, struck by a sudden and mortal blow, and giving out her life in one long deep pang of expiring agony. "Heaven defend us!" exclaimed my mother. "Go you over the hedge, Leary, and save that woman, if she is not yet dead, while we run back to the hut we have just passed, and alarm the village near it." "Woman!" said Leary, beating the horse violently, while his voice trembled, "that's no woman; the sooner we get on, ma'am, the better"; and he continued his efforts to quicken the horse's pace. We saw nothing. The moon was hid. It was quite dark, and we had been for some time expecting a heavy fall of rain. But just as Leary had spoken, and had succeeded in making the horse trot briskly forward, we distinctly heard a loud clapping of hands, followed by a succession of screams, that seemed to denote the last excess of despair and anguish, and to issue from a person running forward inside the hedge, to keep pace with our progress. Still we saw nothing; until, when we were within about ten yards of the place where an avenue branched off to Mr. Bourke's to the left, and the road turned to Spring House on the right, the moon started suddenly from behind a cloud, and enabled us to see, as plainly as I now see this paper, the figure of a tall, thin woman, with uncovered head, and long hair that floated round her shoulders, attired in something which seemed either a loose white cloak or a sheet thrown hastily about her. She stood on the corner hedge, where the road on which we were met that which leads to Spring House, with her face towards us, her left hand pointing to this place, and her right arm waving rapidly and violently as if to draw us on in that direction. The horse had stopped, apparently frightened at the sudden presence of the figure, which stood in the manner I have described, still uttering the same piercing cries, for about half a minute. It then leaped upon the road, disappeared from our view for one instant, and the next was seen standing upon a high wall a little way up the avenue on which we purposed going, still pointing towards the road to Spring House, but in an attitude of defiance and command, as if prepared to oppose our passage up the avenue. The figure was now quite silent, and its garments, which had before flown loosely in the wind, were closely wrapped around it "Go on, Leary, to Spring House, in God's name!" said my mother; "whatever world it belongs to, we

will provoke it no longer." "'Tis the Banshee, ma'am," said Leary; "and I would not, for what my life is worth, go anywhere this blessed night but to Spring House. But I'm afraid there's something bad going forward, or she would not send us there." So saying, he drove forward; and as we turned on the road to the right, the moon suddenly withdrew its light, and we saw the apparition no more; but we heard plainly a prolonged clapping of hands, gradually dying away, as if it issued from a person rapidly retreating. We proceeded as quickly as the badness of the roads and the fatigue of the poor animal that drew us would allow, and arrived here about eleven o'clock last night. The scene which awaited us you have learned from my mother's letter. To explain it fully, I must recount to you some of the transactions which took place here during the last week.

You are aware that Jane Osborne was to have been married this day to James Ryan, and that they and their friends have been here for the last week. On Tuesday last, the very day on the morning of which cousin Mac Carthy despatched the letter inviting us here, the whole of the company were walking about the grounds a little before dinner. It seems that an unfortunate creature, who had been seduced by James Ryan, was seen prowling in the neighbourhood in a moody, melancholy state for some days previous. He had separated from her for several months, and, they say, had provided for her rather handsomely; but she had been seduced by the promise of his marrying her; and the shame of her unhappy condition, uniting with disappointment and jealousy, had disordered her intellects. During the whole forenoon of this Tuesday she had been walking in the plantations near Spring House, with her cloak folded tight round her, the hood nearly covering her face; and she had avoided conversing with or even meeting any of the family.

Charles Mac Carthy, at the time I mentioned, was walking between James Ryan and another, at a little distance from the rest, on a gravel path, skirting a shrubbery. The whole party was thrown into the utmost consternation by the report of a pistol, fired from a thickly planted part of the shrubbery which Charles and his companions had just passed. He fell instantly, and it was found that he had been wounded in the leg. One of the party was a medical man. His assistance was immediately given, and, on examining, he declared that the injury was very slight, that no bone was broken, it was merely a flesh wound, and that it would certainly be well in a few days. "We shall know more by Sunday," said Charles, as he was carried to his chamber. His wound was immediately dressed, and so slight was the inconvenience which it gave that several of his friends spent a portion of the evening in his apartment.

On inquiry, it was found that the unlucky shot was fired by the poor girl I just mentioned. It was also manifest that she had aimed, not at Charles, but at the destroyer of her innocence and happiness, who was walking beside him. After a fruitless search for her through the grounds, she walked into the house of her own accord, laughing and dancing, and singing wildly, and every moment exclaiming that she had at last killed Mr. Ryan. When she heard that it was Charles, and not Mr. Ryan, who was shot, she fell into a violent fit, out of which, after working convulsively for some time, she sprung to the door, escaped from the crowd that pursued her, and could never be taken until last night, when she was brought here, perfectly frantic, a little before our arrival.

Charles's wound was thought of such little consequence that the preparations went forward, as usual, for the wedding entertainment on Sunday. But on Friday night he grew restless and feverish, and on Saturday (yesterday) morning felt so ill that it was deemed necessary to obtain additional medical advice. Two physicians and a surgeon met in consultation about twelve o'clock in the day, and the dreadful intelligence was announced, that unless a change, hardly hoped for, took place before night, death must happen within twenty-four hours after. The wound, it seems, had been too tightly bandaged, and otherwise injudiciously treated. The physicians were right in their anticipations. No favourable symptom appeared, and long before we reached Spring House every ray of hope had vanished. The scene we witnessed on our arrival would have wrung the heart of a demon. We heard briefly at the gate that Mr. Charles was upon his death-bed. When we reached the house, the information was confirmed by the servant who opened the door. But just as we entered we were horrified by the most appalling screams issuing from the staircase. My mother thought she heard the voice of poor Mrs. Mac Carthy, and sprung forward. We followed, and on ascending a few steps of the stairs, we found a young woman, in a state of frantic passion, struggling furiously with two men-servants, whose united strength was hardly sufficient to prevent her rushing upstairs over the body of Mrs. Mac Carthy, who was lying in strong hysterics upon the steps. This, I afterwards discovered, was the unhappy girl I before described, who was attempting to gain access to Charles's room, to "get his forgiveness," as she said, "before he went away to accuse her for having killed him." This wild idea was mingled with another, which seemed to dispute with the former possession of her mind. In one sentence she called on Charles to forgive her, in the next she would denounce James Ryan as the murderer, both of Charles and her. At length she was torn away; and the last words I heard her scream were, "James Ryan, 'twas you killed him, and not I – 'twas you killed him, and not I."

Mrs. Mac Carthy, on recovering, fell into the arms of my mother, whose presence seemed a great relief to her. She wept – the first tears, I was told, that she had shed since the fatal accident. She conducted us to Charles's room, who, she said, had desired to see us the moment of our arrival, as he found his end approaching, and wished to devote the last hours of his existence to uninterrupted prayer and meditation. We found him perfectly calm, resigned, and even cheerful. He spoke of the awful event which was at hand with courage and confidence, and treated it as a doom for which he had been preparing ever since his former remarkable illness, and which he never once doubted was truly foretold to him. He bade us farewell with the air of one who was about to travel a short and easy journey; and we left him with impressions which, notwithstanding all their anguish, will, I trust, never entirely forsake us.

Poor Mrs. Mac Carthy – but I am just called away. There seems a slight stir in the family; perhaps –

The above letter was never finished. The enclosure to which it more than once alludes told the sequel briefly, and it is all that I have further learned of the family of Mac Carthy. Before the sun had gone down upon Charles's seven-and-twentieth birthday, his soul had gone to render its last account to its Creator.

The Wonderful Tune

MAURICE CONNOR was the king, and that's no small word, of all the pipers in Munster. He could play jig and planxty without end, and Ollistrum's March, and the Eagle's Whistle, and the Hen's Concert, and odd tunes of every sort and kind. But he knew one, far more surprising than the rest, which had in it the power to set everything dead or alive dancing.

In what way he learned it is beyond my knowledge, for he was mighty cautious about telling how he came by so wonderful a tune. At the very first note of that tune, the brogues began shaking upon the feet of all who heard it – old or young it mattered not – just as if their brogues had the ague; then the feet began going – going – going from under them, and at last up and away with them, dancing like mad! – Whisking here, there, and every where, like a straw in a storm – there was no halting while the music lasted!

Not a fair, nor a wedding, nor a patron in the seven parishes round, was counted worth the speaking of without "blind Maurice and his pipes". His mother, poor woman, used to lead him about from one place to another, just like a dog.

Down through Iveragh – a place that ought to be proud of itself, for 'tis Daniel O'Connell's country – Maurice Connor and his mother were taking their rounds. Beyond all other places Iveragh is the place for stormy coast and steep mountains: as proper a spot it is as any in Ireland to get yourself drowned, or your neck broken on the land, should you prefer that. But, notwithstanding, in Ballinskellig bay there is a neat bit of ground, well fitted for diversion, and down from it towards the water, is a clean smooth piece of strand – the dead image of a calm summer's sea on a moonlight night, with just the curl of the small waves upon it.

Here it was that Maurice's music had brought from all parts a great gathering of the young men and the young women – *O the darlints!* – for 'twas not every day the strand of Trafraska was stirred up by the voice of a bagpipe. The dance began; and as pretty a rinkafadda it was as ever was danced. "Brave music," said every body, "and well done," when Maurice stopped.

"More power to your elbow, Maurice, and a fair wind in the bellows," cried Paddy Dorman, a hump-backed dancing-master, who was there to keep order. "'Tis a pity," said he, "if we'd let the piper run dry after such music; 'twould be a disgrace to Iveragh, that didn't come on it since the week of the three Sundays." So, as well became him, for he was always a decent man, says he: "Did you drink, piper?"

"I will, sir," says Maurice, answering the question on the safe side, for you never yet knew piper or schoolmaster who refused his drink.

"What will you drink, Maurice?" says Paddy.

"I'm no ways particular," says Maurice; "I drink anything, and give God thanks, barring *raw* water; but if 'tis all the same to you, mister Dorman, maybe you wouldn't lend me the loan of a glass of whiskey."

"I've no glass, Maurice," said Paddy; "I've only the bottle."

"Let that be no hindrance," answered Maurice; "my mouth just holds a glass to the drop; often I've tried it, sure."

So Paddy Dorman trusted him with the bottle – more fool was he; and, to his cost, he found that though Maurice's mouth might not hold more than the glass at one time, yet, owing to the hole in his throat, it took many a filling.

"That was no bad whisky neither," says Maurice, handing back the empty bottle.

"By the holy frost, then!" says Paddy, "'tis but *cowld* comfort there's in that bottle now; and 'tis your word we must take for the strength of the whisky, for you've left us no sample to judge by": and to be sure Maurice had not.

Now I need not tell any gentleman or lady with common understanding, that if he or she was to drink an honest bottle of whiskey at one pull, it is not at all the same thing as drinking a bottle of water; and in the whole course of my life, I never knew more than five men who could do so without being overtaken by the liquor. Of these Maurice Connor was not one, though he had a stiff head enough of his own – he was fairly tipsy. Don't think I blame him for it; 'tis often a good man's case; but true is the word that says, "when liquor's in, sense is out"; and puff, at a breath, before you could say "Lord save us!" out he blasted his wonderful tune.

'Twas really then beyond all belief or telling the dancing Maurice himself could not keep quiet; staggering now on one leg, now on the other, and rolling about like a ship in a cross sea, trying to humour the tune. There was his mother too, moving her old bones as light as the youngest girl of them all; but her dancing, no, nor the dancing of all the rest, is not worthy the speaking about to the work that was going on down on the strand. Every inch of it covered with all manner of fish jumping and plunging about to the music, and every moment more and more would tumble in out of the water, charmed by the wonderful tune. Crabs of monstrous size spun round and round on one claw with the nimbleness of a dancing-master, and twirled and tossed their other claws about like limbs that did not belong to them. It was a sight surprising to behold. But perhaps you may have heard of father Florence Conry, a Franciscan Friar, and a great Irish poet; *bolg an dana*, as they used to call him – a wallet of poems. If you have not he was as pleasant a man as one would wish to drink with of a hot summer's day; and he has rhymed out all about the dancing fishes so neatly, that it would be a thousand pities not to give you his verses; so here's my hand at an upset of them into English:

> *The big seals in motion,*
> *Like waves of the ocean,*
> *Or gouty feet prancing,*
> *Came heading the gay fish,*
> *Crabs, lobsters, and cray fish,*
> *Determined on dancing.*
> *The sweet sounds they follow'd,*
> *The gasping cod swallow'd;*
> *'Twas wonderful, really!*
> *And turbot and flounder,*
> *'Mid fish that were rounder,*
> *Just caper'd as gaily.*
> *John-dories came tripping;*

Dull hake, by their skipping
To frisk it seem'd given;
Bright mackerel went springing,
Like small rainbows winging
Their flight up to heaven.
The whiting and haddock
Left salt-water paddock,
This dance to be put in:
Where skate with flat faces
Edged out some odd plaices;
But soles kept their footing.
Sprats and herrings in powers
Of silvery showers
All number out-number'd;
And great ling so lengthy
Were there in such plenty,
The shore was encumber'd.
The scollop and oyster
Their two shells did roister,
Like castanets fitting;
While limpets moved clearly,
And rocks very nearly
With laughter were splitting.

Never was such an ullabulloo in this world, before or since; 'twas as if heaven and earth were coming together; and all out of Maurice Connor's wonderful tune!

In the height of all these doings, what should there be dancing among the outlandish set of fishes but a beautiful young woman – as beautiful as the dawn of day! She had a cocked hat upon her head; from under it her long green hair – just the colour of the sea – fell down behind, without hinderance to her dancing. Her teeth were like rows of pearl; her lips for all the world looked like red coral; and she had an elegant gown, as white as the foam of the wave, with little rows of purple and red sea-weeds settled out upon it; for you never yet saw a lady, under the water or over the water, who had not a good notion of dressing herself out.

Up she danced at last to Maurice, who was flinging his feet from under him as fast as hops – for nothing in this world could keep still while that tune of his was going on – and says she to him, chaunting it out with a voice as sweet as honey –

"I'm a lady of honour
Who live in the sea;
Come down, Maurice Connor,
And be married to me.

"Silver plates and gold dishes
You shall have, and shall be
The king of the fishes,
When you're married to me."

Drink was strong in Maurice's head, and out he chaunted in return for her great civility. It is not every lady, maybe, that would be after making such an offer to a blind piper; therefore 'twas only right in him to give her as good as she gave herself – so says Maurice,

> *"I'm obliged to you, madam:*
> *Off a gold dish or plate,*
> *If a king, and I had 'em,*
> *I could dine in great state.*

> *"With your own father's daughter*
> *I'd be sure to agree;*
> *But to drink the salt water*
> *Wouldn't do so with me!"*

The lady looked at him quite amazed, and swinging her head from side to side like a great scholar, "Well," says she, "Maurice, if you're not a poet, where is poetry to be found?"

In this way they kept on at it, framing high compliments; one answering the other, and their feet going with the music as fast as their tongues. All the fish kept dancing too: Maurice heard the clatter, and was afraid to stop playing lest it might be displeasing to the fish, and not knowing what so many of them may take it into their heads to do to him if they got vexed.

Well, the lady with the green hair kept on coaxing of Maurice with soft speeches, till at last she overpersuaded him to promise to marry her, and be king over the fishes, great and small. Maurice was well fitted to be their king, if they wanted one that could make them dance; and he surely would drink, barring the salt water, with any fish of them all.

When Maurice's mother saw him, with that unnatural thing in the form of a green-haired lady as his guide, and he and she dancing down together so lovingly to the water's edge through the thick of the fishes, she called out after him to stop and come back. "Oh then," says she, "as if I was not widow enough before, there he is going away from me to be married to that scaly woman. And who knows but 'tis grandmother I may be to a hake or a cod – Lord help and pity me, but 'tis a mighty unnatural thing! – and maybe 'tis boiling and eating my own grandchild I'll be, with a bit of salt butter, and I not knowing it! – Oh Maurice, Maurice, if there's any love or nature left in you, come back to your own *ould* mother, who reared you like a decent Christian!"

Then the poor woman began to cry and ullagoane so finely that it would do anyone good to hear her.

Maurice was not long getting to the rim of the water; there he kept playing and dancing on as if nothing was the matter, and a great thundering wave coming in towards him ready to swallow him up alive; but as he could not see it, he did not fear it. His mother it was who saw it plainly through the big tears that were rolling down her cheeks; and though she saw it, and her heart was aching as much as ever mother's heart ached for a son, she kept dancing, dancing, all the time for the bare life of her. Certain it was she could not help it, for Maurice never stopped playing that wonderful tune of his.

He only turned the bothered ear to the sound of his mother's voice, fearing it might put him out in his steps, and all the answer he made back was –

"Whisht with you, mother – sure I'm going to be king over the fishes down in the sea, and for a token of luck, and a sign that I am alive and well, I'll send you in, every twelvemonth on this day, a piece of burned wood to Trafraska." Maurice had not the power to say a word more, for the strange lady with the green hair, seeing the wave just upon them, covered him up with herself in a thing like a cloak with a big hood to it, and the wave curling over twice as high as their heads, burst upon the strand, with a rush and a roar that might be heard as far as Cape Clear.

That day twelvemonth the piece of burned wood came ashore in Trafraska. It was a queer thing for Maurice to think of sending all the way from the bottom of the sea. A gown or a pair of shoes would have been something like a present for his poor mother; but he had said it, and he kept his word. The bit of burned wood regularly came ashore on the appointed day for as good, ay, and better than a hundred years. The day is now forgotten, and may be that is the reason why people say how Maurice Connor has stopped sending the luck-token to his mother. Poor woman, she did not live to get as much as one of them; for what through the loss of Maurice, and the fear of eating her own grandchildren, she died in three weeks after the dance – some say it was the fatigue that killed her, but whichever it was, Mrs. Connor was decently buried with her own people.

Seafaring men have often heard off the coast of Kerry, on a still night, the sound of music coming up from the water; and some, who have had good ears, could plainly distinguish Maurice Connor's voice singing these words to his pipes:

"Beautiful shore, with thy spreading strand,
Thy crystal water, and diamond sand;
Never would I have parted from thee
But for the sake of my fair ladie."

The Lady of Gollerus

ON THE SHORE of Smerwick harbour, one fine summer's morning, just at daybreak, stood Dick Fitzgerald 'shoghing the dudeen', which may be translated, smoking his pipe. The sun was gradually rising behind the lofty Brandon, the dark sea was getting green in the light, and the mists clearing away out of the valleys went rolling and curling like the smoke from the corner of Dick's mouth.

"'Tis just the pattern of a pretty morning," said Dick, taking the pipe from between his lips, and looking towards the distant ocean, which lay as still and tranquil as a tomb of polished marble. "Well, to be sure," continued he, after a pause, "'tis mighty lonesome to be talking to one's self by way of company, and not to have another soul to answer one – nothing but the child of one's own voice, the echo! I know this, that if I had the luck, or may be the misfortune," said Dick, with a melancholy smile, "to have the woman, it would not be this way with me! And what in the wide world is a man without a wife? He's no more surely than a bottle without a drop of drink in it, or dancing without music, or the left leg of a scissors, or a fishing-line without a hook, or any other matter that is no ways complete. Is it not so?" said Dick Fitzgerald, casting his eyes towards a rock upon the strand, which, though it could not speak, stood up as firm and looked as bold as ever Kerry witness did.

But what was his astonishment at beholding, just at the foot of that rock, a beautiful young creature combing her hair, which was of a sea-green colour; and now the salt water shining on it appeared, in the morning light, like melted butter upon cabbage.

Dick guessed at once that she was a Merrow, although he had never seen one before, for he spied the *cohuleen driuth*, or little enchanted cap, which the sea people use for diving down into the ocean, lying upon the strand near her; and he had heard that, if once he could possess himself of the cap she would lose the power of going away into the water: so he seized it with all speed, and she, hearing the noise, turned her head about as natural as any Christian.

When the Merrow saw that her little diving-cap was gone, the salt tears – doubly salt, no doubt, from her – came trickling down her cheeks, and she began a low mournful cry with just the tender voice of a new-born infant. Dick, although he knew well enough what she was crying for, determined to keep the *cohuleen driuth*, let her cry never so much, to see what luck would come out of it. Yet he could not help pitying her; and when the dumb thing looked up in his face, with her cheeks all moist with tears, 'twas enough to make anyone feel, let alone Dick, who had ever and always, like most of his countrymen, a mighty tender heart of his own.

"Don't cry, my darling," said Dick Fitzgerald; but the Merrow, like any bold child, only cried the more for that.

Dick sat himself down by her side, and took hold of her hand by way of comforting her. 'Twas in no particular an ugly hand, only there was a small web between the fingers, as there is in a duck's foot; but 'twas as thin and as white as the skin between egg and shell.

"What's your name, my darling?" says Dick, thinking to make her conversant with him; but he got no answer; and he was certain sure now, either that she could not speak, or did not understand him: he therefore squeezed her hand in his, as the only way he had of talking to her. It's the universal language; and there's not a woman in the world, be she fish or lady, that does not understand it.

The Merrow did not seem much displeased at this mode of conversation; and making an end of her whining all at once, "Man," says she, looking up in Dick Fitzgerald's face; "man, will you eat me?"

"By all the red petticoats and check aprons between Dingle and Tralee," cried Dick, jumping up in amazement, "I'd as soon eat myself, my jewel! Is it I eat you, my pet? Now, 'twas some ugly ill-looking thief of a fish put that notion into your own pretty head, with the nice green hair down upon it, that is so cleanly combed out this morning!"

"Man," said the Merrow, "what will you do with me if you won't eat me?"

Dick's thoughts were running on a wife: he saw, at the first glimpse, that she was handsome; but since she spoke, and spoke too like any real woman, he was fairly in love with her. 'Twas the neat way she called him man that settled the matter entirely.

"Fish," says Dick, trying to speak to her after her own short fashion; "fish," says he, "here's my word, fresh and fasting, for you this blessed morning, that I'll make you Mistress Fitzgerald before all the world, and that's what I'll do."

"Never say the word twice," says she; "I'm ready and willing to be yours, Mister Fitzgerald; but stop, if you please, till I twist up my hair." It was some time before she had settled it entirely to her liking; for she guessed, I suppose, that she was going among strangers, where she would be looked at. When that was done, the Merrow put the comb in her pocket, and then bent down her head and whispered some words to the water that was close to the foot of the rock.

Dick saw the murmur of the words upon the top of the sea, going out towards the wide ocean, just like a breath of wind rippling along, and, says he, in the greatest wonder, "Is it speaking you are, my darling, to the salt water?"

"It's nothing else," says she, quite carelessly; "I'm just sending word home to my father not to be waiting breakfast for me; just to keep him from being uneasy in his mind."

"And who's your father, my duck?" said Dick.

"What!" said the Merrow, "did you never hear of my father? He's the king of the waves to be sure!"

"And yourself, then, is a real king's daughter?" said Dick, opening his two eyes to take a full and true survey of his wife that was to be. "Oh, I'm nothing else but a made man with you, and a king your father; to be sure he has all the money that's down at the bottom of the sea!"

"Money," repeated the Merrow, "what's money?"

"'Tis no bad thing to have when one wants it," replied Dick; "and maybe now the fishes have the understanding to bring up whatever you bid them?"

"Oh yes," said the Merrow, "they bring me what I want."

"To speak the truth then," said Dick, "'tis a straw bed I have at home before you, and that, I'm thinking, is no ways fitting for a king's daughter; so if 'twould not be displeasing to you, just to mention a nice feather bed, with a pair of new blankets

– but what am I talking about? Maybe you have not such things as beds down under the water?"

"By all means," said she, "Mr. Fitzgerald – plenty of beds at your service. I've fourteen oyster-beds of my own, not to mention one just planting for the rearing of young ones."

"You have?" says Dick, scratching his head and looking a little puzzled. "'Tis a feather bed I was speaking of; but, clearly, yours is the very cut of a decent plan to have bed and supper so handy to each other, that a person when they'd have the one need never ask for the other."

However, bed or no bed, money or no money, Dick Fitzgerald determined to marry the Merrow, and the Merrow had given her consent. Away they went, therefore, across the strand, from Gollerus to Ballinrunnig, where Father Fitzgibbon happened to be that morning.

"There are two words to this bargain, Dick Fitzgerald," said his Reverence, looking mighty glum. "And is it a fishy woman you'd marry? The Lord preserve us! Send the scaly creature home to her own people; that's my advice to you, wherever she came from."

Dick had the *cohuleen driuth* in his hand, and was about to give it back to the Merrow, who looked covetously at it, but he thought for a moment, and then says he, "Please your Reverence, she's a king's daughter."

"If she was the daughter of fifty kings," said Father Fitzgibbon, "I tell you, you can't marry her, she being a fish."

"Please your Reverence," said Dick again, in an undertone, "she is as mild and as beautiful as the moon."

"If she was as mild and as beautiful as the sun, moon, and stars, all put together, I tell you, Dick Fitzgerald," said the Priest, stamping his right foot, "you can't marry her, she being a fish."

"But she has all the gold that's down in the sea only for the asking, and I'm a made man if I marry her; and," said Dick, looking up slily, "I can make it worth anyone's while to do the job."

"Oh! That alters the case entirely," replied the Priest; "why there's some reason now in what you say: why didn't you tell me this before? Marry her by all means, if she was ten times a fish. Money, you know, is not to be refused in these bad times, and I may as well have the hansel of it as another, that maybe would not take half the pains in counselling you that I have done."

So Father Fitzgibbon married Dick Fitzgerald to the Merrow, and like any loving couple, they returned to Gollerus well pleased with each other. Everything prospered with Dick – he was at the sunny side of the world; the Merrow made the best of wives, and they lived together in the greatest contentment.

It was wonderful to see, considering where she had been brought up, how she would busy herself about the house, and how well she nursed the children; for, at the end of three years there were as many young Fitzgeralds – two boys and a girl.

In short, Dick was a happy man, and so he might have been to the end of his days if he had only had the sense to take care of what he had got; many another man, however, beside Dick, has not had wit enough to do that.

One day, when Dick was obliged to go to Tralee, he left the wife minding the children at home after him, and thinking she had plenty to do without disturbing his fishing-tackle.

Dick was no sooner gone than Mrs. Fitzgerald set about cleaning up the house, and chancing to pull down a fishing-net, what should she find behind it in a hole in the wall

but her own *cohuleen driuth*. She took it out and looked at it, and then she thought of her father the king, and her mother the queen, and her brothers and sisters, and she felt a longing to go back to them.

She sat down on a little stool and thought over the happy days she had spent under the sea; then she looked at her children, and thought on the love and affection of poor Dick, and how it would break his heart to lose her. "But," says she, "he won't lose me entirely, for I'll come back to him again, and who can blame me for going to see my father and my mother after being so long away from them?"

She got up and went towards the door, but came back again to look once more at the child that was sleeping in the cradle. She kissed it gently, and as she kissed it a tear trembled for an instant in her eye and then fell on its rosy cheek. She wiped away the tear, and turning to the eldest little girl, told her to take good care of her brothers, and to be a good child herself until she came back. The Merrow then went down to the strand. The sea was lying calm and smooth, just heaving and glittering in the sun, and she thought she heard a faint sweet singing, inviting her to come down. All her old ideas and feelings came flooding over her mind, Dick and her children were at the instant forgotten, and placing the *cohuleen driuth* on her head she plunged in.

Dick came home in the evening, and missing his wife he asked Kathleen, his little girl, what had become of her mother, but she could not tell him. He then inquired of the neighbours, and he learned that she was seen going towards the strand with a strange-looking thing like a cocked hat in her hand. He returned to his cabin to search for the *cohuleen driuth*. It was gone, and the truth now flashed upon him.

Year after year did Dick Fitzgerald wait expecting the return of his wife, but he never saw her more. Dick never married again, always thinking that the Merrow would sooner or later return to him, and nothing could ever persuade him but that her father the king kept her below by main force; "for," said Dick, "she surely would not of herself give up her husband and her children."

While she was with him she was so good a wife in every respect that to this day she is spoken of in the tradition of the country as the pattern for one, under the name of The Lady of Gollerus.

The White Trout
A Legend of Cong

THERE WAS WANST upon a time, long ago, a beautiful lady that lived in a castle upon the lake beyant, and they say she was promised to a king's son, and they wor to be married, when all of a sudden he was murthered, the crathur (Lord help us), and threwn into the lake above, and so, of course, he couldn't keep his promise to the fair lady – and more's the pity.

Well, the story goes that she went out iv her mind, bekase av loosin' the king's son – for she was tendher-hearted, God help her, like the rest iv us! – and pined away after him, until at last, no one about seen her, good or bad; and the story wint that the fairies took her away.

Well, sir, in coorse o' time, the White Throut, God bless it, was seen in the sthrame beyant, and sure the people didn't know what to think av the crathur, seein' as how a *white* throut was never heard av afor, nor since; and years upon years the throut was there, just where you seen it this blessed minit, longer nor I can tell – aye throth, and beyant the memory o' th' ouldest in the village.

At last the people began to think it must be a fairy; for what else could it be? – And no hurt nor harm was iver put an the white throut, until some wicked sinners of sojers kem to these parts, and laughed at all the people, and gibed and jeered them for thinkin' o' the likes; and one o' them in partic'lar (bad luck to him; God forgi' me for saying it!) swore he'd catch the throut and ate it for his dinner – the blackguard!

Well, what would you think o' the villainy of the sojer? Sure enough he cotch the throut, and away wid him home, and puts an the fryin'-pan, and into it he pitches the purty little thing. The throut squeeled all as one as a christian crathur, and, my dear, you'd think the sojer id split his sides laughin' – for he was a harden'd villain; and when he thought one side was done, he turns it over to fry the other; and, what would you think, but the divil a taste of a burn was an it at all at all; and sure the sojer thought it was a *quare* throut that could not be briled. "But," says he, "I'll give it another turn by-and-by," little thinkin' what was in store for him, the haythen.

Well, when he thought that side was done he turns it agin, and lo and behould you, the divil a taste more done that side was nor the other. "Bad luck to me," says the sojer, "but that bates the world," says he; "but I'll thry you agin, my darlint," says he, "as cunnin' as you think yourself"; and so with that he turns it over and over, but not a sign of the fire was on the purty throut. "Well," says the desperate villain – (for sure, sir, only he was a desperate villain *entirely*, he might know he was doing a wrong thing, seein' that all his endeavours was no good) – "Well," says he, "my jolly little throut, maybe you're fried enough, though you don't seem over well dress'd; but you may be better than you look, like a singed cat, and a tit-bit afther all," says he; and with that he ups with his knife and fork to taste a piece o' the throut; but, my jew'l, the minit he puts his knife into the fish, there was a murtherin' screech, that you'd think the life id lave you if you hurd it, and away jumps the throut out av the fryin'-pan into the middle o' the flure; and an the spot where it fell, up riz a lovely lady – the beautifullest crathur that eyes ever seen, dressed in white, and a band o' goold in her hair, and a sthrame o' blood runnin' down her arm.

"Look where you cut me, you villain," says she, and she held out her arm to him – and, my dear, he thought the sight id lave his eyes.

"Couldn't you lave me cool and comfortable in the river where you snared me, and not disturb me in my duty?" says she.

Well, he thrimbled like a dog in a wet sack, and at last he stammered out somethin', and begged for his life, and ax'd her ladyship's pardin, and said he didn't know she was on duty, or he was too good a sojer not to know betther nor to meddle wid her.

"I *was* on duty, then," says the lady; "I was watchin' for my true love that is comin' by wather to me," says she, "an' if he comes while I'm away, an' that I miss iv him, I'll turn you into a pinkeen, and I'll hunt you up and down for evermore, while grass grows or wather runs."

Well the sojer thought the life id lave him, at the thoughts iv his bein' turned into a pinkeen, and begged for mercy; and with that says the lady –

"Renounce your evil coorses," says she, "you villain, or you'll repint it too late; be a good man for the futhur, and go to your duty reg'lar, and now," says she, "take me back and put me into the river again, where you found me."

"Oh, my lady," says the sojer, "how could I have the heart to drownd a beautiful lady like you?"

But before he could say another word, the lady was vanished, and there he saw the little throut an the ground. Well he put it in a clean plate, and away he runs for the bare life, for fear her lover would come while she was away; and he run, and he run, even till he came to the cave agin, and threw the throut into the river. The minit he did, the wather was as red as blood for a little while, by rayson av the cut, I suppose, until the sthrame washed the stain away; and to this day there's a little red mark an the throut's side, where it was cut.

Well, sir, from that day out the sojer was an altered man, and reformed his ways, and went to his duty reg'lar, and fasted three times a-week – though it was never fish he tuk an fastin' days, for afther the fright he got, fish id never rest an his stomach – savin' your presence.

But anyhow, he was an altered man, as I said before, and in coorse o' time he left the army, and turned hermit at last; and they say he *used to pray evermore for the soul of the White Throut*.

[These trout stories are common all over Ireland. Many holy wells are haunted by such blessed trout. There is a trout in a well on the border of Lough Gill, Sligo, that some paganish person put once on the gridiron. It carries the marks to this day. Long ago, the saint who sanctified the well put that trout there. Nowadays it is only visible to the pious, who have done due penance.]

The Soul Cages

JACK DOGHERTY LIVED on the coast of the county Clare. Jack was a fisherman, as his father and grandfather before him had been. Like them, too, he lived all alone (but for the wife), and just in the same spot. People used to wonder why the Dogherty family were so fond of that wild situation, so far away from all human kind, and in the midst of huge shattered rocks, with nothing but the wide ocean to look upon. But they had their own good reasons for it.

The place was just the only spot on that part of the coast where anybody could well live. There was a neat little creek, where a boat might lie as snug as a puffin in her nest, and out from this creek a ledge of sunken rocks ran into the sea. Now when the Atlantic, according to custom, was raging with a storm, and a good westerly wind was blowing strong on the coast, many a richly-laden ship went to pieces on these rocks; and then the fine bales of cotton and tobacco, and such like things, and the pipes of wine, and the puncheons of rum, and the casks of brandy, and the kegs of Hollands that used to come ashore! Dunbeg Bay was just like a little estate to the Doghertys.

Not but they were kind and humane to a distressed sailor, if ever one had the good luck to get to land; and many a time indeed did Jack put out in his little *corragh* (which, though not quite equal to honest Andrew Hennessy's canvas life-boat, would breast the billows like any gannet), to lend a hand towards bringing off the crew from a wreck. But when the ship had gone to pieces, and the crew were all lost, who would blame Jack for picking up all he could find?

"And who is the worse of it?" said he. "For as to the king, God bless him! Everybody knows he's rich enough already without getting what's floating in the sea."

Jack, though such a hermit, was a good-natured, jolly fellow. No other, sure, could ever have coaxed Biddy Mahony to quit her father's snug and warm house in the middle of the town of Ennis, and to go so many miles off to live among the rocks, with the seals and sea-gulls for next-door neighbours. But Biddy knew that Jack was the man for a woman who wished to be comfortable and happy; for, to say nothing of the fish, Jack had the supplying of half the gentlemen's houses of the country with the *Godsends* that came into the bay. And she was right in her choice; for no woman ate, drank, or slept better, or made a prouder appearance at chapel on Sundays, than Mrs. Dogherty.

Many a strange sight, it may well be supposed, did Jack see, and many a strange sound did he hear, but nothing daunted him. So far was he from being afraid of Merrows, or such beings, that the very first wish of his heart was to fairly meet with one. Jack had heard that they were mighty like Christians, and that luck had always come out of an acquaintance with them. Never, therefore, did he dimly discern the Merrows moving along the face of the waters in their robes of mist, but he made direct for them; and many a scolding did Biddy, in her own quiet way, bestow upon Jack for spending his whole day out at sea, and bringing home no fish. Little did poor Biddy know the fish Jack was after!

It was rather annoying to Jack that, though living in a place where the Merrows were as plenty as lobsters, he never could get a right view of one. What vexed him more was that both his father and grandfather had often and often seen them; and he even remembered hearing, when a child, how his grandfather, who was the first of the family that had settled down at the creek, had been so intimate with a Merrow that, only for fear of vexing the priest, he would have had him stand for one of his children. This, however, Jack did not well know how to believe.

Fortune at length began to think that it was only right that Jack should know as much as his father and grandfather did. Accordingly, one day when he had strolled a little farther than usual along the coast to the northward, just as he turned a point, he saw something, like to nothing he had ever seen before, perched upon a rock at a little distance out to sea. It looked green in the body, as well as he could discern at that distance, and he would have sworn, only the thing was impossible, that it had a cocked hat in its hand. Jack stood for a good half-hour straining his eyes, and wondering at it, and all the time the thing did not stir hand or foot. At last Jack's patience was quite worn out, and he gave a loud whistle and a hail, when the Merrow (for such it was) started up, put the cocked hat on its head, and dived down, head foremost, from the rock.

Jack's curiosity was now excited, and he constantly directed his steps towards the point; still he could never get a glimpse of the sea-gentleman with the cocked hat; and with thinking and thinking about the matter, he began at last to fancy he had been only dreaming. One very rough day, however, when the sea was running mountains high, Jack Dogherty determined to give a look at the Merrow's rock (for he had always chosen a fine day before), and then he saw the strange thing cutting capers upon the top of the rock, and then diving down, and then coming up, and then diving down again.

Jack had now only to choose his time (that is, a good blowing day), and he might see the man of the sea as often as he pleased. All this, however, did not satisfy him – "much will have more"; he wished now to get acquainted with the Merrow, and even in this he succeeded. One tremendous blustering day, before he got to the point whence he had a view of the Merrow's rock, the storm came on so furiously that Jack was obliged to take shelter in one of the caves which are so numerous along the coast; and there, to his astonishment, he saw sitting before him a thing with green hair, long green teeth, a red nose, and pig's eyes. It had a fish's tail, legs with scales on them, and short arms like fins. It wore no clothes, but had the cocked hat under its arm, and seemed engaged thinking very seriously about something.

Jack, with all his courage, was a little daunted; but now or never, thought he; so up he went boldly to the cogitating fishman, took off his hat, and made his best bow.

"Your servant, sir," said Jack.

"Your servant, kindly, Jack Dogherty," answered the Merrow.

"To be sure, then, how well your honour knows my name!" said Jack.

"Is it I not know your name, Jack Dogherty? Why, man, I knew your grandfather long before he was married to Judy Regan, your grandmother! Ah, Jack, Jack, I was fond of that grandfather of yours; he was a mighty worthy man in his time: I never met his match above or below, before or since, for sucking in a shellful of brandy. I hope, my boy," said the old fellow, with a merry twinkle in his eyes, "I hope you're his own grandson!"

"Never fear me for that," said Jack; "if my mother had only reared me on brandy, 'tis myself that would be a sucking infant to this hour!"

"Well, I like to hear you talk so manly; you and I must be better acquainted, if it were only for your grandfather's sake. But, Jack, that father of yours was not the thing! He had no head at all."

"I'm sure," said Jack, "since your honour lives down under the water, you must be obliged to drink a power to keep any heat in you in such a cruel, damp, *could* place. Well, I've often heard of Christians drinking like fishes; and might I be so bold as ask where you get the spirits?"

"Where do you get them yourself, Jack?" said the Merrow, twitching his red nose between his forefinger and thumb.

"Hubbubboo," cries Jack, "now I see how it is; but I suppose, sir, your honour has got a fine dry cellar below to keep them in."

"Let me alone for the cellar," said the Merrow, with a knowing wink of his left eye.

"I'm sure," continued Jack, "it must be mighty well worth the looking at."

"You may say that, Jack," said the Merrow; "and if you meet me here next Monday, just at this time of the day, we will have a little more talk with one another about the matter."

Jack and the Merrow parted the best friends in the world. On Monday they met, and Jack was not a little surprised to see that the Merrow had two cocked hats with him, one under each arm.

"Might I take the liberty to ask, sir," said Jack, "why your honour has brought the two hats with you today? You would not, sure, be going to give me one of them, to keep for the *curiosity* of the thing?"

"No, no, Jack," said he, "I don't get my hats so easily, to part with them that way; but I want you to come down and dine with me, and I brought you the hat to dine with."

"Lord bless and preserve us!" cried Jack, in amazement, "would you want me to go down to the bottom of the salt sea ocean? Sure, I'd be smothered and choked up with the water, to say nothing of being drowned! And what would poor Biddy do for me, and what would she say?"

"And what matter what she says, you *pinkeen*? Who cares for Biddy's squalling? It's long before your grandfather would have talked in that way. Many's the time he stuck that same hat on his head, and dived down boldly after me; and many's the snug bit of dinner and good shellful of brandy he and I have had together below, under the water."

"Is it really, sir, and no joke?" said Jack; "why, then, sorrow from me for ever and a day after, if I'll be a bit worse man nor my grandfather was! Here goes – but play me fair now. Here's neck or nothing!" cried Jack.

"That's your grandfather all over," said the old fellow; "so come along, then, and do as I do."

They both left the cave, walked into the sea, and then swam a piece until they got to the rock. The Merrow climbed to the top of it, and Jack followed him. On the far side it was as straight as the wall of a house, and the sea beneath looked so deep that Jack was almost cowed.

"Now, do you see, Jack," said the Merrow: "just put this hat on your head, and mind to keep your eyes wide open. Take hold of my tail, and follow after me, and you'll see what you'll see."

In he dashed, and in dashed Jack after him boldly. They went and they went, and Jack thought they'd never stop going. Many a time did he wish himself sitting at home by the fireside with Biddy. Yet where was the use of wishing now, when he was so many miles, as he thought, below the waves of the Atlantic? Still he held hard by the Merrow's tail, slippery as it was; and, at last, to Jack's great surprise, they got out of the water, and he actually found himself on dry land at the bottom of the sea. They landed just in front of a nice house that was slated very neatly with oyster shells! And the Merrow, turning about to Jack, welcomed him down.

Jack could hardly speak, what with wonder, and what with being out of breath with travelling so fast through the water. He looked about him and could see no living things, barring crabs and lobsters, of which there were plenty walking leisurely about on the sand. Overhead was the sea like a sky, and the fishes like birds swimming about in it.

"Why don't you speak, man?" said the Merrow: "I dare say you had no notion that I had such a snug little concern here as this? Are you smothered, or choked, or drowned, or are you fretting after Biddy, eh?"

"Oh! Not myself, indeed," said Jack, showing his teeth with a good-humoured grin; "but who in the world would ever have thought of seeing such a thing?"

"Well, come along, and let's see what they've got for us to eat?"

Jack really was hungry, and it gave him no small pleasure to perceive a fine column of smoke rising from the chimney, announcing what was going on within. Into the house he followed the Merrow, and there he saw a good kitchen, right well provided with everything. There was a noble dresser, and plenty of pots and pans, with two young Merrows cooking. His host then led him into the room, which was furnished shabbily enough. Not a table or a chair was there in it; nothing but planks and logs of wood to sit on, and eat off. There was, however, a good fire blazing upon the hearth – a comfortable sight to Jack.

"Come now, and I'll show you where I keep – you know what," said the Merrow, with a sly look; and opening a little door, he led Jack into a fine cellar, well filled with pipes, and kegs, and hogsheads, and barrels.

"What do you say to that, Jack Dogherty? Eh! Maybe a body can't live snug under the water?"

"Never the doubt of that," said Jack, with a convincing smack of his under lip, that he really thought what he said.

They went back to the room, and found dinner laid. There was no tablecloth, to be sure – but what matter? It was not always Jack had one at home. The dinner would have been no discredit to the first house of the country on a fast day. The choicest of fish, and no wonder, was there. Turbots, and sturgeons, and soles, and lobsters, and oysters, and twenty other kinds, were on the planks at once, and plenty of the best of foreign spirits. The wines, the old fellow said, were too cold for his stomach.

Jack ate and drank till he could eat no more: then, taking up a shell of brandy, "Here's to your honour's good health, sir," said he; "though, begging you pardon, it's mighty odd that as long as we've been acquainted I don't know your name yet."

"That's true, Jack," replied he; "I never thought of it before, but better late than never. My name's Coomara."

"And a mighty decent name it is," cried Jack, taking another shellfull: "here's to your good health, Coomara, and may ye live these fifty years to come!"

"Fifty years!" repeated Coomara; "I'm obliged to you, indeed! If you had said five hundred, it would have been something worth the wishing."

"By the laws, sir," cries Jack, "*youz* live to a powerful age here under the water! You knew my grandfather, and he's dead and gone better than these sixty years. I'm sure it must be a healthy place to live in."

"No doubt of it; but come, Jack, keep the liquor stirring."

Shell after shell did they empty, and to Jack's exceeding surprise, he found the drink never got into his head, owing, I suppose, to the sea being over them, which kept their noddles cool.

Old Coomara got exceedingly comfortable, and sung several songs; but Jack, if his life had depended on it, never could remember more than:

> *"Rum fum boodle boo,*
> *Ripple dipple nitty dob;*
> *Dumdoo doodle coo,*
> *Raffle taffle chittiboo!"*

It was the chorus to one of them; and, to say the truth, nobody that I know has ever been able to pick any particular meaning out of it; but that, to be sure, is the case with many a song nowadays.

At length said he to Jack, "Now, my dear boy, if you follow me, I'll show you my *curiosities*!" He opened a little door, and led Jack into a large room, where Jack saw a great many odds and ends that Coomara had picked up at one time or another. What chiefly took his attention, however, were things like lobster-pots ranged on the ground along the wall.

"Well, Jack, how do you like my *curiosities*?" said old Coo.

"Upon my *sowkins*, sir," said Jack, "they're mighty well worth the looking at; but might I make so bold as to ask what these things like lobster-pots are?"

"Oh! The Soul Cages, is it?"

"The what? Sir!"

"These things here that I keep the souls in."

"*Arrah!* What souls, sir?" said Jack, in amazement; "sure the fish have no souls in them?"

"Oh! No," replied Coo, quite coolly, "that they have not; but these are the souls of drowned sailors."

"The Lord preserve us from all harm!" muttered Jack, "how in the world did you get them?"

"Easily enough: I've only, when I see a good storm coming on, to set a couple of dozen of these, and then, when the sailors are drowned and the souls get out of them under the water, the poor things are almost perished to death, not being used to the cold; so they make into my pots for shelter, and then I have them snug, and fetch them home, and keep them here dry and warm; and is it not well for them, poor souls, to get into such good quarters?"

Jack was so thunderstruck he did not know what to say, so he said nothing. They went back into the dining-room, and had a little more brandy, which was excellent, and then, as Jack knew that it must be getting late, and as Biddy might be uneasy, he stood up, and said he thought it was time for him to be on the road.

"Just as you like, Jack," said Coo, "but take a *duc an durrus* before you go; you've a cold journey before you."

Jack knew better manners than to refuse the parting glass. "I wonder," said he, "will I be able to make out my way home?"

"What should ail you," said Coo, "when I'll show you the way?"

Out they went before the house, and Coomara took one of the cocked hats, and put it upon Jack's head the wrong way, and then lifted him up on his shoulder that he might launch him up into the water.

"Now," says he, giving him a heave, "you'll come up just in the same spot you came down in; and, Jack, mind and throw me back the hat."

He canted Jack off his shoulder, and up he shot like a bubble – *whirr, whirr, whiz* – away he went up through the water, till he came to the very rock he had jumped off, where he found a landing-place, and then in he threw the hat, which sunk like a stone.

The sun was just going down in the beautiful sky of a calm summer's evening. *Feascor* was seen dimly twinkling in the cloudless heaven, a solitary star, and the waves of the Atlantic flashed in a golden flood of light. So Jack, perceiving it was late, set off home; but when he got there, not a word did he say to Biddy of where he had spent his day.

The state of the poor souls cooped up in the lobster-pots gave Jack a great deal of trouble, and how to release them cost him a great deal of thought. He at first had a mind to speak to the priest about the matter. But what could the priest do, and what did Coo care for the priest? Besides, Coo was a good sort of an old fellow, and did not think he was doing any harm. Jack had a regard for him, too, and it also might not be much to his own credit if it were known that he used to go dine with Merrows. On the whole, he thought his best plan would be to ask Coo to dinner, and to make him drunk, if he was able, and then to take the hat and go down and turn up the pots. It was, first of all, necessary, however, to get Biddy out of the way; for Jack was prudent enough, as she was a woman, to wish to keep the thing secret from her.

Accordingly, Jack grew mighty pious all of a sudden, and said to Biddy that he thought it would be for the good of both their souls if she was to go and take her rounds at Saint John's Well, near Ennis. Biddy thought so too, and accordingly off she set one fine morning at day-dawn, giving Jack a strict charge to have an eye to the place. The coast being clear, away went Jack to the rock to give the appointed signal to Coomara, which was throwing a big stone into the water. Jack threw, and up sprang Coo!

"Good morning, Jack," said he; "what do you want with me?"

"Just nothing at all to speak about, sir," returned Jack, "only to come and take a bit of dinner with me, if I might make so free as to ask you, and sure I'm now after doing so."

"It's quite agreeable, Jack, I assure you; what's your hour?"

"Any time that's most convenient to you, sir – say one o'clock, that you may go home, if you wish, with the daylight."

"I'll be with you," said Coo, "never fear me."

Jack went home, and dressed a noble fish dinner, and got out plenty of his best foreign spirits, enough, for that matter, to make twenty men drunk. Just to the minute came Coo, with his cocked hat under his arm. Dinner was ready, they sat down, and ate and drank away manfully. Jack, thinking of the poor souls below in the pots, plied old Coo well with brandy, and encouraged him to sing, hoping to put him under the table, but poor Jack forgot that he had not the sea over his own head to keep it cool. The brandy got into it, and did his business for him, and Coo reeled off home, leaving his entertainer as dumb as a haddock on a Good Friday.

Jack never woke till the next morning, and then he was in a sad way. "'Tis to no use for me thinking to make that old Rapparee drunk," said Jack, "and how in this world can I help the poor souls out of the lobster-pots?" After ruminating nearly the whole day, a thought struck him. "I have it," says he, slapping his knee; "I'll be sworn that Coo never saw a drop of *poteen*, as old as he is, and that's the *thing* to settle him! Oh! Then, is not it well that Biddy will not be home these two days yet; I can have another twist at him."

Jack asked Coo again, and Coo laughed at him for having no better head, telling him he'd never come up to his grandfather.

"Well, but try me again," said Jack, "and I'll be bail to drink you drunk and sober, and drunk again."

"Anything in my power," said Coo, "to oblige you."

At this dinner Jack took care to have his own liquor well watered, and to give the strongest brandy he had to Coo. At last says he, "Pray, sir, did you ever drink any poteen? – Any real mountain dew?"

"No," says Coo; "what's that, and where does it come from?"

"Oh, that's a secret," said Jack, "but it's the right stuff – never believe me again, if 'tis not fifty times as good as brandy or rum either. Biddy's brother just sent me a present of a little drop, in exchange for some brandy, and as you're an old friend of the family, I kept it to treat you with."

"Well, let's see what sort of thing it is," said Coomara.

The *poteen* was the right sort. It was first-rate, and had the real smack upon it. Coo was delighted: he drank and he sung *Rum bum boodle boo* over and over again; and he laughed and he danced, till he fell on the floor fast asleep. Then Jack, who had taken good care to keep himself sober, snapped up the cocked hat – ran off to the rock – leaped in, and soon arrived at Coo's habitation.

All was as still as a churchyard at midnight – not a Merrow, old or young, was there. In he went and turned up the pots, but nothing did he see, only he heard a sort of a little whistle or chirp as he raised each of them. At this he was surprised, till he recollected what the priests had often said, that nobody living could see the soul, no more than they could see the wind or the air. Having now done all that he could do for them, he set the pots as they were before, and sent a blessing after the poor souls to speed them on their journey wherever they were going. Jack now began to think of returning; he put the hat on, as was right, the wrong way; but when he got out he found the water so high over his head that he had no hopes of ever getting up into it, now that he had not old Coomara to give him a lift. He walked about looking for a ladder, but not one could he find, and not a rock was there in sight. At last he saw a spot where the sea hung rather lower than anywhere else, so he resolved to try there. Just as he came to it, a big cod happened to put down his tail. Jack made a jump and caught hold of it, and the cod, all in amazement, gave a bounce and pulled Jack up The minute the hat touched the water away Jack was whisked, and up he shot like a cork, dragging the poor cod, that he forgot to let go, up with him tail foremost. He got to the rock in no time, and without a moment's delay hurried home, rejoicing in the good deed he had done.

But, meanwhile, there was fine work at home; for our friend Jack had hardly left the house on his soul-freeing expedition, when back came Biddy from her soul-saving one to the well. When she entered the house and saw the things lying *thrie-na-helah* on the table before her – "Here's a pretty job!" said she; "that blackguard of mine – what ill-luck I had ever to marry him! He has picked up some vagabond or other, while I was praying for the good of his soul, and they've been drinking all the *poteen* that my own brother gave him, and all the spirits, to be sure, that he was to have sold to his honour." Then hearing an outlandish kind of a grunt, she looked down, and saw Coomara lying under the table. "The blessed Virgin help me," shouted she, "if he has not made a real beast of himself! Well, well, I've often heard of a man making a beast of himself with drink! Oh hone, oh hone! – Jack, honey, what will I do with you, or what will I do without you? How can any decent woman ever think of living with a beast?"

With such like lamentations Biddy rushed out of the house, and was going she knew not where, when she heard the well-known voice of Jack singing a merry tune. Glad enough was Biddy to find him safe and sound, and not turned into a thing that was like neither fish nor flesh. Jack was obliged to tell her all, and Biddy, though she had half a mind to be angry with him for not telling her before, owned that he had done a great service to the poor souls. Back they both went most lovingly to the house, and Jack wakened up Coomara; and, perceiving the old fellow to be rather dull, he bid him not to be cast down, for 'twas many a good man's case; said it all came of his not being used to the *poteen*, and recommended him, by way of cure, to swallow a hair of the dog that bit him. Coo, however, seemed to think he had had quite enough. He got up, quite out of sorts, and without having the manners to say one word in the way of civility, he sneaked off to cool himself by a jaunt through the salt water.

Coomara never missed the souls. He and Jack continued the best friends in the world, and no one, perhaps, ever equalled Jack for freeing souls from purgatory; for he contrived fifty excuses for getting into the house below the sea, unknown to the old fellow, and then turning up the pots and letting out the souls. It vexed him, to be sure, that he could never see them; but as he knew the thing to be impossible, he was obliged to be satisfied.

Their intercourse continued for several years. However, one morning, on Jack's throwing in a stone as usual, he got no answer. He flung another, and another, still there was no reply. He went away, and returned the following morning, but it was to no purpose. As he was without the hat, he could not go down to see what had become of old Coo, but his belief was, that the old man, or the old fish, or whatever he was, had either died, or had removed from that part of the country.

Flory Cantillon's Funeral

THE ANCIENT BURIAL-PLACE of the Cantillon family was on an island in Ballyheigh Bay. This island was situated at no great distance from the shore, and at a remote period was overflowed in one of the encroachments which the Atlantic has made on that part of the coast of Kerry. The fishermen declare they have often seen the ruined walls of an old chapel beneath them in the water, as they sailed over the clear green sea of a sunny afternoon. However this may be, it is well-known that the Cantillons were, like most other Irish families, strongly attached to their ancient burial-place; and this attachment led to the custom, when any of the family died, of carrying the corpse to the seaside, where the coffin was left on the shore within reach of the tide. In the morning it had disappeared, being, as was traditionally believed, conveyed away by the ancestors of the deceased to their family tomb.

Connor Crowe, a county Clare man, was related to the Cantillons by marriage. 'Connor Mac in Cruagh, of the seven quarters of Breintragh', as he was commonly called, and a proud man he was of the name. Connor, be it known, would drink a quart of salt water, for its medicinal virtues, before breakfast; and for the same reason, I suppose, double that quantity of raw whiskey between breakfast and night, which last he did with as little inconvenience to himself as any man in the barony of Moyferta; and were I to add Clanderalaw and Ibrickan, I don't think I should say wrong.

On the death of Florence Cantillon, Connor Crowe was determined to satisfy himself about the truth of this story of the old church under the sea: so when he heard the news of the old fellow's death, away with him to Ardfert, where Flory was laid out in high style, and a beautiful corpse he made.

Flory had been as jolly and as rollicking a boy in his day as ever was stretched, and his wake was in every respect worthy of him. There was all kind of entertainment, and all sort of diversion at it, and no less than three girls got husbands there – more luck to them. Everything was as it should be; all that side of the country, from Dingle to Tarbert, was at the funeral. The Keen was sung long and bitterly; and, according to the family custom, the coffin was carried to Ballyheigh strand, where it was laid upon the shore, with a prayer for the repose of the dead.

The mourners departed, one group after another, and at last Connor Crowe was left alone. He then pulled out his whiskey bottle, his drop of comfort, as he called it, which he required, being in grief; and down he sat upon a big stone that was sheltered by a projecting rock, and partly concealed from view, to await with patience the appearance of the ghostly undertakers.

The evening came on mild and beautiful. He whistled an old air which he had heard in his childhood, hoping to keep idle fears out of his head; but the wild strain of that melody brought a thousand recollections with it, which only made the twilight appear more pensive.

"If 'twas near the gloomy tower of Dunmore, in my own sweet country, I was," said Connor Crowe, with a sigh, "one might well believe that the prisoners, who were murdered long ago there in the vaults under the castle, would be the hands to carry off the coffin out of envy, for never a one of them was buried decently, nor had as much as a coffin amongst them all. 'Tis often, sure enough, I have heard lamentations and great mourning coming from the vaults of Dunmore Castle; but," continued he, after fondly pressing his lips to the mouth of his companion and silent comforter, the whiskey bottle, "didn't I know all the time well enough, 'twas the dismal sounding waves working through the cliffs and hollows of the rocks, and fretting themselves to foam. Oh, then, Dunmore Castle, it is you that are the gloomy-looking tower on a gloomy day, with the gloomy hills behind you; when one has gloomy thoughts on their heart, and sees you like a ghost rising out of the smoke made by the kelp burners on the strand, there is, the Lord save us! As fearful a look about you as about the Blue Man's Lake at midnight. Well, then, anyhow," said Connor, after a pause, "is it not a blessed night, though surely the moon looks mighty pale in the face? St. Senan himself between us and all kinds of harm."

It was, in truth, a lovely moonlight night; nothing was to be seen around but the dark rocks, and the white pebbly beach, upon which the sea broke with a hoarse and melancholy murmur. Connor, notwithstanding his frequent draughts, felt rather queerish, and almost began to repent his curiosity. It was certainly a solemn sight to behold the black coffin resting upon the white strand. His imagination gradually converted the deep moaning of old ocean into a mournful wail for the dead, and from the shadowy recesses of the rocks he imaged forth strange and visionary forms.

As the night advanced, Connor became weary with watching. He caught himself more than once in the act of nodding, when suddenly giving his head a shake, he would look towards the black coffin. But the narrow house of death remained unmoved before him.

It was long past midnight, and the moon was sinking into the sea, when he heard the sound of many voices, which gradually became stronger, above the heavy and monotonous roll of the sea. He listened, and presently could distinguish a Keen of exquisite sweetness, the notes of which rose and fell with the heaving of the waves, whose deep murmur mingled with and supported the strain!

The Keen grew louder and louder, and seemed to approach the beach, and then fell into a low, plaintive wail. As it ended Connor beheld a number of strange and, in the dim light, mysterious-looking figures emerge from the sea, and surround the coffin, which they prepared to launch into the water.

"This comes of marrying with the creatures of earth," said one of the figures, in a clear, yet hollow tone.

"True," replied another, with a voice still more fearful, "our king would never have commanded his gnawing white-toothed waves to devour the rocky roots of the island cemetery, had not his daughter, Durfulla, been buried there by her mortal husband!"

"But the time will come," said a third, bending over the coffin, "When mortal eye – our work shall spy, and mortal ear – our dirge shall hear."

"Then," said a fourth, "our burial of the Cantillons is at an end for ever!"

As this was spoken the coffin was borne from the beach by a retiring wave, and the company of sea people prepared to follow it; but at the moment one chanced to discover Connor Crowe, as fixed with wonder and as motionless with fear as the stone on which he sat.

"The time is come," cried the unearthly being, "the time is come; a human eye looks on the forms of ocean, a human ear has heard their voices. Farewell to the Cantillons; the sons of the sea are no longer doomed to bury the dust of the earth!"

One after the other turned slowly round, and regarded Connor Crowe, who still remained as if bound by a spell. Again arose their funeral song; and on the next wave they followed the coffin. The sound of the lamentation died away, and at length nothing was heard but the rush of waters. The coffin and the train of sea people sank over the old churchyard, and never since the funeral of old Flory Cantillon have any of the family been carried to the strand of Ballyheigh, for conveyance to their rightful burial-place, beneath the waves of the Atlantic.

Supernatural Forces

Introduction

IRELAND has a long folkloric history involving witches, ghosts, and enchantment. Whether it's bewitched domestic items, people being transformed into animals or objects, or spooky visitations from beyond the grave, the idea of supernatural help or hindrance is a common theme in fairy tale storytelling. Often the purposes or morality of such interference is beyond our control or understanding, making the stories sometimes frightening and often entertaining – as in the memorable examples gathered here.

Bewitched Butter

NOT FAR from Rathmullen lived, last spring, a family called Hanlon; and in a farm-house, some fields distant, people named Dogherty. Both families had good cows, but the Hanlons were fortunate in possessing a Kerry cow that gave more milk and yellower butter than the others.

Grace Dogherty, a young girl, who was more admired than loved in the neighbourhood, took much interest in the Kerry cow, and appeared one night at Mrs. Hanlon's door with the modest request –

"Will you let me milk your Moiley cow?"

"An' why wad you wish to milk wee Moiley, Grace, dear?" inquired Mrs. Hanlon.

"Oh, just becase you're sae throng at the present time."

"Thank you kindly, Grace, but I'm no too throng to do my ain work. I'll no trouble you to milk."

The girl turned away with a discontented air; but the next evening, and the next, found her at the cow-house door with the same request.

At length Mrs. Hanlon, not knowing well how to persist in her refusal, yielded, and permitted Grace to milk the Kerry cow.

She soon had reason to regret her want of firmness. Moiley gave no more milk to her owner.

When this melancholy state of things lasted for three days, the Hanlons applied to a certain Mark McCarrion, who lived near Binion.

"That cow has been milked by someone with an evil eye," said he. "Will she give you a wee drop, do you think? The full of a pint measure wad do."

"Oh, ay, Mark, dear; I'll get that much milk frae her, any way."

"Weel, Mrs. Hanlon, lock the door, an' get nine new pins that was never used in clothes, an' put them into a saucepan wi' the pint o' milk. Set them on the fire, an' let them come to the boil."

The nine pins soon began to simmer in Moiley's milk.

Rapid steps were heard approaching the door, agitated knocks followed, and Grace Dogherty's high-toned voice was raised in eager entreaty.

"Let me in, Mrs. Hanlon!" she cried. "Tak off that cruel pot! Tak out them pins, for they're pricking holes in my heart, an' I'll never offer to touch milk of yours again."

The Horned Women

A RICH WOMAN sat up late one night carding and preparing wool while all the family and servants were asleep. Suddenly a knock was given at the door, and a voice called out, "Open! Open!"

"Who is there?" said the woman of the house.

"I am the Witch of the One Horn," was answered.

The mistress, supposing that one of her neighbours had called and required assistance, opened the door, and a woman entered, having in her hand a pair of wool carders, and bearing a horn on her forehead, as if growing there. She sat down by the fire in silence, and began to card the wool with violent haste. Suddenly she paused, and said aloud, "Where are the women; they delay too long?"

Then a second knock came to the door, and a voice called as before, "Open! Open!"

The mistress felt herself constrained to rise and open to the call, and immediately a second witch entered, having two horns on her forehead, and in her hand a wheel for spinning wool.

"Give me place," she said; "I am the Witch of the Two Horns"; and she began to spin as quick as lightning.

And so the knocks went on, and the call was heard and the witches entered, until at last twelve women sat round the fire – the first with one horn, the last with twelve horns.

And they carded the thread and turned their spinning-wheels, and wound and wove.

All singing together an ancient rhyme, but no word did they speak to the mistress of the house. Strange to hear and frightful to look upon were these twelve women, with their horns and their wheels; and the mistress felt near to death, and she tried to rise that she might call for help, but she could not move, nor could she utter a word or a cry, for the spell of the witches was upon her.

Then one of them called to her in Irish, and said, "Rise, woman, and make us a cake." Then the mistress searched for a vessel to bring water from the well that she might mix the meal and make the cake, but she could find none.

And they said to her, "Take a sieve, and bring water in it." And she took the sieve, and went to the well; but the water poured from it, and she could fetch none for the cake, and she sat down by the well and wept.

Then came a voice by her, and said, "Take yellow clay and moss and bind them together, and plaster the sieve so that it will hold."

This she did, and the sieve held the water for the cake; and the voice said again:

"Return, and when thou comest to the north angle of the house cry aloud three times, and say, 'The mountain of the Fenian women and the sky over it is all on fire.'"

And she did so.

When the witches inside heard the call, a great and terrible cry broke from their lips, and they rushed forth with wild lamentations and shrieks, and fled away

to Slievenamon, where was their chief abode. But the Spirit of the Well bade the mistress of the house to enter and prepare her home against the enchantments of the witches, if they returned again.

And first, to break their spells, she sprinkled the water in which she had washed her child's feet (the feet-water) outside the door on the threshold; secondly, she took the cake which the witches had made in her absence, of meal mixed with the blood drawn from the sleeping family, and she broke the cake in bits, and placed a bit in the mouth of each sleeper, and they were restored; and she took the cloth they had woven, and placed it half in and half out of the chest with the padlock; and, lastly, she secured the door with a great crossbeam fastened in the jambs, so that they could not enter, and having done these things she waited.

Not long were the witches in coming, and they raged and called for vengeance.

"Open! Open!" they screamed. "Open, feet-water!"

"I cannot," said the feet-water; "I am scattered on the ground, and my path is down to the Lough."

"Open, open, wood and trees and beam!" they cried to the door.

"I cannot," said the door, "for the beam is fixed in the jambs, and I have no power to move."

"Open, open, cake that we have made and mingled with blood!" they cried again.

"I cannot," said the cake, "for I am broken and bruised, and my blood is on the lips of the sleeping children."

Then the witches rushed through the air with great cries, and fled back to Slievenamon, uttering strange curses on the Spirit of the Well, who had wished their ruin. But the woman and the house were left in peace, and a mantle dropped by one of the witches was kept hung up by the mistress as a sign of the night's awful contest; and this mantle was in possession of the same family from generation to generation for five hundred years after.

The Witches' Excursion

SHEMUS (RED JAMES) awakened from his sleep one night by noises in his kitchen. Stealing to the door, he saw half-a-dozen old women sitting round the fire, jesting and laughing, his old housekeeper, Madge, quite frisky and gay, helping her sister crones to cheering glasses of punch. He began to admire the impudence and imprudence of Madge, displayed in the invitation and the riot, but recollected on the instant her officiousness in urging him to take a comfortable posset, which she had brought to his bedside just before he fell asleep. Had he drunk it, he would have been just now deaf to the witches' glee. He heard and saw them drink his health in such a mocking style as nearly to tempt him to charge them, besom in hand, but he restrained himself.

The jug being emptied, one of them cried out, "Is it time to be gone?" and at the same moment, putting on a red cap, she added –

> *"By yarrow and rue,*
> *And my red cap too,*
> *Hie over to England."*

Making use of a twig which she held in her hand as a steed, she gracefully soared up the chimney, and was rapidly followed by the rest. But when it came to the housekeeper, Shemus interposed. "By your leave, ma'am," said he, snatching twig and cap. "Ah, you desateful ould crocodile! If I find you here on my return, there'll be wigs on the green –

> *'By yarrow and rue,*
> *And my red cap too,*
> *Hie over to England.'"*

The words were not out of his mouth when he was soaring above the ridge pole, and swiftly ploughing the air. He was careful to speak no word (being somewhat conversant with witch-lore), as the result would be a tumble, and the immediate return of the expedition.

In a very short time they had crossed the Wicklow hills, the Irish Sea, and the Welsh mountains, and were charging, at whirlwind speed, the hall door of a castle. Shemus, only for the company in which he found himself, would have cried out for pardon, expecting to be *mummy* against the hard oak door in a moment; but, all bewildered, he found himself passing through the key-hole, along a passage, down a flight of steps, and through a cellar-door key-hole before he could form any clear idea of his situation.

Waking to the full consciousness of his position, he found himself sitting on a stillion, plenty of lights glimmering round, and he and his companions, with full tumblers of frothing wine in hand, hob-nobbing and drinking healths as jovially and recklessly as if the liquor was honestly come by, and they were sitting in *Shemus's* own kitchen. The red birredh had assimilated *Shemus's* nature for the time being to that of his unholy companions. The heady liquors soon got into their brains, and a period of unconsciousness succeeded the ecstasy, the head-ache, the turning round of the barrels, and the 'scattered sight' of poor Shemus. He woke up under the impression of being roughly seized, and shaken, and dragged upstairs, and subjected to a disagreeable examination by the lord of the castle, in his state parlour. There was much derision among the whole company, gentle and simple, on hearing Shemus's explanation, and, as the thing occurred in the dark ages, the unlucky Leinster man was sentenced to be hung as soon as the gallows could be prepared for the occasion.

The poor Hibernian was in the cart proceeding on his last journey, with a label on his back, and another on his breast, announcing him as the remorseless villain who for the last month had been draining the casks in my lord's vault every night. He was surprised to hear himself addressed by his name, and in his native tongue, by an old woman in the crowd.

"Ach, Shemus, alanna! Is it going to die you are in a strange place without your *cappeen d'yarrag*?" These words infused hope and courage into the poor victim's heart. He turned to the lord and humbly asked leave to die in his red cap, which he supposed had dropped from his head in the vault. A servant was sent for the head-piece, and Shemus felt lively hope warming his heart while placing it on his head. On the platform he was graciously allowed to address the spectators, which he proceeded to do in the usual formula composed for the benefit of flying stationers –

"Good people all, a warning take by me"; but when he had finished the line, "My parents reared me tenderly," he unexpectedly added – "By yarrow and rue," etc., and the disappointed spectators saw him shoot up obliquely through the air in the style of a sky-rocket that had missed its aim. It is said that the lord took the circumstance much to heart, and never afterwards hung a man for twenty-four hours after his offence.

Paddy O'Kelly and the Weasel

A LONG TIME AGO there was once a man of the name of Paddy O'Kelly, living near Tuam, in the county Galway. He rose up one morning early, and he did not know what time of day it was, for there was fine light coming from the moon. He wanted to go to the fair of Cauher-na-mart to sell a *sturk* of an ass that he had.

He had not gone more than three miles of the road when a great darkness came on, and a shower began falling. He saw a large house among trees about five hundred yards in from the road, and he said to himself that he would go to that house till the shower would be over. When he got to the house he found the door open before him, and in with him. He saw a large room to his left, and a fine fire in the grate. He sat down on a stool that was beside the wall, and began falling asleep, when he saw a big weasel coming to the fire with something yellow in his mouth, which it dropped on the hearth-stone, and then it went away. She soon came back again with the same thing in her mouth, and he saw that it was a guinea she had. She dropped it on the hearth-stone, and went away again. She was coming and going, until there was a great heap of guineas on the hearth. But at last, when she got her gone, Paddy rose up, thrust all the gold she had gathered into his pockets, and out with him.

He had not gone far till he heard the weasel coming after him, and she screeching as loud as a bag-pipes. She went before Paddy and got on the road, and she was twisting herself back and forwards, and trying to get a hold of his throat. Paddy had a good oak stick, and he kept her from him, until two men came up who were going to the same fair, and one of them had a good dog, and it routed the weasel into a hole in the wall.

Paddy went to the fair, and instead of coming home with the money he got for his old ass, as he thought would be the way with him in the morning, he went and bought a horse with some of the money he took from the weasel, and he came home riding. When he came to the place where the dog had routed the weasel into the hole in the wall, she came out before him, gave a leap, and caught the horse by the throat. The horse made off, and Paddy could not stop him, till at last he gave a leap into a big drain that was full up of water and black mud, and he was drowning and choking as fast as he could, until men who were coming from Galway came up and drove away the weasel.

Paddy brought the horse home with him, and put him into the cow's byre and fell asleep.

Next morning, the day on the morrow, Paddy rose up early, and went out to give his horse hay and oats. When he got to the door he saw the weasel coming out of the byre and she covered with blood.

"My seven thousand curses on you," said Paddy, "but I'm afraid you've done harm."

He went in and found the horse, a pair of milch cows, and two calves dead. He came out and set a dog he had after the weasel. The dog got a hold of her, and she got a hold of the dog. The dog was a good one, but he was forced to loose his hold of her before Paddy could come up. He kept his eye on her, however, all through, until he saw her creeping

into a little hovel that was on the brink of a lake. Paddy came running, and when he got to the little hut he gave the dog a shake to rouse him up and put anger on him, and then he sent him in. When the dog went in he began barking. Paddy went in after him, and saw an old hag in the corner. He asked her if she saw a weasel coming in there.

"I did not," said she; "I'm all destroyed with a plague of sickness, and if you don't go out quick, you'll catch it from me."

While Paddy and the hag were talking, the dog kept moving in all the time, till at last he gave a leap and caught the hag by the throat. She screeched and said:

"Paddy Kelly, take off your dog, and I'll make you a rich man."

Paddy made the dog loose his hold, and said:

"Tell me who you are, or why did you kill my horse and my cows?"

"And why did you bring away my gold that I was gathering for five hundred years throughout the hills and hollows of the world?"

"I thought you were a weasel," said Paddy, "or I wouldn't touch your gold; and another thing," says he, "if you're for five hundred years in this world, it's time for you to go to rest now."

"I committed a great crime in my youth," said the hag, "and now I am to be released from my sufferings if you can pay twenty pounds for a hundred and three-score masses for me."

"Where's the money?" said Paddy.

"Go and dig under a bush that's over a little well in the corner of that field there without, and you'll get a pot filled with gold. Pay the twenty pounds for the masses, and yourself shall have the rest. When you'll lift the flag off the pot, you'll see a big black dog coming out; but don't be afraid before him; he is a son of mine. When you get the gold, buy the house in which you saw me at first. You'll get it cheap, for it has the name of there being a ghost in it. My son will be down in the cellar. He'll do you no harm, but he'll be a good friend to you. I shall be dead a month from this day, and when you get me dead, put a coal under this little hut and burn it. Don't tell a living soul anything about me – and the luck will be on you."

"What is your name?" said Paddy.

"Mary Kerwan," said the hag.

Paddy went home, and when the darkness of the night came on, he took with him a spade and went to the bush that was in the corner of the field, and began digging. It was not long till he found the pot, and when he took the flag off of it a big black dog leaped out, and off and away with him, and Paddy's dog after him.

Paddy brought home the gold, and hid it in the cow-house. About a month after that he went to the fair of Galway, and bought a pair of cows, a horse, and a dozen sheep. The neighbours did not know where he had got all the money; they said that he had a share with the good people.

One day Paddy dressed himself, and went to the gentleman who owned the large house where he first saw the weasel, and asked to buy the house of him, and the land that was round about.

"You can have the house without paying any rent at all; but there is a ghost in it, and I wouldn't like you to go to live in it without my telling you, but I couldn't part with the land without getting a hundred pounds more than you have to offer me."

"Perhaps I have as much as you have yourself," said Paddy. "I'll be here tomorrow with the money, if you're ready to give me possession."

"I'll be ready," said the gentleman.

Paddy went home and told his wife that he had bought a large house and a holding of land.

"Where did you get the money?" says the wife.

"Isn't it all one to you where I got it?" says Paddy.

The day on the morrow Paddy went to the gentleman, gave him the money, and got possession of the house and land; and the gentleman left him the furniture and everything that was in the house, into the bargain.

Paddy remained in the house that night, and when darkness came he went down to the cellar, and he saw a little man with his two legs spread on a barrel.

"God save you, honest man," says he to Paddy.

"The same to you," says Paddy.

"Don't be afraid of me, at all," says the little man. "I'll be a friend to you, if you are able to keep a secret."

"I am able, indeed; I kept your mother's secret, and I'll keep yours as well."

"Maybe you're thirsty?" said the little man.

"I'm not free from it," said Paddy.

The little man put a hand in his bosom and drew out a gold goblet. He gave it to Paddy, and said: "Draw wine out of that barrel under me."

Paddy drew the full up of the goblet, and handed it to the little man.

"Drink yourself first," says he.

Paddy drank, drew another goblet, and handed it to the little man, and he drank it.

"Fill up and drink again," said the little man. "I have a mind to be merry tonight."

The pair of them sat there drinking until they were half drunk. Then the little man gave a leap down to the floor, and said to Paddy:

"Don't you like music?"

"I do, surely," said Paddy, "and I'm a good dancer, too."

"Lift up the big flag over there in the corner, and you'll get my pipes under it."

Paddy lifted the flag, got the pipes, and gave them to the little man. He squeezed the pipes on him, and began playing melodious music. Paddy began dancing till he was tired. Then they had another drink, and the little man said:

"Do as my mother told you, and I'll show you great riches. You can bring your wife in here, but don't tell her that I'm there, and she won't see me. Any time at all that ale or wine are wanting, come here and draw. Farewell, now; go to sleep, and come again to me tomorrow night."

Paddy went to bed, and it wasn't long till he fell asleep.

On the morning of the day on the morrow, Paddy went home, and brought his wife and children to the big house, and they were very comfortable. That night Paddy went down to the cellar; the little man welcomed him and asked him did he wish to dance?

"Not till I get a drink," said Paddy.

"Drink your fill," said the little man; "that barrel will never be empty as long as you live."

Paddy drank the full of the goblet, and gave a drink to the little man. Then the little man said to him:

"I am going to the Fortress of the Fairies tonight, to play music for the good people, and if you come with me you'll see fine fun. I'll give you a horse that you never saw the like of him before."

"I'll go with you, and welcome," said Paddy; "but what excuse will I make to my wife?"

"I'll bring you away from her side without her knowing it, when you are both asleep together, and I'll bring you back to her the same way," said the little man.

"I'm obedient," says Paddy; "we'll have another drink before I leave you."

He drank drink after drink, till he was half drunk, and he went to bed with his wife.

When he awoke he found himself riding on a broom near Doon-na-shee, and the little man riding on another besom by his side. When they came as far as the green hill of the Doon, the little man said a couple of words that Paddy did not understand. The green hill opened, and the pair went into a fine chamber.

Paddy never saw before a gathering like that which was in the Doon. The whole place was full up of little people, men and women, young and old. They all welcomed little Donal – that was the name of the piper – and Paddy O'Kelly. The king and queen of the fairies came up to them, and said:

"We are all going on a visit tonight to Cnoc Matha, to the high king and queen of our people."

They all rose up then and went out. There were horses ready for each one of them, and the *coash-t'ya bower* for the king and queen. The king and queen got into the coach, each man leaped on his own horse, and be certain that Paddy was not behind. The piper went out before them, and began playing them music, and then off and away with them. It was not long till they came to Cnoc Matha. The hill opened, and the king of the fairy host passed in.

Finvara and Nuala were there, the arch-king and queen of the fairy host of Connacht, and thousands of little persons. Finvara came up and said:

"We are going to play a hurling match tonight against the fairy host of Munster, and unless we beat them our fame is gone for ever. The match is to be fought out on Moytura, under Slieve Belgadaun."

The Connacht host cried out: "We are all ready, and we have no doubt but we'll beat them."

"Out with ye all," cried the high king; "the men of the hill of Nephin will be on the ground before us."

They all went out, and little Donal and twelve pipers more before them, playing melodious music. When they came to Moytura, the fairy host of Munster and the fairy men of the hill of Nephin were there before them.

Now it is necessary for the fairy host to have two live men beside them when they are fighting or at a hurling match, and that was the reason that little Donal took Paddy O'Kelly with him. There was a man they called the '*Yellow Stongirya*' with the fairy host of Munster, from Ennis, in the County Clare.

It was not long till the two hosts took sides; the ball was thrown up between them, and the fun began in earnest. They were hurling away, and the pipers playing music, until Paddy O'Kelly saw the host of Munster getting the strong hand, and he began helping the fairy host of Connacht. The *Stongirya* came up and he made at Paddy O'Kelly, but Paddy turned him head over heels. From hurling the two hosts began at fighting, but it was not long until the host of Connacht beat the other host. Then the host of Munster made flying beetles of themselves, and they began eating every green thing that they came up to. They were destroying the country before them until they came as far as Cong. Then there rose up thousands of doves out of the hole, and they swallowed down the beetles. That hole has no other name until this day but Pull-na-gullam, the dove's hole.

When the fairy host of Connacht won their battle, they came back to Cnoc Matha joyous enough, and the king Finvara gave Paddy O'Kelly a purse of gold, and the little piper brought him home, and put him into bed beside his wife, and left him sleeping there.

A month went by after that without anything worth mentioning, until one night Paddy went down to the cellar, and the little man said to him: "My mother is dead; burn the house over her."

"It is true for you," said Paddy. "She told me that she hadn't but a month to be in the world, and the month was up yesterday."

On the next morning of the next day Paddy went to the hut and he found the hag dead. He put a coal under the hut and burned it. He came home and told the little man that the hag was burnt. The little man gave him a purse and said to him: "This purse will never be empty as long as you are alive. Now, you will never see me more; but have a loving remembrance of the weasel. She was the beginning and the prime cause of your riches." Then he went away and Paddy never saw him again.

Paddy O'Kelly and his wife lived for years after this in the large house, and when he died he left great wealth behind him, and a large family to spend it.

There now is the story for you, from the first word to the last, as I heard it from my grandmother.

Smallhead and the King's Sons

LONG AGO THERE LIVED in Erin a woman who married a man of high degree and had one daughter. Soon after the birth of the daughter the husband died.

The woman was not long a widow when she married a second time, and had two daughters. These two daughters hated their half-sister, thought she was not so wise as another, and nicknamed her Smallhead. When the elder of the two sisters was fourteen years old their father died. The mother was in great grief then, and began to pine away. She used to sit at home in the corner and never left the house. Smallhead was kind to her mother, and the mother was fonder of her eldest daughter than of the other two, who were ashamed of her.

At last the two sisters made up in their minds to kill their mother. One day, while their half-sister was gone, they put the mother in a pot, boiled her, and threw the bones outside. When Smallhead came home there was no sign of the mother.

"Where is my mother?" asked she of the other two.

"She went out somewhere. How should we know where she is?"

"Oh, wicked girls! You have killed my mother," said Smallhead.

Smallhead wouldn't leave the house now at all, and the sisters were very angry.

"No man will marry either one of us," said they, "if he sees our fool of a sister."

Since they could not drive Smallhead from the house they made up their minds to go away themselves. One fine morning they left home unknown to their half-sister and travelled on many miles. When Smallhead discovered that her sisters were gone she hurried after them and never stopped till she came up with the two. They had to go home with her that day, but they scolded her bitterly.

The two settled then to kill Smallhead, so one day they took twenty needles and scattered them outside in a pile of straw. "We are going to that hill beyond," said they, "to stay till evening, and if you have not all the needles that are in that straw outside gathered and on the tables before us, we'll have your life."

Away they went to the hill. Smallhead sat down, and was crying bitterly when a short grey cat walked in and spoke to her.

"Why do you cry and lament so?" asked the cat.

"My sisters abuse me and beat me," answered Smallhead. "This morning they said they would kill me in the evening unless I had all the needles in the straw outside gathered before them."

"Sit down here," said the cat, "and dry your tears."

The cat soon found the twenty needles and brought them to Smallhead. "Stop there now," said the cat, "and listen to what I tell you. I am your mother; your sisters killed me and destroyed my body, but don't harm them; do them good, do the best you can for them, save them: obey my words and it will be better for you in the end."

The cat went away for herself, and the sisters came home in the evening. The needles were on the table before them. Oh, but they were vexed and angry when they saw the twenty needles, and they said someone was helping their sister!

One night when Smallhead was in bed and asleep they started away again, resolved this time never to return. Smallhead slept till morning. When she saw that the sisters were gone she followed, traced them from place to place, inquired here and there day after day, till one evening some person told her that they were in the house of an old hag, a terrible enchantress, who had one son and three daughters: that the house was a bad place to be in, for the old hag had more power of witchcraft than anyone and was very wicked.

Smallhead hurried away to save her sisters, and facing the house knocked at the door, and asked lodgings for God's sake.

"Oh, then," said the hag, "it is hard to refuse anyone lodgings, and besides on such a wild, stormy night. I wonder if you are anything to the young ladies who came the way this evening?"

The two sisters heard this and were angry enough that Smallhead was in it, but they said nothing, not wishing the old hag to know their relationship. After supper the hag told the three strangers to sleep in a room on the right side of the house. When her own daughters were going to bed Smallhead saw her tie a ribbon around the neck of each one of them, and heard her say: "Do you sleep in the left-hand bed." Smallhead hurried and said to her sisters: "Come quickly, or I'll tell the woman who you are."

They took the bed in the left-hand room and were in it before the hag's daughters came.

"Oh," said the daughters, "the other bed is as good." So they took the bed in the right-hand room. When Smallhead knew that the hag's daughters were asleep she rose, took the ribbons off their necks, and put them on her sister's necks and on her own. She lay awake and watched them. After a while she heard the hag say to her son:

"Go, now, and kill the three girls; they have the clothes and money."

"You have killed enough in your life and so let these go," said the son.

But the old woman would not listen. The boy rose up, fearing his mother, and taking a long knife, went to the right-hand room and cut the throats of the three girls without ribbons. He went to bed then for himself, and when Smallhead found that the old hag was asleep she roused her sisters, told what had happened, made them dress quickly and follow her. Believe me, they were willing and glad to follow her this time.

The three travelled briskly and came soon to a bridge, called at that time 'The Bridge of Blood'. Whoever had killed a person could not cross the bridge. When the three girls came to the bridge the two sisters stopped: they could not go a step further. Smallhead ran across and went back again.

"If I did not know that you killed our mother," said she, "I might know it now, for this is the Bridge of Blood."

She carried one sister over the bridge on her back and then the other. Hardly was this done when the hag was at the bridge.

"Bad luck to you, Smallhead!" said she, "I did not know that it was you that was in it last evening. You have killed my three daughters."

"It wasn't I that killed them, but yourself," said Smallhead.

The old hag could not cross the bridge, so she began to curse, and she put every curse on Smallhead that she could remember. The sisters travelled on till they came to a King's castle. They heard that two servants were needed in the castle.

"Go now," said Smallhead to the two sisters, "and ask for service. Be faithful and do well. You can never go back by the road you came."

The two found employment at the King's castle. Smallhead took lodgings in the house of a blacksmith near by.

"I should be glad to find a place as kitchen-maid in the castle," said Smallhead to the blacksmith's wife.

"I will go to the castle and find a place for you if I can," said the woman.

The blacksmith's wife found a place for Smallhead as kitchen-maid in the castle, and she went there next day.

"I must be careful," thought Smallhead, "and do my best. I am in a strange place. My two sisters are here in the King's castle. Who knows, we may have great fortune yet."

She dressed neatly and was cheerful. Everyone liked her, liked her better than her sisters, though they were beautiful. The King had two sons, one at home and the other abroad. Smallhead thought to herself one day: "It is time for the son who is here in the castle to marry. I will speak to him the first time I can." One day she saw him alone in the garden, went up to him, and said:

"Why are you not getting married, it is high time for you?"

He only laughed and thought she was too bold, but then thinking that she was a simple-minded girl who wished to be pleasant, he said:

"I will tell you the reason: My grandfather bound my father by an oath never to let his oldest son marry until he could get the Sword of Light, and I am afraid that I shall be long without marrying."

"Do you know where the Sword of Light is, or who has it?" asked Smallhead.

"I do," said the King's son, "an old hag who has great power and enchantment, and she lives a long distance from this, beyond the Bridge of Blood. I cannot go there myself, I cannot cross the bridge, for I have killed men in battle. Even if I could cross the bridge I would not go, for many is the King's son that hag has destroyed or enchanted."

"Suppose some person were to bring the Sword of Light, and that person a woman, would you marry her?"

"I would, indeed," said the King's son.

"If you promise to marry my elder sister I will strive to bring the Sword of Light."

"I will promise most willingly," said the King's son.

Next morning early, Smallhead set out on her journey. Calling at the first shop she bought a stone weight of salt, and went on her way, never stopping or resting till she reached the hag's house at nightfall. She climbed to the gable, looked down, and saw the son making a great pot of stirabout for his mother, and she hurrying him. "I am as hungry as a hawk!" cried she.

Whenever the boy looked away, Smallhead dropped salt down, dropped it when he was not looking, dropped it till she had the whole stone of salt in the stirabout. The old hag waited and waited till at last she cried out: "Bring the stirabout. I am starving! Bring the pot. I will eat from the pot. Give the milk here as well."

The boy brought the stirabout and the milk, the old woman began to eat, but the first taste she got she spat out and screamed: "You put salt in the pot in place of meal!"

"I did not, mother."

"You did, and it's a mean trick that you played on me. Throw this stirabout to the pig outside and go for water to the well in the field."

"I cannot go," said the boy, "the night is too dark; I might fall into the well."

"You must go and bring the water; I cannot live till morning without eating."

"I am as hungry as yourself," said the boy, "but how can I go to the well without a light? I will not go unless you give me a light."

"If I give you the Sword of Light there is no knowing who may follow you; maybe that devil of a Smallhead is outside."

But sooner than fast till morning the old hag gave the Sword of Light to her son, warning him to take good care of it. He took the Sword of Light and went out. As he saw no one when he came to the well he left the sword on the top of the steps going down to the water, so as to have good light. He had not gone down many steps when Smallhead had the sword, and away she ran over hills, dales, and valleys towards the Bridge of Blood.

The boy shouted and screamed with all his might. Out ran the hag. "Where is the sword?" cried she.

"Someone took it from the step."

Off rushed the hag, following the light, but she didn't come near Smallhead till she was over the bridge.

"Give me the Sword of Light, or bad luck to you," cried the hag.

"Indeed, then, I will not; I will keep it, and bad luck to yourself," answered Smallhead.

On the following morning she walked up to the King's son and said:

"I have the Sword of Light; now will you marry my sister?"

"I will," said he.

The King's son married Smallhead's sister and got the Sword of Light. Smallhead stayed no longer in the kitchen – the sister didn't care to have her in kitchen or parlour.

The King's second son came home. He was not long in the castle when Smallhead said to herself, "Maybe he will marry my second sister."

She saw him one day in the garden, went toward him; he said something, she answered, then asked: "Is it not time for you to be getting married like your brother?"

"When my grandfather was dying," said the young man, "he bound my father not to let his second son marry till he had the Black Book. This book used to shine and give brighter light than ever the Sword of Light did, and I suppose it does yet. The old hag beyond the Bridge of Blood has the book, and no one dares to go near her, for many is the King's son killed or enchanted by that woman."

"Would you marry my second sister if you were to get the Black Book?"

"I would, indeed; I would marry any woman if I got the Black Book with her. The Sword of Light and the Black Book were in our family till my grandfather's time, then they were stolen by that cursed old hag."

"I will have the book," said Smallhead, "or die in the trial to get it."

Knowing that stirabout was the main food of the hag, Smallhead settled in her mind to play another trick. Taking a bag she scraped the chimney, gathered about a stone of soot, and took it with her. The night was dark and rainy. When she reached the hag's house, she climbed up the gable to the chimney and found that the son was making stirabout for his mother. She dropped the soot down by degrees till at last the whole stone of soot was in the pot; then she scraped around the top of the chimney till a lump of soot fell on the boy's hand.

"Oh, mother," said he, "the night is wet and soft, the soot is falling."

"Cover the pot," said the hag. "Be quick with that stirabout, I am starving."

The boy took the pot to his mother.

"Bad luck to you," cried the hag the moment she tasted the stirabout, "this is full of soot; throw it out to the pig."

"If I throw it out there is no water inside to make more, and I'll not go in the dark and rain to the well."

"You must go!" screamed she.

"I'll not stir a foot out of this unless I get a light," said the boy.

"Is it the book you are thinking of, you fool, to take it and lose it as you did the sword? Smallhead is watching you."

"How could Smallhead, the creature, be outside all the time? If you have no use for the water you can do without it."

Sooner than stop fasting till morning, the hag gave her son the book, saying: "Do not put this down or let it from your hand till you come in, or I'll have your life."

The boy took the book and went to the well. Smallhead followed him carefully. He took the book down into the well with him, and when he was stooping to dip water she snatched the book and pushed him into the well, where he came very near drowning.

Smallhead was far away when the boy recovered, and began to scream and shout to his mother. She came in a hurry, and finding that the book was gone, fell into such a rage that she thrust a knife into her son's heart and ran after Smallhead, who had crossed the bridge before the hag could come up with her.

When the old woman saw Smallhead on the other side of the bridge facing her and dancing with delight, she screamed:

"You took the Sword of Light and the Black Book, and your two sisters are married. Oh, then, bad luck to you. I will put my curse on you wherever you go. You have all my children killed, and I a poor, feeble, old woman."

"Bad luck to yourself," said Smallhead. "I am not afraid of a curse from the like of you. If you had lived an honest life you wouldn't be as you are today."

"Now, Smallhead," said the old hag, "you have me robbed of everything, and my children destroyed. Your two sisters are well married. Your fortune began with my ruin. Come, now, and take care of me in my old age. I'll take my curse from you, and you will have good luck. I bind myself never to harm a hair of your head."

Smallhead thought awhile, promised to do this, and said: "If you harm me, or try to harm me, it will be the worse for yourself."

The old hag was satisfied and went home. Smallhead went to the castle and was received with great joy. Next morning she found the King's son in the garden, and said: "If you marry my sister tomorrow, you will have the Black Book."

"I will marry her gladly," said the King's son.

Next day the marriage was celebrated and the King's son got the book. Smallhead remained in the castle about a week, then she left good health with her sisters and went to the hag's house. The old woman was glad to see her and showed the girl her work. All Smallhead had to do was to wait on the hag and feed a large pig that she had.

"I am fatting that pig," said the hag; "he is seven years old now, and the longer you keep a pig the harder his meat is: we'll keep this pig a while longer, and then we'll kill and eat him."

Smallhead did her work; the old hag taught her some things, and Smallhead learned herself far more than the hag dreamt of. The girl fed the pig three times a day, never thinking that he could be anything but a pig. The hag had sent word to a sister that she had in the Eastern World, bidding her come and they would kill the pig and have a great feast. The sister came, and one day when the hag was going to walk with her sister she said to Smallhead:

"Give the pig plenty of meal today; this is the last food he'll have; give him his fill."

The pig had his own mind and knew what was coming. He put his nose under the pot and threw it on Smallhead's toes, and she barefoot. With that she ran into the house for a stick, and seeing a rod on the edge of the loft, snatched it and hit the pig.

That moment the pig was a splendid young man.

Smallhead was amazed.

"Never fear," said the young man, "I am the son of a King that the old hag hated, the King of Munster. She stole me from my father seven years ago and enchanted me – made a pig of me."

Smallhead told the King's son, then, how the hag had treated her. "I must make a pig of you again," said she, "for the hag is coming. Be patient and I'll save you, if you promise to marry me."

"I promise you," said the King's son.

With that she struck him, and he was a pig again. She put the switch in its place and was at her work when the two sisters came. The pig ate his meal now with a good heart, for he felt sure of rescue.

"Who is that girl you have in the house, and where did you find her?" asked the sister.

"All my children died of the plague, and I took this girl to help me. She is a very good servant."

At night the hag slept in one room, her sister in another, and Smallhead in a third. When the two sisters were sleeping soundly Smallhead rose, stole the hag's magic book, and then took the rod. She went next to where the pig was, and with one blow of the rod made a man of him.

With the help of the magic book Smallhead made two doves of herself and the King's son, and they took flight through the air and flew on without stopping. Next morning the hag called Smallhead, but she did not come. She hurried out to see the pig. The pig was gone. She ran to her book. Not a sign of it.

"Oh!" cried she, "that villain of a Smallhead has robbed me. She has stolen my book, made a man of the pig, and taken him away with her."

What could she do but tell her whole story to the sister. "Go you," said she, "and follow them. You have more enchantment than Smallhead has."

"How am I to know them?" asked the sister.

"Bring the first two strange things that you find; they will turn themselves into something wonderful."

The sister then made a hawk of herself and flew away as swiftly as any March wind.

"Look behind," said Smallhead to the King's son some hours later; "see what is coming."

"I see nothing," said he, "but a hawk coming swiftly."

"That is the hag's sister. She has three times more enchantment than the hag herself. But fly down on the ditch and be picking yourself as doves do in rainy weather, and maybe she'll pass without seeing us."

The hawk saw the doves, but thinking them nothing wonderful, flew on till evening, and then went back to her sister.

"Did you see anything wonderful?"

"I did not; I saw only two doves, and they picking themselves."

"You fool, those doves were Smallhead and the King's son. Off with you in the morning and don't let me see you again without the two with you."

Away went the hawk a second time, and swiftly as Smallhead and the King's son flew, the hawk was gaining on them. Seeing this Smallhead and the King's son dropped down into a large village, and, it being market-day, they made two heather brooms of themselves. The two brooms began to sweep the road without anyone holding them, and swept toward each other. This was a great wonder. Crowds gathered at once around the two brooms.

The old hag flying over in the form of a hawk saw this and thinking that it must be Smallhead and the King's son were in it, came down, turned into a woman, and said to herself:

"I'll have those two brooms."

She pushed forward so quickly through the crowd that she came near knocking down a man standing before her. The man was vexed.

"You cursed old hag!" cried he, "do you want to knock us down?" With that he gave her a blow and drove her against another man, that man gave her a push that sent her spinning against a third man, and so on till between them all they came near putting the life out of her, and pushed her away from the brooms. A woman in the crowd called out then:

"It would be nothing but right to knock the head off that old hag, and she trying to push us away from the mercy of God, for it was God who sent the brooms to sweep the road for us."

"True for you," said another woman. With that the people were as angry as angry could be, and were ready to kill the hag. They were going to take the head off the hag when she made a hawk of herself and flew away, vowing never to do another stroke of work for her sister. She might do her own work or let it alone.

When the hawk disappeared the two heather brooms rose and turned into doves. The people felt sure when they saw the doves that the brooms were a blessing from heaven, and it was the old hag that drove them away.

On the following day Smallhead and the King's son saw his father's castle, and the two came down not too far from it in their own forms. Smallhead was a very beautiful woman now, and why not? She had the magic and didn't spare it. She made herself as beautiful as ever she could: the like of her was not to be seen in that kingdom or the next one.

The King's son was in love with her that minute, and did not wish to part with her, but she would not go with him.

"When you are at your father's castle," said Smallhead, "all will be overjoyed to see you, and the king will give a great feast in your honour. If you kiss anyone or let any living thing kiss you, you'll forget me for ever."

"I will not let even my own mother kiss me," said he.

The King's son went to the castle. All were overjoyed; they had thought him dead, had not seen him for seven years. He would let no one come near to kiss him. "I am bound by oath to kiss no one," said he to his mother. At that moment an old grey hound came in, and with one spring was on his shoulder licking his face: all that the King's son had gone through in seven years was forgotten in one moment.

Smallhead went toward a forge near the castle. The smith had a wife far younger than himself, and a stepdaughter. They were no beauties. In the rear of the forge was a well and a tree growing over it. "I will go up in that tree," thought Smallhead, "and spend the night in it." She went up and sat just over the well. She was not long in the tree when the moon came out high above the hill tops and shone on the well. The blacksmith's stepdaughter, coming for water, looked down in the well, saw the face of the woman above in the tree, thought it her own face, and cried:

"Oh, then, to have me bringing water to a smith, and I such a beauty. I'll never bring another drop to him." With that she cast the pail in the ditch and ran off to find a king's son to marry.

When she was not coming with the water, and the blacksmith waiting to wash after his day's work in the forge, he sent the mother. The mother had nothing but a pot to get the water in, so off she went with that, and coming to the well saw the beautiful face in the water.

"Oh, you black, swarthy villain of a smith," cried she, "bad luck to the hour that I met you, and I such a beauty. I'll never draw another drop of water for the life of you!"

She threw the pot down, broke it, and hurried away to find some king's son.

When neither mother nor daughter came back with water the smith himself went to see what was keeping them. He saw the pail in the ditch, and, catching it, went to the well; looking down, he saw the beautiful face of a woman in the water. Being a man, he knew that it was not his own face that was in it, so he looked up, and there in the tree saw a woman. He spoke to her and said:

"I know now why my wife and her daughter did not bring water. They saw your face in the well, and, thinking themselves too good for me, ran away. You must come now and keep the house till I find them."

"I will help you," said Smallhead. She came down, went to the smith's house, and showed the road that the women took. The smith hurried after them, and found the two in a village ten miles away. He explained their own folly to them, and they came home.

The mother and daughter washed fine linen for the castle. Smallhead saw them ironing one day, and said:

"Sit down: I will iron for you."

She caught the iron, and in an hour had the work of the day done.

The women were delighted. In the evening the daughter took the linen to the housekeeper at the castle.

"Who ironed this linen?" asked the housekeeper.

"My mother and I."

"Indeed, then, you did not. You can't do the like of that work, and tell me who did it."

The girl was in dread now and answered:

"It is a woman who is stopping with us who did the ironing."

The housekeeper went to the Queen and showed her the linen.

"Send that woman to the castle," said the Queen.

Smallhead went: the Queen welcomed her, wondered at her beauty; put her over all the maids in the castle. Smallhead could do anything; everybody was fond of her. The King's son never knew that he had seen her before, and she lived in the castle a year; what the Queen told her she did.

The King had made a match for his son with the daughter of the King of Ulster. There was a great feast in the castle in honour of the young couple, the marriage was to be a week later. The bride's father brought many of his people who were versed in all kinds of tricks and enchantment.

The King knew that Smallhead could do many things, for neither the Queen nor himself had asked her to do a thing that she did not do in a twinkle.

"Now," said the King to the Queen, "I think she can do something that his people cannot do." He summoned Smallhead and asked:

"Can you amuse the strangers?"

"I can if you wish me to do so."

When the time came and the Ulster men had shown their best tricks, Smallhead came forward and raised the window, which was forty feet from the ground. She had a small ball of thread in her hand; she tied one end of the thread to the window, threw the ball out and over a wall near the castle; then she passed out the window, walked on the thread and kept time to music from players that no man could see. She came in; all cheered her and were greatly delighted.

"I can do that," said the King of Ulster's daughter, and sprang out on the string; but if she did she fell and broke her neck on the stones below. There were cries, there was lamentation, and, in place of a marriage, a funeral.

The King's son was angry and grieved and wanted to drive Smallhead from the castle in some way.

"She is not to blame," said the King of Munster, who did nothing but praise her.

Another year passed: the King got the daughter of the King of Connacht for his son. There was a great feast before the wedding day, and as the Connacht people are full of enchantment and witchcraft, the King of Munster called Smallhead and said:

"Now show the best trick of any."

"I will," said Smallhead.

When the feast was over and the Connacht men had shown their tricks the King of Munster called Smallhead.

She stood before the company, threw two grains of wheat on the floor, and spoke some magic words. There was a hen and a cock there before her of beautiful plumage; she threw a grain of wheat between them; the hen sprang to eat the wheat, the cock gave her a blow of his bill, the hen drew back, looked at him, and said:

"Bad luck to you, you wouldn't do the like of that when I was serving the old hag and you her pig, and I made a man of you and gave you back your own form."

The King's son looked at her and thought, "There must be something in this."

Smallhead threw a second grain. The cock pecked the hen again. "Oh," said the hen, "you would not do that the day the hag's sister was hunting us, and we two doves."

The King's son was still more astonished.

She threw a third grain. The cock struck the hen, and she said, "You would not do that to me the day I made two heather brooms out of you and myself." She threw a fourth grain. The cock pecked the hen a fourth time. "You would not do that the day you promised not to let any living thing kiss you or kiss anyone yourself but me – you let the hound kiss you and you forgot me."

The King's son made one bound forward, embraced and kissed Smallhead, and told the King his whole story from beginning to end.

"This is my wife," said he; "I'll marry no other woman."

"Whose wife will my daughter be?" asked the King of Connacht.

"Oh, she will be the wife of the man who will marry her," said the King of Munster, "my son gave his word to this woman before he saw your daughter, and he must keep it."

So Smallhead married the King of Munster's son.

The Pudding Bewitched

"MOLL ROE RAFFERTY was the son – daughter I mane – of ould Jack Rafferty, who was remarkable for a habit he had of always wearing his head undher his hat; but indeed the same family was a quare one, as everybody knew that was acquainted wid them. It was said of them – but whether it was thrue or not I won't undhertake to say, for 'fraid I'd tell a lie – that whenever they didn't wear shoes or boots they always went barefooted; but I heard afthewards that this was disputed, so rather than say anything to injure their character, I'll let that pass. Now, ould Jack Rafferty had two sons, Paddy and Molly – hut! what are you all laughing at? – I mane a son and daughter, and it was generally believed among the neighbours that they were brother and sisther, which you know might be thrue or it might not: but that's a thing that, wid the help o' goodness, we have nothing to say to. Troth there was many ugly things put out on them that I don't wish to repate, such as that neither Jack nor his son Paddy ever walked a perch widout puttin' one foot afore the other like a salmon; an' I know it was whispered about, that whinever Moll Roe slep', she had an out-of-the-way custom of keepin' her eyes shut. If she did, however, for that matther the loss was her own; for sure we all know that when one comes to shut their eyes they can't see as far before them as another.

"Moll Roe was a fine young bouncin' girl, large and lavish, wid a purty head o' hair on her like scarlet, that bein' one of the raisons why she was called *Roe*, or red; her arms an' cheeks were much the colour of the hair, an' her saddle nose was the purtiest thing of its kind that ever was on a face. Her fists – for, thank goodness, she was well sarved wid them too – had a strong simularity to two thumpin' turnips, reddened by the sun; an' to keep all right and tight, she had a temper as fiery as her head – for, indeed, it was well known that all the Raffertys were *warm*-hearted. Howandiver, it appears that God gives nothing in vain, and of coorse the same fists, big and red as they were, if all that is said about them is thrue, were not so much given to her for ornament as use. At laist, takin' them in connection wid her lively temper, we have it upon good authority, that there was no danger of their getting blue-moulded for want of practice. She had a twist, too, in one of her eyes that was very becomin' in its way, and made her poor husband, when she got him, take it into his head that she could see round a corner. She found him out in many quare things, widout doubt; but whether it was owin' to that or not, I wouldn't undertake to say *for fraid I'd tell a lie*.

"Well, begad, anyhow it was Moll Roe that was the *dilsy*. It happened that there was a nate vagabone in the neighbourhood, just as much overburdened wid beauty as herself, and he was named Gusty Gillespie. Gusty, the Lord guard us, was what they call a black-mouth Prosbytarian, and wouldn't keep Christmas-day, the blagard, except what they call 'ould style'. Gusty was rather good-lookin' when seen in the dark, as well as Moll herself; and, indeed, it was purty well known that – accordin' as the talk went – it was in nightly meetings that they had an opportunity of becomin' detached to one another. The quensequence was, that in due time both families began to talk very seriously as to what was to be done. Moll's brother, Pawdien O'Rafferty, gave Gusty the best of two choices. What they were it's not worth spakin' about; but at any rate *one* of them was a poser, an' as Gusty knew his man, he soon came to his senses. Accordianly everything was deranged for their marriage, and it was appointed that they should be spliced by the Rev. Samuel M'Shuttle, the Prosbytarian parson, on the following Sunday.

"Now this was the first marriage that had happened for a long time in the neighbourhood betune a black-mouth an' a Catholic, an' of coorse there was strong objections on both sides aginst it; an' begad, only for one thing, it would never 'a tuck place at all. At any rate, faix, there was one of the bride's uncles, ould Harry Connolly, a fairy-man, who could cure all complaints wid a secret he had, and as he didn't wish to see his niece married upon sich a fellow, he fought bittherly against the match. All Moll's friends, however, stood up for the marriage barrin' him, an' of coorse the Sunday was appointed, as I said, that they were to be dove-tailed together.

"Well, the day arrived, and Moll, as became her, went to mass, and Gusty to meeting, afther which they were to join one another in Jack Rafferty's, where the priest, Father M'Sorley, was to slip up afther mass to take his dinner wid them, and to keep Misther M'Shuttle, who was to marry them, company. Nobody remained at home but ould Jack Rafferty an' his wife, who stopped to dress the dinner, for, to tell the truth, it was to be a great let-out entirely. Maybe, if all was known, too, that Father M'Sorley was to give them a cast of his office over an' above the ministher, in regard that Moll's friends were not altogether satisfied at the kind of marriage which M'Shuttle could give them. The sorrow may care about that – splice here – splice there – all I can say is, that when Mrs. Rafferty was goin' to tie up a big bag pudden, in walks Harry Connolly, the fairy-man, in a rage, and shouts out – 'Blood and blunderbushes, what are yez here for?'

"'Arrah why, Harry? Why, avick?'

"'Why, the sun's in the suds and the moon in the high Horicks; there's a clipstick comin' an, an' there you're both as unconsarned as if it was about to rain mether. Go out and cross yourselves three times in the name o' the four Mandromarvins, for as prophecy says: – Fill the pot, Eddy, supernaculum – a blazing star's a rare spectaculum. Go out both of you and look at the sun, I say, an' ye'll see the condition he's in – off!'

"Begad, sure enough, Jack gave a bounce to the door, and his wife leaped like a two-year-ould, till they were both got on a stile beside the house to see what was wrong in the sky.

"'Arrah, what is it, Jack,' said she; 'can you see anything?'

"'No,' says he, 'sorra the full o' my eye of anything I can spy, barrin' the sun himself, that's not visible in regard of the clouds. God guard us! I doubt there's something to happen.'

"'If there wasn't, Jack, what 'ud put Harry, that knows so much, in the state he's in?'

"'I doubt it's this marriage,' said Jack: 'betune ourselves, it's not over an' above religious for Moll to marry a black-mouth, an' only for –; but it can't be helped now, though you see not a taste o' the sun is willin' to show his face upon it.'

"'As to that,' says the wife, winkin' wid both her eyes, 'if Gusty's satisfied wid Moll, it's enough. I know who'll carry the whip hand, anyhow; but in the manetime let us ax Harry 'ithin what ails the sun.'

"Well, they accordianly went in an' put the question to him:

"'Harry, what's wrong, ahagur? What is it now, for if anybody alive knows, 'tis yourself?'

"'Ah!' said Harry, screwin' his mouth wid a kind of a dhry smile, 'the sun has a hard twist o' the cholic; but never mind that, I tell you you'll have a merrier weddin' than you think, that's all'; and havin' said this, he put on his hat and left the house.

"Now, Harry's answer relieved them very much, and so, afther calling to him to be back for the dinner, Jack sat down to take a shough o' the pipe, and the wife lost no time in tying up the pudden and puttin' it in the pot to be boiled.

"In this way things went on well enough for a while, Jack smokin' away, an' the wife cookin' and dhressin' at the rate of a hunt. At last, Jack, while sittin', as I said, contentedly at the fire, thought he could persave an odd dancin' kind of motion in the pot that puzzled him a good deal.

"'Katty,' said he, 'what the dickens is in this pot on the fire?'

"'Nerra thing but the big pudden. Why do you ax?' says she.

"'Why,' said he, 'if ever a pot tuck it into its head to dance a jig, and this did. Thundher and sparbles, look at it!'

"Begad, it was thrue enough; there was the pot bobbin' up an' down and from side to side, jiggin' it away as merry as a grig; an' it was quite aisy to see that it wasn't the pot itself, but what was inside of it, that brought about the hornpipe.

"'Be the hole o' my coat,' shouted Jack, 'there's something alive in it, or it would never cut sich capers!'

"'Be gorra, there is, Jack; something sthrange entirely has got into it. Wirra, man alive, what's to be done?'

"Jist as she spoke, the pot seemed to cut the buckle in prime style, and afther a spring that 'ud shame a dancin'-masther, off flew the lid, and out bounced the pudden itself, hoppin', as nimble as a pea on a drum-head, about the floor. Jack blessed himself, and Katty crossed herself. Jack shouted, and Katty screamed. 'In the name of goodness, keep your distance; no one here injured you!'

"The pudden, however, made a set at him, and Jack lepped first on a chair and then on the kitchen table to avoid it. It then danced towards Kitty, who was now repatin' her prayers at the top of her voice, while the cunnin' thief of a pudden was hoppin' and jiggin' it round her, as if it was amused at her distress.

"'If I could get the pitchfork,' said Jack, 'I'd dale wid it – by goxty I'd thry its mettle.'

"'No, no,' shouted Katty, thinkin' there was a fairy in it; 'let us spake it fair. Who knows what harm it might do? Aisy now,' said she to the pudden, 'aisy, dear; don't harm honest people that never meant to offend you. It wasn't us – no, in troth, it was ould Harry Connolly that bewitched you; pursue *him* if you wish, but spare a woman like me; for, whisper, dear, I'm not in a condition to be frightened – troth I'm not.'

"The pudden, bedad, seemed to take her at her word, and danced away from her towards Jack, who, like the wife, believin' there was a fairy in it, an' that spakin' it fair was the best plan, thought he would give it a soft word as well as her.

"'Plase your honour,' said Jack, 'she only spaiks the truth; an', upon my voracity, we both feels much oblaiged to your honour for your quietness. Faith, it's quite clear that if you weren't a gentlemanly pudden all out, you'd act otherwise. Ould Harry, the rogue, is your mark; he's jist gone down the road there, and if you go fast you'll overtake him. Be me song, your dancin' masther did his duty, anyhow. Thank your honour! God speed you, an' may you never meet wid a parson or alderman in your thravels!'

"Jist as Jack spoke the pudden appeared to take the hint, for it quietly hopped out, and as the house was directly on the road-side, turned down towards the bridge, the

very way that ould Harry went. It was very natural, of coorse, that Jack and Katty should go out to see how it intended to thravel; and, as the day was Sunday, it was but natural, too, that a greater number of people than usual were passin' the road. This was a fact; and when Jack and his wife were seen followin' the pudden, the whole neighbourhood was soon up and afther it.

"'Jack Rafferty, what is it? Katty, ahagur, will you tell us what it manes?'

"'Why,' replied Katty, 'it's my big pudden that's bewitched, an' it's now hot foot pursuin' –'; here she stopped, not wishin' to mention her brother's name – '*someone* or other that surely put *pishrogues* an it.'

"This was enough; Jack, now seein' that he had assistance, found his courage comin' back to him; so says he to Katty, 'Go home,' says he, 'an' lose no time in makin' another pudden as good, an' here's Paddy Scanlan's wife, Bridget, says she'll let you boil it on her fire, as you'll want our own to dress the rest o' the dinner: and Paddy himself will lend me a pitchfork, for purshuin to the morsel of that same pudden will escape till I let the wind out of it, now that I've the neighbours to back an' support me,' says Jack.

"This was agreed to, and Katty went back to prepare a fresh pudden, while Jack an' half the townland pursued the other wid spades, graips, pitchforks, scythes, flails, and all possible description of instruments. On the pudden went, however, at the rate of about six Irish miles an hour, an' sich a chase never was seen. Catholics, Prodestants, an' Prosbytarians, were all afther it, armed, as I said, an' bad end to the thing but its own activity could save it. Here it made a hop, and there a prod was made at it; but off it went, an' someone, as eager to get a slice at it on the other side, got the prod instead of the pudden. Big Frank Farrell, the miller of Ballyboulteen, got a prod backwards that brought a hullabaloo out of him you might hear at the other end of the parish. One got a slice of a scythe, another a whack of a flail, a third a rap of a spade that made him look nine ways at wanst.

"'Where is it goin'?' asked one. 'My life for you, it's on its way to Meeting. Three cheers for it if it turns to Carntaul.' 'Prod the sowl out of it, if it's a Prodestan',' shouted the others; 'if it turns to the left, slice it into pancakes. We'll have no Prodestan' puddens here.'

"Begad, by this time the people were on the point of beginnin' to have a regular fight about it, when, very fortunately, it took a short turn down a little by-lane that led towards the Methodist praichin-house, an' in an instant all parties were in an uproar against it as a Methodist pudden. 'It's a Wesleyan,' shouted several voices; 'an' by this an' by that, into a Methodist chapel it won't put a foot today, or we'll lose a fall. Let the wind out of it. Come, boys, where's your pitchforks?'

"The divle purshuin to the one of them, however, ever could touch the pudden, an' jist when they thought they had it up against the gavel of the Methodist chapel, begad it gave them the slip, and hops over to the left, clane into the river, and sails away before all their eyes as light as an egg-shell.

"Now, it so happened that a little below this place, the demesne-wall of Colonel Bragshaw was built up to the very edge of the river on each side of its banks; and so findin' there was a stop put to their pursuit of it, they went home again, every man, woman, and child of them, puzzled to think what the pudden was at all, what it meant, or where it was goin'! Had Jack Rafferty an' his wife been willin' to let out the opinion they held about Harry Connolly bewitchin' it, there is no doubt of it but poor Harry might be badly trated by the crowd, when their blood was up. They had sense enough, howandiver, to keep that to themselves, for Harry bein' an' ould bachelor, was a kind friend to the Raffertys. So, of coorse, there was all kinds of talk about it – some guessin' this, and some guessin' that –one party sayin' the pudden was of there side, another party denyin' it, an' insistin' it belonged to them, an' so on.

"In the manetime, Katty Rafferty, for 'fraid the dinner might come short, went home and made another pudden much about the same size as the one that had escaped, and bringin' it over to their next neighbour, Paddy Scanlan's, it was put into a pot and placed on the fire to boil, hopin' that it might be done in time, espishilly as they were to have the ministher, who loved a warm slice of a good pudden as well as e'er a gintleman in Europe.

"Anyhow, the day passed; Moll and Gusty were made man an' wife, an' no two could be more lovin'. Their friends that had been asked to the weddin' were saunterin' about in pleasant little groups till dinner-time, chattin' an' laughin'; but, above all things, sthrivin' to account for the figaries of the pudden; for, to tell the truth, its adventures had now gone through the whole parish.

"Well, at any rate, dinner-time was dhrawin' near, and Paddy Scanlan was sittin' comfortably wid his wife at the fire, the pudden boilen before their eyes, when in walks Harry Connolly, in a flutter, shoutin' – 'Blood an' blunderbushes, what are yez here for?'

"'Arra, why, Harry – why, avick?' said Mrs. Scanlan.

"'Why,' said Harry, 'the sun's in the suds an' the moon in the high Horicks! Here's a clipstick comin' an, an' there you sit as unconsarned as if it was about to rain mether! Go out both of you, an' look at the sun, I say, and ye'll see the condition he's in – off!'

"'Ay, but, Harry, what's that rowled up in the tail of your *cothamore* (big coat)?'

"'Out wid yez,' said Harry, 'an' pray aginst the clipstick – the sky's fallin'!'

"Begad, it was hard to say whether Paddy or the wife got out first, they were so much alarmed by Harry's wild thin face an' piercin' eyes; so out they went to see what was wondherful in the sky, an' kep' lookin' an' lookin' in every direction, but not a thing was to be seen, barrin' the sun shinin' down wid great good-humour, an' not a single cloud in the sky.

"Paddy an' the wife now came in laughin', to scould Harry, who, no doubt, was a great wag in his way when he wished. 'Musha, bad scran to you, Harry –.' They had time to say no more, howandiver, for, as they were goin' into the door, they met him comin' out of it wid a reek of smoke out of his tail like a lime-kiln.

"'Harry,' shouted Bridget, 'my sowl to glory, but the tail of your cothamore's a-fire— you'll be burned. Don't you see the smoke that's out of it?'

"'Cross yourselves three times,' said Harry, widout stoppin', or even lookin' behind him, 'for, as the prophecy says –Fill the pot, Eddy –' They could hear no more, for Harry appeared to feel like a man that carried something a great deal hotter than he wished, as anyone might see by the liveliness of his motions, and the quare faces he was forced to make as he went along.

"'What the dickens is he carryin' in the skirts of his big coat?' asked Paddy.

"'My sowl to happiness, but maybe he has stole the pudden,' said Bridget, 'for it's known that many a sthrange thing he does.'

"They immediately examined the pot, but found that the pudden was there as safe as tuppence, an' this puzzled them the more, to think what it was he could be carryin' about wid him in the manner he did. But little they knew what he had done while they were sky-gazin'!

"Well, anyhow, the day passed and the dinner was ready, an' no doubt but a fine gatherin' there was to partake of it. The Prosbytarian ministher met the Methodist praicher – a divilish stretcher of an appetite he had, in throth – on their way to Jack Rafferty's, an' as he knew he could take the liberty, why he insisted on his dinin' wid him; for, afther all, begad, in thim times the clargy of all descriptions lived upon the best footin' among one another, not all as one as now – but no matther. Well, they had nearly finished their dinner, when Jack Rafferty himself axed Katty for the pudden; but, jist as he spoke, in it came as big as a mess-pot.

"'Gintlemen,' said he, 'I hope none of you will refuse tastin' a bit of Katty's pudden; I don't mane the dancin' one that tuck to its thravels today, but a good solid fellow that she med since.'

"'To be sure we won't,' replied the priest; 'so, Jack, put a thrifle on them three plates at your right hand, and send them over here to the clargy, an' maybe,' he said, laughin' – for he was a droll good-humoured man – 'maybe, Jack, we won't set you a proper example.'

"'Wid a heart an' a half, yer reverence an' gintlemen; in throth, it's not a bad example ever any of you set us at the likes, or ever will set us, I'll go bail. An' sure I only wish it was betther fare I had for you; but we're humble people, gintlemen, and so you can't expect to meet here what you would in higher places.'

"'Betther a male of herbs,' said the Methodist praicher, 'where pace is –.' He had time to go no farther, however; for much to his amazement, the priest and the ministher started up from the table jist as he was goin' to swallow the first spoonful of the pudden, and before you could say Jack Robinson, started away at a lively jig down the floor.

"At this moment a neighbour's son came runnin' in, an' tould them that the parson was comin' to see the new-married couple, an' wish them all happiness; an' the words were scarcely out of his mouth when he made his appearance. What to think he knew not, when he saw the ministher footing it away at the rate of a weddin'. He had very little time, however, to think; for, before he could sit down, up starts the Methodist praicher, and clappin' his two fists in his sides chimes in in great style along wid him.

"'Jack Rafferty,' says he – and, by the way, Jack was his tenant – 'what the dickens does all this mane?' says he; 'I'm amazed!'

"'The not a particle o' me can tell you,' says Jack; 'but will your reverence jist taste a morsel o' pudden, merely that the young couple may boast that you ait at their weddin'; for sure if *you* wouldn't, *who* would?'

"'Well,' says he, 'to gratify them I will; so just a morsel. But, Jack, this bates Bannagher,' says he again, puttin' the spoonful o' pudden into his mouth; 'has there been dhrink here?'

"'Oh, the divle a *spudh*,' says Jack, 'for although there's plinty in the house, faith, it appears the gintlemen wouldn't wait for it. Unless they tuck it elsewhere, I can make nothin' of this.'

"He had scarcely spoken, when the parson, who was an active man, cut a caper a yard high, an' before you could bless yourself, the three clargy were hard at work dancin', as if for a wager. Begad, it would be unpossible for me to tell you the state the whole meetin' was in when they seen this. Some were hoarse wid laughin'; some turned up their eyes wid wondher; many thought them mad, an' others thought they had turned up their little fingers a thrifle too often.

"'Be goxty, it's a burnin' shame,' said one, 'to see three black-mouth clargy in sich a state at this early hour!' 'Thundher an' ounze, what's over them at all?' says others; 'why, one would think they're bewitched. Holy Moses, look at the caper the Methodis cuts! An' as for the Recther, who would think he could handle his feet at such a rate! Be this an' be that, he cuts the buckle, and does the threblin' step aiquil to Paddy Horaghan, the dancin'-masther himself? An' see! Bad cess to the morsel of the parson that's not hard at *Peace upon a trancher*, an' it of a Sunday too! Whirroo, gintlemen, the fun's in yez afther all – whish! more power to yez!'

"The sorra's own fun they had, an' no wondher; but judge of what they felt, when all at once they saw ould Jack Rafferty himself bouncin' in among them, and footing it away like the best o' them. Bedad, no play could come up to it, an' nothin' could be heard but laughin', shouts of encouragement, and clappin' of hands like mad. Now the minute Jack Rafferty left the chair where he had been carvin' the pudden, ould Harry Connolly comes over and claps himself down in his place, in ordher to send it round, of coorse; an' he was scarcely sated, when who should make his appearance but Barney Hartigan, the piper. Barney, by the way, had been sent for early in the day, but bein' from home when the message for him went, he couldn't come any sooner.

"'Begorra,' said Barney, 'you're airly at the work, gintlemen! But what does this mane? But, divle may care, yez shan't want the music while there's a blast in the pipes, anyhow!' So sayin' he gave them *Jig Polthogue*, an' after that *Kiss My Lady*, in his best style.

"In the manetime the fun went on thick an' threefold, for it must be remimbered that Harry, the ould knave, was at the pudden; an' maybe he didn't sarve it about in double quick time too. The first he helped was the bride, and, before you could say chopstick, she was at it hard an' fast before the Methodist praicher, who gave a jolly spring before her that threw them into convulsions. Harry liked this, and made up his mind soon to find partners for the rest; so he accordianly sent the pudden about like lightnin'; an' to make a long story short, barrin' the piper an' himself, there wasn't a pair o' heels in the house but was as busy at the dancin' as if their lives depinded on it.

"'Barney,' says Harry, 'just taste a morsel o' this pudden; divle the such a bully of a pudden ever you ett; here, your sowl! Thry a snig of it – it's beautiful.'

"'To be sure I will,' says Barney. 'I'm not the boy to refuse a good thing; but, Harry, be quick, for you know my hands is engaged, an' it would be a thousand pities not to keep them in music, an' they so well inclined. Thank you, Harry; begad that is a famous pudden; but blood an' turnips, what's this for?'

"The word was scarcely out of his mouth when he bounced up, pipes an' all, an' dashed into the middle of the party. 'Hurroo, your sowls, let us make a night of it! The Ballyboulteen boys for ever! Go it, your reverence – turn your partner – heel an' toe, ministher. Good! Well done again – Whish! Hurroo! Here's for Ballyboulteen, an' the sky over it!'

"Bad luck to the sich a set ever was seen together in this world, or will again, I suppose. The worst, however, wasn't come yet, for jist as they were in the very heat an' fury of the dance, what do you think comes hoppin' in among them but another pudden, as nimble an' merry as the first! That was enough; they all had heard of – the ministhers among the rest – an' most o' them had seen the other pudden, and knew that there must be a fairy in it, sure enough. Well, as I said, in it comes to the thick o' them; but the very appearance of it was enough. Off the three clargy danced, and off the whole weddiners danced afther them, everyone makin' the best of their way home;

but not a sowl of them able to break out of the step, if they were to be hanged for it. Throth it wouldn't lave a laugh in you to see the parson dancin' down the road on his way home, and the ministher and Methodist praicher cuttin' the buckle as they went along in the opposite direction. To make short work of it, they all danced home at last, wid scarce a puff of wind in them; the bride and bridegroom danced away to bed; an' now, boys, come an' let us dance the *Horo Lheig* in the barn 'idout. But you see, boys, before we go, an' in ordher that I may make everything plain, I had as good tell you that Harry, in crossing the bridge of Ballyboulteen, a couple of miles below Squire Bragshaw's demense-wall, saw the pudden floatin' down the river – the truth is he was waitin' for it; but be this as it may, he took it out, for the wather had made it as clane as a new pin, and tuckin' it up in the tail of his big coat, contrived, as you all guess, I suppose, to change it while Paddy Scanlan an' the wife were examinin' the sky; an' for the other, he contrived to bewitch it in the same manner, by gettin' a fairy to go into it, for, indeed, it was purty well known that the same Harry was hand an' glove wid the *good people*. Others will tell you that it was half a pound of quicksilver he put into it; but that doesn't stand to raison. At any rate, boys, I have tould you the adventures of the Mad Pudden of Ballyboulteen; but I don't wish to tell you many other things about it that happened – *for fraid I'd tell a lie*."

Morraha

MORRAHA ROSE IN THE MORNING and washed his hands and face, and said his prayers, and ate his food; and he asked God to prosper the day for him. So he went down to the brink of the sea, and he saw a currach, short and green, coming towards him; and in it there was but one youthful champion, and he was playing hurly from prow to stern of the currach. He had a hurl of gold and a ball of silver; and he stopped not till the currach was in on the shore; and he drew her up on the green grass, and put fastenings on her for a year and a day, whether he should be there all that time or should only be on land for an hour by the clock. And Morraha saluted the young man courteously; and the other saluted him in the same fashion, and asked him would he play a game of cards with him; and Morraha said that he had not the wherewithal; and the other answered that he was never without a candle or the making of it; and he put his hand in his pocket and drew out a table and two chairs and a pack of cards, and they sat down on the chairs and went to card-playing. The first game Morraha won, and the Slender Red Champion bade him make his claim; and he asked that the land above him should be filled with stock of sheep in the morning. It was well; and he played no second game, but home he went.

The next day Morraha went to the brink of the sea, and the young man came in the currach and asked him would he play cards; they played, and Morraha won. The young man bade him make his claim; and he asked that the land above should be filled with cattle in the morning. It was well; and he played no other game, but went home.

On the third morning Morraha went to the brink of the sea, and he saw the young man coming. He drew up his boat on the shore and asked him would he play cards. They played, and Morraha won the game; and the young man bade him give his claim. And he said he would have a castle and a wife, the finest and fairest in the world; and they were his. It was well; and the Red Champion went away.

On the fourth day his wife asked him how he had found her. And he told her. "And I am going out," said he, "to play again today."

"I forbid you to go again to him. If you have won so much, you will lose more; have no more to do with him."

But he went against her will, and he saw the currach coming; and the Red Champion was driving his balls from end to end of the currach; he had balls of silver and a hurl of gold, and he stopped not till he drew his boat on the shore, and made her fast for a year and a day. Morraha and he saluted each other; and he asked Morraha if he would play a game of cards, and they played, and he won. Morraha said to him, "Give your claim now."

Said he, "You will hear it too soon. I lay on you bonds of the art of the Druid, not to sleep two nights in one house, nor finish a second meal at the one table, till you bring me the sword of light and news of the death of Anshgayliacht."

He went home to his wife and sat down in a chair, and gave a groan, and the chair broke in pieces.

"That is the groan of the son of a king under spells," said his wife; "and you had better have taken my counsel than that the spells should be on you."

He told her he had to bring news of the death of Anshgayliacht and the sword of light to the Slender Red Champion.

"Go out," said she, "in the morning of the morrow, and take the bridle in the window, and shake it; and whatever beast, handsome or ugly, puts its head in it, take that one with you. Do not speak a word to her till she speaks to you; and take with you three pint bottles of ale and three sixpenny loaves, and do the thing she tells you; and when she runs to my father's land, on a height above the castle, she will shake herself, and the bells will ring, and my father will say, 'Brown Allree is in the land. And if the son of a king or queen is there, bring him to me on your shoulders; but if it is the son of a poor man, let him come no further.'"

He rose in the morning, and took the bridle that was in the window, and went out and shook it; and Brown Allree came and put her head in it. He took the three loaves and three bottles of ale, and went riding; and when he was riding she bent her head down to take hold of her feet with her mouth, in hopes he would speak in ignorance; but he spoke not a word during the time, and the mare at last spoke to him, and told him to dismount and give her her dinner. He gave her the sixpenny loaf toasted, and a bottle of ale to drink.

"Sit up now riding, and take good heed of yourself: there are three miles of fire I have to clear at a leap."

She cleared the three miles of fire at a leap, and asked if he were still riding, and he said he was. Then they went on, and she told him to dismount and give her a meal; and he did so, and gave her a sixpenny loaf and a bottle; she consumed them and said to him there were before them three miles of hill covered with steel thistles, and that she must clear it. She cleared the hill with a leap, and she asked him if he were still riding, and he said he was. They went on, and she went not far before she told him to give her a meal, and he gave her the bread and the bottleful. She went over three miles of sea with a leap, and she came then to the land of the King of France; she went up on a height above the castle, and she shook herself and neighed, and the bells rang; and the king said that it was Brown Allree was in the land.

"Go out," said he; "and if it is the son of a king or queen, carry him in on your shoulders; if it is not, leave him there."

They went out; and the stars of the son of a king were on his breast; they lifted him high on their shoulders and bore him in to the king. They passed the night cheerfully, playing and drinking, with sport and with diversion, till the whiteness of the day came upon the morrow morning.

Then the young king told the cause of his journey, and he asked the queen to give him counsel and good luck, and she told him everything he was to do.

"Go now," said she, "and take with you the best mare in the stable, and go to the door of Rough Niall of the Speckled Rock, and knock, and call on him to give you news of the death of Anshgayliacht and the sword of light: and let the horse's back be to the door, and apply the spurs, and away with you."

In the morning he did so, and he took the best horse from the stable and rode to the door of Niall, and turned the horse's back to the door, and demanded news of the death of Anshgayliacht and the sword of light; then he applied the spurs, and away with him. Niall followed him hard, and, as he was passing the gate, cut the horse in two.

His wife was there with a dish of puddings and flesh, and she threw it in his eyes and blinded him, and said, "Fool! Whatever kind of man it is that's mocking you, isn't that a fine condition you have got your father's horse into?"

On the morning of the next day Morraha rose, and took another horse from the stable, and went again to the door of Niall, and knocked and demanded news of the death of Anshgayliacht and the sword of light, and applied the spurs to the horse and away with him. Niall followed, and as Morraha was passing, the gate cut the horse in two and took half the saddle with him; but his wife met him and threw flesh in his eyes and blinded him.

On the third day, Morraha went again to the door of Niall; and Niall followed him, and as he was passing the gate, cut away the saddle from under him and the clothes from his back. Then his wife said to Niall:

"The fool that's mocking you, is out yonder in the little currach, going home; and take good heed to yourself, and don't sleep one wink for three days."

For three days the little currach kept in sight, but then Niall's wife came to him and said:

"Sleep as much as you want now. He is gone."

He went to sleep, and there was heavy sleep on him, and Morraha went in and took hold of the sword that was on the bed at his head. And the sword thought to draw itself out of the hand of Morraha; but it failed. Then it gave a cry, and it wakened Niall, and Niall said it was a rude and rough thing to come into his house like that; and said Morraha to him:

"Leave your much talking, or I will cut the head off you. Tell me the news of the death of Anshgayliacht."

"Oh, you can have my head."

"But your head is no good to me; tell me the story."

"Oh," said Niall's wife, "you must get the story."

"Well," said Niall, "let us sit down together till I tell the story. I thought no one would ever get it; but now it will be heard by all."

The Story

When I was growing up, my mother taught me the language of the birds; and when I got married, I used to be listening to their conversation; and I would be laughing; and my wife would be asking me what was the reason of my laughing, but I did not like to tell her, as women are always asking questions. We went out walking one fine morning, and the birds were arguing with one another. One of them said to another:

"Why should you be comparing yourself with me, when there is not a king nor knight that does not come to look at my tree?"

"What advantage has your tree over mine, on which there are three rods of magic mastery growing?"

When I heard them arguing, and knew that the rods were there, I began to laugh.

"Oh," asked my wife, "why are you always laughing? I believe it is at myself you are jesting, and I'll walk with you no more."

"Oh, it is not about you I am laughing. It is because I understand the language of the birds."

Then I had to tell her what the birds were saying to one another; and she was greatly delighted, and she asked me to go home, and she gave orders to the cook to have breakfast ready at six o'clock in the morning. I did not know why she was going out early, and breakfast was ready in the morning at the hour she appointed. She asked me to go out walking. I went with her. She went to the tree, and asked me to cut a rod for her.

"Oh, I will not cut it. Are we not better without it?"

"I will not leave this until I get the rod, to see if there is any good in it."

I cut the rod and gave it to her. She turned from me and struck a blow on a stone, and changed it; and she struck a second blow on me, and made of me a black raven, and she went home and left me after her. I thought she would come back; she did not come, and I had to go into a tree till morning. In the morning, at six o'clock, there was a bellman out, proclaiming that everyone who killed a raven would get a fourpenny-bit. At last you could not find man or boy without a gun, nor, if you were to walk three miles, a raven that was not killed. I had to make a nest in the top of the parlour chimney, and hide myself all day till night came, and go out to pick up a bit to support me, till I spent a month. Here she is herself to say if it is a lie I am telling.

"It is not," said she.

Then I saw her out walking. I went up to her, and I thought she would turn me back to my own shape, and she struck me with the rod and made of me an old white horse, and she ordered me to be put to a cart with a man, to draw stones from morning till night. I was worse off then. She spread abroad a report that I had died suddenly in my bed, and prepared a coffin, and waked and buried me. Then she had no trouble. But when I got tired I began to kill everyone who came near me, and I used to go into the haggard every night and destroy the stacks of corn; and when a man came near me in the morning I would follow him till I broke his bones. Everyone got afraid of me. When she saw I was doing mischief she came to meet me, and I thought she would change me. And she did change me, and made a fox of me. When I saw she was doing me every sort of damage I went away from her. I knew there was a badger's hole in the garden, and I went there till night came, and I made great slaughter among the geese and ducks. There she is herself to say if I am telling a lie.

"Oh! You are telling nothing but the truth, only less than the truth."

When she had enough of my killing the fowl she came out into the garden, for she knew I was in the badger's hole. She came to me and made me a wolf. I had to be off, and go to an island, where no one at all would see me, and now and then I used to be killing sheep, for there were not many of them, and I was afraid of being seen and hunted; and so I passed a year, till a shepherd saw me among the sheep and a pursuit was made after me. And when the dogs came near me there was no place for me to escape to from them; but I recognised the sign of the king among the men, and I made for him, and the king cried out to stop the hounds. I took a leap upon the front of the king's saddle, and the woman behind cried out, "My king and my lord, kill him, or he will kill you!"

"Oh! He will not kill me. He knew me; he must be pardoned."

The king took me home with him, and gave orders I should be well cared for. I was so wise, when I got food, I would not eat one morsel until I got a knife and fork. The man told the king, and the king came to see if it was true, and I got a knife and fork, and I took the knife in one paw and the fork in the other, and I bowed to the king. The king gave orders to bring him drink, and it came; and the king filled a glass of wine and gave it to me.

I took hold of it in my paw and drank it, and thanked the king.

"On my honour," said he, "it is some king or other has lost him, when he came on the island; and I will keep him, as he is trained; and perhaps he will serve us yet."

And this is the sort of king he was – a king who had not a child living. Eight sons were born to him and three daughters, and they were stolen the same night they were born. No matter what guard was placed over them, the child would be gone in the morning. A twelfth child now came to the queen, and the king took me with him to watch the baby. The women were not satisfied with me.

"Oh," said the king, "what was all your watching ever good for? One that was born to me I have not; I will leave this one in the dog's care, and he will not let it go."

A coupling was put between me and the cradle, and when everyone went to sleep I was watching till the person woke who attended in the daytime; but I was there only two nights; when it was near the day, I saw a hand coming down through the chimney, and the hand was so big that it took round the child altogether, and thought to take him away. I caught hold of the hand above the wrist, and as I was fastened to the cradle,

I did not let go my hold till I cut the hand from the wrist, and there was a howl from the person without. I laid the hand in the cradle with the child, and as I was tired I fell asleep; and when I awoke, I had neither child nor hand; and I began to howl, and the king heard me, and he cried out that something was wrong with me, and he sent servants to see what was the matter with me, and when the messenger came he saw me covered with blood, and he could not see the child; and he went to the king and told him the child was not to be got. The king came and saw the cradle coloured with the blood, and he cried out "where was the child gone?" and everyone said it was the dog had eaten it.

The king said: "It is not: loose him, and he will get the pursuit himself."

When I was loosed, I found the scent of the blood till I came to a door of the room in which the child was. I went back to the king and took hold of him, and went back again and began to tear at the door. The king followed me and asked for the key. The servant said it was in the room of the stranger woman. The king caused search to be made for her, and she was not to be found. "I will break the door," said the king, "as I can't get the key." The king broke the door, and I went in, and went to the trunk, and the king asked for a key to unlock it. He got no key, and he broke the lock. When he opened the trunk, the child and the hand were stretched side by side, and the child was asleep. The king took the hand and ordered a woman to come for the child, and he showed the hand to everyone in the house. But the stranger woman was gone, and she did not see the king – and here she is herself to say if I am telling lies of her.

"Oh, it's nothing but the truth you have!"

The king did not allow me to be tied any more. He said there was nothing so much to wonder at as that I cut the hand off, as I was tied.

The child was growing till he was a year old. He was beginning to walk, and no one cared for him more than I did. He was growing till he was three, and he was running out every minute; so the king ordered a silver chain to be put between me and the child, that he might not go away from me. I was out with him in the garden every day, and the king was as proud as the world of the child. He would be watching him everywhere we went, till the child grew so wise that he would loose the chain and get off. But one day that he loosed it I failed to find him; and I ran into the house and searched the house, but there was no getting him for me. The king cried to go out and find the child, that had got loose from the dog. They went searching for him, but could not find him. When they failed altogether to find him, there remained no more favour with the king towards me, and everyone disliked me, and I grew weak, for I did not get a morsel to eat half the time. When summer came, I said I would try and go home to my own country. I went away one fine morning, and I went swimming, and God helped me till I came home. I went into the garden, for I knew there was a place in the garden where I could hide myself, for fear my wife should see me. In the morning I saw her out walking, and the child with her, held by the hand. I pushed out to see the child, and as he was looking about him everywhere, he saw me and called out, "I see my shaggy papa. Oh!" said he; "Oh, my heart's love, my shaggy papa, come here till I see you!"

I was afraid the woman would see me, as she was asking the child where he saw me, and he said I was up in a tree; and the more the child called me, the more I hid myself. The woman took the child home with her, but I knew he would be up early in the morning.

I went to the parlour-window, and the child was within, and he playing. When he saw me he cried out, "Oh! My heart's love, come here till I see you, shaggy papa." I broke the window and went in, and he began to kiss me. I saw the rod in front of the chimney, and I jumped up at the rod and knocked it down. "Oh! My heart's love, no one would give me the pretty rod," said he. I hoped he would strike me with the rod, but he did not. When I saw the time was short I raised my paw, and I gave him a scratch below the knee. "Oh! You naughty, dirty, shaggy papa, you have hurt me so much, I'll give you a blow of the rod." He struck me a light blow, and so I came back to my own shape again. When he saw a man standing before him he gave a cry, and I took him up in my arms. The servants heard the child. A maid came in to see what was the matter with him. When she saw me she gave a cry out of her, and she said, "Oh, if the master isn't come to life again!"

Another came in, and said it was he really. When the mistress heard of it, she came to see with her own eyes, for she would not believe I was there; and when she saw me she said she'd drown herself. But I said to her, "If you yourself will keep the secret, no living man will ever get the story from me until I lose my head." Here she is herself to say if I am telling the truth. "Oh, it's nothing but truth you are telling."

When I saw I was in a man's shape, I said I would take the child back to his father and mother, as I knew the grief they were in after him. I got a ship, and took the child

with me; and as I journeyed I came to land on an island, and I saw not a living soul on it, only a castle dark and gloomy. I went in to see was there anyone in it. There was no one but an old hag, tall and frightful, and she asked me, "What sort of person are you?"

I heard someone groaning in another room, and I said I was a doctor, and I asked her what ailed the person who was groaning.

"Oh," said she, "it is my son, whose hand has been bitten from his wrist by a dog."

I knew then that it was he who had taken the child from me, and I said I would cure him if I got a good reward.

"I have nothing; but there are eight young lads and three young women, as handsome as anyone ever laid eyes on, and if you cure him I will give you them."

"Tell me first in what place his hand was cut from him?"

"Oh, it was out in another country, twelve years ago."

"Show me the way, that I may see him."

She brought me into a room, so that I saw him, and his arm was swelled up to the shoulder. He asked me if I would cure him; and I said I would cure him if he would give me the reward his mother promised.

"Oh, I will give it; but cure me."

"Well, bring them out to me."

The hag brought them out of the room. I said I should burn the flesh that was on his arm. When I looked on him he was howling with pain. I said that I would not leave him in pain long. The wretch had only one eye in his forehead. I took a bar of iron, and put it in the fire till it was red, and I said to the hag, "He will be howling at first, but will fall asleep presently, and do not wake him till he has slept as much as he wants. I will close the door when I am going out." I took the bar with me, and I stood over him, and I turned it across through his eye as far as I could. He began to bellow, and tried to catch me, but I was out and away, having closed the door. The hag asked me, "Why is he bellowing?"

"Oh, he will be quiet presently, and will sleep for a good while, and I'll come again to have a look at him; but bring me out the young men and the young women."

I took them with me, and I said to her, "Tell me where you got them."

"My son brought them with him, and they are all the children of one king."

I was well satisfied, and I had no wish for delay to get myself free from the hag, so I took them on board the ship, and the child I had myself. I thought the king might leave me the child I nursed myself; but when I came to land, and all those young people with me, the king and queen were out walking. The king was very aged, and the queen aged likewise. When I came to converse with them, and the twelve with me, the king and queen began to cry. I asked, "Why are you crying?"

"It is for good cause I am crying. As many children as these I should have, and now I am withered, grey, at the end of my life, and I have not one at all."

I told him all I went through, and I gave him the child in his hand, and "These are your other children who were stolen from you, whom I am giving to you safe. They are gently reared."

When the king heard who they were he smothered them with kisses and drowned them with tears, and dried them with fine cloths silken and the hair of his own head, and so also did their mother, and great was his welcome for me, as it was I who found them all. The king said to me, "I will give you the last child, as it is you who have earned him best; but you must come to my court every year, and the child with you, and I will share with you my possessions."

"I have enough of my own, and after my death I will leave it to the child."

I spent a time, till my visit was over, and I told the king all the troubles I went through, only I said nothing about my wife. And now you have the story.

And now when you go home, and the Slender Red Champion asks you for news of the death of Anshgayliacht and for the sword of light, tell him the way in which his brother was killed, and say you have the sword; and he will ask the sword from you. Say you to him, "If I promised to bring it to you, I did not promise to bring it for you"; and then throw the sword into the air and it will come back to me.

* * *

He went home, and he told the story of the death of Anshgayliacht to the Slender Red Champion, "And here," said he, "is the sword." The Slender Red Champion asked for the sword; but he said: "If I promised to bring it to you, I did not promise to bring it for you"; and he threw it into the air and it returned to Blue Niall.

The Greek Princess and the Young Gardener

THERE WAS ONCE A KING, but I didn't hear what country he was over, and he had one very beautiful daughter. Well, he was getting old and sickly, and the doctors found out that the finest medicine in the world for him was the apples of a tree that grew in the orchard just under his window. So you may be sure he had the tree well minded, and used to get the apples counted from the time they were the size of small marbles.

One harvest, just as they were beginning to turn ripe, the king was awakened one night by the flapping of wings outside in the orchard; and when he looked out, what did he see but a bird among the branches of his tree. Its feathers were so bright that they made a light all round them, and the minute it saw the king in his night-cap and night-shirt it picked off an apple, and flew away. "Oh, botheration to that thief of a gardener!" says the king, "this is a nice way he's watching my precious fruit."

He didn't sleep a wink the rest of the night; and as soon as anyone was stirring in the palace, he sent for the gardener, and abused him for his neglect.

"Please your Majesty!" says he, "not another apple you shall lose. My three sons are the best shots at the bow and arrow in the kingdom, and they and myself will watch in turn every night."

When the night came, the gardener's eldest son took his post in the garden, with his bow strung and his arrow between his fingers, and watched, and watched. But at the dead hour, the king, that was wide awake, heard the flapping of wings, and ran to the window. There was the bright bird in the tree, and the boy fast asleep, sitting with his back to the wall, and his bow on his lap.

"Rise, you lazy thief!" says the king, "there's the bird again, botheration to her!"

Up jumped the poor fellow; but while he was fumbling with the arrow and the string, away was the bird with the nicest apple on the tree. Well, to be sure, how the king fumed and fretted, and how he abused the gardener and the boy, and what a twenty-four hours he spent till midnight came again!

He had his eye this time on the second son of the gardener; but though he was up and lively enough when the clock began to strike twelve, it wasn't done with the last bang when he saw him stretched like one dead on the long grass, and saw the bright bird again, and heard the flap of her wings, and saw her carry away the third apple. The poor fellow woke with the roar the king let at him, and even was in time enough to let fly an arrow after the bird. He did not hit her, you may depend; and though the king was mad enough, he saw the poor fellows were under *pishtrogues*, and could not help it.

Well, he had some hopes out of the youngest, for he was a brave, active young fellow, that had everybody's good word. There he was ready, and there was the king watching him, and talking to him at the first stroke of twelve. At the last clang, the brightness

coming before the bird lighted up the wall and the trees, and the rushing of the wings was heard as it flew into the branches; but at the same instant the crack of the arrow on her side might be heard a quarter of a mile off. Down came the arrow and a large bright feather along with it, and away was the bird, with a screech that was enough to break the drum of your ear. She hadn't time to carry off an apple; and bedad, when the feather was thrown up into the king's room it was heavier than lead, and turned out to be the finest beaten gold.

Well, there was great *cooramuch* made about the youngest boy next day, and he watched night after night for a week, but not a mite of a bird or bird's feather was to be seen, and then the king told him to go home and sleep. Everyone admired the beauty of the gold feather beyond anything, but the king was fairly bewitched. He was turning it round and round, and rubbing it against his forehead and his nose the live-long day; and at last he proclaimed that he'd give his daughter and half his kingdom to whoever would bring him the bird with the gold feathers, dead or alive.

The gardener's eldest son had great conceit of himself, and away he went to look for the bird. In the afternoon he sat down under a tree to rest himself, and eat a bit of bread and cold meat that he had in his wallet, when up comes as fine a looking fox as you'd see in the burrow of Munfin. "Musha, sir," says he, "would you spare a bit of that meat to a poor body that's hungry?"

"Well," says the other, "you must have the divil's own assurance, you common robber, to ask me such a question. Here's the answer," and he let fly at the *moddhereen rua*.

The arrow scraped from his side up over his back, as if he was made of hammered iron, and stuck in a tree a couple of perches off.

"Foul play," says the fox; "but I respect your young brother, and will give a bit of advice. At nightfall you'll come into a village. One side of the street you'll see a large room lighted up, and filled with young men and women, dancing and drinking. The other side you'll see a house with no light, only from the fire in the front room, and no one near it but a man and his wife, and their child. Take a fool's advice, and get lodging there." With that he curled his tail over his crupper, and trotted off.

The boy found things as the fox said, but *begonies* he chose the dancing and drinking, and there we'll leave him. In a week's time, when they got tired at home waiting for him, the second son said he'd try his fortune, and off he set. He was just as ill-natured and foolish as his brother, and the same thing happened to him. Well, when a week was over, away went the youngest of all, and as sure as the hearth-money, he sat under the same tree, and pulled out his bread and meat, and the same fox came up and saluted him. Well, the young fellow shared his dinner with the *moddhereen*, and he wasn't long beating about the bush, but told the other he knew all about his business.

"I'll help you," says he, "if I find you're biddable. So just at nightfall you'll come into a village.... Goodbye till tomorrow."

It was just as the fox said, but the boy took care not to go near dancer, drinker, fiddler, or piper. He got welcome in the quiet house to supper and bed, and was on his journey next morning before the sun was the height of the trees.

He wasn't gone a quarter of a mile when he saw the fox coming out of a wood that was by the roadside.

"Good morrow, fox," says one.

"Good morrow, sir," says the other.

"Have you any notion how far you have to travel till you find the golden bird?"

"Dickens a notion have I – how could I?"

"Well, I have. She's in the King of Spain's palace, and that's a good two hundred miles off."

"Oh, dear! We'll be a week going."

"No, we won't. Sit down on my tail, and we'll soon make the road short."

"Tail, indeed! That 'ud be the droll saddle, my poor *moddhereen*."

"Do as I tell you, or I'll leave you to yourself."

Well, rather than vex him he sat down on the tail that was spread out level like a wing, and away they went like thought. They overtook the wind that was before them, and the wind that came after didn't overtake them. In the afternoon, they stopped in a wood near the King of Spain's palace, and there they stayed till nightfall.

"Now," says the fox, "I'll go before you to make the minds of the guards easy, and you'll have nothing to do but go from lighted hall to another lighted hall till you find the golden bird in the last. If you have a head on you, you'll bring himself and his cage outside the door, and no one then can lay hands on him or you. If you haven't a head I can't help you, nor no one else." So he went over to the gates.

In a quarter of an hour the boy followed, and in the first hall he passed he saw a score of armed guards standing upright, but all dead asleep. In the next he saw a dozen, and in the next half a dozen, and in the next three, and in the room beyond that there was no guard at all, nor lamp, nor candle, but it was as bright as day; for there was the golden bird in a common wood and wire cage, and on the table were the three apples turned into solid gold.

On the same table was the most lovely golden cage eye ever beheld, and it entered the boy's head that it would be a thousand pities not to put the precious bird into it, the common cage was so unfit for her. Maybe he thought of the money it was worth; anyhow he made the exchange, and he had soon good reason to be sorry for it. The instant the shoulder of the bird's wing touched the golden wires, he let such a *squawk* out of him as was enough to break all the panes of glass in the windows, and at the same minute the three men, and the half-dozen, and the dozen, and the score men, woke up and clattered their swords and spears, and surrounded the poor boy, and jibed, and cursed, and swore at home, till he didn't know whether it's his foot or head he was standing on. They called the king, and told him what happened, and he put on a very grim face. "It's on a gibbet you ought to be this moment," says he, "but I'll give you a chance of your life, and of the golden bird, too. I lay you under prohibitions, and restrictions, and death, and destruction, to go and bring me the King of *Morōco's* bay filly that outruns the wind, and leaps over the walls of castle-bawns. When you fetch her into the bawn of this palace, you must get the golden bird, and liberty to go where you please."

Out passed the boy, very down-hearted, but as he went along, who should come out of a brake but the fox again.

"Ah, my friend," says he, "I was right when I suspected you hadn't a head on you; but I won't rub your hair again' the grain. Get on my tail again, and when we come to the King of Morōco's palace, we'll see what we can do."

So away they went like thought. The wind that was before them they would overtake; the wind that was behind them would not overtake them.

Well, the nightfall came on them in a wood near the palace, and says the fox, "I'll go and make things easy for you at the stables, and when you are leading out the filly,

don't let her touch the door, nor doorposts, nor anything but the ground, and that with her hoofs; and if you haven't a head on you once you are in the stable, you'll be worse off than before."

So the boy delayed for a quarter of an hour, and then he went into the big bawn of the palace. There were two rows of armed men reaching from the gate to the stable, and every man was in the depth of deep sleep, and through them went the boy till he got into the stable. There was the filly, as handsome a beast as ever stretched leg, and there was one stable-boy with a currycomb in his hand, and another with a bridle, and another with a sieve of oats, and another with an armful of hay, and all as if they were cut out of stone. The filly was the only live thing in the place except himself. She had a common wood and leather saddle on her back, but a golden saddle with the nicest work on it was hung from the post, and he thought it the greatest pity not to put it in place of the other. Well, I believe there was some *pishrogues* over it for a saddle; anyhow, he took off the other, and put the gold one in its place.

Out came a squeal from the filly's throat when she felt the strange article, that might be heard from Tombrick to Bunclody, and all as ready were the armed men and the stable-boys to run and surround the *omadhan* of a boy, and the King of Morōco was soon there along with the rest, with a face on him as black as the sole of your foot. After he stood enjoying the abuse the poor boy got from everybody for some time, he says to him, "You deserve high hanging for your impudence, but I'll give you a chance for your life and the filly, too. I lay on you all sorts of prohibitions, and restrictions, and death, and destruction to go bring me Princess Golden Locks, the King of Greek's daughter. When you deliver her into my hand, you may have the 'daughter of the wind', and welcome. Come in and take your supper and your rest, and be off at the flight of night."

The poor boy was down in the mouth, you may suppose, as he was walking away next morning, and very much ashamed when the fox looked up in his face after coming out of the wood.

"What a thing it is," says he, "not to have a head when a body wants it worst; and here we have a fine long journey before us to the King of Greek's palace. The worse luck now, the same always. Here, get on my tail, and we'll be making the road shorter."

So he sat on the fox's tail, and swift as thought they went. The wind that was before them they would overtake it, the wind that was behind them would not overtake them, and in the evening they were eating their bread and cold meat in the wood near the castle.

"Now," says the fox, when they were done, "I'll go before you to make things easy. Follow me in a quarter of an hour. Don't let Princess Golden Locks touch the jambs of the doors with her hands, or hair, or clothes, and if you're asked any favour, mind how you answer. Once she's outside the door, no one can take her from you."

Into the palace walked the boy at the proper time, and there were the score, and the dozen, and the half-dozen, and the three guards all standing up or leaning on their arms, and all dead asleep, and in the farthest room of all was the Princess Golden Locks, as lovely as Venus herself. She was asleep in one chair, and her father, the King of Greek, in another. He stood before her for ever so long with the love sinking deeper into his heart every minute, till at last he went down on one knee, and took her darling white hand in his hand, and kissed it.

When she opened her eyes, she was a little frightened, but I believe not very angry, for the boy, as I call him, was a fine handsome young fellow, and all the respect and love that ever you could think of was in his face. She asked him what he wanted, and he stammered, and blushed, and began his story six times, before she understood it.

"And would you give me up to that ugly black King of Morōco?" says she.

"I am obliged to do so," says he, "by prohibitions, and restrictions, and death, and destruction, but I'll have his life and free you, or lose my own. If I can't get you for my wife, my days on the earth will be short."

"Well," says she, "let me take leave of my father at any rate."

"Ah, I can't do that," says he, "or they'd all waken, and myself would be put to death, or sent to some task worse than any I got yet."

But she asked leave at any rate to kiss the old man; that wouldn't waken him, and then she'd go. How could he refuse her, and his heart tied up in every curl of her hair? But, bedad, the moment her lips touched her father's, he let a cry, and every one of the score, the dozen guards woke up, and clashed their arms, and were going to make *gibbets* of the foolish boy.

But the king ordered them to hold their hands, till he'd be *insensed* of what it was all about, and when he heard the boy's story he gave him a chance for his life.

"There is," says he, "a great heap of clay in front of the palace, that won't let the sun shine on the walls in the middle of summer. Everyone that ever worked at it found two shovelfuls added to it for every one they threw away. Remove it, and I'll let my

daughter go with you. If you're the man I suspect you to be, I think she'll be in no danger of being wife to that yellow *Molott*."

Early next morning was the boy tackled to his work, and for every shovelful he flung away two came back on him, and at last he could hardly get out of the heap that gathered round him. Well, the poor fellow scrambled out some way, and sat down on a sod, and he'd have cried only for the shame of it. He began at it in ever so many places, and one was still worse than the other, and in the heel of the evening, when he was sitting with his head between his hands, who should be standing before him but the fox.

"Well, my poor fellow," says he, "you're low enough. Go in: I won't say anything to add to your trouble. Take your supper and your rest: tomorrow will be a new day."

"How is the work going off?" says the king, when they were at supper.

"Faith, your Majesty," says the poor boy, "it's not going off, but coming on it is. I suppose you'll have the trouble of digging me out at sunset tomorrow, and waking me."

"I hope not," says the princess, with a smile on her kind face; and the boy was as happy as anything the rest of the evening.

He was wakened up next morning with voices shouting, and bugles blowing, and drums beating, and such a hullibulloo he never heard in his life before. He ran out to see what was the matter, and there, where the heap of clay was the evening before, were soldiers, and servants, and lords, and ladies, dancing like mad for joy that it was gone.

"Ah, my poor fox!" says he to himself, "this is your work."

Well, there was little delay about his return. The king was going to send a great retinue with the princess and himself, but he wouldn't let him take the trouble.

"I have a friend," says he, "that will bring us both to the King of Morōco's palace in a day, d— fly away with him!"

There was great crying when she was parting from her father.

"Ah!" says he, "what a lonesome life I'll have now! Your poor brother in the power of that wicked witch, and kept away from us, and now you taken from me in my old age!"

Well, they both were walking on through the wood, and he telling her how much he loved her; out walked the fox from behind a brake, and in a short time he and she were sitting on the brush, and holding one another fast for fear of slipping off, and away they went like thought. The wind that was before them they would overtake it, and in the evening he and she were in the big bawn of the King of Morōco's castle.

"Well," says he to the boy, "you've done your duty well; bring out the bay filly. I'd give the full of the bawn of such fillies, if I had them, for this handsome princess. Get on your steed, and here is a good purse of guineas for the road."

"Thank you," says he. "I suppose you'll let me shake hands with the princess before I start."

"Yes, indeed, and welcome."

Well, he was some little time about the hand-shaking, and before it was over he had her fixed snug behind him; and while you could count three, he, and she, and the filly were all the guards, and a hundred perches away. On they went, and next morning they were in the wood near the King of Spain's palace, and there was the fox before them.

"Leave your princess here with me," says he, "and go get the golden bird and the three apples. If you don't bring us back the filly along with the bird, I must carry you both home myself."

Well, when the King of Spain saw the boy and the filly in the bawn, he made the golden bird, and the golden cage, and the golden apples be brought out and handed to him, and was very thankful and very glad of his prize. But the boy could not part with the nice beast without petting it and rubbing it; and while no one was expecting such a thing, he was up on its back, and through the guards, and a hundred perches away, and he wasn't long till he came to where he left his princess and the fox.

They hurried away till they were safe out of the King of Spain's land, and then they went on easier; and if I was to tell you all the loving things they said to one another, the story wouldn't be over till morning. When they were passing the village of the dance house, they found his two brothers begging, and they brought them along. When they came to where the fox appeared first, he begged the young man to cut off his head and his tail. He would not do it for him; he shivered at the very thought, but the eldest brother was ready enough. The head and tail vanished with the blows, and the body changed into the finest young man you could see, and who was he but the princess's brother that was bewitched. Whatever joy they had before, they had twice as much now, and when they arrived at the palace bonfires were set blazing, oxes roasting, and puncheons of wine put out in the lawn. The young Prince of Greece was married to the king's daughter, and the prince's sister to the gardener's son. He and she went a shorter way back to her father's house, with many attendants, and the king was so glad of the golden bird and the golden apples, that he had sent a waggon full of gold and a waggon full of silver along with them.

The Three Crowns

THERE WAS ONCE a king, some place or other, and he had three daughters. The two eldest were very proud and uncharitable, but the youngest was as good as they were bad. Well, three princes came to court them, and two of them were the moral of the two eldest ladies, and one was just as lovable as the youngest. They were all walking down to a lake one day that lay at the bottom of the lawn, just like the one at Castleboro', and they met a poor beggar. The King wouldn't give him anything, and the eldest princes wouldn't give him anything, nor their sweethearts; but the youngest daughter and her true love did give him something, and kind words along with it, and that was better nor all.

When they got to the edge of the lake, what did they find but the beautifulest boat you ever saw in your life; and says the eldest, "I'll take a sail in this fine boat"; and says the second eldest, "I'll take a sail in this fine boat"; and says the youngest, "I won't take a sail in that fine boat, for I'm afraid it's an enchanted one." But the others overpersuaded her to go in, and her father was just going in after her, when up sprung on the deck a little man only seven inches high, and he ordered him to stand back. Well, all the men put their hands to their soords; and if the same soords were only thraneens they weren't able to draw them, for all sthrenth was left their arms. Seven Inches loosened the silver chain that fastened the boat and pushed away; and after grinning at the four men, says he to them: "Bid your daughters and your brides farewell for awhile. That wouldn't have happened you three, only for your want of charity. You," says he to the youngest, "needn't fear; you'll recover your princess all in good time, and you and she will be as happy as the day is long. Bad people, if they were rolling stark naked in gold, would not be rich. Banacht lath!" Away they sailed, and the ladies stretched out their hands, but weren't able to say a word.

Well, they were crossin' the lake while a cat'd be lickin' her ear, and the poor men couldn't stir hand nor foot to follow them. They saw Seven Inches handing the three princesses out of the boat, and letting them down by a nice basket and winglas into a draw-well that was convenient, but king nor princes never saw an opening before in the same place. When the last lady was out of sight the men found the strength in their arms and legs again. Round the lake they ran, and never drew rein till they came to the well and windlass, and there was the silk rope rolled on the axle, and the nice white basket hanging to it. "Let me down," says the youngest prince; "I'll die or recover them again."

"No," says the second daughter's sweetheart, "I'm entitled to my turn before you."

"And," says the other, "I must get first turn, in right of my bride." So they gave way to him, and in he got into the basket, and down they let him. First they lost sight of him, and then, after winding off a hundred perches of the silk rope, it slackened, and they stopped turning. They waited two hours, and then they went to dinner, because there was no chuck made at the rope.

Guards were set till morning, and then down went the second prince, and, sure enough, the youngest of all got himself let down on the third day. He went down perches and perches, while it was as dark about him as if he was in a big pot with the cover on. At last he saw a glimmer far down, and in a short time he felt the ground. Out he came from the big lime-kiln, and lo and behold you, there was a wood and green fields, and a castle in a lawn, and a bright sky over all. "It's in Tir-na-n Oge I am," says he. "Let's see what sort of people are in the castle." On he walked across fields and lawn, and no one was there to keep him out or let him into the castle; but the big hall door was wide open. He went from one fine room to another that was finer, and at last he reached the handsomest of all, with a table in the middle; and such a dinner as was laid upon it! The prince was hungry enough, but he was too mannerly to go eat without being invited. So he sat by the fire, and he did not wait long till he heard steps, and in came Seven Inches and the youngest sister by the hand. Well, prince and princess flew into one another's arms, and says the little man, says he, "Why aren't you eating?"

"I think, sir," says he, "it was only good manners to wait to be asked."

"The other princes didn't think so," says he. "Each of them fell to without leave nor license, and only gave me the rough side o' his tongue when I told them they were making more free than welcome. Well, I don't think they feel much hunger now. There they are, good marvel instead of flesh and blood," says he, pointing to two statues, one in one corner and the other in the other corner of the room.

The prince was frightened, but he was afraid to say anything, and Seven Inches made him sit down to dinner between himself and his bride, and he'd be as happy as the day is long, only for the sight of the stone men in the corner. Well, that day went by, and when the next came, says Seven Inches to him, "Now, you'll have to set out that way," pointing to the sun, "and you'll find the second princess in a giant's castle this evening, when you'll be tired and hungry, and the eldest princess tomorrow evening; and you may as well bring them here with you. You need not ask leave of their masters; they're only housekeepers with the big fellows. I suppose, if they ever get home, they'll look on poor people as if they were flesh and blood like themselves."

Away went the prince, and bedad it's tired and hungry he was when he reached the first castle at sunset. Oh, wasn't the second princess glad to see him! And if she didn't give him a good supper it's a wonder. But she heard the giant at the gate, and she hid the prince in a closet. Well, when he came in, he snuffed, and he snuffed, an' says he, "Be (by) the life, I smell fresh mate."

"Oh," says the princess, "it's only the calf I got killed today." "Ay, ay," says he, "is supper ready?"

"It is," says she; and before he ruz from the table he hid three-quarters of the calf and a kag of wine.

"I think," says he, when all was done, "I smell fresh mate still."

"It's sleepy you are," says she; "go to bed."

"When will you marry me?" says the giant; "you're puttin' me off too long."

"St. Tibb's Eve," says she. "I wish I knew how far off that is," says he; and he fell asleep with his head in the dish.

Next day he went out after breakfast, and she sent the prince to the castle where the eldest sister was. The same thing happened there; but when the giant was snoring, the princess wakened up the prince, and they saddled two steeds in the stables, and magh go bragh (the field for ever) with them. But the horses' heels struck the stones outside the gate, and up got the giant, and after them he made. He roared, and he shouted, and the more he shouted the faster ran the horses; and just as the day was breaking he was only twenty perches behind. But the prince didn't leave the Castle of Seven Inches without being provided with something good. He reined in his steed, and flung a short, sharp knife over his shoulder, and up sprung a thick wood between the giant and themselves. They caught the wind that blew before them, and the wind that blew behind them did not catch them. At last they were near the castle where the other sister lived; and there she was, waiting for them under a high hedge, and a fine steed under her.

But the giant was now in sight, roaring like a hundred lions, and the other giant was out in a moment, and the chase kept on. For every two springs the horses gave the giants gave three, and at last they were only seventy perches off. Then the prince stopped again and flung the second skian behind him. Down went all the flat field, till there was a quarry between them a quarter of a mile deep, and the bottom filled with black water; and before the giants could get round it the prince and princesses were inside the domain of the great magician, where the high thorny hedge opened of itself to everyone that he chose to let in.

Well, to be sure, there was joy enough between the three sisters till the two eldest saw their lovers turned into stone. But while they were shedding tears for them Seven Inches came in and touched them with his rod. So they were flesh and blood and life once more, and there was great hugging and kissing, and all sat down to a nice breakfast, and Seven Inches sat at the head of the table.

When breakfast was over he took them into another room, where there was nothing but heaps of gold and silver and diamonds, and silks and satins; and on a table there was lying three sets of crowns: a gold crown was in a silver crown, and that was lying in a copper crown. He took up one set of crowns and gave it to the eldest princess; and another set, and gave it to the second princess; and another set, and gave it to the youngest princess of all; and says he, "Now you may all go to the bottom of the pit, and you have nothing to do but stir the basket, and the people that are watching above will draw you up, princesses first, princes after. But remember, ladies, you are to keep your crowns safe, and be married in them all the same day. If you be married separately, or if you be married without your crowns, a curse will follow – mind what I say."

So they took leave of him with great respect, and walked arm-in-arm to the bottom of the draw-well. There was a sky and a sun over them and a great high wall, and the bottom of the draw-well was inside the arch. The youngest pair went last, and says the princess to the prince, "I'm sure the two princes don't mean any good to you. Keep these crowns under your cloak, and if you are obliged to stay last, don't get into the basket, but put a big stone, or any heavy thing, inside, and see what will happen."

So when they were inside the dark cave they put in the eldest princess first, and she stirred the basket and up she went, but first she gave a little scream. Then the basket was let down again, and up went the second princess, and then up went the youngest; but first she put her arms round her prince's neck and kissed him, and cried a little. At last it came to the turn of the youngest prince, and well became him – instead of going into the basket he put in a big stone. He drew on one side and listened, and after the basket was drawn up about twenty perch down came itself and the stone like thunder, and the stone was made brishe of on the flags.

Well, my poor prince had nothing for it but to walk back to the castle; and through it and round it he walked, and the finest of eating and drinking he got, and a bed of bog-down to sleep on, and fine walks he took through gardens and lawns, but not a sight could he get, high or low, of Seven Inches. Well, I don't think any of us would be tired of this way of living for ever! Maybe we would. Anyhow, the prince got tired of it before a week, he was so lonesome for his true love; and at the end of a month he didn't know what to do with himself.

One morning he went into the treasure room and took notice of a beautiful snuff-box on the table that he didn't remember seeing there before. He took it in his hands and opened it, and out Seven Inches walked on the table. "I think, prince," says he, "you're getting a little tired of my castle?"

"Ah!" says the other, "if I had my princess here, and could see you now and then, I'd never see a dismal day."

"Well, you're long enough here now, and you're wanting there above. Keep your bride's crowns safe, and whenever you want my help open this snuff-box. Now take a walk down the garden, and come back when you're tired."

Well, the prince was going down a gravel walk with a quick-set hedge on each side and his eyes on the ground, and he thinking on one thing and another. At last he lifted his eyes, and there he was outside of a smith's bawn gate that he had often passed before, about a mile away from the palace of his betrothed princess. The clothes he had on him were as ragged as you please, but he had his crowns safe under his old cloak.

So the smith came out, and says he, "It's a shame for a strong big fellow like you to be on the sthra, and so much work to be done. Are you any good with hammer and tongs? Come in and bear a hand, and I'll give you diet and lodging and a few thirteens when you earn them."

"Never say't twice," says the prince; "I want nothing but to be employed." So he took the sledge and pounded away at the red-hot bar that the smith was turning on the anvil to make into a set of horse-shoes.

Well, they weren't long powdhering away, when a stronshuch (idler) of a tailor came in; and when the smith asked him what news he had, he got the handle of the bellows and began to blow to let out all he had heard for the last two days. There were so many questions and answers at first that, if I told them all, it would be bedtime before I'd be done. So here is the substance of the discourse; and before he got far into it the forge was half filled with women knitting stockings and men smoking.

Yous all heard how the two princesses were unwilling to be married till the youngest would be ready with her crowns and her sweetheart. But after the windlass loosened accidentally when they were pulling up her bridegroom that was to be, there was no more sign of a well or a rope or a windlass than there is on the palm of your hand. So the buckeens that were coortin' the eldest ladies wouldn't give peace nor ease to their lovers nor the King till they got consent to the marriage, and it was to take place this morning. Myself went down out of curiosity; and to be sure I was delighted with the grand dresses of the two brides and the three crowns on their heads – gold, silver, and copper – one inside the other. The youngest was standing by, mournful enough, in white, and all was ready. The two bridegrooms came walking in as proud and grand as you please, and up they were walking to the altar rails when, my dear, the boards opened two yards wide under their feet, and down they went among the dead men and the coffins in the vaults. Oh, such screeching as the ladies gave! And such running and racing and peeping down as there was; but the clerk soon opened the door of the vault, and up came the two heroes, and their fine clothes covered an inch thick with cobwebs and mould.

So the King said they should put off the marriage, "For," says he, "I see there is no use in thinking of it till my youngest gets her three crowns and is married along with the others. I'll give my youngest daughter for a wife to whoever brings three crowns to me like the others; and if he doesn't care to be married, some other one will, and I'll make his fortune."

"I wish," says the smith, "I could do it; but I was looking at the crowns after the princesses got home, and I don't think there's a black or a white smith on the face of the earth could imitate them."

"Faint heart never won fair lady," says the prince. "Go to the palace, and ask for a quarter of a pound of gold, a quarter of a pound of silver, and a quarter of a pound of copper. Get one crown for a pattern, and my head for a pledge, and I'll give you out the very things that are wanted in the morning."

"Ubbabow," says the smith, "are you in earnest?"

"Faith, I am so," says he. "Go! Worse than lose you can't."

To make a long story short, the smith got the quarter of a pound of gold, and the quarter of a pound of silver, and the quarter of a pound of copper, and gave them and the pattern crown to the prince. He shut the forge door at nightfall, and the neighbours all gathered in the bawn, and they heard him hammering, hammering, hammering, from that to daybreak, and every now and then he'd pitch out through the window bits of gold, silver, or copper; and the idlers scrambled for them, and cursed one another, and prayed for the good luck of the workman.

Well, just as the sun was thinking to rise he opened the door and brought the three crowns he got from his true love, and such shouting and huzzaing as there was! The smith asked him to go along with him to the palace, but he refused; so off set the smith, and the whole townland with him; and wasn't the King rejoiced when he saw the crowns! "Well," says he to the smith, "you're a married man, and what's to be done?"

"Faith, your majesty, I didn't make them crowns at all; it was a big shuler (vagrant) of a fellow that took employment with me yesterday."

"Well, daughter, will you marry the fellow that made these crowns?"

"Let me see them first, father." So when she examined them she knew them right well, and guessed it was her true love that had sent them. "I will marry the man that these crowns came from," says she.

"Well," said the King to the eldest of the two princes, "go up to the smith's forge, take my best coach, and bring home the bridegroom." He was very unwilling to do this, he was so proud, but he did not wish to refuse. When he came to the forge he saw the prince standing at the door, and beckoned him over to the coach. "Are you the fellow," says he, "that made them crowns?"

"Yes," says the other.

"Then," says he, "maybe you'd give yourself a brushing, and get into that coach; the King wants to see you. I pity the princess." The young prince got into the carriage, and while they were on the way he opened the snuff-box, and out walked Seven Inches, and stood on his thigh. "Well," says he, "what trouble is on you now?"

"Master," says the other, "please to let me back in my forge, and let this carriage be filled with paving-stones." No sooner said than done. The prince was sitting in his forge, and the horses wondered what was after happening to the carriage.

When they came to the palace yard the King himself opened the carriage door to pay respect to the new son-in-law. As soon as he turned the handle a shower of stones fell on his powdered wig and his silk coat, and down he fell under them. There was great fright, and some tittering, and the King, after he wiped the blood from his forehead, looked very cross at the eldest prince. "My liege," says he, "I'm very sorry for this accidence, but I'm not to blame. I saw the young smith get into the carriage, and we never stopped a minute since."

"It's uncivil you were to him. Go," says he to the other prince, "and bring the young prince here, and be polite."

"Never fear," says he.

But there's some people that couldn't be good-natured if they were to be made heirs of Damer's estate. Not a bit civiller was the new messenger than the old, and when the King opened the carriage door a second time it's a shower of mud that came down on him; and if he didn't fume and splutter and shake himself it's no matter. "There's no use," says he, "going on this way. The fox never got a better messenger than himself."

So he changed his clothes and washed himself, and out he set to the smith's forge. Maybe he wasn't polite to the young prince, and asked him to sit along with himself. The prince begged to be allowed to sit in the other carriage, and when they were half-way he opened his snuff-box. "Master," says he, "I'd wished to be dressed now according to my rank."

"You shall be that," says Seven Inches. "And now I'll bid you farewell. Continue as good and kind as you always were; love your wife, and that's all the advice I'll give you." So Seven Inches vanished; and when the carriage door was opened in the yard, out walks the prince, as fine as hands and pins could make him, and the first thing he did was to run over to his bride and embrace her very heartily.

Everyone had great joy but the two other princes. There was not much delay about the marriages that were all celebrated on the same day, and the youngest prince and princess were the happiest married couple you ever heard of in a story.

The Story-Teller at Fault

AT THE TIME WHEN the Tuatha Dé Danann held the sovereignty of Ireland, there reigned in Leinster a king, who was remarkably fond of hearing stories. Like the other princes and chieftains of the island, he had a favourite story-teller, who held a large estate from his Majesty, on condition of telling him a new story every night of his life, before he went to sleep. Many indeed were the stories he knew, so that he had already reached a good old age without failing even for a single night in his task; and such was the skill he displayed that whatever cares of state or other annoyances might prey upon the monarch's mind, his story-teller was sure to send him to sleep.

One morning the story-teller arose early, and as his custom was, strolled out into his garden turning over in his mind incidents which he might weave into a story for the king at night. But this morning he found himself quite at fault; after pacing his whole demesne, he returned to his house without being able to think of anything new or strange. He found no difficulty in 'there was once a king who had three sons' or 'one day the king of all Ireland', but further than that he could not get. At length he went in to breakfast, and found his wife much perplexed at his delay.

"Why don't you come to breakfast, my dear?" said she.

"I have no mind to eat anything," replied the story-teller; "long as I have been in the service of the king of Leinster, I never sat down to breakfast without having a new story ready for the evening, but this morning my mind is quite shut up, and I don't know what to do. I might as well lie down and die at once. I'll be disgraced for ever this evening, when the king calls for his story-teller."

Just at this moment the lady looked out of the window.

"Do you see that black thing at the end of the field?" said she.

"I do," replied her husband.

They drew nigh, and saw a miserable looking old man lying on the ground with a wooden leg placed beside him.

"Who are you, my good man?" asked the story-teller.

"Oh, then, 'tis little matter who I am. I'm a poor, old, lame, decrepit, miserable creature, sitting down here to rest awhile."

"An' what are you doing with that box and dice I see in your hand?"

"I am waiting here to see if anyone will play a game with me," replied the beggar man.

"Play with you! Why what has a poor old man like you to play for?"

"I have one hundred pieces of gold in this leathern purse," replied the old man.

"You may as well play with him," said the story-teller's wife; "and perhaps you'll have something to tell the king in the evening."

A smooth stone was placed between them, and upon it they cast their throws.

It was but a little while and the story-teller lost every penny of his money.

"Much good may it do you, friend," said he. "What better hap could I look for, fool that I am!"

"Will you play again?" asked the old man.

"Don't be talking, man: you have all my money."

"Haven't you chariot and horses and hounds?"

"Well, what of them!"

"I'll stake all the money I have against thine."

"Nonsense, man! Do you think for all the money in Ireland, I'd run the risk of seeing my lady tramp home on foot?"

"Maybe you'd win," said the bocough.

"Maybe I wouldn't," said the story-teller.

"Play with him, husband," said his wife. "I don't mind walking, if you do, love."

"I never refused you before," said the story-teller, "and I won't do so now."

Down he sat again, and in one throw lost houses, hounds, and chariot.

"Will you play again?" asked the beggar.

"Are you making game of me, man; what else have I to stake?"

"I'll stake all my winnings against your wife," said the old man.

The story-teller turned away in silence, but his wife stopped him.

"Accept his offer," said she. "This is the third time, and who knows what luck you may have? You'll surely win now."

They played again, and the story-teller lost. No sooner had he done so, than to his sorrow and surprise, his wife went and sat down near the ugly old beggar.

"Is that the way you're leaving me?" said the story-teller.

"Sure I was won," said she. "You would not cheat the poor man, would you?"

"Have you any more to stake?" asked the old man.

"You know very well I have not," replied the story-teller.

"I'll stake the whole now, wife and all, against your own self," said the old man.

Again they played, and again the story-teller lost.

"Well! Here I am, and what do you want with me?"

"I'll soon let you know," said the old man, and he took from his pocket a long cord and a wand.

"Now," said he to the story-teller, "what kind of animal would you rather be, a deer, a fox, or a hare? You have your choice now, but you may not have it later."

To make a long story short, the story-teller made his choice of a hare; the old man threw the cord round him, struck him with the wand, and lo! A long-eared, frisking hare was skipping and jumping on the green.

But it wasn't for long; who but his wife called the hounds, and set them on him. The hare fled, the dogs followed. Round the field ran a high wall, so that run as he might, he couldn't get out, and mightily diverted were beggar and lady to see him twist and double.

In vain did he take refuge with his wife, she kicked him back again to the hounds, until at length the beggar stopped the hounds, and with a stroke of the wand, panting and breathless, the story-teller stood before them again.

"And how did you like the sport?" said the beggar.

"It might be sport to others," replied the story-teller looking at his wife, "for my part I could well put up with the loss of it."

"Would it be asking too much," he went on to the beggar, "to know who you are at all, or where you come from, or why you take a pleasure in plaguing a poor old man like me?"

"Oh!" replied the stranger, "I'm an odd kind of good-for-little fellow, one day poor, another day rich, but if you wish to know more about me or my habits, come with me and perhaps I may show you more than you would make out if you went alone."

"I'm not my own master to go or stay," said the story-teller, with a sigh.

The stranger put one hand into his wallet and drew out of it before their eyes a well-looking middle-aged man, to whom he spoke as follows:

"By all you heard and saw since I put you into my wallet, take charge of this lady and of the carriage and horses, and have them ready for me whenever I want them."

Scarcely had he said these words when all vanished, and the story-teller found himself at the Foxes' Ford, near the castle of Red Hugh O'Donnell. He could see all but none could see him.

O'Donnell was in his hall, and heaviness of flesh and weariness of spirit were upon him.

"Go out," said he to his doorkeeper, "and see who or what may be coming."

The doorkeeper went, and what he saw was a lank, grey beggarman; half his sword bared behind his haunch, his two shoes full of cold road-a-wayish water sousing about him, the tips of his two ears out through his old hat, his two shoulders out through his scant tattered cloak, and in his hand a green wand of holly.

"Save you, O'Donnell," said the lank grey beggarman.

"And you likewise," said O'Donnell. "Whence come you, and what is your craft?"

"I come from the outmost stream of earth,
From the glens where the white swans glide,
A night in Islay, a night in Man,
A night on the cold hillside."

"It's the great traveller you are," said O'Donnell.

"Maybe you've learnt something on the road."

"I am a juggler," said the lank grey beggarman, "and for five pieces of silver you shall see a trick of mine."

"You shall have them," said O'Donnell; and the lank grey beggarman took three small straws and placed them in his hand.

"The middle one," said he, "I'll blow away; the other two I'll leave."

"Thou canst not do it," said one and all.

But the lank grey beggarman put a finger on either outside straw and, whiff, away he blew the middle one.

"'Tis a good trick," said O'Donnell; and he paid him his five pieces of silver.

"For half the money," said one of the chief's lads, "I'll do the same trick."

"Take him at his word, O'Donnell."

The lad put the three straws on his hand, and a finger on either outside straw and he blew; and what happened but that the fist was blown away with the straw.

"Thou art sore, and thou wilt be sorer," said O'Donnell.

"Six more pieces, O'Donnell, and I'll do another trick for thee," said the lank grey beggarman.

"Six shalt thou have."

"Seest thou my two ears! One I'll move but not t'other."

"'Tis easy to see them, they're big enough, but thou canst never move one ear and not the two together."

The lank grey beggarman put his hand to his ear, and he gave it a pull.

O'Donnell laughed and paid him the six pieces.

"Call that a trick," said the fistless lad, "anyone can do that," and so saying, he put up his hand, pulled his ear, and what happened was that he pulled away ear and head.

"Sore thou art; and sorer thou'lt be," said O'Donnell.

"Well, O'Donnell," said the lank grey beggarman, "strange are the tricks I've shown thee, but I'll show thee a stranger one yet for the same money."

"Thou hast my word for it," said O'Donnell.

With that the lank grey beggarman took a bag from under his armpit, and from out the bag a ball of silk, and he unwound the ball and he flung it slantwise up into the clear blue heavens, and it became a ladder; then he took a hare and placed it upon the thread, and up it ran; again he took out a red-eared hound, and it swiftly ran up after the hare.

"Now," said the lank grey beggarman; "has anyone a mind to run after the dog and on the course?"

"I will," said a lad of O'Donnell's.

"Up with you then," said the juggler; "but I warn you if you let my hare be killed I'll cut off your head when you come down."

The lad ran up the thread and all three soon disappeared. After looking up for a long time, the lank grey beggarman said: "I'm afraid the hound is eating the hare, and that our friend has fallen asleep."

Saying this he began to wind the thread, and down came the lad fast asleep; and down came the red-eared hound and in his mouth the last morsel of the hare.

He struck the lad a stroke with the edge of his sword, and so cast his head off. As for the hound, if he used it no worse, he used it no better.

"It's little I'm pleased, and sore I'm angered," said O'Donnell, "that a hound and a lad should be killed at my court."

"Five pieces of silver twice over for each of them," said the juggler, "and their heads shall be on them as before."

"Thou shalt get that," said O'Donnell.

Five pieces, and again five were paid him, and lo! The lad had his head and the hound his. And though they lived to the uttermost end of time, the hound would never touch a hare again, and the lad took good care to keep his eyes open. Scarcely had the lank grey beggarman done this when he vanished from out their sight, and no one present could say if he had flown through the air or if the earth had swallowed him up.

He moved as wave tumbling o'er wave
As whirlwind following whirlwind,
As a furious wintry blast,
So swiftly, sprucely, cheerily,
Right proudly,
And no stop made
Until he came
To the court of Leinster's King,
He gave a cheery light leap
O'er top of turret,
Of court and city
Of Leinster's King.

Heavy was the flesh and weary the spirit of Leinster's king. 'Twas the hour he was wont to hear a story, but send he might right and left, not a jot of tidings about the story-teller could he get.

"Go to the door," said he to his doorkeeper, "and see if a soul is in sight who may tell me something about my story-teller."

The doorkeeper went, and what he saw was a lank grey beggarman, half his sword bared behind his haunch, his two old shoes full of cold road-a-wayish water sousing about him, the tips of his two ears out through his old hat, his two shoulders out through his scant tattered cloak, and in his hand a three-stringed harp.

"What canst thou do?" said the doorkeeper.

"I can play," said the lank grey beggarman.

"Never fear," added he to the story-teller, "thou shalt see all, and not a man shall see thee."

When the king heard a harper was outside, he bade him in.

"It is I that have the best harpers in the five-fifths of Ireland," said he, and he signed them to play. They did so, and if they played, the lank grey beggarman listened.

"Heardst thou ever the like?" said the king.

"Did you ever, O king, hear a cat purring over a bowl of broth, or the buzzing of beetles in the twilight, or a shrill tongued old woman scolding your head off?"

"That I have often," said the king.

"More melodious to me," said the lank grey beggarman, "were the worst of these sounds than the sweetest harping of thy harpers."

When the harpers heard this, they drew their swords and rushed at him, but instead of striking him, their blows fell on each other, and soon not a man but was cracking his neighbour's skull and getting his own cracked in turn.

When the king saw this, he thought it hard the harpers weren't content with murdering their music, but must needs murder each other.

"Hang the fellow who began it all," said he; "and if I can't have a story, let me have peace."

Up came the guards, seized the lank grey beggarman, marched him to the gallows and hanged him high and dry. Back they marched to the hall, and who should they see but the lank grey beggarman seated on a bench with his mouth to a flagon of ale.

"Never welcome you in," cried the captain of the guard, "didn't we hang you this minute, and what brings you here?"

"Is it me myself, you mean?"

"Who else?" said the captain.

"May your hand turn into a pig's foot with you when you think of tying the rope; why should you speak of hanging me?"

Back they scurried to the gallows, and there hung the king's favourite brother.

Back they hurried to the king who had fallen fast asleep.

"Please your Majesty," said the captain, "we hanged that strolling vagabond, but here he is back again as well as ever."

"Hang him again," said the king, and off he went to sleep once more.

They did as they were told, but what happened was that they found the king's chief harper hanging where the lank grey beggarman should have been.

The captain of the guard was sorely puzzled.

"Are you wishful to hang me a third time?" said the lank grey beggarman.

"Go where you will," said the captain, "and as fast as you please if you'll only go far enough. It's trouble enough you've given us already."

"Now you're reasonable," said the beggarman; "and since you've given up trying to hang a stranger because he finds fault with your music, I don't mind telling you that if you go back to the gallows you'll find your friends sitting on the sward none the worse for what has happened."

As he said these words he vanished; and the story-teller found himself on the spot where they first met, and where his wife still was with the carriage and horses.

"Now," said the lank grey beggarman, "I'll torment you no longer. There's your carriage and your horses, and your money and your wife; do what you please with them."

"For my carriage and my houses and my hounds," said the story-teller, "I thank you; but my wife and my money you may keep."

"No," said the other. "I want neither, and as for your wife, don't think ill of her for what she did, she couldn't help it."

"Not help it! Not help kicking me into the mouth of my own hounds! Not help casting me off for the sake of a beggarly old –"

"I'm not as beggarly or as old as ye think. I am Angus of the Bruff; many a good turn you've done me with the King of Leinster. This morning my magic told me the difficulty you were in, and I made up my mind to get you out of it. As for your wife there, the power that changed your body changed her mind. Forget and forgive as man and wife should do, and now you have a story for the King of Leinster when he calls for one"; and with that he disappeared.

It's true enough he now had a story fit for a king. From first to last he told all that had befallen him; so long and loud laughed the king that he couldn't go to sleep at all. And he told the story-teller never to trouble for fresh stories, but every night as long as he lived he listened again and he laughed afresh at the tale of the lank grey beggarman.

The Fate of Frank M'Kenna

THERE LIVED a man named M'Kenna at the hip of one of the mountainous hills which divide the county of Tyrone from that of Monaghan. This M'Kenna had two sons, one of whom was in the habit of tracing hares of a Sunday whenever there happened to be a fall of snow. His father, it seems, had frequently remonstrated with him upon what he considered to be a violation of the Lord's day, as well as for his general neglect of mass. The young man, however, though otherwise harmless and inoffensive, was in this matter quite insensible to paternal reproof, and continued to trace whenever the avocations of labour would allow him. It so happened that upon a Christmas morning, I think in the year 1814, there was a deep fall of snow, and young M'Kenna, instead of going to mass, got down his cock-stick – which is a staff much thicker and heavier at one end than at the other –and prepared to set out on his favourite amusement. His father, seeing this, reproved him seriously, and insisted that he should attend prayers. His enthusiasm for the sport, however, was stronger than his love of religion, and he refused to be guided by his father's advice. The old man during the altercation got warm; and on finding that the son obstinately scorned his authority, he knelt down and prayed that if the boy persisted in following his own will, he might never return from the mountains unless as a corpse. The imprecation, which was certainly as harsh as it was impious and senseless, might have startled many a mind from a purpose that was, to say the least of it, at variance with religion and the respect due to a father. It had no effect, however, upon the son, who is said to have replied, that whether he ever returned or not, he was determined on going; and go accordingly he did. He was not, however, alone, for it appears that three or four of the neighbouring young men accompanied him. Whether their sport was good or otherwise, is not to the purpose, neither am I able to say; but the story goes that towards the latter part of the day they started a larger and darker hare than any they had ever seen, and that she kept dodging on before them bit by bit, leading them to suppose that every succeeding cast of the cock-stick would bring her down. It was observed afterwards that she also led them into the recesses of the mountains, and that although they tried to turn her course homewards, they could not succeed in doing so. As evening advanced, the companions of M'Kenna began to feel the folly of pursuing her farther, and to perceive the danger of losing their way in the mountains should night or a snow-storm come upon them. They therefore proposed to give over the chase and return home; but M'Kenna would not hear of it.

"If you wish to go home, you may," said he; "as for me, I'll never leave the hills till I have her with me." They begged and entreated of him to desist and return, but all to no purpose: he appeared to be what the Scotch call *fey* – that is, to act as if he were moved by some impulse that leads to death, and from the influence of which a man cannot withdraw himself. At length, on finding him invincibly obstinate, they left him pursuing the hare directly into the heart of the mountains, and returned to their respective homes.

In the meantime one of the most terrible snow-storms ever remembered in that part of the country came on, and the consequence was, that the self-willed young man, who had equally trampled on the sanctities of religion and parental authority, was given over for lost. As soon as the tempest became still, the neighbours assembled in a body and proceeded to look for him. The snow, however, had fallen so heavily that not a single mark of a footstep could be seen. Nothing but one wide waste of white undulating hills met the eye wherever it turned, and of M'Kenna no trace whatever was visible or could be found. His father, now remembering the unnatural character of his imprecation, was nearly distracted; for although the body had not yet been found, still by everyone who witnessed the sudden rage of the storm and who knew the mountains, escape or survival was felt to be impossible. Every day for about a week large parties were out among the hill-ranges seeking him, but to no purpose. At length there came a thaw, and his body was found on a snow-wreath, lying in a supine posture within a circle which he had drawn around him with his cock-stick. His prayer-book lay opened upon his mouth, and his hat was pulled down so as to cover it and his face. It is unnecessary to say that the rumour of his death, and of the circumstances under which he left home, created a most extraordinary sensation in the country – a sensation that was the greater in proportion to the uncertainty occasioned by his not having been found either alive or dead. Some affirmed that he had crossed the mountains, and was seen in Monaghan; others, that he had been seen in Clones, in Emyvale, in Five-mile-town; but despite of all these agreeable reports, the melancholy truth was at length made clear by the appearance of the body as just stated.

Now, it so happened that the house nearest the spot where he lay was inhabited by a man named Daly, I think – but of the name I am not certain – who was a herd or care-taker to Dr. Porter, then Bishop of Clogher. The situation of this house was the most lonely and desolate-looking that could be imagined. It was at least two miles distant from any human habitation, being surrounded by one wide and dreary waste of dark moor. By this house lay the route of those who had found the corpse, and I believe the door of it was borrowed for the purpose of conveying it home. Be this as it may, the family witnessed the melancholy procession as it passed slowly through the mountains, and when the place and circumstances are all considered, we may admit that to ignorant and superstitious people, whose minds, even upon ordinary occasions, were strongly affected by such matters, it was a sight calculated to leave behind it a deep, if not a terrible impression. Time soon proved that it did so.

An incident is said to have occurred at the funeral in fine keeping with the wild spirit of the whole melancholy event. When the procession had advanced to a place called Mullaghtinny, a large dark-coloured hare, which was instantly recognised, by those who had been out with him on the hills, as the identical one that led him to his fate, is said to have crossed the roads about twenty yards or so before the coffin. The story goes, that a man struck it on the side with a stone, and that the blow, which would have killed any ordinary hare, not only did it no injury, but occasioned a sound to proceed from the body resembling the hollow one emitted by an empty barrel when struck.

In the meantime the interment took place, and the sensation began, like every other, to die away in the natural progress of time, when, behold, a report ran abroad like wild-fire that, to use the language of the people, "Frank M'Kenna was *appearing*!"

One night, about a fortnight after his funeral, the daughter of Daly, the herd, a girl about fourteen, while lying in bed saw what appeared to be the likeness of M'Kenna, who had been lost. She screamed out, and covering her head with the bed-clothes, told her father and mother that Frank M'Kenna was in the house. This alarming intelligence naturally produced great terror; still, Daly, who, notwithstanding his belief in such matters, possessed a good deal of moral courage, was cool enough to rise and examine the house, which consisted of only one apartment. This gave the daughter some courage, who, on finding that her father could not see him, ventured to look out, and she *then* could see nothing of him herself. She very soon fell asleep, and her father attributed what she saw to fear, or some accidental combination of shadows proceeding from the furniture, for it was a clear moonlight night. The light of the following day dispelled a great deal of their apprehensions, and comparatively little was thought of it until evening again advanced, when the fears of the daughter began to return. They appeared to be prophetic, for she said when night came that she knew he would appear again; and accordingly at the same hour he did so. This was repeated for several successive nights, until the girl, from the very hardihood of terror, began to become so far familiarised to the spectre as to venture to address it.

"In the name of God!" she asked, "what is troubling you, or why do you appear to me instead of to some of your own family or relations?"

The ghost's answer alone might settle the question involved in the authenticity of its appearance, being, as it was, an account of one of the most ludicrous missions that ever a spirit was despatched upon.

"I'm not allowed," said he, "to spake to any of my friends, for I parted wid them in anger; but I'm come to tell you that they are quarrelin' about my breeches – a new pair that I got made for Christmas day; an' as I was comin' up to thrace in the mountains, I thought the ould one 'ud do betther, an' of coorse I didn't put the new pair an me. My raison for appearin'," he added, "is, that you may tell my friends that none of them is to wear them – they must be given in charity."

This serious and solemn intimation from the ghost was duly communicated to the family, and it was found that the circumstances were exactly as it had represented them. This, of course, was considered as sufficient proof of the truth of its mission. Their conversations now became not only frequent, but quite friendly and familiar. The girl became a favourite with the spectre, and the spectre, on the other hand, soon lost all his terrors in her eyes. He told her that whilst his friends were bearing home his body, the handspikes or poles on which they carried him had cut his back, and *occasioned him great pain*! The cutting of the back also was known to be true, and strengthened, of course, the truth and authenticity of their dialogues. The whole neighbourhood was now in a commotion with this story of the apparition, and persons incited by curiosity began to visit the girl in order to satisfy themselves of the truth of what they had heard. Everything, however, was corroborated, and the child herself, without any symptoms of anxiety or terror, artlessly related her conversations with the spirit. Hitherto their interviews had been all nocturnal, but now that the ghost found his footing made good, he put a hardy face on, and ventured to appear by daylight. The girl also fell into states of syncope, and while the fits lasted, long conversations with him upon the subject of God, the blessed Virgin, and Heaven, took place between them. He was certainly an excellent moralist, and gave the best advice. Swearing, drunkenness, theft, and every evil propensity of our nature, were declaimed against with a degree of spectral eloquence quite surprising. Common fame had now a topic dear to her heart, and never was a ghost made more of by his best friends than she made of him.

The whole country was in a tumult, and I well remember the crowds which flocked to the lonely little cabin in the mountains, now the scene of matters so interesting and important. Not a single day passed in which I should think from ten to twenty, thirty, or fifty persons, were not present at these singular interviews. Nothing else was talked of, thought of, and, as I can well testify, dreamt of. I would myself have gone to Daly's were it not for a confounded misgiving I had, that perhaps the ghost might take such a fancy of appearing to *me*, as he had taken to cultivate an intimacy with the girl; and it so happens, that when I see the face of an individual nailed down in the coffin – chilling and gloomy operation! – I experience no particular wish to look upon it again.

The spot where the body of M'Kenna was found is now marked by a little heap of stones, which has been collected since the melancholy event of his death. Every person who passes it throws a stone upon the heap; but why this old custom is practised, or what it means, I do not know, unless it be simply to mark the spot as a visible means of preserving the memory of the occurrence.

Daly's house, the scene of the supposed apparition, is now a shapeless ruin, which could scarcely be seen were it not for the green spot that once was a garden, and which now shines at a distance like an emerald, but with no agreeable or pleasing associations. It is a spot which no solitary schoolboy will ever visit, nor indeed would the unflinching believer in the popular nonsense of ghosts wish to pass it without a companion. It is, under any circumstances, a gloomy and barren place; but when looked upon in connection with what we have just recited, it is lonely, desolate, and awful.

Andrew Coffey

MY GRANDFATHER, Andrew Coffey, was known to the whole barony as a quiet, decent man. And if the whole barony knew him, he knew the whole barony, every inch, hill and dale, bog and pasture, field and covert. Fancy his surprise one evening, when he found himself in a part of the demesne he couldn't recognise a bit. He and his good horse were always stumbling up against some tree or stumbling down into some bog-hole that by rights didn't ought to be there. On the top of all this the rain came pelting down wherever there was a clearing, and the cold March wind tore through the trees. Glad he was then when he saw a light in the distance, and drawing near found a cabin, though for the life of him he couldn't think how it came there. However, in he walked, after tying up his horse, and right welcome was the brushwood fire blazing on the hearth. And there stood a chair right and tight, that seemed to say, "Come, sit down in me." There wasn't a soul else in the room. Well, he did sit, and got a little warm and cheered after his drenching. But all the while he was wondering and wondering.

"Andrew Coffey! Andrew Coffey!"

Good heavens! Who was calling him, and not a soul in sight? Look around as he might, indoors and out, he could find no creature with two legs or four, for his horse was gone.

"ANDREW COFFEY! ANDREW COFFEY! Tell me a story."

It was louder this time, and it was nearer. And then what a thing to ask for! It was bad enough not to be let sit by the fire and dry oneself, without being bothered for a story.

"ANDREW COFFEY! ANDREW COFFEY!! Tell me a story, or it'll be the worse for you."

My poor grandfather was so dumbfounded that he could only stand and stare.

"ANDREW COFFEY! ANDREW COFFEY! I told you it'd be the worse for you."

And with that, out there bounced, from a cupboard that Andrew Coffey had never noticed before, *a man*. And the man was in a towering rage. But it wasn't that. And he carried as fine a blackthorn as you'd wish to crack a man's head with. But it wasn't that either. But when my grandfather clapped eyes on him, he knew him for Patrick Rooney, and all the world knew *he'd* gone overboard, fishing one night long years before.

Andrew Coffey would neither stop nor stay, but he took to his heels and was out of the house as hard as he could. He ran and he ran taking little thought of what was before till at last he ran up against a big tree. And then he sat down to rest.

He hadn't sat for a moment when he heard voices.

"It's heavy he is, the vagabond."

"Steady now, we'll rest when we get under the big tree yonder." Now that happened to be the tree under which Andrew Coffey was sitting. At least he thought so, for seeing a branch handy he swung himself up by it and was soon snugly hidden away. Better see than be seen, thought he.

The rain had stopped and the wind fallen. The night was blacker than ever, but Andrew Coffey could see four men, and they were carrying between them a long box. Under the tree they came, set the box down, opened it, and who should they bring out but – Patrick Rooney. Never a word did he say, and he looked as pale as old snow.

Well, one gathered brushwood, and another took out tinder and flint, and soon they had a big fire roaring, and my grandfather could see Patrick plainly enough. If he had kept still before, he kept stiller now. Soon they had four poles up and a pole across, right over the fire, for all the world like a spit, and on to the pole they slung Patrick Rooney.

"He'll do well enough," said one; "but who's to mind him whilst we're away, who'll turn the fire, who'll see that he doesn't burn?"

With that Patrick opened his lips: "Andrew Coffey," said he.

"Andrew Coffey! Andrew Coffey! Andrew Coffey! Andrew Coffey!"

"I'm much obliged to you, gentlemen," said Andrew Coffey, "but indeed I know nothing about the business."

"You'd better come down, Andrew Coffey," said Patrick.

It was the second time he spoke, and Andrew Coffey decided he would come down. The four men went off and he was left all alone with Patrick.

Then he sat and he kept the fire even, and he kept the spit turning, and all the while Patrick looked at him.

Poor Andrew Coffey couldn't make it all out at all, at all, and he stared at Patrick and at the fire, and he thought of the little house in the wood, till he felt quite dazed.

"Ah, but it's burning me ye are!" says Patrick, very short and sharp.

"I'm sure I beg your pardon," said my grandfather "but might I ask you a question?"

"If you want a crooked answer," said Patrick; "turn away or it'll be the worse for you."

But my grandfather couldn't get it out of his head; hadn't everybody, far and near, said Patrick had fallen overboard. There was enough to think about, and my grandfather did think.

"ANDREW COFFEY! ANDREW COFFEY! IT'S BURNING ME YE ARE."

Sorry enough my grandfather was, and he vowed he wouldn't do so again.

"You'd better not," said Patrick, and he gave him a cock of his eye, and a grin of his teeth, that just sent a shiver down Andrew Coffey's back. Well it was odd, that here he should be in a thick wood he had never set eyes upon, turning Patrick Rooney upon a spit. You can't wonder at my grandfather thinking and thinking and not minding the fire.

"ANDREW COFFEY, ANDREW COFFEY, IT'S THE DEATH OF YOU I'LL BE."

And with that what did my grandfather see, but Patrick unslinging himself from the spit and his eyes glared and his teeth glistened.

It was neither stop nor stay my grandfather made, but out he ran into the night of the wood. It seemed to him there wasn't a stone but was for his stumbling, not a branch but beat his face, not a bramble but tore his skin. And wherever it was clear the rain pelted down and the cold March wind howled along.

Glad he was to see a light, and a minute after he was kneeling, dazed, drenched, and bedraggled by the hearth side. The brushwood flamed, and the brushwood crackled, and soon my grandfather began to feel a little warm and dry and easy in his mind.

"ANDREW COFFEY! ANDREW COFFEY!"

It's hard for a man to jump when he has been through all my grandfather had, but jump he did. And when he looked around, where should he find himself but in the very cabin he had first met Patrick in.

"Andrew Coffey, Andrew Coffey, tell me a story."

"Is it a story you want?" said my grandfather as bold as may be, for he was just tired of being frightened. "Well if you can tell me the rights of this one, I'll be thankful."

And he told the tale of what had befallen him from first to last that night. The tale was long, and maybe Andrew Coffey was weary. It's asleep he must have fallen, for when he awoke he lay on the hill-side under the open heavens, and his horse grazed at his side.

The Beresford Ghost

"**THERE IS** at Curraghmore, the seat of Lord Waterford, in Ireland, a manuscript account of the tale, such as it was originally received and implicitly believed in by the children and grandchildren of the lady to whom Lord Tyrone is supposed to have made the supernatural appearance after death. The account was written by Lady Betty Cobbe, the youngest daughter of Marcus, Earl of Tyrone, and granddaughter of Nicola S., Lady Beresford. She lived to a good old age, in full use of all her faculties, both of body and mind. I can myself remember her, for when a boy I passed through Bath on a journey with my mother, and we went to her house there, and had luncheon. She appeared to my juvenile imagination a very appropriate person to revise and transmit such a tale, and fully adapted to do ample justice to her subject-matter. It never has been doubted in the family that she received the full particulars in early life, and that she heard the circumstances, such as they were believed to have occurred, from the nearest relatives of the two persons, the supposed actors in this mysterious interview, viz., from her own father, Lord Tyrone, who died in 1763, and from her aunt, Lady Riverston, who died in 1763 also.

"These two were both with their mother, Lady Beresford, on the day of her decease, and they, without assistance or witness, took off from their parent's wrist the black bandage which she had always worn on all occasions and times, even at Court, as some very old persons who lived well into the eighteenth century testified, having received their information from eyewitnesses of the fact. There was an oil painting of this lady in Tyrone House, Dublin, representing her with a black ribbon bound round her wrist. This portrait disappeared in an unaccountable manner. It used to hang in one of the drawing-rooms in that mansion, with other family pictures. When Henry, Marquis of Waterford, sold the old town residence of the family and its grounds to the Government as the site of the Education Board, he directed Mr. Watkins, a dealer in pictures, and a man of considerable knowledge in works of art and vertu, to collect the pictures, etc., etc., which were best adapted for removal to Curraghmore. Mr. Watkins especially picked out this portrait, not only as a good work of art, but as one which, from its associations, deserved particular care and notice. When, however, the lot arrived at Curraghmore and was unpacked, no such picture was found; and though Mr. Watkins took great pains and exerted himself to the utmost to trace what had become of it, to this day (nearly forty years), not a hint of its existence has been received or heard of.

"John le Poer, Lord Decies, was the eldest son of Richard, Earl of Tyrone, and of Lady Dorothy Annesley, daughter of Arthur, Earl of Anglesey. He was born 1665, succeeded his father 1690, and died 14th October, 1693. He became Lord Tyrone at his father's death, and is the 'ghost' of the story.

"Nicola Sophie Hamilton was the second and youngest daughter and co-heiress of Hugh, Lord Glenawley, who was also Baron Lunge in Sweden. Being a zealous Royalist, he had, together with his father, migrated to that country in 1643, and returned from it at the Restoration. He was of a good old family, and held considerable landed property in the county Tyrone, near Ballygawley. He died there in 1679. His eldest daughter and co-heiress, Arabella Susanna, married, in 1683, Sir John Macgill, of Gill Hall, in the county Down.

"Nicola S. (the second daughter) was born in 1666, and married Sir Tristram Beresford in 1687. Between that and 1693 two daughters were born, but no son to inherit the ample landed estates of his father, who most anxiously wished and hoped for an heir. It was under these circumstances, and at this period, that the manuscripts state that Lord Tyrone made his appearance after death; and all the versions of the story, without variation, attribute the same cause and reason, viz., a solemn promise mutually interchanged in early life between John le Poer, then Lord Decies, afterwards Lord Tyrone, and Nicola S. Hamilton, that whichever of the two died the first, should, if permitted, appear to the survivor for the object of declaring the approval or rejection by the Deity of the revealed religion as generally acknowledged: of which the departed one must be fully cognisant, but of which they both had in their youth entertained unfortunate doubts.

"In the month of October, 1693, Sir Tristram and Lady Beresford went on a visit to her sister, Lady Macgill, at Gill Hall, now the seat of Lord Clanwilliam, whose grandmother was eventually the heiress of Sir J. Macgill's property. One morning Sir Tristram rose early, leaving Lady Beresford asleep, and went out for a walk before breakfast. When his wife joined the table very late, her appearance and the embarrassment of her manner attracted general attention, especially that of her husband. He made anxious inquiries as to her health, and asked her apart what had occurred to her wrist, which was tied up with black ribbon tightly bound round it. She earnestly entreated him not to inquire more then, or thereafter, as to the cause of her wearing or continuing afterwards to wear that ribbon; 'for,' she added, 'you will never see me without it'. He replied, 'Since you urge it so vehemently, I promise you not to inquire more about it'.

"After completing her hurried breakfast she made anxious inquiries as to whether the post had yet arrived. It had not yet come in; and Sir Tristram asked: 'Why are you so particularly eager about letters today?' 'Because I expect to hear of Lord Tyrone's death, which took place on Tuesday.' 'Well,' remarked Sir Tristram, 'I never should have put you down for a superstitious person; but I suppose that some idle dream has disturbed you.' Shortly after, the servant brought in the letters; one was sealed with black wax. 'It is as I expected,' she cries; 'he is dead.' The letter was from Lord Tyrone's steward to inform them that his master had died in Dublin, on Tuesday, 14th October, at 4 p.m. Sir Tristram endeavoured to console her, and begged her to restrain her grief, when she assured him that she felt relieved and easier now that she knew the actual fact. She added, 'I can now give you a most satisfactory piece of intelligence, viz., that I am with child, and that it will be a boy'. A son was born in the following July. Sir Tristram survived its birth little more than six years. After his death Lady Beresford continued to reside with her young family at his place in the county of Derry, and seldom went from home. She hardly mingled with any neighbours or friends, excepting with Mr. and Mrs. Jackson, of Coleraine. He was the principal personage in that town, and was, by his mother, a near relative of Sir Tristram. His wife was the daughter of Robert Gorges, LL.D. (a gentleman of good old English family, and possessed of a considerable estate in the county Meath), by Jane Loftus, daughter of Sir Adam Loftus, of Rathfarnham, and sister of Lord Lisburn. They had an only son, Richard Gorges, who was in the army, and became a general officer very early in life. With the Jacksons Lady Beresford maintained a constant communication and lived on the most intimate terms, while she seemed determined to eschew all other society and to remain in her chosen retirement.

"At the conclusion of three years thus passed, one luckless day 'Young Gorges' most vehemently professed his passion for her, and solicited her hand, urging his suit in a most passionate appeal, which was evidently not displeasing to the fair widow, and which, unfortunately for her, was successful. They were married in 1704. One son and two daughters were born to them, when his abandoned and dissolute conduct forced her to seek and to obtain a separation. After this had continued for four years, General Gorges pretended extreme penitence for his past misdeeds, and with the most solemn promises of amendment induced his wife to live with him again, and she became the mother of a second son. The day a month after her confinement happened to be her birthday, and having recovered and feeling herself equal to some exertion, she sent for her son, Sir Marcus Beresford, then twenty years old, and her married daughter, Lady Riverston. She also invited Dr. King, the Archbishop of Dublin (who was an intimate friend), and an old clergyman who had christened her, and who had always kept up a most kindly intercourse with her during her whole life, to make up a small party to celebrate the day.

"In the early part of it Lady Beresford was engaged in a kindly conversation with her old friend the clergyman, and in the course of it said: 'You know that I am forty-eight this day'. 'No, indeed,' he replied; 'you are only forty-seven, for your mother had a dispute with me once on the very subject of your age, and I in consequence sent and consulted the registry, and can most confidently assert that you are only forty-seven this day.' 'You have signed my death-warrant, then,' she cried; 'leave me, I pray, for I have not much longer to live, but have many things of grave importance to settle before I die. Send my son and my daughter to me immediately.' The clergyman did as he was bidden. He directed Sir Marcus and his sister to go instantly to their mother; and he sent to the archbishop and a few other friends to put them off from joining the birthday party.

"When her two children repaired to Lady Beresford, she thus addressed them: 'I have something of deep importance to communicate to you, my dear children, before I die. You are no strangers to the intimacy and the affection which subsisted in early life between Lord Tyrone and myself. We were educated together when young, under the same roof, in the pernicious principles of Deism. Our real friends afterwards took every opportunity to convince us of our error, but their arguments were insufficient to overpower and uproot our infidelity, though they had the effect of shaking our confidence in it, and thus leaving us wavering between the two opinions. In this perplexing state of doubt we made a solemn promise one to the other, that whichever died first should, if permitted, appear to the other for the purpose of declaring what religion was the one acceptable to the Almighty. One night, years after this interchange of promises, I was sleeping with your father at Gill Hall, when I suddenly awoke and discovered Lord Tyrone sitting visibly by the side of the bed. I screamed out, and vainly endeavoured to rouse Sir Tristram. "Tell me," I said, "Lord Tyrone, why and wherefore are you here at this time of the night?" "Have you then forgotten our promise to each other, pledged in early life? I died on Tuesday, at four o'clock. I have been permitted thus to appear in order to assure you that the revealed religion is the true and only one by which we can be saved. I am also suffered to inform you that you are with child, and will produce a son, who will marry my heiress; that Sir Tristram will not live long, when you will marry again, and you will die from the effects of childbirth in your forty-seventh year." I begged from him some convincing sign or proof so that when the morning came I might rely upon it, and feel satisfied that his appearance had been real, and that it was not the phantom of my imagination. He caused the hangings of the bed to be drawn in an unusual way and impossible manner through an iron hook. I still was not satisfied, when he wrote his signature in my pocket-book. I wanted, however, more substantial proof of his visit, when he laid his hand, which was cold as marble, on my wrist; the sinews shrunk up, the nerves withered at the touch. "Now," he said, "let no mortal eye, while you live, ever see that wrist," and vanished. While I was conversing with him my thoughts were calm, but as soon as he disappeared I felt chilled with horror and dismay, a cold sweat came over me, and I again endeavoured but vainly to awaken Sir Tristram; a flood of tears came to my relief, and I fell asleep.

"'In the morning your father got up without disturbing me; he had not noticed anything extraordinary about me or the bed-hangings. When I did arise I found a long broom in the gallery outside the bedroom door, and with great difficulty I unhooded the curtain, fearing that the position of it might excite surprise and cause inquiry. I bound up my wrist with black ribbon before I went down to breakfast, where the agitation of my mind was too visible not to attract attention. Sir Tristram made many anxious inquiries as to my health, especially as to my sprained wrist, as he conceived mine to be. I begged him to drop all questions as to the bandage, even if I continued to adopt it for any length of time. He kindly promised me not to speak of it any more, and he kept his promise faithfully. You, my son, came into the world as predicted, and your father died six years after. I then determined to abandon society and its pleasures and not mingle again with the world, hoping to avoid the dreadful predictions as to my second marriage; but, alas! In the one family with which I held constant and friendly intercourse I met the man, whom I did not regard with perfect indifference. Though I struggled to conquer by every means the passion, I at length yielded to his solicitations, and in a fatal moment for my own peace I became his wife. In a few years his conduct fully justified my demand for a separation, and I fondly hoped to escape the fatal prophecy. Under the delusion that I had passed my forty-seventh birthday, I was prevailed upon to believe in his amendment, and to pardon him. I have, however, heard from undoubted authority that I am only forty-seven this day, and I know that I am about to die. I die, however, without the dread of death, fortified as I am by the sacred precepts of Christianity and upheld by its promises. When I am gone, I wish that you, my children, should unbind this black ribbon and alone behold my wrist before I am consigned to the grave.'

"She then requested to be left that she might lie down and compose herself, and her children quitted the apartment, having desired her attendant to watch her, and if any change came on to summon them to her bedside. In an hour the bell rang, and they hastened to the call, but all was over. The two children having ordered everyone to retire, knelt down by the side of the bed, when Lady Riverston unbound the black ribbon and found the wrist exactly as Lady Beresford had described it – every nerve withered, every sinew shrunk.

"Her friend, the Archbishop, had had her buried in the Cathedral of St. Patrick, in Dublin, in the Earl of Cork's tomb, where she now lies."

* * *

The writer now professes his disbelief in any spiritual presence, and explains his theory that Lady Beresford's anxiety about Lord Tyrone deluded her by a vivid dream, during which she hurt her wrist.

Of all ghost stories the Tyrone, or Beresford Ghost, has most variants. Following Monsieur Haureau, in the Journal des Savants, I have tracked the tale, the death compact, and the wound inflicted by the ghost on the hand, or wrist, or brow, of the seer, through Henry More, and Melanchthon, and a mediaeval sermon by Eudes de Shirton, to William of Malmesbury, a range of 700 years. Mrs. Grant of Laggan has a rather recent case, and I have heard of another in the last ten years! Calmet has a case in 1625, the spectre leaves

> *The sable score of fingers four on a board of wood.*
> *Now for a modern instance of a gang of ghosts with a purpose!*

When I narrated the story which follows to an eminent moral philosopher, he remarked, at a given point, "Oh, the ghost spoke, did she?" and displayed scepticism. The evidence, however, left him, as it leaves me, at a standstill, not convinced, but agreeably perplexed. The ghosts here are truly old-fashioned.

My story is, and must probably remain, entirely devoid of proof, as far as any kind of ghostly influence is concerned. We find ghosts appearing, and imposing a certain course of action on a living witness, for definite purposes of their own. The course of action prescribed was undeniably pursued, and apparently the purpose of the ghosts was fulfilled, but what that purpose was their agent declines to state, and conjecture is hopelessly baffled.

The documents in the affair have been published by the Society for Psychical Research (Proceedings, vol. xi., p. 547), and are here used for reference. But I think the matter will be more intelligible if I narrate it exactly as it came under my own observation. The names of persons and places are all fictitious, and are the same as those used in the documents published by the S.P.R.

The Talking Head of Donn-Bo

THERE IS AN OLD TALE told in Erin of a lovable and bright and handsome youth named Donn-bo, who was the best singer of 'Songs of Idleness' and the best teller of 'King Stories' in the world. He could tell a tale of each king who reigned in Erin, from the 'Tale of the Destruction of Dind Righ', when Cova Coelbre was killed, down to the kings who reigned in his own time.

On a night before a battle, the warriors said, "Make minstrelsy tonight for us, Donn-bo."

But Donn-bo answered, "No word at all will come on my lips tonight; therefore, for this night let the King-buffoon of Ireland amuse you. But tomorrow, at this hour, in whatsoever place they and I shall be, I will make minstrelsy for the fighting men." For the warriors had said that unless Donn-bo would go with them on that hosting, not one of them would go.

The battle was past, and on the evening of the morrow at that same hour Donn-bo lay dead, his fair young body stretched across the body of the King of Ireland, for he had died in defending his chief. But his head had rolled away among a wisp of growing rushes by the waterside.

At the feasting of the army on that night a warrior said, "Where is Donn-bo, that he may make minstrelsy for us, as he promised us at this hour yesternight, and that he may tell us the 'King Stories of Erin'?"

A valiant champion of the men of Munster answered, "I will go over the battle-field and seek for him." He enquired among the living for Donn-bo, but he found him not, and then he searched hither and thither among the dead.

At last he came where the body of the King of Erin lay, and a young, fair corpse beside it. In all the air about there was the sound of minstrelsy, low and very sweet; dead bards and poets reciting in faint whispers old tales and poems to dead chiefs.

The wild, clear note of the battle-march, the dord fiansa, played by the drooping hands of slain warriors upon the points of broken spears, low like the echo of an echo, sounded in the clump of rushes hard by; and, above them all, a voice, faint and very still, that sang a song that was sweeter than the tunes of the whole world beside.

The voice that sang was the voice of the head of Donn-bo. The warrior stooped to pick up the head.

"Do not touch me," said the head, "for we are commanded by the King of the Plains of Heaven to make music tonight for our lord, the King of Erin, the shining one who lies dead beside us; and though all of us are lying dead likewise, no faintness or feebleness shall prevent us from obeying that command. Disturb me not."

"The hosts of Leinster are asking thee to make minstrelsy for them, as thou didst promise yesternight," said the messenger.

"When my minstrelsy here is done, I will go with thee," saith the head; "but only if Christ, the Son of God, in whose presence I now am, go with me, and if thou takest me to my body again."

"That shall be done, indeed," saith the messenger, and when it had ceased chanting for the King of Erin he carried away the head.

When the messenger came again amongst the warriors they stopped their feasting and gathered round him. "Hast thou brought anything from the battle-field?" they cried.

"I have brought the head of Donn-bo," said the man.

"Set it upon a pillar that we may see and hear it," cried they all; and they said, "It is no luck for thee to be like that, Donn-bo, and thou the most beautiful minstrel and the best in Erin. Make music, for the love of Jesus Christ, the Son of God. Amuse the Leinster men tonight as thou didst amuse thy lord a while ago."

Then Donn-bo turned his face to the wall, that the darkness might be around him, and he raised his melody in the quiet night; and the sound of that minstrelsy was so piteous and sad that the hosts sat weeping at the sound of it. Then was the head taken to his body, and the neck joined itself to the shoulders again, and Donn-bo was at rest.

The Enchanted Island

ON THE AFTERNOON of Sunday, July 7, 1878, the inhabitants of Ballycotton, County Cork, were greatly excited by the sudden appearance, far out at sea, of an island where none was known to exist. The men of the town and island of Ballycotton were fishermen and knew the sea as well as they knew the land. The day before, they had been out in their boats and sailed over the spot where the strange island now appeared, and were certain that the locality was the best fishing-ground they had.

"And still they gazed, and still the wonder grew", for the day was clear and the island could be seen as plainly as they saw the hills to the north. It was rugged, in some parts rocky, in others densely wooded; here and there were deep shadows in its sides indicating glens heavily covered with undergrowth and grasses. At one end it rose almost precipitously from the sea; at the other, the declivity was gradual; the thick forest of the mountainous portion gave way to smaller trees, these to shrubs; these to green meadows that finally melted into the sea and became indistinguishable from the waves.

Under sail and oar, a hundred boats put off from the shore to investigate; when, as they neared the spot, the strange island became dim in outline, less vivid in color, and at last vanished entirely, leaving the wonder-stricken villagers to return, fully convinced that for the first time in their lives they had really seen the Enchanted Island. For once there was a topic of conversation that would outlast the day, and as the story of the Enchanted Island passed from lip to lip, both story and island grew in size till the latter was little less than a continent, containing cities and castles, palaces and cathedrals, towers and steeples, stupendous mountain ranges, fertile valleys, and wide spreading plains; while the former was limited only by the patience of the listener, and embraced the personal experience, conclusions, reflections, and observations of every man, woman, and child in the parish who had been fortunate enough to see the island, hear of it, or tell where it had been seen elsewhere.

For the Enchanted Island of the west coast is not one of those ordinary, humdrum islands that rise out of the sea in a night, and then, having come, settle down to business on scientific principles, and devote their attention to the collection of soil for the use of plants and animals. It disdains any such commonplace course as other islands are content to follow, but is peripatetic, or, more properly, seafaring, in its habits, and as fond of travelling as a sailor. At its own sweet will it comes, and, having shown itself long enough to convince everybody who is not an innocent entirely of its reality, it goes without leave-taking or ceremony, and always before boats can approach near enough to make a careful inspection. This is the invariable history of its appearance. No one has ever been able to come close to its shores, much less land upon them, but it has been so often seen on the west coast, that a doubt of its existence, if expressed in the company of coast fishermen, will at once establish for the sceptic a reputation for ignorance of the common affairs of everyday life.

In Cork, for instance, it has been seen by hundreds of people off Ballydonegan Bay, while many more can testify to its appearance off the Bay of Courtmacsherry. In Kerry, all the population of Ballyheige saw it a few years ago, lying in Tralee Bay, between Kerry Head and Brandon's Head, and shortly before, the villagers of Lisneakeabree, just across the bay from Ballyheige, saw it between their shore and Kerry Head, while the fishermen in Saint Finan's Bay and in Ballinskelligs are confident it has been seen, if not by themselves, at least by some of their friends. It has appeared at the mouth of the Shannon, and off Carrigaholt in Clare, where the people saw a city on it. This is not so remarkable as it seems, for, in justice to the Enchanted Island, it should be stated that its resemblance to portions of the neighboring land is sometimes very close, and shows that the 'enchanter' who has it under a spell knows his business, and being determined to keep his island for himself changes its appearance as well as its location in order that his property may not be recognized nor appropriated.

In Galway, the Enchanted Island has appeared in the mouth of Ballinaleame Bay, a local landlord at the time making a devout wish that it would stay there. The fishermen of Ballynaskill, in the Joyce Country, saw it about fifteen years ago, since when it appeared to the Innisshark islanders. The County Mayo has seen it, not only from the Achille Island cliffs, but also from Downpatrick Head; and in Sligo, the fishermen of Ballysadare Bay know all about it, while half the population of Inishcrone still remember its appearance about twenty years ago. The Inishboffin islanders in Donegal say it looked like their own island, "sure two twins couldn't be liker", and the people on Gweebarra Bay, when it appeared there, observed along the shore of the island a village like Maas, the one in which they lived. It has also appeared off Rathlin's Island, on the Antrim coast, but, so far as could be learned, it went no further to the east, confining its migrations to the west coast, between Cork on the south and Antrim on the north.

Concerning the island itself, legendary authorities differ on many material points. Some hold it to be "a rale island sure enough", and that its exploits are due to "jommethry or some other inchantmint", while opponents of this materialistic view are inclined to the opinion that the island is not what it seems to be, that is to say, not "airth an' shtones, like as thim we see, but only a deludherin' show that avil sper'ts, or the divil belike, makes fur to desave us poor dishsolute craythers." Public opinion on the west coast is therefore strongly divided on the subject, unity of sentiment existing on two points only; that the island has been seen, and that there is something quite out of the ordinary in its appearance. "For ye see, yer Anner," observed a Kerry fisherman, "it's agin nacher fur a rale island to be comin' and goin' like a light in a bog, an' whin ye do see it, ye can see through it, an' by jagers, if it's a thrue island, a mighty quare wan it is an' no mishtake."

On so deep and difficult a subject, an ounce of knowledge is worth a pound of speculation, and the knowledge desired was finally furnished by an old fisherman of Ballyconealy Bay, on the Connemara coast, west of Galway. This individual, Dennis Moriarty by name, knew all about the Enchanted Island, having not only seen it himself, but, when a boy, learned its history from a 'fairy man', who obtained his information from 'the good people' themselves, the facts stated being therefore, of course, of indisputable authority, what the fairies did not know concerning the doings of supernatural and enchanted circles, being not worth knowing. Mr. Moriarty was stricken in years, having long given up active service in the boats and relegated himself to lighter duties on shore. He had much confidence in the accuracy of his information on the subject of the island, and a glass of grog, and "dhraw ov the pipe", brought out the story in a rich, mellow brogue.

"Faith, I'm not rightly sure how long ago it was, but it was a good while an' before the blessed Saint Pathrick come to the counthry an' made Crissans av the haythens in it. Howandiver, it was in thim times that betune this an' Inishmore, there was an island. Some calls it the Island av Shades, an' more says its name was the Sowls Raypose, but it doesn't matther, fur no wan knows. It was as full av payple as it could howld, an' cities wor on it wid palaces an' coorts an' haythen timples an' round towers all covered wid goold an' silver till they shone so ye cudn't see for the brightness.

"And they wor all haythens there, an' the king av the island was the biggest av thim, sure he was Satan's own, an' tuk delight in doin' all the bloody things that come into his head. If the waither that minded the table did annything to displaze him, he'd out wid a soord the length av me arrum an' cut aff his head. If they caught a man shtaling, the king 'ud have him hung at wanst widout the taste av a thrial, 'Bekase,' says the king, says he, 'maybe he didn't do it at all, an' so he'd get aff, so up wid him,' an' so they'd do. He had more than a hunderd wives, ginerally spakin', but he wasn't throubled in the laste be their clack, for whin wan had too much blasthogue in her jaw, or begun gostherin' at him, he cut aff her head an' said, beways av a joke, that 'that's the only cure fur a woman's tongue.' An' all the time, from sun to sun, he was cursin' an' howlin' wid rage, so as I'm sure yer Anner wouldn't want fur to hear me say thim blastpheemies that he said. To spake the truth av him, he was wicked in that degray that, axin' yer pardon, the owld divil himself wouldn't own him.

"So wan time, there was a thunderin' phillaloo in the king's family, fur mind ye, he had thin just a hunderd wives. Now it's my consate that it's aisier fur a hunderd cats to spind the night in pace an the wan thatch than for two wimmin to dhraw wather out av the same well widout aitch wan callin' the other wan all the names she can get out av her head. But whin ye've a hunderd av 'em, an' more than a towsand young wans, big an' little, its aisey to see that the king av the island had plinty av use fur the big soord that he always kept handy to settle family dishputes wid. So, be the time the row I'm tellin' ye av was over an' the wimmin shtopped talkin', the king was a widdy-man just ten times, an' had only ninety wives lift.

"So he says to himself, 'Bedad, I must raycrout the force agin, or thim that's left 'ull think I cant do widout 'em an' thin there'll be no ind to their impidence. Begorra, this marryin' is a sayrious business,' says he, sighin', fur he'd got about all the wimmin that wanted to be quanes an' didn't just know where to find anny more. But, be pickin' up wan here an' there, afther a bit he got ninety-nine, an' then cud get no more, an' in spite av sendin' men to ivery quarther av Ireland an' tellin' the kings' dawthers iverywhere how lonesome he was, an' how the coort was goin' to rack an' ruin entirely fur the want av another quane to mind the panthry, sorra a woman cud be had in all Ireland to come, fur they'd all heard av the nate manes he tuk to kape pace in his family.

"But afther thryin' iverywhere else, he sent a man into the Joyce Counthry, to a mighty fine princess av the Joyces. She didn't want to go at first, but the injuicemints war so shtrong that she couldn't howld out, for the king sint her presints widout end an' said, if she'd marry him, he'd give her all the dimunds they cud get on a donkey's back.

"Now over beyant the Twelve Pins, in the Joyce Counthry, there was a great inchanter, that had all kinds av saycrets, an' knew where ye'd dig for a pot av goold, an' all about doctherin', and cud turn ye into a pig in a minnit, an' build a cassel in wan night, an' make himself disappare when ye wanted him, an' take anny shape he plazed, so as to look to be a baste whin he wasn't, an' was a mighty dape man entirely. Now to him wint the princess an' axed him phat to do, for she didn't care a traneen for the king, but 'ud give the two eyes out av her head to get the dimunds. The inchanter heard phat she had to say an' then towld her, 'Now, my dear, you marry the owld felly, an' have no fear, fur av he daars to touch a hair av yer goolden locks, I'll take care av you an' av him too.'

"So he gev her a charm that she was to say whin she wanted him to come an' another wan to repate whin she was in mortial danger an' towld her fur to go an' get marr'ed an' get the dimunds as quick as she cud. An' that she did, an' at foorst the king was mightily plazed at gettin' her, bekase she was hard to get, an' give her the dimunds an' all she wanted, so she got on very well an' tuk care av the panthry an' helped the other wives about the coort.

"Wan day the king got up out av the goolden bed he shlept an, wid a terrible sulk an him, an' in a state av mind entirely, for the wind was in the aiste an' he had the roomytisms in his back. So he cursed an' shwore like a Turk an' whin the waither axed him to come to his brekquest, he kicked him into the yard av the coort, an' wint in widout him an' set down be the table. So wan av the quanes brought him his bowl av stirabout an' thin he found fault wid it. 'It's burned,' say he, an' threw it at her. Then Quane Peggy Joyce, that hadn't seen the timper that was an him, come in from the panthry wid a shmile an her face an' a big noggin o' milk in her hand. 'Good morrow to ye,' she says to him, but the owld vagabone didn't spake a word. 'Good morrow,' she says to him agin, an' thin he broke out wid a fury.

"'Howld yer pace, ye palaverin' shtrap. D' ye think I'm to be deefened wid yer tongue? Set the noggin an the table an' be walkin' aff wid yerself or I'll make ye sorry ye come,' says he.

"It was the first time he iver spake like that to her, an' the Irish blood ov her riz, an' in a minnit she was as mad as a gandher and as bowld as a lion.

"'Don't you daar to spake that-a-way to me, Sorr,' she says to him. 'I'll have ye know I won't take a word av yer impidince. Me fathers wore crowns ages afore yer bogthrottin' grandfather come to this island, an' ivery wan knows he was the first av his dirthy thribe that had shoes an his feet.' An' she walked strait up to him an' folded her arrums an' looked into his face as impidint as a magpie. 'Don't think fur to bully me,' she says. 'I come av a race that niver owned a coward, and I wouldn't give that fur you an' all the big soords ye cud carry,' says she, givin' her fingers a snap right at the end av his nose.

"Now the owld haythen niver had anny wan to spake like that to him, an' at first was that surprised like as a horse had begun fur to convarse at him, no more cud he say a word, he was that full o' rage, and sat there, openin' and shuttin' his mouth an' swellin' up like he'd burst, an' his face as red as a turkey-cock's. Thin he remembered his soord ah' pulled it out an' stratched out his hand fur to ketch the quane an' cut aff her head. But she was too quick for him entirely, an' whin he had the soord raised, she said the charm that was to purtect her, an' afore ye cud wink, there stood the blood-suckin' owld villin, mortified to shtone wid his arrum raised an' his hand reached out, an' as stiff as a mast.

"Thin she said the other charm that called the inchanter an' he come at wanst. She towld him phat she done an' he said it was right av her, an' as she was a purty smart woman he said he'd marry her himself. So he did, an' bein' that the island was cursed be rayzon av the king's crimes, they come to Ireland wid all the payple. So they come to Connemara, an' the inchanter got husbands fur all the king's wives an' homes fur all the men av the island. But he inchanted the island an' made it so that the bad king must live in it alone as long as the sun rises an' sits. No more does the island stand still, but must go thravellin' up an' down the coast, an' wan siven years they see it in Kerry an' the next siven years in Donegal, an' so it goes, an' always will, beways av a caution to kings not to cut aff the heads av their wives."

Biographies

D.L. Ashliman
Foreword: Irish Fairy Tales
D.L. Ashliman, an emeritus professor at the University of Pittsburgh, taught folklore, mythology, German, and comparative literature at that institution for thirty-three years. He also served as guest professor at the University of Augsburg in Germany. He is the editor of the *Aesop's Fables* volume in the Barnes and Noble *Classics* series. His book-length publications include two volumes in the Folklore Handbooks series of Greenwood Press: *Folk and Fairy Tales* (2004) and *Fairy Lore* (2005). He authored numerous articles in the four-volume encyclopedia *Folktales and Fairy Tales* (Greenwood Press, 2016).

John D. Batten
John D. Batten (1860–1932) was an English painter that excelled in oils, tempera, and fresco. A book illustrator and printmaker, he had studied under the French artist and sculptor Alphonse Legros. He began displaying his work at the Royal Academy in 1891, as well as the Grosvenor Gallery, the New Gallery, and the Arts and Crafts Exhibition Society. His paintings frequently contained mythological and allegorical motifs, as can be seen in his contributions to various fairy tale books.

T. Crofton Croker
T. Crofton Croker (1798–1854) was born in Cork as the son of an army major. Although he had little education, he always made time to read while working in merchant trade. When his father died in 1818, Croker moved to London where he held a position in the Admiralty. Throughout his youth, Croker collected Irish legends, folk songs, and keens, some of which he sent to the poet Thomas Moore. This collection formed the basis of Croker's first major publication, *Researches in the South of Ireland* (1824). His next work, *Fairy Legends and Traditions of the South of Ireland*, was so greatly received he decided to write a second series. Passionate about his findings, Croker's Fairy Tales are filled with his notes, emphasising the similarities between Irish legends and those of other countries.

Alfred Perceval Graves
Alfred Perceval Graves (1846–1931) was an Anglo-Irish poet, songwriter, and folklorist. Born in Dublin, he was educated in England at Windermere College, Westmoreland, and Trinity College, Dublin. He dabbled in several careers besides writing. He entered the Civil Service in 1869 as a clerk in the British Home Office and later became an Inspector of Schools in 1874. He greatly contributed prose and verse to *The Spectator*, *Athenaeum*, *John Bull*, and *Punch*, but he is known for having a leading role in the 19th-century revival of Irish literature. He published *Songs of Ireland* (1882) with Charles Villiers Stanford, and *Irish Songs and Ballads* (1893). These ballads stirred public interest in the old folk-songs of Ireland, Wales, and the Highlands, encouraging musicians and singers to become interested as well.

Joseph Jacobs
Joseph Jacobs (1854–1916) was born in Australia and settled in New York. He is most famous for his collections of English folklore and fairy tales including 'Jack and the Beanstalk' and

'The Three Little Pigs'. He also published Celtic, Jewish and Indian fairytales during his career. Jacobs was an editor for books and journals centered on folklore and a member of The Folklore Society in England.

Andrew Lang

Poet, novelist and anthropologist Andrew Lang (1844–1912) was born in Selkirk, Scotland. He is now best known for his collections of fairy stories and publications on folklore, mythology and religion. Inspired by the traditional folklore tales of his home on the English-Scottish border, Lang compiled twelve coloured fairy books which collected 798 stories from French, Danish, Russian and Romanian sources, amongst others. This series was hugely popular and had a wide influence on increasing the popularity of fairy tales in children's literature.

Edmund Leamy

Edmund Leamy (1848–1904) was an Irish journalist, barrister, author of fairy tales, and nationalist politician. Born in Waterford, Ireland, he became a Member of Parliament in the House of Commons of the United Kingdom of Great Britian and Ireland, where he represented various Irish seats from 1880 until his death in 1904. During his life, he wrote several fairy tales such as 'The Golden Spears' and 'The Enchanted Cave'. After they gained popularity, they were reprinted several times throughout the UK and Ireland. His main collection of stories was called *Irish Fairy Tales* (1890).

D.R. McAnally

D.R. McAnally Jr. (1847–1909) is known for his collection *Irish Wonders*, which brings together the best of the country's fables. The written word, paired with sixty-five beautiful pen-and-ink drawings, allowed the work to thoroughly appreciate the folklore of the culture.

Arthur Rackham

Arthur Rackham (1867–1939) was one of the most renowned and beloved illustrators of his day. The English artist brought countless stories and fairytales to life with his imagination and creative eye for detail. Born in Lewisham as one of twelve children, Rackham's first serious commission was in 1894 for *The Dolly Dialogues*, a collection of sketches by Anthony Hope who later went on to write *The Prisoner of Zenda*. Rackham's career as a book illustrator immediately took off. He developed a reputation of pen and ink fantasy illustration with works such as *Gulliver's Travels* (1900), *Fairy Tales of the Brothers Grimm* (1900), and *Rip Van Winkle* (1905), which brought him fully into the public's attention. Rackham is still regarded today as one of the leading illustrators of the 'Golden Age' of British Book illustration.

W.B. Yeats

William Butler Yeats (1865–1939) was an Irish poet and is considered one of the greatest writers from the twentieth century. He played an important role in the Celtic Twilight, a revival of Irish literature focused on Gaelic heritage and Irish nationalism. Yeats was fascinated by Irish legends, including many Irish heroes in his works and focusing his poetry on Irish folklore. Alongside his poetry he is famous for writing short stories and plays. Yeats set up the Abbey Theatre in 1899, which held Irish and Celtic performances. In recognition of Yeats' important work he received a Nobel Prize in 1923.

Illustrations

The illustrations throughout this book are based on a range of sources, including fairy tales illustrated by Arthur Rackham and John D. Batten. The main illustrations are by the following artists:

John D. Batten: p62, 67, 71, 73, 81, 85, 167, 171, 176, 177, 189, 197, 199, 228, 279, 282, 295, 330, 335, 392, 395, 400, 402, 409, 420, 425, 427, 431, 434, 436, 438, 449, 458, 459
George Denham: p149, 165, 186, 202, 241, 313, 423, 442
S. Fazoin: p33, 43, 249, 269
H.R. Heaton: p216, 219, 223, 288, 305, 307, 340, 343, 387, 470, 472
Arthur Rackham: p12 13, 25, 26, 90, 91, 93, 130, 181, 193, 224, 245, 246, 247, 260, 266, 280, 293, 317, 337, 358, 360, 364, 368, 369, 381, 382, 473, 476, 477
James Torrance: p57, 211, 265, 352, 385, 413
Corinne Turner: p20, 36, 274, 320

Images courtesy Shutterstock.com and © the following contributors:
basel101658 58; GrAI 388; Alexey Pushkin 408.

Sources

The stories in this book are largely reproduced from collections of fairy tales published around the turn of the twentieth century, whose authors and editors either gathered tales or rewrote material to produce their own variations. The list of sources for this book are as follows:

Crofton, T. Croker, *Fairy Legends and Traditions of the South of Ireland* (1825)
Graves, Alfred Perceval (ed.), *The Irish Fairy Book* (1909)
Contributors from the book used here: Jeremiah Curtin, Eleanor Hull, Patrick Kennedy.
Jacobs, Joseph, *Celtic Fairy Tales* (1891)
Jacobs, Joseph, *More Celtic Fairy Tales* (1894)
Lang, Andrew, *Red Fairy Book* (1890)
Lang, Andrew, *Lilac Fairy Book* (1910)
Lang, Andrew, *The Book of Dreams and Ghosts* (1897)
Leamy, Edmund, *Irish Fairy Tales* (1906)
McAnally, Jr, D.R., *Irish Wonders* (1888)
Rolleston, T.W., *The High Deeds of Finn* (1910)
Yeats, W.B. (ed.), *Fairy and Folk Tales of the Irish Peasantry* (1888)
Contributors from the book used here: William Carleton, T. Crofton Croker, Patrick Kennedy, Samuel Lover, Miss Letitia Maclintock, Abraham McCoy (trans. Nicholas O'Kearney), J. Todhunter, Lady Wilde.
Yeats, W.B. (ed.), *Irish Fairy Tales* (1892)
Contributors from the book used here: T. Crofton Croker, Standish O'Grady.

The Cattle-Raid of Cualnge text is taken from the **L. Winifred Faraday** version published by David Nutt in 1904.

FLAME TREE PUBLISHING
Short Story Series
New & Classic Writing

Flame Tree's Gothic Fantasy books offer a carefully curated series of new titles, each with combinations of original and classic writing:

Chilling Horror • Chilling Ghost • Science Fiction
Murder Mayhem • Crime & Mystery • Swords & Steam
Dystopia Utopia • Supernatural Horror • Lost Worlds
Time Travel • Heroic Fantasy • Pirates & Ghosts
Agents & Spies • Endless Apocalypse • Alien Invasion
Robots & AI • Lost Souls • Haunted House • Cosy Crime
Urban Crime • American Gothic • Epic Fantasy

Also, new companion titles offer rich collections of classic fiction, myths and tales in the gothic fantasy tradition:

H.G. Wells • Lovecraft • Sherlock Holmes
Edgar Allan Poe • Bram Stoker • Mary Shelley
African Myths & Tales • Celtic Myths & Tales
Chinese Myths & Tales • Norse Myths & Tales
Greek Myths & Tales • Japanese Myths & Tales
King Arthur & The Knights of the Round Table
Alice's Adventures in Wonderland • The Divine Comedy
The Wonderful Wizard of Oz • The Age of Queen Victoria • Brothers Grimm

Available from all good bookstores, worldwide, and online at
flametreepublishing.com

See our new fiction imprint
FLAME TREE PRESS | FICTION WITHOUT FRONTIERS
New and original writing in Horror, Crime, SF and Fantasy

And join our monthly newsletter with offers and more stories:
FLAME TREE FICTION NEWSLETTER
flametreepress.com

GOTHIC FANTASY

For our books, calendars, blog
and latest special offers please see:
flametreepublishing.com